WELCOME TO THE VOID

WELCOME TO THE VOID

STAKED
REVAMPED

J.F. LEWIS

SFBC
FANTASY

STAKED   Copyright © 2008 by Jeremy F. Lewis
   Publication History: Pocket Books mass market, July 2009
REVAMPED   Copyright © 2009 by Jeremy F. Lewis
   Publication History: Pocket Books mass market, October 2010

First SFBC Fantasy Printing: August 2012

Selected by Rome Quezada, SFBC Senior Editor

Published by arrangement with
Pocket Books
A Division of Simon & Schuster, Inc.
1230 Avenue of the Americas
New York, NY 10020

Visit The SFBC online at http://www.sfbc.com

ISBN # 978-1-62090-457-2

Printed in the United States of America.

CONTENTS

STAKED

The book is dedicated to four very special women:
My mom, Martha
My wife, Janet
My mother-in-law, Virginia
and
My good friend, Mary Ann

ACKNOWLEDGMENTS

The author would like to acknowledge every single person who made this book possible, but he's quite certain he left someone out. If it was you . . . oops.

With that said, I'd like to thank my writing group, WTF (Write the Fantastic): Janet, Rob, Mary Ann, Dan, Karen, and Virginia. Thank you for the many Tuesdays you've sacrificed on my behalf and for letting me go out of order every single time I was up against a deadline. Mom and Dad, thanks for the child care that made those editing sessions possible. Sandra and Rachel, I know you aren't technically in the group, but for your feedback and general ability to put up with me, I thank you. Rich and Shea, I know editing's not your thing, but thanks for your support during the whole process. Having friends helps.

Thank you to my agent, Shawna McCarthy, for rescuing me from the slush pile and letting me know what genre I was actually writing. Your advice was invaluable.

Thanks to my editor, Jennifer Heddle, not just for buying *Staked* but for going above and beyond the call, sanding the rough edges, and making the novel shine.

Thanks also to my copyeditor, Chris Fuller, for his detailed character sketches, time line, and especially fine attention to detail.

And thanks to you, the reader, for picking up this book. I hope you enjoy it. (Buy two!)

1

ERIC:

THE ALLEY

Somewhere in the middle of my rant it occurred to me that I'd killed whoever it was I'd been yelling at, so arguing was no longer important. I looked down at my victim's broken headless body and winced at the unnatural odor of rapidly rotting flesh. It never smells right to me when a vampire dies. I've always chalked it up to bowels. If you don't eat, you don't shit, and death just doesn't smell right without it.

Whoever this guy was, he'd obviously been a Master vampire, because Drones and Soldiers don't get the quick rot treatment. They turn to dust and blow away . . . which smells even less natural. And if he'd been a Vlad like me, he'd still be kicking.

I glanced around the dingy back alley where we'd been arguing and couldn't remember exactly where I was, what we'd been fighting about, or what I'd done with the guy's head. From the way the neck muscles had been ripped, I was guessing I'd torn it off. If he'd been human, I would have been soaked in blood, but vampires don't bleed easily; my fingers were barely damp.

Out of curiosity, I went looking for What's His Name's head and found it lying next to the Dumpster at the back of the alley. I figured I ought to see if I recognized him. In spite of the unnaturally rapid decay, he looked vaguely familiar, like I might have seen him around town. Other than that his face didn't ring any bells.

A homeless man was curled up against the wall of the alley, shaking like a leaf and staring at me. I tucked Dead Guy's head under my arm and slipped the bum a twenty, mostly to screw with his mind, but also because I was sorry he'd seen whatever it was he'd seen. Besides, the homeless guy kind of looked like Alex Trebek and *Jeopardy!* is a damned good show.

"Do you want me to tell the police somethin' in particular?" asked the bum.

"Don't talk to me, you dirty little fucker," I snarled. I flashed my fangs at him and let my eyes do the whole glowing red bit. "I'm not paying you to do anything. The body will burn up when the sun hits it. Tell the cops whatever you want. If they believe you at all, they're well paid to do the right thing. This is Void City, sweetheart."

Norms don't notice the supernatural here unless they aren't really normal. The spell that hangs over this city doesn't work on crazies, though. In this case I suspected the bum might remember what actually happened rather than thinking he'd seen a mugging or a gang fight or something.

I can't see magic, but I know that's how the spell is supposed to work. Your average Joe or Jane will forget the undead, the werewolves, even the demons that roam Void City and call it home . . . or sometimes they remember it wrong, their memories haphazardly replaced or jumbled by the spell. To see vampires and remember it later, you have to be crazy, be supernatural yourself, or be part of the scene, focused on being "in" with the undead crowd.

The cops all work for some high society fang I've never met and have no interest in meeting. I forget his name. If the police in his pocket have to cover up your crimes, you get a bill in the mail or a demand via phone from Captain Stacey with the VCPD. Everybody calls it the fang fee, because vampires get hit with the most of them. It's just one of the extra headaches of being a vampire, right alongside having to drink blood, staying away from holy objects, avoiding sunlight. . . .

Sunlight. I looked at my watch and cursed angrily. You'd think a vampire could remember to be in by sunrise, but my time sense has always sucked. Dropping the vamp's head and ignoring the bum, I dashed for my car only to see the driver's side door already glowing cheerily with the first lovely rays of dawn. I stopped for a moment in the shade of the alley to watch the sun's reflection in my Hummer's windshield. I used to love the sun. I still do, but now she doesn't like me so much. Which makes her not that much different from any number of women I dated back during my living years.

I strolled back down the alley and glared disapprovingly at the bum. In the increasing illumination I could see him much better, and he didn't look a damn thing like Alex Trebek. "You could have told me how close to sunrise it was," I complained.

The bum smiled, and began to grow fur.

It rippled across his body, fingertips first, in a wave so fast the brown hair breaking the skin made little musical tinkling sounds like a giant rainstick. In the movies, the transformation always looks painful, but the bum's eyes rolled back in his head, eyelids fluttering in what looked more like pleasure than pain.

"If I'd have done that, it would've been a fair fight, dead boy." He growled, his skeleton distending with a sound like a hundred knuckles popping all in order, smallest to largest. The human teeth fell out of his muzzle as it lengthened, replaced by a mouthful of sharp pointy teeth. The better to blah blah blah me with.

"If you put those under your pillow, does the tooth fairy still pony up?" I asked.

"She pays more for vampire fangs," he retorted.

What a pistol, that guy! I was laughing even as I picked up the Dumpster and emptied its contents over his head. Two more dead vamps rolled out to join No-Name. Their bodies weren't like Headless Guy's. They were little more than skeletons, the quick rotting flesh having bubbled away, leaving only a thin layer of gray scum. The bones had been gnawed on; the rib cages were splintered, gaping open where their hearts had been ripped out. They stunk even worse than Headless Guy did.

Normal animals won't touch vampire remains, which left Werewolf Bum the obvious culprit. I'd have guessed even a low-level Master to be equal to one werewolf, so either this guy'd had help or he was really something special.

The werewolf launched himself from beneath the garbage, sending gouts of filth into the air and scattering refuse everywhere. The dead vamps' peculiar odor problem ceased to be an issue. Now the whole alley smelled like human waste of all types, foreign and domestic. I smiled, though. After all, Wolfy had to have a much more acute sense of smell than me. Heh.

"Damn it!" he roared, then sneezed pathetically and swatted at his nose.

I've always had trouble taking werewolves seriously. They all look like one of Ray Harryhausen's stop-motion creature effects to me; you know, fake looking. I keep expecting Sinbad to show up and pretend to duel with them, like he did with the skeletons in *Sinbad and the Eye of the Tiger*. Normally I could probably take on four or five of them. This guy had no chance. I was still thinking that when Wolfy sank his fangs into my shoulder. The Dumpster fell backward out of my hands. He should have bitten my head or my neck; he wouldn't get another shot.

Time seemed to slow as I reached up and grabbed the werewolf's jaws, forcing them apart until I felt the joint give. Then I let go and rolled backward, coming up beneath the falling Dumpster, and catching it before it landed. It always makes me feel like a superhero when my vampire speed kicks in. Some vamps are able to use that speed all the time, but mine has always been sporadic for some reason.

I knew that I should kill Wolfy, but I really wasn't interested. Werewolves tend to stick together. Kill one and you might wind up fighting the whole pack, or worse. Besides, I didn't care about the other two vamps he'd killed. Wolf Bum was just doing what came naturally to him, so if I could, I'd let him go with a warning. I swung the Dumpster in an arc and knocked him into the air with it.

Time sped up again. I watched the blood spurt from his jaws, splattering when he hit the wall of the alley with a wet cracking noise. Bones had broken when he landed. Some of them sounded important. My twenty-dollar bill hit the ground and I dropped the Dumpster to pick it up, the crash of metal on concrete reverberating in my ears.

Wolfy was still breathing, but he was down for the count. With a grimace, I walked over and tucked the cash into his hand, then added another twenty to it. His jaw was really going to hurt if it healed that way and had to be re-broken. Adding a third twenty, I shook my head.

"Walk away," I told him. "You gave it a good try."

At least the buildings on either side of me were tall enough to keep most of the alley safe from the sun, but not for long. I had to get out of here somehow. I ripped off the lid of the Dumpster and dropped the bin down over myself. "God, this stinks," I complained.

The front page of the *Void City Echo* was stuck to one wall of the Dumpster. I could make out a headline about the decrease in crime, the record drop in the murder rate on East Side. It was bullshit, of course. There's a reason the paper is called the *Echo*. It's a fang rag, heavily influenced by vampires who want to keep Void City's human populace fat and happy. On the plus side, the captions jogged my Swiss cheese memory and I suddenly remembered where I was, and for that matter, which alley I was in. My club wasn't far from here.

I put my hands on the brownish sludge caking the walls of the Dumpster and felt it squish between my fingers as I began to push my makeshift sunblock toward the end of the alley.

Tabitha was going to find me so appealing when I got back to the club. The thought of her pretty little nose turned up in disgust brought a smile to my lips. A wet clump of refuse fell from the Dumpster's up-turned bottom, slapping me messily across my hairline. "Shit!" If it wasn't, it certainly smelled like it. I wiped whatever it was from my face, leaving a trail of brown sludge in its place.

I put my hands back on the Dumpster wall and began to push, leaving long scratches in the road as I went. The sound of metal on asphalt was earsplitting, but I picked up speed anyway. The strip club was only three blocks away and all I could think about was washing this shit off and making Tabitha help. Tabitha was one of a long line of human girlfriends I'd had. There were always girls willing to do anything a vampire might want as long as they thought there was a chance they might get immortality out of it.

My Dumpster-pushing progress came to a sudden halt as I slammed into my Hummer. It was new; only a couple of weeks old. My car alarm started going off. It was the last straw. The next thing I knew, I was punching holes through the Dumpster with my bare hands. It came apart like tissue paper. It was all very satisfying until I caught fire. Note to self: The big burning ball of gas in the sky is the sun.

I walked back into the alley, rolled on the ground, and beat my head against the wall to put out the remaining flames. Then I checked on Wolfy. He was still unconscious, so I pulled out my cell phone and called my club.

Roger answered the phone. "How refreshing! Did you actually remember the phone number or did you have to look it up?" He sounded tired and angry, as if he'd answered the phone only because he'd recognized the name on the caller ID. I decided to let it slide. After all, Roger needed more sleep than I do and he was my best friend. I also needed a ride.

"Remembered," I said.

"Thank heavens!" Roger's voice dripped with sarcasm. "It's Eric," he called to someone else on the other end. "Safe and sound, our lost little lamb. We were all so worried about you." In the background I heard a woman let out one scornful "Ha!" I ignored it.

"I'm three blocks away, in the alley at Thirteenth Street and Fifth Avenue. Bring the party van around to pick me up."

"Sun's up, pal. I can't come get you," he said more seriously. "I'll send Candice over."

Candice is the kind of golden-hearted stripper other strippers pretend to be. She's working on her nursing degree, and if I were still human I'd be all over her. As it is, I just pay for her college and watch her dance naked in the club. And, okay, sometimes I pretend I'm with her when I'm with Tabitha. It's just better for all involved.

"I smell pretty bad. Is Lillian still around?" I asked. Lillian had come in late three days in a row, just in time for the evening rush. If she thought early afternoons were shit duty, I'd show her shit duty.

"Yes," Roger answered, laughing. "Don't want to smell bad in front of your little groupie?"

"Lillian's more deserving," I said. "Send her over, then tell Talbot he's going to need to get the van cleaned up after we're done with it."

Roger hung up and I waited for the van, admiring my handiwork on the Hummer. From the damage, I must have really picked up some speed before impact. I took a perverse joy in having demolished the shiny new SUV. Roger had talked me into buying it, but to be honest, I hated the thing. I'm only comfortable in my Mustang. It's old, but so am I, and we both have plenty of miles left in us.

A few minutes later, the party van rounded the corner, screeching to a halt just inches into the shade. Lillian glared at me through the windshield, bleary-eyed through her half-removed makeup. She looked really pissed. As I walked toward the van, I found out the hard way that the werewolf had been playing possum for the last few minutes. I'd never known what it was like to be picked up by the ankles and slammed face-first into a brick wall. The experience isn't much to write home about.

He swung me back around to repeat the process and I felt time begin to slow down once more. I was giving Wolfy too many chances to kill me. I'm pretty damn hard to wipe out, but I supposed he could get lucky. After all, he'd killed those other two vamps somehow.

I bent backward at an angle usually reserved for circus acrobats and grabbed his jaw. He would have whimpered if he'd had the time. The jaw had healed broken; each portion pointed in opposite directions at odd angles. I re-broke it for him and slammed it shut on his lolling tongue.

As time shifted back to normal, he screamed. It was part pain, part fear; a real little-girl scream. He dropped me, and I rolled to the ground and came up facing him. Wolfy smelled scared. I guess he finally realized the first round hadn't been a fluke and the little five-foot-ten bastard he was up against actually could kick his ass up and down the alley. He held up both paws and backed away from me. My twenties had scattered across the alley, mixing like dried leaves with the trash. For some reason, it pissed me off.

The edges of my vision began to blur. It happens sometimes when I get really angry. The werewolf tried to say something despite his mangled tongue, but I couldn't quite make it out. It was too late for talk; I was too far gone to rein the anger in.

The next thing I knew, I was knee-deep in werewolf, shoving bloody twenty-dollar bills into my jeans. His chest had been cracked open like an oyster and gutted. I was standing where his organs ought to have been, but they were scattered about the alley like mismatched socks. I never remember what happens when I'm really mad. I black out.

I couldn't decide whether the scene would be more or less disturbing when the sun rose high enough to fill that portion of the alley and his corpse turned human. A dead werewolf reverts to human form in the light of day. Too bad it doesn't do the same to live lycanthropes. Part of his stomach was under my left shoe, the bile already staining it beyond recognition. At least the blood had washed some of the garbage off. Lillian, her face contorted in disgust, climbed out of the van, opened the back, and threw me a towel.

Sometimes being a vampire is truly fucked up. If you don't believe me, ask the poor vamp I'd killed in the alley earlier. I couldn't remember why the hell I'd killed him, much less why we'd been arguing. For all I knew, it was about football. Definitely fucked up.

2

ERIC:

DEMON HEART

My strip club, the Demon Heart, is in downtown Void City in a district lovingly referred to as East Side. I couldn't tell you why, because it's actually on the south side of town. The club sits on the corner of Thirteenth Street and Eighth Avenue, across from the old Pollux Theater. The Pollux is a beautiful art nouveau popcorn palace that dates back to the days when there was a cartoon and a sing-along before the movie and a nosebleed section for the folks white people didn't want to see.

I bought both buildings cheap since hardly anybody gives a damn about East Side anymore. Roger says Sable Oaks is where all the high society vamps want to build. If you ask me, it's too far from Void City. I'm not commuting an hour into town to hunt.

The Demon Heart kept me close to people nobody would miss and the Pollux gave me a place to be by myself. Besides, I hate society vamps. We have a nonaggression pact. If I don't see them and they don't see me, then there's no need for aggression.

I considered buying a pizza parlor once, but I decided I would go crazy from the smell. I love pizza. If I smell pizza, I have to stop and take a good whiff; I have to look at it, see what kind it is, and watch a lucky bastard take a few bites. Chicago pizza, Italian pizza, brick-oven pizza, anchovies, pepperoni, olives, mushrooms, peppers, kiwi, it doesn't matter to me, so long as it's pizza. I think I miss pizza more than I miss the sun.

I smelled pizza the instant Lillian smuggled my lightly toasted, stinking, quilt-covered ass in through the back entrance of the Demon Heart. The tangy Sicilian aroma made my mouth water, by which I mean blood filled my mouth, a poor imitation of saliva. It's Mother

Nature's way of reminding me that I'm a walking corpse that hasn't fallen down yet. Thanks, Mom. Shower forgotten, I followed the smell of the pizza down the hall to the girls' dressing room behind the stage.

I opened the door and found Candice eating a slice of pepperoni. She was mostly naked, and when she saw me, she began ostentatiously licking the side of the pizza to remove the excess cheese. My fangs came out and a certain lower portion of my anatomy paid attention, too. If she had been wearing her glasses or her contacts I think she would've had a harder time keeping up the act. Even so, when the smell hit her, the revulsion was hard for her to mask. "Good Lord, Eric. What have you been doing?"

"Eat your pizza," I snapped. It was all I could do not to jump on her, so I left the room and headed for my shower. Maybe I'd been rude to Candice, but it was better that way. If she was smart, she'd quit in a huff and go start a normal life somewhere the hell away from me. In the end, a friendship between a vampire and a human is like a friendship between a dog and a chicken nugget. Sooner or later, the nugget is going to get eaten; the only real question is how many bites it will take.

On my way down the hallway, I caught Tabitha's scent. Fresh out of the shower, she smelled like fizzy citrus-scented soap. She opened the door of our bedroom wearing nothing but a bathrobe. I don't know if she was on her way across the hall to borrow some lotion or to see if she could score a slice of pizza, but it didn't matter since she wasn't going to do either.

I kissed her, filled with the need for sex and blood. She didn't even mention the smell, answering the urgency of my kisses with her own, pushing me out into the hall, pressing my back against the wall. When we kissed, her heat washed over me all at once. Her robe came open, revealing the smooth surface of her sex. She'd just waxed.

"Are you okay, baby?" She asked the question between kisses, but I didn't answer. She didn't ask again, didn't complain or wrinkle her nose as I left trails of blood and grime along her breasts. I would have had sex with her right there, but I was afraid the gunk from the Dumpster might make her sick. I carried her into the bathroom, the tile still slick with moisture, mirror still cloudy, and got into the shower.

Tabitha was the only kind of girlfriend I let myself have anymore. She had a great body, a bad attitude, and extremely low self-esteem. She wasn't dumb, but she wasn't smart, and she thought that she wanted to be a vampire when she grew up. I knew she had a sister named Rachel whose photo she carried in her billfold, and I guessed she had parents, but they never seemed to be around. In short, if I broke her by accident I wouldn't feel too bad about it and no one would really miss her. It's cruel, I know, but I am a vampire, remember?

I meant to have sex, but that's not what happened. We made love instead. It was passionate, tender. It was a mistake. When we got out of the shower, Tabitha wore that stupid look she gets when she thinks she's being sly. I turned away and rolled my eyes; my memory, for once, clear as crystal.

It was like a formula with her. Before she even opened her mouth I knew the basic ploy. She would compliment me on the act, even though I'd know she was faking it for my benefit. Even when she wasn't, she always put on a big show. I guess the whole preternatural senses thing hadn't clued her in to the fact that I could tell. I didn't blame her for faking it a little; unless blood turns you on, having it stand in for all the normal bodily fluids can get a little nasty, especially during sex.

After the compliments, I predicted she'd snuggle for a minute and then ask me how old I am. I'd answer and she'd pretend like she'd forgotten. She'd tell me how cool it is to be immortal, how wonderful it must be to know that no matter what happens to the rest of the world, you will go on, forever. I'd attempt to disabuse her of the notion. She would tell me that she heard one of any number of a recycled little list of activities is much better when it's between two vampires. She'd insist it would make us feel so much closer, claim we'd be able to read each other's minds. I'd disagree.

She'd say it would be different with us because we're in love. I'd point out that I don't love her and then I'd wait to see if she cried or started yelling. If she cried, I'd leave. If she yelled, I'd leave. So predictable.

"You are so good at that, you know," she started up. I sighed. She walked across the room still damp from the shower and I thought about taking her again to see if she would take another shower and leave me alone when we were done. I let her rub up against me.

Tabitha was an extremely attractive woman; she was big where she was supposed to be big and narrow where narrow is good. Her long and luxurious hair was the same dark black I dyed mine, only hers wasn't a dye job. Cutting it would have been a crime. She had the sexiest green eyes I'd ever seen, though she claimed she wished they were blue like mine. Tabitha's smiles took complete advantage of her full red lips. Other girls had to use makeup to achieve the qualities she already possessed.

Tabitha would go to great lengths to vary her soaps and perfumes, to wear just enough that I would notice, but little enough that it rarely annoyed me. She even got a tattoo at the base of her spine where I once mentioned one might look sexy. I designed it for her: a multicolored butterfly. She'd be a great woman if she didn't act so dumb.

". . . and I mean my legs were so totally shaking." Oops, I missed part of it. It sounded like we were still in the "what a sex god" section, though. She hugged me from behind and I felt her breasts against my back. Her warmth overwhelmed me again. Vampires don't generate any body heat so we're always cold unless we've just fed. Even then, humans feel warm by comparison.

Despite her flaws, she was so *alive*. Maybe it was that I could still smell pizza in the distance, or maybe it was her perfume, but I began to feel a knot of panic in my chest.

"How old are you?" she asked.

"I'm not even a hundred, Tabitha," I told her halfheartedly. "You know that."

She kissed my neck tenderly. It wasn't a sexual kiss, more a touch of possessiveness. *Oh, shit.*

"I always forget. You seem so much older. God, it must be so cool to be immortal. Time wears down mountains and changes the flow of mighty rivers, but not you. To be changeless, forever . . ."

I felt caught, trapped. It was like a snare closing in around me. What the fuck was wrong with me? This crap didn't work on me. I'd heard it a thousand times. It was all bullshit. I didn't believe a damn word of it. I knew she didn't believe it either. Then I realized that this morning had been different. I could hear her breath, her heartbeat. She'd meant it all, and it was too late to do a damn thing about it.

"Maybe," I said finally. There is nothing more terrifying than the heartbeat of a woman in love. It complicates everything.

I could hear the muscles in her face draw her lips into a smile. Her heartbeat sped up and I felt it as if it were pounding in my own chest. Her breath was a little faster, too. She knew something was different. Was it the way she helped clean me up after the fight?

She hadn't looked disgusted once. Not when I'd walked in covered with blood and filth, not when I'd pulled her close before we'd even made it to the shower and not when the act was complete and my blood swirled down the drain. She was into it. It hadn't been fake this time. If it wasn't love, it was a close cousin. I was so fucked.

"I want us to be together, Eric. I've heard that—"

She was so alive, so warm, and I was so dead, so cold.

"Shut up," I said softly.

"What?" I felt her heart skip a beat.

It won't be what you're expecting, I wanted to say. If I make you a vampire, you won't be warm anymore; you won't smell like you anymore.

Before long, you won't even act like you. Just looking at you will be a painful reminder of what I am and what you used to be. And then you'll have to leave.

Instead, even more softly, I said, "I'll do it."

When women truly fall in love with me, I can't say no. It's like a sickness.

She hugged me so tightly her entire body seemed pressed against mine, squealing as she did so. I smelled her excitement for almost the last time. I was so stupid. I was dumber than she was. I knew better. I'd seen what happens. The transformation changes people. Even when they turn out just the way you want, there are problems. Like with Greta . . .

"Can we do it right here, in the bed?" she asked.

"Hell, no." I scowled. "I don't want your crap all over everything." I shook free of her and picked her up in my arms like a damned newlywed, as though the act could make murdering someone romantic rather than monstrous. "We do it in the bathroom, on the pot, so there's less to clean up."

My inner voice told me exactly what I needed to hear. I didn't love this woman. I only cared about her because she was a moist warm tightness with the appropriate attachments. She wouldn't be the same. She'd be a dead thing like me, a walking would-be body bag occupant.

I wouldn't be able to live vicariously through her. I wouldn't be able to feel and smell the sun's heat on her skin when she came in from outdoors. No more making her eat the food I craved just so I could watch her eat it. I wouldn't even be able to listen to her breathe while she slept because she wouldn't breathe autonomously anymore. I tried to think of everything she'd be giving up, all the things I'd miss, and none of it mattered because she loved me. How twisted is that?

I should have just broken her neck and found a new girlfriend, but I didn't have the balls to do it. Somebody should have put a stake in me, or better yet, gotten a good strong muzzle . . . one of those masks like Hannibal Lecter wore in the movies. It was all wrong, but that morning I no longer cared enough not to do it, or perhaps I cared too much, wanted both of us to live her crazy fantasy, though I knew damn well giving her undeath wouldn't just shatter those illusions, it would grind them into the dirt.

3

ERIC:

EVENING AFTER

I usually wake early. In fact, as far as I can tell, I barely sleep more than an hour or two each day. Even then it's easy to wake me. I rolled over and was momentarily surprised to find Tabitha beside me. I was even more surprised to see the time display on my alarm clock—18:43 . . . after six o'clock. I never sleep until six. I knew why I'd overslept today, though. The reason was still lying next to me.

She was pale, a little thinner than she'd been, but not unattractively so. The sudden additional slenderness made her breasts look bigger than they actually were and the skin and muscle all over her body had tightened a bit as the transformation took hold. She looked better than she ever had in life. I could picture how pleased she would be when she woke up. I smelled a strong odor from the bathroom and rolled out of bed. There was blood caked to my lips, trailing down my face, across my neck, and down my chest. It had dried there during the day.

I opened the bathroom and retched at the stink. The transformation flushes the body clean. That's twenty-five feet of intestines with five to ten pounds of solid waste. The process isn't pleasant or comfortable, either; I had a vague memory of Tabitha screaming. The toilet clogged when I flushed. Hastily grabbing the plunger, I took care of it before the putrid brown water poured out onto the floor.

A narrow trail of fluids led from the toilet to the sink, but I left it alone for the moment and opened the shower door. My clothes from earlier were already piled in there. I must have rinsed them out before I went to bed. I didn't remember doing it, but I was glad that I had. Most of them looked recoverable.

When I'm in top form, I can usually shapeshift into an animal, and then use a little of the residual transformation mojo to fix my clothes when I change back, but it can be very draining. The worse the damage is to the clothes, the greater the drain. This morning it had been worth the possible loss of the clothes to save that energy, to make sure I only woke up hungry, not starving. I had no desire to go on a feeding frenzy after the blood-and-energy-intensive cost of turning Tabitha.

I turned the shower on hot and washed myself, scratching at the dried blood with my fingernails to get it all off, and as the water turned scalding, I started to feel better.

I got out of the shower and squared away the rest of the room using the cleaning supplies Marilyn kept under the sink. Marilyn and I had been lovers before . . . when I'd been alive. We'd come within three weeks of getting married.

My wallet sat on the edge of the sink; I checked it quickly to make sure it hadn't gotten wet. When I opened it, Marilyn's picture smiled up at me. She wore a leather biker's jacket and sat with casual disdain on Roger's motorcycle, a 1964 Harley-Davidson Duo-Glide. In shades of sepia, the photo didn't show her red hair, but it captured her look, smoldering like Cyd Charisse, a Marlboro at the corner of her lips.

Forty-three years doesn't seem like a long time for a vampire, until you look at one of your living contemporaries. My Marilyn was more like my nanny now.

I laughed, imagining Marilyn's reaction to the whole Tabitha thing. At least it would get a rise out of her, and that was always fun.

I wasn't looking forward to telling the others, though. Candice's feelings would probably be hurt and Talbot wouldn't say a word; he'd just glare at me. Roger, on the other hand . . . Roger would probably never let me hear the end of it. He still gave me shit about turning Irene some twenty years ago.

Greta would probably take it all in stride, if she ever found out about it. Greta's my daughter. There was a picture of her in my wallet, too, but I kept it behind Marilyn's. Once I'd decided to make my own little vampire children: a girl and a boy. Greta and Kyle. It hadn't worked out. Greta took to vampirism just fine, I guess because I'd raised her, more or less, from the time she was nine, but I'd only known Kyle for a year or two when I'd turned them both. After the change Kyle wasn't the same anymore: the jaunty step he'd had in life disappeared, leaving him a shadow of his former self, a Drone, so hard to look at that I eventually sent them both away. Thinking of Greta and wondering how she was doing, I looked at the bathroom mirror and wiped off the condensation with a towel.

Nope, still no reflection.

A longing in the back of my throat told me I was hungry. It was followed quickly by a fiery pain in my gut. Turning someone takes a lot out of you even if they don't drink very much. The wound you feed them with can grow dark and inflamed; sometimes they even scar.

It takes a lot out of me to make a vampire. In the movies, it's simple: you just drain a human and then have her drink your blood. If it really worked that way, I had no doubt that Tabitha would have saved up some of my blood, slit her wrists, and turned herself a long time ago. For starters, draining the human is just common sense, not a requirement. Drinking their blood first gives you more blood to spare, but the change, making the human become a vampire, requires an act of will. It doesn't happen by accident.

I left Sleeping Beauty on the bed and walked out into the hallway before I realized I was naked. Back in my room I pulled on jeans and one of my favorite T-shirts. A few years back the Void City Music Festival swapped suppliers; instead of *Welcome to the Void City Music Festival* all ten thousand T-shirts said *Welcome to the Void* in white letters on black material. The misprint was so popular they claimed it was intentional and kept right on printing them that way every year. I have dozens of them.

Sitting on the edge of the bed, I tugged on a pair of dark socks and my work boots. My favorite belt was still lying in the shower so I went without one even though it irks me. It's a hang-up I have. Maybe I got pantsed once too often as a child. I don't know. After a little searching, I found my watch under my nightstand and slipped it on my wrist.

I checked the backstage dressing room on my way down the hall. Sheena and Desiree both gave me polite smiles. Sheena was dressed for work, ready to go onstage in a perky cheerleader uniform complete with pom-poms. Desiree, having finished her set, was slipping into a slinky French maid's outfit to wear while selling drinks and lap dances. I gave them a half smile in return and walked back out into the hall, then out into the club itself. Often the sounds and lights make me feel better. Even though the music usually hurts my ears, it excites everyone else and the more alive they feel the more I can leech off of their excitement.

I didn't see Marilyn, which only vaguely concerned me. Maybe she was at another doctor's visit. Old people get sick a lot, and Marilyn had grown old. We'd known each other since we were kids. We'd been friends, lovers, fiancées. I've been told that when I rose as a vampire, she was there, standing over my grave crying. I don't remember any of it, but it must be true, 'cause she's been with me ever since.

She's the one woman I've ever really wanted to turn, but she's always said no. Something about her immortal soul, which is odd, since she claims to be an atheist. The real reason is probably a secret. All Marilyn's secrets are safe from me. I can't even make her tell me what she's getting me for Christmas. When she dies, I'm pretty sure I'll go crazy, but only time will tell.

I looked around the room, soaking up the atmosphere. Sarah was doing an uninspired bit of stripping while Kelly and Lillian worked the tables. Talbot stood off to the right of the stage. There were a lot of people in the club for a Wednesday. I glanced at my watch and realized it was Saturday. Damn. My sense of time was getting worse. I think that's why Marilyn bought me a watch that displayed the time, date, and day of the week. Talbot headed my way and I headed back the way I'd come, straight toward the nearest exit. Talbot was big, black, bald, and too well dressed to be a bouncer in a place like mine.

The Demon Heart was no dump, but it didn't pretend to be anything it wasn't. Clean but faded, it was the kind of club that looks better in dim light. The outside still looked like a department store, which is what it had been, I guess, back when the Pollux was open across the street. I'd had the interior redone in red, black, and chrome. It reminded me of a 1950s burger joint gone wrong.

Talbot sped up to catch me and I let him. It would look a little silly to run away from my own employee, wouldn't it? Even if that was exactly what I wanted to do? I was ashamed of what I'd let happen and I didn't want to face it yet, not until I'd eaten, maybe not even then.

He reached me just as I started down the hall toward the back door. "Tabitha didn't come up to help open the club," he said abruptly.

I turned to look at him and couldn't say it. "Hire someone else," I snapped, instead. "Get one of the other girls to fill in for now."

He waited for an explanation and I just stared at him. Figure it out, damn it! Talbot has been with me for close to twenty years. By now, I expected him to know when the boss has fucked up. Then I saw it in his eyes. The bastard knew exactly what had happened. He just wanted to make me say it, to watch me be uncomfortable, the bastard.

"I fucking turned her last night, okay? And I'm too hungry to snack on anyone here. I'd drain them down too far and I don't want to have to deal with a dead body in the club tonight, so get back there and keep an eye on her for me. If she wakes up before I get back, you can damn well feed her yourself!"

His brown eyes turned green for a moment and his pupils narrowed into slits. Cats' eyes. He took a couple of breaths and his eyes turned back to normal. I usually knew not to goad him like that, but I was fucking up so consistently that I didn't want to interrupt my streak.

"I can do that, sir," he rumbled. Then he smiled, regaining his composure. "I was just talking to Roger about a rumor he heard . . . supposedly a vampire killed a werewolf three blocks from here . . . around dawn . . . down at Thirteenth and Eleventh Avenue."

"Good for him," I growled.

"He said that was where Lillian picked you up last night. Is that so?" Talbot asked.

I didn't remember. It sounded right. "Maybe." I sighed.

"Rumor also has it that the dead wolf was important to his pack," Talbot added.

I looked away for a moment and rubbed my eyes. I could feel the beginnings of a nice happy migraine coming on. "How important?"

He pursed his lips and made a whistling noise. "Pretty darn."

"Yeah, well, that's just wonderful! With my luck, it was the fucking Alpha."

He laughed. "Actually, it was William's eldest son."

"William's the Alpha?"

He nodded.

"Shit."

Enjoying my dismay, Talbot continued, "The van cleaned up well, but the Hummer will be in the shop for a while."

"Sell it for scrap," I said harshly. "I don't even know why I let Roger talk me into buying it."

Talbot has one of those infectious laughs that can make anyone laugh in return. It didn't work this time, maybe because I felt he was laughing at me, at the mess I'd made. When I didn't share in his amusement, Talbot grimaced. "What else are you not telling me, Eric?"

I waved him off and walked out the door. My Mustang was waiting for me. Even though Ford didn't make a distinction between the 1965 and the 1964½, I could tell. I'd bought it new in late April 1964, and had it loaded with options. I don't know if it was the first vehicle with a power convertible top, but for fifty-four dollars and ten cents, I'd said hell, yes. That Mustang was the first car I ever owned that had an air conditioner.

I ran my hand along the long blunt hood and grinned from ear to ear, picturing the 271 horsepower V-8 engine underneath. I understood why Roger wanted me to get used to a new car. The Mustang couldn't last forever, but I wouldn't let it go yet. Marilyn's first time was in that car. They don't make cars like that anymore.

"Hey, asshole," Roger shouted from the club's rear door. That I hadn't sensed him only slightly surprised me. The first and second tier of vampires can sense each other when they come into range. Roger's second tier, a Master. I'm a Vlad and a Vlad trumps a Master. My not sensing him meant that he'd been within my range before I woke up. Technically, I must have sensed him in my sleep, but since it was Roger, it hadn't woken me.

He was dressed better than me, as usual, but he looked harried, every hair out of place. "I just heard that guy who owns the Demon Heart turned another one of his girlfriends last night."

"What a prick," I said dryly. If Roger was trying to cheer me up, he was going about it the wrong way.

"Tell me about it." He walked over to the car, thoroughly enjoying pissing in my Cheerios. "I hear he crashed his new Humvee, too."

"Sounds like a real fuckup. What do you want, Roger? I'm hungry."

"I hear he's eating out tonight."

"I figure I'm on a roll . . ."

". . . so why not let it ride?" he said, finishing my sentence. The last time I could remember Roger being all buddy-buddy like this was in Vegas. We'd hit it big, or I had, and I'd taken care of his losses, paid for the whole damn trip, actually. Roger's always happier when he's spending someone else's money.

"You want to come with?" I asked.

He shook his head no, the prospect unthinkable. "Look, buddy, I know it's not my place to say—"

"But you're going to anyway." That drew a smile, but not the friendly one for which I'd hoped.

"Why don't you go ahead and end Tabitha? Spare yourself a little heartache and get it over with, huh? She's not worth it." It was Roger's same old song and dance. He was right, of course, but that didn't mean I wanted to hear it.

"Speaking of girlfriends," I said, "are you still fucking Froggy?" It was nasty and I shouldn't have said it, but I wanted him to go away. If he didn't want to be teased about having a girlfriend vamp who could only turn into a frog, he should know better than to start poking at me and mine.

Besides, I needed to eat. No vampire is hungry and nice. Nice and hungry, sure, but . . .

"Look, just hunt away from the club tonight, okay?" he said.

"I was planning to."

"Oh, you were planning?" Roger smirked. "Where were you planning on going then, if I might ask?" He emphasized *planning* like it had air quotes around it. Still, I'd asked for it, by mentioning Froggy.

"North Side," I blurted.

"Any particular spot?"

"I'll figure it out when I get there."

"Right, 'cause you're so good at winging it. Why don't you come inside and drink some blood from the fridge, just to take the edge off? The way you look, you might go all Black Out Boy any minute and—"

"'Bye," I said brusquely. I slid into my Mustang and started her up, gunning the V-8 before peeling out toward North Side. I don't normally hunt over there, but I craved a change of pace and it was the first place that had come to mind when Roger asked.

A vampire can get tired of eating the same old people. Tonight I wanted to eat someone upscale who worked out every day and smelled like expensive perfume. By the time I reached the tony neighborhood, my head had cleared a little. I parked my car on the street and began prowling the specialty coffee shops.

I passed up two college students and a cop before I started to get desperate. I had to pick a victim soon or I might not have much of a choice—sheer need would make me grab whoever was closest. Just then a woman in a Jag pulled up and parked in front of the hydrant across from Starbucks, then got out of the car. Her perfume smelled like heaven, and her skin looked soft and supple. Finally. The street was empty for a moment and I dashed out from my spot in the shadows.

Everything dropped into slow motion. I was glad now that I'd decided to hunt away from my normal territory. Basically all vampires are monsters and I'm no exception. I'm not proud of it, and I try to keep myself well fed so that most of the time my prey are spared the worst of it, but bad nights do happen. Feeding was going to be bad tonight and I knew it. Roger might have known it, too. Maybe he'd been trying to help in his own weird passive-aggressive way. I was too hungry to hunt carefully.

She barely knew what hit her. I had her back in the alley and on the ground in the twinkling of an eye. The perfume was expensive stuff: delicate, but arousing. She'd even dabbed a little down below, on the nape of her neck, and between her breasts. Someone called a woman's name, so I leapt to the fire escape, dragging her up to the roof in spite of her struggles. She bit me, which always pisses me off (I'm the biter, not the bitee), so I slapped her. I didn't want to, but it happened. The worse the hunger is, the less time there is for thinking, and the more primal those few thoughts become. The slap dazed her, but she still tried to scream when she saw my fangs. Fingernails clawed at my face, hard and lacquered. I threw her down on the roof and unwrapped her like a Christmas present, shreds of fabric scattering as I ripped and tore.

Her lingerie told me I was screwing up someone else's evening. It was a lacy purple number, expensive and luxurious. She'd shaved her legs for someone who would never know. Some vampires like the jugular, but I prefer the vein at the inner thigh when I'm drinking a woman. Another hunger stirred and I fought it like a drowning man. *No*, I told myself. *Finish it.*

Normally I would have broken her neck first, but right now I wanted the blood hot and alive. She screamed so loud my eyes crossed. I wish I could say she tasted special, but the truth is all blood tastes the same. She bled out in little under a minute. When I was sated, I ripped her head off to make sure she wouldn't rise as a wampyre.

My memory's not great, but I did remember reading about wampyres—they're what happens when a human dies from a vampire bite. Wampyres are mindless rotting corpses that drink blood. They're kind of the black sheep of the undead family, just above zombies.

I dropped her body down a city drain and left her car illegally parked. It wasn't smart, but then again this wasn't my week for smart. In the end, all I'd done was kill her. I'd roughed her up some, too, but as hungry as I'd been, not doing more was a victory. A hungry vampire is capable of anything.

I was willing to forgive myself a little carelessness. Besides, in a town like Void City, you can get away with being careless if you've got the money. Despite the enchantment over the city, most of us take additional precautions. Various flesh-eating types can be brought in for corpse disposal. Some pay to have the norms' memories professionally rearranged, just in case. We can even get a mage or shaman to come in and move along any angry spirits we leave behind. It's a hassle and it costs more than I like to think about. In my case, it would also result in a few hours of listening to Roger bitch and moan about the expense.

No wonder I prefer to eat in.

On the way home, my cell phone rang and I nearly wrecked the Mustang trying to find the damn thing. It was in the car charger. As I answered it, it occurred to me that it would have really pissed me off to wreck the Mustang.

"What?" I spat into the phone.

"Hey, buddy," Roger oozed.

"Yeah?"

"Did Brian tell you where he was headed last night?" He sounded concerned and more than a little weird.

"Fuck Brian," I snarled. "I don't even know why you keep bringing him out with us. If he doesn't learn to keep his mouth shut about the Void City Howlers I'm going to wind up shutting it for"—oh, shit. That was how I knew the headless vampire in the alley's face. It was fucking Brian. Damn it!—"him."

I swerved around on the road for a minute and slammed my fist into the console.

Roger's voice sounded even more distant, and I could hear faint music in the background. "Okay, well, just let me know if you hear from him. He was supposed to meet me here at the Artiste Unknown."

"Fine."

"What?" he asked incredulously. "You wanted to come?"

How the hell had Roger gotten that from "fine"?

"Um, have I even heard of that place?" I asked, trying to figure out how the hell I was going to tell Roger that I'd offed his buddy.

"It's Ebon Winter's club, very exclusive. Vampires have to bring a human date." He paused. "The only place more exclusive than the Irons Club?"

Have I mentioned that my memory is shit? "Doesn't ring a bell, but you and Brian have fun."

"I was supposed to meet him at eight. It is now eight thirty."

"Then I guess he's late." In the corner of my mind, an alarm was going off. I eyed the spotless white truck behind me, but didn't see anything strange about it. I checked all my mirrors, but still saw nothing suspicious. The hairs on the back of my neck stood up anyway and a cold shiver went down my spine. My body thinks it knows better than me whether I'm in trouble or not. It's usually right.

"I don't think so," Roger said, sounding pissed. "You're the only one who ever keeps me waiting."

"Get over yourself." I laughed. Roger certainly had an ego. If I hadn't known him from my living days, there was no way I would have put up with his crap.

I've always thought it was kind of weird that we both became vampires at about the same time. Roger's never given me a good answer about it either. If we'd had the same sire it would have been less confusing to me, but Roger's sire was from Atlanta and we have no idea who sired me. He told me not to worry about it, but I do. Marilyn tried to explain it away once. She had this whole sob story about Roger being distraught over my death and arranging his own; she seemed to believe it, but I didn't.

In my rearview mirror, the same spotless white truck was pacing me. A red truck pulled up beside it. Same make, same model, same year . . . my alarm kept going off. I shifted my attention from Roger's past to the present. "Look, he's probably just running late. I'm sure he'll show up. Why don't you go on in and have a good time. I've gotta go."

"Why? Have some other important werewolves to piss off tonight? Watch out for William, by the way. I hear he's not your average fare."

"What do you mean?" I asked, trying to sound nonchalant while keeping an eye on the trucks in my rearview mirror.

"He's supposed to be a real badass, one heck of an Alpha." Roger covered the phone for three or four seconds and then continued talking. "He's probably as hard to kill as you are. You'll have to use blessed silver, the whole nine yards."

I told him to go screw himself and hung up before I meant to, but he deserved it. This wasn't really my fault. If the werewolf from last night was so damn important then he should have been wearing a doggie collar and a tag. And he should have been warned not to hunt vampires so close to my club.

Before I could decide what to do about my suspicious tailgaters, my cell phone rang again. As soon as I said, "Hello?" the shit hit the fan. Another truck, a black one, pulled off of a side street and swerved to a sideways halt in front of me. The other two trucks sped up and rammed me from behind, knocking my Mustang into a skid.

I spun sideways, smashing into the truck in front of me. My Mustang flipped up and over. Metal scraped on concrete as it cartwheeled down the street. Loud music was coming from the cell phone. As the car rolled, I was dumped unceremoniously onto the concrete (seat belt anyone?) and the cell phone flew out of my hand. Through the crunching death knell of my Mustang, I still managed to hear Sheena's whiny voice. "Boss, did Veruca say anything to you about coming in late, or taking the night off? Oh, and Talbot said to warn you . . ."

4

TABITHA:

MIDWIFE

When I awoke in Eric's bed, the first thing I felt was hunger. I was also cold, colder than I'd ever been. Nothing felt right. Noises were too loud, my skin felt too tight, and there was a really strong odor. It smelled like crotch. I realized Talbot was standing over in the corner. I snarled at him without meaning to, and suddenly my gums felt like they were on fire. The sensation was a cutting, jabbing, tearing feeling. I fell off the bed and smacked my head against the floor. That hurt, too.

I was on my feet again in an instant. The pain left, but my mouth still felt strange. Frightened, but excited, I ran my fingers along the inside of my mouth and there they were—fangs! Oh my God! He had really done it. I was a vampire! I looked back in Talbot's direction; he was still there, silently watching.

Low, thumping, and filled with what I needed, Talbot's heart called to me. All other sounds faded into the background, a distant buzz. Talbot's features blurred until I recognized him only by his scent. I'd always thought Talbot was human, but no human could have a scent like his, tangy and wild. His skin grew semitranslucent and I don't know if it was an illusion or not, but I seemed to be able to see the blood coursing through his body. It wanted out. I wanted in.

So I charged him. Surely Eric wouldn't mind if I ate Talbot. Eric loved me and I was hungry. Thoughts that were not mine warred in my brain. Thinking rationally hurt. I didn't need to think, I needed to feed.

I can't eat Talbot, I told myself unconvincingly.

Of course you can, I disagreed. *He's food.*

No . . . he's . . . I wasn't even sure it really was Talbot now; his scent was gone, replaced with an odor that I couldn't describe. It was what food smells like, what blood smells like.

Talbot lashed out with his right hand and knocked me to the floor. I reacted instinctively, trying to scratch him, bite him, anything that would draw blood. He just laughed. God, how that pissed me off! Faster than I could understand, he was on top of me, straddling my thighs. One hand was on my throat and the other was on my chest pushing me down. He was so warm. My emotions went wild. Images passed through my head that would have made me retch the night before. I wanted him. I wanted him inside me and at the same time I wanted to rip his throat out. I wondered if I could have both if I was on top.

I don't know how long it took me to recognize the sound of my own name, but from the look on Talbot's face he'd been using it for a while. I opened my eyes, not realizing that I had closed them, and saw fresh scratches on his face. He was holding both of my wrists in one hand above my head while he squeezed my throat with the other. I was writhing and bucking under him trying to get free. He was surprisingly strong. I could smell his excitement; the scent mingled with that of the blood pumping through his veins . . . so close, just under the skin. I think I started screaming then, because he tightened his grip on my throat and told me to stop.

"One more scream out of you, Tabitha, and I don't care how put out Eric will be, I'll abort this little experiment. Now please try to be quiet. My hearing is better than yours and you're hurting my head. I'm going to feed you."

I went still, but I was keening. I think that's the word for what I was doing. I couldn't help it. I was so hungry. "I need it," I gasped. It was hard to speak with him choking me.

"I know you do." He sounded almost sympathetic. "But you have to be a good girl, or I really will kill you."

Staring at the slight trickle of blood running down his cheek, I strained to try and reach it with my tongue, even though his face was a foot or more from mine. I was vaguely conscious of a stream of babble coming from somewhere, as I stared at the blood. Someone was offering to perform a string of sexual acts ranging from simple to wild to outright depraved. Then I realized I was doing the offering. I would do anything for blood, or at least promise anything. I made myself stop. I hadn't expected it to be like this.

Talbot's light brown eyes turned green; the pupils became slits again. I remembered walking outside the lion cages at the zoo, the smell of the great cats. That was the smell of him. Shock flooded me at the realization he wasn't human, but then I was overcome by new images, dead lions, me crawling naked in their blood, lapping it up on all fours.

I shuddered in revulsion. "What's happening to me?"

"You're a vampire, princess, just like you wanted. You ever read 'The Monkey's Paw'?"

I shook my head. My books were about vampires, not monkeys. My sister had been the bookish type, not me.

"Why am I not surprised?" He laughed. I kept expecting his eyes to change back. They didn't. Instead, I watched fangs grow in his mouth, uppers and lowers, different than Eric's and mine. Ours were uppers only. Talbot's fangs looked like an animal's teeth had grown in, replacing his canines. It was hard not to keep staring at the blood on his cheek.

"Here's how this is going to work," Talbot said. "I'm not going to release you until I can trust you not to go into a feeding frenzy. . . ."

His voice faded away as I turned my attention to the door. Outside I could smell more blood. I could hear it calling me. There was a heartbeat to go with it and another smell, a bathroom smell that was dreadful. It reminded me of the women's restroom when I'd worked retail. Those women had been real skanks, but this smell was worse. My nostrils flared and I curled my upper lip. Another delicious heartbeat joined the first, but it brought with it even more yucky smells: age, smoke, and something else, something that reminded me of a hospital . . . some kind of sickness.

Talbot slapped me. I tried to bite him, but his hand was off my throat and back on it before I could react.

"Smell bad?" he purred. I nodded. I started keening again in spite of myself. So hungry. "I bet I smell pretty good, don't I?" I nodded again. I was having thoughts about Talbot that I'd never had before. If I could have put those thoughts on film I was pretty sure a whole lot of horny guys would have ordered it on pay-per-view. Talbot shifted his grip from my throat to the top of my head and slammed it into the floor two quick hard times. I saw stars, but I tried to bite him anyway, so he did it again. Dazed, I simply lay back and waited for what would happen next. I'd be damned before I let myself cry in front of him.

"It's simple, Tabitha. Marilyn and Desiree are each outside with a pint of blood. They are going to come in one at a time and feed it to you. It will be cold."

I began to shake my head violently. "No. Hot! I need it hot! I want it from the vein. Let me rip their throats open. We can share. I can drink them and you can fuck them—or me if you want. You can take me from behind and—"

"Shut! Up!" Talbot screamed and I tried to cover my ears. It was as if a gun had been fired next to my head. My ears rang. I thought he'd deafened me. I realized I was crying. The tears came rushing out and I couldn't stop them. As I cried, I could smell more blood, and I knew it was coming from me.

"Where's Eric?" I whined. "I want Eric! He'd feed me. He wouldn't let you do this to me. Let me go! When he finds out what you're doing—"

Talbot shouted again and all I could do was cry harder. Bastard. Didn't he know how it hurt? Couldn't he feel how I needed warmth as badly as I needed blood?

"Eric knows what I'm doing. He sent me in here to feed you because all it would take is one slipup from him and you'd be one short-lived little vampire. You get two pints of blood and you get them cold because if you had it warm you'd lose control of yourself and I might have to kill you in self-defense. Two pints ought to dull the pain and clear your head. Then I can educate you a little and answer your questions, but here's the thing. You have to keep the blood down and you have to drink both pints. Once the hunger starts to fade you're going to want to stop drinking, but you can't. I need you to have both pints in you so that you'll have a little self-control. Okay?"

I nodded. Two pints? God! Give me three pints. Give me a gallon! Let me drink the whole bar, every patron. Two pints. Ha!

Talbot called for Desiree and she came in. The smell of her grew stronger. She really did smell like a bathroom stall that needed cleaning. I realized that she must have just finished a set, because a sickening sweet smell of sweat and deodorant rolled off of her in waves, but as she drew near, the scent of the blood overwhelmed all of that. It wasn't that it smelled good or bad, it was just blood and blood was what I needed more than any junkie has ever needed any drug. My muscles strained as I tried to pull free of Talbot to get to the blood.

Desiree kept walking. In her hands, she held a blood bag. It moved back and forth, almost hypnotizing me as it bounced gently from side to side with the rocking motion of her strides. Talbot must have been giving her instructions, but I couldn't hear them. Everything, my entire being, was centered on that pint of fluid. She knelt next to Talbot and opened one end of the bag before placing it over my open, eager mouth. I barely even tasted it. It didn't matter that it was cold or what type it was, all that mattered was that I needed it.

Before I knew it, I was finished with the bag and Marilyn was walking in while Desiree was hurrying out the door past her. Marilyn looked even more fragile than she had when I had last seen her. Her skin was wrinkled, her gray hair was unkempt, and she was wearing the same old-woman clothes she always wore. Her glasses made her eyes look huge and I could hear her labored breathing and the not quite steady beat of her heart. She smelled like smoke and I coughed as she came near. She gave me a disapproving look.

"You were so afraid of dying that you had him do this to you?" She shook her head, then attached one end of some IV tubing to the blood bag. Unlike Desiree, Marilyn seemed practiced at this. She knelt next to me and gently slid the tube between my lips like a drinking straw. She wasn't afraid at all, but I did notice that she was careful to keep her fingers out of reach. As I sucked greedily at the tube, she took a handkerchief from her pocket and began to wipe the bloody tears from my face. "Are you in love with him?"

A growing calm spread out from the center of my body, slowly moving through each limb, filling me, sating my thirst. It had nothing to do with Marilyn's words and everything to do with the blood. My senses seemed to dim slightly. Smells were still strong, but more bearable. I could still hear the beating of Talbot's heart, but it was a faint rhythm, reassuring in its presence.

Slowly, I began to notice the taste and texture of the blood. Before, I'd needed it and it wouldn't have mattered if it had tasted like battery acid. It wasn't bad, but it wasn't good, either; it reminded me of milk, but with a strong copper taste, sort of like sucking on a penny—a cold penny. It certainly wasn't the grossest thing I'd ever put in my mouth, and it definitely wasn't my first taste of the stuff. Vampire boyfriend, remember? I kept drinking and Talbot smiled at me from behind friendly brown eyes. Whatever he'd been expecting, I'd proved him wrong.

When I was done, Marilyn stood back. Talbot was still on top of me and I finally noticed that I was naked, on the floor, being straddled by a large man who was noticeably excited. Oh my God. I tried to cover myself and Talbot laughed as he let me up. "Oh, so now we're modest," he said jovially. "After all the things you were just offering to do to me?"

I expected myself to blush, but nothing happened. I rushed over to the closet, grabbed one of Eric's shirts, and ran into the bathroom. I looked into the mirror and saw nothing. I gasped. I should have expected this; I knew it would happen. But somehow it's different when it's you.

Marilyn opened the door behind me, carrying my underwear and one of my dresses. "You look better than ever, Tabitha," she said sadly. "You'll just never be able to look in the mirror for reassurance. You might find your clothes are a little loose."

I got dressed under her watchful eye. The silence was uncomfortable. "I'll just have to watch Eric's reaction to see how good I look now, I guess. It won't be so bad."

Marilyn shook her head and left the room. Dressed but shoeless, I followed her. "What? Is there something I don't know? Did something happen to him?"

Marilyn ignored me, walking out of the bedroom and shutting the door behind her. Talbot was leaning against the door frame with his arms crossed over his chest. "What's her problem?" I asked him.

"One thing you need to know about Eric, Tabitha. I've known him a long time and I know you think that this is going to be some wonderful eternal love thing, but I've seen this happen before and odds are—"

"Odds are?" I asked.

He let out a long breath before continuing. "Odds are he'll ask you to leave."

What? That wasn't possible. Talbot was playing some sort of sick game with me. My fangs came out and so did his. They didn't hurt as much the second time. The sensation was more of an uncomfortable distension combined with a jaw-popping feeling that was nowhere near my jaw.

"I love him," I said. "I would do anything for him. I did this for him, so that we could be together."

Talbot's voice was calm and steady like a judge delivering a death sentence. "I've only ever known Eric to love one woman, Tabitha, and she just walked out that door."

"Marilyn? But he can't even sleep with her," I argued. "She's old! She's nothing. I'm forever young. Look at me. I've got the body of a goddess. I can do things to him now that no human woman could ever imagine."

Talbot just stared at me. I tried to convince myself that he was lying, but there was a look in his eyes that wounded me. It wasn't sadness, but a look of familiarity, like he'd heard it all before and some of it twice.

"Did Eric ever say he loved you?" Talbot asked finally.

"No," I whispered.

"What did he tell you when you asked?"

"He . . . he would . . ." I could feel my lower lip begin to tremble. Whether it was rage, sadness, or despair, I didn't know. Maybe all three.

"He would say I was a moist warm tightness with all the necessary parts." I was crying again. Talbot turned away.

"One thing about Eric, he doesn't hide his feelings. If he loved you, he'd have told you." As he opened the door, Talbot looked back. "I'll be right outside when you're ready to learn the ropes."

He left me alone and all I felt was the cold.

5

ERIC:

DEAD CAR

They'd killed my Mustang. It lay on its back in the road, a dead metal cockroach leaking oil and antifreeze onto the asphalt. One of the wheel covers rolled across the road, the three-pronged center of the simulated knockoff hub blurring like a propeller until it hit the base of a streetlight with an insulting clang.

The trucks skidded into a circle around the Mustang, completely blocking off the intersection. Two men stepped out of each truck. As I watched, long lupine claws pushed out through their fingernails and their human teeth dropped to the ground. The werewolves' muzzles flowed forward, fangs bared. I'm sure they meant the display to be impressive, but it still looked to me more like bad special effects. At least they weren't all the same generic brown as Wolfy from the alley. These six must have come out of the variety pack; there were two gray, two black, and two that looked more like werehuskies than were-wolves.

"So which two are the Cool Ranch?" I asked. They charged at me, and I fought for control. The red tinge to my vision faded even as I popped my fangs. This was important. I wanted to remember killing the bastards that had murdered my Mustang.

The two gray wolves were a little faster than the others, so they reached me first. I caught one by the muzzle, flinging him across the intersection and through the glass front of an antique shop. The shop's burglar alarm sounded as the other guy sank his fangs into my shoulder. I wondered if there was a little werewolf handbook that insisted the shoulder was the best place to bite a vampire. It hurt like an old wound, a remembered pain.

The werewolf I'd thrown into the storefront recovered quickly and raced back to help his partner. When he ripped my belly open I definitely felt it, but I know what it's like to be engulfed in flame and staked through the heart. In comparison, this was nothing. Pain is fleeting for the undead. Our nerve endings don't work the same as those of the living. The initial damage registers, but unless the weapons are blessed or something, the ache doesn't last.

As the fight went on, I gained a little more respect for their methods. They worked well together, a real team. It made me miss fighting alongside Greta.

"You assholes know you can't kill me, right?" I tightened my grip on the muzzle of the gray that had gutted me and listened to his teeth crack. He kept right on tearing into me with his claws and his buddy kept chewing on my shoulder.

They wanted me to scream or beg for mercy, but it wasn't going to happen. The injuries didn't annoy me that much. Vlads heal quickly and I heal quicker than most, but healing is hungry work and it did mean that I would need to feed again before dawn.

I planted a foot on each of the grays' chests, but before I could try to push off, the two black werewolves joined the fray and grabbed my legs. Still, I was winning, not the fight against the werewolves, but the fight against myself. The more I reined in my anger, bit it back, choked on it, the more I realized that I needed to talk to these guys, to see if I could stop this before it got even more out of hand and I was facing down twenty or thirty of them.

Just then two more werewolves showed up in another matching truck. The werewolves that got out of it were brown. "You two must be the corn chips," I told the newcomers. They didn't get the joke, but one of the huskies hovering on the sidelines chuckled. I guess the huskies were the Cool Ranch.

"Do you have anything to say for yourself, vampire?" asked one of the black-furred pair.

I considered trying to bite the gray to get him off of my shoulder, but I answered the question instead. "Yeah, take me to your leader." Once again only the huskies seemed to get the joke. Maybe my humor was too old. "Seriously, I want to talk to your Alpha . . . Willard or whatever his name is." I sighed. "Why else do you think I'm not turning to mist right now?"

Actually the real reason I wasn't turning to mist is that I couldn't, didn't know anyone who could. Animals, yes. Mist, no. I'd tried it once and instead of turning into a cloud, I'd gone translucent blue like Obi-Wan Kenobi in *The Empire Strikes Back*. It had felt like dying, all the life-force draining out of me, the world changing colors, blurring. Turning back had been hard, too. It had taken the better part of an hour, and once my body finally re-formed, I promised myself never to screw around with it again.

Roger was the only one who'd seen me do it and we'd both agreed that I shouldn't try it again. "It looked like you almost died, Eric," Roger had told me. "I'd be scared of getting stuck that way."

I shuddered at the memory and came back to the present. Eight pairs of eyes stared at me from unconvincing giant Harryhausen-esque wolf heads.

I tried talking again, but this time I spoke slowly and clearly. "Will you take me to your Alpha? Maybe we can work something out." I felt a sharp blow to the back of my head.

"What the hell are you doing back there?" I asked angrily.

Two more whacks and my vision blurred; out of the corner of my eye, I saw the stake. It wasn't one of those fancy things with a real weapon grip like proper vampire hunters use. A long jagged splinter jutted out from a mahogany spindle with a dark finish, like someone had snapped the stretcher off of an old rocking chair. Either these guys didn't usually hunt vampires, or they weren't used to taking prisoners. As the stake arced toward my chest, I tried to transform.

I didn't care what I turned into: bat, cat, snake, rat, frog, wolf, or raven. I can do them all, which is unusual. I even managed a flea once. The problem is that changing into anything takes concentration, and I didn't have any to spare.

My other option was to just give in to my anger and let myself go berserk. But going berserk would mean more dead werewolves and I needed to keep the body count down if I was going to find a way to make peace with the Alpha.

Before I could think up Plan C, someone hit me again. My vision stretched and the lights went out as I felt the stake slide home. You learn something new every day. My lesson for today was: If you knock a vampire out before you stake him, you can drag him around in the back of your new pickup truck and he won't know what's happening.

Even in my unconscious state, letting them beat me grated on my nerves. I should have been able to take them. It's not like there was a full moon or anything. I know myths and legends talk about werewolves going crazy and eating people during the full moon, but as far as I can tell all the full moon does is make them bigger and meaner. I can't ever remember which one is waxing or waning, but the moon looked like a sideways grin, so I figured these boys were at about half power.

I decided to enjoy the nap. My night was fucked anyway. I'd already lost my Mustang. I didn't want to lose anything else. Fighting were-wolves isn't like dealing with vampires. They travel in packs. The idea of two dozen werewolves tearing through the Demon Heart wasn't pretty. If they had me, then they'd leave the club alone; they'd leave Marilyn and Roger and Tabitha alone.

If I was lucky, they'd do what I was hoping and actually take me to their Alpha. Maybe we could work this out. I'd probably killed his son; he'd definitely killed my Mustang. It was an even trade from my per-spective.

I don't know how long I was out, but my world came back in a sud-den rush of pain. I swear stakes hurt worse coming out than they do going in. I was in a bag that smelled kind of like feathers, but there was flannel and something synthetic there, too. A sleeping bag. Cute. A ragged hole gaped in the bag over my chest where someone, one of my captors, I guessed, had ripped it open to remove the stake. I wasn't on fire, which meant it was either still night out or I was in a covered area someplace.

I fumbled with my watch, finally managing to hit the right button. A soft blue glow showed the time as 03:03, just after three in the morn-ing. Still dark.

Fangs and claws at the ready, I ripped my way out of the sleeping bag and looked around. Pickup truck. Parking lot. Woods. The smell of water filled my nostrils. It smelled clean . . . untainted . . . no chlorine. There was no sign of whoever had unstaked me.

It was extremely dark . . . a real look-out-behind-you kind of dark, perfect for vampire vision. I took a few minutes to explore my sur-roundings. Crickets chirped loudly, a distant frog splashed down into lake water, and somewhere out in the night an owl hooted. The gravel lot was almost full of cars and trucks. A small building off to one side smelled like it contained a couple of poorly maintained restrooms. A concrete boat launch sloped gently down to the lake, and a set of con-crete steps led down to a little marina where thirty or forty boat slips served as a waterside parking lot. There were only a few boats parked at the moment: a couple of pontoon boats, a speedboat, and a rickety-looking fishing boat made of aluminum.

Dense woods covered the lakeshore opposite the marina and I could only make out one house, old but in good repair, its short wooden dock poking out into the lake, a moored pontoon boat bobbing gently with the natural rise and fall of the water.

I remembered this place. It was called Orchard Lake. My family used to come out here when I was a kid. It was part of the county water supply, not exactly a state park, but a public lake. The homes were only accessible from the water; the absence of boats at the marina meant most of the residents were home.

Far to the left of the marina, Orchard Dam kept the lake fat and happy. It also kept all that water from destroying the expensive developments that had sprung up downstream. Below the dam, only a little creek tumbled away through the woods, while the lake itself ran some fifteen miles in the other direction.

Orchard Lake was old, a sprawling gem tucked away in a pocket of forest and mountains, slowly being encroached upon by overpriced suburbia. Sable Oaks, Greymont, and Harvest Estates bordered the Orchard Lake area, but none of them came within a mile of the lake itself. The lake homes were older houses, passed down through the families of blue collar workers, real salt of the earth folks.

Back when we were alive, every time we'd get a little plastered, Roger would talk about how he was going to be rich one day and buy up Orchard Lake. He wanted to turn it into a hoity-toity community for rich old farts and politicians. A lot of people had the same idea. Over the years, countless developers had tried to purchase the land, but nobody would sell. The news always seemed to show the same old guy claiming, "My grandpa built this house with his own two hands," and refusing to give in even at outlandish prices.

I shook my head to clear it, wondering where the werewolf variety pack had gone. It was three in the morning. I'd been out for six hours or more, and Orchard Lake was only an hour or so from town.

"Hello?" I called out. Silence.

Why go through all the trouble of ambushing me only to unstake me in an abandoned marina and run away? Clearly, I did not understand the modern werewolf. All four trucks could be accounted for amid the other vehicles. Gravel crunching under my feet, I scouted the place a little more.

As I followed the drive down to the boat launch, the scent of gunpowder and blood drifted over to me from the nearby woods. Werewolf blood. I followed the smell up and over the half of the mountain that the parking lot hadn't claimed and found the werewolves easily enough.

They'd been cut to ribbons, dead for at least an hour. It was worse than what I'd done to the werewolf in the alley the night before. I was pretty sure there were enough pieces to make most of eight werewolves.

Just to check, I sifted through the bodies, stacking the heads in a neat little row. Two of them had obvious bullet holes. One shot had been close range to the temple; the fur was badly powder burned. Not the most pleasant of smells. The second one had been shot through the back of the head, and I didn't see an exit wound.

Morbid curiosity got the better of me and I cracked the skull open. The bullet wasn't hard to find; I just followed the trail of blackened gray matter from the back of the skull to where the bullet had lodged in the side of the frontal bone, above the nasal cavity and between the eyes.

I'm not a big gun person, but the bullet looked weird even to me. On *CSI* when they pull the bullet out of a dead guy it looks like a little metal rock, but this one looked whole, casing included.

My brain was fuzzy and my head hurt. *Concentrate*, I told myself. Each werewolf's body had long jagged claw marks, and one had had his heart ripped out. Aside from the bullet wounds, the werewolves looked like they'd been torn apart by a vampire. It would look even more gruesome in daylight, when the remains reverted from wolf form to human.

I leaned in closer, examining the wounds. They looked familiar. Damn. Resting my hand atop one of the ragged cuts, I extended my claws. They weren't quite a match, but they were close, and now the whole area probably smelled like me, too.

If not for the bullet holes, someone might have convinced me that I'd blacked out and done it, but I don't own a pistol and these boys hadn't been killed with vampire claws. Now that I was suspicious, I could find bullet holes in several other body parts. No more bullets, though.

I'd been framed.

Unable to discern anything more from the bodies, I walked back down to the boat launch. Brains and blood washed off of the single silver bullet I'd retrieved, leaving it looking bright and new. It was warm to the touch even after I cleaned it off in the cool lake water. Little markings glowed faintly in the dark.

Magic bullet. Bodies cut up to look like I did it. . . . But why go through all the trouble to dig out the other bullets and leave this one behind—unless I was supposed to find it? I put the bullet in the pocket of my jeans and knelt by the water. *Somebody doesn't want me and the Alpha werewolf to kiss and make up, but they don't have the nerve to kill me themselves.*

It didn't particularly bother me that the variety pack had been killed, but something in the back of my head (my brain, maybe) was telling me that I'd been outsmarted. Someone had figured out that I would go with them to try to see Willard or Wilbur, or whatever his name was, and had arranged this mess to ensure that didn't happen, taking a fucked-up set of circumstances and boosting them to a whole new level of suckage.

That meant it was political and possibly out of my league. But I did know a guy who might know a guy. Roger knew all the bigwigs in town, the annoying seedy little assholes who pretended to be royalty.

I reached for my cell phone before I remembered it was littering the street back in Void City. By my watch, I'd wasted forty minutes wandering around the parking lot. For once, I remembered the sun. I did not want to be caught hiding in the restrooms here if the pack managed to locate their buddies, and it was over an hour's drive back to Void City.

There were no keys in the truck and I've never learned how to hot-wire a vehicle. Unless I absolutely had to do it, I didn't relish the idea of breaking into one of the lake homes; too many windows, no base-ments. There had to be a gas station around here somewhere. I might be able to make it to a pay phone. Maybe Talbot could drive out here and pick me up before dawn. It wasn't a good plan, but it was the best I had.

I made it halfway up the mountain before I realized I'd make bet-ter time flying than I would on foot. Orchard Dam Road was a wind-ing curving thing and the shortest distance between two points . . . I concentrated on what it was like to be a bat. To the observer, it's pretty quick, but to the vampire doing it, transforming into something that small is painful. It's like having cold-water shrinkage so bad your testicles retract, taking refuge in the pelvis.

Some vampires leave their clothes behind when they change. My daughter is one of them. I'm not. My clothes folded in with me as I sprouted leathery wings and launched skyward.

Bat radar gives me headaches, so I rely mostly on my bat vision. Bats have good eyesight at long distances, so it wasn't too bad. I felt very cold, though. A smaller body meant the cold went to my core faster, and even though it was a sultry summer evening at ground level, it's always colder in the air.

The trees stretched out below me as I flew, heading south to avoid crossing too close to Sable Oaks. County Road 58 was hard to miss, but every time I tried to cross it, something interfered with my senses, making everything hazy and wavering. I don't know if it was residual heat from the asphalt or what, but it was bad enough that I stuck to the forest edge.

A few miles down the road, I had a thought, and if I'd had a human throat, I'd have cursed. As it was, I made a little squeaky irate bat sound. Who the hell had unstaked me and where had he gone? How had he gotten far enough away to escape my notice in the time it took me to rip my way out of a sleeping bag? It didn't seem to make sense.

6

TABITHA:

VAMPIRE 101

Halfway through the lesson, I was having a hard time listening to Talbot. We were over in the Pollux Theater across from the club, alone. I loved every inch of its elaborately detailed elegance, from the real velvet of the curtains to the leather-covered seats to the sweeping balconies and carved balustrades.

There was no orchestra pit. I sat in the front row only a few feet from the wooden stage, a massive structure that appeared to be about three feet high, though I knew there was a whole basement underneath, still filled with props and pieces of scenery, and a little room where the pipe organ was stored when it wasn't onstage.

It wasn't that I didn't want to know how the whole vampire thing worked; it was more that I couldn't get a handle on Talbot and it was driving me crazy. I'm a focused girl. I set a goal for myself, a man I want or a dress or whatever, and I go out and do what it takes to get it.

Talbot was driving me nuts by refusing to do one simple thing. He was leaning casually against the stage in front of me, and I knew he must have had a good view from there, but no matter what I did, I could not get him to stare at my breasts. I'd never tried when I was alive because I didn't want to lead him on, but now that I was a vampire, it was like my brain had been restructured. My thoughts were still mine, I hadn't exactly stopped being me, but there was a predatory urge coloring everything.

I'd assumed it would be hard getting used to people as food, but it wasn't. The best way I can describe it is that it's like dreaming. You're in the center of a little make-believe universe. Everything around you is for your amusement, pleasure, or dismay. Nothing you do in a dream has any real consequences. For me, that was how being undead felt.

The red tones in the Pollux's velvet curtains were vibrant even though I knew there was a layer of dust covering them. The wind blew through the air ducts with a musical tone so distinct that I would recognize it anywhere. Talbot droned on, but his words weren't important. I watched his eyes, his skin, his pulse, and inhaled his scent.

Finally, he stopped trying to explain whatever it was he had been talking about, stalked up to my seat, and put his big hands right over my breasts. "If I stare at these will it make you pay attention to what I'm saying?" He jiggled them briefly as he spoke and then let go.

I was mortified. Had I really been that obvious? "Because," he continued, "I could do that, but I want you to know right now that neither you nor any other human is of any interest to me in that way."

So he was a pervert, a real pervert. I wondered what exactly he did like. Sheep? "Wait a minute," I protested. "You were really excited back in the bedroom. That wasn't fake. I could smell it, not to mention the way you were poking me with that thing."

Talbot laughed. It wasn't a mean laugh, more like he'd just heard a hilarious joke, but it felt mean anyway. I don't like to be laughed at. My fangs came out. It was only the third time, but it already felt natural. There was the same stretching jaw-popping feeling, but it was a good sort of hurt. I hissed at him, and he grinned crookedly at me. "Let's just say that it's a dominance thing. You were trying to get away and you couldn't. I like that. It's perfectly natural for one of my kind."

"Are you a were-something?" I asked. It was hard to believe he wasn't human. Then again, it wasn't like I paid close attention to any of the guys here, other than Eric.

"No," he answered. "Now listen; we aren't here to learn about me. We are here to learn about your new lifestyle. Your unlifestyle. You with me?"

I nodded. I knew that I could get him to tell me what he was eventually, or maybe get Eric to tell me. It was simply a matter of time.

"What," asked Talbot, "is the last thing you remember?"

"You told me about the whole mirror thing, which I'd pretty much figured out. You said I should stay out of sunlight, which I already knew. You covered the garlic thing and holy symbols, blessed weapons, and not getting my heart or head ripped out, off, destroyed, or whatever. That pretty much covers what I heard. I don't remember what was last. It all ran together."

"Okay," Talbot said. He slipped back into lecture mode, and I tried to pay attention this time. "The number one thing to remember about being a vampire is that the biggest threat that you have is yourself. When you feed, try not to kill anyone. The best way to do that is to eat before you get too hungry. The more ravenous you are, the harder it will be for you to control yourself. If you don't want to act like you did earlier, when you were totally out of control, don't skip meals.

"If you do kill someone, then remove the head or the heart to keep them from rising as bloodsucking zombies. Eric calls them wampyres because he's read too much crap on the Internet, but they're just zombies.

"Don't get sloppy. When you kill a human, you have to dispose of the body or have it done for you. It costs twice as much if the city has to take care of it."

"Costs more?"

"Void City is vampire owned and operated. The Council of High Magic makes them use guild mages for most disposal services, so they get a nice tidy kickback every month. It drives the prices up.

"What else? Oh, if one of your snacks comes back as a ghost, tell me or Eric about it. We'll get Magbidion to move them along. He's cheaper than a guild mage and he's pretty good at keeping under their radar. In addition, ghosts are less likely if you destroy the corpse completely. Don't get caught and don't leave any evidence behind.

"Eric does a piss-poor job of getting rid of bodies, which is one of the reasons that he likes to eat in and one of the reasons he keeps Magbidion around. Eric tends to eat a little bit from several different people and he tends to prefer his employees. You already know that, but what you don't know is that once you start feeding directly from the vein, it gets hard not to drink it all at once.

"Blood bags are good, if you don't mind it being cold or room temp. Eric usually feeds that way once or twice a week. Most vampires loathe cold blood. Eric doesn't and you don't seem to have that issue either, which puts you one up on a lot of them.

"You can even try animal blood. Eric can't drink it, his body rejects it rather violently, but most vampires can and some do so exclusively. If you choose to feed by killing people, Eric will be likely to make you leave sooner than he might otherwise. You may notice that he breaks his own rules. I wouldn't suggest pointing the double standard out to him. He already knows.

"For the first few months you may feel like you have to go to the bathroom. Don't. The phantom sensations will fade more quickly if you don't indulge them. Some vampires do continue those functions because it makes them feel more normal, but all that comes out is blood and it's better not to waste it that way. You may also have bouts of panic when you feel like you're suffocating. You don't have to breathe anymore, but your mind can and will play tricks on you. After all, you're used to breathing automatically and it can be disquieting once it sinks in that you only breathe when you consciously think about it."

Feeling a little bit like I was back in high school, I raised my hand. "When do you get to the powers part?" I asked when he acknowledged me. "I mean, I know I still need to know all this other stuff, but I should be able to do cool stuff, too. What can I do?"

I don't know how to describe Talbot's look. He clearly disapproved, but there was something else in his eyes that made me feel there was more to it. "That kind of attitude can get you killed, but to answer your question: I don't know. Eric has a lot of powers, real Dracula-type stuff. He's a Vlad."

"Vlad?"

"Vamps come in four flavors: Drones, Soldiers, Masters, and Vlads. They used to be called Serfs, Knights, Barons, and Kings." He hopped up onto the stage, pacing back and forth along the very edge. "Remind you of anything?"

"Should it?"

"It should remind you of the feudal system. Vampire society is slow to change, but as time goes by the names get updated by the new recruits."

"So Eric is like a king?"

"It's not literal. It's a classification of power levels. Vlads have all the powers in the book and tend to keep coming back no matter what you do to them, just like Dracula."

I knew my Eric was special . . . and as the offspring of a King, I should be special, too. "So that makes me a Queen, right?"

"It has nothing to do with bloodline, and everything to do with personality, the strength of an individual's character. I've always thought of it as a supernatural Rorschach test."

"Then what am I?"

"I don't know," Talbot said, hopping off the stage and landing adroitly on his feet in front of me. "You'll find out, in time, through experimentation. Roger could tell you for sure. He's a Master."

"A master of what?" I smirked.

"A Master vampire. Masters and Vlads can sense each other, tell who is who. Vlads can also announce themselves to other vampires, kind of like a psychic challenge, but it's rude, so even if you are a Vlad, you don't want to go around announcing yourself."

"Can't Eric just tell me what I am when he gets back?"

"You'd think so," Talbot said, "but a sire can't usually sense his offspring's power level."

"Why not?"

"I don't know. I didn't make the rules. What I know mostly comes from what I've observed with Eric. In some areas, I'm just as uninformed as he is. Thralls are a good example. I know very little about them other than that they are humans that serve vampires and that Eric refuses to make one or to allow his offspring to make them. For now, though, let's only worry about the basics."

I looked him in the eye to show I was paying attention, but I think he took it the wrong way.

"Don't try to mesmerize me either. Vampires can't entrance c— my kind."

"I wasn't," I protested.

"No harm done, but be careful looking other vampires in the eyes unless you trust them. As Melville said, 'The eyes are the gateway to the soul.' With vampires, he wasn't kidding."

"So I can take over people's minds?" I giggled.

"You can," Talbot replied, "but a human with strong will can resist you and a vampire with a stronger will than yours can take you over instead."

I yawned. I didn't care about Talbot, didn't want to be with him, didn't need to know this stuff. I wanted Eric. I did try to listen as Talbot began to lecture on what he called "the second biggest threat to vampires," but visions of Eric filled my mind. Despite what Talbot and Marilyn had told me, I had to see him. Even more so, I needed him to see me.

Marilyn had been right about my clothes feeling loose. After I'd been fed the cold blood and Talbot had left the bedroom, I had wound up borrowing clothes out of Amanda's trunk. Amanda was a charity case who'd overdosed on crack about a week before I'd moved in with Eric, and no one had ever come to claim her things.

She'd had this whole black leather temptress thing going on and she'd been frighteningly thin. I dug through her outfits and put together an ensemble I thought Eric would go for. It wasn't all that revealing, but it was what I call a highlighter outfit. What it didn't show, it highlighted and underlined. I was wearing it now. Since it was made for the stage, it came off in sections and I could barely wait to see which parts Eric would want to take off and which ones he would want to leave on. Kelly and Desiree had both assured me I looked sexy beyond belief. They had also helped me with my hair and makeup; I already missed mirrors.

Even the thought of Eric made me tremble in a way I hadn't been sure that I would be able to as an undead. I ached for him. He could say all of the terrible things he wanted about me and claim I was nothing more to him than a sex toy, but I knew the passion he showed when we were together, the way he needed me, the way he sometimes just held me close for hours.

If Eric didn't love me, then why was I the only one he took into his bed? Candice wanted him and I knew he wanted her, but he had never been with her. He was faithful. Sure, sometimes he would have me dress up as other women, now and then even call me by their names, but that was just his way of spicing up the bedroom.

All guys have fantasies, and Eric held none of them back from me. He trusted me with all of his darkest urges and most of them I was happy to fulfill, even if a few of them were a little nasty. Eric loved me, he had to love me, and what he'd said didn't matter.

"Anyone who says otherwise is a liar!"

It dawned on me that I had spoken that last sentence aloud. Color was slowly bleeding back into my vision, replacing the red tint that I hadn't even noticed until it started to fade. My fangs were out and as I looked down at my hands, I could see that my fingernails were longer than they had been. They were sharp and a little curved at the ends, like claws or talons. My skin had grown even paler than before, virtually a true white. Someone was growling. It was me. A rapid drumbeat pounded in my ears, throbbing.

Talbot clapped. "Well, now we know that you have claws, you can make your eyes glow red, and you haven't been listening to a word I've been saying unless you really do agree so vehemently about the third biggest threat to vampires."

I nodded. "Yes . . . I mean, no, I wasn't listening." As I calmed down, I noticed that I was standing up and that the pounding in my head was Talbot's heartbeat. My claws retracted into fingernails again. It felt much weirder than the fangs had, the physical equivalent of the sound fingernails make on a chalkboard. My vision returned to normal, too, although my skin tone didn't. Interesting. "I'm sorry, Talbot. It's just that I want to see him. I need him."

"I know you do," he said softly.

"He does love me," I insisted.

"I hope you're right, little girl." In an unexpected move, Talbot put his arms around me and gave me a hug. The warmth of him encompassed me as if his heart beat inside my own chest. I fought the urge to sink my teeth into his flesh, but it was one of the hardest things I'd ever done. The hug must have lasted less than a second, but when he stepped away I was trembling. He looked into my eyes and I saw what I thought was compassion.

"Very good. You pass."

"Pass?" I asked, confused.

"Do I look like a touchy-feely guy to you?" His eyes went slit-pupiled again and he roared at me, his bestial fangs looming large and dangerous between his jaws. This time he flashed claws, too, curved feline things, sharper than mine, with needle-thin points. His other smell resurfaced, too: jungle cat musk. "If you'd bitten me, I'd have ended you and told Eric you were too stupid to keep around."

"I'd like to see you try," I shot back with more defiance than confidence.

"I'd succeed." He chuckled and let his features become human again. "I don't know why I'm trying to impress you. I've been human-oid too long." He sighed abruptly. "We'll pick this up a little later. Why don't we see if we can round you up another couple pints of blood and then you can experiment with your powers."

I nodded and followed him back across the street to the club. Powers. I'd show him powers.

✦ 7 ✦

ERIC:

LITTLE SISTER

Dawn was beautiful. The fiery tendrils of morning crimson bathed me in their warm glow. The sun, with typical brilliance, cast its loving gaze in my direction. Had I been alive, I would have turned to face it with joy, or more likely put on my shades to prevent my usual hangover from getting worse. Either way, I wouldn't have fallen out of the sky and into the woods on account of it. I told you my time sense sucked. Admittedly, being ignited two mornings in a row was a bit unusual for me. It wasn't my record—there had been a really strange week in El Segundo—but it was unusual.

Flailing my fiery bat wings wasn't helping the situation, so I turned human again as I fell. Strictly speaking, I suppose I should have been naked since I'd certainly been a naked bat, but it never works that way for me. I re-formed with all my clothes on just before I hit the root system of an oak tree. Fortunately for me, the trees would keep me shaded from the sun until it rose higher . . . a couple of hours, at least. My eyes started to close and I shook myself awake.

Shit like this never seemed to happen to vampires in the movies. Where were my vampire groupies, my loyal henchlings? Where was fucking Renfield? I didn't want to break into anyone's house, but I didn't want to be burned to ash, either.

There were other options. I could hide under a car, or in a doghouse, or in a mailbox. I could dig a hole and bury myself, technically, but what I really wanted was for Talbot to somehow sense that I needed him and to come pick my burnt ass up and take me home.

I walked through the woods, grateful that I lived in the South, where civilization and forest intermingle from the mountains to the beach. Lots of subdivisions extended right into the woods. Through the trees up ahead, I could see a long line of houses, the leading edge of suburbia.

It had recently become highly fashionable to cut down as few trees as possible; in some areas, contractors built sidewalks and even porches right around existing trees. This subdivision was older, but at least the contractor had let the trees run right up to the property line of the houses, especially where the natural slope of the terrain made building a little more difficult.

One guy was starting his car on my side of the street in the shadows while a woman was doing the same thing on the other side of the street in full sunlight. There were people in the houses. I could sense them. Some were asleep and others were waking, showering, getting ready, brushing their teeth. There were two people still in the nearest house, the one the man had just left. Both of them sounded female, one younger than the other: a mother and daughter.

I moved from house to house along the shady side of the street, concealed by the trees. The houses were all two stories, most with vinyl siding, and each house had somebody home.

I looked at my watch. It was 6:50 on a nice Sunday morning. Didn't any of these assholes go to church? Back when I was alive, it had seemed like I was the only one who didn't go to church on Sunday. How long had this been going on? What time did church service start now? Eight o'clock? Nine? I couldn't wait that long; the sun would be really most sincerely up and this whole stupid subdivision would be bathed in light.

I started toward the closest house, even though it had a family of four inside, but the same strange vibe I'd gotten last night, the odd discomfort that kept me from flying across the county road, repulsed me. It wasn't the same feeling a blessed house gives off, it was something else, and it almost had a smell, like badly burned toast. It could have been anything, an amateur mage, a botched breakfast attempt . . . I was too tired to figure it out.

Through the haze, one of the houses suddenly looked perfect. It smelled like freshly baked cinnamon rolls, and the aroma drew me closer nearly against my will. I'd never liked cinnamon rolls in life, but this was intoxicating, almost as much as pizza. If I'd been a cartoon, the scent might have lifted me off of my feet and carried me along.

The wooden privacy fence was short enough to jump and there was an obliging shade tree that completely bridged the gap from fence to garage; only one person was home, plus the house had blacked-out windows in one of the second-story rooms. An amateur photographer would have just the sort of room I could use as shelter until Talbot could come pick me up.

The door to the garage was locked. Rather than force it, I turned into a mouse and crawled under the space between the garage door and the concrete. I turned human again on the other side and looked around for a light switch. The garage smelled of old gasoline and bagged grass. Despite the noxiousness of the smell, I felt a twinge in the back of my throat. I was getting hungry. In the warmth and humidity of the garage, I caught myself falling asleep again. Being exposed to the sun by a goofball with a garage-door opener didn't sound like fun to me, though, so I shook myself awake again.

I usually go to sleep a few hours after dawn, but I can make it to early afternoon if necessary. Once or twice I'd managed to stay up all day, but each time, I'd passed out at sunset and slept clear through to the next one.

The bulb blew when I tried to turn the lights on. I had almost been expecting it. It was the way things had been going since Friday night: one big fuckup after another. The inside door was locked. My foot did a pretty good job of opening it before I remembered that I was trying to be sneaky. Upstairs I heard a girl sit up in bed. It sounded like she was grabbing something off of the floor. "Mom?" she cried out. "Dad?"

"Nope," I said under my breath. "Not quite."

I heard footsteps. Hungry though I was, I didn't want to eat this teenage kid, home alone on a Sunday morning. Wasn't she supposed to be watching cartoons? Or was that Saturday? The door from the garage opened up into a little eating space adjoining the kitchen. I sped across the linoleum and into a sitting room that had been converted into a home office. Hanging blinds over the bay window were all that stood between me and an instant sunburn. A small stream of sunlight scorched my leg where one of the blinds was askew.

Where to hide? I considered my options quickly, racing the footsteps overhead. There were no good hiding places. I could smell her now. Her scent was familiar, somehow, and afraid. She also smelled a little excited, which got me a little excited, too, but if I wasn't going to kill her, it was unlikely that I was going to force myself on her either.

I'd always thought vampires turned into black cats, but it never seemed to work that way for me. Slowly but surely she came down the stairs. A white long-furred kitty waited for her. Of the various creatures I could turn into, it was usually a good bet that the cat would get the most sympathetic reaction. She came around the corner, saw me, and shrieked. Now, what kind of person is afraid of cats?

She was a beautiful girl, dark haired, with smooth skin and bright green eyes. She looked like a younger, more attractive Tabitha. She was wearing a white tank top and panties. Despite the baseball bat in her hands, I was noticing things that I shouldn't have been. And then I recognized her. She was the girl in the battered photo Tabitha carried in her purse. I cursed in whatever language it is that cats speak and turned into myself again.

She froze, midscream. "So," I said casually, "you must be Rachel."

She cocked her head to one side and began slowly backing away from me. "I'm Eric," I offered lamely. "Your sister's boyfriend?"

She stopped and looked at me. Her fear was subsiding and I smelled something that it would have been better if I hadn't. Was Tabitha's whole family a big mob of vampire junkies? I wondered what would happen if I got Tabitha, Rachel, and their mother all in a room together. It was yet another image to be added to my internal wall of shame. Did all men have thoughts like these? If so, why wasn't I smart enough to keep them to my subconscious?

Roger had once told me that all I had to do if I wanted to rule the world was keep my mouth shut, my pants on, and my temper under control. "What about sunlight?" I'd asked him. He'd laughed at me and said that if I was strong enough to rein in the first three things, he was pretty sure even sunlight wouldn't be a problem for me.

"Holy shit! And you really are a vampire? What are you doing here? Is Tab with you?" Rachel asked. She'd gotten closer to me in the brief moment I'd been lost in thought. I shook my head, backing toward the door.

She continued to walk toward me and I considered running out the front door and into the sunlight. She had the same look in her eye that Tabitha had had when she'd first approached me at the club. Maybe one of the other houses had a pack of werewolves in it or a few vampire hunters . . . something safe. Anything but this. My eyes were glowing against my will and my fangs had dropped down in full-on vampire munch mode. She should have been running away at this point. Instead, she was taking off her tank top. She was certainly pierced in interesting places.

Closing my eyes, I fought back either a yawn or a snarl. I could not eat, sleep with, or otherwise enact upon Tabitha's sister. Even though I couldn't see her anymore, her scent still plagued me. There hadn't been any cinnamon rolls in the oven when I'd passed, yet their tantalizing aroma mingled with hers. What was I doing here?

With supreme effort, I mustered enough concentration to turn back into a cat. Lower to the ground, I struggled to keep my gaze on her ankles. A low rumbling echoed from my chest. I was purring at her. Damn it.

Sunlight was beginning to reach the side windows of the house, so I darted past her and up the stairs. She yelped as I brushed by her in transit, and if cats could smile, I would have. Now all I had to do was figure out a way to call Talbot and explain my situation without being the jumper or the jumpee with regard to Rachel.

My memory really sucks, but even so, I knew that I had never encountered this kind of problem in my living years. What was it about vampires that attracted these women? Surely they couldn't all be necrophiliacs. When I'd died I had been in my thirties. I didn't remember much, but I did recall that I hadn't been particularly handsome. I wasn't Quasimodo either, but . . .

Focus, Eric. Drowsiness was making me punchy. I skidded on the hardwood flooring at the top of the stairs and slid into the wall. Rachel sprinted up the stairs behind me. A phone and a door, that's what I needed.

Mom must have been a great housekeeper, because I couldn't smell anyone but Rachel. Everything else smelled new. Maybe they'd just redecorated?

Photographs of Rachel, Tabitha, and their parents lined the hallway in cheap frames, plastic that was meant to imitate wood. I passed the bathroom in my mad feline dash down the hall. There were two bedrooms upstairs, one with a "No cats!" warning symbol and the other with a two-drink-minimum sign.

I surmised that the second room might have been Tabitha's and darted toward it. Changing back to human form felt like coughing up the world's largest hairball, but without thumbs, I couldn't turn the doorknob. I vaguely remembered Tabitha having told me once that she spray-painted her windows black when she was a teenager. They must have been the windows I'd noticed from outside.

"Thanks for not scraping the paint off the windows, Mom," I muttered. Rachel reached the top of the stairs as I closed the door behind me and locked the dead bolt. I hoped she didn't have the key. Why had Tabitha needed a dead bolt on her bedroom door? Rachel slapped the door with a perturbed grunt, then her footsteps disappeared back in the direction of the stairs.

Tabitha's room was done in black and crimson. No wonder she liked the color scheme at the Demon Heart. She had crosses mounted to the walls and a blacklight bulb hung in the overhead lamp. Little Goth dolls lined a shelf on her wall where I still laughably expected a teenage girl to have wooden horses, old Barbies, and pretty glass knickknacks.

It looked like Tabitha had cleared out all of the stuff she really wanted and left the junk she didn't want for her parents to throw away. That sounded like the Tabitha I knew. When I saw her queen-size bed, piled with fluffy black pillows, I almost went to sleep on it. Instead, I slapped myself a few times. I heard Rachel's footsteps pounding back up the stairs. Either she was quicker than I thought, or I'd just spent a minute or two staring into space.

Phone! There didn't seem to be a phone. In one corner, I saw a huge pile of books and an empty cordless phone charger. All the books appeared to be about vampires. That explained a lot. I heard a key in the exterior lock on the dead bolt and leapt for the door. It was impossible that Rachel could have been fast enough to open it before I could reach her, but it happened anyway. There was probably a fancy psychological term for it, but the only way she could have been faster than me was if I subconsciously wanted her to be faster. Then again, maybe it was just sleep slowing me down.

She was still topless and determined. I tried to ignore her body heat. The warmth of her as she entered the room called to me almost as much as the blood coursing through her veins. I had just healed from major injuries and I needed blood. I needed a phone. I needed Talbot. He could make things simple. He could handle things. That was his job. I needed Marilyn to slap my face for me and tell me to control myself, to act like the man she'd agreed to marry. Every time she told me that I wasn't a monster, for a few minutes, a few hours, I wouldn't be.

I grabbed Rachel by both arms and pulled her against me. She was afraid, but willing, just like her sister. I threw her down on the bed and straddled her thighs. Shifting my grip, I trapped her arms above her head. She leaned up and we kissed. Her tongue was pierced. Roger once told me that it's always the younger sister that you have to watch out for. He must have been talking about girls like Rachel.

"I need . . ." I struggled to find the words.

"I need you too, baby. It's okay. I want you." It was her turn to purr.

I pictured Rachel lying cold and dead on her sister's bed or worse, rising the next night, like her sister had, only eighteen instead of twenty-three. It was enough.

"What I need is a telephone," I managed.

"After," she whispered. She turned her head to one side. "Drink first. I want to feel it. I want to feel the pleasure and the pain."

"I need to use the telephone. I need to call the Demon Heart and have someone come pick me up." I was proud of myself. Total control was mine. I could resist the young woman underneath me. She started kissing me again. Her breath smelled like those cinnamon buns they sell in the mall. Her heartbeat filled my ears and then I did the only thing that I could think of that would keep me from doing exactly what she wanted me to do. I fell asleep.

8

ERIC:

PRICE TAGS

When I woke up, I was in the back of the party van. The party van had two seats up front and two benches along the sides in the back, with heavy shutters separating the driver from the people in back. It had originally been a paddy wagon, but I'd bought it a few years ago and had it fixed up to suit my needs.

The shutters were adorned with crosses. It wasn't anything that would keep a vampire at bay for long, more of an attention-getter to help jar me back to my senses in case I was ever out of control. Talbot had also replaced the rear doors with windowless ones. The other additions we'd made included a good air conditioner and a stereo system.

I realized belatedly that I was not alone. Rachel was in the back with me; my head was resting on her lap. I don't know what it is about the hour or two of sleep that I get each day, but I wake up hungry, much hungrier than I am after twenty some-odd waking hours. Combined with the hunger from before, I didn't stand a chance against it. Rachel was going to get bitten whether I wanted it or not.

Faster than humanly possible, she found herself on the floor of the van as I spread her legs and bit into her femoral artery. As soon as I started drinking, I was trying to stop. Rachel's fear was real. It made things harder to control. It was obvious to the thinking part of me that she had expected it to feel good. Why anyone would expect puncture wounds to feel good is beyond me, but I'd been around long enough to know that the pain often takes humans by surprise.

Fighting the hunger is like being in a wrestling match with a bigger, badder version of yourself; like getting a starving man to slowly sip broth a little bit at a time, only the starving man is ten times stronger than you and at least twice as mean.

I tried to hear Marilyn's voice in my head. *You are not a monster. You are the strongest man I know. When you rose for the first time, I was standing right there and you didn't touch me. Roger himself told you that a newly risen vampire has no self-control. If you could control yourself then, you can control yourself at any time.* Over and over, I repeated it in my head like a mantra.

I still don't remember rising. Marilyn has told me the story, but I don't remember doing any of it. According to her, I rose in full daylight. She was standing over my grave, but I did not attack her. I stood there for a minute in the sunlight, thick black smoke pouring off my exposed skin. Then, I took refuge in the cemetery's chapel. When she followed me inside, I supposedly said, "Am I late for something?" and passed out.

My memory has been like Swiss cheese ever since. I've always blamed it on having been embalmed. Sometimes I forget what happened yesterday, or five minutes ago, but just then, for a moment, I remembered what it was like to control myself. I remembered the calm and ease of my early days as a vampire. I remembered a different me, just long enough to take my teeth out of Rachel and hold her close.

"That was so fucking incredible," she gasped weakly, "and it hurt so fucking much! Holy shit!" She laughed as I held her. The danger was lost on her. She wouldn't believe how close she had come to death, or maybe she didn't care. I shouldn't have cared, but I did. I knew Rachel. I had a connection to her, through our kisses, through her sister. If I murdered her, she wouldn't be a faceless woman who died in the night, soon forgotten. Knowing the victim makes it more real, makes it harder to forget, and I damn sure don't want to remember.

By the time we got to the club, Rachel was sleeping. Talbot gave me the hairy eyeball as I carried her out of the van, under the awning into the club's rear entrance. Marilyn met me at the door. She looked and smelled old, but if I half closed my eyes, let my vision blur, I could almost see her like she used to be, the red-haired vixen on the motorcycle.

My Marilyn stared at me from behind a mask of age, her hair cut short and grown gray, the once luscious lips dry and stern. Her eyes were the same, though, blue as an ocean and every bit as tempest tossed. Old as she had become, I still wanted her as badly as I had on the day I'd died, but she wouldn't have anything to do with me, not like that, not since my death, not once.

She studied the girl I was carrying. Rachel looked like a trollop in her hip-huggers and white tank top. There was a bloody rip where I'd bitten through her jeans. The blood was making the material stick to her leg. "Who is that?" Marilyn asked.

"It's Tabitha's little sister," I said, handing her to Talbot. That was all I got out before Marilyn slapped me hard across the face. "She . . ." I let my voice trail off as she slapped me again.

"For heaven's sake, what is the matter with you?" she yelled. The pain was nice. It was nice to receive any physical sensation from Marilyn. Not only had she refused to sleep with me since I'd become a vampire, she rarely touched me. A psychologist could have probably written volumes regarding what that said about my getting into trouble. They'd say I was like a child who did bad things to get my mama's attention. Maybe they'd be right.

I caught Marilyn's arm when she tried to slap me a third time. It was something I'd never done before. "The third slap is foreplay, M," I said. It didn't even sound like me. It was half growl, half scorn. "Unless you're up for it, I suggest you leave it to the younger ones." I let go of her arm. She winced.

Talbot stepped between us and inwardly I thanked some higher power for small favors. "Where's Tabitha?" I asked.

"She's in your bedroom," Talbot answered. "She's a late riser. Most vamps rise early on their first night and she didn't get up until eight. She went to bed a full hour before sunrise. She's looking at maybe eight or nine hours of wakefulness a night; more if she manages to break schedule."

My short daytime sleep requirement often got me twenty hours or more out of a day-and-night cycle. Maybe I could put up with her for eight hours a night. Maybe not. I checked my watch. It was nine in the morning. I walked back toward the rear entrance and gestured with my head for Talbot to follow me. As we moved past Marilyn again, I could feel anger coming off of her in waves. No fear, though, just anger. When I knew she couldn't see my face, I grinned. "That's my girl," I whispered.

"We're going to spend the day over at the Pollux," I told no one in particular. "Have someone bring Rachel orange juice and a big breakfast."

"I'll take care of it," Talbot said gruffly. As he fell into step behind me, carrying Rachel, he mumbled something else under his breath. "In for a penny . . ."

No shit, I told myself. *No shit.*

If Tabitha was going to sleep until eight this evening then I had eleven hours to figure out what to do about Rachel, not to mention the damn werewolves. The notion that I was forgetting something rolled around in my head. Talbot helped me get Rachel back into the van and across to the Pollux without incident.

Of the two movie palaces that had once been in Void City, the Pollux was the only one still standing. The Freemont may have been a little more stylish, but it had been turned into a parking deck twenty years ago, so I guess the Pollux won. The projector still works and I own a large collection of old films.

I'd kept the original glass entryway, even the old-fashioned central ticket booth, but beyond that, the new doors were reinforced steel, well-decorated, but secure. Beyond the doors, the foyer was still brightly lit by the original crystal chandelier, its glow magnified by the mirrors lining both walls. Rachel took in my absence of reflection without comment, paying more attention to the chandelier.

I'd moved several of the couches and tables from the downstairs lounges to the lobby, creating a sitting area for guests. Rachel plopped down on a burgundy velvet sofa and stared up at the painted art nouveau ceiling. A grand marble stair led up to the mezzanine and my offices.. There were more offices and some dressing rooms behind the stage, but I only used them for storage.

"You like it?" I asked.

She nodded. "It's awesome. How do you afford it?"

"I get by," I told her gruffly. "Guys like nudity and I don't waste much money on groceries." How long would it take Talbot to get breakfast? If he went to Jackie's on the corner, he could be back in ten minutes. I didn't want to be alone with Rachel for much longer than that.

"If you're thirsty, the soda fountain still works. I only keep the Coke and the lemonade refilled, though. Everything else will get you water. I tried to put in a blood dispenser, but it clogs the machine."

Rachel watched me with smug contentment. She had just opened her mouth to speak when my rescue arrived. I could smell the food before Talbot opened the door. He was early. I don't pay him enough.

Muscling past the steel doors, Talbot backed into the foyer, carrying two covered breakfast plates. The scent pulled at my stomach. I craved breakfast only slightly less than pizza. One plate had scrambled eggs, crispy bacon, and a side of hash browns. The other had two fried eggs (sunny-side up), link sausage, and cheese grits.

"Rachel, isn't it? Do you like your eggs scrambled or fried?" Talbot asked.

"Which does he like?" She asked the question with purpose. To a vampire, that question is a signal, a sign that the woman he's with knows a little about vampires. Talbot remained valiantly smirkless, but he noticed.

"You'll want this plate." Talbot sat the tray before her, poured some orange juice in a glass, and laid a straw across the top. "I think I'll take my breakfast at the club," he said, walking right back out the door with the other tray of food. *Bon apéritif.*

Bon apéritif. Happy before-dinner drink. Fucking Talbot. I pay him too much. I wanted to protest, but the words stuck in my throat. In the split second I'd been distracted by Talbot, Rachel had taken the lid off of her tray, picked up one of the sausage links and commenced licking the grease off of the underside. For lack of a better word, she nearly fellated it.

"Less sexual, more sensual," I corrected. A rookie mistake most women make is equating eating to sex. For a living, breathing man, that would be correct, but for vampires it isn't about sex, it's about the food . . . about what we can't have and watching someone else have it. In polite circles, they call it voyeuristic dining, but food porn is more honest.

Criticism made her nervous. Each bite came a bit too quickly and her *mmmms* and *ahs* sounded forced. She had raw talent, though, and unlike Tabitha, she didn't forget that I was watching her. She purposefully let little beads of egg yolk gather at the corner of her mouth, then asked me to wipe it away. When I did, she seized my wrist, sucking the egg yolk from my finger, peering up into my eyes for approval. Long after the yolk was gone, her tongue danced along the bottom of my index finger, the curious stud on her tongue providing an erotic counterpoint to the softness of her flesh. It felt strange and wonderful. I approved.

After breakfast, Talbot sauntered back in and cleared away the dishes. For me, the next quarter hour passed like time-lapse photography. I didn't think there'd been cinnamon in any of the food, but I certainly smelled it. Maybe it was a breath mint or a new perfume. Talbot and Rachel blurred around me, politely avoiding each other in an elaborate dance, while I sat perfectly still, trying to remember whatever it was I'd forgotten. The image of Rachel sucking a little drop of golden egg yolk from my finger haunted my thoughts, making it harder than usual to think straight.

"I killed Brian," I said suddenly.

"What?" Talbot and Rachel spoke in unison.

"Brian. You know; the guy Roger met through that real estate thing, the one who was always talking crap about the Void City Howlers, trying to start a fight. I don't remember exactly what happened, but I think I ripped his head off."

"Rage blackout, huh?" Rachel asked.

Talbot and I both looked at her funny. "How the hell do you know about my rage blackouts?" I asked.

She laughed and rolled her eyes. "Sorry. I guess everyone who knows anything about vampires in this city knows about your rage blackouts." Her pulse quickened, but I couldn't decide whether she was lying or nervous.

"She's got you there." Talbot walked over to the door. "I just want to know how you're going to break it to Roger. He and Brian seemed pretty tight."

"Yeah, well, Roger isn't renowned for his choice of acquaintances," I said, "present company included."

"Depends on what you're looking for in a friend," Talbot countered. "He certainly attracts the powerful, wealthy, and influential. Present company included." He added that last bit with a mocking nod. Talbot had a smirk on his lips and he cut his eyes toward Rachel as he left. "I'll be across the street. Call me if you need anything."

Rachel squirmed under his gaze. As the door closed, she seemed comfortable again. Too comfortable. "What are you going to do about the werewolves?" She slunk toward me and the vibe was suddenly very different than it had been with Tabitha. This wasn't about sex. I could smell that sex was an option, but this was something different. She was teasing me, flirting with me, manipulating me.

"So . . . you know about the rage blackouts and the werewolf fiasco. You're pretty well informed."

"I'm just lucky." She moved close to me. I couldn't help but notice that her breasts were nearly touching my chest. "I heard some of your employees talking about it." She closed the gap between us. "That's okay, isn't it?"

It was more than okay, but more because of how she was touching me than the answers she was giving. She could read me better than Tabitha ever could and we'd known each other less than a day. She was extremely dangerous, a very good liar. She hadn't heard my employees talking about the werewolves; she couldn't have. I reminded myself to be careful.

"You're standing a little closer than I think your sister would approve." I took a step back, mentally applauding my fortitude.

She put a hand on my chest and I found myself staring down her tank top.

"You like it," she said, following my gaze.

"She wouldn't." I pushed her hand away.

"No, Tab would be mortified. If she even knows what mortified means," Rachel said.

"Look, what's going on between me and your sister is complicated and I'm not sure I want to complicate it any further than it—"

"I know," she said, "you're trying to be a good boy, but if you want a girl who really gets the whole vampire thing, who can give a vampire everything he wants and make him go all weak and kitteny . . ."

"That would be you?"

She nodded again.

"Not interested." Now I was lying. I decided to give Rachel the benefit of the doubt. We all lie sometimes. Maybe if I were a eunuch, I mused, things would be easier.

I left the seating area, passing the old refreshment stand as I crossed the lobby. At the top of the stairs, to the left of the mezzanine access, a long hall led to a row of offices. She followed me to the stairs. I held out a hand behind me to stop her. "No one comes up to my offices uninvited."

"Can I send somebody home to get my clothes?" Rachel asked. "Do you have any movies?"

"Why don't I just get Talbot to take you home, period?" That was my first good idea of the night. "Won't your parents be looking for you?"

She laughed. "Not likely."

I turned to face her. "If I were your dad, I'd be worried sick."

Rachel moved in close, too close, and kissed me. "Don't stress over it." I wasn't supposed to be kissing her back, but I was. Maybe it was the perfume she was wearing. Something about the cinnamon smell made me want to keep her around. Sure that was it. It was the cinnamon. It had nothing to do with my desire to throw her on the ground and tear her clothes off.

"Let me worry about my parents," she said, pulling away briefly and rubbing at her thigh where I'd bitten her. "I'm still kind of sore. You should at least let me hang out for the rest of the day."

"Fine," I said. "Get one of the girls to take you shopping. Tell Talbot I said it was okay. I don't care what you spend. I just don't want one of my employees having to explain to your dad why they need to pick up a change of clothes."

She squealed; I turned into a bat and flew up the stairs. I was showing off for her. It was not a good sign.

9

ERIC:

DAMAGE REPORT

Sitting at my desk with a small stack of notes, I looked at the bricked-up windows and shook my head. The first two notes were from Talbot. One said that Carl needed to know what to do about the Mustang. He hadn't done a complete assessment yet, but most of the interior looked salvageable. The rest of the car was a mess and Carl's best guess was that repairing it wasn't worth the effort or the money. Talbot noted that he'd told Carl to protect the interior of the car, and to start looking for replacement parts, but to do nothing further without calling first.

His second note was attached to a clipping from that morning's *Void City Echo*. The headline read "Local News Anchor Found Dead in Sewer." I *would* have had to drop my victim down a drain someone was going to start working on in the morning. Her name had been Evelyn Courtney-Barnes. Lots of people were going to miss her, blah blah blah.

The third note was from Roger telling me that he'd given Veruca the night off again and asking me to get Tabitha to cover. Veruca. Veruca. It took me a moment to recognize the name, because I always called her Froggy. She was Roger's girlfriend. She could only transform into one creature: a frog. Her other vampire powers were fine, but it seemed to piss her off that all she could change into was an amphibian. According to Roger's note, she might need the next several nights off. I wondered if this was some kind of payback for me having turned Tabitha . . . making my vampire girlfriend work so his wouldn't have to.

The last note was an invitation to a hockey game, though, also from Roger. For the last decade or so Roger and I hadn't exactly been bosom buddies. We didn't hang out much anymore, and when we did, he almost always brought some new friend or other along. Lately, it'd been Brian.

Our business relationship hadn't been much better. Roger had been big in real estate when he was alive. Now that he had more time, I think he aspired to be an undead Donald Trump. Roger always picked what stocks we would buy and how much of each we needed. He'd made us both rich men. He had also been the one who'd figured out how to transfer our wealth back to ourselves once we'd officially died.

But time changes things, and it had certainly changed Roger. I knew he didn't like the way I was running the club, though I'd noticed it didn't stop him from taking payouts from the register whenever he needed petty cash. My guess was that the whole operation made him look bad to his high society buddies. I kind of missed the way things had been between us. Maybe he did, too. On the other hand, I'd just whacked his buddy Brian . . . and it was probably Brian's ticket to the hockey game that Roger was offering me.

Stacking the notes to one side of my desk, I looked around my office. Except for the modern conveniences, it looked like it had jumped fully formed out of *The Maltese Falcon*. The door in the outer office had my name stenciled on it in nice black letters. The secretary's desk was vacant. Sometimes when I was working I'd have Tabitha come up and sit at that desk. I'd have her run errands for me to and from the Demon Heart. I could have used the telephone, or even e-mail, but I liked the illusion that it created. For a time it let me pretend that the world was still the same place where I'd once walked in sunshine, a world in which area codes were new and there were some numbers that you just couldn't dial without operator assistance.

"What the hell am I going to do?" I asked the room. I put my head down on my desk like I was a little boy in school and the teacher was mad at me. I wasted an hour or more that way before I noticed the burning sensation in my pocket and remembered the bullet.

"Son of a bitch." I picked up the phone and the number for the Demon Heart went right out of my head. I could remember the first three digits, but the last four . . . well, I knew it had a six in it. One quick flip through the phone book later, I called over to the Demon Heart.

Roger answered, but I wasn't in the mood to talk to him. Having ripped his friend's head off and lied to him about it made me a little uncomfortable.

"Get Marilyn on the phone," I said brusquely.

"She's kinda busy, Eric," Roger snapped. Why was he being so bitchy lately? Was all this really over the damn Froggy crack? Was this my fault? Maybe I should go to the hockey game after all.

"Look, just get her on the phone," I answered.

"She's not here because you broke her arm, tough guy." He sounded so smug about it that if he hadn't just invited me to a hockey game, I'd have walked across the street and wiped the accompanying look off of his face. "She's old and fragile. You can't just push her around like that. She didn't want you to know, but she's gone to the emergency room."

Cursing, I hung up on Roger. Sometimes it seemed like Roger was closer to Marilyn than I was. Then again, maybe that was a good thing. Why did she even stay around a guy like me? Couldn't she see I was dangerous? I told myself that what happened was her fault, that she shouldn't have slapped me. I was lying to myself again. I wondered if I'd ever get any better at it.

If I concentrated, I could hear Rachel talking to Sally downstairs, their words vibrating along the air ducts and the building's central vacuum system. I went downstairs and found them in one of the dressing rooms behind the stage.

Tabitha had a tendency to dress like a sex doll. Her sister had better taste. She was wearing a floor-length backless evening gown. The green set off her eyes beautifully. Her hair was up and she'd replaced her nose ring with a small silver stud that was barely noticeable. Even her makeup was right. Have I mentioned how dangerous I thought she was? I had no idea where she had gotten the dress, but it was beautiful. She was beautiful.

"Goldman's opens at ten and it's not that far from here," she explained. "Sally went down with me and we picked up a few options." Rachel twirled and the dress rose off the floor a little, enough for me to see her matching shoes and a glimpse of ankle. Sally looked proud of herself. I was proud of her, too.

"We spent almost five thousand dollars," Sally told me.

"Why the hell did you buy a prom dress?"

"Because we all know what happens after prom," Rachel whispered.

"Yeah." Sally giggled with amusement. "You kids have fun." She winked at me on her way out the door. What the hell had Rachel told her?

Rachel smiled. I checked my fucked-o-meter. The gauge was set firmly on "Seven ways from Sunday." That seemed about right.

Rachel pulled up her dress and showed me her thigh. The wound was gone.

"It's already healed," she said.

"Mine always do," I told her. "I don't know why. Roger's bites don't heal like mine. Talbot tells me it's an unusual ability for a vampire."

She looked at me quizzically, dropping her dress back into place. "Talbot tells me that about most of my abilities, though," I added.

She walked over to me casually. "Have you asked him about it?"

"No," I answered. She was leaning close to me again. Her smell was different, less musky, and I couldn't smell cinnamon anymore. I decided it wasn't a perfume that she'd been wearing; it was something else, something that came and went. I didn't ask, for the same reason I didn't ask a lot of things. I was afraid that she might tell me, or worse, lift up her dress and show me.

"Why not?"

"Because I was worried that he might tell me." I backed away from her, pausing at the doorway.

"You want to know about that bullet, don't you?" She was just full of surprises.

"What bullet?" I asked.

"The magic one you're holding in your hand." Rachel pointed. "Or is it just a party favor?"

I looked down and sighed. The bullet glowed even more brightly now, like it was charging back up, replenishing itself.

"I was going to call Magbidion. He's kind of my mage on retainer."

"Can I see it?" She held out her hand. Since I had no reason other than blatant paranoia not to hand it over, I gave her the bullet. She held it up to her eye and put a hand on my shoulder. We both got popped by static electricity. "Ow. Yep, it's magic. I'm no expert on magic bullets, but it's made of silver. My guess is that it's enchanted to kill lycanthropes. One of those swirly symbols kind of looks like a rune I've seen used to represent them."

"How do you know all this?"

There was mischief in her eyes. "Because, unlike some people, I ask questions."

"Yeah, but I'm a vampire. How come you know more about it than me?"

"I don't jump blindly into anything. I do research. There's a place called the Irons Club. It's really exclusive and a lot of vampire thralls meet down there and play golf when their Masters are asleep."

"And they just told you all this stuff?"

"It took a little doing," she said, leaning in close to nuzzle my neck, "but you know how persuasive I can be and how curious I am."

"Remember what curiosity did to the cat."

"I'm not a cat," she answered. "I hate cats."

"I'd noticed. You know, your sister is going to wake up about an hour after sunset. I should talk to her about things." Rachel opened her mouth, but I shushed her. "Not about us, if there is an us . . . which there isn't." *Shit.* "I need to explain. I have to break up with her. She's dead now and I don't date corpses. I've tried it and it doesn't work."

"She talked you into it, huh? What an idiot. There is no quicker way to lose your undead boyfriend than turning off the body heat." Rachel turned her back to me and looked over her shoulder in my direction. "Unzip me? I want to change out of this before I get it dirty." Reluctantly, I did as she asked. She was wearing a strange-looking bra underneath it.

"What is that?"

She looked down. "A backless bra," she said with a smirk. "I can't go braless all the time, silly. I'd sag."

"What was I just talking about?" I sighed.

"My sister," Rachel answered. She bit her bottom lip thoughtfully and then stepped out of the dress. I watched her put it on a hanger and pull a plastic bag over it. I was still staring at her when she took off her shoes. She had a small frog tattoo just above her ankle. It was cute and dainty and I seemed to remember it from somewhere, as if I had previously seen one just like it.

"You like frogs?" I asked.

"Better than cats," she answered mysteriously. She glanced at me as if waiting to see if I had any other questions, then pulled on a new pair of jeans and a silk blouse.

"You were talking about my sister," she repeated. "She's going to be really pissed off when you dump her. Does she have any idea that it's coming?"

"It's what happened to the one before her," I answered defensively. "Look, I think she knows, but either way I'm sure Talbot will have told her that it's likely."

Rachel shook her head as she pulled a pair of socks out of a shopping bag. They were followed by a pair of new tennis shoes. "So in other words, she's probably in denial. You're not one of those guys who tosses 'I love you' grenades around, are you?"

"I told her she was a moist warm tightness with the right attachments."

Rachel looked exceedingly amused. "Holy shit! You did not tell my sister that." She stopped laughing and looked up at me. "You did tell her that? Oh my God!" She sat down on the dressing chair and tried to catch her breath. Amusement was not the reaction I had been expecting. Anger would have been my bet, maybe a little dash of outrage, but not this. It was a clear sign that I did not understand the modern teenager.

"What does she expect?" Rachel continued. "You're a fucking vampire. You eat people." Her comments weren't accusations. I might have felt better about it if they had been.

"I have to go across to the club and talk to Roger," I said, changing the subject. I needed to ask him about the hockey game, maybe find some way to mention Brian. I also wanted to be there whenever Tabitha woke up. "Look, just hang out here. Watch a movie, listen to CDs, just . . . whatever. I'll be back." Applauding my mental fortitude, I left, walking up the stairs, out through the lobby, and across to the Demon Heart without a backward glance.

Since it was a few minutes before noon, I caught fire again on the way. Catching fire always reminds me of that one horrible week in California, a week full of demons and hellfire. "Fricking El Segundo," I griped.

10

TABITHA:
RELATIONSHIP ISSUES

When I awoke, I was in Eric's bed again and he was standing over me. "You're up early," he remarked.

"Hello to you too," I said with a smile. I expected him to kiss me. Instead he pointed at the shower. "You smell," he said bluntly. "Go take a shower."

There was an odor in the air, like natural gas or methane mixed with pee. I sniffed my forearm. "That's me?"

Eric pulled me off of the bed by my arm and dragged me to the shower. Too stunned to react, I just lay there while he turned the shower on and pushed me inside. I was still wearing my leather outfit. He didn't notice. Instead, he stripped off his shoes and stepped into the shower. The cold water slowly became warmer as he removed my clothing. I closed my eyes and imagined him delicately unsnapping each snap and kissing the soft white flesh underneath.

"My darling," my imaginary Eric said. "I love you. Now we can be together, creatures of the night, unstoppable, unquenchable; the world is ours."

I opened my eyes and looked at the real Eric as he roughly undressed me.

He met my gaze. "These clothes are ruined. You won't be able to get the smell out."

I closed my eyes again and resumed my fantasy. In my mind, we made love passionately, more passionately than ever before and as we reached climax, Eric said he loved me again and again. He whispered it in my ear and then we both sank our fangs into each other, our minds touched, we were one.

In reality, I could feel him rubbing a bar of soap over me. It might have been sensuous except that his touch was coarse and businesslike. His hands did not linger and no gentle kisses were forthcoming. He washed my hair three times and I began to smell blood. I'd started crying without realizing it. I was getting tired of crying.

"Stop crying," Eric ordered. Out of reflex, I did. "It's called corpse sweat," he continued. "Did it happen last night? I mean, last day . . ." Frustration filled his voice. "I mean when you woke up last night did you stink?"

At first I didn't answer. Talbot's voice was playing in my head repeating all the things he had said the night before and I didn't like what he was saying. I must have started moving my head from side to side, because Eric took it as a response and continued talking.

"Good. Then it might not happen again. You were probably playing with your powers. Most vampires only get the sweats when they discover new talents. Some get them every night. I don't get them at all. Anybody I've ever heard of that had corpse sweat on the first night has to deal with it every night. Still, it's too early to tell. You probably ought to sleep naked on a plastic sheet or get one of the girls to move you once you fall asleep. Otherwise you might get corpse sweat on your sheets and whatever you're wearing."

He picked me up in his arms and carried me to the bed. Thankfully, someone had already changed the sheets. The Eric behind my closed eyelids made love to me again on that bed and promised to never leave me. In reality, though, I felt myself being toweled off and opened my eyes. The look on Eric's face said everything I needed to know. There I was, naked, in all my glory. According to the other girls, I looked better than I ever had, and he looked at me like I was a chore. There was no hunger there at all. He turned away from me and dropped the towel on the floor, then began to remove his shirt, peeling the wet cloth from his body. I guess that was a chore too.

Rage came over me. He'd treated me and the shirt with equal disdain, as if I were no more than an article of clothing to be tossed away and forgotten. Nobody forgets me! I leapt at him, my vision tinting red, claws and fangs at the ready.

One moment he was there and the next he wasn't. I had no idea where he had gone until I felt him behind me. Both his arms went underneath mine and he locked his fingers behind my neck. Smiling, I popped my claws and scratched his face, opening four short furrows in his cheek. He released me more out of shock than surprise and I snarled at him.

The wounds on his cheek healed as he began to do his little fast-moving trick, only this time I did it too. He was still faster than me, but I was quick enough to keep him from getting a good grip.

"You do look nice," he told me.

"What?"

"You look very pretty." He looked deep into my eyes, and suddenly I couldn't move; I couldn't react. I was frozen, staring into his eyes, mesmerized like any number of Dracula's victims in the movies. Had Talbot told me vampires could do that? I couldn't remember. I pushed back, tried to grab Eric the way he had me, but either I was too inexperienced or he was too strong. Those beautiful blue eyes sucked at my mind, pulling me deeper. They seemed to glow and flash, not a red glow, but a strange warm blue overwhelming color. I struggled, but his hold on me felt like a vise. He moved with casual menace and the look was back . . . that look that said I was no more important than ruined bedsheets, possibly less.

He wrapped his hands around my throat and squeezed. I couldn't move. He forced me down onto the clean silk sheets, never breaking eye contact. Inside I was screaming at myself, trying to move a finger, a toe, anything.

"In case you have forgotten," he began in a calm and steady voice far more frightening than any time he'd ever yelled, "I am the biggest, baddest motherfucking vampire that you will ever meet. Nothing has changed just because you have claws. Any stupid crap you think up has already been tried. I created you. I made you undead and I can make you 'dead' dead, too. I am your vampiric father or sire or whatever lame-ass little tagline you wannabes use. Any vampire power you can think of, I have it and I either use it better than you or I don't need to use it because I have a better way of doing the same thing. Do you understand me?"

At first I couldn't speak, and then it was like a ghostly force had relaxed its hold on my body, but just enough for me to answer the question. "Let me go, you . . . you bastard!"

"Say, 'Yes, Eric.'"

"Yes, Eric," I replied. What was I doing? I felt my jaws lock again, but I tried to scream anyway. Nothing happened.

"Now I want you to pay attention to what I'm going to tell you." His words trailed off; sadness suddenly filled his eyes. As quickly as he had evaded my claws, he was on the other side of the room. He leaned up against the dresser, cursing. After testing myself gingerly to make sure I could move, I sat up slowly, confused.

"This is not how I want to do this, Tabitha."

I got up and walked toward him. He tensed, but I kept coming. When I reached him, he glared at me.

"Look, Tabitha, just back off."

"You're standing between me and my underwear, Eric. Do I have to be naked the whole time I listen to you? If I am, will this end differently?" I tried to keep calm, but I was certain he could hear the anger in my voice. That sorry son of a bitch was going to dump me. What the hell was wrong with him? Hadn't I performed every sick act that his dirty little mind could think of? Did I do too much, too little? It was beyond me. The idea of it was too much for me to wrap my brain around. I felt like this all had to be happening to another person.

Eric slid away from the dresser and I opened the top drawer, my panty drawer. The smell of lilacs hit me as I opened it. I kept lilac-scented sachets in my underwear drawers to keep my underwear smelling nice. With my heightened senses most of them now smelled too strongly of lilacs for me to put on.

I stopped, taking a good look at the open drawer. It was filled with panties that were exactly what a man would like to see me wear. None of them were comfortable. They were lingerie, not real underwear. Digging through them, I found one pair of white panties that weren't crotchless, lacy, or a thong. I put them on. The next drawer down had my bras in it. It was like déjà vu. I had the same problem with the bras. They all seemed to have snap-off cups, too much lace, or no support whatsoever. A little digging revealed one plain beige bra. I put that on too.

"Your underwear doesn't match."

I glared at Eric; my expression must have spoken volumes because he literally flinched. "What the hell did you just say?"

He flinched again and walked to the far side of the room. I suddenly realized this was no different from all the times he'd insisted he wouldn't turn me, sworn that he didn't make vampires anymore. I knew exactly how to handle him. I grabbed a see-through bra out of the second drawer and threw it on the bed. I grabbed the matching pair of panties out of the top drawer and threw them on the bed too. I added a pair of black high-heeled shoes and a little leather choker the same color. "Is that what you want me to put on? What you'd like to see me in? Is that what you want?"

Eric shrugged.

"Because all you have to do is say it. You don't even have to tell me you're sorry. You just have to tell me what to do!"

I started crying again, this time on purpose, though the smell made me hungry. Streaks of red ran down my face and onto the bra. I took it off and threw it down on the floor. His eyes went involuntarily to my breasts. Poor Eric.

"Tell me you want me to wear something sexy tonight! Tell me you want to screw me, to sink your fangs into my jugular and drink my blood when you come. Tell me why we can't do that anymore. The only thing that's changed is I'm like you now. I'm a vampire. I'm not warm and alive, but I am still here. If you want a living girl to join us so that there will be some body heat, tell me and I'll go out and find one. You can pick one, it doesn't matter . . . just tell me . . ."

I threw myself into his arms, half worried he would push me away, but some emotion, some feeling of shame or guilt, possibly even some strange version of love kept him from doing so. He closed his arms around me.

His chest was damp and cold against my skin, but I didn't care. The world was a cold place anyway now that I was a vampire. I had thought it would be the other way around despite what Eric had always said, that I'd feel hot because I was at room temperature, but it definitely didn't work that way and I didn't know or care why. After a long moment, he kissed me on the forehead.

"Wear the lacy black set with fishnet stockings and a garter belt. Wear white over the top of it. I know it will show through; that's okay. Wear those strappy high-heeled shoes you have and that little white jacket thing with the short sleeves. Roger and I are going out tonight. You can't come. It's a guy thing, so don't freak out on me."

I didn't smile, because he might have thought I was laughing at him, at the way he'd given in, but I was definitely smiling on the inside. Talbot could say whatever he wanted, but Eric loved me. He just needed to talk tough, make demands, and be in control . . . typical male.

"You may be asleep again before I get back, but if so," he paused, "if so you'll wake up next to me tomorrow."

Eric could be as macho as he wanted, but when it came down to it, he'd give in. He wanted to give in; he was just afraid . . . and he loved me. I wanted him to say it, but I knew he wouldn't. Not yet. He kissed me again. This time he kissed my cheeks where the blood had begun to dry.

"I want you to help Talbot keep an eye on things tonight. I broke Marilyn's arm earlier and I need you to help out. You might have to dance tonight because Roger's happy ass keeps giving Froggy the night off. Can you handle that?"

I nodded. I wasn't sure if I could or not, but for him I would try almost anything that might give him time to realize what I already knew. It might take longer than it had to convince him to turn me, but

I had time, buckets of time. When I was human, time had been the enemy; now, time was on my side.

He held my arms and pushed me slowly away from him, as far as he could without letting go. "Maybe this will work out, Tabitha. It probably won't. It never has before, but . . . but I suppose that it might be possible. We can try a human in the bed with us, but it will have to be a girl. I don't like to feed on guys."

"Fine," I agreed eagerly. I'm not afraid of other women; the only girl who ever managed to steal a boyfriend from me was my sister Rachel, before she got sick. I felt a pang of grief when I thought of her. If only I'd been a vampire then, I could have brought her over, but it had taken too long.

"And I get to feed off of the girl. You will have to eat before or after."

"Okay," I said. If he needed to feel like he was in control that was okay with me. He began taking off his wet things and I toweled him off with the driest parts of the towel he'd used on me. "And you don't get to bite me," he added. "Ever. Not unless I explicitly say so. I don't like to be bitten."

I helped Eric dress in jeans and one of those *Welcome to the Void* T-shirts he usually wore; then he kissed me one more time. "Don't leave the room until you've eaten."

I nodded. As the door closed behind him, I could hear him muttering, "I bet Dracula never had to put up with this shit."

I laughed. "Dracula had three wives, honey," I whispered. "It was probably much worse."

11

ERIC:

THE VOID CITY HOWLERS

My to-do list was a mile long. I needed to look up Magbidi-on's number and get him to take a look at the silver bullet I'd dug out of the werewolf skull over at Orchard Lake. Roger might appreciate it if I found a way to tell him I'd accidentally whacked his buddy Brian. Werewolves were apparently out for my blood. If I had half a brain, I would be out there now, look-ing for a way to get them off my ass.

With that same half a brain, I should have turned around, walked back into my bedroom, and told Tabitha that it was over. Since I appar-ently wasn't going to do that, I needed to put Rachel in a cab and send her home. Yes, there were a lot of things I should have been doing.

Instead, I was going to a hockey game. C'mon—front row, center ice. Who could turn that down? Believe me when I say that, up to the last minute, I tried.

"I can't go to the game, Roger."

"What are you even talking about? You know you're going. Brian already stood me up. I'm not getting stood up by you too."

Ah, guilt. "Yeah, sorry about Brian."

"It's not your fault the guy turned out to be a flake," Roger spat. "Screw him."

He trailed after me from the front door of the Demon Heart to the Pollux. Rachel was waiting just inside the door. She'd changed into hip-huggers and a crop top. When I was born, seeing a girl in her bloomers was indecent. Now, my girlfriend and most of the women I knew were strippers. You might say that I've changed with the times. Even so, I stared at Rachel's pelvic bone. A hint of her thong peeked out over her hip-huggers and the only thing that stopped me from at-tacking her on the spot was Roger's hand on my shoulder.

"If she's why you can't go to the hockey game, you have my bless-ing," Roger whispered.

"Hockey?" Rachel perked up. "I love hockey."

Roger bit his lip. "Brian's a no-show, so we do have an extra ticket." He'd bought one for Brian and one for me, so he wasn't just giving me Brian's unused seat. I suddenly felt better about having accepted.

"I thought you liked high society gals," I teased.

"Just because you like orchids," Roger said, taking Rachel's hand, "doesn't mean you ignore the wild-flowers." She blushed when he kissed her hand. The light in the room took on a crimson tinge and Roger backed off.

"Don't go all flashy-eyes at me, buddy." He held up both hands in supplication. "I was just being friendly."

I counted to ten in my head and reminded myself that Roger was my best friend. Slowly, the red receded. Rachel looked on with a be-mused pout. I didn't like the look of accomplishment that I saw blazing in her eyes. At least with Roger, we'd have a chaperone along.

I *should* have sent Rachel home and invited Tabitha to the hockey game, but there just wasn't time. We'd miss the whole first half argu-ing. So I went to the hockey game with Roger and Rachel.

The Void City Howlers weren't all that good, but they were the home team and they could usually be counted on for a fight. They didn't win very often, but when they took to the ice someone always got hurt, and that's all I wanted to see anyway. My favorite player was Sparky Parker, the Howlers' power forward. Without fail, he always started a fight in the last seven minutes of the game. He used to do it at five minutes until the NHL screwed it up with all those crappy penalties. Even so, he was the king of the Gordie Howe hat trick, pulling off the goal, assist, fight trio in most matches to the exclusion of all else, even winning.

Roger led us down to the front row, where the cold from the rink seeps up through the floor. Rachel was already freezing when we got to our seats, and the souvenir jersey that I'd bought her wasn't helping much. I took off the jacket I always wore to hockey games and hung it on her shoulders.

"Thanks." She touched my hand and the world went black, white, and red. It can happen when the bloodlust gets bad. Thing is, I didn't think I was hungry enough to justify it. Before I had time to give it much thought, Rachel whispered, "Later," in my ear and snuggled up under my arm, a warm little cinnamon-scented angel. Her proximity, the sheer physical closeness, should have made things worse, but color slowly bled back into my vision. That was weird.

"How did you—" I began to ask, but Roger cut me off.

"So, does Tabitha know about your new girlfriend yet?" asked Roger.

"No." I looked down at Rachel. "She's not my . . . look, just drop it." Roger just smiled and scanned the crowd.

"Looking for someone?" I asked.

"Something like that." He waved at a blond guy who was dressed to the nines. He couldn't have been much older than twenty. The blond came over, carrying two boxes carefully in his arms. He handed the boxes to Roger with a curt nod.

"With Lady Gabriella's compliments, Lord Roger."

"New boyfriend?" I asked Roger.

"Yeah, yeah. Go screw yourself." Roger slipped him five one-hundred-dollar bills, holding on to his hand when the boy accepted. Five hundred dollars and Roger didn't even flinch. Must not have been his own money. I wondered if I checked the receipts back at work, whether I'd find a five-hundred-dollar payout with Roger's name on it. "And, Dennis, the other thing?"

"It's been arranged, Lord Roger," Dennis responded. "If there will be nothing else?"

Roger barely noticed him. He had released Dennis's hand and was busy opening one of the boxes. "Huh? Oh, yeah, we're good. Run on."

"Seriously," I continued, "you pitching or catching, Rodge? I bet you're catching."

"Shut up." Roger pulled a dark bottle out of the box and handed it to me. It said *Horace Gibson—1922—AB negative* on the label. "If you keep giving me the business, I won't share."

"Giving you the business? Who the hell says that anymore?"

"I'm serious, Eric."

"Fine." I handed the bottle back. "I can get my own blood. I don't need to have it delivered."

"Yeah, but can you ferment yours?" He broke the seal and popped the cork.

"What?"

"Blood booze." He took a swig from the bottle, shuddered, and then coughed. "Smooth."

"How does it taste?" I asked.

"Like blood," he admitted, "but with a serious kick."

"Can I try it?" asked Rachel.

Roger agreed and I disagreed in unison.

"She doesn't need to start drinking blood, Roger."

"Oh, like that won't be part of this evening's festivities for you two." Roger handed the bottle back to me. "Blood is the only bodily fluid we've got."

Rachel raised an eyebrow. "Come on, Eric. What do you think it tastes like when I kiss you?"

"Fine." I handed her the bottle. She took two small sips and passed it back to me.

"Not bad," Roger told her, "but save the rest for the vampires, if you please. It cost me more than you know. They don't just sell this stuff at the local liquor store."

"Where'd your boyfriend get it?" I asked. Roger's eyes lit up from within, a dull orange pinpoint encompassed by his pupils. The fading brown pigment in his irises set it off nicely. He normally wore contacts to conceal the fade. Plenty of vamps do. Vamp irises typically lose their hue with age, resulting in a washed-out shade of the original color.

Talbot once told me that truly ancient vampires have red irises, and sometimes even the whites of their eyes go permanently crimson. Mine hadn't faded at all, but most Vlads have weird traits that set them apart, like my ability to turn into a white cat instead of a black one. My guess was that my blue eyes were like that. I once heard a rumor about a Vlad who can eat hamburgers. I'd have rather had the hamburgers and worn contacts.

"Well?" asked Roger.

"I drifted off there for a second," I told him. "I was thinking about hamburgers."

He tossed his head back and laughed. "You could drive a saint to murder, you know that?"

"Game's starting," I answered. "Are we going to fight or watch the game?"

The row behind us was enthralled by our conversation. I looked at the fat guy behind me and bared my fangs. "Don't mind us," I told him. "We're vampires."

"My son plays that game," he replied. "Aren't you guys a little old?"

I turned my attention to the start of the game without answering him. Halfway through the first period I took a swig of the fermented blood. My taste buds couldn't tell the difference. Maybe they had all died, or perhaps my palate is unrefined. I enjoyed the kick, though. It burned going down my throat and every swallow sent a dagger of heat into my heart, like heartburn would feel if it involved real fire.

"Good?" Roger asked.

"It's different," I shrugged. "Anything different . . ." I yawned. "When are they going to start playing?" I asked.

"They are playing," said Roger.

"Not that I can see."

"It's not that bad," Roger said.

"Which game are you watching?" I took another pull off of the bottle and realized that it was empty. Roger opened the other box and handed me a second bottle.

"This is total crap. Sparky hasn't even crosschecked anybody."

"You can tell him about it after the game." Roger smirked. "I have a friend who knows the owner. We've got permission to go and talk with the team."

"Cool." I offered Roger a drink from bottle number two. It had a red label on it with *Unidentified Female—1982—O positive* written on it in bold black letters. If anything, the burn was worse with the second bottle, but there was a taste to it, acidic and bitter.

Sparky Parker played like he was more intent on ice-skating than cross-checking anybody. In the second period, Fordman, the Howlers' left winger, had about as much chance of scoring as a hippo in a full-body condom. They weren't even trying. Halfway through the third period, I finished the bottle.

"Let's just go," I told Roger.

"What about meeting the team?"

"Screw 'em." My tongue felt heavy and things were a little blurry. I was completely wasted.

"Please, can we stay and meet the team?" Rachel asked.

"Fine." I cupped her breast. She didn't seem to mind. "Anything you want." We kissed and time rolled away. She moved onto my lap, grinding against me. Some parts of my body became more engorged with blood than others. The little voice in my head that normally would have thought twice and worried about consequences had passed out in the middle of that first bottle of blood booze. In his place was a horny little voice that I hadn't heard since college. He didn't care if we got caught or if security threw us out. All that mattered to him was getting inside Rachel's jeans.

The world blurred around us like time-lapse photography. Only Rachel and I were still, cocooned in cinnamon bliss. I wondered if it was some kind of magic or just the booze, but I couldn't bring myself to care.

"Guys?" Roger whistled in my ear, then thumped me in the forehead.

The game was over, the crowd all gone. It was just the three of us.

Rachel got to her feet, blushing sweetly as she straightened her outfit. What the hell had happened? Without her to hold on to, I fell backward and began sliding off the bleachers. Maybe blood booze had been a bad idea. Roger pulled me to my feet.

"Jesus, you are totally crocked," Roger told me. "Let's go meet the team."

Resting one arm on Rachel and the other on Roger, I stumbled in the direction that they led me. "You're my best friend, Roger," I slurred. He didn't answer.

12

ERIC:

BISCUIT IN THE BASKET

Arm in arm, Roger, Rachel, and I stumbled down a long hallway behind the bleachers. I vaguely remember singing at one point. Then, suddenly we were in the locker room, meeting the Void City Howlers.

My vision cleared long enough for me to see Sparky Parker, my former hero, the king of the ten-minute penalty, transform into a werewolf. A snarl started at the base of his toes and ran up his entire body, leaving hair, fur, and muscle in its wake. The only signs of his human form were the green and white Howlers jersey he was wearing and the hockey stick gripped tightly in his left paw.

You'd think I'd have put it all together. After all, the team was called the Void City Howlers. In my own defense, though, the Mighty Ducks had never turned into mallards on ice. So the deductive reasoning wasn't as intuitive as it might seem. Plus, I was totally wasted for the first time in forty years.

Autograph book in hand, I looked around the room. It was just me, Sparky, and the other Howlers . . . no sign of Roger or Rachel. "Where did they go?" I asked.

"Your friends just ditched you, vampire," Sparky growled. "They ran."

"That's good." I blinked. "Did I run away too?"

"You shouldn't have done it, vamp," he growled.

"You've got spots." He did have spots. Wolf Sparky looked sillier than any werewolf I'd ever seen. Coarse white fur covered most of his body, but it was speckled with dark black spots. He blurred. A large Dalmatian-spotted blob hit me in the face with something long and thin with a curved end: a hockey stick. I was grateful, because when the world stopped spinning everything was a little clearer.

He grabbed me by the face, palming my head like a basketball, and tossed me through the double doors that led out to the rink.

Other blobs expanded. They were angry fuzzy blobs with white and green middles, kind of cute, really. My vision cleared a little and a very wavery Wolf Sparky loomed over me. A long trail of drool dangled from his muzzle and pooled on the souvenir jersey I was wearing. I wondered if it was the one I'd bought for Rachel, and if so, how I'd ended up in it.

"You have a droopy ear," I observed. "Did you know that you had . . . have a droopy ear? I think your mom got a little drunk one night and . . . oof."

That time he grabbed my leg and tossed me out onto the ice. I felt kind of bad about mentioning the whole parentage thing. I'm kind of a happy chatty drunk and my mouth gets away from me. Cold hard ice broke my fall and I slid along the freshly resurfaced rink. The top layer hadn't quite refrozen and the glacial water soaked into my clothes.

No crowd cheered the Howlers when they took to the ice this time, but I was impressed. "You guys just skate around me, okay?" I told them. "I don't think I can get up."

I don't know who took the next several shots at me, but they must have been pissed off about something, or maybe . . . "I'm starting to think you guys don't like me," I complained.

"He's totally hosed," growled a dark black one with a bobbed tail and brown highlights like a Doberman's. "Just stake him and get it over with."

Trying to roll over, I lost my balance and fell to the ground with a loud crack.

"Lookit. One of his eyes is blinking." Strobelike red light flashed rapidly on and off, upsetting my stomach.

"I think I'm going to be sick," I said to no one in particular.

"He's gonna yack," one of them said, gliding past me.

"Vampires can't yack," called number 45 from one side. Each of them moved as easily on the ice bare-pawed as they had with skates, but in wolf form their strides were more confident, their reflexes better.

"You guys ought to skate like this all the time," I said. "Then you might win a game or two." That didn't come out the way I had meant it.

A sharp pain in my side sent me spinning along the ice quickly. Sparky was driving me down the rink, a human-size hockey puck, across the blue line, straight through center ice, and toward the goal.

"Yeah, Sparky!" someone shouted.

Two of the other Howlers, Fordman and Hartaff judging by the jerseys, skated in to try and steal me from Sparky with more resounding thuds. One of my arms gave way with a crack and pain lanced up to my shoulder, my blood was smeared all over the ice.

"Okay, fellas," I said. "That's enough."

Sparky brought me in, shoving me across the goal line and into the boards. About that time, I realized they weren't just playing, they were fighting. My growl was louder than Sparky's.

"Stake him!" Fordman shouted. Sparky's custom stick plunged into my back and out through the front of my souvenir jersey. I didn't want to think about how much strength it took to jam a blunt handle completely through a man's torso. Red illumination flashed on the boards in spurts. Off. On. Off. On. Blood wine erupted violently from my throat. It ran down the stick and onto the ice. The glow from my eyes blinked twice more and stayed on.

"Biscuit in the basket, baby!" several of them roared.

"Get the cooler." The hockey stick wasn't made of real wood, but I was still moving far too slowly. Two of them ran off of the ice and then came back toward me with a cooler.

"This ain't football," I complained. "What the hell are you guys—" They dumped the cooler over my head. It burned like acid. Holy water. I think they thought it would kill me. It was a good try. It would have worked on a Soldier, or possibly on a Master, but as I keep trying to remind everyone, I'm a Vlad and we are damn near indestructible.

"I am so fucking killing you guys," I said as my skin peeled away and caught fire. Holy water is powerful stuff. It ate right through my clothes, my skin, through the bone, mixing with my liquid remains and flowing out onto the ice like gruesome pancake batter.

The blood wine I'd spewed mixed with the puddle of water and with, well, me, turning the mixture into a bubbling red mess, with smoke pouring off the top as I sizzled and popped like a fried egg. I knew I was going to survive, but a vampire who has been melted is in bad shape even if it doesn't send him to the great beyond. We need blood to re-form. Fortunately for me, I was lying in a puddle of it.

As the holy water boiled away, the smoke stopped and bit by bit the grotesque liquefied mass developed solid chunks, drawing in on itself. I floated above the ice, looking down on my body, detached and clearheaded, glowing that same ghostly blue I'd been the one time I tried to turn to mist.

Being melted was pretty damn low on my list of sobriety quick fixes, but it did the job. My bones reformed first. One of the werewolves rammed another hockey stick through my ribs where my heart was going to be. I guess he thought the stick was made of wood, but it was some high-tech plastic. Plastic doesn't do dick.

My body lay naked on the ice and I found myself drawn back into it, momentarily disoriented, but regaining my senses just fast enough to pull the stick out of my chest before my clothes came back.

It's good to be a badass. Using my anger as a focus, I turned into a bat. It took longer than usual and felt different, like when your dick falls asleep because your underwear is too tight and there is that long agonizing wait followed by a pins and needles sensation exactly where you never want one. I flew out over the rink and landed in the stands. When I changed shape again, my clothes were back. I'd instinctively regenerated my usual outfit, but at the high price of what felt like every last drop of blood in my body.

I missed the Howlers jersey, but it was okay. I was over them. Now these assholes had it coming. They'd lured me back to the locker room with Roger's unwitting help, used me as a hockey puck, and been the first group of people to ever melt me down with holy water. Worst of all, they'd made me sit through a piss-poor game of hockey. There is no excuse for bad hockey.

They'd make it up to me though. I was hungry.

This time, I wouldn't make the mistake of holding back like I had with the guys who'd wrecked my Mustang. I was tired of talking, and at this point the hunger wouldn't have let me hold back anyway. I felt the blackout coming, bitter and cold like winter rain. Yep, these jerks had it coming. They had it coming Dracula style.

As my vision started to blur, I hovered at the edge of awareness just long enough to make one last taunt. "So are you motherfuckers going to come and get me or do I have to hang a steak around my neck?"

✦ 13 ✦

TABITHA:

HIDDEN DEPTHS

The whole no-reflection thing was really starting to grate on my nerves. I needed mirrors. There is only so much a girl can tell about how she looks by craning her neck and bending over backward. The other girls were busy, so I did the best I could on my own and then called up front to ask Talbot if he had a few minutes to come to the back.

"Why?"

"I need someone to check my makeup and stuff; the other girls were busy, so I tried to do it myself, but—"

"Ten minutes." He laughed and hung up.

While I waited, I finished up the second pint of blood he'd brought me earlier. It tasted a little funny, but I didn't want to have to argue with Talbot over it when he came back to check me out. I was tired of being cooped up in the club and I wanted to go outside for a while after my set. After I finished the blood, I still had five minutes to wait, so I practiced popping my claws and making my eyes glow. It was cool and all, but I wanted to know more about what I could do. I wondered what would happen if I used a power that I didn't know how to undo. What if I turned into a bat and got stuck that way?

When Talbot came into the bedroom, I retracted my claws and let my eyes turn back to normal.

His smell wasn't human and it was thrilling to be near him, to not know what he was. He looked me up and down and I studied him in return.

"You look fine," he said. He turned and started to leave again.

"Wait. Talbot, do you have a few minutes?"

He looked at me over his shoulder. "Why?"

"I wanted to try and figure out what other powers I have." I walked over to the dresser and fiddled with my hairbrush. He showed up clearly in the mirror even though my reflection would have been blocking his.

He closed the door and turned back to me. "You don't need me to do that."

I looked down at the brush in my hand. It was silver. For a moment, I was lost in the shiny surface. My grandmother had left it to me when she'd died. She had always intended it for Rachel, but cancer had taken my sister away from us earlier than anyone could have expected. She was so angry at the end, she blamed me for not finding a way to save her.

"I'm afraid," I admitted.

Talbot came closer, put his hand near my shoulder, and then pulled it away. I could feel the heat of him behind me. It was like standing with my back to the fire on a cold winter day. I leaned into him involuntarily and closed my eyes. "You feel so warm."

Gentle, but firm, he pushed me away from him. I was off balance and I almost didn't catch myself. Something was wrong. "You don't want to play the kind of games I like, Tabitha," he told me softly.

How embarrassing! Did I have to throw myself at every warm-bodied man that crossed my path? I shivered. "I'm sorry. It just feels so cold."

"You'll get used to it." He sat down on the edge of the bed and I realized that it was the first time that I had ever seen Talbot sit down. He was always leaning on things, but never actually sitting.

"So how do I do it?" I asked.

"Do what?"

I put down the brush and threw my hands up in the air. "Do anything! I've read lots of books, but it isn't something that Eric ever talked about. I could ask Roger, but—"

"You don't want Eric to get jealous." He nodded. "I get you. Which do you like best: bats, cats, fleas, wolves, frogs, or do you want to try for something funky, like a virus?"

I turned around and leaned up against the dresser. "What?"

"You don't know yet how powerful you are. If you're a Soldier or a Drone, you might only be able to do the first one you try, or you might not be able to do any of them. You might not get a choice, but if you do get a choice and you can only do one . . ." He shrugged. "Well, they say that's what happened to Froggy."

"So, it'd better be one that I like," I mused. "Okay. Wait, a virus?"

He laughed. When he did, I could tell that even with his fangs retracted, his canines were a little longer than normal. "It's been done.

I guess it was a good way to avoid hunters back in the day, but it sounds kind of gross to me."

"Can I try something else weird? Is there a bird, like a raven or something?"

"Try it and see," he urged.

"Do I need to take my clothes off?"

"Some do, but why don't you just go ahead and try it with clothes for now." He got up and walked around the room, arms outstretched like a big kid playing airplanes. "Close your eyes and think of yourself as a bird. See yourself flying over the city, like in a helicopter ride only the wind is underneath your wings. You aren't in some metal cockpit. There is no glass between you and the air, no metal. It's you, just you."

I spread my arms like he had done. At first I felt silly, but gradually, I really could see it. My body tightened, wrenching painfully in on itself, my skin an overfilled balloon that might pop any second, and then the wind was beneath my wings; I was free! It was so sudden that I screamed in surprise, but no human sound escaped my lips. It was a bird's cry. I had done it! Of course, I didn't know how to fly, so I fluttered to the ground. When I landed, I felt dizzy and confused, sick to my stomach. Talbot pounced, catching me between his hands and eyeing me closely with his fangs out and his cat eyes flashing. "Gotcha!"

Willing myself back to human size didn't work. I flapped my wings ineffectually and started pecking at his fingers with my beak. If I'd had fangs I would have bitten him. As it was, I tried for his eyes, but he was too far away.

"If you're a Master vampire," he gloated, "you'll be able to turn back even though I have you trapped. Just concentrate. Think about being humanoid. Picture yourself biting my hand or something."

It didn't work. I couldn't focus.

"Try it. Picture yourself dancing onstage."

Nope.

"All right," he said as he set me down on the bed. "Try it now."

Instantly, I was myself again. "You bastard!"

"The test isn't definitive, but you're probably a Soldier." He stood up and grinned. "Care to try for a mouse?"

I did not care to try for a mouse. Instead I tried for a cat. I pictured myself as a large gray kitty I'd had as a little girl. I loved that cat more than anybody in my family. I used to sit and pet him for hours and listen to him purr. He was the only thing that was mine and mine alone. He never let anyone else touch him, especially not Rachel. It was almost as if Mr. Fuzzy Bottom had some kind of never-ending feud with her. Cats in general didn't like her; maybe they knew something I didn't.

The change was not as sudden as before; quick, but not instant, like a slow collapse into a nice warm ball of fur. It was a relief to be warm again. Talbot took a step away from the bed, his eyes wider than usual and his mouth open. I looked down at my paws. They were gray, just like Mr. Fuzzy Bottom's. I preened myself at Talbot and gazed at him haughtily.

"Okay, so maybe you are a Master vampire," he allowed. "You could have been too panicked to make the change before."

Master vampire or not, I could turn into a bird and I could turn into a cat. My chest felt funny, though. It sort of vibrated. "Meow," I told Talbot. "My chest feels funny," is what I had meant to say. My heart was beating! I was breathing! I stumbled and accidentally sat down.

"I'll just bet it does," Talbot whispered. He reached over and grabbed me, holding up my kitty-cat self to the mirror so that I could see my reflection.

I could see my reflection!

"Meow!" I said, meaning "Holy shit!"

"Holy shit, indeed," he said as he put me down on the dresser, in front of the mirror. I put a paw against the mirror and stared at myself. Even though it wasn't the human me, just being able to show up in a mirror, to see a reflection that belonged to me, made me feel safe and warm inside. I rubbed up against the mirror and purred at myself.

"Meow," I said to myself, meaning "Hello, me."

Veruca opened the door and glanced around the room. Her makeup was sloppy and her shoes didn't go with her dress. I could tell that she wasn't happy.

"What's a cat doing in here?" Veruca asked. Talbot just looked at her. Veruca's lip curled. "Tell Tabitha not to get too full of herself, Talbot. Just because she's been turned, she's nothing special. She's supposed to go on in half an hour. Then it's serving drinks and doing lap dances just like everybody else. I'm taking the night off."

"A little hard on your new sister in undeath, aren't you?" Talbot asked. "As a matter of fact, since you're here, she doesn't have to go onstage at all. . . ."

Veruca flipped Talbot off and pulled up her shirt. Claw marks criss-crossed her stomach and from the look of them, they went around to the back.

"What happened?" I meowed.

"What happened?" Talbot repeated for me. Interesting. Talbot understood cat speak and Veruca didn't. Was he a werecat? A weretiger? What else could he be?

"None of your business, asshole!" Veruca slammed the door and stalked off down the hall. The sound echoed in my head. My vision blurred and for a moment there were two furry "me"s in the mirror.

"Meow?" I said, and I had no idea what I meant. Something was definitely wrong.

I rolled over on my back and swatted at the pretty rainbows and the colored lights that had appeared in the air. There was that same funny taste in my mouth, like the second pint of blood. In the distance I heard Talbot's voice calling my name.

The rainbows started moving faster and I tried harder to catch them. Then, I heard someone barfing. I wondered if it was me. At some point, I fell off of the dresser. Talbot caught me. The psychedelic swirling stopped, replaced by a vibration deep in my skull. There was a sound like when a monitor blinks out. My skin went numb all at once and little sparks danced in front of my eyes. Talbot blurred in hazy motion lines, faded, and then was gone completely.

14

TABITHA:

THE SHOW MUST GO ON

When I woke up, Talbot was snapping his fingers in front of my eyes and calling my name. I was wet and I was still a cat. The lights were too bright and my heart was beating in my ears. Was I drunk? Did vampires get drunk? Did cats get drunk? For that matter, why was my heart beating? I was breathing too fast and my skin was all tingly.

"C'mon, Tabitha. Get up!" Talbot told me. I sneezed a pitiful cat sneeze at him and it made my head pound.

"Meow," I said, meaning, "God, I feel awful."

"It's probably just transformation sickness," Talbot explained. "Try turning back to normal and see if that helps."

It was hard to concentrate with my head pounding, but I managed it. It was even slower than before, my body chilling and expanding like a balloon slowly being filled with cold water. After a few minutes, I was myself again, panting on the floor. I even had clothes on. The dull ache in my head eased up and the world stopped spinning in circles.

I blinked a few times, steadied myself, and stood up. "Okay. That was both awesome and shitty at the same time. So, what? I can turn into a cat, but only if I want to start tripping and then barf?"

Talbot looked at my eyes closely. "Your eyes are dilated." He held my right eye open with his fingers. "Okay, better. They're normal now."

I started to rub my eye, but stopped myself when I remembered my eye shadow. I touched my cheek and looked reflexively to the mirror to check my makeup. No reflection. An inexplicable rage welled up inside of me and I turned on Talbot.

"You better not have fucked up my makeup, asshole!" My claws were out before I even thought about extending them. I wanted to tear him apart, drink his blood, drain him dry, and then tear the pieces up when I was done. I knew my reaction was over the top, but I couldn't explain what was happening. Talbot seemed just as surprised as I was, even more so because I had actually slashed his forearm with my claws, moving too fast for even Talbot to avoid. We both looked down at the blood.

"I—" I didn't know what I was going to say, but I opened my mouth to say it. Talbot wasn't interested in listening.

"Your makeup is fine. Get your ass out there and do your job." He walked into the bathroom and began washing the cuts out with soap and water.

"Talbot?" I followed him into the bathroom, reaching out to him.

"Just go, Tabitha!" he yelled. Closing his eyes, he let out a sigh. "Just go out and dance. We'll talk about this later. I probably pushed you too hard."

Of course it was his fault, I cursed inwardly. Talbot was the one with experience. Talbot was supposed to know better, to teach me. I left the room and headed toward the stage. "Dumb, fucking asshole," I said aloud.

My emotions were a mess. Edginess does not even begin to describe what I was feeling. Imagine that someone ran over your cat, and then backed into your new car trying to get away. Imagine that when the police came, the officer laughed and told you to buy a new cat. Picture how angry that would make you. I was that mad at everyone and everything, and I could not understand why.

In the dressing room behind the stage, Candice and Sharon were getting ready to go serve drinks and sell lap dances. Sharon said hello and I flipped her off in response. She shrugged it off, but I could smell her anger.

Candice looked up at me with that stupid innocent look she always gave to Eric. "Did somebody wake up on the wrong side of the grave this morning?"

I don't even remember hitting her. She just seemed to lift up out of her chair and fly backward through the air of her own accord. One of the mirrors shattered as she hit it and there was a blinding flash as the lights around it exploded. Bouncing off of the wall, she landed face-down on the floor. Shards of glass landed all around and over her, like glittery sprinkles. It was pretty in a violent, deadly sort of way. It was too much trouble to get to her throat with all the glass in the floor, so I leapt over her and landed on the steps leading up to the stage.

I smiled back at Sharon and she froze, evidently hoping that if she stayed still, I'd leave her alone. "One word and I'll put you right fucking next to her." She was used to being around vampires and it probably saved her life. I'm sure she was terrified, but she knew better than to show it. It was one of the first things Eric told new girls. I'd been with him long enough to know how true it was: Fear was like a good marinade to a vampire. Running could get you killed. Hold still, submit, and you might have a chance.

A weird taste played across my tongue, bitter and sweet at the same time. I knew I had tasted it before, but I couldn't think clearly enough to figure out where. By the time I hit the stage I had all but forgotten about Candice. Jasmine was out there doing her Little Red Riding Hood routine, managing to look innocent and sexy all at once. Her long brown hair trailed behind her, down over the hood and cape. The light creamy texture of her skin stood out in perfect contrast to the bright red cape, a thin layer of baby oil glistening on her skin, her pink nipples hard and erect.

I decided to play the Big Bad Wolf. When I walked out from behind the stage, I could hear the emcee asking Marilyn what was going on. I couldn't remember what his name was; only that he was a pig who always tried to get us to suck him off. Tonight, I decided, he would get his wish.

I hit the stage and Jasmine looked back at me, pretty brown eyes wide in surprise. She was down to her G-string and the little red cape. I strutted up to her and pulled the G-string off. It was what the guys really wanted to see anyway. Jasmine protested, but I was having fun. Excitement emanated from the audience. The scent filled my nostrils and made it even harder to think. I showed my fangs to the crowd and they cheered. As far as they knew, this was all part of the show. Jasmine's scent was the most thrilling of all: fear and uncertainty, combined with sweat and a hint of sex.

It woke the inner predator in me. I began a routine of my own. I danced around her, stripping; Jasmine relaxed and started to dance with me, closer than I would have normally found comfortable. When the tips started rolling in, she whispered her thanks into my ear.

But Jasmine's terror started to return when she realized that I wasn't going to let her leave the stage. By the time I was down to my own G-string, we had collected more money than I normally did in an entire night, but I didn't want money. Talbot had made his way to the edge of the stage and was whispering just loudly enough for me to hear him.

"Let her off the stage, Tabitha! Let Jasmine go backstage and then follow her. Something is very wrong here and we'll figure it out. Just don't hurt her."

I wanted, no, needed, Jasmine to run, but she wouldn't do it; she'd been trained too well. Like Sharon, she knew running from a vampire would get you killed for sure. If you didn't run, then you had a chance. I pulled her close to me, pressing her back to my chest, and whispered in her ear, "Let me taste you and you can leave."

She nodded slightly and I sank my teeth into her neck. Fresh blood touched my tongue and it felt hot enough to burn. It was more than a taste. The liquid warmth ran down my throat, into my core, spreading like traces of fire along my veins. She sagged in my arms, another trick, designed to cue a vampire that she'd had enough. The audience went wild.

Somehow, I let her go. She stumbled toward the rear of the stage and into someone's waiting arms. I didn't care who. That one taste of fresh blood unleashed a monster inside me. I hesitated momentarily in the calm before the storm. Sounds grew even louder than before. I could hear people all around the club, both voices I knew and those I did not know.

"Didn't I tell you this was an awesome club?"

"Fake blood, you can tell by the way . . ."

"Lap dance . . ."

"What the hell is she doing, Marilyn . . ."

"Get off the stage, Tabitha."

"Don't know, boss. I haven't seen him, but his ex is going nuts . . ."

Music flickered brightly above the speakers, wave after wave of electric blue. I heard rather than felt the terror of those around me, high-pitched and frantic like a mad guitar solo. Sensory confusion. In a detached way, I realized I was tripping again.

One sound flashed red, more enticing than the others, a sensual pulse: a summons, pulsing faster. Heartbeats. I was the monster and the monster was me. It felt like I was gaining control over myself, like I was winning. All sense of right and wrong flowed away to be replaced by the new morality: drinking blood, good; not drinking blood, bad.

I remember shoving Talbot to one side, leaping for the emcee. People screamed as I bit through the emcee's pants into his femoral artery.

"How's that for a suck job, asshole?"

Claws raked down my back and I kicked in my vampire speed without having to concentrate, fluidly, as easy as sneezing. I remember laughing, long purple streams of laughter rising over my shoulder. Power over life and death was mine. Killing led to drinking blood. Not killing led to not drinking blood. Killing became a virtuous act.

Even Talbot was too slow to stop me. I moved like a whirlwind, dancing through the crowd. His attempts to stop me were like cheap scares in a haunted house. He could jump out at me, growl at me, but he couldn't touch me any more than a dancing plastic skeleton with glowing eyes could. A series of bleeding lines on backs, faces, necks, and chests slid beneath my claws and it was fun, like finger-painting.

I felt warm inside and out. These stupid perverts didn't need their lives. I did. I needed all that they had to give and more. I deserved it. They were cattle, little more than fast-food wrappers. And I . . . I faltered. The new morality flickered, replaced by my former sense of right and wrong. I saw what I had done and it sickened me. I staggered backward.

Twang.

Pain lanced through my chest as I fell to the floor. In the distance, across the club, I saw Marilyn. She had taken her arm out of its sling so she'd have both hands for the crossbow. Beyond her, people were pounding on the doors, but they wouldn't open. Talbot was beside me, picking me up, charging through the crowd to get me out of there.

"Use the crystal, Marilyn!" he yelled behind him, and instantly there was silence. Then, I heard the unmistakable sound of bodies hitting the floor.

I blacked out, not comprehending exactly what had happened.

When I came to, I couldn't see. Someone had closed my eyes, but I could hear voices. It sounded like they were in another room. Unable to move, I listened carefully. Bugs skittered inside the walls and what sounded like a larger thing, a mouse, probably, thumped its leg against the floor as it scratched at a flea. There were birds on the roof. A man was chanting over the speaker system in the main club. His words were nonsense mixed with what might have been Latin. I also heard Marilyn.

"I want you to have Magbidion check her out as soon as he's done with the mind job on the customers, Talbot. I want him to check her and everything she's touched. She's a stupid girl, but I looked into her eyes after she'd turned. She's still too human inside to do something like that."

Liquid splashed against the sides of a mug. I couldn't smell what it was. They were too far away. "Thanks," said Marilyn.

"Look, he's just going to have to put her down," Veruca said. "There is something wrong with him. Whenever he turns a new slut, she winds up defective."

"No," Marilyn disagreed. "It isn't that. Something happened to her." She stopped talking abruptly.

Talbot paced back and forth across the floor. It sounded like he was walking on wood. They had to be in the office, since I doubted they were on the stage. "Do you think it was a spell?" he asked. "You know

Eric pissed off the local Alpha. I wouldn't think a religious type like William would stoop to this, though."

Marilyn sipped her drink carefully. The aroma of coffee, strong and bitter, reached my nostrils.

"I couldn't say, Talbot, but you tell Magbidion that I'm not paying his fee until he finds out what on God's green earth happened." She fiddled with a package that crackled and when she next spoke she sounded like she had a cigarette in her mouth. "Could you?"

A mechanical lighter clicked and Marilyn inhaled deeply. "Thanks," she told him.

"I think I'll spare myself the secondhand smoke, Marilyn." Talbot coughed. "I'll get back to you when Magbidion has more information."

I heard the door open and close and then open again.

"Talbot," Marilyn called down the hallway.

"Yes?"

"She didn't drink a junkie or anything tonight, did she?"

"No," he answered. "I brought her some of Eric's stash from the fridge in the break room. I meant to ask you to check your ledger and see whose turn it is to give more this week so that I could replace it."

"Not from here in the office?" Marilyn asked.

"No," Talbot answered. "According to Veruca, Roger pitched a shit fit when you fed Tabitha some of his stock last night, said for us to stay out of the office fridge . . ."

"Like he ever drinks cold blood," Marilyn snapped.

"And that Tabitha should have to hunt, like Veruca," Talbot finished.

"Well," Veruca interjected defensively, "that's what he said."

"The stash in the break room is all Eric's, though," Talbot continued, "so I thought that'd be okay."

Marilyn took a long drag off her cigarette and blew smoke into the hallway. "Have Magbidion check the blood. All of it."

"Will do," Talbot replied.

I knew that blood had tasted funny.

15

ERIC:

SPIKED

It was a warm August night so I didn't mind flying home. Roger had been right to get Rachel out of there, but I was still a little pissed that he hadn't come back to give me a ride. He did know I was going to win, right?

It didn't take as long as I thought it would for me to fly back to the Pollux. I landed on the old theater's roof. Across the street, the Demon Heart's large neon sign was off and a *Closed* sign hung on the front doors. My watch had stopped, but I didn't think it was closing time yet.

The scent of blood hit me before I had made it halfway across the street. The smell wasn't quite as strong at the back door, but when I walked in I had to pause, allow myself to adjust. Whatever had happened, I was relatively certain that going into a feeding frenzy wouldn't help. Down the hall, in the business office, Marilyn and Talbot were talking. They looked my way when I opened the door.

Marilyn looked stressed, puffing away at a cigarette, her arm in a sling. Talbot was pretty well banged up. His shirt was shredded, and I could see scratches on his arms, chest, and back. The ones on his back looked particularly deep. The sorcerer Magbidion was with them. Sometimes I call him Mag because it gets on his nerves. He wasn't with the local mages' guild, so he was free to work for vampires; I'd used him before. In fact, I'd been meaning to call him. I made a mental note to have Mag look at the silver bullet while he was here.

"I was just telling them they did the right thing when they used the Somnolence Crystal," Magbidion told me. "I was able to fix all the humans out there, but you'll need a new Somnolence Crystal. I can have it ready tomorrow for fifteen grand."

"Fifteen thousand?" I asked incredulously. I seemed to recall the last one costing less than that.

"Pay it," Marilyn snapped. "And I don't want to hear any complaints about the fifty thousand we owe him for cleaning up the mess tonight. It was worth every penny."

"What the hell happened?" I walked past them into the office and slid the company checkbook out of the drawer. The carbon copy above the check I was writing caught my attention.

"Who the fuck is Fergus Jenkins and why did we write him a check for thirty thousand dollars?"

Talbot shrugged. Marilyn's eyes narrowed, but her mouth stayed firmly shut. "Anyone?" I asked again.

"Who wrote the check?" Veruca asked innocently.

I looked closely at the signature. Roger had signed my name. He never dots his *i*'s. He also made the *E* in *Eric* look more like a *c* and connected it to the *r*. When I write my name the *E* stands alone.

"Roger," I said flatly, "I'll ask him about it." I sniffed the air. It was hard to tell over the carnage, but I didn't smell him. "Isn't he back yet?"

Veruca shook her head. "I don't think so. I'm headed out, though. If I see him, I'll ask him to call you."

"Fine." Someone was going to have to explain this to me eventually, but in the meantime I wrote Magbidion a check. He reached for it, but I held back.

"What am I paying sixty-five thousand dollars for?" I asked.

"Fifteen thousand for the new crystal. I could do it for five, but then it wouldn't put paranormals to sleep. It costs ten to cover werewolves, ogres, those kinds of things, and another five to make sure that it doesn't put any of the Demon Heart staff to sleep along with the riffraff. I have to key them in individually."

"I know that. I mean the rest of it."

"Ask them." Mag pointed at Talbot and Marilyn. "You don't want to pay me to explain it to you." I held the check back out to him. He took it, shook my hand, and started to leave. "You know," he called over his shoulder, "you'd save a lot of money if you just agreed to be my champion."

Ever since Mag had seen me fight that demon in El Segundo he'd been after me to champion his cause when the time came. Magbidion hadn't been born with magic; he'd cut a deal to get it. He was going to lose his soul unless he had a champion who could kill whatever demon it was that he'd made the deal with. Mag lived in fear of repo day, and I wanted no part of it.

"Let's keep it cash and carry for now," I told him. He headed for the exit and then I remembered the silver bullet in my pocket.

"Mag," I said, following him out to the hallway, "let me ask you something."

He stopped and peered at me from beneath bushy brown eyebrows. As far as I knew, it was the only hair on his body and that was why he let them grow a little wild. "What is it?" Mag asked.

"I found this bullet out at Orchard Lake in the skull of a werewolf. You ever see anything like it?" I handed him the bullet. He promptly dropped it.

"You can't just hand somebody a thing like that!" Mag wiped his hands off on his pants. "It's a soul stealer."

I knelt next to it. "I've been carrying it around in my pocket."

"You can hold it safely." He emphasized the *you*. "You're a dead thing."

"Sorry." I picked it up and held it out in my palm. He bent over to examine it more closely. Lines of blue shone on his face, cast by the runes carved into the bullet. "If death wasn't enough to pull your soul out of your body," Magbidion continued, "then this won't be a problem for you."

He took a ratty-looking pair of wire-framed reading glasses out of his shirt pocket and put them on. Magbidion traced his finger over one of the symbols, the same symbol Rachel had recognized. "It only kills werewolves." He sighed. "You want to be careful, though. It's not made to kill vampires, but it shape-locks anything supernatural that it hits. You get hit with one of these and there'll be no turning to a bat and flying back to the crypt until you get the bullet out. The silver would probably set you on fire too. Hell, I didn't have anything to worry about."

"Then you hold it." I handed it to him. The way I dumped the bullet into his hand made me remember having handed it to Rachel. Good thing it only worked on werewolves.

"It has souls inside of it, too." He crossed his eyes. "Two, four, six . . . hold still . . . eight . . . nine . . . Lot of 'em in there. Fella could make some impressive wards with these guys."

"Wards?"

"Are you kidding me?" Magbidion tapped the bullet. "Werewolf souls are perfect for wards. They're supernatural and mundane at the same time. . . . Human, yet not human. Perfect for keeping normals and paranormals at bay. I hear it took about thirty to erect the wards over at the Highland Towers and they're damn near impregnable."

He made a series of motions in the air.

"Looks like you're trying to adjust the focus on an invisible camera," I told him.

"I am." Mag paused. "Well, kind of."

He kept motioning and my stomach turned. The sound of finger-nails on a chalkboard rose from the bullet. "It's a tricky artifact," Mag explained. "I nearly missed it, but this bullet is linked to something . . . some things. More bullets, maybe? I could tell for sure if I saw the gun."

With each adjustment he made, the sound got worse until with a final twist it stopped. Seven little blue cables of light extended three feet from the bullet's base. Magbidion touched one of them and bit his lip. "It's no good. Someone would have to follow the trail and you don't have enough money to pay me to do that." He perked up. "Un-less, of course, you want to be my champion."

"I'll think about it." I took the bullet back. "For now, why don't you tell me what you can."

"This bullet is connected . . . it has five little brother bullets, and all of them are tied to one another and more importantly, to one hell of a gun." He took off his glasses and put them away. "It's powerful magic. I couldn't make something like that. Whoever made it is either real bad juju or had a demon to help them."

"Now I just have to find a tracker, right?" I put the bullet back in my pocket. "How much do I owe you for the info?"

"I'll put it on your tab."

"I'd rather write you another check."

"Just let me know if you decide to make any wards with that stuff. I've always wanted to work with the real thing."

"It's a deal," I agreed.

He started to leave, then stopped himself. "Can I park my RV in the Pollux parking deck tonight? The first floor is tall enough."

"Anytime," I told him, meaning it. I followed him out the back door and watched as he walked over to a ragtag RV with what looked like a decade's worth of dust and grime on it. He unlocked it and looked over his shoulder at me.

"You know Talbot could probably follow the bullet's trail back to the gun if he knew to look for it." He tapped his temple. "Cat's eyes." He climbed in and the vehicular behemoth came to life, spewing a cloud of black smoke from the tailpipe.

I walked back inside and returned to the office. Marilyn hopped out of my chair as I approached, moving to a folding chair across the room. Talbot loomed near the door as usual. They gave me a rundown on what had happened and it didn't make me the happiest boy in the world to find out that my newly turned girlfriend had gone batshit and tried to kill every human in my club. "How's Candice?"

"They're keeping her overnight for observation," Talbot said matter-of-factly. "Broken clavicle, cracked sternum, a pretty good concussion, and a fair assortment of cuts and bruises; I wouldn't expect her to work for a while even if she does decide to come back. We had six girls working when it happened. Jasmine will be okay in a day or two. She's weak from the blood loss. Kaylee got off with bumps and bruises, and Sharon and Desiree were just scared half to death. Lil's dead, though, and that emcee you were trying out, Rick . . . we'll need to find a replacement. He's dead too."

"Fuck! That stupid bitch!" I stood up, brushing past Talbot to stick my head out into the hall. Tabitha's new scent drifted toward me from the dressing room.

"It wasn't her fault, Eric." Marilyn sighed. I turned to look at her, my hand still on the door. "Magbidion was surprised that she lasted as long as she did before exploding."

The question I was about to ask must have been betrayed by my expression, because Talbot answered it. "I fed her cold blood again tonight. I got it out of your emergency stash in the break room fridge because I didn't have much time."

"And?"

"And Magbidion said somebody spiked your blood," he concluded. "Not the blood in the office fridge that you and Roger share. Just the stuff in the break room . . . just yours."

"It's easier to get to," I said. "Anybody can get into that break room."

"Call the girls and tell them that the Demon Heart is closed until I get this all sorted out. Everyone still gets paid," I told Marilyn.

It's not like I need the money anyway, which I've tried to explain to Roger more than once. It doesn't matter if we turn a profit. The Demon Heart's all about food supply, not money. Managed properly, the club could lose twenty grand a month and we'd still be fine. As it was, we usually made money anyway, assuming we didn't have to shell out for a lot of high-priced magical stuff. Maybe it would have been cheaper to be Magbidion's champion. I just didn't know exactly what it entailed, aside from killing the demon, and as usual, I didn't want to know.

"Damn werewolves," I griped. "Do you think they could be behind this? I mean I get the attack at the hockey game, but—"

"You got attacked at a hockey game?" Marilyn wheezed. She'd walked around behind the desk and started dialing, receiver in hand.

"Yeah. I killed the Void City Howlers." I shrugged. "They were werewolves. Didn't Roger and Rachel tell you about it?"

"Veruca told you they aren't back yet," Talbot reminded me.

"Shit. They left first. They really should have gotten back first." Marilyn hung up the phone and the three of us walked back to the fridge in the break room. Talbot slid past me and opened it. I kept five pints of blood in there for emergencies and weekends, in addition to the supply Roger and I share in the office mini-fridge. There was generally at least one night each week when I wound up drinking blood out of the fridge, usually when all the girls were busy and I just didn't feel like going out. There were two left, pushed to the back behind various salad dressings, bottled water, diet sodas, and the remains of Candice's pizza; Magbidion had marked both bags with a big red X. Marilyn reached past me for a bottle of water with a large M etched into the cap.

I picked up one of the blood bags and shook it at Talbot. "What the hell did he say is in these things?"

Marilyn set her water on top of the fridge, took the bag from me, put it back in the fridge, and closed the door. She stood facing me, but her eyes were on the floor. "Someone tried to slip you the be-all-end-all of Mickey Finns, Eric. Magbidion did two thousand dollars worth of mojo over it and said it was something mixed with werewolf blood. He took one with him to study it, but we already know it makes the vampire who drinks it go berserk. He thinks that at the beginning it gives the victim a mild euphoria and erodes their self-control, but when the drinker next tastes human blood, warm blood, from the source—"

"They go apeshit," Talbot concluded. "We're just lucky that it wasn't you."

"I'd have killed everyone," I said softly. "Is there any way to know who did it?"

"No." Marilyn shook her head. "All of the girls use this room, and our security's not all that tight to start with." She grabbed her water bottle and took a drink. There was a bruise on her right arm, like it had been grabbed too hard, but it was her left arm in the sling. I thought back to the slap. Had I grabbed both arms? I didn't think so, not that I could ask. "Hey, did I do that, too?" seemed a little insensitive.

Talbot seemed to be considering something.

"Spit it out," I said.

"Well, Veruca was back here even though she had the night off. That struck me as a little odd."

"I think that blood's been in there all week. Could have been anyone. Go make your calls, and if you get any leads from the girls, let me know," I told Marilyn. "I'll check on Tabitha." Pushing past both of them,

I headed down the hall toward the dressing room. Tabitha was inside lying on the floor. A crossbow bolt protruded from the side of her left breast. Dried blood covered her from knee to earlobe. Combined with the unnatural pallor, she looked like a murder victim.

I sniffed. Most of the blood was human, though some of it smelled like Talbot's. She was also naked except for a G-string. The whole scene reminded me of a little kid looking at his favorite toy broken on the floor, but I knew that Tabitha was more than a plaything, whether I wanted to believe it or not.

Scooping her up, I carried her into the bedroom and kicked the door shut behind me. I sat down on the bed and held her tight against me. She was limp, cold, and lifeless, but not "dead" dead. A piece of wood through the heart kills Drones, Soldiers, and some of the wimpier Masters, but it only paralyzes the rest of us.

I kissed her forehead and silently thanked anybody that was listening for letting her be powerful enough to survive. For a few more minutes I just sat there with her, holding her, then I laid her on the bed and straddled her. Her eyes were closed. I pushed them open so that I could see them.

Any vampire can use telepathy if they have eye-to-eye contact with someone, but it opens you up to being mesmerized by the other vampire . . . unless you're their sire, or have a stronger psychic fortitude than they do. Using my power over her as her sire, I reached into her mind. She was awake and aware. She could feel everything, hear everything, but she couldn't move.

I'm going to pull the bolt out, I thought to her. *If you can't keep control of yourself, I'll have to put it back in.*

Okay, she thought at me, weakly.

I tried pulling the bolt out backward, tearing muscle, but in the end, I rolled her up on her side and slowly pushed the bolt through far enough to snap off the bloodied head. I let her fall back, locking eyes with her again, and extracted the bolt, a foot-long shaft of thin wood covered in blood.

She cried out and grabbed my shoulders. "Ow! Fuck!" She clutched at the gaping hole in her chest. "That really hurts! Shit!"

She seemed fine. The wound was already closing; her healing worked about as quickly as mine, which was a good thing. I tossed the bolt aside and kissed her, happy she was alive, undestroyed, whatever. I wanted to lick the blood from her breasts, but stopped myself, afraid it might be tainted with whatever had drugged her. It was then, as I leaned down, tongue hovering over Tabitha's breast, that Marilyn walked in.

"I've called all the girls," she said in a disapproving tone. "If you're going to lick that blood off, let me reload the crossbow first, just in case."

Why did I feel like my wife had walked in on me and the other woman? "No, that's okay," I told her. "We'd both better get cleaned up."

Tabitha and I headed into the bathroom and two minutes later, Marilyn joined us with the crossbow. "Just in case."

16

ERIC:

BUYING A CLUE

Talbot, Marilyn, and Tabitha sat across the table from me back in Marilyn's office. The tableau reminded me of a bunch of escaped prisoners trying to decide how to get out of the country. Everyone expected me to have the answers, but my think tank was running low.

"Okay, so we've got Willard's werewolf pack," I said.

Talbot coughed. "William."

"What?"

"William, not Willard. I found out a little more about him, too. He's trouble."

"So am I."

"I know, but not this kind of trouble. He's not just any werewolf."

"Yeah, Roger told me. He's an Alpha. It takes blessed silver to kill him."

"Roger said that?" Talbot cracked his knuckles. "Did he tell you that silver doesn't always work? You might need a specific type of blessed silver, something that's also magic, or maybe inherited. In rare cases, silver doesn't work at all and you have to make them drink mercury."

"Oh for Christ's sake," said Tabitha. "How is he supposed to find out something like that?"

I tossed the bullet to Talbot. He sniffed it gently, then popped it in his mouth and rolled it around. A few seconds later, he spat it back into his hand and studied it with all the intensity that a cat might give a mouse.

"Blessed, magic, and silver," Talbot said. He held it next to my hand. "Hold still."

His pupils changed from round to oblong. He whistled appreciatively. "Your auras are similar. It might even be inherited."

"My aura and the bullet's?"

"Yes," he said, serious despite my incredulous tone. I wanted to throw a flag on that play and give him a fifteen-yard bullshit penalty, but Talbot doesn't lie about things like that.

"One of my ancestors owned a magic gun custom-made for killing werewolves? You'd think Dad would have mentioned something."

"Like you even remember your father's name," Marilyn muttered under her breath.

"Sure, I do." I paused. "It was . . . Dad."

Marilyn laughed.

"John Albert Courtney," she said in bittersweet tones. "It's okay, Eric, that's why you have me." I wanted to kiss her for that, but I knew she wouldn't let me. She'd made that abundantly clear, time and again.

Talbot leaned forward, breaking the uncomfortable silence as Marilyn and I looked at each other. "It's news to me too."

"It's almost like somebody wants me in a fight with Willard. I mean William," I said. "Who would want me to kill him?"

"Why do you say that?" Tabitha asked.

"I don't know." I ran my hand along the desk and stared at my lack of reflection in the computer monitor. "I . . . I think . . . the day they murdered my Mustang . . . I was out hunting and I didn't stumble on one werewolf or two, I got jumped by eight of them while I was hunting in a part of town I don't even usually go to." I felt close to figuring it out and then it tumbled away from me, a lost thought.

"Who would want William dead?" I asked again.

"Who wouldn't?" Tabitha tossed up her hands. "He's a werewolf."

"Most werewolves have learned to stay out of the public eye," Talbot told her. "They form large packs, stick together in groups or communities. Some of them hunt vampires or humans, but those are mostly outcasts. William's group is a little different."

"How so?"

"Well . . . his pack believes they have been given lycanthropy for a reason."

"What reason is that?"

"Whatever William tells them it is, but basically it's to defeat the servants of Satan. Fight fire with fire. Use their unnatural powers for good."

"Oh, give me a break," I put in.

"William himself is a fanatic, or so I've heard," Talbot assured me.

"His wolves tend to pick off lone vamps and leave groups alone, but when you get him on the warpath, everything turns into a crusade. He also has connections to the Lycan Diocese."

I held my head. See, this is why you leave werewolves alone.

"Diocese?" Tabitha snorted with laughter. "What, like the Furry Roman Catholic Church or something?" The laughter died on her lips when no one joined in.

"If by Rome, you mean Rome, Georgia," Talbot answered, "then yes. They aren't part of any human church, though; they don't exactly report to the pope."

"Why spike my blood?" I asked. "If William's a real in-your-face kind of guy and he has access to heavy hitters like the Lycan Diocese—"

"If the Diocese pissed off the high society vamps they might run the risk of starting a turf war. Maybe they wanted to make you look out of control . . . so that no one would take it badly if they vanished you," Talbot said. That made sense. "Or maybe the blood spiking was done by someone else entirely."

"I don't like it being someone else," I said.

"Why?" Talbot held the silver bullet out to me, but I didn't accept it.

"Because it complicates things." According to the clock, it was just past midnight, meaning today was technically tomorrow . . . a Monday. "How do I find this Will guy?"

"I can ask around, but if you're thinking about buying him off, I doubt you'll get anywhere. Last time I heard, he had ninety werewolves running with him, but it could be more. And like I said, he's a real power, not just in the city, but in the whole state, Eric. He could be a problem even for you . . . and he has no reason to make a deal."

"Okay. Talbot, I want you to get out there and try to find the magic gun that belongs to that." I pointed at the bullet. "Magbidion says the bullet will lead you to the gun and the other bullets. They're connected. Tabitha, I want you to back him up in case he runs into any vamps that have issues with . . . his kind."

Talbot nodded and Tabitha's eyes widened.

"Marilyn, I want you to forward the calls from here to your apartment in case Mag calls back with any information." She nodded. I like it when everyone agrees with me.

"What are you going to do?" asked Tabitha.

"I'm going to see if I can't clear up the damn werewolf mess. See if I can set up a meeting with Wilbur . . . I mean William. Maybe we can just get a tape measure and settle it. I'm also going to try to look up Greta to see if she'll help hold down the fort for a few nights."

The only one of them who didn't seem to immediately dislike that idea was Tabitha. I guessed that was only because she didn't know who Greta was.

"I don't think that's such a good idea, boss," Talbot said.

Marilyn shook her head. It didn't take vampiric senses to feel her anger. "You just keep reeling her back into this, don't you?" She snatched up her purse and headed toward the hall. At the door she stopped and looked back at me. Her arm was still in a sling, but she looked fierce, not frail, challenging me with what I had done to her. I tended to forget how long it takes humans to heal. I tried not to look at it. My avoidance amused her. "You can't tell her to stay away from you and then expect her to come running whenever you need her." Head held high, Marilyn stalked out of the room.

"Who's Greta?" Tabitha asked.

"Vampirically speaking," I told her, "she's your older sister. She and her brother are the only children I've made that I haven't . . . that are still with us."

"So your old girlfriend and boyfriend?" Tabitha looked scandalized. "I had no idea you were so broadminded."

"No, it's not like that. They're my son and daughter. I tried to start a family. It didn't work, or maybe it worked too well."

"What went wrong?" she asked.

"See," I said to Talbot. "This is why it's better just to kill them. It saves on aggravation." I regretted it immediately. "I didn't mean that," I said hastily to Tabitha, "or I did, but not about you."

"How many have you killed?" she asked quietly.

"More than you'd like to know about." Tabitha looked a little sickened by that, but she pushed it down deep and plastered on a smile even I could tell she didn't feel inside.

I looked over at Talbot. His body language was tight and coiled underneath a stony exterior. As he headed for the door, I said, "Before you go, is there a way to check my cell phone voice mail on a regular phone? I want to know if Roger left a message."

Talbot walked over to Marilyn's desk and grabbed a blank piece of computer paper out of her printer. He wrote the instructions down and left them on the desk. "Anything else?"

I shook my head. "Head on out. You know what I need you to do." There was more that I wanted to tell Tabitha, but it wasn't the time, especially not with the possibility that she might still be experiencing a few side effects from the blood. Hell, it was probably a bad idea to send her with Talbot, but I definitely didn't want her there with me. Besides, I wasn't ready to tell her about Rachel, and I couldn't risk Tabitha popping over to the Pollux and finding her.

Tabitha nodded and left with Talbot, but the look on his face let me know that I'd be hearing about this later. He didn't like Greta or Kyle, he never had, but he also knew what they meant to me.

Maybe I knew too. I had their damn pictures in my wallet, right behind Marilyn's: family photos from the night I'd turned them; their last moments among the living. It was almost like carrying around an ultrasound in an odd sort of way. After all, you can't take pictures of a vampire, not without more magical assistance than I could easily pay for, and carrying around an artist's representation just didn't seem right. I picked up Talbot's calling instructions, folded them and put them in my pocket.

Feeling conflicted, I walked over to the Pollux. Rachel was waiting for me in a white bustier with lacy white panties, stockings, garters, and high heels. She wore a little black choker with a cameo on it. Dressed that way, she looked even more like Tabitha. Rachel pouted when she saw me, beckoning me with one finger.

I knew why I wanted her. She was young and alive. I could only guess about her desire for me. Maybe it was an adrenaline rush, the thrill of near-death, the danger that I might lose control. Maybe she just liked pain and knew from her sister's experiences that a relationship with me was a good way to get hurt. Either way, her passion and eagerness rubbed off on me. Vampires are like that.

Her excitement fed mine as we kissed. It was a bad idea.

My kisses moved from her lips across her jaw and down the side of her neck. She tensed slightly when I kissed her throat, afraid perhaps that I was going to dispense with the pleasantries and feed. She needn't have worried; I knew it wasn't time for the fangs yet. It hadn't taken me long to discover that women like it best if I feed right as they climax. The pleasure deadens the pain and the pain enhances the pleasure. Sex with a vampire is a monumentally bad idea, but I try to make sure it has its benefits.

Of course, having sex with Rachel was somewhere around a nine out of ten on the stupid scale, which was actually surprisingly low for me based on the evening's events.

Maybe, if I had actually broken up with Tabitha, I would have felt better about it, less guilty. I wondered if I really loved Tabitha. If I loved her, then wouldn't I be faithful? Yet, there I was. . . .

My jacket fell to the floor and I grinned as Rachel tugged at my shirt. Grabbing her by the shoulders, I pushed her down onto the rich red-and-gold carpet of the Pollux and knelt between her legs.

We kissed again, nipping at each other playfully and not so playfully, before she tore my shirt off and ran her hands over my chest. I had been in good shape when I died; I supposed I would remain that way until I died again. Just as she knew I could smell the scent of her excitement, I knew she could feel mine. She undid my belt while I kicked my shoes off onto the floor behind me. For an awkward moment, I was off balance and thought I might fall on top of her, but it didn't happen. I regained my center, but not my composure, and rolled the top of her bra down. Her piercings were simple but fascinating, two golden hoops. I couldn't help but think how painful they must have been. Even so, the effect was quite appealing and I lingered there in my affections before continuing downward.

A single diamond stud pierced her belly button, and she giggled involuntarily when I kissed it. "I'm sorry," she laughed, "but that tickles."

I moved lower, removing barriers and discovering yet another piercing. There were no giggles accompanying my kisses there. "Does that tickle?" I asked.

"Don't stop," was her answer, "that's amazing."

Of course it was; I had been doing this for over fifty years. The difference in our ages surfaced briefly in my mind and I did my best to put it aside. Her heartbeat sped up; oddly it did not encourage my bite, but rekindled a lower passion instead.

She rolled me over on my back and straddled me. I could smell her blood; it surprised me that I didn't feel its pull as strongly as usual. Her body heat flowed over me, strong and vibrant, but it didn't call to me the way it usually did. I wasn't ungrateful for the extra restraint, but at the same time, it felt controlled, artificial. Why couldn't I stop this? It almost felt like magic.

I chalked it up to all the fresh blood I'd been drinking over the last few days, but that didn't fully explain it. Rachel crawled backward over my legs, pulling my pants with her and forcing me to lift my hips to accommodate her motion.

"Socks, off or on?" she asked.

"Off."

She pulled them off and kissed her way up my legs. I don't know why women get their tongues pierced, but why men like it became self-evident. Before I had a chance to think, I was on top of her, our movements urgent and impassioned. I'm not necessarily quiet in bed, but Rachel was very vocal. As we moved together she began a steady stream of soft little nonsense words, a rhythmic chant that sounded almost like another language, and dug her fingernails into my back, drawing blood. Our pace increased and she put both hands on the sides of my head turning it to face hers. We locked eyes and the smell of cinnamon filled my nostrils.

"Bite me!" she commanded. "Bite me, now!"

We both climaxed as I bit into her neck. For the first time in my unlife, the blood had a taste beyond that monotonous sameness to which I had become accustomed. Sweet and bitter all at once, it burned my throat as I swallowed. With each mouthful, the sensation grew. My mind was on fire and my skin was awash with heat. I felt the sun on my face, but there was no sun.

Then, all at once, I was full, completely sated even though I couldn't have had more than a few ounces of her blood. Inside my chest, my heart stirred once, twice, three times before growing cold and still once more. Collapsing on top of her, I panted like a human, as if I actually had to catch my breath.

"What . . . what was that? How?" Sex had never been that way for me before, and neither had feeding. I'd never experienced the easy fullness, the beating heart, such complete satisfaction.

Rachel kissed my forehead and rolled me onto my back before resting her head on my chest. My heart beat one last time and I could see her smile. "How many times did it beat?"

"Four," I answered. My panting slowed and my skin began to cool.

Laughing, Rachel bent her neck back and kissed me once more. "How long has it been since you felt your heartbeat?"

"The day I died," I said softly.

"I can't believe Tabitha hasn't done that for you, baby." Her voice held a note of reproach in it, but she didn't say anything else. Instead, she laid her head back on my chest and sighed. "You wore me out."

"How did you do that?" I asked again.

"It's easy," she said sleepily. "It's a thrall thing. The thralls at the Irons Club told me. If I was your thrall . . ."

I didn't know how to make a thrall. I only vaguely understood what they were, and from Roger's explanation, it sounded too much like slavery to me. I used humans for a little while and let them go. Okay, so sometimes I killed them, but I didn't *enslave* them, had no interest in even knowing how to do so. In my opinion, thralldom was more high society vampire bullcrap to make the wannabe Dracula types feel like kings and queens of the universe. I pictured Rachel eating insects like Renfield in the movies and shuddered. "No."

"Maybe I can do better next time, but I've never actually done it before and it took more out of me than I thought it would. Can we try again in the morning?"

"Maybe. Let's get you to bed."

She muttered a soft assent and slowly started to get up. I stood more quickly, swept her off her feet and carried her into the next room. I'd had the office next to mine converted into a bedroom for when I wanted to spend time away from the club and my employees. It wasn't much, but the windows had been bricked up and the sound system was excellent. There was no bathroom, but there was a sink in the corner with a towel rack next to it. I laid Rachel down on the bed and walked over to the sink. She fell asleep the second her head hit the pillow.

It took a while for the water to heat up, but once it was warm I wet a washcloth and went over to the bed. There was blood caked on her thighs and I gently wiped it away before drying her off with the towel that had been hanging next to the sink. She didn't stir.

"What have you gotten yourself into, Eric?" I asked myself aloud.

I watched her sleep for a while then climbed into bed next to her, feeling like one of those old kings in the Bible who'd been given young girls to warm their beds, except that I was making love to my human bed warmer and drinking her blood.

Guilt wasn't what I was feeling. It was more a sense of profound stupidity. There was more to Rachel than there appeared to be, but I couldn't bring myself to care. I wanted to bite her again, to taste anything other than the coppery taste of blood, to feel my heart beating, to feel alive for even a matter of seconds.

It was selfish and dumb and any number of things, but none of that mattered. I needed her. She made me feel like I was in control, or at least in control of being out of control.

And yet, if I was very still, I could sense an inner conflict. Deep down, I knew that being with Rachel was a *loss* of control, even if it did seem to bring momentary calming of my inner storm.

A little voice inside me told me otherwise. It argued that if I could maintain control of my emotions, even if I lost control to Rachel in the process, then I had an advantage. That didn't make any sense, but the harder I tried to think about it, to analyze it, the murkier it became, as if my thoughts were being deliberately clouded.

The only reason I could come up with for the werewolves spiking the blood supply in the Demon Heart was that they wanted me out of my mind, needed me to go berserk.

If I wanted to stop them, then I not only had to maintain control, I also needed the help of a human who could handle herself when it came to the supernatural, someone who could walk around in the sunshine. Rachel certainly seemed like the best woman for the job. I was going to have to be careful not to feed off of her for the next few days, though. I normally had a once-a-week rule for feeding on my girls, to help them stave off anemia, and I'd already violated that with Rachel.

Before I let myself fall asleep, I checked the time on the wall clock. It was a quarter to four. I shook my head and rolled out of bed. Time was getting away from me and I hadn't even checked my messages yet.

I went into my office, took the paper out of my pocket, and followed Talbot's instructions. I had five voice mails. The first was from Talbot and dealt with the Mustang. There was a message from Carl that told me how long fixing the Mustang would take and how much it would cost. He wanted me to call him on Monday and let him know what to do. I fast-forwarded through the details. The cost didn't matter. Fixing the Mustang was imperative.

Message number three was from Roger. "Hey, pal. Sorry about ditching you back at the game, but I'm betting you had it handled. I dropped Rachel off at the Pollux, but listen: a pack of werewolves jumped Veruca and she's all freaked out. I'm going over there now to see if she's okay. She's a slow healer, so I'm going to give her another few nights off. She can't dance with claw marks all over her. I'll catch you tomorrow."

The last two messages took me by surprise. I listened to them one after the other and then sat down at my desk and listened to them again. The first one was from Kyle.

"No one answered at the club, Pops, so I guess something is going down. Just had a weird feeling and thought I should check in. You didn't close the club, did you? I think Greta would have let me know, but you know how she is when she's mad, so if it happened, you know, recently or something, then I understand why she wouldn't tell me, because you know, she's busy and everything, being mad and all, but if it isn't that maybe you could call me back, because I've been getting these freaky phone calls from a guy named William. He said he's coming for me and I kinda want to know what it's about because—"

Crashing sounds and shattering glass interrupted him; I could hear a scuffle and growling. Werewolves. Kyle never screamed, but I heard him die. It was a whooshing rush of air. Drones always turn to dust when they die. It sounds just like that. Soldiers usually turn to dust as well, but beyond that it's all based on power level, as if a vamp's extra power bought better special effects. Kyle had been a Drone; no special effects for him.

As I listened to the recording, I could tell when one of the werewolves picked up the phone. "You and your vampire whore have a lot to answer for, dead boy," he said. "You killed my son. You and your bitch killed eight more out at the lake. Did you think I wouldn't be able to smell your stench through hers? I was willing to negotiate, but you don't get that chance anymore. I'm coming for you. I'm going to tear down your unholy family and wipe your allies from the face of the earth. You, your unholy spawn, your den of immorality, even the humans that you've tainted with your presence will be wiped clean. Amen." Damn werewolves.

The last message was from Greta wanting to know why she'd just had to kill three werewolves. She gave me her new cell number and asked me to call her soon. Greta was a Vlad, like me. Three werewolves were no problem for her.

Kyle's death was more of a relief than anything else. Just because I hadn't killed him myself didn't mean that I was a big fan. He had just been too stupid to bother killing. What irked me was the part about my "bitch" killing people out at the lake. It couldn't have been Greta because she'd said three werewolves, not eight; and anyway, she'd have let me out of the sleeping bag. It couldn't have been Tabitha, because she had been with Talbot, and, well, the werewolves would've won that fight.

I slapped my palm into my forehead. "I am so fucking stupid!"

Froggy. Veruca didn't have an alibi for last night or for the night before. She had constant access to the break room fridge, and could easily have spiked my blood supply. Veruca wouldn't have been fast enough to unstake me and run, but—an image of a frog hopping away from the driver's side door of the truck flashed up in my mind's eye— she was definitely fast enough to unstake me, turn into a frog, and slowly hop away while I wandered around like a jackass trying to figure out what the hell was going on. It had to be her, but how had she managed to kill eight werewolves by herself?

The silver bullets. They certainly would have evened the odds. If Magbidion had been right (and I had no reason to doubt him) all it took was a single bullet to kill a normal werewolf, to steal its soul. With six bullets, she could have killed six werewolves and only had to fight the other two. I may make fun of her for only being able to turn into a frog, but she's a mean little fighter. She's fast for a Soldier, and she has claws. She could believably have taken on two werewolves.

She'd covered up her scent or maybe I'd missed it, but werewolves have a better sense of smell than vampires. William's phone call meant that he hadn't been fooled, which put him one up on me. The only thing that bothered me was why she'd left one of the bullets behind for me to find. Had she been in a hurry? Had trouble finding the last bullet? It didn't seem that way. It felt purposeful.

I picked up the phone and called Talbot on his cell. When I told him about Veruca, he agreed that it was possible, even likely. I told him about Kyle, too.

"Sure sounds like he's dead," Talbot allowed.

"Par for the course, I guess."

"Are you going to call Roger?" Talbot asked the question carefully, not wanting to imply anything. He knew how long we'd been friends. Just because Roger's girlfriend was mixed up in all this didn't mean Roger'd been in on it too. He'd been with me at the hockey rink when the werewolves had attacked. Sure, he had run away, but he'd just been taking care of Rachel. I still hadn't told him about Brian . . . how was I going to tell him my suspicions about Froggy?

"Not yet. Look, I gotta go. Be careful, Talbot."

Grunting his assent, he hung up.

I still needed to call Greta, but couldn't think of what to say. She hadn't done anything wrong, exactly, but I had sent her away. It had seemed like the right thing to do at the time, even though she thought of me as her father. She also called me Dad; one more reason I had come to find her presence disturbing. Greta looked up to me and genuinely cared about me, which always makes me want to push people away. There was also her eating problem. Compulsive eaters make bad vampires.

I played back her message and scribbled the number down on a piece of paper. The number stared at me. I stared back. My finger finally punched in the digits and to my relief, my call went straight to voice mail. "This is . . . this is Dad. Head over to the Pollux. I'll explain about the werewolves and then we can go kill their boss . . . or talk things over with him . . . or whatever. Oh, and you may know about your brother already, but they got him. Fuck. I don't know. Just come to the Pollux." I carried the handset into the bedroom and set it on the floor by the bed before climbing under the covers and snuggling up with Rachel.

Maybe Tabitha and Talbot would end Froggy, tell Roger about Brian, and make peace with William while I slept. That would be nice.

17

TABITHA:

FINDING FROGGY

Moving on four legs had been uncomfortable at first, but now that I was getting used to it, the warmth and the heartbeat were addictive. I changed into a cat as soon as we got into Talbot's Jag XKR and stayed that way for the whole trip to West Side.

West Side is all high-end apartment buildings and high-rise businesses. Roger's apartment was in the Highland Towers. You couldn't even get near the parking garage without an ID and a pass card. Talbot parked on the street and I forced myself to get out of the car, abandoning the comfort of the soft leather seats.

"This is it," Talbot said. "The trail leads right to the front door."

"How can you tell?" I meowed.

"The eyes of a cat see things the eyes of a human can't," he answered mysteriously. "Can't you see it? It'll be easier to spot when we get closer."

With Talbot leading the way, we walked over to the security gate. Actually, I sauntered. If I squinted and held my head just right, I could see the thin blue line from the bullet, brighter now that we were close to the source.

The Highland Towers loomed before us. I'd never been to the high-rise before, never even driven past it. Close up, it looked huge and imposing, a building that would have been more at home in Gotham City, very noir.

"Somebody's compensating," I meowed.

"Most of these people don't need to compensate. It's a status symbol to live here. That's probably one of the reasons Roger picked this place. Roger is conscious of appearances; it's why he keeps trying to get Eric to close the Demon Heart. His pals in the upper crust probably bust his balls on a regular basis about being a partner in a strip club."

I could smell the security guard even before we reached his booth. A few steps later, I paused in the street. Three faces leapt into my brain, and I yowled, hackles rising. No one had warned me about seeing things in my head. At least, I think they were in my head. They hovered like phantoms, or effects in a 3-D movie, right in front of my nose, but when I swatted at the images, my paw passed through them.

There were two men and a woman. The woman was gorgeous, blond hair hanging down to the middle of her back. Her body was soft and curvy like Marilyn Monroe's. She dressed like one of those old-school movie starlets and she felt old, lots older than me, like she'd seen the passing of centuries, even though we appeared to be physically the same age. She noticed me, and I got the feeling that my presence irked her. I knew why, too. She was less powerful than me. I can't describe how I knew; I could just feel it in my gut.

As my attention shifted, the woman vanished and the first man came into better focus. He was good-looking, but he was dressed more than a decade out of style. It looked good on him, but still, his friends ought to tell him to update his wardrobe. He was old, vampirically, but not as ancient as the actress. I was more powerful than him, too. He seemed startled by my age and power. I actually caught a glimpse of myself in his mind. He saw me as a cat and he couldn't quite tell whether I was a boy or a girl. It unnerved him, and he seemed relieved when my attention moved on to the third and final image.

The other man was short, fat, and balding. He felt just as powerful as me. Physically, I guessed he had been in his fifties when he had been turned, but he hadn't been a vampire very long—maybe thirty years or so. He smiled at me when I sensed him, spread his arms and gave a short bow. "A pleasure," he whispered in my mind and then vanished from the air as the others had, but before I was done examining him. It was less like I had dismissed him and more like he'd dismissed me.

I blinked rapidly, clearing my head. I was still standing in my cat form in the middle of the street. Looking up, I saw Talbot, arms outstretched, blocking traffic, so I darted up onto the sidewalk. He followed me and the cars moved on, their drivers cursing angrily.

"Next time, I might let you get run over," Talbot muttered.

"What the hell was that?" I meowed. "Who were those people? What where they doing in my head? What was I doing in their heads?"

I turned human and grabbed Talbot by his jacket. "Talbot, what the hell is going on here?"

"What people in your head?" he asked. "Tell me exactly what

happened." Concern filled his voice, but he looked more amused than worried.

"I saw three people: two men and a woman. They were floating right in front of my face, Talbot, like holograms or something!" I shook him once and then let go of him. "Sorry. I . . . It's just . . . I could feel how old they were and whether they were more or less powerful than me . . ."

Talbot looked down his nose at me. "Less powerful?"

"Well, yes. Two of them were less powerful and one of them was the same as me." That stopped him for a second and then he grinned. I liked the way his teeth seemed to shine in the dark. It wasn't anything supernatural, just the contrast between his oh-so-white teeth and his dark skin.

Both of us were too distracted to notice the approaching guard until he announced himself. I didn't like him. He was too plain. Even though he was a vampire, he had a semivacant look, like he wasn't awake.

Talbot turned to respond, but I brushed past him. "What?" I said icily.

He recoiled from my question like it had been a slap. I wondered if he would rub his cheek. He didn't, but he did take a step back. Outraged. I was *outraged* that he had dared to speak to me. That wasn't like me. Was it spiked blood again? Or transformation sickness? Was I about to lose it? I didn't feel like I was losing it. . . .

Talbot started to speak again but I gestured for him to be quiet. "You wanted something," I said to the guard. "I know you did, because you walked over in the middle of my conversation." My voice came out louder than I'd meant it to. "So now that you've interrupted me, you might as well tell me what you wanted! What is it?"

He bowed. "My deepest apologies, Lady Bathory. Lord Phillip wishes to invite you and your servant to join him for a drink, if it pleases you. If you are not inclined to join him, then I am to tell you that it is his great hope that you will accept his offer at a later date. I am to await a response." The words were nice enough, but his delivery was off. He might as well have been reading from a cue card.

"Why did he call me Lady Bathory?" I asked Talbot.

"It's a polite name older vampires use for the female equivalent of a Vlad. Nowadays most vamps use Vlad, regardless of gender, but you might still run into a few vamps who will call you a queen vampire, or Lady Bathory."

"Holy shit!" I looked at the security goober. He was waiting patiently, eyes looking at the sidewalk. "Holy shit." Leaning in closer to Talbot, I whispered, "But I thought you said I was a Soldier or at best a Master."

"I thought you were," he answered softly. "It's not an exact science."

"How does this guy know when you didn't?"

"I'm not a vampire." Talbot touched my arm and the contact surprised me, my skin oversensitive to his. "Phillip is a very influential Vlad."

"How influential is very?"

"This is his city."

"So, with a capital 'V' then."

"All caps," Talbot confirmed.

"Right." The guard was still waiting patiently, gaze politely averted. "Which one is Lord Phillip?" I asked the guard.

"I'm sorry, Mistress, but I don't know how to answer that."

I sighed. "Is he the tall good-looking one or the little balding fat one?"

That time I got an incredulous look from the guard, but he covered it up quickly. "What Lord Phillip lacks in height, he makes up for in stature. He is—"

Talbot took two steps backward.

"Impressed that you made the effort, Hollister, but it isn't strictly necessary." The light tenor voice seemed to come from all directions at once. Mist flowed through the security gate and the little man who had bowed to me in my mind coalesced before us. "I am indeed the little balding fat one."

"I am *so* sorry about that," I told him.

"Think nothing of it, Lady—?"

"Tabitha," I answered. He took my hand and brought it to his lips.

"A beautiful name; it has its roots in Hebrew, meaning gazelle. How appropriate." He released my hand and offered me his arm. I placed my hand on the crook of his elbow so that I wouldn't have to stoop. Hollister opened the gates for us as Phillip led me toward the building.

"My name is actually Phillipus," he continued. "It means friend of horses, though I've never much liked them. In recent days, it has behooved me to accept the name Phillip, which both shortens my name and also strengthens, by meaning, my relationship with horses . . . from friend to lover."

"I guess it had to happen eventually," I offered, not quite knowing what to say.

Phillip looked at me questioningly. "Well, you know," I continued, "sometimes when you've been friends with someone for a long time, it's only natural for the relationship to blossom . . ."

"Yes, exactly," my host said with a chuckle, "exactly so."

Two glass doors slid open before us. A tingle spread across my skin as I crossed the threshold. Turning my head, I watched Talbot step through the field without incident. "Pay no attention to that annoying ward," Phillip explained with mild embarrassment. "The less supernaturally adept tenants insist on it for protection. It's paranoia, if you ask me, but then again, most are not as capable of defending themselves as we are. Are they, my dear?"

I said something that I hoped didn't sound impolite, but it was hard to concentrate on what Phillip was saying. I didn't have the words to describe what I was seeing. The building was beautiful, all stone, marble, wood, and stained glass. I can't tell Frank Lloyd Wright from Andrew Lloyd Webber, but this place was perfect. Paintings hung on the walls in just the right light, while sculptures graced the alcoves and hallways.

The elevator was manned by a human attendant, who smiled and spoke to us as if we were royalty. He knew Phillip on sight and pressed an elevator button marked with a strange symbol. "Don't forget that sunrise will be at six eighteen, Lord Phillip," the young man said cheerfully.

"Thank you, Dennis," Phillip answered. "This charming young woman is Lady Tabitha. I'd like you to treat her and her escort as my guests." His lip curled briefly as he said *escort*; he'd come close to being less polite. As he continued, I wondered what he'd almost said. "They are welcome without chaperone in the common areas, the lounge, the elevator, on the roof, and of course, in the waiting area outside my own quarters. See to it and let me know immediately upon completion."

"Of course, sir." Dennis smiled at Talbot and me. "I'm pleased to make your acquaintance, Lady Tabitha. Could I trouble you for a drop of blood?"

"It's for the security system only, I assure you," Phillip explained. I held out my finger and Dennis produced a tiny golden needle with a small crystal on one end. He pricked my finger and the crystal turned red. It flashed once then faded to white again. Dennis repeated the procedure for Talbot. As the crystal turned white for the second time, the doors opened and Dennis ushered us politely out of the elevator.

"It shouldn't be longer than ten minutes, Lord Phillip," Dennis called after us.

When the elevator closed, Phillip led us toward a large wooden door. The wood looked like it had been stained purple. Outside the door was a large sitting area that I mistook for a library at first. To one side of the elevator stood a midsize wine rack filled with bottles labeled with dates, ethnicities, and blood types. Phillip must have noticed my interest.

"Oh, this is my waiting area. I'm an erratic sleeper, so one can never be sure if I'll be receiving guests or snoring the morning, evening, or afternoon away. This is just my little way of apologizing to guests for the inconvenience. Of course, Dennis can arrange for food to be brought up to the more broad-dieted, the humans, werewolves, and whatnot"—he glanced at Talbot as he said the last—"but since I understand firsthand how quickly the thirst can come upon our kind, I like to keep a wide selection of appropriate vintages at hand."

The grand door opened as we approached it and Phillip welcomed us inside. "Enter of your own free will."

"Isn't that what Dracula says?" I asked, pausing in the doorway.

"My apologies," he said, shaking his head. "I thought I was being clever. Please, do come in. I promise my intentions are not malevolent."

"It's okay," Talbot said softly.

I went in. There were even more books inside than in the waiting area. Lovely oak bookshelves lined the walls and wrapped around the oddly shaped room. The interior of Phillip's apartment was humongous; he seemed to have the floor to himself. Glass cases contained displays that ranged from a suit of samurai armor to an actual vampire with a wooden stake through his heart. Startled, I backed away from the glass case and bumped into Talbot.

"Talbot, that's—"

"You mustn't mind Percy." Phillip ran his hand along the glass as he passed, without ever actually touching it. "He's being punished."

For what? I thought. Percy was supported by a metal stand extending up from the bottom of the case and passing concealed under the rear of his jacket. He wore a tweed suit, gold-rimmed spectacles with round lenses, and a thin little mustache. The expression on his face reminded me of the Mona Lisa, a smirk perhaps, or bemused disapproval.

Age hadn't worn away his good looks; in fact, vampirism had frozen him at the magic moment before men stop looking distinguished and become simply old. He was the first vampire I'd seen with eyes so thoroughly faded, the irises gone from whatever color they had once been to the slightly gray off-white of recycled paper. He was trapped in there, frozen by the stake that had entered at an angle, piercing his tie neatly through the middle several inches above a diamond tie tack.

I gave myself a quick mental biology lesson—the stake had pierced Percy's heart.

The plaque at his feet read "My dear Percy, who serves as a remembrance to all that I do not bluff, I do not make empty threats, and there are indeed worse fates than death."

"He was such a naughty vampire." Phillip chuckled.

"He's dead, then? Or he's a Soldier or whatever?" I couldn't imagine him being anything less than a Vlad or a Master, but I hadn't sensed him. "I thought a stake would dust a Soldier."

"Oh, no, my dear," Phillip answered merrily. "Percy's no mere Knight. The stake masks his presence. He can see everything, hear, feel, smell, but he cannot move. He cannot reach beyond his body, even if you stare him in the eye."

I shuddered. Phillip raised a finger in a just-a-moment gesture and vanished around a corner of the room. I wandered about, admiring his collection of miniature antique statues, vases, and expensive knick-knacks until he returned with two glasses and a bottle of what looked like wine.

"Care to join me?" he asked.

"Yes," I answered, smiling.

✦ 18 ✦

TABITHA:

AN AUDIENCE WITH INFAMY

It kind of bothered me that Phillip hadn't offered Talbot anything, but once I tasted the "wine" I knew why. It wasn't exactly wine. The texture, taste, and smell of it were like wine, but my body knew that it was blood. Surely if Eric knew about this, he would have had some at the club; especially with all the bitching he did about not being able to taste anything.

"This is nice," I told Phillip. "Is it a family secret? Because I've never heard of it before."

"Begging your pardon, Lady Tabitha, but you *were* born yesterday."

I must have blushed because he almost dropped his wineglass and I felt a familiar warmth in my checks.

"Extraordinary! A blush response. You have no idea what a priceless jewel you are."

My cheeks grew warmer and I looked away. Part of it was real and the other part was a test. I wanted to know how he would react. He touched my cheek briefly and then withdrew his hand.

"To answer your question, it is not a family secret, at least, not my family. Most of my stock is made up of gifts from other creatures, tokens of respect or appreciation . . . an occasional peace offering. What we're drinking, for example, was made from the blood of Carmella Goshaunt's late lover, Emil. She interfered with my most recent attempt at ascension. The poor dear failed, obviously, but her machinations did prove a distinct inconvenience. . . ."

"Ascension?" I asked, taking another sip of the blood wine.

"Of course, my dear . . . from Master to King, or Vlad, if you prefer."

Talbot pretended not to react, but I could see him stiffen.

"I didn't know that you could do that."

"One can do many things with the correct ingredients. Why, I was commenting on a similar subject some months ago to a young Master vampire who has rather amusing ideas regarding werewolf souls. I think perhaps you may know him." Phillip smiled a genteel smile and put the cork back in the bottle. He hurried off again and Talbot and I shared a look.

"Roger?" I mouthed.

Talbot nodded, but before he could say anything Phillip returned with a small black container roughly the size and shape of a cigar box, made of some kind of stone. "Volcanic glass," he informed me. "Percy made it for me when we were . . . on better terms."

He offered me the box and I handed my wineglass to Talbot. The box itself felt warm to the touch, but it wasn't real heat. It felt more like what I imagined magic might feel like. Inside the box, six items were carefully arranged on black velvet: a thumbnail-size red crystal, possibly a ruby, with a crack in it; a silver ring molded in the shape of a snake; a golden amulet; a pair of yellowish dice; and a small black stone.

"Each of these items was a part of a ritual or ceremony that allowed me to become a vampire or to grow in power."

"Become a vampire? Didn't you have a sire?"

"Not everyone travels an identical path to immortality," Phillip explained. "Vampires have always been reluctant to embrace wizards. As I could locate none to aid me willingly, I was forced to improvise." Trapped by a memory or an old thought, he looked off into space, sighing wistfully before his attention returned to the box.

"The Stone of Aeternum is the only one I haven't used, but it requires a vampire so rare that even a *belluo librorum*, a bookworm, such as myself has read of only a few. It's not as if one meets such a creature every day."

He held his hand out for the box and I handed it back to him. He looked fondly at its contents and then shut the lid. "It's of no true consequence, however; I must wait at least another seventy years before I can attempt an additional ascension. And I'd have to contact the right demons. . . ."

He walked off around the corner of his room again and called back over his shoulder. "That is a lesson worth remembering, my dear. Never try to ascend more than once a century or you may undo the work you've done. None of those soul-thirsty power brokers will tell you that either, so take my word for it."

He returned quickly, his glass in one hand and a necklace case in the other. "Now, this," he said with a smile, "you will appreciate."

He handed the case to me and took a sip of his wine. "Open it," he said eagerly. "It won't bite."

I did as he requested. Inside was a diamond necklace. I could tell it was real just by the way it sparkled in the light. A double ring of round-cut diamonds set in platinum formed the base of the necklace and alternating strands of one or two smaller pear-cut diamonds dangled like priceless teardrops at regular intervals. Queen Elizabeth might have worn such a necklace, or maybe the real Lady Bathory, but I had never seen anything like it, not up close.

"Try it on," he said. Suddenly self-conscious, I looked down at my clothes. I'd changed into a sequined black tank top, a pair of black knit leggings, and running shoes after Eric had unstaked me back at the club. I'd worn it to be comfortable, but it didn't go with a necklace like this. This necklace deserved to be worn with a gown.

"Do try it on," he urged. "It will look gorgeous on you."

"Okay." Just holding the necklace in my hand made me feel beautiful and extravagant. Trying it on was better and worse at the same time. From the look on Phillip's face, I knew that it must have looked wonderful, but not being able to see it for myself was unbearable.

"Oh, you simply must look at yourself. It's astonishing!" He toddled off again, mumbling to himself, then glanced back at me. "Oh, by all means, follow me. I never move the mirror, it's too delicate."

Around the corner he'd so frequently darted past was a large ornate desk with a gold reading lamp shaped like a dragon. Light poured out of the dragon's open mouth, illuminating an old book with pretty little pictures around the words. A leather case containing an assortment of pens lay open on the desk and a slim silver laptop rested in an overstuffed reading chair directly across from the desk.

Phillip brushed past the desk and over to a pair of doors set back between two bookcases. He opened them to reveal a full-length mirror held by a crystal frame that was decorated with fanciful flowers and artful designs. In the mirror I could see not just Phillip's reflection, but my own. I looked better than I ever had in life.

Everything about being a vampire rushed in on me at once—the rampage in the Demon Heart, the blood, Eric, Lillian's terrified face as I struck her down, all of it, my mind seared like bacon in a hot frying pan.

Then, almost as if the mirror had a will of its own, I sensed that it wasn't satisfied with what it had made me feel. I guess I hadn't been dead long enough to truly horrify myself with what I had done, so the mirror rummaged through my life for ammunition. The last conversation I'd had with Rachel had been a fight. Our words rang out in my ears.

Each mistake I'd made, each humiliation I'd ever endured, the mirror latched onto, multiplied, and distilled. All the times I'd ever been hurt, by Rachel, by my parents, by Eric, crashed back on me as one exaggerated assault.

You want to see how pretty you look? the mirror's whispering not-quite voice wheedled in my thoughts. *I'll show you what you look like on the outside, but only if you can endure what you are on the inside.*

Turning into a vampire had made my emotions more volatile than they'd been when I was alive. I'd been crying right and left since the change, like having PMS all the time. I was easy prey for the mirror: the tears came quickly, pouring red down my cheeks, a deluge of self-loathing, self-pity, and remorse. I turned away.

Doors clicked shut behind me as Phillip covered the glass. The mirror's taunting voice slowly faded, but having once peered into it, I could feel it there, behind the thin paneled doors, watching me, waiting for me to take another look.

Talbot rushed to my side, but I waved him away. I didn't want to be comforted; I was too busy being mad at myself for crying. I was tired of crying. I hadn't cried when my grandmother had passed away or when Rachel had died, and the mirror had exploited that, thrown it back at me in a horrible way. Phillip offered me his handkerchief and I took it, soaking the red silk with my blood as I tried to stop the tears.

"Damn it," I said between sobs.

"It's my fault," Phillip said, sounding genuinely angry with himself. "The mirror allows a vampire to see his reflection, but it takes its toll in other ways. We who gaze within that mirror must face the things we've done as vampires, our hidden sins, the things that would make us cringe and weep were we still human. I'm so used to it that I had forgotten the effect it can have. I shan't show it to you again without giving you time to prepare."

"Is it alive?" I asked.

"There is a demon trapped inside to power it," Phillip answered, "if that's what you mean. It's only a small one."

Talbot took my arm and we walked out of Phillip's study and back into the main room of his chambers. "If there is anything I can do to make it up to you," Phillip offered, "I would be most pleased if you would tell me. You may keep the necklace, of course. I knew at once that you should have it."

"No, I can't, it's too much."

"Bah," Phillip protested. "It was a gift from so long ago that I no longer remember who gave it to me. It's yours whether you take it or leave it, though I'd rather you took it. I have collected so many things over the years that I could give half of it away and never notice."

I smiled, and my tears began to subside. "How long have you been alive—I mean, how old are you? You seemed—that is, you felt kind of young, you know, outside."

"Oh, not quite a thousand . . . each time I ascend it makes other vampires sense me as though I were younger, but my mind has not forgotten the truth that the magic conceals."

"And you really used those things in the box to become a vampire—to ascend?"

"You will, in time, learn not to question my veracity, my dear." Phillip's eyes hardened briefly before softening once again. "But you are new and I can't bring myself to hold it against you, so yes. Oh, yes. Vampires have always been reluctant to grant immortality to wizards, are strictly forbidden to do so now, unless it is done via a thralldom, which is a capricious immortality at best. So, yes, I had to find alternatives.

"I used those 'things in the box' along with rituals, demons, and of course, vampires of the required power level. . . . Does it concern you? I'm already a Vlad; you have nothing to worry about from me on that account. I've no further need for sacrifices from those of our rank; my final ascension will be much more difficult to arrange. Besides, I've made it a habit to expend only those I found distasteful, and I find you anything but." He waved a hand. "Enough talk of me, though, I am still waiting to know how to make it up to you—my faux pas with the mirror."

"But the necklace—"

"The necklace is a gift, my dear, not an apology. I gave it to you because I wanted you to have it." He gestured around the room. "Excepting the Stone of Aeternum and my own existence, you may choose from anything I have. Even Percy. Please, take your pick. I insist."

His eyes sparkled mischievously. "I could dispel the enchantment on the city. I used a Veil of Scrythax, you know. Have you seen one? Oh, they're ghastly-looking things, but incredibly effective and oh, so delicate. There are nights when I'm gripped with the urge to rush to the vault, seize the hideous thing and smash it to pieces, to let the humans see us for what we really are and remember all the things I've hidden from them. Think of the panic! It would be impossible for the Council of High Magic to contain it. Another war with the humans would be such . . . fun. It's always so interesting to see how the human rulers choose to conceal it from their constituents."

Uh . . . no. There was nothing that I saw in Phillip's house that I really wanted and a war was not my idea of fun. There were plenty of things that it might be nice to have, but . . . I wondered what Percy had done and whether I ought to ask for him and let him go. Then Talbot mouthed *werewolves* at me and I remembered that I was supposed to be finding out about the magic gun thing.

I held my hand out to Talbot and he handed me the silver bullet. Phillip's eyes lit up when I showed it to him. He delicately took it from my outstretched palm and held it up to one eye.

"A bullet from *El Alma Perdida*, meaning in Spanish 'the Lost Soul.' I wonder where he found it."

"I was . . . we were looking for the rest of it, the other bullets, and the gun. Talbot tracked it here for me."

"Ah," Phillip said excitedly, "information, the most valuable gift of all! Do you realize how rare it is for one of my new acquaintances to ask me for information? They all ask for money or power—"

A knock at the door interrupted him. "That should be Dennis," Phillip said as he walked to the door. "He is one of my applicants, you know. An intern . . . as it were." Phillip looked through a small eye-hole, midway up the door and smiled. "It is he."

He opened the door and invited Dennis inside, but the man declined. "I just wanted to let you know that the lady and her companion have been added to the ward matrix, sir. I apologize for taking so long, but Mistress Gabriella was quite interested in your new guest."

"What did you tell her?" Phillip asked eagerly. He seemed giddy, childlike in his delight.

"As per your standard request, sir, I told her only that the lady and her companion were your guests and that they were to be given access to all of the common areas."

"Was she vexed?"

"Quite vexed," Dennis replied.

"Excellent as always, Dennis," said Phillip. "You may go."

He closed the door and walked back over to me. "Please, excuse the interruption. Gabriella has been a bit wroth with me for the last few decades. She recently relocated from Atlanta in hopes that she might be the agent of my eventual demise. How quickly my offspring turn against me. But you wanted to know about *El Alma Perdida*; you thought you might find it here?"

"Yes. We think a female vampire, a Soldier, has it and we think she's in the building. Her name is Veruca."

"Meaning wart . . . such an unpleasant name for a lady."

I'd been taking one last sip of blood wine when he said that and it shot out my nose as I tried to stifle my laughter. I caught the blood with the handkerchief I was still holding, but I continued to cough and sputter. My nose and sinuses started burning and I would have dropped to my knees if Talbot hadn't caught me.

"I'm sorry," I said, coughing, "that's just too funny. Her name means wart? Eric calls her Froggy."

More blood tears formed in the corners of my eyes and even Phillip chuckled. "That is indeed an unfortunate nickname for one whose name comes from the Latin *verruca*, meaning wart. At least he doesn't call her *acuminata*. *Verruca accuminata* would be just too terrible. . . ."

Only Phillip laughed that time. He quickly controlled himself and sat down in one of the armchairs. They were slightly undersize for a person of average height, but they suited Phillip quite well. He smiled in my direction and motioned for me to sit. Instead, I walked over and knelt next to him. It let us look at each other eye-to-eye and I was tired of looming over him.

"And you believe her to be in possession of *El Alma Perdida?*" he asked.

"I do."

He caressed the air about the bullet with his fingertips, but his eyes did not leave mine. "No one by the name of Veruca lives here, I'm afraid, but that doesn't mean she isn't staying here with someone else. Did she have any other acquaintances who might have a residence here?"

I nodded. "Her boyfriend, Roger."

"Ah, yes, Germanic, meaning quiet . . . or famous spearman. And this Roger, would he be a Master vampire?"

I nodded again.

"I spoke with him several months ago," Phillip said as he stroked his chin with his left hand. "Utterly ignorable. He tried to engage me in no less than three business transactions. He wanted to buy the Stone of Aeternum from me. I didn't sell it to him, of course. You don't sell those sorts of things; they are given or sought. I am not in retail. I think I suggested that he talk to one of the local demons, though. It's in my log." He raised both hands in a dismissive gesture. "I can always check it later."

"Do you remember the other transactions?" I asked.

"Oh, he had some foolish notion about my backing him in the Orchard Lake acquisition. Naturally, I declined. Vampires like him will be the ruin of us." He trailed off and his eyes focused on someplace far away and probably long ago. Eric has that look sometimes. "Let's see if your Wart is sleeping over, shall we?" He walked over to an old-fashioned wall phone, lifted the earpiece, and held it at arm's length. "Dennis?"

I could hear Dennis easily, one of the benefits of being a vampire. "Yes, my lord?"

"I want you to check on a Master vampire named Roger. See what suite he is in and find out whether or not he has another vampire by the name of Veruca visiting him. Ring me back as soon as you know anything, would you?"

"Of course, sir," Dennis answered.

A barely audible click signaled the end of the connection on Dennis's end.

"He's going to find out and get back to us," Phillip explained. "He's such a clever boy; he's the current leader amongst the male applicants."

"Applicants?" I asked.

He laughed. "I do hope you will excuse me for not explaining earlier. Every decade I have a contest to determine my next two children: one boy and one girl. It keeps me busy, and some of them make wonderfully entertaining opponents after a few centuries.

"But enough of that. Dennis should be back soon and I don't like to let them hear too much about who is in the lead. It makes them insufferable. While we wait, could I get you another glass of wine? Perhaps your mouser is hungry? I'm certain Dennis could scrounge up a rodent or two."

I stared at him blankly. "I'm fine, Lady Tabitha," Talbot told me.

"He's fine, thank you," I said with a puzzled look on my face.

Phillip nodded absentmindedly, then snapped his fingers. "I could play the violin for you. I've only been playing for a century, though, so I haven't mastered it yet."

Talbot cleared his throat. "Maybe you could tell Lady Tabitha about the Lost Soul? What's it for?"

Phillip set the bullet down on a table and dashed off. It sounded like he was wrestling with a box of Christmas lights. When he returned, it was with a beautifully crafted violin case. "Perhaps I shall do both?"

I nodded and he opened the case.

19

ERIC:
GRETA

I woke to a cacophonous mix of werewolf howls and trucks revving their engines outside the Demon Heart. I was getting tired of fucking around with these stupid werewolves. The door to my bedroom in the Pollux swung open and Greta stepped inside. She'd cut her hair. It was short now, but still blonde. Dressed in running shoes, jogging shorts, and a sports top, she looked none the worse for wear. The only sign of her recent conflict with the werewolves outside was the remains of a tiny media player still clipped to her shorts; there wasn't much left of it.

"Up and at 'em, Dad. There are werewo—" She paused in midsentence as she spotted Rachel. "So that's Tabitha," she said awkwardly. "She's certainly . . . um, pierced, isn't she? Those cannot have felt good."

"Her name's Rachel," I muttered as I rolled out of bed. "I turned Tabitha. This is her little sister."

"Jesus, Dad," Greta complained. "That's screwed up even for you." Greta blanched at her own sentence, worried that she'd criticized me too harshly, that I might have taken her seriously, missed the teasing tone in her voice. She looked purposefully away from Rachel's nakedness and cocked a thumb toward the door, hiding her dismay behind a jaunty smile. "Let's kill the werewolves across the street and then you can tell me all about it." She looked back at Rachel and sighed. "Or better yet, you could just not."

I rolled my eyes and headed for the door. "Did you have a nice trip?"

"Oh, yes," Greta quipped. "It's been great. Those werewolves have been chasing me all night. I probably could take them, except they've got crosses and stuff. How's Mom?"

We headed out of my room and down the stairs.

"I think she suspects that the Demon Heart is really a strip joint," I joked.

Greta jumped over the rail and landed next to the door. Why hadn't I thought of that? "That whole 'interpretive dance school for nudists' story couldn't hold up forever," she tossed back at me.

That, in a nutshell, was my problem with Greta. I liked her too much and we got along too well. She fell into the father-daughter role easily and could make it seem so normal when it definitely isn't. She accepted me. Even when she snarked about my lifestyle, her complaints were usually voiced as lighthearted teasing.

If we were a real family, when I grew old, Greta would have never sent me to an old folks' home; she would have kept me close and taken care of me. That kind of devotion was scary, especially coming from a cold-blooded killer even more amoral than me. Greta viewed me as a hero growing up, justified my every mistake, and lionized my flaws. She took my dislike of other vampires to another level, too; sometimes, she even hunted them.

Greta opened the front door and one of those fake-looking werewolves was there waiting for us. His hair could have been badly dyed rabbit fur glued over latex rubber skin, and his smooth tan teeth reminded me of a botched resin model kit. He snarled, snapping at Greta.

"Bad dog!" she admonished. "No biscuit!" Greta caught him by the muzzle, snapping his jaws shut with a pop and giggling when he whined. "Can I keep him, Dad?"

Roger likes to tell me I don't think before I act. Compared to Greta, I'm well-reasoned, insightful, and reserved. The werewolf swiped at Greta with his claws and she laughed, popping him twice in the forehead with her right fist. While he was stunned, she grabbed his neck and pulled the beast down into a headlock.

"Well, can I?" Greta asked insistently.

"I don't care if he did follow you home," I said as I grabbed either side of his head and twisted. "You're not keeping him." The wolf's neck broke and Greta let him drop to the floor. He wasn't dead, but the broken neck would keep him out of the fight.

Behind him, I could see about a dozen of his companions strutting across the street like some kind of inner-city gang, clearly confident that we'd be no problem for them. The four in the middle of the pack seemed to be the ones in charge. Two of those wore cross-studded collars around their hulking necks, their fur a uniform dark brown. The third was larger than the rest, a mottled gray werewolf with a pug-nose muzzle more befitting a bulldog than any wolf I'd ever seen. He hefted a large wooden cross made from two interlocking railroad ties. Next to him, a black wolf with a priest's collar stared directly at me, rosary beads wrapped around his right paw.

"William?" I asked.

"The flock calls me Reverend." His voice was light and airy, a complete contrast to the wolf's hulking black form. The sound didn't even synch up with his lips, like a badly dubbed kung fu movie or spaghetti western. Maybe he was using some big magic mojo to translate snarls and growls into English for the wolf-speech-impaired. Quite possibly I should have been impressed, but it only served to enhance the goofy unreality that I experience whenever I run into a werewolf.

I glanced at Greta. She had a hungry look in her eyes. I imagined it was the same look that I had in mine when I woke up each morning, ready for my next drink of the red stuff. That's the other problem with Greta. She's always hungry.

"What about one of these?" she asked with mock sincerity.

We walked out into the street side by side. I stopped to lock the door behind me, casually, as if there was no rush.

"Sorry, honey. You know the rules. No pets."

We were both smiling; it seemed to confuse the werewolves. They outnumbered us five to one and they expected trepidation at the least, outright terror at the most. Cocksure bravado was not in their list of likely prey responses. Unfortunately for them, we weren't prey.

A wave of holy power hit me as they crossed the center lane. The four in the middle were true believers; no wonder they felt confident. I realized immediately why Greta hadn't wanted to fight them on her own. She doesn't heal from holy wounds easily. The more powerful the vampire, the more quirks he or she has. That was one of hers.

The true believers were going to be the real problem. Most werewolves just charge in without thinking, but these guys held back, waiting, I supposed, on the good reverend's word.

"Let's not do this, Reverend," I said. "I'm not a bad guy. Ask Jackie, down at the—"

Reverend made the sign of the cross with his rosary-clad paw and spoke Latin: *"In nòmine Patris, et Filii, et Spìritus Sancti."*

"Amen," the other werewolves said in unison. My teeth went numb, my fangs retracted, and I took two involuntary steps backward. You only feel power like that every once in a while, and generally not from locals. These guys were from the Lycan Diocese, or the one with the rosary was; he had to be. What the Inquisition was to witches the

Lycan Diocese is to vampires and other things that might threaten the therianthropic flock. Your average skinchanger can't go to them for help, but William obviously had some pull.

This was exactly the sort of attention I'd wanted to avoid.

"William was right to call us," said the big one with the giant cross. He unlimbered the heavy thing as he spoke and swung it like a giant hammer. Greta screamed, but I couldn't move, as if a spell were fixing me in place. The cross hit me midchest, igniting the front of my *Welcome to the Void* T-shirt and hurling me back into the brick next to the *Casablanca* poster at the side of the Pollux's main entrance.

"I was kind of disappointed when Deacon sent you instead of coming himself. I see that I was wrong," one of the other werewolves told him. Three werewolves on the left teamed up on Greta, grabbing her as the one called Reverend advanced. He placed his rosary-wrapped paw at her throat. The sizzle and pop of her flesh was all I could hear, the smell of the rosary charring her flesh.

She screamed out one word, "Daddy," and then, suddenly, I was free. I could move again.

Speed. Most vampires have it all the time. Mine comes and goes. Sometimes I can control it, but usually it just kicks in and out. This time, it kicked in. Each sizzling pop of Greta's flesh resounded like a gunshot. My whole body began to vibrate. I felt like I was going to lose control, go into one of my rage blackouts, but then, somehow, I didn't. In a wave of remembered cinnamon scents, my proximity to Rachel, even asleep upstairs in the Pollux, gave me reins for my rage. I took a deep breath and charged.

In an instant I was on the three werewolves holding Greta, bypassing the two werewolves with the cross-studded collars that were headed toward me. I cocked my hands back and plunged my claws through the backs of two of Greta's captors. My hands closed around their hearts and I let them each beat a single time before I tore them out.

It must have broken Reverend's concentration or something, because suddenly Greta could move, too. Greta's claws were out and I couldn't stifle my laughter when she gave Reverend a knuckle-deep two-finger eye poke, Three Stooges style, accompanied by an imitation of Curly's famous "Nyuk nyuk."

I tossed the two hearts I was holding down onto the pavement. The remaining werewolf with a grip on Greta let her go and threw up. Weak stomach, I guessed.

Reverend drew back howling, clutching at his ruined eyes, blood matting the fur around them. The sight distracted me, and the two collared werewolves took the opportunity to sink their fangs into either shoulder. The shoulder bite I'd gotten on Friday had hurt; two hurt more than twice as bad. The added sizzle of their collars against my cheeks didn't help either. I grabbed them both by the scruffs of their necks like oversize puppies and flung them across the street. The movement didn't do my shoulders any good, but I didn't have much choice.

"Don't fucking bite me," I snarled furiously. "I'm the vampire! I bite you. You do not get to fucking bite me!"

I pointed my finger at the remaining combatants. "You can claw me. You can hit me. Hell, run me over with a truck, but no biting or I'm going to stop dicking around here and you won't even have time to run away."

Everybody stopped.

"And another thing, your fight is with me and me alone. You touch my little girl again and when I'm done with you, I'll get your scent from the pieces, I'll track it back to your home and I'll bring the fight to your kids, your family. Does that sound fucking fair to you, assholes?"

They seemed to suddenly shrink before me, or maybe I was expanding. I could feel a familiar burning in my chest. I wasn't just standing on the brink of a blackout, I had jumped off the cliff and now everyone was waiting to see if I would catch the rope dangling behind me.

"Oh, great!" Greta sighed. "You guys went and pissed him off! Now he's going to go all uber vamp and I'm not going to get to play anymore."

"Okay," Reverend said softly, his paws still pressed to his eyes.

"Okay what?"

"Just let us leave. We heard what happened to the Howlers, but we assumed you'd had help. Lots of help. We couldn't believe that you'd done it alone. I can see we were wrong. So just let us take Jim and leave."

"Who the hell is Jim?" I asked.

He pointed blindly in the direction of the werewolf with the broken neck.

"Okay, Reverend." I smiled. "You have a deal. You grab your boy Jim and get the hell out of here. Anybody that wants to go can go, but if I see you around here again, you die. Oh, and I want you to tell your boss something for me."

"You can't do that, Reverend!" one of the collar-wearing fuzzies protested. "They've killed Bruce and Annie. We can't just walk away. They are unholy monsters. We have to kill them, now!" One of them had been a girl? I glanced down at the bodies, but they were too furry for me to tell. Dead werewolves do change back to human form, but only when the sun hits them.

The Reverend seemed to think it over before answering his pack-mate. He didn't take long. "I'm sorry, Paul, but William is going to have to come out here with us if he's going to send us up against something like this. That isn't a normal vampire. It can't be. A normal vampire could not have broken free of my spell like that. You can stay here if you want, but the rest of us are going." Eyes still covered, he turned blindly back toward me. "What is it you wanted me to tell William?"

"Tell him I know who killed the werewolves out at the lake and it wasn't me or any of my people. I'll admit to having killed his son, but he killed my son, not to mention my car, so I'm willing to call it even and let things blow over. If Willy Boy won't go for that, then I'm even willing to find the ones responsible for what happened out at the lake and gift wrap them for your boss. You got all that?"

Reverend nodded.

"One more thing. Tell him I'll need an answer by tomorrow night." I pulled Greta back to the sidewalk, trying not to pay attention to how badly burned her neck had gotten.

I shouldn't have spent so much time talking. Reverend pulled his hands away from freshly healed peepers, a bit bloodshot but clearly functional. This time my speed didn't kick in. Damn it. Before I could react, the two werewolves next to him grabbed me, one furry bastard on each arm. Reverend reached up and put the paw with the rosary over my eyes. An eye for an eye. It was even less fun than El Segundo, but this time I had Greta at my side. I heard the slight jingle of were-wolf collars as they ran for her, but she was already in motion.

I heard the swoosh of Pug Nose's big hammer-cross thing, and felt the displacement of air brush past my face as it just missed me, con-necting with Reverend instead. His skull caved in with the sound of a smashing watermelon, music to my ears.

"You missed," Greta taunted.

Two sets of claws I couldn't see tore into my belly, spilling my guts onto the concrete about the same time I heard the sickening tear of a werewolf's head being torn from his neck.

"Grow that back, Rev." Greta laughed again, but the laugh turned into a shriek and a sizzle. Damn it. Not sure of what to do, I jumped backward, carrying my two captors with me, shattering the glass doors at the front of the Pollux and landing with a crash in what used to be the ticket booth.

The werewolf on my left arm relaxed his grip and I used the mo-ment to tear free of him; then I pulled in the one on my right and sank my fangs into his throat. Werewolf blood doesn't taste much different than human blood. The tricky part is not getting any fur stuck in your teeth.

I didn't have time for a prolonged snack, just enough to speed my healing. Blood is both food and medicine for us. I tore out enough of his throat to put him out of the fight, and rubbed my eyes against the wound. Gross, but effective. My vision returned, but it was still cloudy, like viewing the world through a sheet of wax paper. Lucky for me, werewolf silhouettes are easy to recognize.

I turned on the second werewolf just in time to get a claw slash to the chest as he extricated himself from the ruined ticket booth. Cuts and scrapes from the glass dotted his hide. Behind him, I could see Greta going toe to toe with pug-face and the others in the middle of the street.

A minivan sped by, swerving to avoid the melee, and I could only imagine what the driver would remember. Greta used the distraction to snatch the railroad-tie cross away from Bulldog and concuss him with it, her hands igniting even as she touched the wood. She sank her flaming claws into Bulldog, using his blood to extinguish the flames, and then latched onto his neck with her fangs.

I pulled myself upright and boxed my opponent's ears. He howled in pain and I did it again. The second time, I heard the pops I was waiting for and he dropped to his knees.

I saw that Greta was now on her own against the collared were-wolves that had been helping Bulldog, so I simply wrenched my opponent's jaws apart, taking the top half of his skull with me as I turned away, hastily stuffing guts into my rapidly healing torso.

I charged toward Greta only to get pulled off my feet by Jim, the werewolf with the no-longer-broken neck. He had the same fighting style as the wolf from the alleyway, and I had terrible déjà vu as he battered my head first into the concrete, then the brick, then the bench in front of the Pollux.

I caught a *fwoosh* of flame out of the corner of my eye as Wolfboy kept swinging, applying the tiger by the tail principle. One of the were-wolves had removed his collar and strapped it around Greta's neck. He and his companions were holding her down as she burned.

So much for keeping my temper. My vision blurred, and then everything went dark, but I could still hear the screaming. Usually, a rage blackout was a hole in time that I could never get back, but this time was different. I heard flesh rending and tearing. I heard bones break and smelled fur charring. Underneath it all, there was another noise, like wings flapping in the night. Finally, when everything was silent, I could see again. Greta was in my arms and the fuzzies were scattered in piles across the street. One of them was impaled on the massive railroad-tie cross, his ribs splayed open by the massive wooden center beam protruding from his chest. The rosary beads and cross-studded collars were nowhere to be seen. I was pretty sure I didn't want to know what had happened to them.

I took Greta inside the Pollux and called Tiko. He's an oni—sort of a Japanese ogre. His kind are body-disposal specialists. They eat them. Sometimes they play with them first. I don't ask any questions as long as the corpses go away and don't show up again.

"I need you to get out here," I said when he answered. "I've got a bunch of dead werewolves for you . . . and the good news is that some of them had shiny new trucks."

Tiko said he'd get there as quickly as he could, but that he was going to have to charge extra. "I have a few cousins over in Georgia who could help," he offered, "if you're going to keep killing off werewolves left and right. We can only eat so much."

"Yeah. Call 'em," I said, sighing. "There may be seventy more where those came from and who knows what else."

I hung up before he said anything else and carried Greta up to my office. She was pretty badly burned. There would be no talking to William now. Son for son, I was willing to accept. I was even close to overlooking the Mustang. But now he'd fucked with my little girl and there was going to be hell to pay.

20

ERIC:

EYE OF THE . . . ?

One of the things Roger taught me was that a sire, if he or she is powerful enough, can heal their offspring with their blood. Not that he'd meant to teach me on purpose, but near the end of the whole El Segundo thing, the only way we found to heal the cross-shaped burns Roger received was to take him home to mommy. He, like Greta, had difficulty healing wounds inflicted with holy implements. I'd thought the burns were pretty darn funny, myself. Anyway, we'd looked up Roger's sire in Atlanta and she had taken care of his wounds.

I didn't get to meet her; Roger made me wait outside. For weeks afterward, I had to hear how she'd had this whole ritual that I thought was her way of making sure Roger knew what a pain in the ass it was to do the healing for him. Roger had been impressed, but I was pretty sure that it was little more than the strategically placed flour women get on their faces in the movies. You know, so the audience can tell they've been toiling for hours to bake those instant cookies?

As far as I could tell, the ritual was like that, all pomp and circumstance, and highly unnecessary. Fortunately for Greta, she had me for a sire; trust me, I'm powerful enough, and I have no use for ritualistic ass kissing.

I tore my wrist open with my fangs and bled directly onto her ruined face, working the blood into the remaining skin, smearing it across bare bone where necessary. Skin bubbled back into place, like burning in reverse. Greta's hair grew back long and blonde, the same as when I had embraced her. My blood bubbled like thick red hydrogen peroxide over the marks on her neck, only when the bubbling was over, the wounds weren't just disinfected, they were gone.

I moved on to her injured hands, withered stick fingers crackling as I doused them liberally with blood. It started to work immediately. The claw marks on her side and a nasty bite she had taken to the left calf healed just as quickly after a similar treatment.

When I was done with the front, I rolled her over and checked her back. There were a few claw marks, but they had already started healing, so I left them alone. My own wounds were gone by the time I finished with hers, but I didn't feel the hunger I thought I should. Between my own healing and bleeding all over Greta, I should have been ravenous. Instead, I felt nothing.

I washed myself off using the sink in my Pollux bedroom and changed into jeans, tennis shoes, and a fresh *Welcome to the Void* T-shirt. By the time I was done Greta was waking up. The clock in my office read four o'clock. That meant I'd slept for a good hour before the fight, maybe more. I should have been feeling the daily hunger as well, but I wasn't. True, I'd ingested a little werewolf blood, but that didn't account for everything.

"Dad?"

Greta stood up, covered in blood, and looked down at what was left of her clothes. The running shoes were okay and her panties had survived (they were soaked with blood, but technically intact); the rest was in a desperate state. "Okay, either you healed me or you thought it would be fun to blood wrestle your unconscious naked daughter."

I averted my eyes. My first thought was to send her down to the dressing room Rachel had appropriated, but Greta was taller than Rachel and more endowed. "You can probably find some clothes across the street in the club, but if Tiko is out there, I'm going to want to walk over with you. Oni have two favorite pastimes: eating people and raping them. Tiko is a good guy as far as oni go, but—"

"Seeing me naked and covered in blood might stretch his self-control a little?"

"Yeah, something like that. And you can't kill him. . . . I need him right now."

She walked out and I waited, listening. I heard her footsteps on the stairs, the door opening and closing, but I didn't hear her go outside. I couldn't hear Tiko working, but I assumed that was why she had stopped. Finally her footsteps echoed on the stairs again, then down the hall to my office door.

"Is he out there?"

"Yep."

"So you came back to get me." She nodded and I headed out with her. "Good girl."

"Dad?" she asked on the stairs.

"Yes?"

"Is there something wrong?" She bit her lip nervously. "Did I do something wrong? Are you mad at me?"

"What? Where the hell did that come from?" We stopped midway down the stairs and she put a hand on my shoulder. She looked genuinely concerned.

"No, nothing, it's okay, it's just, you know, your eyes . . ."

I didn't know. "No. What about my eyes?"

"They're still . . . doing the thing."

The thing? I held a hand up in front of my eyes, but there was no red light shining on them. "What thing?"

She exhaled and I was a little taken back. Greta never breathed unless she was talking; even then, she took only the necessary breaths. Breathing was like pacing for her; she only did it when she got nervous. "You know . . . your angry eyes."

"My angry eyes? Am I supposed to be Mr. Potato Head all of a sudden? They aren't glowing red. I just checked."

She looked away and removed her hand from my shoulder. "I'm sorry. It's nothing. I shouldn't have brought it up."

"No," I said quickly. "It's okay; I just don't know what you're talking about. Seems like everyone mentions it but no one will talk about it. You act like I'm going to chomp you or something. Can we please talk about it?"

"Okay," she said, "but let me shower and dress first. This blood is starting to congeal on me."

I took off my shirt, right there on the stairs and slipped it over her head. Why hadn't I thought of that before? The hem of the T-shirt only came down to mid-hip on her, but it concealed most of her nudity. We crossed the street to the club uneventfully. Tiko stared at her, hunger in his eye, but looked away when he realized I was with her.

Greta showered and dressed quickly. The clothes came from a stash Marilyn had been keeping for her, but hiding from me. She walked straight to Marilyn's office and pulled them out of a small travel bag stored in the bottom drawer of the filing cabinet. I wondered absently what other secrets Marilyn was keeping from me.

When she was finished, Greta met me back in Marilyn's office. She was wearing jeans and a black T-shirt that read *Welcome to the Void*. It was similar to mine, only hers showed a fair amount of midriff and had pink lettering.

"Are they still doing it?" I asked.

"Your eyes?"

"Yes, my eyes."

She sighed. "Yes, Dad, they're still doing it."

"Describe it to me."

She got up and crossed the room, knelt in front of me and rested her arms across my lap as she stared into my face. One thing that I find unnerving about other vamps is the lack of heartbeat. If she had been human, there would have been all sorts of signs to give me insight into what she was feeling, whether she was scared and trying to look calm, or vice versa.

"I've never gotten a good close look like this before," she said, sounding fascinated, "but it's actually kind of cool. The whites have turned black and the veins in your eyes . . . from a distance I couldn't see it, but up close they're dark, dark purple. Your irises are purple too, but sort of crimson at the same time. They're shifting back and forth slowly from one color to the other, with a kind of subtle glow. When you get totally furious they glow more and more brightly until there are actual beams of light shining out of them. I've only seen that once, but I didn't stick around. I've never been too sure about how safe you are when you're like that."

"Like what? Angry?" I asked. Greta scooted back away from me across the floor and climbed backward up into her chair.

"No, Dad," she said quietly. "I mean when you go all uber vamp, with the wings and all."

I stood up so quickly my feet nearly left the floor. "What do you mean 'wings'?"

✦ 21 ✦

TABITHA:

WAYS AND MEANS

Phillip's violin was made of a beautiful dark-colored wood and so was his bow. I could tell it was old and probably expensive. The light dimmed as he began to play, and underneath the music, outside the range of human hearing, disembodied voices moaned along with the song. I didn't like classical music; pissed-off girl rock was more my style. But Phillip's music, indescribably beautiful and sad, captured even my attention, although it was still a little too loud for my enhanced hearing.

Talbot listened with rapt attention. His eyes were half lidded and subtle movements of his chest and head suggested that he was in full-blown musical bliss. Finally, Phillip put down his bow and bowed to us. Talbot and I clapped with an appreciation that wasn't feigned on my part. I was glad that Phillip wanted to spend time with me. It was very flattering, and I had to admit that the whole violin playing deal was pretty romantic.

"That was beautiful," I told him.

"Too shrill for your ears, though, I fear," Phillip said sadly. "I forget how sound-sensitive newborns can be."

I blushed again. "I'm sorry, Phillip. It truly was beautiful, my ears just aren't"—I struggled to find the right word—"refined enough to really appreciate it yet."

"The fault is mine," he said as he put his instrument away. Even the case was lovely. It also looked expensive. Everything around Phillip looked expensive.

Phillip glanced at the wall clock and frowned. "It's after four and I promised to tell you about *El Alma Perdida*." The fire in the fireplace turned blue, then green, and the lights dimmed even further. Phillip either had the coolest dynamic lighting setup I'd ever heard of, or he was using magic.

"The Lost Soul is the Colt Peacemaker used by John Paul Courtney in his misguided quest not only to kill werewolves, but to save their souls. Oh, it's such a remarkable story. No one knows how Courtney came by the weapon, but many know its description. *El Alma Perdida* is a pearl-handled six-shooter with silver crosses worked into the grip to help ensure that his enemies, vampires and werewolves, could not use it against him."

Phillip flicked his wrist and a translucent image of the gun appeared in front of him. It just looked like any old gun to me, but Talbot leaned in closely. Must be a guy thing. "Made in 1873, it was lost when Courtney died in 1925 at the ripe old age of one hundred and two. Few knew he was that old. You wouldn't have suspected that he was a day over fifty." Phillip's expression became dark and mysterious. "Some say his soul was bound to his weapon and resides there to this day." He smiled. "If one is inclined to believe in ghost stories."

Another gesture from Phillip caused the gun to transform into the shape of a man. He wasn't handsome, but something about his eyes, the confidence there, reminded me of a lion. They were a startling shade of blue. "He looks familiar."

"You might find he resembles your sire. I tried to turn Courtney," Phillip mentioned casually. "Do you know his blood actually burned my mouth? I had to snap his neck—twice. Such a waste. He would have made a most interesting foil for those long boring nights. I had such hopes. . . ." Phillip must have noticed my confusion, because he smiled sweetly. "You're so young, Lady Tabitha, but trust this wizened old vampire when I tell you that eternity, after a time, begins to wear on one's nerves."

"What would a vampire want with his gun, though?" I asked.

"Guns are generally used for two purposes: one is display, the other killing. It's the motive that always interests me. How did you come by the bullet?"

"It was found."

"By whom?"

"Eric."

"Eric. Hmmm. Scandinavian, I think, meaning kingly, honorable ruler, or even ever-powerful. How interesting. Did you know that in the hands of Eric, your sire, this gun could be used to kill nearly any werewolf?"

"Because its bullets are blessed—" I started.

"Magical, silver, and, in his case, inherited," Phillip completed. "It's made for lycanthropes, but it will work on any type of therianthrope that walks this mortal earth excepting one."

"Which one?"

"Snakes," Talbot answered too quickly. "Reptilian skin-changers are vulnerable to gold, not silver."

Phillip wrinkled his nose. "Yes, snakes. These bullets would still hurt them, though, lock their form."

"Magbidion already told us about that part." I clapped my hands over my mouth. Lord Phillip didn't appreciate interruptions and Talbot and I had both managed to cut him short, back to back.

"Then I won't bore you further." Phillip snapped his fingers and the room brightened so swiftly that spots danced in front of my eyes. "Surely Dennis won't be much longer," he added.

I looked at the clock and suppressed a yawn. It was only 04:17 and I was already starting to feel tired. Shit! What was going to happen to me when the sun came up? Would I just pass out? I gave Talbot a concerned look, but he gave a slight shake of his head. Did he mean I shouldn't mention it or that it was okay and he'd take care of everything? I stared at him for a few more seconds until he finally nodded toward Phillip. Not knowing what to do, I turned my attention back to the elder vampire.

"So," I began, "based on what you said earlier, you're kind of your own sire? How does that work?"

Phillip stiffened for a moment, but then chuckled and relaxed. "After a fashion, you could say that, yes. I was a wizard during my human days, but as I grew older, I became obsessed with immortality. The prospect of what lay waiting for me in the great beyond was a bit too chilling. At first, I sought out a true immortal, one of those lucky souls who walk the earth born to immortality: human, but unending. I spent decades searching, but never found one. I had a ritual, you see, that would have allowed me to steal his immortality. Along the way, I made certain discoveries about vampirism and as time grew shorter for me, I decided that vampiric immortality was better than none at all and so, here I am."

"That's interesting," I said. I stilled another yawn as I stretched.

"How about you?" Phillip asked gently. "I assume you were sired in the more conventional manner?"

"Yes, by Eric," I answered.

"Oh, yes. If I'm not being too bold, are the two of you involved?"

"I'm in love with him," I blurted. I hadn't meant to say that, but it came out anyway.

Phillip didn't look surprised. He smiled warmly and closed his eyes. He stood and waltzed himself in a little circle. "Ah, young love." He put his hand to his heart. "I hope it lasts. Lady Gabriella and I were in love once. Now we are waging a merry little war of intrigue against each other."

There was a knock at the door and Phillip rushed over to it. "That should be Dennis," he pronounced. Checking the little peephole, he clapped his hands together excitedly. "It is!"

He opened the door and invited the man in. As he had the last time, Dennis declined.

"What do you have for me?" Phillip asked.

"It seems that the Gryphon Suite houses a Master vampire named Roger. According to security, Master Roger hasn't been home since Friday, but his girlfriend, who answers to the name Veruca, has been in and out of the apartment at odd hours for several days."

"How interesting," Phillip said gleefully.

"She returned Friday in the early evening with an assortment of bites and scratches that prompted the security guard to ask if she needed help. According to his report she responded with a rude gesture. She went out again on Saturday. On both days she carried a pistol Master Roger had registered with security."

Outrage washed over me. That bitch! She was a part of it. And Roger . . . what an asshole! How could he do something like this to his best friend?

"And why, may I ask, did security not alert me to the presence of *El Alma Perdida*?" Phillip asked.

"Greed, milord."

"Greed?" I asked.

"He was bribed," Dennis explained.

"His name wasn't Fergus Jenkins, by any chance?" Talbot asked.

"No, sir. Salvadore Belino," the man replied. Shifting his attention back to Lord Phillip, Dennis smiled. "He awaits your pleasure in the lower galleries, milord. I've also taken the liberty of sending a car around to collect his family."

Thinking about Veruca, the spiked blood, and the way I'd had to cover her set made me really mad. My eyes flashed red, but I shut them down quickly. Dennis was a little taken aback, but Phillip just laughed it off. "Ah, the impetuousness of the young."

"I'm sorry; it's Veruca . . . not you." I looked at Dennis. "Did she come back here?"

Dennis looked questioningly at Phillip before answering my question. When Phillip nodded, he proceeded. "She returned just after dawn looking much worse for the wear. More scratches, I'm told, and some burns."

"Is she still here?" I asked.

The same series of looks was exchanged between man and vampire, and then Dennis hesitantly answered my question. I guess he didn't want to ruin his chances of being Phillip's newest son. "As a matter of fact, she is still here. She hasn't left Master Roger's apartments since she returned this . . . that is, yesterday evening."

"How do I get to the Gryphon Suite?"

"Not so fast, milady," Phillip said, holding up his hand. "Everything in its own time." He walked around to his desk, opened a drawer and came back holding five one-hundred-dollar bills. He folded them carefully and handed them to Dennis. "Thank you, Dennis; that will be all."

Phillip closed the door, turned and leaned against it with a tired look on his face. "I'm afraid I can't allow you to go rampaging through my building, knocking down doors and dragging people from their apartments, my dear. Neither you nor your mouser will be allowed to behave that way within these walls without earning my most sincere reproach, as did my dear friend Percy." He gestured to the vampire in the glass case, the one with the stake through his heart.

"Then why even bother to tell us she's here?" I complained, stomping my foot. "God, that's infuriating!"

Phillip clasped his hands. "Anyone who has been granted access to the common areas of the Highland Towers may call upon any resident by simply approaching their rooms, wings, apartments, or floors, whichever is appropriate, and knocking upon the door in a polite manner.

"It is forbidden for one of my guests to physically assault a resident." He acted like I was supposed to be going "A-ha!" From his tone, I knew he was trying to give me a hint, but I sure as hell didn't know what it was.

Talbot walked over to me and put his hands on my shoulders. "We've taken enough of Lord Phillip's time, milady. Perhaps you could assure him that we wouldn't dream of physically assaulting any residents of the Highland Towers, but would be quite happy to pay a call on a good friend of ours by the name of Veruca. Perhaps we'll find we see eye-to-eye on a few things."

Talbot stressed the word *residents* and the phrase *eye-to-eye* when he spoke, but I still didn't get it. Still, Phillip seemed to understand and he carefully explained how to go about getting an elevator to the Gryphon Suite. I gave Phillip a kiss on the cheek and, by virtue of our comparative heights, a really good look down my top, and walked out wearing the diamond necklace he had given me. As the door closed, I stifled a yawn and started to ask Talbot what was going on, but he shushed me and walked over to the elevators. We waited a few seconds for the doors to open. Dennis was not inside. Talbot pressed the correct button and when the doors closed he winked at me.

"Not bad, Tab. I think he wants to go steady."

"Whatever!" I liked Phillip, but I wasn't going to date a balding little short dude no matter how much money he had, not unless I was in love with him; and since I was currently in love with an attractive, not to mention quite wealthy in his own right, vampire, things didn't look good for Phillip.

"He told you everything you need to know to get Veruca out of this place and wherever you want her."

The elevator slowed and we walked out into one of the building's elegant waiting rooms, crossed to a set of elevators that served the correct floors, and waited for another elevator to show up. After the doors closed and the button was pushed, I asked Talbot what the hell he was talking about.

"You're a Vlad and she's a Soldier. All you have to do is lock eyes with her and you can make her leave with us."

"Oh. If you wanted to make me feel stupid, you succeeded," I told him.

Now all I had to do was get Veruca to answer the door, lock eyes with her, get her into the car, and restrain her somehow before I passed out from vampiric sleep deprivation. Great.

So there I was, a few minutes later, in front of Roger's door, doing my impersonation of Mr. Fuzzy Bottom. It was a silly plan, but I didn't have a better one. If Veruca hadn't eaten, then a cat might seem like a tasty treat to take the edge off. On the other hand, if she didn't want to eat a cat, she might want to cuddle with one and enjoy the body heat. Heck, she might even like cats for all I knew. It was worth a shot.

Talbot was waiting down the hall next to the television playing in Roger's waiting area. Which, incidentally, was nothing compared to Phillip's. There were no comfy chairs, no stashes of bottled blood. It looked like a waiting room in a doctor's office, right down to the magazines that nobody interesting would want to read. They were all about money, or people who have money, or what was happening to other people's money. Even the station the television was turned to was all about money. I wondered what Eric's waiting room would have looked like if he'd decided to live here. Lots of strippers, maybe, or a giant neon sign that said, *Go away!*

Stifling a yawn, I meowed at the door and rubbed up against it. Pacing in little circles, I rubbed against the door eight or nine times, meowing, before the sounds of someone stirring in the apartment reached the doorway. Footsteps started for the door, followed by cursing and the sound of something clattering down to tile and shattering. Yet more cursing and then the handle on the door began to turn. I stopped and sat in front of the door flipping my tail back and forth. No wonder cats do that; it's fun. The doorknob stopped turning.

"Meow," I complained, by which I meant, "Open the door, you stupid bitch!"

Veruca stood on the other side of the door and waited. "I know it's you, Tabitha," she gloated. "And tell Talbot that I can smell him, too."

I turned human and looked incredulously at Talbot. "Any other bright ideas, Sensei?"

"Just one. She's not really a resident." He grinned and walked closer to the door. "Here, Froggy, Froggy, Froggy. Here, Froggy!"

"Stop it, Talbot!" Veruca snarled.

"I've got a hundred-dollar bill out here if you'll give me a lap dance, Froggy. Here, Froggy, Froggy, Froggy!" With each "Froggy" Talbot grew incrementally louder.

"I'm serious, Talbot," Veruca shouted. "I'll call security."

"You know, Froggy," Talbot continued. "I was just talking to Lord Phillip about you. Did you know Veruca means wart? I thought warts were what you got from frogs and toads, not—"

That did it. She charged out at us in a rage.

22

TABITHA:
CAT FIGHT

I expected Talbot to do all of the fighting, so I hung back, watching as he and Veruca tore at each other. Talbot's claws popped right out of the tips of his fingers like a cat's. Veruca's were scarier; her fingers curved and hardened, like talons. Talbot tore a chunk out of her side and smoke billowed up from the wounds. He tried to pull her in close, using the leverage to bite her, but she spun free, slashing open his forehead.

"What the hell?" Veruca yelled. She fell back into a crouch, gripping her side. "You burned me!"

"My claws are holy." Talbot took a step closer. "I'm a noble hunter, a sacred guardian. You're just a damn vampire."

"Hey, watch it," I blurted, slightly offended. "I'm just a damn vampire, too."

"It's just an expre—" His attention left his opponent for only a second, eyes flickering in my direction, but Veruca took advantage. She dove between his legs, rolling to her feet on the other side and flaying open his back with her claws. Talbot stumbled forward away from the door, cursing loudly. I stood in front of Veruca, hands out in front of me to ward her off.

"Stop her," Talbot ordered. "Don't let her back in the apartment."

"Look, uh . . . Froggy—" I shouldn't have said that. It slipped out. Naturally, it pissed her off even more.

"You think it's fucking funny, huh? That you can do a kitty cat and I can't?" She barreled into me, face contorted with rage, literally tackling me through the apartment door.

"Look out, damn it!" Talbot reached for my arm, but we fell, entangled, into the apartment and down on a throw rug in the center of what seemed to be a sitting room, with tacky chairs and a coffee table. Veruca kicked the door shut with her foot.

"Lock!" she shouted, and the door flashed blue for an instant. Talbot hit it from the outside and the wall shook, but it didn't give. "Tabitha! The rooms are warded; I can't get in."

"Unlock! Unlock!" I shouted at the door, but it didn't want to take orders from me.

"Talbot may be too much for me to handle," Veruca snarled, baring her fangs, "but I can still end you!" Time slowed as she stalked toward me, claws at the ready. I slid across the floor, got to my feet and tried to force the door from the inside. It wouldn't budge.

"It won't open!" I yelled.

"Not until she or Roger opens it." Talbot's voice sounded like he was leaning against the door. "Just fight."

I turned in time to see Veruca's claws slashing my way again. I dodged in the nick of time, but only because I don't think she expected me to have time to react. Her claws slashed the door, leaving large furrows in the dark wood.

Veruca growled, then spun with terrible speed and lunged at me again. Her claws were larger than mine and the tips were hooked. Brawling wasn't my thing; I misjudged her range. Both sets struck home. Getting hurt felt weird: an initial shock of pain that immediately faded, as though the nerve endings registered it once, then forgot about it.

"Get off of me," I screamed. My own claws came out and I used them as best I could, scratching at her eyes with one hand and her neck with the other. She might know how to kill, but I knew how to hurt a woman like her. She'd always been vain and petty. If she didn't have her looks, then, at least as far as she was concerned, she had nothing. Flesh ripped away from her face in jagged ribbons.

Veruca rolled away from me as we both howled in agony. Vampires aren't supposed to bleed much, but the chunks of flesh she ripped from my sides as her claws pulled free sent a shower of bloody spray across the living room, dappling the ceiling and the walls. This time the pain was jagged, raw and angry, pulsing.

"My face!" she screamed, launching herself back at me.

I moved with vampiric alacrity. Heartbeats faster than she could strike, I rolled backward and to my feet with a grace I hadn't had since ballet class, pressing my back against the door.

"Your claws may be bigger, but the wounds mine make don't heal," I lied. "When I'm done with you, you'll be lucky if you can pay a man to look at you, much less touch you."

I took a step forward, claws raised to strike. She reared back, feinting with her right hand. I dodged to the left to avoid her deadly claws, and fell right into her trap. As I moved, she dropped into a low crouch, knocking my feet out from under me with a leg sweep. She got in two more slashes before I landed. The first slash caught me in the belly and wasn't too deep, but the second dug into my left breast and I heard her claws scratching against my breastbone.

I hit the floor right on top of the broken vase and then rolled up into a ball, clutching my breast. Veruca slashed at my back, cutting easily through my sequined top and flaying me open to the spine. I knew Eric could take injuries like this and laugh them off, but I wasn't Eric and it hurt more than anything I had ever felt.

"How do you like that, pussycat?" Veruca taunted.

I didn't like it at all, not that I could have replied anyway. Pain was my world and I wallowed in it. Veruca continued to slash at my exposed back, but the more she hurt me, the more I began to drift away from the pain. It was there, but it was being replaced with another feeling. Outrage, maybe? I was a queen, after all, and she was merely a Soldier.

Then a funny new sensation rose in my chest, the outrage mixed with something else: disdain. Before, when I had lashed out verbally at the Drone, I had felt the same thing. I lashed out with it again, now, but not verbally; more than voice and yet less. My mental voice screamed, not in terror, but in utter fury that a lesser vampire would dare to treat me this way. Me—her better! *I may be only two days old*, my mental voice proclaimed, *but a queen is still a queen!*

She paused for three seconds and three seconds only, but three seconds can be an eternity when you're fighting a vampire. It was more than enough time for me to roll over and lock eyes with her. "Who's the badass now?" I shouted.

My vision tinged with red and I knew my eyes were glowing. I pushed my will right in through her eyes and down into her little brain, just like Eric had done to me the night before. In my mind's eye, tiny invisible strings affixed themselves to her arms, legs, and head. She fought back, but she had no depth. There was hardly anything to fight.

We stayed there, eyes locked, while my wounds healed. I don't know how long it took, a minute, two minutes, five, but once I felt whole again, I stood slowly, making sure to keep eye contact with Veruca the entire time. I grabbed the sides of her head and pulled her to her feet, willing her to stand. I walked us over to a large framed photograph of a marina that hung on one wall, feeling like a puppeteer working a life-size marionette.

Talbot was saying something outside, but I didn't have time to answer. I could feel Veruca fighting me, trying to buy a second or two of freedom so she could tear out my throat. Smashing the picture with my left hand, I snapped the bottom of the wooden frame loose and thrust it through Veruca's heart to immobilize her. Or at least, that was the plan.

It didn't work like in the movies, though, and my first thrust hadn't been hard enough to penetrate all the way to her heart. I glanced down at the stake, remembering Percy and mentally checking biology. I'd rammed it against her sternum, splintering the shard of wood and deflecting it into the side of her breast. I instantly realized my mistake. Stake jutting through the ripped front of her shirt, Veruca head-butted me and shoved me away from her. I grabbed for her shirt to steady myself, but it ripped, coming free in my hand, and I landed on my ass.

"You are so dead, bitch!" Veruca yelled. She kicked at my face and I twisted away, catching a glancing blow to my cheek. I threw her tattered shirt back in her face as she stumbled, put off balance by the kick. I got a good look at the cute little frog tattoo she had above her pelvis when I grabbed her leg and hurled her across the room.

Vampire strength is fun for the whole family. She flew over the coffee table and crashed through a pressed-wood closet door, bringing coats and jackets down on top of her. I glanced around the room for something wood, something sturdier than the picture frame. The coffee table was glass and the chair legs looked like metal. Damn it.

In the closet, Veruca roared, clawing at the jackets as she got to her feet. Her head bumped the top shelf in the closet, sending a shoe box tumbling and spilling its contents—a pair of leather gloves with scorched palms and an unmistakable pearl-handled six-shooter—onto the floor.

Veruca grabbed for the gun, wincing as the crosses on the butt smoked against her skin. I launched myself over the coffee table at her, grabbing for the stake, but she pulled away from me and it popped free of her chest.

She fired once, twice, missing both times either because the pain in her hands threw off her aim, or because I was moving too quickly. I darted in low, under the gun, thrusting the stake in at an angle under her ribs. The gun barked again, pain lanced through my shoulder, and she froze, hands flaming as *El Alma Perdida* tumbled from her limp fingers. The little frog tattoo flashed bright white and vanished. I was afraid that she might do the same. Her skin began to melt away, followed by the muscle underneath. Her skull opened its mouth in a silent scream and then her entire skeleton exploded into ashes with a loud *fwoosh*. I'd killed her. I felt sick to my stomach.

At least I'd found the gun. Eric would be pleased with me. Smoke poured out of a nice neat hole in my shoulder where the third bullet had passed clean through. Talbot and I were going to have to dig three bullets out of the wall.

Dropping the stake, I walked over to the door. "Unlock?" I asked it tentatively, wondering how the hell we were going to get the door open if Veruca's death hadn't reset it. I guessed killing her had broken the spell, or maybe it was that I still had her dust on my hands, but when I touched the doorknob, the door pulsed blue and opened easily.

Talbot stepped inside and looked at the pile of ash, the broken bit of picture frame, and the blood covering the floor. Finally he looked at me, my clothes in shreds and covered in blood, most of it mine.

"A stake through the heart kills Soldiers and Drones," he observed. "Bet she wishes she'd made Master."

"Yeah," I agreed numbly. I kept expecting her to reform like Dracula did in the movies, and while I knew that was possible for me, since I was a Vlad, for her *poof* seemed to pretty much mean *poof*. "I wonder when security's going to get here."

"They won't." Talbot smirked. "Veruca swung first, and she's not a resident." He picked up *El Alma Perdida*. "Eric will be glad to see this." Gun in hand, he walked across the room and dug three perfectly preserved bullets, casings and all, out of the wall. "That's just weird," he said after reloading the gun and returning it to the shoe box.

I sat down in one of the chairs, the bullet wound still throbbing. It was healing very slowly, not like the other wounds, where I could literally feel them closing. Talbot looked down at me, his eyes softening. "You did good. Are you hungry?"

I noticed his heart speeding up as he asked me. Sexual excitement rolled off of him in waves. Talbot ripped open his already ruined shirt, exposing his muscular, chocolate-colored chest. Watching me intently, he popped a claw, drawing it lazily down his body, blood welling up along the wound.

His blood smelled strong and powerful, but more importantly, it was warm and so was he. My hunger awoke with a need almost as overwhelming as when I'd first risen. "I thought I didn't have anything you were interested in," I said coyly.

Three magic words left his mouth, almost as strong and powerful as *I love you*. "I was wrong."

The need for blood permeates everything when you're hungry, gets confused with other hungers. At that moment there was no difference between the hunger for blood and the hunger for sex. I leapt on him with animal glee, licking the long line of blood off his chest. He shivered and his excitement ignited mine. I wanted him inside me and he didn't resist as I fumbled with his belt, lapping at his bloody chest while I pushed down his pants.

He slipped off my pants and panties, awkwardly because I wouldn't lift my lips from his chest. I dove for the artery pulsing in his thigh, but he caught my head and forced me up to his neck. I pushed him back onto the coffee table, following him down, and it shattered, but I didn't care. Talbot began to protest, but I sank down onto him and he snarled with pleasure.

His hands cupped my breasts and he seemed only slightly startled when I sank my fangs into his neck, penetrating him in my own way.

When he tired, I made him keep going and he did everything I asked and more, like a dying man following the orders of the one person who can give him water. Sex with a warm, breathing person was more than I could have explained. No wonder Eric liked to sleep with the living. They are so alive, so hot, and so full of blood. When I was finally sated, I lay sprawled on his chest, wearing nothing but my diamond necklace, and listened to him breathe, wondering when we'd left the remains of the glass table and found our way to Roger's bed. Tiny wisps of smoke rose from the little scratches Talbot had given me.

"I bet you've never done that with Eric," I teased.

"Definitely not," he laughed. "He's even less my type than I thought you were."

"Why do you stay with him?" I asked.

Talbot's beautifully massive chest rose and fell deeply. "He's a unique individual—worth protecting. You could say he awakens in me an infinite curiosity."

"And me?"

He blinked and smiled, showing me his fangs. "You're unique, too. I find you almost as curious as I find Eric."

"I still love Eric, you know," I told him seriously.

His eyes flashed and the pupils became slits. "I'm glad. If you fell in love with me, it would end badly for one of us. Eric would kill me or perhaps eventually you would kill me. After all, my kind is incapable of the kind of love you more human types feel for each other. Our bonds are based on dominance, mutual need, and, at most, a deep and abiding fondness."

I still didn't understand what Talbot was, but I felt I understood him. Maybe he was some strange cat-human hybrid, or perhaps he had lied about not being a lycanthrope. The romantic in me liked to think it was a spell. Anything was possible. I'd met a wizard, become a vampire. Perhaps Lord Phillip himself had trapped Talbot in the body of a man, as punishment, like with Percy. No, that didn't sound right. Talbot had described himself as a sacred guardian, a noble hunter. To me, that said: cat. Obviously not a normal cat, but a magic one. I wondered absently if it counted as bestiality if you had sex with an animal that had been turned humanoid.

I lay there, trying to bask in his warmth, in the afterglow of our intimacy, but the moment was gone. A final curl of smoke drifted up from the shallow scratches around my breasts and my pale skin was whole once more, as if the act itself had not taken place, leaving me empty and restless. Talbot had been a nice substitute, but I craved Eric.

I got up, found Roger's shower and washed the last traces of combat from my body. Once I was dry, I started going through Veruca's clothes. She'd been smaller than me, in every way, and her clothes tended to be one size too small for her already. Not having to breathe enhances a vampire's ability to dress for effect, but it also meant that there wasn't anything in her closet that fit me. Which left me my panties, my shoes, and my diamond necklace. The pants had long rents in them and I didn't want to put back on what was left of the sequined top.

"What the hell am I supposed to wear?" I asked, holding the remains of my clothes and shaking them in Talbot's general direction.

"I think that outfit suits you just fine," Talbot murmured throatily from where he was sprawled on the bed.

I rolled my eyes and changed into a cat.

"That suits you even more." He wasn't teasing.

I changed back, in further exasperation. *Poof* . . . clothes. Yay me! The clothes I'd been wearing were new again and I wasn't holding them in my hands anymore, I was wearing them. The magic that had repaired them left them feeling right-out-of-the-dryer warm.

"Now, that's something I've seen only Eric do." Talbot rolled out of the bed, naked. He stretched and yawned, his fangs and claws popping out midway through and retracting at the end. He flexed at me and I admired him openly. He was taller than Eric and more heavily muscled. His dark skin was sleek, almost glossy, and stood out in perfect contrast to the red satin sheets. The picture he made was incredibly alluring, and I considered taking off my newly created clothes. Just because I was in love with Eric didn't mean I couldn't enjoy a little companionship from the living. What was good for the goose . . .

"How does it work?" I asked softly, placing my hand on Talbot's shoulder.

"With Eric it seems to work automatically," he told me. "When he changes shape, unless he's paying close attention, it changes whatever he was wearing into the same jeans and T-shirt outfit he prefers. I mentioned it to him in El Segundo, but I'm sure he's forgotten by now. Not that it matters much since he wears the same damn thing every day."

"I think he looks nice," I said defensively.

Talbot laughed at that, and I couldn't help but join in.

23

ERIC:

NO GOOD NEWS

With no music playing in the Demon Heart, no crowd, not even Marilyn or one of the girls getting ready to open the club or shut it down, the silence ate at my nerves. I needed something to block out the sound of the oni out front jabbering back and forth at each other in Japanese in between mouthfuls of dead werewolf.

I thought about ordering a pizza—Italian sausage, black olives, mushrooms, and daikon—just so I could smell it, look at it, feel the warmth of the box.

I don't know what daikon tastes like, but I'm fond of the smell and I'm curious. Few things are more annoying than a curious vampire. If the smell of a particular food entices us, we want to make people eat it, so they can describe the taste to us. The best description I'd gotten of daikon was "kind of like a pickle, but not." How can something that looks like a big white carrot taste like a pickle, but not? Did they do something to it first? The question vexed me.

Greta sat across Marilyn's desk from me, playing with a staple remover, pretending it was a shark or a vampire, something with fangs. The phone rang in my office across the street and Rachel stirred in her sleep, but didn't wake. On the third ring, Greta heard it too.

"Phone's ringing," she told me.

"I know."

"You want me to go and—"

"No," I said too quickly. "Just wait a minute." My brain wouldn't process what she'd told me about my "uber vamp" form. How could I have been turning into a giant, black-skinned, leather-winged beast thing off and on since 1965 and not know it, not even have had an inkling beyond the understanding that I blacked out when I got really mad? It was like Bruce Banner not knowing about the Hulk.

I didn't want to think about who was setting me up, either. If I'd known where the investigation had been likely to lead, I never would have looked into it. I would have taken on the werewolves without question. A wise man once said "Ignorance is bliss," and he was right. I wanted Veruca to be behind everything, needed it. I wanted to forget about the check I'd seen where Roger had forged my name. I wished Roger had dotted his damn *i*'s.

So I concentrated on the pizza. If I gave up on the daikon, I could call one of the big pizza chains, but if I wanted the daikon, I had to wait until Jackie's opened at six. I could get Jackie to put anything I wanted on a pizza, even if he had to run down to the Asian market. Jackie knows about vampires, and if you let him know that your order is for eating in front of one of us, he tacks on an extra 50 percent surcharge and makes it look like it does in the pictures on the menu.

I remembered sitting in his diner with Roger watching Froggy, still Veruca then, eat a Reuben. It's a big deal for vampires to share their food porn like that, proof of our long friendship.

The phone rang in Marilyn's office and I jumped, startled. It wasn't supposed to do that. I glanced at it suspiciously. For all I knew the phone was undergoing a demonic transformation. It certainly seemed like the week for it. It rang a second and a third time before I answered it. It was Talbot; I recognized his breathing.

"How did you get through to this phone?" I asked. "Didn't Marilyn transfer the calls to her home number?"

"Star six eight," he answered.

"Huh?"

"It forwards the call, but only if the number dialed is busy or there's no answer. . . . Look, don't worry about it. I tried you at the Pollux first."

He sounded upset. Tough shit, it wasn't all blow jobs and balloons for me either. "Did you know that I turn into some sort of rampaging berserker flying vampire thing when I lose my temper?"

Talbot scoffed. "Of course."

"Even Talbot knows! Am I the only fucking person around who doesn't know I've got go-go gadget bat wings?" I yelled, holding the receiver about a foot from my face. I hung up the phone and threw up my hands.

Greta acted sympathetic, but I could tell that she was trying to hold back her laughter.

"Who else knows?" I asked her. Before she could respond, the phone rang again. It was Talbot. "Does Marilyn know?" I asked him.

"I . . . I think so," Talbot answered. I hung up on him again and cast a disparaging look at Greta.

"Even Marilyn knows! Why does nobody tell me these things?" Greta watched me as I paced the room angrily. Small snorts of nasal laughter escaped despite her best attempts to hold them back. "It's not funny, damn it!"

Greta couldn't even speak. Tears of blood rolled down the sides of her face and she burst out laughing. Loud obnoxious guffaws filled the room punctuated by a periodic "I'm so sorry" or "I know it's not funny." She clutched her sides, sliding farther down in her chair, leaving me staring at her in impotent rage and disbelief.

The phone rang and I picked it up before the first ring finished. "I swear to God, Talbot, if Tabitha knows, I am going to fucking kill somebody!"

"I don't think she d—" Talbot began.

I hung up the phone again and put my hands on my hips. "Well, at least there is one person who is as clueless as me. Of course it's frickin' Tabitha."

More laughter erupted from Greta and she began to gasp for air in a way that looked absolutely human.

"It's not that funny!" I yelled, standing over her.

She nodded her head. "Yes, it is," she gasped. "Hello, Talbot? Blah blah blah. Click."

I didn't get it. Maybe that was funny in a women-are-from-Venus way, but here on Mars, it didn't make a whole lot of sense. The phone rang again and I picked it up. "Talbot, I think Greta has gone loopy. She's over here laughing her head off like it's some big joke. I've been a vampire for over forty years and nobody bothered to—"

"You have a collect call from 'Talbot,'" interrupted a mechanical voice. "Will you accept the charges?"

"Yes," I answered. Why was Talbot calling collect?

"Talbot?" I asked.

"Yes," he answered, drawing out the word. He sounded pretty ticked off.

"Why the hell are you calling collect?"

"Because, if you'll pardon my language, some asshole keeps hanging up on me and I thought that if you had to listen to the operator first, you might actually stop and pay attention!"

Talbot didn't usually yell. Greta stopped laughing and climbed back into her chair. Her chest was still heaving a little, but she had control of herself. I breathed in and out deeply a few times to calm myself. I don't need oxygen, but the act of breathing triggered a physical memory, giving it much the same effect. "Okay, sorry. I'm ready to pay attention now; it's just a big shock to find out something like that."

"I'm sure it was," he interrupted, enunciating slowly and clearly. "I'm sorry none of us knew how to tell you, but I need you to listen right now. Okay?"

"Sure."

"If you hang up on me again, I'm going to come over there while you're asleep and put a big 'jackass' tattoo on your forehead. Do you understand?"

I rolled my eyes. "Yes."

"Okay. Good. The good news is that we found the gun."

I slapped Marilyn's desk. "Hot damn!"

"Veruca had it."

"What did she have to say for herself?"

"Not much, but it's pretty clear she's the one who shot the werewolves you found at Orchard Lake."

"Did you get her to tell you why she left one of the bullets behind?"

"No, and I don't quite know how to tell you this, Eric, but we found her at Roger's place."

"Was he all right?" I asked.

"He wasn't there," Talbot answered. "But you have to consider the possibility that he is wrapped up in all of this."

"That's crap, Talbot," I said, determined to deny it.

"He's been covering for her," Talbot said patiently. "He took you to a hockey game, got you drunk, and let eighteen werewolves try to kill you."

"Yeah, but—"

"Eric," Talbot said. "Where is he right now? Did you call him?"

"No, I haven't called him yet. Greta and I ran into some werewolves here at the club. Real Lycan Diocese types that William called in."

"You both okay?" he asked.

"Yeah, no problems here. Tiko and some of his cousins are taking care of the bodies for us."

"Good. Now listen. I want you to go back to the alley where you fought the Alpha's son. He was killed at Thirteenth Street and Eleventh Avenue. I want you to go there and see if you recognize it."

"Why?"

"Because I don't trust Roger, damn it!" he snapped. I heard him take a deep breath and his next words were calmer. "He gave Veruca that night off and she had the gun with her. We can't ask Lillian where she picked you up, because Tabitha killed her when she went loco."

"Talbot, I did kill a werewolf in an alley."

"I believe you, boss." He sighed. "I just want to make sure you killed the werewolf that you think you killed."

"Ask Froggy," I said. "Make her tell you."

"I would if I could, Eric, but Tabitha put a stake through her heart."

"*Poof*, huh?"

"*Poof*," he confirmed. "We found the gun before Tabitha fell asleep. It looks like Veruca was wearing leather gloves in order to fire it. They're scorched through on the palms. The silver crosses on the grip must have burned her even through the leather."

"It can happen," I said noncommittally.

"I think I'll hole up here with Tabitha until she wakes up tomorrow."

"And what if Roger comes home?"

"I don't think he will," Talbot said. "The sun will be up too soon. Roger takes a lot more sleep than you do and he'd never cut it this close. Wherever he is, I think he'll stay there until sunset. Besides, he hasn't been here since Friday. I don't think he's going to come back until this whole thing is over."

"Why?"

"Because he's setting you up. Veruca was the fall guy in case anything went wrong."

"I don't believe that," I said flatly.

"If you don't believe it, then check the alley."

"I—"

"Eric, please. Will you check the damn alley?"

No, Talbot, I can't, I wanted to say. I don't want to look in the damn alley. If Roger set me up, I don't want to frickin' know about it.

"Fine," I answered, "and thanks."

Greta and I walked back across to the Pollux. The bodies and trucks were all gone. Tiko and his crew had worked fast. "So, who else knows?" I asked her as we walked.

"About the alley?"

"No," I said. "About the super vamp thing."

"Dad, I don't know." She put her arm around my shoulders, emphasizing the fact that she was over two inches taller than me. "But look on the bright side. Most of the people who knew got killed before they could tell anyone. I'll bet Roger doesn't even know, with the way he runs away from fights so fast."

Reminded of Roger, I plopped down onto the sofa in the Pollux's lobby and punched buttons on my cell phone until it decided to dial his number for me.

"Hello?" The voice on the other end sounded strange, like he was whispering into the receiver from the bottom of a giant tin bucket.

"Roger?"

"Yeah. Dude. I've been trying to call you. Why the hell did you close the club? Marilyn says you sent everyone home with pay."

"You talked to Marilyn?"

"I'm at her place now. She needed a little help. Seems some asshole broke her arm."

"Yeah," I mumbled. It was a classic Roger deflection. Question: Roger, why are you trying to put my club out of business? Answer: Hey, do you remember that time you broke Marilyn's arm?

"Same asshole killed Brian," I blurted.

"What?" he demanded. "You killed Brian? Why?"

Why? What an interesting question. I didn't know why. Another good question was why Roger didn't seem more upset about it.

"Because he annoyed me, I guess," I said vaguely. "I don't remember."

"It's all right, man. He was always picking fights with you and it wasn't like he hadn't been warned."

"He was your friend, though. I'm sorry."

"Don't worry about it," Roger assured me. "He was just a Soldier."

Huh. I wonder if he would've responded the same way if he'd known Tabitha had killed Froggy. Besides, Brian hadn't been a Soldier, he'd been a Master. What the fuck?

I tried another tack. "Do you know anything about a check for thirty thousand dollars to some guy named Fergus?" I asked.

"I'd been meaning to ask you about it," Roger countered. "You can't just spend money like that without clearing it first. We're flush and it's not a problem this time, but what if I hadn't had enough money in that account to cover it? The money moves around, man. I gotta keep it working for us, not just sitting in an account in case you overspend."

You fucking liar, I wanted to scream, *you're behind everything!* Then, again, this was Roger and he could have been covering up for something else, maybe just some run-of-the-mill embezzlement. If that was the case, I didn't care. He'd always taken a little without asking. When an investment deal paid off later, he'd slip it back in and tell me I'd okayed everything. It usually worked out.

"Yeah," I whispered, "my mistake." *Please just be embezzling money*, I thought at him.

"Gotta let you go, pal," he said. "I want to hunt before I turn in."

"Which gives you what," I said, checking the clock, "fifteen minutes?" Roger had to be lying to me. He always hunts first thing. "You're going to hunt and make it back to your place in fifteen minutes from Marilyn's?" I willed him to say yes. If he said yes then—

"No," he answered. "Not that it's any of your business, but I have a place nearby. Look, don't worry about it, Mom. I'll be fine, but I've got to go if I'm going to hunt. Like you said, fifteen minutes."

"How close by?" I asked, but he was already off the line.

Rachel was up and moving; I could hear her rummaging around downstairs in the dressing room she'd confiscated. "Sounds like the Pierced Princess is awake," Greta said snidely.

I shushed her and walked upstairs to my office, opened my desk drawer, and pulled out a pair of sunglasses to conceal my eyes, since I didn't want to scare anyone without meaning to do so. Eyes safely covered, I went back down to the dressing room and checked on Rachel.

She was naked except for a pair of lacy white panties. Her scent filled my nostrils and I pulled her into my arms. God, she was warm. She kissed me and I caught a faint hint of cinnamon.

"You smell nice," I told her. "I keep smelling cinnamon around you, but only sometimes."

"It's a special trick for girls with vampire boyfriends."

I let her step back and playfully tugged one of her piercings. "More fun facts from the Irons Club?"

She let out a little sigh followed by a wicked grin. "Do we have any plans or do we get to play all day?"

It was tempting, but I walked away from her, toward the door. "As much as I'd like to, I need you to take me for a walk."

"Does it have to be right now?" Rachel ran her hands suggestively over her breasts.

"Yes," I insisted, ignoring the part of my anatomy that disagreed. "You can get a shower over at the Demon Heart if you need one."

She raised an eyebrow. "Do I?"

I shook my head. "No, but I thought I'd offer."

She smiled. "Are we taking a cab?"

"It's only three blocks," I answered. "Get dressed and bring your purse."

I walked out past Greta, who was leaning against the wall in the hallway.

"Do I need a shower, Dad? Can I use the one over at the Demon Heart? Can I? Please?"

Ignoring her as best I could, I went back to my office to wait for

Rachel. Soon I heard a loud thump, the sound a body makes when it hits the floor. "Sun's up," I muttered to myself. Out in the hall, Greta lay in a heap. Dawn always hits her hard and like me, she never seems to remember that it's coming. I don't know if she does it on purpose to be more like me or not, but I find it endearing in a dysfunctional sire sort of way. Unlike me, she's impossible to wake up during the day. At least when she wakes each evening she's cheerful and well rested. Some days I envy her. I picked her up in my arms and carried her back to my Pollux bedroom, tucked her in, and kissed her on the forehead.

"You ready?" Rachel called from the doorway. "How am I walking with you somewhere, anyway? You're not going to turn into a virus and infect me are you?" Her heart rate sped up. "I mean, it's okay if you are, I guess. It's just that . . ."

I turned into a mouse and back again, the rapid transition feeling only slightly more comfortable than a shot to the nuts. I really needed to stop showing off for this girl. "I want you to jog up to the intersection of Thirteenth Street and Eleventh Avenue with me in your purse."

She knelt down and opened her purse on the floor. It was smaller than I was happy with, but it was leather and I doubted enough sun would get through the material to be a problem. I admired the view down Rachel's top before transforming. Rachel zipped me up in her purse and away we went.

I really wanted Talbot to be wrong, but in the back of my furry little undead mind, I already knew that he wasn't. Roger had betrayed me. Froggy was too stupid to come up with a plan so complex on her own. I don't know if he wanted me dead—I hoped he didn't—but he definitely wanted me at odds with William. Maybe that's all there was to it. Maybe he wanted me to kill William and knew that I wouldn't do it just for shits and giggles, so he'd arranged for William to come after me, knowing that I'd be able to defend myself.

But why?

Deep down, it didn't matter why he'd done what he'd done. He'd betrayed me and I'd found out about it. I silently hated him for not being clever enough to slip it all past me. *Dot your damn i's,* I thought again. If only he'd done a better job of forging the check. If only he hadn't lied about it. If only we could go back to being best friends, like none of this had ever happened. . . .

24

ERIC:

THE OTHER SHOE

Checking out the alley took about an hour, but only because I made Rachel investigate all four intersections that were three blocks from the club. If Talbot's suspicions were correct, then two werewolves had been killed three blocks from the Demon Heart at the same time. I'd killed one and Froggy had killed the other.

We found the place where I'd killed Brian first. I knew it was the right alley because long scratches in the concrete showed where I'd dragged the Dumpster to the sidewalk. I examined the scene from the safety of the shadows. That alley, at Thirteenth Street and Fifth Avenue, had been completely cleaned. The Dumpster wasn't there anymore, but the wall still bore a scorch mark from where I'd beat my head out when I'd caught fire.

We checked Thirteenth Street and Eleventh Avenue last. The odor of gunpowder and werewolf permeated the site. It wasn't the scent of the werewolf I'd killed. This one smelled stronger, more primal. I smelled Veruca in the alley, too, and sex. What pissed me off the most, though, was the smell of my own blood. Someone had siphoned some off of me and sprayed it on the walls. Werewolves have a better sense of smell than vampires; I wondered momentarily if William thought I'd slept with Froggy there, rolling around in his son's remains.

"Son of a bitch," I said, standing in a shadow. "Talbot was right. Roger played me. Why the fuck would he do that?"

"Maybe it isn't what it looks like," Rachel offered. "Maybe he didn't know what to do. Maybe he knew that the werewolves were after his girlfriend. He could have been scared."

"So he set them on my trail because he knew they couldn't kill me?" I asked.

"Maybe," Rachel said with a shrug.

"Nah, I don't think so. He sent Veruca out here to kill Willie Junior so that Willie Senior would come after me. He sent Veruca to kill the werewolves at Orchard Lake because he wanted to make sure I didn't talk it over with William and make peace. He's behind everything. I wonder if he's still over at Marilyn's."

Cars whizzed past dangerously on Eleventh Street heading for the interstate on-ramp one block down. I stood along the edge of the shadows and watched the people inside. Were any of their best friends trying to screw them over? Fucking their spouses, cheating on them, framing them for murder? What would Roger say if I confronted him? And why did the thought of him having a place close to Marilyn's apartment suddenly make me queasy? *She'll be fine*, I told myself. Besides, like a lot of vampires, Roger slept all day, every day.

I was going to ask Rachel to drive me over there when horns honked on the street outside the mouth of the alley and two identical trucks, one black and the other blue, peeled past on the wrong side of the road, within ten feet of me. In the back of one of the trucks, I saw a big metal box studded with crosses, secured to the bed of the truck with elastic cords. I thought I heard a scream.

Instinctively, I took off after them, running right out of the shadows into the sun.

"Shit!" I jumped back into the shadows, on fire again. "Fuck!"

"We need to get back to the Pollux," I growled after I'd dropped and rolled to put out the flames. "Run."

The Pollux felt wrong. I knew it the moment Rachel panted across the threshold and let me out of her purse. Old buildings have moods, especially those full of personality, like the Pollux. She had once been a grand affair, a celebrated showplace, and the center of attention. Now she had been reduced to a quaint old memory of better days. She was distressed about something; a palpable sense of anxiety resonated through her. Something was out of place. Something was wrong. Rachel seemed to feel it too. It was as if, while we were away, the proverbial other shoe had dropped.

"Greta," I said under my breath. Rachel and I both hit the stairs running, but I was in full-on combat mode and had already thrown open the door to my bedroom by the time Rachel was clearing the fifth step. My bed had been made and the sink had been cleaned. It even looked like my towel had been washed and dried. Maybe Greta had woken up early and headed out, but it wasn't like her to clean stuff up and she'd only been asleep for an hour, tops. She had to have been taken.

I went into my office, and noticed some stuff had been moved around. The light on my answering machine was blinking. I pushed PLAY as Rachel walked in and closed the door behind her.

"I have your whore," growled a voice. It was the same voice I'd heard on the answering machine when Kyle died: William. "Your Jezebel is with me. Is it true that you make her call you Daddy? How can you compare this twisted unholy family you have created to the son you stole from me? The brethren you killed? Their souls cry out for vengeance. 'Vengeance is mine,' sayeth the Lord, but I am his instrument. Through me you will be returned unto the dust from which you came.

"This time you will come to me, vampire. You will walk into the sunlight and face us in a place of our own choosing. Come for your so-called daughter to Bald Mountain State Park, Campground B. If you are not here by five p.m., I will end her miserable sinful existence once and for all, freeing her soul from its cage so that God may judge her and she may receive her eternal damnation."

Rachel hugged me from behind and cinnamon filled the air. I didn't even feel angry, just empty. She whispered her sweet nonsense words into my ear and told me everything was going to be okay. I turned to her and before I knew it we were kissing. My daughter needed me. I didn't have time for this, but I couldn't stop myself. Rachel helped me out of my clothes, undressing herself in the process. I was lost in her warmth, her need, and the beating of her heart. Her own natural smell blended with the cinnamon on her breath and I couldn't stop myself.

As we neared climax, writhing on top of my desk, she put both hands on my chest to support herself and looked deep into my eyes. "Bite me, Eric. I need it and you need it."

I held back. She seemed okay, but I had never fed on the same person so many times in succession, not even Tabitha. "It'll be okay, baby," she said. She ran her left hand across the top of my head. "You'll know when to stop." Her hand moved over my forehead. "I trust you." She touched my throat. Her hands wandered lower, touching lightly over my heart and on my belly. She reached between us to cup the base of my testicles.

It wasn't right. It felt completely wrong. A line of heat shot through my body from the crown of my head to my groin where she still moved, grinding against me. Internal alarms were going off in my head, but I couldn't interpret them properly. She kept moving on top of me, but slowed her rhythm, prolonging the inevitable. "Please," she whispered. The smell of cinnamon replaced everything; it was the only odor in the room, overwhelming all else. I bit into her neck, white pinpricks of light searing my vision. My teeth went numb, fangs retracting, and my taste buds awoke, assaulted by stimuli to all their receptors, as if I'd bitten into a jalapeño rather than an eighteen-year-old girl.

My heart spurred to life, beating as if it might burst from my chest. I couldn't breathe properly; each breath came fast and furious, too short and too quick. Heat spread across my body from the core outward. I stopped drinking and we both cried out in unison, reaching completion.

In Rachel's eyes, I could see a vague reflection of myself. Hazy, but me. I didn't want to look at myself, not in her eyes, not in a mirror. Purple light flickered from my eyes and the reflection faded. An urge to hurl her against the wall, to break her in half, to fight her, fight something, came out of nowhere, but I suppressed it. Cinnamon was replaced by the smell of sweat and sex. She looked down at me, her wide eyes torn between terror and exhilaration.

"Are you going to eat me, baby?" she cooed.

"What are you doing to me?" I asked breathlessly.

"Making you feel alive," she said as she collapsed on my chest. Her heart was racing too. Mine began to slow to a stop. "It's what I'm supposed to do. I want to be your thrall. A thrall does her best to make her master forget the things he has lost in order to gain immortality. A good thrall is supposed to train several replacements and then join the master in unlife, but I don't want to be a vampire, Eric. I just want to be yours."

"Bullshit," I mouthed.

We lay there for a while without moving and I felt my body grow cold once more. The clock said 09:43. We had wasted over an hour, basking in the aftermath of my inability to resist Rachel's advances. This wasn't like me and I knew it.

Well, *inappropriate sex* was all me, but usually, when things need killing or my friends are in danger, sex takes a backseat. I told myself that I had hours to spare and that was why I went ahead with it, but I was lying to myself.

My little cinnamon girl was more than she appeared to be and the whole "it's a thrall thing" excuse was wearing thin. If all thralls could do what Rachel could do, then Roger would have had one. Hell, it had been Roger who'd told me that thralls were little more than slaves, that any human who became a thrall descended into madness, like Renfield. I wondered if he'd lied, and why.

"Thralls." I gently pushed her up and she rolled off of me. "Is there a way to tell who is a thrall and who isn't?"

"Sure," Rachel answered, surprised. "You should be able to tell just by looking at them and thinking about it."

I started putting my clothes back on and Rachel did the same. "Really? How? Do they have big glowing signs over their heads that say 'I belong to X,' or what?"

Rachel looked puzzled as she slipped her bra back on. She put it on backward, fastened up the hooks, and then slid them around to the back. She flipped the cups up to cover her breasts and put her arms through the straps before pulling them up onto her shoulders. I'd never paid attention to how women got dressed. I wondered if Tabitha did it the same way. I'd probably seen her get dressed a thousand times and I didn't know how she did it.

"I think it's supposed to be similar to the way Vlads and Masters sense each other, except that even Soldiers can have thralls. Only Drones can't."

Which was not what Roger had told me. "I thought only Vlads could make thralls."

"Who told you that?" She looked like it was the dumbest thing she'd ever heard.

"Roger." Rachel's heart skipped a beat when I answered. She continued getting dressed, but I stood there in my underwear, watching her. "So I should get a sense of age and power, but it would be the thrall's master I was sensing?"

"Yes, you should get a sense of the vampire, probably a mental image of the master overlaid on an image of the thrall."

For forty years, I'd gotten all that I knew about vampires from talking to Roger. Big mistake. "So do a lot of high society vampires have thralls?"

"Sure," she said. "They're a status symbol. Who has the most attractive, the most talented, that sort of thing."

So Roger would have known. He hadn't just been mistaken; his had been a deliberate deception.

"You've really never sensed a thrall before?" Rachel asked.

My attitude toward other vampires meant that I didn't know many of them, but Roger knew all the most important ones around. I had steered clear of vampire society . . . or had Roger steered me clear of it? I had trouble remembering which way it had been. But how had I never sensed even one thrall before? "No, I haven't. Not that I've noticed."

She shrugged and slipped her blouse on. "Maybe you have to make one before you can sense them."

"No," I said immediately, stepping into my jeans.

"No what?" she asked innocently.

"I'm not making you my thrall. You seem to be doing just fine with what you've learned from those friends of yours at the Irons Club." I looked around for my shirt, found it in the wastebin next to my desk. I shook the little bits of paper off of it and slid it over my head.

"You need me, Eric," she said as she put a hand on my chest. I brushed her hand away and finished pulling my shirt on. She took a step away, but I could still feel the warmth where she'd touched me. "What if it would help you find Greta? You might be able to sense vampires better, too . ... those that are yours, anyway."

"How does that follow?"

"You know how sires don't sense their children?"

"Uh-huh."

"Well, that's not strictly true. When you sense another vampire, you don't sense them all the time, right?"

"Just until you've acknowledged each other," I agreed.

"Yep, and then when you get out of each other's range and come back into contact . . ."

"You sense each other again."

"Well, the reason sire and offspring don't sense each other is that they're always linked."

"But if that's true, then I should be able to sense something, shouldn't I? Because I can't sense Greta or Tabitha."

"You need to practice. Which is why you need to make me your thrall. Thralls help focus a vampire's mental abilities. In time, the most powerful vampires can learn to see, hear, and in rare occasions even taste through their thralls."

"No," I insisted. She sat down on the edge of my desk, crestfallen.

"Not even if it can help you find Greta?"

"I know where Greta is! She's in Bald Mountain State Park, Campground B, like the man said."

"He could have been lying," Rachel argued. "What werewolves always tell the truth? What if Greta is already dead and—"

I put my hand over her mouth. "Be quiet and let me think."

She nodded, eyes wide.

Rachel had been right about everything so far and she seemed to genuinely want to help, but no one dates a vampire unless they want something. It was possible she was just in it for the danger and the thrill, but I doubted it. She had to have an ulterior motive. Or was I just being paranoid? It wouldn't be the first time.

And yet—when we'd had sex, why had I suddenly viewed her as a threat? And what was that feeling that made me want her incessantly? It was something more than lust, but much less natural than love. It probably had something to do with cinnamon.

Still—I didn't see how it could hurt to bind her to me. And, most importantly, I'd do anything for Greta. Even this.

I took my hand away from her mouth. "Okay."

Rachel let out an exhilarated yip and began bouncing up and down. If it was an act, it was a good one. She seemed genuinely excited. Then again, bouncing up and down like she was doing would accelerate her heart rate. I looked at Rachel in a whole new light and waited to smell cinnamon. "Can we do it now?" she said, rushing into my arms.

"How do we do it?" I kissed her neck. "Does it involve sex?" I tugged at her blouse and she removed it with a laugh. Still no cinnamon.

"No, but I'm ready any time you are, lover." Damn.

I lifted her off the desk and kissed her breasts through her bra. She wrapped her legs around me and I smelled her desire. Double damn. "How do we do it?" I asked again.

"You smear your blood on my head and over my heart, then put a single drop on my tongue and we kiss. You look into my eyes and push your mind into mine, like when you control other vampires. We'll both feel it when it happens. I've been told that it hurts a little for you and a lot for me, but when we're done, I'll be able to do even more for you."

She pulled at my shirt. "Of course, there's no reason we can't do it while we have sex."

"I don't know," I said. "Maybe I should just—"

"Oh, please, baby." Still no cinnamon. Maybe I *was* being paranoid.

"Fine," I relented, telling myself it was for Greta. "Let's do it."

25

ERIC:

THIRD EYE OPEN AND READY FOR BUSINESS

Rachel hadn't been kidding. It hurt like a motherfucker, but when it was done, I could feel her with my mind. Without looking, I could sense where she was and how she was doing. It wasn't telepathy, in that her thoughts were closed to me, but her general mood was clear.

She wasn't the only new presence in my mind, either. I felt them all, my "children," including three who were supposed to be dead. To be honest, it was kind of nice to see them.

I don't stay mad long. Usually, I'd rather wish someone a long happy life the hell away from me. It's just that so often, they won't oblige. I'd staked the first two and left them to greet the dawn. I'd taken care of Irene in El Segundo; her survival proved she really was a heartless bitch.

They felt me too.

My oldest, Lisa, squirmed in her sleep, long blonde hair cascading over her breasts. She'd fallen asleep with her jeans on, the flared bottoms finally back in style. Lisa had been my rebound girl, once I'd given up on Marilyn ever taking me back. It felt like she was in the back of a plane. Someone was playing acoustic guitar softly in the background; they stopped and I felt a presence near her, a human. He wanted to know if she was okay.

Nancy was Lisa's replacement. She was sleeping not far away, no farther than Sable Oaks. She still slept in a coffin with dirt in the bottom, the interior lit with blacklight bulbs. She'd always been superstitious. Nancy wore a white silk teddy, her supple chestnut-colored skin standing out in sensuous contrast.

In the quasiviolet light, her eyes flashed open briefly, the once-black irises now faded close to gray, flaring red before she surrendered again to the sleep of the dead. Nancy and I had had a falling out over Greta. Nancy believed that teenage girls shouldn't talk back to vampires. I didn't disagree, but held an even firmer conviction that nobody got to slap my little girl around.

Irene was awake, smiling, and in the act. She still got me hot. Irene had been wild, too wild, and she'd dyed her hair red, really red, like a Porsche. She climbed off of her lover and gripped his member, smiling at me. "It's longer," she mouthed, before beginning to fellate the lucky bastard. Irene was the farthest away of all, miles and miles across the ocean.

I gestured to Rachel. "She's younger," I mouthed, but Irene was gone, replaced by Tabitha, asleep in a bed in the Highland Towers. Talbot was curled up next to her on the bed, in his natural form, a little black ball of fur, purring. He'd never curled up to me that way.

Last came Greta. She was immobilized, but not by a stake. A metal box enclosed her, the sides lined with little crosses. Even if she'd been one of the chosen few who can turn to mist, the box was airtight. She twisted and turned, trying to position herself so that the crosses no longer burned her skin. Each time she found a moment's peace, sleep claimed her, and she fell back against the sizzling signs of faith.

I waited to feel angry, but the most I could manage was irritation. The werewolves were dead either way, but it would be trickier if I couldn't go berserk on them. Just hours ago, seeing Greta in agony had been enough to send me directly over the edge. I was in control, but I shouldn't have been. I should have been a raging black-winged terror, tearing ass across the country to save my little girl.

"Shit." I rolled off of Rachel and sat on the edge of the bed. We'd moved the whole thing to the bedroom because she'd asked nicely and I hadn't cared.

"Are you okay?" she asked. There was a slight tremor in her voice. "Did something go wrong? It's supposed to hurt me more."

"It's not that," I said. "Just some unfinished business. A few of my children, ones I thought I'd disposed of, are still around. It worked; I can sense them."

I walked over to the sink and started sponging off, thinking about Irene, Lisa, and Nancy.

Irene might try to start a fight eventually, but none of this current mess was hers. She wasn't very subtle. She would have just blown up the Demon Heart with me in it. Lisa wasn't a threat; she was big, beautiful, and about as smart as Kyle had been. Roger had assured me once that she wasn't a Drone, but she certainly acted like one. Nancy could have come up with a plan like this, but she never would have been able to execute it. Besides, she would have been up in my face gloating by now.

Tabitha was safe, but asleep. Greta was my only real concern.

I went back into my office and dialed Marilyn's number.

"Hello?" she answered.

"Any messages?" I asked.

"I got a call from our friend Captain Stacey with the VCPD. He says that he hopes you can afford to keep paying for the cover-up. He wanted to make sure you knew that you have had him, two folks in dispatch, and six other officers working double duty to cover up your—and I'm quoting—'bullshit shenanigans' this weekend."

"Can I afford it?" I asked.

"For a while." Marilyn sounded like she was speaking to a delinquent teenager. Rachel walked in wearing tennis shoes, short shorts, and a baby-doll T-shirt that said *Boy Toy*. She approached the desk, pointing happily to a new necklace she was wearing; it was a black choker with a tiny golden padlock.

"I've also been meaning to talk to you about the money that you've been spending on clothes. I assume that Sally told me the truth about your little shopping spree?" Marilyn choked out the words.

"She did."

"Were those clothes for your new little trollop? Will I be meeting that one again or do you already have a different one?"

I wanted to tell her she was wrong about me, but I didn't know whether that was true anymore. There had been a line that I had been trying not to cross, the line between being a man who was monstrous and an actual monster. Now I couldn't even see the line. I had passed it without realizing it some time ago.

"I have a couple of things to do tonight," I said, ignoring her questions and my own guilt. "So I might be late. I have to go rescue Greta. Then I might have to kill Roger."

"Serves him right." Her voice was acid.

That took me by surprise. "Is he still over there? Stake him for me."

"No, he wouldn't be that stupid, although I imagine he isn't far. I'm sorry I can't stake him for you."

"I was kidding." I wasn't kidding.

"Me, too." And the funniest thing was that for the first time in the half century or so I'd known Marilyn, I could tell that she was lying to me.

"No," I said in stunned amazement. "You weren't."

"Leave it alone, Eric. Please."

"Marilyn, if something's going on—"

"It's nothing. I'm just tired. You said something happened to Greta?" She sounded more concerned about Greta than she usually did about me. "What happened?"

"Werewolf trouble. I'm going to take care of it now."

"But it isn't even noon, yet. What about the sun?"

I played with the lock on Rachel's necklace. "Hey," I spoke into the phone. "This is Greta we're talking about here. Fuck the sun. Me and my new thrall are going to get creative."

I hung up the phone and Rachel put her arms around me. She was nervous and curious at the same time. "Creative?"

"Yeah," I told her as I walked back to the bedroom. "Creative."

I emerged from the bedroom a few minutes later with my clothes on. "How do my eyes look?"

"They're back to normal," she said. "I guess a little blood was all you needed."

"I need you to go shopping for me," I told her. "I need a jumpsuit that covers up as much skin as possible and a full-face motorcycle helmet with one of those little thingies that covers up the neck. Get the helmet visor as dark as you can. I have boots, but I need a pair of gloves in my size. Call a cab. Get the stuff and meet me back here by two o'clock. I want to be up on Bald Mountain by four."

"Okay," Rachel said. "What's the rest of the plan?"

"Leave that to me." I kissed her. "Oh, and buy a bigger purse, it might need to hold two."

I gave her the money from the safe and she laughed at the amount. "When I get back from Vegas, will you still love me?"

"You head anywhere near Vegas," I said, tapping my temple, "and I'll know, remember?"

"Only if you think to check," she teased.

We kissed a long, lingering kiss. She let her hands wander across my chest and lower still. It was then that I smelled the cinnamon. I was ready for it this time. Thoughts and feelings that were not quite mine danced gently through my brain like little puffs of cotton candy. "Trust Rachel," a sweet tender voice ordered my mind. "Love Rachel. Need Rachel." Riding the wave of sensation, I let my hands drift across her breasts and down her back. I grabbed her butt and started kissing her harder. She pushed gently away from me and I didn't let her go, kissing my way down her neck instead.

"Not that I'm complaining, Eric, but if you want me to get everything done in time to leave . . ."

I let her go reluctantly.

I had Magbidion's phone number written down on a blue sticky note stuck to the bottom of my desk drawer. It came free easily and I stuck it on the desk. Did I care if Rachel was trying to use magic on me to enhance our sex, to calm me down, to make my heart beat? The sad and sorry answer is that I didn't.

Roger was in the same category as Rachel. I didn't really care that he had set me up. I wanted to know why he'd done it and if we could resolve things, but basically, he was my best friend. Sure, he was an asshole, but so was I. He was also the only person still around, other than Marilyn, that I'd known when I was alive. Like my Mustang, I wouldn't give up on him unless I had no choice.

So what if Roger had sicced some werewolves on me. I could kill the werewolves. I would rescue Greta. Hell, if he wanted the Demon Heart shut down bad enough to spike my blood supply, maybe I ought to just shut it down. I knew that it embarrassed him, that he was afraid his upper-crust pals would look down on him. What if this all could have been avoided by my buying out his interest in the Demon Heart? I hate questions like that—what-ifs. They can drive you crazy.

I wasn't proud of it, but it all boiled down to the bliss of ignorance. If I knew for sure what was going on with Rachel, or with Roger, then I might have to take action and the truth was that I just didn't want to do that. Why would I? Let's say your spouse is good to you, treats you right, and you have a long happy life together. Do you really want to find out fifty years down the road that she hated your guts the whole time or that for thirty of those years she'd been banging the milkman every Monday and Wednesday? If it were me, I wouldn't. Does that make me a bad person?

A little voice in my head told me that I was a bad person regardless. Everything else was just a bonus.

26

ERIC:

AGORANAUT

Bald Mountain wasn't much of a mountain compared to the Rockies or the Smokies, but it was big enough to count. Oak, dogwood, and pine trees made up most of the surrounding forest. The bulk of the land had been designated a state park in the late thirties or early forties. For two dollars, anyone could get a day pass to visit the park from about seven a.m. until sunset. They also had overnight passes for campers and areas set aside for RV parking. I hadn't been out to Bald Mountain since Marilyn and I had been dating. The picnic area was different and there was a conservation center, but the park itself looked surprisingly familiar.

Rachel looked beautiful in the light that poured between the trees and in through the windshield. If I squinted just right, I could pretend she was Marilyn. It took me back to my last picnic. Roger, Marilyn, and I had gone to the park in my Mustang, top down, the wind blowing through our hair. Marilyn drove that day and I'd let Roger ride up front. The ice chest sat next to me on the bench seat. Back then, the grilling stations in the picnic area had been new. All we had to supply was the food, the charcoal, and the fire.

The fire. I'd caught Marilyn looking at me in the rearview mirror. I'd forgotten it on purpose, that look . . . a sad look with I-don't-know-how-to-tell-you eyes. I buried it again.

Rachel looked over at me, the way you look at an angry dog who's cornered you. Her hand touched my leg tentatively. "Is there something wrong?"

"Why?"

"You just . . . um, the link, it goes both ways a little and, I don't know, you felt lost."

I turned my head. Outside the window, the leaves were rich and green. "Only for the last forty-three years," I whispered.

It had never occurred to me before, but I'd now been undead longer than I'd been alive. My vampiric existence had eclipsed my human life, and it seemed like each year beyond that balance eroded me more. Forty-three years of undeath. It seemed longer. My watch was still broken. "What month is it?" I asked.

"It's August, Eric," Rachel told me.

The leather outfit she'd brought me would have looked more natural on a rock star like Marilyn Manson. It did cover my whole body, though, and it was real leather, so it could probably take a beating. The mask had zippers where I thought it ought to have holes, but it wasn't noticeable with the helmet on. Over the suit's gloves, I wore a pair of work gloves secured with duct tape. I had the legs of the jumpsuit tucked into a pair of steel-toed work boots, secured like the gloves. Between the tinted goggles and the tinted visor, the sun didn't hurt my eyes that much, but my vision was restricted to whatever was directly in front of me.

"What day?" I asked.

"Monday," she answered.

"Monday the what?"

"Monday the ninth," she answered, looking over at me. "Why so interested?"

I watched the trees go by, noting each hiking trail we passed. Rachel was doing a good job playing chauffeur. After I'd hung up with Magbidion, I'd had Carl drive a loaner out to me. It was a rusted-out hunk of junk with no air conditioner, but that just showed Carl's intelligence.

It was always a crapshoot when it came to me and loaners. He knew that I would pay for damages, but we both felt better about it if he loaned me cheap cars . . . just in case. No sense in throwing money away. The heat didn't bother me, but Rachel was covered in a thin sheen of sweat and her deodorant wasn't keeping pace with demand.

"Roger will have something big planned for tomorrow. Something drastic . . . probably his big finale."

She looked confused. "How do you figure that?"

"It's my birthday," I told her.

"That's great! How old will you be?"

My sense of Greta grew stronger as we passed a turn and then started to grow fainter. "Turn around and go back," I ordered. "She's down that road." Rachel made a three-point turn and headed down the road I had indicated.

"This way?" she asked.

I nodded. "Yeah, we're getting close."

"How old are you going to be?" she asked again.

"I don't remember," I said distractedly. I was turning forty again. I turn forty every year, but it never sticks.

Greta was screaming in a metal box. Rage reached up into my chest. I could see the box clearly. Men—werewolves in human form—were taking turns rolling the box over and shaking it back and forth. Greta's cries were louder than my thoughts. Something inside me roared, but made no sound.

"Sweet Jesus!" Rachel swore. I guessed she'd felt that one along our link.

"Stop the car," I commanded.

Brakes squealed as Rachel slammed her foot to the floor and the car turned sideways, sliding as it went. We came to a halt at the edge of a drainage ditch that directed the camping area's runoff under the road as it ran downhill. The car had rotated one hundred and eighty degrees from where we had started, facing back down the way we'd come. I stepped out of the car and looked back at Rachel. "If I'm not back in fifteen minutes, go home."

I didn't wait for an answer. Instead, I ran down the slope into the drainage ditch and started scrambling up the rise in front of me. Greta was on the other side of the hill.

My mental picture of the campground grew clearer and clearer the closer I got. As I topped the hill, I saw the first werewolf, a lookout. He looked human, but even through the visor of my helmet, I could smell him. He'd been a wolf recently. We both froze, momentarily stunned. He couldn't have been more than sixteen, an inexperienced fighter, so it was no surprise that I recovered first. I put my fist through his chest and it came out on the other side holding his heart. Young or old, these werewolves were my enemies and anyone who wanted to live had better change sides quickly.

His body rolled halfway down the hill and stopped when it hit the base of a pine tree. His pack would smell the blood soon. I broke into a run and hit the campsite as soon as I cleared the tree line. A group of tents was arranged in a circle around one large tent. Garlic cloves hung on ropes over the entrances and each tent had a cross painted on all four sides. It was definitely not a vampire-friendly zone.

On the far side of the camping area, RVs with out-of-state tags were parked in double rows. Not a good sign. I'd already seen the kind of help William was rounding up and I didn't want to get in a fight with more fun-loving representatives of the Lycan Diocese.

Two men—werewolves—saw me walk into the camp. I staggered like I'd been injured and they rushed toward me. Before they reached me, the taller one slowed down, his eyes widening. "Chuck, no! It's a—" I grabbed Chuck by the shoulder blades, hooking my fingers into his collarbone for leverage, and tore him open at the chest, his sternum popping, ribs gaping apart. His buddy staggered away from me.

It was probably the sunlight that confused him. Even though I was expected, vampires are creatures of the night. The werewolves were used to hunting us inside houses, sewers, crypts, or apartments during the day. Was it possible that I was more frightening in the light? I wiped my visor with the back of Chuck's shirt and charged his pal.

"Vampire!" he yelled at the top of his lungs. We ran at each other full tilt. He transformed as he ran, shedding teeth. He swiped at me with his claws and the blow caught me just right, turning my leaping dodge into an out-of-control tumble through the air. I cannonballed into one of the tents, crumpling it, tent poles snapping. The fabric wrapped around me completely, blocking my vision of all but bright blue tent flap. I'd landed within a few feet of the metal box; I could feel Greta inside.

I struggled out from under the tent as the werewolf landed next to me. Reaching out, I grabbed him by the muzzle and threw him hard and high into the bough of a nearby oak.

The box. I spun quickly, searching, and saw it. They had welded the box shut, and it looked like a professional job. I also found the folks who had been rolling it around. Six men and two women were gathered around the metal container, taking turns rocking it from side to side. A handful of children stopped playing and ran for the big tent. The adults started to change and more werewolves began pouring out of the other tents and the RVs. I counted at least forty. There was no way I could outfight them all, not in the daytime. I grabbed a little boy and a little girl by the scruffs of their necks and I felt like scum when I did it.

They both screamed for their mommy and one of the female werewolves turned human again. "Please, no!" It was a standoff. The males started circling, but kept their distance as I walked toward the box. The females who were still in werewolf mode backed slowly away from me, but the one in human form stayed put. I heard the tent flaps flutter behind me and I spun around.

"Don't make me hurt them!" I shouted.

I hoped they would buy it, because I already knew I wouldn't do anything to the kids. The little boy might have been as old as eight, and the little girl was only four or five. I couldn't have killed either of them.

A tall man stepped out of the tent. He was six foot five and had dusty blond hair. I couldn't tell the color of his eyes, but he looked like a real mountain man. A foot-long wooden cross hung from his belt, the base sharpened to a point. A smaller metal cross hung from his neck over a flannel shirt.

"What in God's name is going on here?" he spat.

"You called," I said acidly. "I came."

William didn't look fake when he transformed. No weird latex-looking skin, no fur turned all the wrong way, and when he moved, it was smooth, not the jerky stop-motion effect I'd seen so often. That alone would have earned him the Alpha title in my book. Pure white fur covered him from head to toe, and he stared at me angrily from behind ice-blue eyes. "How dare you threaten children?" The voice rang more in my head than in my ears and it was angry.

"Fuck you, pal," I shouted back. "You see, believe it or not, I haven't done a damn thing to you. Your son got lured into an alleyway by a vampire stripper and, as weird as it sounds, she used a magic gun to kill him. I wound up playing the scapegoat. I think her boss wants me to kill you, but I'm still working on why.

"As for the stripper who killed your son, not to mention your pack-mates out at Orchard Lake—she's dead now. I had my girlfriend track her down and kill her. If you want, you can have her ashes. All I want is my daughter back and for you guys to back off."

"Liar!" William's huge clawed hands shook with rage as he bared his fangs at me. "My son was pure. He would never consort with some vampire whore."

"Have you ever gotten a blow job from a woman who doesn't have to breathe? Trust me, he'd consort."

"No more of your lies, vampire. I know what you want and we will never surrender our land to one of your kind. No matter how many dead you lay on our doorstep, we will not give in."

"Land? What do you think this is, the Louisiana fucking Purchase? Let's try it this way. I don't want to kill you. I didn't even bring any silver with me. Hell, I didn't even bring the magic gun with me." Which, by the way, I was already regretting. "I just want to be left alone. If you can't do that, then we have a problem and if we have a problem, I'm going to have to put you and your little wolf pack down."

"Those two children you hold in your hands are sinless, vampire. If you kill them, we shall not be sad, but shall rejoice. They will fly to their Heavenly Father and join him forever in paradise. We, unlike you, are living, breathing creatures of God. We worship in many ways, but we all worship, and he will send us more soldiers to fill our ranks and more pups to fill our hearts." He looked meaningfully at his pack when he spoke, trying, I thought, more to convince them than to persuade me.

I saw grim commitment in the eyes of the gathering pack, some of them wearing crosses, some clutching crucifixes, even a few wielding Stars of David. They didn't like it, but most of them would do whatever he told them.

"Kill it," he shouted.

I mouthed an obscenity as he struck. I wouldn't have had time to break the children's necks even if I'd been willing to do it. He was faster than anything I'd ever seen, faster than me, faster than Talbot. His huge white paws smacked my helmet with lightning speed and it shattered. The Beatles' "Here Comes the Sun" played through my mind. Now I had definitely beaten El Segundo.

ERIC:

POWERHOUSE

I'd been on fire before and it usually made me feel like an idiot. Often, when I ignited, it was a result of forgetting what time it was or watching an impending sunrise just a little too long. This time it made me angry. Claws tore at my clothes, and as each strip of fabric fell away, new pain erupted. But hey, at least I was warm.

Part of me wondered if it wasn't better this way, to die on Bald Mountain, in the sun on a breezy day in August. The other part of me told the suicidal part to shut the fuck up and fight.

It only took a few seconds for the flames to completely engulf me. I wondered if I looked anything like the Human Torch or if it was more like one of those movie stuntmen. Several werewolves were laughing and the mama werewolf was fussing over her children. I was just as glad as she was that they were safe. Then I heard a single word that changed everything.

"Daddy!" It was Greta. She could feel me burning, even through her own pain. People say that monsters only come out at night. Mine came out right then. Rage doesn't even begin to cover it. Steel bands snapped inside my chest and chains pulled free of their wall mounts.

Suddenly, I could see. The flames were out and everyone looked a little shorter. Tendrils of smoke rose off dark black skin that I didn't recognize as mine. It didn't look charred. It was smooth and sizzled softly in the sun. I tried to move, but couldn't. My whole body had gone numb and useless, as if I'd been staked through the heart, but then it started moving of its own accord. I could see and hear, but something else was in the driver's seat.

The thing I had become held up its arm and high-pitched squealing filled the air, joined by the sound of a few thousand wings. Clouds of bats and birds swarmed overhead, blocking out the sun. My opponents looked on in silence as the sky turned black. My new skin stopped sizzling. William looked up at me and crossed himself. Several of the others presented their holy symbols and began to pray in Latin, Hebrew, Spanish, and English. The super vamp I had become roared and started toward them.

No! Wait! I started yelling inside my head. *Get Greta, jackass!*

There was no response from Ericzilla. It was more like watching the demo for a first-person shooter video game than actually being me. Two werewolves jumped at me in slow motion. Uber vamp speed was unbelievable. I darted forward, plucking both werewolves from the air and tearing them into quarters, not just killing them, but mangling them with a purpose. If this was what happened when I blacked out, then I wished I would black out again, because I really didn't want to see this.

Blood jetted in lazy streams from the werewolves' remains as I struggled with all my might to regain control. If I could even just turn my head toward Greta . . . Instead, I was forced into the skies as the uber Eric darted down at another unlucky werewolf, pulling it up into the air and tearing off its head with talon-tipped fingers.

There was no doubt that I could destroy the entire pack this way, but if I did that and then suddenly found myself back at the wheel, standing over the bodies, the living curtain of wings would probably disperse, and Greta and I would both be fried. My death would have been fast, and right now I almost welcomed it, but hers would be prolonged and torturous. I couldn't abide that.

Stop screwing with the werewolves and get Greta out of the box, you dumb fucker! I yelled at Ericzilla. *She's going to die in there if you blow this! If you can even pick up a single thought, you cave-brained bastard, then open the damn box!*

Another werewolf entered the shredding zone and went from living thing to flesh-chunk confetti with bright red liquid streamers. Either I had slowed or the pack was speeding up. They were doing their best to fight against me, and so was I. Then, the two little kids wolfed out and my uber vamp body turned on them. I tried with every bit of mental strength to stay the death that awaited those children; *They're just kids,* I shouted mentally. *We are here to get Greta, shit-for-brains! So get Greta and get us the fuck out of here!*

I pictured myself standing in front of the uber Eric, blocking the children and pointing at the box. My mental image head-butted the black-skinned beast and kicked it in the groin. When that didn't work, I fought dirty. I showed him the night I'd first found Greta, lying bruised and bloody in her foster father's bed. She'd been nine. The uber vamp howled. *You remember that?* I shouted. *You want to be like that, like the human so evil I wouldn't even bite him?*

Greta is in that damn metal box right over there and she needs me! Comprendez? I had my mental image walk over to the box and rip it open. Greta was inside and I imagined myself ripping open a vein and spraying blood like my arm was a fire hose to heal her wounds.

Uber Eric paused and time returned to normal. Ten werewolves piled onto me, clawing and biting like mad to take my uber vamp body down. Had I gotten through? Did it, whatever was driving, understand? I began to suspect that it had, because it slowly turned, ignoring the wounds and the werewolves, looking for the box. Black blood flowed down one of my arms from a multitude of cuts and bites. I couldn't feel it, but it looked painful.

Uber me turned its head to look at the blood, swatting the werewolves away on autopilot, using both wings and the less-injured arm. Then, I got a look at the box with Greta inside and heard my own voice say, "Hold tight, sweetheart. We're getting the hell out of Dodge!"

I still wasn't in control, but that certainly sounded like a step in the right direction. The uber vamp grabbed the box and leapt into the air.

Gunshots sounded from below and the twang of arrows filled the air. The arrows made me laugh on the inside, but Supervamp must not have thought it was funny. Real wooden arrows are much more useful than bullets against a vampire, and William's werewolves knew it.

I wanted to see how many werewolves were down there, but uber me wasn't interested. A mass of bats poured out of the sky, diving toward the werewolves, and the uber vamp's black skin began to sizzle again in the now imperfect screen created by the remaining bats above.

I spotted Rachel in the loaner car. My uber vamp body made a beeline for the vehicle, landing a few feet from the front bumper. Rachel screamed, but she didn't hit the gas.

Crouching low over the box, shielding it with tenebrous wings as if afraid an arrow or stray beam of sunlight might strike Greta, the uber vamp and I punched through the seam of the metal box with one black talon. Metal screeched as the weld gave way, little curlicue strands falling to the grass as we peeled back the top. Tilting the box to the side, we let Greta roll out onto the ground. She looked pretty bad, like charred hamburger, but she was still with us.

As soon as I saw my girl, the whole transformation happened in reverse. My nerve endings woke up. It would have been just fine with me if they had waited awhile. I had multiple gunshot wounds, cuts, scratches, bites, and two or three arrows in me. One of the arrows was close enough to my heart that I was afraid to move too quickly lest it wiggle those last few centimeters and leave me paralyzed midrescue.

"Rachel!" I shouted. "Get over here and pull these arrows out!"

She stared at me motionlessly for a moment before springing into action. "How did you do that?" she asked.

"Arrows. Out. Now!"

Rachel grabbed the first arrow and jerked it out of my shoulder with a loud grunt. It came free, red blood mixing with the black blood already covering the shaft. She grabbed the next and pulled with all her might. I gritted my teeth against the pain as the shaft came free. Rather than pulling out the arrow in my left side, she thrust it the rest of the way through. My legs buckled and I fell to one knee. But when she grabbed the last arrow I couldn't stand it anymore. It was too deep.

"Leave it," I said.

"I've almost got it." Rachel put her knee in my back for more leverage and I shouted as the arrow twisted in my chest.

"Just leave the damn thing in and start the car!"

More spots of sunlight appeared on the grass as she dove straight through the open window of the car and into the driver's seat. Overhead and back near the camp, the mass of winged minions was beginning to disperse. A core group of gray bats struggled to maintain formation, but was losing the battle. As Rachel kicked open the passenger's side door, dozens of werewolves, no longer blinded by the horde of bats, howled a battle cry and began loping toward us.

I gashed my wrist open with my fangs and bled into Greta's eyes. When they flickered open I pushed my thoughts into her head. "Turn into a mouse."

"Can't, Dad," she replied. "Too tired."

I latched ahold of her thoughts, but they were hazy, jumbled, and confused. So were mine. I tried to block out the sound of the approaching werewolves and pushed harder, so hard she screamed. She managed the change, then went limp again.

She was a sad, burnt-looking mouse. Talbot would have thought her an hors d'oeuvre gone wrong, but she was still my Greta and she was still undead, which was all that mattered to me. I jumped into the car, holding her carefully in my fist, and yowled as sunlight hit the exposed flesh on my back where claws, bullets, and arrows had torn through the leather. Rachel gunned the engine and started pulling away.

As the first wolf cleared the hill I tucked Greta into Rachel's purse, turned into a mouse, and jumped in after her. Rachel reached over, closed the purse flap, and drove hell-bent toward the park exit. Inside the bag, I cuddled against Greta and hoped William's pack didn't catch up with us.

I had no idea how the whole uber vamp thing actually worked, but I knew it was tied to my anger. If I got angry enough to have a rage blackout, then I did my own little version of the Incredible Hulk or Super Dracula, whatever you wanted to call it. Freud would have said that it was pure id, unleashed and given form, not unlike Dr. Jekyll and Mr. Hyde, but that was a little too easy an answer for me. No one was lining up to explain why I'd been aware this time either, why I'd heard and seen what happened, though I'd never remembered any of it before.

Could it be that making Rachel my thrall had been responsible? If it allowed me to sense my offspring, and to supposedly recognize the thralls created by other vampires . . . who knew if it helped control the part of me that went berserk? Was it a good thing or a bad thing? I couldn't decide.

I'd been a vampire for over forty years, and all along I'd been turning into this thing right, left, and sideways, whenever people pissed me off. Why had nobody said anything? Talbot said he hadn't told me because he thought I knew. I believed that. How do you not know you turn into a giant vampire blender and puree things when you're mad? Maybe Marilyn had never seen it. No one ever had to tell me that I turned into a bat, a cat, or anything else. Why would they assume I didn't know? But Roger knew me better than that.

In fact, I'd bet Roger knew the most about it, and I couldn't ask him about it. Not right now. What if we'd already had that discussion before, or after one of my blackouts, and I'd forgotten? What if I'd "figured it out" any number of times, but, unable to control it, had forgotten?

What's your father's name? Marilyn's question from earlier rose, a disturbing specter in my thoughts. I'd already forgotten what she'd said. The last name started with a C, I thought.

Take it from me: If you're going to die in a car crash and miraculously rise as one of the living dead, don't let them embalm you. I was starting to think maybe it had screwed with my head. As I lay puzzling out the complexity of my life, the thrum of the motor and the exertion of the day lulled me gently to sleep.

28

TABITHA:

PMS

Void City was quiet and brooding that Monday night. Every traffic light glared bright red before allowing Talbot's Jaguar to weave its way homeward. Halfway there, the two of us realized that it was Eric's birthday, or at least, it would be after midnight, so we went shopping.

Talbot bought him a new cell phone and I made do with a selection from Victoria's Secret, Frederick's of Hollywood, and Sahid's Adult Books and Novelties. I spent too much money, but I felt guilty about sleeping with Talbot. Eric would have slept with a human and not called it cheating. Maybe he already had. I hoped he had. It would make me feel better about what I'd done.

I stood up on all fours, turned in a circle, and sat back down on the seat fitfully. I liked being a cat, feeling warm, having a heartbeat, breathing autonomically, things that my human body no longer provided. Even as a cat, though, I was increasingly on edge. "Damn him, that man has me wrapped around his little finger!" I hissed.

"I would hesitate to refute that," Talbot said as he glanced down at me.

"I have never cheated on him, not once! There is no telling how many times he's screwed around on me, but I'm the one who feels guilty."

Streetlamps and skyscrapers passed by the windows and Talbot did not comment. "Well?" I meowed.

"Well what?" he answered. Eyes on the road, he reached down and silenced the classical music on the radio. I hadn't even noticed there had been music until he turned it off. "Eric never made any pretense at being faithful. You did. Maybe you took pride in it? It kept you in the right as the long-suffering faithful member of the relationship. Now you're not the martyr anymore and it's eating away at you."

Turning human, I crossed my arms and stared out the side window. "That is so totally screwed up! I don't even know how you said it with a straight face."

"Oh, so now you're mad at me?" he said with a grin.

"I was vulnerable and hungry, and I'm still new to this. You're used to dealing with newborn vamps." I kept my eyes focused on the window, staring out at the city. "You should have stopped me. I wasn't in control of myself."

"Buckle your seat belt," he ordered. Outside the window, a little boy in dirty jeans and a ratty T-shirt stood on the street corner. He smiled at someone across the street. I rolled down the window as we passed. Wind hit my face, tousling my hair. Craning my neck out of the window, I watched the woman the boy was smiling at cross the street. "What happened to your jeans?" she asked him.

The rest was lost to me as we sped past. Remorse struck me by surprise and I blinked back tears. "I can never have kids."

"And this didn't occur to you before you decided you wanted to be a vampire?"

"It did. I thought I didn't want kids, but now that I can't have them . . ."

"Buckle your seat belt if you're going to be in human form," he said patiently. "I don't want to have to pay my way out of a ticket."

"What do you mean? Couldn't you just flash your fangs or go all cat-eyed so they'd let you go?"

"And then I'd have to pay for the ticket in cash later when one of Lord Phil's cronies called me up to talk about the fang fee."

"Fang fee."

"Hey," Talbot said more cheerfully. "Now that you know Lord Phil, maybe you can get him to fix my tickets."

"What are you even talking about?" Rushing in on the end of my thoughts about children, I thought about my last sunset. Shouldn't I have looked at the sun one last time, to say good-bye?

"I'm talking about you buckling your seat belt so that I don't get a ticket. Void City cops love to pull people over, particularly if they think you're undead."

Drops of blood flew off of my cheeks when I jerked around to face him. "I don't want to wear a fucking seat belt!" Fingernails elongated into claws at the end of my hands and my jaw popped to accommodate the fangs that slid out of their sheaths in my gums. Refusing to flinch, Talbot remained blasé.

"Turn back into a cat if you don't want to wear a seat belt. There is a cop up ahead."

"Would you shut up about the damn cop?" I yelled, not sure why I was reacting this way. "If he pulls us over I'll rip his fucking head off, okay? Just forget about it! I'm not wearing a damn seat belt, you stupid motherfucker, and you can't make me! I'm the boss here! I'm the vampire, not you. I'm Lady Bathory and you're just some . . . some . . . mouser, whatever that is. A cat, or a human that used to be a cat, or whatever the fuck you are. You're not even human. You probably don't even have a soul. You probably never had one . . . and . . . and you raped me, you bastard!"

The officer in question eyed us warily as we passed, saw my fangs, and mouthed "Fuck that" to himself. Smarter than the rest of us, he knew when to mind his own business.

A twinge of pain squeezed my chest. With it came other thoughts, emotions, a flood of regret. If Rachel hadn't died, I'd never have become so obsessed with death. I never would have gotten wrapped up in the vampire scene. I'd have stayed in college like my parents had wanted instead of rebelling and deciding life was too short to waste.

I wouldn't have even met Eric, I wouldn't be in love with him, and I wouldn't have spent the last two years praying that he loved me back. I'd probably have been off somewhere, hopelessly in love with some asshole who just wanted my body, but he would have been a human asshole. Maybe I'd even be pregnant.

The tight ragged pain spread out from my chest, up into my skull, and down my arms and legs. My insides felt tight and shrunken. At the back of my eyes, the pain and pressure increased, as if my eyes were going to jerk through the sockets and become recessed in my braincase.

"It hurts," I yelled.

"What?" Talbot asked.

"It hurts!"

I grabbed the sides of my head with full vampiric acceleration. My elbow touched the window with what would have been a light bump, but the increased velocity magnified the force of the blow, shattering the passenger's side window. Glass cut into my elbow and I started to scream. I needed to get out of the car, to run; I felt trapped, as if the car were attacking me, or keeping me prisoner, or both. I attacked back.

Brakes squealed and the Jaguar swerved into an alley. The driver's side door flew open, and I lost sight of Talbot as I lashed out at the upholstery, leather shredding easily under my claws. Something was wrong with me again and it was worse than the drugged blood. Euphoric anger had detached me from my actions in the Demon Heart, but this was real.

Pain lanced through my hand as I punched through the dash and into the glove compartment. Metal and plastic cut me, but I jerked my hand free, leaving blood and skin behind, before kicking away from the dash, breaking my seat, and flailing into the back of the car, my claws tearing at the ceiling and smashing out the rear window.

Suddenly my lungs started working and went into overdrive, pumping air in and out with such urgency it might have been trying to atone for all the breaths it had missed over the last couple of nights.

Once, in high school biology class, we'd had to dissect a frog. I had been so afraid I'd hyperventilated and passed out. This felt a lot like that. Rapid, shuddering booms shook my chest and I realized my heart was beating. Not only was it beating, it was beating far too fast. Gritting my teeth, I managed to stop actually screaming, but a high keening sound escaped my throat.

Talbot rounded the car, put his hand on the passenger's side door, and I hit it from the inside with both feet, ripping the door loose of its hinges and sending Talbot and the door flying into the concrete wall of the building. He was still holding on to the door when he hit the ground. "Get away from me," I screamed through chattering teeth. "Don't touch me!"

Color leached out of my vision, the world sliding to black and white, to grayscale, and then to shades of red. Waves of heat rushed over me and my entire body began to vibrate. Staggering out of the Jag, I pressed my head against the cool metal on the roof. Beating loudly in my ears, the sound of my heartbeat was joined by another sound, a loud *whooshing* sound; I realized it was the blood rushing through my veins once more. The pain left my chest, the inner tightening faded as blood flowed. Color vision came back, but the colors were too bright, blindingly kaleidoscopic. "What's happening to me?" I demanded.

"Turn back into a cat," Talbot choked out as he shoved the door off onto the sidewalk.

I tried. Desperately. I couldn't.

Panic continued to swell inside me. I felt like my heart was about to tear itself out of my chest like a baby alien from that space movie with Sigourney Weaver.

He got to his feet and took a deep breath. "It's probably autonomic function return brought on by postmortem stress, maybe even a panic attack. It's rarely this bad, but I've seen it before."

None of that made sense to me. My body was too loud. At the end of my fingers, claws extended and retracted, rhythmically gouging holes into the roof. "Don't touch me," I panted. "Get away from me." Bottom fangs pushed their way into my mouth from between the teeth in my lower jaw, blood filling my mouth as the gums ripped open, a long searing pain. I shouldn't even have bottom fangs. What was happening to me? "Your blood must have done this to me," I spat out, shaking so hard I could barely talk. "It's poisonous or something."

"It's not my blood, Tabitha, it's you. Your body is reacting to stress the only way it remembers how. Turn back into a cat," he urged, "and it will stop. You have a pulse as a cat. Your body will remember what it's supposed to be doing." He didn't sound mad at all, but there was a tone in his voice that I didn't recognize, a tinge of concern or wonder. "Trust me, Tabitha. Turn into a cat."

Hugging my arms tightly around myself and closing my eyes, I finally managed to turn into a cat. The panic and anxiety were still there, but my body was calm and controlled. Normal heartbeat. Normal breath. Normal blood flow. Everything felt right, natural, as it should be.

Talbot leaned in through the passenger's side door, turned off the engine, and pulled his keys out of the ignition. Leaning up against his poor Jaguar, he asked, "Better now?"

I nodded.

He looked down at the keys in his hand and mumbled, "Ninety-three thousand dollars. Damn, you're high maintenance."

Angry, sad, and terrified all at once, I curled up into a ball of fur, pressing myself against the brick wall of the alley, not knowing what to say, what to do, or how to react. Why had I let Eric do this to me? No more sun. No more mirrors. No food but blood. How could I have wanted this? Liquid diets had never worked for me, and now I was on the ultimate liquid diet. Not just for six to eight months, either. No, I had signed up for the infinity plan. Immortality was all fun and games until you read the fine print.

"What's happening to me?" I meowed.

"PMS," he said, stone-faced.

I glared at him.

"Postmortem stress," he continued. "It happens to the newly undead. There comes a point when you stop thinking of yourself as human and accept your new self. You let go of who you were and become what you are. When it happens, your body freaks out. Your mind freaks out. So essentially, you're freaking out," he answered. "Eric is the only vampire I know of who never did it. I meant to tell you about it first thing. I guess it slipped my mind." It hadn't, though; I could tell from the smug cat grin on his face. He'd worn the same self-satisfied expression when he'd held me down at the Demon Heart while Marilyn and Desiree fed me cold blood.

"Bullshit," I meowed. "You guess it slipped your mind? You wanted to see me freak. You got off on it."

"Told you I wasn't human," Talbot said without remorse or shame.

I rose to all fours, pacing back and forth, my tail twitching furiously. "PMS when I'm alive and PMS when I'm dead. Retaining water may have made my ankles swell, but it never made me rip a sports car apart."

I turned human again and it no longer felt strange or otherworldly. The change was as natural as stepping out of one dress and into another: a momentary vulnerability, followed by comfort in my new outfit. My body was still warm and my heartbeat was steady. I was still breathing. Blood pumped through my veins, but the sound was muted. Now that I expected it, none of it was so alarming.

"One in a mill—" Talbot reached for my cheek and I slapped him so hard it knocked him across the alley. When he landed, I was there, claws out and waiting. It was a cheap shot and it left him too dazed to react.

"I told you not to touch me, Talbot!" I sank my right-hand claws into his chest, just above the heart. Crouched on his chest, the claws of my left hand at his throat, I said, "I'm very grateful for all your help. I needed it. I needed your knowledge and experience. I really, really did, but I swear to God that if you ever touch me again I will rip your heart out with my bare hands, throw it in the street and back over it with Eric's Mustang! Do you understand?"

Fur puffed up under my fingertips as Talbot's ears slid upward and extended, pointed, like a cat's. I made a move to claw him with my left hand, as a threat rather than to rip his throat out, but he caught it with a hand covered in sable fur. His voice echoed in my head, his jaws unmoving as he spoke.

Tabitha, you do not want me as your enemy. Cat's eyes glared at me from his handsome face as his nose broadened and whiskers erupted from his cheeks. The first three buttons on his shirt popped loose as his chest expanded, the material drawing tight and ripping where my claws pierced it. *I can make your life a living hell.*

"Too late!" I spat. "Don't you understand that? Everything is totally fucked up now. Eric will never want me now that I've been with you and you should have known better, Talbot. You should have fucking stopped me. You're supposed to be my damn babysitter!"

"It had been a long time for me, Tabitha. A very long time, and if I took advantage of you, if you think I did, then I'm sorry." He took hold of my right hand and gently pulled my claws from his chest. I let him.

Even with my hand poised to hurt him, possibly kill him, I was afraid. His claws were holy. He was some kind of sacred hunter. I was just a vampire, a queen, sure, but . . .

His expression softened as my claws came free, the fur subsiding, his pantherlike features not quite melting into human ones, but fading, like an illusion. He stared at me with human eyes that were too cute, too endearing, and I let him up.

"My kind does not apologize, Tabitha. We don't have to, because we are never wrong. . . ." I bared my fangs, arms crossed, standing against the brick, away from him, as he continued, "Or we claim we aren't. I'm different." He straightened his clothes, brushing at the dirt, and the rips disappeared. I wondered if they were really gone or if it was an illusion. Did he really look human at all or did everyone simply see what he wanted them to see?

"I am willing to admit that it is remotely possible that I share part of the blame, but not all of it." He leaned in close, his lips a breath away from mine. Despite myself I wanted to kiss him. "You did not smell out of control," he continued. His left hand traced the outline of my body, almost, but not quite touching me. "You smelled like you knew exactly what was going on and I trusted that."

He looked me straight in the eyes, dared me to make contact, to pit my will against his.

"Now I'm going to smell like you," I said, looking away.

"Most people only get one chance with me, Tabitha. You've already had two; this makes it three. I let it go the first time you jumped me, because you didn't know any better. I let the second one go because you were drugged. I'm going to let this one go because of the postmortem stress and the extenuating circumstances, but don't try for a fourth chance. I'll tear you apart and swallow all the pieces. Unless you've made a pact with a demon that I don't know about, you won't be coming back from that."

Angry with myself and with Talbot, I brushed past him, stopping near the car. Little dots of light reflected up at me from the Jag's passenger's side mirror, which lay cracked in the alley. I picked it up and looked at my reflection. I was a mess. My new blouse was ruined; grime and blood spotted it in multiple places and there was even a small rip where glass had cut it. My hair—

I don't think I could have been more surprised if I went to my folks' house and Rachel answered the door. I dropped the mirror, stumbling away from it in denial. "My reflection. How . . ."

After a moment, I picked the mirror up again. I did look beautiful, even with the grime and dirt. Then, my image slowly faded, along with the body heat and my other renewed bodily functions. It was more depressing than the ruined blouse, like dying all over again, without the promise of immortality.

"Damn." I shivered, cold again, as my fingertips caressed the glass. "Come back." With unbearable slowness, my face reappeared in the glass. "How is this possible?" I whispered.

"I suspected it when you first turned into a cat, and appeared to be alive," Talbot said from across the alley. "Eric seems to draw vamps that defy the norm. Every one he creates comes prepackaged with pain and wonder. Maybe one in ten thousand, possibly one in a hundred thousand vampires can turn their bodies back on, choose to cast a reflection in animal form or human form. The number of vamps who can do both? I couldn't even begin to calculate. Maybe one in a million? My guess? No more than five and possibly just you."

"What?" I asked. I'd heard what he said, but it wasn't sinking in.

"They're called Dolls. They are vampires that can seem completely lifelike. You can stop worrying about whether he'll want you or not. He'll probably fall head over heels for you. You're immortal, you're beautiful, and you will never change. You can have body heat, a heartbeat . . . even blood coursing through your veins. You can even cast a reflection when you wish. You'll probably even be able to have saliva and, um, other appropriate fluids after a little practice." He let out a long breath again.

"But I tried that earlier and it didn't work—"

"The first time you tried to transform into a bird it didn't work either. It takes practice, like anything else." Talbot reached out as if to touch my cheek again, but checked the impulse before I swatted him, though I don't think I would have.

"If you think Veruca was angry that you could turn into a cat," he continued, "you should know that there will be plenty of vampires that will hate you for what you can do. Just stop worrying about your boyfriend. The only way another girl could compete with you now is with magical breasts and an enchanted crotch. He's yours for the taking, if you still want him."

I smiled. "Oh, no; he'll have to earn it." If he wanted this Snow White, then first he was going to have to kiss my cold dead lips. I didn't want him to want me because I could be warm and lifelike, his precious little doll. First he had to want me for me.

And then . . . I forced blood to run through my veins, watched as my pale perfect skin grew pink and pretty. Mine for the taking. I liked the sound of that.

29

ERIC:
PICTURE PERFECT

Have you ever slept through an entire day and woken up at night thinking it was still the same day? That's kind of what happened to me. I woke in my own bed at the Pollux, with Rachel paying me some not unwanted attention below the waist. Disorienting—but nice. I don't know how it is for girls, but for guys, when something like that happens, you go with it. Everything else is immaterial. For instance, the rainbow wig completely escaped my attention at first. As did the *Happy Birthday* banner hung on the wall opposite the bed and the balloons tied to the bedposts.

"Are you wearing clown makeup?" I asked.

Rachel looked up. Though bereft of white paint, she wore thick black mascara mixed with blue, strategically smudged at the corners of her eyes. The big red clown nose was obscene in contrast to her nakedness and the black choker around her neck. I wondered if the tiny gold padlock held some special meaning.

"Happy birthday!" Rachel straddled me and doffed the wig and nose, going from clown to Goth as easy as smiling. While I'd been asleep, she'd apparently highlighted her dark hair with streaks of reds and blondes.

I don't like clowns. I'm not afraid of them, but I've never found them amusing. This, the Goth thing, was more my style. We kissed, smearing her black lipstick. My heart began beating in time with our rhythm. As birthday surprises go, this was near the top of the chart.

It isn't hard to get up there though; my birthdays are usually a disaster. Or at least as far as I can remember. Ninety percent of the women who have ever dumped me chose my birthday as the magical day. When I was alive, two of the three wrecks I'd been in were birthday related. My mom died of a heart attack on my nineteenth birthday. You get the idea.

Maybe, I thought, maybe this will be one of the good ones. The knob on the bedroom door began turning, almost in slow motion. Have you ever had your girlfriend walk in on you while you were screwing her sister on your birthday? Yeah, I thought not.

Tabitha wore a midnight-blue dress that clung to her curves. A diamond necklace sparkled at her throat in the partial light from the hallway. The necklace accentuated her cleavage even more than the dress's plunging neckline. Her skin took on a golden tone, little bits of glitter catching the light. She was beautiful. She looked almost human. Her expression was exactly the sort of complex blend of shock and embarrassment I might expect her to have worn if she'd walked in on her parents having sex.

A package rested in the crook of her arm. It tumbled to the ground as she turned and ran. A gun I supposed to be *El Alma Perdida* was visible for a microsecond, flipping through the air.

It was a single-action pistol. They call them single-action because you cock the hammer back manually and all the trigger does is let the hammer fall. It can go off accidentally if the hammer strikes the round in the chamber hard enough to discharge the bullet. In the Old West, most folks would only put five rounds in the gun to keep accidents from happening. Tabitha must have put in all six.

I don't get shot very often. All the vampire hunters I'd ever met used arrows, holy water, and crosses. Bullets hurt, but they don't generally give any vamp but a Drone much trouble. The bullet went through the side of the mattress at an angle, lodging itself in my right butt cheek. It sizzled like fire. I yowled in pain. Rachel rolled off of me. I know I'm not a werewolf, but the bullet clearly did not like me.

"Get it out!" I shouted. "It's magic."

Just when I thought things couldn't get worse, my ass caught fire. Flames literally jetted out of the bullet hole in my butt. Rachel laughed uncontrollably while I fumbled with the sink. She laughed even harder when I sat in it. Cracks formed in the plaster around the corners. My ass still stung, but the lack of fire made things more bearable.

I tried to pop my claws to dig the bullet out, but nothing happened. Shapeshifting didn't work either. I even tried misting. I was that desperate, but I couldn't change. Rachel ran out of the room and came back with a letter opener. She dug the bullet out, periodically splashing water on the wound to keep it from reigniting. Several agonizing minutes later she handed me a perfect little bullet with no signs of damage, just like the one I'd found out at the lake.

"It's not funny." I dropped the bullet on the bed. She didn't stop laughing and I realized I wanted to snap her neck. The anger was so sudden, so visceral that had I been another vampire, one who had the speed all the time, who didn't have to hope it kicked in when he needed it, I think she would have been lying broken on the floor without my ever consciously deciding to act.

"Oh, it's funny all right," she said, sobering slightly. She was going to get herself killed acting that way around me. At least that's how I justified it in my head when I grabbed her left arm.

"If you thought that was funny, you're gonna love this."

"What are you doing?" she asked, a tinge of fear in her tone. Her heartbeat sped up. *Don't be mad*, said a voice in my head that wasn't mine. *Forgive Rachel. Love Rachel.* The smell of cinnamon hit me, enough to make blood tears well up around my eyes. I wasn't mad anymore; but I was still mean.

"Feeding," I answered. I sank my fangs into her inner elbow, hitting the ulnar artery. It's inefficient and painful for the donor, but it works. Rachel cried in short gasping sobs, but she didn't fight me. Instead, she wiggled her feet nervously.

"I'm sorry," she said. Taste hit my tongue, sweet and bitter like before. *Leave, damn it*, I thought at her. *Don't you understand, this is what I am? I'm a monster. You don't want this.*

"Yes, I do," Rachel whispered. "Yes, I do."

I let her go. She cupped her hand over the wound and her teeth dug into her bottom lip. *Good one, Eric*, I thought. *Just beat the crap out of her next time, you fucking moron.*

"Did you get enough?" she asked. "Do you need the other one?" She let go of the wound and held out her uninjured arm.

"No." My voice cracked when I spoke. "That was . . . Look, I'm sorry. Do you need a doctor?"

"I'm a thrall now," she said through gritted teeth and indicated the choker and the golden padlock with her uninjured arm. "I can take care of it. Just give me ten or fifteen minutes and I'll be good as new."

"Right." I pushed open the bedroom door and slunk away, grabbing my jeans off the floor as I went. I slipped them on in the hallway and rested my head against the door. You'd think there was a monster inside me, a creature that wanted to hurt people, a creature to whom violence was the most favorable answer to all of unlife's problems. Oh, right—a vampire!

But to be honest, I don't think just any vampire would have felt guilty about what I'd done, would have recognized the monstrosity. I did, and it didn't feel much different than it might have felt when I was alive. You do what you have to do to get by. You try to stay out of trouble, but when life or unlife throws you lemons, you don't make lemonade, you warm up your pitching arm and you throw them right back.

There were presents lined up along the concession counter, each wrapped in different paper and bows. It looked more like Christmas than a birthday. I looked down over the rail to see Tabitha waiting for me in the sitting area below. I'd half expected to find her sitting there with blood running down her cheeks, ruining her makeup, but her cheeks were dry. She was upset, but she wasn't crying. She was almost smiling, her lips pressed against each other in a thin severe line. I walked down the stairs, and sat down on the coffee table, my knees on either side of her.

"Sorry you walked in on that," I told her.

"It's your birthday," she said matter-of-factly. "Besides, I told you that you could sleep with whoever you wanted. I was just . . . surprised, that's all."

"I noticed that you found the gun." I leaned closer, resting my hand on her knee. She was wearing too much perfume and her skin smelled like two or three different types of soap. She was covering up an odor she didn't want me to notice. Probably corpse sweat again. She needn't have worried.

"I hope it didn't hit the girl when it went off." Tabitha's words were faint, less than whispers. She hadn't recognized Rachel. Thank God!

"Nah, it hit me in the ass." I laughed. "It was pretty funny."

"It didn't sound funny."

"It wasn't funny when it happened, but it's funny now."

"Oh." She looked left and right, anywhere but at me. "Do you want to open your presents?"

"If you want." I walked over to the concession stand with Tabitha in tow.

"You don't have to," she whispered. "I did tell you that I'd try, you know, it, with a human and you. We could go upstairs."

"No," I said too quickly. "No, let's . . . do you know what I really want to do?"

"What?" She had calmed down a bit, her body language more relaxed, more like the Tabitha I knew.

"I want to get Greta and go kill those fucking werewolves." I pulled her close. "Wanna come?"

"You're joking." Her face lit up like New Year's Eve. "Can I?"

"You'll want to change clothes first, but I can help you with that."

We exchanged a quick kiss. Her cold dead lips couldn't match her sister's heat, but I still cared for her.

"Sounds like a plan," she agreed with a slow smile.

"You run across to the Demon Heart and get changed," I said. "I'll find out where Greta went off to."

"I thought you were going to help me change clothes," Tabitha pouted.

"I will," I promised. "Just let me round up Greta and I'll be right over."

Her eyes lingered on the stairs. "Okay," she said slowly.

Upstairs, Rachel was curled under the covers. She didn't say anything when I walked in or when I slipped on the rest of my clothes. The silence was a relief.

Without thinking, I picked up *El Alma Perdida*. It didn't burn my hand. I took the barrel in my left hand and touched the cross on the grip to my forearm, and it didn't burn that either. It was hot, but not hot enough to burn. The bullets didn't like me, but the gun seemed to think I was okay. Weird. I put it back in the box and tucked the box under my arm.

"I'll be back later," I said.

"Okay." Rachel sounded tired and hurt. I fought the impulse to say anything else. Anything I said would have just made things worse. I'd never had a woman like her. She didn't want to be a vampire and she liked being hurt, wanted it. I was going to have to get used to that.

Thanks to the new thrall sense, I could feel Greta nearby, in the parking deck attached to the Pollux. When I reached her, she was sitting on the hood of a Pinto looking up at the moon. Dried blood clung to her chin and throat and the matted tangle of her hair was plastered to the side of her head. Two half-naked teenagers lay in the backseat; their disembodied heads stared with sightless eyes from the roof of the car.

"I was really hungry, Dad," Greta offered apologetically.

A cat, two pigeons, and a rat lay on the concrete next to the car. Greta's eating problem in a nutshell.

"It's fine. No lectures tonight." I took off my shirt and wiped gently at the blood on her neck. "It's my birthday."

"The girl was supposed to be your present," Greta sulked.

The blood wouldn't come off. She needed a shower and a change of clothes. "Why don't you get cleaned up and then as part of my present you can help me do something important."

"Really?" Her expression was a mirror of Tabitha's. Why do so many beautiful women think so highly of me? It's like a kind of brain damage.

"Yeah." I dropped the shirt on the car hood and put an arm around her. "I want to go kill those werewolves and put an end to this whole mess. It'll be just the three of us: me, you, and your new mom."

"Okay." Greta got up slowly, uncertainly. "Where are the werewolves? I wouldn't think they'd still be hanging around the park."

They wouldn't? No, I guessed not. The campground at the State Park couldn't have been a long-term living arrangement. They probably went there just to set up the confrontation with me.

"Why do you think they picked the park?" I asked myself aloud.

"Because they like the woods?" Greta offered.

"No," I said, still rolling the idea around in my head. "Because it's not the city. It's exposed. A vampire could take cover from the sun, but not the same way he might in the city. There are no sewers to hide in, no people to hide among, no way to diffuse the scent."

We will never surrender our land to one of your kind. That's what William had said. No *matter how many dead you lay on our doorstep, we will not give in.*

Our doorstep . . . the only place . . . no, damn it; I couldn't remember. It was somewhere . . . somewhere . . . I'd been out there. I found the bullet that went in the magic gun, the one that led to the Highland Towers . . . Yesterday I knew, I'd remembered it, known it.

"Son of a bitch," I shouted. "What the hell do you call it, the place with the big lake . . ." I barely noticed the smell of cinnamon and then I remembered. "Orchard Lake. William said I left dead werewolves at his doorstep. If he was talking about the ones Froggy killed, then he meant Orchard Lake. That's where they are," I finished triumphantly.

"Will there be fish?" Greta asked.

Will there be fish? What the hell kind of question was that? "Yes, sweetheart," I assured her. "There will be fish, but we'll be there for the wolves."

✦ 30 ✦

ERIC:

ORCHARD DAM ROAD

The drive out to Orchard Lake can take anywhere from an hour to ninety minutes, depending on traffic. The trip takes you from interstate to highway to County Road 58 where you wind through Keener and Tartarus, cutting through broad areas of wooded acreage and low mountains punctuated by small townships and the occasional empty strip mall.

I pulled off of 58 onto Orchard Dam Road and parked in the driveway of an abandoned house. I was still driving Carl's loaner. The car's rear bumper was somewhere back at Bald Mountain State Park, or maybe the werewolves kept it as a trophy.

There was a farm across the road, boasting a small herd of cattle and horses, a hobby farm by the looks of it. The entrance to Sable Oaks was just beyond, a broad stone arch lit by ground lights so that it blazed formidably. Two vampires dressed like Secret Service men, in earpieces and black suits, stood on either side of the entrance to the gated community. I'd flown south when I'd left Orchard Lake the other night, partially to avoid the place. Sable Oaks was for high society fangs, not me.

I'd half expected to find two werewolves on this side, standing guard over Orchard Dam Road from the empty house where we'd parked. A weathered piece of cardboard announced that the house was for sale, but the number had been washed away by rain or bleached out by the sun. If it had really been for sale, then the same vampires who owned Sable Oaks would have undoubtedly snapped it up. I could easily imagine the reason the werewolf community had abandoned it. Too close to the undead.

I waved cheerily at the two vampires, but they stared straight ahead, ignoring me.

Greta unfolded out of the backseat and stretched her arms. "God, it's nice to be out of there," she said.

"You could have traveled as something smaller." I stepped out and closed the door, slamming it so it would catch. It bounced back open and fell off. Vampire strength: gotta love it.

"No thanks," Greta said. "I'll leave the shapeshifting to you."

"Why?" asked Tabitha. She still looked happy to have been invited. She'd even dressed appropriately. Her jeans, tennis shoes, and old T-shirt weren't as glamorous or sexy as the clothes she usually wore, but were much more sensible for fighting werewolves. I wondered if she would still be happy once the killing started. So far, she had killed only when under the influence of the doped blood Froggy had slipped into my reserve at the Demon Heart. As far as I knew, she hadn't ever killed to feed.

"I'm not an animal," Greta answered.

"So?" Tabitha walked around the car and stood next to me, her hand tucked possessively into the back pocket of my jeans.

"So, I don't like being anything I'm not," said Greta. "It feels weird." She rubbed her left arm, taking in her surroundings.

"Being a cat feels awesome," Tabitha said.

"Not to me."

"Are you two done?" I asked. "It's half past one and sunrise is at six eighteen."

"You checked?" Greta's hands flew to her cheeks in exaggerated shock.

"Ha. Ha," I replied dryly. "Yes, I checked." *El Alma Perdida* was in the glove compartment. I leaned across the interior of the car, flipped open the compartment, and pulled out the gun, measuring its heft in my hand. The gun hummed, its grip warm, but the crosses still didn't bother me.

"That is so odd," said Tabitha. "I barely touched the thing and it burned the crap out of me. Why doesn't it hurt you?"

"Talbot told me that my aura and the gun's looked the same, that the gun might be inherited. Did you find anything else out about it?" I asked.

"Just that it was used by a guy named John Paul Courtney back in the Wild West."

Greta laughed.

"What's so funny?" asked Tabitha.

"That's Dad's real last name, Mom," Greta told her.

"Could you not do that? Call me Tabitha."

Greta shook her head. "I can't do that, Mom. That would just be too weird."

Tabitha looked at me for assistance, but I couldn't help on this one. Anytime I turned a girlfriend, Greta started calling her "Mom" until we broke up. The only exception was Marilyn. She had always called her "Mom" or "old Mom." Maybe in Greta's head, even though we'd never married, Marilyn counted as my first wife and that made her Greta's real mother. Marilyn had certainly helped raise her, taken her to school, made her lunches, and picked her up at the end of the day.

Marilyn had been furious when I turned Greta at twenty-one, but I'd had my reasons. Most humans don't know what they're getting into if they become a vampire, but Greta had known better than most. She'd spent twelve years with a vampire for a dad, watching what I did, how I was.

I kept very little hidden from her, hoping that if she saw everything, if I took away the mystique, she'd change her mind. I'd expected her to grow to hate me, but she didn't. To Greta, I'd always be her knight in shining armor, the hero who came in through the window one night and killed the bad guy. She didn't care that if she'd been older, I might have also killed her.

"I thought your last name was Jones," said Tabitha, snapping me out of my fugue.

"Alias," I said. "Roger says we have to roll everything into a new identity every three or four decades so that no one at the federal level gets suspicious."

Courtney sounded familiar, but a lifetime away. "I used to be a Courtney, I guess. Marilyn would know."

What's your father's name? Marilyn asked again in my head. The truth was, I didn't want to remember. I knew Marilyn's name, though: Marilyn Amanda Robinson. It should have been Marilyn Robinson Courtney . . .

"How can you not remember your last name?" asked Tabitha in amazement. Her hand was no longer in my pocket. She stood beside me, gesturing as she spoke.

"I haven't used it in forty years," I replied defensively. I didn't have time for this conversation. Talking about the past wakes up all the ghosts in my head. My brother, my parents—they were all better half remembered. I hadn't made them proud when I'd been alive, hadn't been what they wanted me to be. Even if I still had nieces and nephews out there, I didn't want to know about them and they didn't need to know about me. We weren't part of the same world anymore.

I began to walk up the road toward the marina. Greta fell in step beside me, but Tabitha blocked my path, hand on my chest. "But it's your name," she insisted.

"So?" I stepped around her.

"What do you mean 'so'?" Tabitha moved to intercept me again. Her white T-shirt looked red in the sudden light from my eyes.

"Why is it important to you that I remember it?" Now that I was away from Rachel, I felt more like my old self, my anger closer to the surface, harder to control. Tabitha couldn't possibly understand the difference, but now that she had no heartbeat, it was difficult for me not to think of her as a thing, not a person, not a woman. She'd gone through the change, and she wasn't my Tabitha anymore, just a convincing fake. The urge to crush that impostor, to tear it apart, brought my claws out. But then a look of surprise in her eyes that reminded me of the Tabitha I had given in to pushed that urge away and dimmed the red light in my own eyes.

"It just is," Tabitha said. "You can't forget who you really are." But she already had. She didn't realize it, but she had. The Tabitha I knew would have screamed at me when she walked in on the birthday sex at the Pollux, or fled the room in tears.

"Are you hunting werewolves?" I asked, exasperated. "Because Greta and I are hunting werewolves."

"Yes, but—"

"Good," I interrupted. "Everyone who's hunting werewolves is walking this way." I pointed at the rough paved road that ran up the hill and down the other side to the marina.

Tabitha moved to my right side and walked with us in silence. The night was quiet, any sound absorbed by the stands of oak and pine that flanked the road. A half mile from the intersection, the road turned twice. I stopped next to the yellow sign warning drivers of the sharp curve and looked down the hill at the creek forty feet below.

"You okay?" Tabitha asked.

"No," I answered. I'd been thinking about Brian, the vampire I'd decapitated, wondering why we'd both been in the alleyway. If Roger was behind this, then it meant he'd talked Brian into it. Or had he scammed Brian too, knowing that we couldn't get along, that my losing my temper in a fatal way was inevitable? "But it doesn't matter."

We walked about another mile, the road continuing up a steep climb and then angling down at an equally steep incline toward the parking lot.

We walked carefully along the downward slope and stopped about fifty yards from the parking lot, where the pavement turned into an uncertain mixture of gravel and dirt. A large blue Dumpster hulked in the corner of the lot, obscuring the sight of us from the small brick utility building that housed the restrooms. The werewolves had posted a guard outside the building. I smelled him on the wind as it blew both his scent and that of the Dumpster our way.

Trucks, RVs, and all manner of off-road vehicles filled the parking lot, many more than when I'd last been here. The werewolves had regrouped.

I set *El Alma Perdida* on the lid of the Dumpster for safekeeping and turned into a white cat, then picked my way along the gravel quietly until I got a better look at the guard. He was sitting in a lawn chair on the sidewalk that ran across the water side of the parking lot, near the steps that led down to the long bridge connecting the marina's floating docks to the shore. His back was to the utility building, his eyes gazing out over the parking lot to the hillside where Froggy had left the bodies of the werewolves she'd killed. Hard rock classics played on a small portable radio, Pink Floyd's "Hey You" suggesting ironically that the guard not give up without a fight.

A small gray cat settled next to me. "What do we do?" Tabitha meowed.

I looked back to where Greta crouched low and ready next to the Dumpster and gave her a nod. She darted across the parking lot, little more than a blur. The werewolf barely had time to blink before Greta picked him up by the feet and slammed his head against the wall of the utility building.

She was back at my side before he hit the ground, blood and brain matter splattering. Tabitha and I morphed back to our human bodies and I stepped out onto the concrete, looking down the long set of steps to the boat slips below. I couldn't smell or sense anyone down there. If anyone else was keeping watch, they were doing it from one of the lake houses.

"We're not allowed to eat until we find the werewolves," said Greta. She looked pointedly at Tabitha when she said it. "Then we can eat anyone we want. Dad just doesn't want us getting carried away."

"Oh, God." Tabitha sounded like she might be ill. I guess she'd never seen brains on brick before.

"Do you need to wait in the car?" I asked quietly.

"No," she forced out past clenched teeth.

"Try to remember what it feels like when you're hungry," I advised. "Think of them as food, just blood sources, not people."

"That makes it worse." Huh. Maybe there was more Tabitha still in there than I wanted to believe. What if I didn't *want* her to be Tabitha, wanted her to be a monster like me, because that made it easier not to feel guilty about being with Rachel?

"Then go back to the car," I said sharply. The Tabitha I knew was squeamish about killing a mouse in a trap. She'd killed Veruca, yes, but that had been self-defense more than anything else. A straightforward werewolf slaughter was another matter.

"It'll be all right, Mom." Greta tried to put her arm around Tabitha, but Tabitha pulled away. "Dad and I can handle it. We don't need you."

"I can do this," Tabitha insisted.

"Then stop acting like a prissy little bitch," I said as I walked back to the Dumpster and retrieved *El Alma Perdida*. I hadn't meant to say that, it just jumped out there.

"I said I can do it!"

"Fine." *If you can, then you really aren't my Tabitha anymore*, I thought. I tucked the gun into the back of my pants and tried to turn into a bat, but nothing happened except an angry hum from *El Alma Perdida*. The Lost Soul didn't seem to like vampire games. I couldn't leave it behind; I was going to need it if I had to kill William. Only in my hands was the gun blessed, magical, silver, and inherited. As a bonus, I liked the idea of trapping William's soul inside one of the bullets. For all I knew, death didn't hold anything scary for him and I certainly didn't wish him a happy afterlife.

"You want to be helpful?" I asked Tabitha.

"Yes. I said I could do this and I—"

"Can you turn into a bat or a bird, mist, maybe?"

"Yes."

"Which?" I asked with a slightly impatient sigh.

"I can do a bird. I can probably do a bat."

"Good, then turn into a bat and go find the werewolves," I said. "Don't fight them, just find them and come back."

"Why?" she asked.

"Just do it," I said.

She shifted into a bat just fine, but fluttered to the ground and flapped weakly. Greta giggled, but I kept a straight face. It isn't easy to fly the first time out. Tabitha got the hang of it after the radio played through two more songs and finally took off over the gentle waves of Orchard Lake, three bars into "Magic Carpet Ride."

I waited until I knew she was out of earshot, but still spoke quietly. "There are some kids with the werewolves."

"Kids or puppies?" Greta asked.

"They're werewolves, too."

She kissed me fondly on the cheek. "You old softy. Don't worry, Daddy; I'll kill them for you." I let the music from the portable radio fill in the silence. I told you that there are other reasons Greta makes me uncomfortable.

I don't like hurting children. Hell, even though this whole outing had been my idea, I would have preferred not to have to kill *any* werewolves. I much preferred just beating them up enough so that they knew they couldn't take me and then letting them go. Unless I went into a rage blackout, of course.

Even the werewolf I had killed in the alley when all this crap started might have survived if I hadn't been trapped by the sun. Killing werewolves tended to be more trouble than it was worth. As the last few days had shown, once you start killing werewolves, your wolf problems multiply. The pack gets angry. The pack comes after you. There's more killing. The pack calls in reinforcements, maybe from the Lycan Diocese, maybe from one of the other freaky-ass skinchanger cults out there, but either way there's even more killing. If you leave the cubs alive, then all you've done is buy yourself a brief respite, because cubs grow up and when they do, they remember the vampire who slaughtered their pack and the process starts all over again.

I picked up the guard's lawn chair that lay half-folded on its side. Underneath it on the concrete was a sheet of paper, a list of names, all checked off. The lake houses didn't have addresses per se. Mail was delivered in a drop box at the utility building. The local paper got left in an old vending machine with a note on it that said "For Subscribers Only."

On the sheet, each werewolf residence was recorded by family name and dock number. It looked like the guard had tracked who had come and gone and the license plates of the vehicles that had been driven in or out of the lot. For some of them, he'd listed their driver's license number too.

William's name wasn't on the list, but I was pretty sure that if I started killing whole families of werewolves, he was bound to show up sooner or later.

31

TABITHA:

BAT GIRL

rissy little bitch, huh? Well excuse me for not being used to seeing some guy's brains splattered on the wall! I should have told him about Talbot and me. I should have turned on the bodyworks and shown him what I could do, that I could have body heat, a heartbeat, even a reflection. I bet that would have wiped the smile off of his face. *Prissy little bitch* would turn into *honey, baby, sweetie pie* pretty damn quick then. At this point I didn't know why I'd been so excited to come out to Orchard Lake in the first place.

Most of the houses I saw looked run-down or cobbled together, built along the slanted lakeside with boat docks sticking out into the lake, and irregular steps leading from the docks to the houses. I flew a quick loop around the inlet closest to the marina. There were three houses there, one on the same side of the water as the marina, the other two staring at it across the inlet.

There were no numbers on the docks and I wondered how they got their mail. I saw power lines but no phone lines, and the only air conditioners were window units. At the far side of the lake, where it narrowed, continuing in a wide ribbon upstream, two fishermen sat on an old wooden dock, kept afloat by what looked like white plastic barrels under the water. They each dangled their feet off the edge of the dock, beer and fishing poles close at hand.

One of them let a flashlight shine out over the lake. It cut a blue-green swath through the water and the fish went crazy, striking at the light. The two guys thought that was hilarious; then one of them sniffed the air. "You smell something?"

The one with the light turned it off. "No."

An old wooden ramp rose from the dock to cinderblock steps

leading up a steep incline to an even older house. The smell of coffee carried on the breeze. Two older women and two teenagers sat on the porch playing some game with lots of little multicolored plastic pyramids.

One of the women got up and walked halfway down the steps. "We're about to turn in, Lucas," said the woman. "How long are you boys going to sit out there playing with that flashlight?"

"William said to keep an extra eye out tonight just in case," one of the men, evidently Lucas, replied.

"And then I suppose you'll sleep all day?"

"No," said Lucas. "No, then I'm going to drive into town and work first shift. One sleepless night isn't going to kill me."

These were the werewolves? They were just like normal people. Okay, normal hicks, but normal just the same. I'd expected monsters who went crazy under the light of the full moon . . . not real people. I flew farther down the lake, finding similar scenes. At one house, a couple lay asleep on a futon set out on the middle of their screened porch. A mother sat in a rocking chair in a different house nursing a baby who kept restlessly shifting from puppy to human. "Bert," she called over her shoulder. "Did you find that teething medicine?"

"No, I must have left it in the truck," Bert's voice replied. "Let me get some clothes on and I'll take the boat back and get it."

I flew back to the marina. Eric and Greta were out on the pier untying a canoe. I landed in the center and resumed my human shape, the canoe wobbling as I did. "Are you sure these are the right people?" I whispered.

"Yes," said Eric, climbing into the canoe.

"But they seem . . . normal."

"They are normal." They each took a paddle and we began moving quietly toward the shore. "That doesn't mean they aren't werewolves. Look, I'll try talking to them, but they're not going to listen. We'll have to fight them sooner or later . . . and the only way to keep you and Greta safe is to opt for sooner."

"And we have to kill all of them?"

"No, Mom," Greta said. "You can go home. Dad and I will handle it."

Again with the "Mom" thing. "No, I can deal, but some of them are only teenagers."

"And some of them are younger," said Eric. "But I didn't start this; they did. I tried to make peace. It didn't work."

"Do I need to take care of the teenagers, too, Dad?" Greta asked.

"Not exclusively, just the little guys."

"Little guys?" I asked, a chill running up my spine.

"The children." Eric shipped his paddle and bowed his head, letting us drift upstream on his momentum. He looked defeated and annoyed. "We can't just kill their parents and leave them. They don't stay small and cute, you know. They grow up into big bad werewolves who want revenge for what happened to their pack. If you don't like it, go home."

"I'm just trying to understand." I didn't buy the whole we'll-try-talking-first thing, and killing, not for food, but just flat-out murdering these people, werewolves or not . . . there was no difference between that and . . . I don't know. It seemed monstrous.

"Well, stop trying!" Eric threw down his paddle. "Just stop. It's harder if you think about it. God, you make everything so damned difficult. Part of being a vampire is turning off the piece of you that gives a damn. You do whatever it takes to feed and care for yourself or you go crazy. Tonight it means that I have to murder a whole bunch of people who might just have more right than I do to be walking the planet in the first place, but I can't worry about that. It's you or them. Who would you pick?"

I wanted to say "them" to disagree, but the words lodged in my throat. Deep inside, the same part of my brain that was offended by Drones, that became angry when lesser vampires spoke to me without permission, reared its ugly head. It would kill any of them if survival required it. The vampire within twitched inside my head and peeked out from behind my eyes. "Me," I said quietly. "I'd pick me."

"That's what I thought," Eric said. "Don't try to pretend otherwise. It just makes things . . . shit!"

A mini spotlight hit Eric, lighting him up bright enough for anyone to see. Greta rolled noiselessly over the side into the water the instant before the light would have given her away. She didn't even make a splash. I turned into a cat. Eric pulled his sunglasses off of his T-shirt collar and slid them on. The light came from the same two men I'd seen on the dock. Now Lucas held a crossbow and the other guy held the flashlight.

Eric picked up his paddle and began to row toward the dock. "Either of you rednecks know a guy named William?" he asked as the canoe came closer to their little wooden dock.

"Who wants to know?" asked Lucas.

Eric smiled, his fangs preternaturally white against the darkness. "I'm Roger Malcolm." He spoke with easy confidence, though he was easing the magic gun out of his pants with his right hand. Eric slid it onto the bottom of the canoe. "I just wanted to stop by one more time and talk to William."

"William already told you that we aren't selling," said Flashlight Man.

"What the hell are you talking about?" I meowed.

Greta's head broke the surface in the water beneath their dock, her eyes watching them predatorily through the gaps in the boards.

"You just get on out of here, mister." The man gestured back to the marina with his light. "William will be here soon enough if you don't. We're not selling, to you or anyone else."

"So that's what this is about." Eric nodded to Greta. "Now!"

I ducked back under the lip of the canoe.

"Hi." Greta sounded perky and upbeat when she grabbed their dangling legs. "Whatcha doing?"

They vanished from the dock, the flashlight clattering momentarily on the wood before falling into the water. Shadows moved frantically beneath the surface of the lake and Eric paddled to the dock as quickly as he could, stepping out of the canoe with *El Alma Perdida* in his hand.

"Lucas? Henry?" On the porch, one of the old women gripped the porch rail. "Vampire!"

Darkness came over the canoe. I poked my head back out. Eric leveled the gun at the old woman. "Get William," he said evenly.

"Jimmy, Lisa, run for help!" someone shouted from the porch. The teen wolves charged off howling into the night.

A large black werewolf broke the water behind Eric, as if he'd been fired from an underwater cannon.

"Lucas!" the old woman yelled triumphantly as she too began to change. Eric spun and caught Lucas, slamming him against the dock and latching onto his back. *El Alma Perdida* skidded out of Eric's hand toward the water, but I leapt out of the canoe and onto the dock, trapping it by the barrel with my paws.

Lucas struggled with Eric on his back biting into his shoulder. "How do you like it?" Eric yelled between bites. "How do you like it when I sink my teeth into your fucking shoulder?"

"Better'n a stick in the eye." Lucas shrugged him off and leapt from the dock. I couldn't see the churning underwater battle between Greta and her opponent, but Lucas must have thought his friend needed help. Eric caught him in midleap and smashed him back first onto the wooden dock. Boards cracked, but the dock held.

Greta bobbed up out of the water, clinging to the body of a large brown werewolf who floated facedown. She swam for the dock and pulled herself up out of the water with one hand.

Eric delivered a double-fisted blow to Lucas's temple and the werewolf went still.

Both women from the porch charged down the hill, but only one of them had transformed into a wolf. The other woman was human. I could smell it. Greta met the werewolf halfway and they rolled around together on the hillside. Greta's laughter echoed out over the water. She was having too much fun.

The old woman swung her open hand at Eric. He caught it with no effort at all and tossed her over his shoulder into the lake. She landed with a splash.

"Help! Vampires! Help!" The teenagers' voices carried clear out over the water. I dove back down into the boat. None of this was happening like it was supposed to happen. Now there were humans here, too?

"Grandma," Greta said, gripping the werewolf's upper and lower jaws and forcing them open too wide. "What big teeth you have."

"Just kill her," Eric said impatiently.

Greta frowned, but did as she was told.

I leapt back up onto the dock and resumed my human shape, complete with jeans and T-shirt. "Both of you, stop this," I cried.

"Go home, Tabitha." Eric grabbed me by the chin, squeezing my cheeks. "Just go the fuck home. I'm sorry I asked you here." He pushed me away. "I never should have turned you. I knew it wouldn't work out. You can't handle this."

"I can do anything I need to do! But this doesn't need to be done. It's stupid. It's murder, not self-defense, not feeding."

"Looks like you got another dud, Dad," Greta said, walking up to the porch of the house.

The woman Eric had thrown in the water floated in the darkness, watching us. Eric pointed at her. "Don't be stupid," he said. "Swim off to the marina or something."

He watched her swim away, looking relieved that he didn't need to kill her. "What do you want from me, Tabitha?"

"I want . . ." *I want you not to push me away,* I thought. *I want you to understand that I'm still me, and then I want to show you what I can do, that I can be like a live girl for you, that I can be warm and sexy and still hunt with you. I want you to be the same reluctant romantic that you always were, the man who isn't always in the right, but tries.*

"Do you want me to be all sexy and dangerous?" He sniffed the air, checking for werewolves. "Am I supposed to be Tom Cruise?"

"No. I . . ." *Did he really want me to leave? Was he pushing me away on purpose?*

"Am I supposed to go fight crime with you? Open a detective

agency? Look for a cure? Because it's not happening. You wanted a monster and you got one!" Waving his gun around as he spoke, Eric came toward me, his intemperate footsteps causing the dock to creak in protest. One of the white plastic barrels supporting it floated out from underneath, dropping the dock closer to the water's surface on one side.

"You're not a monster!" I shouted.

"I'm not?" His voice cracked as he asked. *El Alma Perdida* hummed angrily, but Eric's eyes blazed brightly just the same. His claws came out, and with them, the fangs. He snarled at me, doing everything he could to be less than what he was.

"No. Not really. You're the man I love."

"Oh, please," Eric said, his features becoming human once again. "Maybe you loved me when you were alive, but now you're dead. You don't even smell like you anymore."

"But I—" But I can, I tried to say. Eric cut me off.

"Just shut up, Tabitha," he yelled in a voice so loud that my ears rang. "Listen," he snapped, grabbing me by the shoulder. "Do you hear that?" Howl after howl rang out into the night. "Do you see those?" He pointed out over the water to werewolves in pontoon boats heading our way, some swimming in the lake. "I do not have time to talk about this right now. Some things are more important than how you feel."

And he was right. He was right. This wasn't the time or place. In truth, it was way past time for this discussion, but he hadn't been ready for it, and probably never would be. He didn't like to think about things too hard, especially not emotional things. He didn't want to admit that he loved me, but I knew that he did. He had to.

But I had to rethink my tactics. Chasing him wasn't working. Rolling over and letting him act however he wanted just made things worse. He had to realize that he loved me, had to be willing to admit it to me and to himself. And he couldn't do that with me giving in to him over and over again.

Which left only one way to get his attention.

"I hate you!" My claws raked down his face, leaving behind furrows of ravaged white flesh. He didn't react, didn't yell or scream. He just stood there, an inhuman statue.

"That makes two of us," he spat.

"If you love me, come find me. Otherwise . . . we're finished," I said. I turned into a bat and flew off into the night. I could pick up my things at the Demon Heart and make it to the Highland Towers by morning.

Phillip would take care of me. I knew he would. He knew how to treat a lady. He was nice and sweet . . . and short, fat, and bald, but he would do for starters. If Eric couldn't get a grip on his feelings for me, refused to acknowledge them, never came to get me . . . then a vampire queen deserved better. I deserved better.

32

ERIC:

ILL MET BY MOONLIGHT

Greta and I waited for William on the front porch. We didn't talk about Tabitha. Out in the dark, pawfalls sounded on the damp evening soil. A small armada of pontoon boats and speedboats floated in the middle of the lake, biding their time. Smart puppies. They wanted me surrounded before attacking. Overhead, the crescent moon watched our little war games. I pretended not to hear the rustle of seventy-plus werewolves panting in the night. Greta found an old transistor radio and turned it on.

"I forget," I asked Greta, "is it waxing or waning that's bad news for them, good news for us?" She shrugged.

The same classic rock station popped and hissed to life, treating us all to a little Led Zeppelin.

A wolf, white as snow and large as a lion, rounded the corner of the house.

"Waning is good for you," he snarled. "Tonight's moon is waxing crescent." Huh. Even the moon was out to screw me.

"What kept you?" I asked.

"A meeting."

"It would have saved you three packmates and a guard if you'd been at the marina."

"They are with the Lord now, just as you will soon be with your master the devil."

"Has anybody ever told you how cool it is that you guys talk in wolf form? I wish I could speak English when I change, but it all comes out like animal talk."

"You think this is funny."

"Not really." I pulled the pistol out of the back of my jeans and scratched my temple with the barrel. "I think us fighting each other is pretty damn stupid though. You might be able to hurt me, but I have *El Alma Perdida.*"

If he didn't know what *El Alma Perdida* was, then I was screwed and the rest of my night was going to be like the bloodbath at the docks. Tabitha was right about killing them being murder, but wrong about it being needless. Murder can be necessary. If I looked weak to the wolves, like I wouldn't carry out any threat I made, there was no way William would listen.

William didn't blink. "If I shoot you with this," I warned, "you don't go to your reward. You get trapped by the gun. You don't want to spend eternity in a bullet, William. I know you don't."

The other werewolves began to close in, jumping out of boats and onto the embankment. Others came out of the woods.

"You killed my son!" William bellowed.

"No, but you did kill mine," I replied calmly. "I'm still willing to overlook that."

"Dad!" Greta crossed her arms with a loud *humph.* "Can't we just kill them all? They tortured me and they killed Kyle."

"Not yet, sweetheart." My eyes never left William's. "I killed a bunch of werewolves for that already."

William blurred, a mass of growling angry white fur charging at me, going for my throat. If I hadn't had the gun out, I'd never have managed to bring it to bear.

His jaws touched my throat and the barrel of the gun touched his forehead. It charred his fur slightly and he drew back. I had almost been too slow.

"How?" said William. "A vampire can't hold—"

"They can if they wear gloves and don't mind it burning the crap out of them."

"You aren't wearing gloves."

"I'm an exception," I said. "I have it on good authority that John Paul Courtney was my great, great, great-granddad or granduncle . . . or something like that.

"You see, someone has been trying pretty damn hard to maneuver us into this position. At first, I thought it was because I killed your son, but actually I didn't. I don't know who I killed. He was dressed like a bum, had already killed two other vamps, and jumped me in an alley."

"Fergus." William spat the name out like it tasted bad. "No wonder I couldn't get in touch with him. He's no packmate of ours. He's an outcast and a murderer. He'll do anything for money."

"Greta," I called over my shoulder to her. "I'm supposed to remember that name, for some reason. Do you—" Then it clicked. The check! Thirty thousand dollars written to a Fergus . . . something . . . a check on which Roger forged my name. Bastard. "Well, that explains that. So Roger hired Fergus to jump me in the alley. He got Brian to maneuver me into position and . . . Where was I?"

"You didn't do it," Greta answered from the porch.

"Right. I . . . Do you mind backing up a few steps?" I asked William. "Your breath smells like Alpo."

William withdrew slightly, growling low, ears flattened against his head. "You cannot escape."

"I know, I know," I said. "You and your pack will call up more goons from the Lycan Diocese to hunt me down. Blah blah blah."

"Do not mock me, vampire."

"Sorry," I said. I cleared my throat. "Okay, so then I thought that I was being used as a fall guy, that the boyfriend of the vampire who killed your son had framed me to protect his girlfriend, the theory being that I would probably kill you and even if I didn't . . . well, once you killed me you would think the whole deal was over and move on with your life.

"But then I found out about *El Alma Perdida*." I leaned against the wall. It was hard to read William's expression, but since he was listening I kept on talking. "How likely is it that I just happened to stumble into a mess involving an Alpha werewolf, one that I might need all different sorts of silver to kill—blessed, magic, inherited, cherry-flavored, the whole bit, and then wind up with all of it neatly packaged in one gun?

"Now . . . I happen to believe the whole John Paul Courtney thing. I kind of like the idea that I'm related to a badass cowboy werewolf hunter. But that someone would just happen to be using his special gun, that they would just happen to leave a bullet behind so that I could find that gun? It's just too much coincidence."

"You have another explanation?" he growled.

"Yeah, yeah, I do. You know a vampire named Roger, right?"

William growled low in his throat. "Roger Malcolm. He dared to come here, to ask us to sell him our land. He—"

I cut him off. "That's the guy. I think the whole reason I'm down here is because Roger wants me to kill you and enough of your pack that he can bring in some hired muscle and dispose of the rest, snatch the property out from under any relatives you might have, and build his little fancy-schmantsy vampire lake resort."

"And are you here because you wish to protect this 'friend'? Because he is also the one who told us where we could find you the other night."

"Me?" I asked. "Hell, no! Yes, I was planning to kill you, but that's only because after the stunts you've pulled trying to get back at me, I didn't think we'd be able to talk things over. I expected to kill you with the magic gun and then to have to kill your pack so that they'd leave me alone." He bristled at that.

"Now that we're talking, though, we've got options. I figure we can do this one of two ways. Way one I call 'the bad plan.' You don't believe me and I see how many of you I can kill before you take me down. Then, being a Vlad, I keep coming back over and over again. You get the idea.

"Way two, which I must say I prefer, I call 'the give the bastard what he deserves plan.' About forty of your pack members keep Greta as collateral, unharmed, and the rest of us go pay Roger a little visit."

"Dad," Greta protested. "You can't trust them. They'll try to eat me."

"Not if he promises they won't," I told her.

"Dad, no."

"Do it and I'll let you move back into the Pollux," I said cajolingly. "You can have one of the dressing rooms all to yourself."

Greta bit her lip, considering it. With Kyle gone, if I let her move in, she knew I'd let her stay. "And I get to hunt for a whole week, however I want, and you won't complain or be mad about how much I eat."

"Deal," I told her. I inclined my head slightly toward William. "What do you say?"

William resumed his human form. I'd seen other werewolves change back before, the fangs receding and new teeth growing in to fill the bloody holes. In contrast, William's reversion seemed painless. The fur around his eyes lit up from within, spreading outward across his body until the only thing not illuminated were those fierce eyes, the glow obscuring the rest of him. The outline changed, became that of a man. The glow receded and he stood before me in jeans and a white T-shirt, wearing loafers without socks. Very cool. "Assuming I agree to this, what happens after?"

"You let Greta go, deliver her safely to the Pollux—at night," I emphasized, "and agree to stay out of my way in exchange for me staying out of yours."

"In other words, a return to the status quo."

"Yes."

"I can't speak for the Lycan Diocese," William replied, "but I can attempt to explain. I can call off my pack, but you killed Reverend. He was a member of Deacon's pack. Even if the Lycan Diocese decides to forgive you . . ."

"I'll burn that bridge when I come to it," I told him.

"William," one of the others snarled in protest. "He killed Lucas and—"

"Silence," William snapped. "He will pay for his sins. All we do here is agree to let the Lord handle his punishment. If what he says is true, then we attacked him mistakenly."

They argued for twenty minutes, but eventually he convinced them. He convinced me that he could be trusted, too, especially when the packmates he picked to keep an eye on Greta were all wolves who had raised their voices in support of his plan.

The werewolves ferried us to the marina in a pontoon boat, then William let me ride in the back of his pickup, intending to drop me off at my car. We had to make new plans when we got to the abandoned house, though. It seemed Tabitha had decided to take the car with her when she left.

I waved again at the security guards still standing in front of Sable Oaks. This time I got a reaction. They stared openmouthed and called for backup. I think they thought we were invading. With a mutual laugh shared between me and my temporary allies, we drove on.

Which left me with one last problem: Did I really want to help these werewolves kill Roger?

✦ 33 ✦

TABITHA:

TIDYING UP

No one was supposed to be at the Demon Heart, but when I pulled around back to park, I saw Marilyn's old Buick in its usual spot, second closest to the door. She always saved the first spot for Eric. I pulled into his parking place and wondered how the fight was going. Had Eric and Greta slaughtered all the werewolves yet? I couldn't imagine the werewolves winning.

Inside the club, all the lights were off except for a narrow band shining out from underneath the door in the main office. The weak thud of Marilyn's heartbeat thumped in my ears, the acrid smell of her cigarette assaulting my nostrils. The door to Eric's bedroom was open. The light snapped on at a touch and I started unpacking my things from Eric's chest of drawers.

I pulled my suitcase from his closet, but I knew everything wouldn't fit. I'd accumulated too much stuff. He'd been so free with money that I now had six times the number of outfits I'd moved in with. My lingerie alone could have filled the suitcase. Packing up my favorites and my jewelry seemed the best way to go. I set aside the blue dress that I'd worn for Eric's birthday and the diamond necklace. I wanted to be wearing them when I saw Phillip.

I went into the bathroom and willed myself to seem alive, my heart to beat, my blood to flow, and most of all for my reflection to appear in the mirror. Doing so diminished my other senses, the sound of my own heart and the blood rushing through my veins drowning out external sounds to near-human levels.

I stripped out of my clothes and studied the figure in the glass. No fat. No cellulite. My breasts were firm and full, and, unlike some dancers, completely natural. The slight sag that gravity normally gave them had been banished by vampirism. My tummy was flat, my muscles toned, and looking over my shoulder verified that my butt was tight and heart-shaped. My long black hair was healthy; it had body and bounce. What was not to love?

I didn't hear her come into the room, but I smelled the smoke.

"That's not the problem," Marilyn said. Her cigarette was out, but the scent clung to her, a cloud of stench.

"Don't you knock?" I reached down for my panties, embarrassed by her presence even though I'd shown my body to thousands of perfect strangers.

"When I feel like it," she said, cackling. "I'm old. People overlook things when you're old."

"Well, I don't. I—"

"You decided to leave him?" she asked, pointing to the suitcase. Her eyes loomed large behind her glasses. She wasn't wearing her false teeth, and it changed the timbre of her voice.

"Yes." *Not for long, though,* I thought. *He'll come after me.* I walked past her and retrieved my blue dress.

"He won't." Marilyn sat on the edge of the bed, a withered old woman, a witch reading my mind. She smiled a pursed-lip toothless smile at my surprise.

"How did you—"

"I know him better than anybody," Marilyn told me, crossing her arms. There was no sling, no cast. "Better than Roger ever suspected." A cough took her, a series of long wracking painful rasps. "I know you, too, because you're a woman who loves him. We have that in common." She stood up, slow and creaking. "So I feel I should tell you this. He won't chase you, but he does love you."

We had that in common?

"But you hate him," I protested, forgetting the dress in my hand as I gestured with it. "He disgusts you."

"You don't know me," Marilyn said. She started folding some of my things, putting them neatly into the suitcase. "And you don't know him, either.

"Do you know what his hopes and dreams were when he was alive? Did you see him come back from the Second World War, a man who hadn't believed in killing, but who had believed in doing what was right? We were just friends, then. He was too stupid to realize that when I said I was saving myself for marriage, what I really meant was saving myself for him."

She didn't cry; as emotional as her words were, she snapped them off bitterly. "Did you ever hear him play the piano? Did you even know he could? Did you hold his head in your lap on the day you were supposed to be married to him and cry because he'd been ruined, too?"

"You know I haven't. I wasn't even born then."

"I know." Marilyn's head sagged. "You're young and you're stupid and you think you can treat an eighty-two-year-old man like a teenager. You expect him to run after you, but he can't."

"I don't know what else to do," I shouted. "It's like he wants me to leave, but I know he still cares about me. I've seen him decide to be cruel on purpose and push me away—"

Marilyn slapped me and I slapped her back, the blow spinning her all the way around before she dropped to the ground like a sack of old laundry. Her glasses landed on the bed and I thought that I had killed her.

"Oh my God. Marilyn." I touched her shoulder. "I'm so sorry. I—" And then she slapped me again, her laugh sharp and abrasive, cawing crowlike laughter. I reeled away from her and she grinned, her fierce eyes challenging me. My fingernails had cut her skin when I'd struck her, but the wounds weren't bleeding, they were creeping closed.

"You have to stay and fight for him and you have to win. You have to get Greta on your side and you have to protect him, like I tried to do, but you have to succeed."

"Protect him from what? Himself?" I asked.

Marilyn pulled herself up and reached for the top of her blouse. I thought she was hiding a cross, that she was going to use it on me, but instead, she opened the top button, baring part of a wrinkled, drooping breast, upon which she had a small tattoo of a frog. "Do you see?" she asked. "Talbot told me you killed Veruca. You might have seen, when she died."

"She turned to dust, Marilyn."

"Never mind." Marilyn closed her blouse, deflated, as she spoke. "I can't . . . he won't let me say more."

"Who won't?" I asked. As if in answer to my question, Roger popped up in my mind, seemingly holographic like the vampires at the Highland Towers. He was less powerful than me and had been a vampire for forty-three years. He was shocked to see me, but not as shocked as I was to see his companion. He was walking down Thirteenth Street talking to a young woman who was the spitting image of Rachel. They were arguing and he seemed nervous, almost afraid.

"Nice tits," he said to me and I broke the contact.

"I've gotta go," I told Marilyn. I slipped the blue dress over my head and darted barefooted out the front door.

They'd reached the front of the Pollux by the time I got there. The girl who looked like Rachel wore tight black hip-huggers and a midriff top. A small gold padlock hung from her choker and she wore a jade bracelet on her left wrist. Except for the hair, which had been highlighted in blondes and reds, she was Rachel's twin. She smirked when she saw me.

"Hi, slut," she said. "Where ya been?"

Even her voice was Rachel's. But I'd seen her open casket. I'd watched them lower her into the ground.

"Rachel?" I whispered. "But . . . but you died."

"Anyone can get a second chance aboveground, Tab. You just have to be willing to do absolutely anything to get it. Third chances are harder. But I died human, so my path didn't require any special ingredients that I didn't have with me. It's not easy to close the deal when your soul is already hellbound and on-site, but it can be done."

"Rachel wouldn't have gone to hell," I told the look-alike. "She was just a kid."

The smile on her lips was in that uncertain territory between sweet and malicious. "That's cute, Tab. I'm flattered." She turned to Roger. "She gets to leave."

"Like you could stop me anyway," I snapped.

"Kill her," Roger suggested.

I honestly don't know whether he was talking to her or to me, but the Rachel look-alike answered him. "If I do, he'll know I did it, because you insisted that I link with him, make him think he'd made me his thrall. I'm not like your wrinkled-up old fuck puppet, Roger. I'm a witch and you're just a frickin' Master vampire. You can't control me."

Roger opened his mouth to reply, but I beat him to it. "So that's how you look like my sister? You used magic?" I popped my claws. "Well, stay back, witch, because I'm not just a 'frickin' Master.' I'm a Vlad."

The witch laughed like a wicked child, eyes sparkling as if she enjoyed a challenge. "Don't tempt me, sis."

"Do it," Roger urged her. He reached out to her, but drew his hand back before he made contact. He feared her. She sensed it and her nostrils flared. He stammered, "I didn't—"

Her eyes narrowed. "Watch it, dead boy. I'm only helping *you* out because it will help pay my debt. My real boss got me out of hell. You did squat. He said to help you with Eric. Tabitha is not part of the deal."

"You guys are going to try and take Eric on?" I asked incredulously. "The two of you?"

"Roger thinks he is," the woman who claimed to be Rachel answered. "Which is a total joke. I mean, let's be serious. In a fight, even you would kick Roger's ass."

"That's why you're here," Roger said angrily. "You have to help me."

"Not in a fight. Your contract for assistance specifies noncombat. If you want more, you'll have to work it out with my boss." The witch tapped Roger on the nose with her index finger like he was a particularly dumb child. "If he was really just a Vlad, then I might've helped you out. My magic would have had him wrapped around my little finger in under a minute." She ran her hand along Roger's shoulder and he relaxed visibly. The scent of freshly baked cinnamon rolls washed over me, but I couldn't tell where it came from. "But as it is, I have to go all out to influence him even a little bit. I could barely keep him from flying to the other side of the interstate after that mess at the lake. He nearly didn't make it to the right house. So, I'm sorry, but you're on your own."

"Which," the woman turned her attention to me and began massaging Roger's shoulders as she spoke, "is why Roger, here, is going to get his undead ass handed to him tonight."

"He won't kill me," Roger objected, shoving her away with some difficulty, trying to regain his composure.

"Oh yes, he will," the witch countered. "Because you refuse to believe that Eric is an Emperor, not a Vlad. I get why. Accepting what he is means you have to accept that you helped Eric become more powerful than you will ever be, even though you didn't mean to do it."

Emperor, my ass. "You're both nuts," I said finally. "And you," I added, pointing at the Rachel look-alike. "I don't know who you are, witch, or what spell you're using, but you are definitely not my sister."

I stormed back into the Demon Heart and locked the door. Marilyn sat behind the bar, my packed suitcase propped up on top of it next to a bottle of Jack Daniel's. Lord Phillip's diamond necklace sparkled on top of the suitcase. The shoes that went with my dress were sitting on a bar stool.

"You'd better go," Marilyn said after she took a shot of Jack.

"Who is that girl?" I asked.

"I don't know for sure," Marilyn replied, "but she's bad business and that's all I can say. I'm only able to say this much to you because he's careless with the details."

"Who is?" I wondered if she was being infuriating on purpose.

Marilyn cursed under her breath. I know she thought I was stupid, the look in her eyes told me as much, but there was another emotion there that I couldn't read: not fear, but frustration, perhaps? "Don't let her touch you, and stay away from Roger. If you try to hurt him, I'll have to defend him."

"What? Why? Defend Roger? You're just as nuts as they are. You're all in on it!"

"Just go." Marilyn sighed. "Go to Eric. He might not figure it out either, but he can protect you, as he has me."

"I'm not going to Eric!" I shouted. "He's coming to me!"

Marilyn made a hand-washing motion and reached into her purse for a pack of cigarettes. "Do what you want then, Tabitha. I hope you're right about him. I truly do."

Rachel, or the thing that looked like Rachel, knocked on the door. "You still in there, slut?"

Marilyn tore a match out of a Demon Heart matchbook, lit her cigarette and coughed on the smoke. "I hate these things," she told me, "but if you smoke enough of them they can kill you."

"Stop talking to her, Marilyn," Roger shouted from the other side of the door. As if by magic, Marilyn's mouth snapped shut. Her eyes spoke volumes and I finally got it. Somehow Roger was controlling Marilyn. But really, what did that have to do with me? I was leaving.

I slipped on my shoes, put on my necklace, and glared at Marilyn, suitcase in hand. If . . . no, *when* Eric came after me, I'd tell him about all the weird shit that had been going on behind his back, but until then, he was on his own.

I heard Roger fumble with his keys, followed by the metallic click of the lock. I waited until they stepped through the front door.

"Give Eric a message for me?" I asked, looking from Roger to the witch and back to Marilyn. "Whichever one of you is in charge?"

"I'm not giving him any mess—," Roger said. Rachel shut him down with an elbow to the side.

"What's the message?" she asked.

"Tell him I'm going to Lord Phillip's at the Highland Towers."

Roger's lip twitched, but he didn't say anything.

"Fine," Rachel told me.

I nodded and headed out the back way, to Eric's loaner, smiling as I loaded my suitcase into the trunk. Marilyn thought Eric wouldn't come for me, but she didn't know him like I did. She'd only really known him when he'd been alive. My knowledge was more recent. Death had changed him, changed both of us. It might take him a while, but he'd made me immortal. I had nothing but time.

Even when the loaner broke down four blocks from the Demon

Heart, it didn't put a dent in my good mood. Carrying my suitcase, I headed toward the Highland Towers, a strong, single, attractive vampire queen. My only thought was how jealous Eric would be when he found out where I'd gone.

✦ 34 ✦

ERIC:

UNFINISHED BUSINESS

I had William drop me off a few blocks from the Demon Heart and I walked them slowly. Roger and I sensed each other half a block away. He popped into my head and I into his, but we acknowledged each other too fast to allow the other to gain much insight into our emotions. We both had things to hide.

Roger was waiting for me at the Pollux. He sat on a wrought-iron bench to the left of the door in front of the marquee. The *Casablanca* title was clearly visible on the poster above his head.

When I was sixteen, I saw *Casablanca* at the Pollux. Rick said good-bye to Ilsa in the end, even though he loved her. He didn't know that he was just a character. He didn't know that Bogart would be in other movies and that on one of those movie sets, Humphrey Bogart would meet Lauren Bacall and fall in love, real love, not celluloid make-believe.

By leaving me, Tabitha had proved herself. Even as a vampire, she loved me, or she wouldn't have been so angry when she stormed off. She was better off without me. If I went after her, I'd regret it. If not today or tomorrow, then soon, and for the rest of my unlife.

"You look like shit." Roger blew a smoke ring from one of his expensive cigars. He offered me one and I shook my head.

"I can't taste them," I told him.

"Neither can I, but I still enjoy the aroma." He put the extra back into the inside pocket of his suit. Roger's lips pursed together, the hazy fragrant smoke flowing lazily from his nostrils. He looked so cocky, so self-assured, daring me to call him on what he'd been doing, to accuse him.

"How'd it go with the werewolves?" Roger took another longer pull on his cigar and held it.

"They're dead," I lied casually. We looked at each other. I stared him in the eye, but his attention was focused on my eyebrows, my chin, somewhere over my shoulder, my shoes, and lastly the concrete.

"Tabitha?" he asked, the words pushing the smoke back out of his lungs.

"Dumped me. It seems that I'm a murderer and an asshole. I pull the wings off flies and glue them back on upside down . . . the whole nine yards."

The ember at the end of his cigar glowed brighter as he took a long steady draw. "That sucks."

I laughed bitterly. "Yeah, it sucks."

"What about the wildflower . . . what's her name?" He looked up, still careful to avoid my gaze.

"Rachel? She's still around. It'll probably take me a month or two to screw that up." I sat next to him on the bench. He suppressed the urge to flinch, thought I didn't notice it, but I did.

"I'm still sorry about Brian." He smirked when I said the name. "I killed him the same night you framed me."

"You were meant to. That's why I befriended him." Another series of smoke rings slipped from his lips, perfect, each inside the other, the way only years of practice can achieve. Damn! And the Cold-Blooded Bastard Award goes to Roger Malcolm.

"So how much is it going to cost me to buy into this Orchard Lake thing?" I asked, trying to make it sound like a real interest. Here was a man I thought I'd known, a man I'd called *friend* since 1937. I wanted to know how long he'd been playing me false. After he became a vampire? Before?

"I underestimated you." He said it thoughtfully and with a complete lack of shame. No remorse at all.

"Maybe you just overestimated the werewolves," I said, trying to match his tone, his total lack of emotion. It was easier, because I could feel Rachel nearby and her influence crept in. Aware of it this time, having been outside her field of influence, I noticed how my control came back in some areas, fled in others: much of my anger was replaced with a desire for her.

Moving the cigar from one side of his mouth to the other, Roger closed his eyes. "Maybe you were just lucky."

"Could be," I allowed. "I always have been."

Roger threw the cigar to the ground. The cherry, still lit, rolled free and lay burning on the concrete. We both watched it burn. "That's something I've always hated about you." He slapped his hands on his knees and rose to his feet. "You get everything you want. You didn't even care about being a vampire." He made an effort to stop himself, to bottle up whatever it was that had been boiling up inside him, but it bubbled out anyway, the rant making him look more alive than he'd been in years. "God, I mean, do you even understand how hard I worked to find just the right sire for myself, to arrange things carefully, to slowly win her trust and work my way in?"

"I bet she really made you work, too," I said, remembering the rituals he had told me about, the ones she made him go through before she would bleed on his cross-inflicted wounds and heal him. "You must have had it rough. Poor Roger." Sarcasm bled into my voice. I couldn't keep up the act anymore. Neither, apparently, could Roger.

"Damn it!" he shouted at me, fists clenched, eyes burning with a light matching the dying ember from his discarded cigar. "I'm a Master vampire. A Master fucking vampire! Sure it's not the top. Not the same as being a Vlad. But it's still the big time. And you, you die in a goddamn car accident . . . and . . . and . . . destiny says screw it! Eric is important. I like Eric. Eric can't be dead. Let's make him a Vlad! He's a good boy! He deserves it!"

"It could have been anybody, one of the ambulance drivers, a passing bum," I offered. "What does it matter? What does that have to do with anything?"

"There was no ambulance, you dumb shit. No hospital. I watched you lie there bleeding for a damn hour before you stopped breathing and then I watched you for another hour just to be sure. And when I was certain you were good and dead, I bribed the cops, paid the fang fee to have you taken directly to the mortician, and had your ass embalmed so that there would be no doubt, because I was tired of you being so much better than me and you getting everything I ever wanted!"

Cold. Icy cold is how I felt—too astonished or appalled to be mad. "Roger? What the hell, man?" I felt sore and tired. I pushed myself up off of the bench like an old man. "That's what this was all about? You're jealous?"

"Oh. It's funny to you, huh? Poor jealous Roger." I had never seen him like this. Not ever in all our fights had he looked at me with such hatred. It was like walking in on your mother-in-law in the bathroom and realizing she's a guy in drag. It just didn't fit. What had I ever done to Roger? Who cared if he was a Master and I was a Vlad? "You won't think it's funny for long."

"Look," I said soothingly. "Maybe we should get you a vampire therapist or something and just move on."

"God! You'd do it, too, wouldn't you?" He took two agitated steps away from me and spun back around, flailing his arms. "You'd just forget all about it. I bet that if I told you I was sorry you'd forgive me. Inside a month you probably wouldn't remember it ever even happened."

"Pretty much," I answered truthfully. My words hit him hard and it was clear from the insane look in his eyes that he couldn't quite grasp how that could be possible. I didn't want our friendship to be over. I was willing to believe that he was going through some kind of vampiric midlife crisis, that what he was saying about watching me die was bullshit or that he'd been in shock. I wanted him to have a reason, any reason, other than stupid jealousy. *C'mon, Roger,* I thought at him, *just make something the fuck up!*

I didn't see him move. The stake ripped through my T-shirt and lodged in my heart, a familiar feeling for me. Every time it feels exactly the same. Some vampires say it hurts, but to me, it only hurts on the way in and out. While the stake is in there, I just have an overwhelming urge to burp.

"You thought I'd share it with you, that I'd let you buy into the project? After all the shit I've put up with, do you really think I'd let you in? When Orchard Lake becomes Midnight Lake it's going to be the next Highland Towers, Eric, and I can't have you fucking it up. I'm going to be the next big thing! The big kahuna!" Drops of blood stood out on Roger's brow, rivulets of vampire sweat.

Nope, I thought at him, overwhelmed more with apathy than sadness, *what you get to be is dinner.*

He heard the first howl and staggered away from me. The wolves romped in like the Magnificent Seven and the Seven Samurai all rolled up into one big bad case of old-school whoop ass. All wore their human forms, but with lupine grins. William strolled out of the entrance to the Pollux parking deck holding *El Alma Perdida*.

Roger backed away slowly, not running. Was he expecting backup? Ten more of the pack walked out of the deck behind him and another ten stalked from around the corner of the Pollux, all dressed in exactly what they'd worn at their Orchard Lake homes, everything from sweatpants to jeans.

William yanked the stake out of my chest and pressed the gun into my hands. He grinned at Roger. "Hello again, Mr. Malcolm."

"You can't kill me, Eric. I've got connections." Roger stepped into the road, fighting off panic, keeping all of the werewolves in his field of vision. "And I may not be able to kill you, but now I know what you are and I'm going to take that, too—"

I fired *El Alma Perdida*. The bullet struck him in the shoulder and the wound began to sizzle.

"I've been waiting all night to shoot somebody with this gun, Roger," I said. "And there's just nobody I'd rather shoot with it than you."

"I—" Roger tried to speak, but I shot him twice more, the reports ringing out sharp, clear, and satisfying. You see, I've never liked vampires, not even myself. I've never made any bones about that. While I thought Roger was my friend, I'd made exceptions, but now . . . that made him just one more high society vamp in my territory, on my front fucking doorstep. The impact spun him around and he hit the asphalt. His arms flapped up and down as if he were a bat. "Can't change . . ."

"Same thing happened to me earlier," I explained, not the least bit sympathetic as I walked over to him. "Magbidion explained it to me."

"The bullets from *El Alma Perdida* shape-lock anyone they strike," William said. "It kept any werewolves Courtney killed from reverting to human form when the sun hit them."

"He made sure to leave one bullet in the werewolf until the local law enforcement showed up. He'd let them see the monster, and then dig the last bullet out so they could watch it change back into a human with their own eyes," I explained. "That way he could get hailed as a monster killer, not hanged as a murderer." Flames licked out of Roger's wound, and I kept talking as he swatted frantically at the fire. "It was a nice touch when you had Froggy leave one bullet behind to make it look like *El Alma Perdida* was back in Courtney hands. Too bad the bullets are all linked. Talbot and Tabitha followed the trail right to your bedroom door. Oh, and it's official . . . Froggy was a Soldier. When Tabitha staked her: *Poof.*"

Roger tried to speak. "I have a hos—" Tongues of fire climbed up his chest and his words were choked off by cries of pain. Once the flames began to spread, they quickly engulfed him, and the pack, now in werewolf forms, descended on him, heedless of the fire, tearing still-smoking chunks of flesh free with their teeth. Does getting eaten by werewolves count as total destruction? I assumed so. He didn't stop screaming even when he no longer had a throat, the sound echoing out of the empty space at his neck where his throat had been.

Absent the meat, Roger's skeleton writhed on the ground. Several of the werewolves drew back, but William and his core followers devoured even the bones. Roger's cries finally ceased when William crushed his skull between those massive jaws and started chewing. I guess he couldn't have tasted too bad, because they didn't leave anything behind. Note to self: That is not the way I want to go out.

William's pack loped away to their trucks, leaving William alone with me. He laughed when I put the barrel of *El Alma Perdida* against his furry chest. "Now, about Greta."

"Your spawn will be returned to you unharmed," he replied. "I am as good as my word."

"Fair enough." I lowered the gun. "I'm sorry about—"

"Don't come back to Orchard Lake."

So much for apologies. "Keep your pack away from Void City and you've got a deal."

"What would you have done if I hadn't listened to you back at the lake and your magic gun didn't kill me?" he asked.

"I've got an old mercury thermometer in my back pocket," I lied.

William smiled. "And if that failed you?"

"I'd have figured something out," I assured him. "Don't you worry about that."

"I believe you," William said, nodding. "Out at the park, when you commanded the bats to block out the sun, I was afraid you would destroy us all."

"Nah, I only wanted my little girl back."

"She's a monster," he protested.

"Now you're just being mean. Besides, she's no worse than I am."

"I beg to differ," William said. "I didn't see it until I watched you gun down your friend."

"Friend?"

"Fellow vampire, then," he amended. "The look in your eye was the same look I see in the eyes of my pack when they exterminate a vampire. You know they are monsters."

"It's kind of a no-brainer."

"So you say, Eric of the revenant's eyes."

"Huh?" I asked, startled. "Revenant's eyes?"

"When you grow angry, angry enough to grow wings of hate and a skin black with rage, the purple eyes from which you stare are not the eyes of a vampire, but of a revenant, a murdered soul."

"Murdered?" I echoed, not wanting to think about it too closely.

"I only tell you what I saw, Eric."

"All right, so maybe I was murdered, but I'm a vampire, not a frickin' revenant, okay?"

"As you say, vampire. May the Lord have mercy on your soul." I watched him lope off into the distance.

Not a bad birthday, all in all. The werewolves weren't after me anymore, my best friend who really hadn't been my best friend was dead, and I could go back into the Pollux and have my way with Rachel guilt-free, more or less.

"Revenant's eyes," I scoffed and sat down on the bench where old what's-his-name had admitted his betrayal. Roger. Forget him, I told myself. Just let him go. But my memories of Roger were too tangled up with memories of Marilyn. I couldn't let go of one without sacrificing the other.

Her familiar heart beat across the street at the Demon Heart, a weary skittish beat in comparison to the steady rhythmic thump of Rachel's. I let them both serenade me, Rachel upstairs in my bed at the Pollux and Marily—What was Marilyn doing at the Demon Heart this early?

I crossed the street at a trot and unlocked the front door of the club. She was probably getting things ready for our grand reopening. We could open back up tomorrow, I thought.

Serves me right for being optimistic.

The hair on the back on my neck stood up. Cold white light from the street illuminated Marilyn, tied to a chair in the middle of the room. Blood trickled down her arms and legs where piano wire had cut into her wrinkled flesh. A large band of duct tape covered her mouth. It was frayed along the bottom, tucked under and stuck to itself on the upper right corner. All the little details.

Her eyes screamed at me to run, but I didn't. I'm stupid like that. I never know when to run or when to leave someone behind. That I do, on occasion, manage to do one or the other just goes to prove the age-old adage. "The sun even shines on a dog's ass some days."

Stuck to her chest was a Post-It note with the words: *Happy Birthday, you stupid fuck!* It was signed *Hugs and kisses—Roger.* My vampire speed kicked in and I think I might have made it if Roger hadn't been the one who'd set the trap for me. He'd known me too well.

My claws raked through the piano wire, severing it on both sides simultaneously. I clutched Marilyn close, the smell of stale cigarettes and old age filling my nostrils. The intro music from the old *Superman* radio show flashed through my head. I heard an electronic whine that didn't sound like the alarm system. I rolled away from it, hoping to shield Marilyn from the blast. More than one bomb went off.

I'd never moved with such urgent speed before. We shot past the first explosion as it happened, outrunning it like in the movies, dodging over the runway and into the dressing room. The next explosion went off in there, my every move anticipated, creating a circle of fire, shaped charges designed to hit me from all angles. It wasn't normal fire, either; the way it burned and pierced was a sensation I associate only with crucifixes and holy water.

He'd paid someone to bless the damn explosives. Even so, I lasted longer than Marilyn, watched her burn away. The only thing that eased the pain was knowing that I got Roger first. He was a Master, easy to kill. I'm not.

We Vlads keep coming back unless you find that one special way that will take us out forever. It didn't feel like Roger's method was it for me, but it felt damn close. My body was completely gone; not even a speck of ash remained. I'd been melted before, but there, in the goop, I'd still had a body, just an icky liquid one. Now, I was totally disconnected, a floating ghost.

I hate ghosts.

I hovered over the burning ruins of the Demon Heart, pleasantly surprised to see that the explosion hadn't harmed the Pollux Theater across the street, waiting for my body to re-form and wondering how long it would take. And waiting. And waiting. You know, when I get my self back together, I'm going to find the guy who thought up blessed C-4 and kick his ass.

Happy fucking birthday to me.

REVAMPED

The book is dedicated to four very special guys:
My dad, Ferrell
My grandfather, C.M.
My friend & unpaid researcher, Rob
and
My good buddy, Rich

ACKNOWLEDGMENTS

Welcome back to the Void!

The author would like to acknowledge every single person who made this book possible, but he is quite certain (yet again) that he's left someone out. If it was you . . . oops . . . again.

First and foremost, my thanks go out to you, the reader. Whether you're here for a return visit to Void City or are a first time guest, I'm glad you came and I hope you enjoy your stay.

I owe a debt of gratitude to my writing group, the WTF (Write the Fantastic): Rob, Mary Ann, Dan, Karen, Janet, and Virginia. Literarily speaking, they are murderous bastards yet they still manage to be good friends with enough mad baking skills between them that I am often the bearer of cookies at late night convention panels.

Thanks are also owed to Mom, Dad, Shea, Rich, Sandra, Rachel, Daniel, and the Lawleys (Jimmy, Linda, and Hunter) for support and friendship above and beyond the call of duty.

These acknowledgments would not be complete without mentioning two mighty women: my agent, Shawna McCarthy, and my editor, Jennifer Heddle. Without them, you wouldn't be reading this. Plus, they both let me keep Fang, a character that I was (perhaps unreasonably) worried might not survive the editing process.

Thank you to Gene Mollica for the wonderful cover . . . I really like the way you incorporated Fang.

An additional "You rock" goes out to the many podcasters who happily agreed to run audio promos for the series, in particular: J. C. Hutchins, Mur Lafferty, Rick & Anne Stringer, Kimi, Michael R. Mennenga, Summer Brooks, and Shaun Farrell.

Last, but certainly not least, thank you to my wife and my sons . . . just because.

1

ERIC:

WELCOME BACK TO THE VOID

If you've never been blown up before, I can't recommend it. I suggest it even less if the perpetrators are using blessed shaped charges of C-4. Being atomized by that kind of firepower would have ended most vampires, but I'm not that lucky. I'm *special*.

In ice cream terms, vampires come in three flavors: chocolate, strawberry, and vanilla. I'm grape sherbet—hard to come by and much more likely to give you brain freeze. Technically there's one more type of vampire, Drones, but they're barely even immortal—the vampire equivalent of ice milk—and they certainly wouldn't have survived what happened to me.

My name is Eric Courtney and up until several minutes ago, I was a vampire. Now . . . ? Let's just say I'm working on it.

The only good thing about being explosively deconstructed was that the sensation was new and different, two essential requirements for keeping an immortal from getting too bored. Being blown up by my best friend, having my body destroyed, and seeing my strip club obliterated weren't what I would have chosen to shake things up, but I've learned to roll with the punches, even the sucker ones.

For the first few seconds I actually thought I might be really most sincerely dead. Ended. Gone for good. I hovered over the still blazing ruin of my strip club, a glowing blue specter wearing jeans and a *Welcome to the Void* T-shirt; unseen, unheard, and utterly unamused. The neon sign flared impressively before melting into slag. Shards of glass covered the street between the Demon Heart and the old Pollux Theater, where the *Casablanca* poster in the display began to wither under the intense heat, browning at the edges as it curled. I owned both buildings, having bought them inexpensively after, of all things, a fire.

Security alarms from the buildings on the block adjoining mine rang out into the night. I ran a hand over my spectral face.

How do I get my body back?

That was the first question. I'd been reduced to ashes before, but Talbot (my . . . bouncer) or one of my other employees had always been around to pour blood on my remains. Vampires run on blood, so blood plus vampire ashes meant poof—instant vampire, kind of like the instant Martians in those old Looney Tunes animated shorts. I had no idea how Talbot and the gang could bring me back this time, though. No ashes.

Being a ghost wasn't all bad, at least. As a ghost, my thoughts were clearer than they'd ever been, and the hunger for blood, that ever-present inner dark that had driven me to do most of the questionable things I'd done in my unlife, was gone. It was as if, for once, my brain worked like everybody else's; no memories seemed to hover just out of reach. Even my attitude had shifted. I'm an angry guy, but searching my feelings, I found my anger replaced by pain and more grief than I'd ever felt before, a sense of endless loss.

The world of the living was a faded watercolor painting seen through my noncorporeal eyes, blurry and surreal. Most of the Demon Heart's side of the street burned, flames devouring the place hungrily.

Firefighters and police showed up in time to save the Pollux. Distorted figures in half-recognized uniforms sprayed water on the ancient movie palace. It bothered me that I couldn't smell the smoke or feel the heat of the fire. Even with all the hustle and bustle, the heartbeats of the humans responding to the emergency did not echo in my ears. Instead, their voices were muted and far away.

I stared at the fire engine. They had parked it in the middle of the street, right over the spot where my former best friend Roger had been eaten by werewolves. I saw a flash of him in my mind's eye, reduced to a skeleton, still screaming as the Orchard Lake pack consumed him in his entirety. I felt a pang of guilt for siccing them on Roger, even though he'd betrayed me, but it was a brief pang. Intellectually, I knew he hadn't really been my friend.

For the last forty years Roger had plotted my downfall, but with my memory functioning properly, it was hard not to hear his screams echoing through my brain. Worse, though, were the memories of Marilyn, watching as the explosion ripped through her, seeing her die . . . Her death had been Roger's parting birthday present to me. What a pal.

At least Tabitha hadn't been at the club when it had happened. If there's a good time to ditch your boyfriend, I'd say right before he gets incinerated is a good pick. So, kudos to her for timing.

"It's all so eerily beautiful," said a voice. Marilyn was standing next to me. Young again, red hair hanging down past her shoulders, she sported the same leather jacket she'd worn in the photograph I'd carried in my wallet before it got torched with the rest of me. If Ann-Margret or Maureen O'Hara had been blessed with more attractive younger sisters, they might have looked almost as sensational as my Marilyn. She'd been the bait for the trap Roger had set for me. I had to give him high marks for effectiveness there. Picking the love of my life (if not the love of my death) to lure me to my final destruction was primo angst material.

"Like a Van Gogh painting," Marilyn continued. *"The Starry Night* or *The Café Terrace on the Place du Forum, Arles, at Night."*

"'Starry, Starry Night' is an old Don McLean song, right?"

Marilyn laughed. "That song's called 'Vincent,' but 'Starry Night' is in the chorus."

I was born in 1926 and Marilyn was a few years my senior. When I turned into a vampire, she stayed human, wouldn't let me turn her . . . so I'd watched her age for over forty years. I had missed her so much without even realizing it. The person she had become, the one who was old and sick and smoked too much, bore almost no resemblance to the Marilyn I remembered, the one who was here now.

"I'm sorry," she said softly. "I am so sorry, Eric."

Ghosts, as it turns out, can hug one another. I took her in my arms, crushed her to my chest. We probably looked like long-lost lovers in some old black-and-white movie, but given our ages, I guess that shouldn't have come as a big surprise. Her breasts pressed against me, without warmth. It didn't matter. I covered her with kisses and she laughed again, despite herself, before she pulled away.

"What is it?" I asked.

"I need to tell you something." I didn't need an orchestral cue to know it was bad news. Marilyn is not a timid woman. She could stare down an angry vampire, blow smoke in his face, and laugh when he snarled. I couldn't count the number of times she'd done exactly that . . . to me. I had never seen her so scared.

"Tell me," I said. "Look. It's okay. I mean, we may be forced to haunt the remains of a strip club for eternity, unless our bus is just late or something, but I don't see how this is your fault."

Shaking her head, she walked away from me, passing unthinkingly through a firefighter.

"I'm not staying," she said. "I can feel it"—she placed her hand over her bosom—"inside. I just . . . I have to tell you something before I . . . go."

Go? Going sounded like a bad idea. Marilyn walked back and put her arms around me. "I didn't know about it, I swear. When Roger told me, I was shocked and horrified, and when you rose, I knew that I couldn't go through with it. So he . . ."

A babbling Marilyn was an even bigger warning sign. My girl didn't babble. She didn't mince words, and she sure as hell didn't let her words trail off into nothingness.

"When I rose . . . as a vampire?"

As far as I knew, I'd died in a car wreck. Coming back as a vampire had surprised me as much as it had anyone else. When I rose, it was two weeks after the crash at two in the afternoon on the day Marilyn and I were supposed to have been wed. "Am I late for something?" I'd asked her before bursting into flames. The look in her ghostly eyes, there in the remains of my club, was the same as the look she'd had back then standing over my grave. And I was afraid of that look, that not-only-did-I-not-get-what-I-wanted-for-my-birthday-but-the-gifts-that-I-did-get-prove-no-one-really-understands-me-at-all look—full of hurt and disappointment and . . . fear.

I did not want to know. Call me King Avoidance. I have a sixth sense for things I don't want to know and her manner pegged this as top of the scale ignorance-is-bliss material. Her confession or revelation or whatever was best left unsaid, best taken into the grave and left there. All the bad ones are.

No one wants to hear that you never really loved them, that it was you who ran over their pet dog, that you forgot to pull out, or that you actually did nail your secretary that one time in New York when you claimed you were in separate rooms.

You've got to understand . . . being blown up was not the most traumatic thing that has happened to me lately. When it turned out Roger was behind all the attempts on my unlife, the one who set me up to fight the werewolves, the one who tried to spike my blood supply . . . I hadn't wanted to know that, either, would have given almost anything to change things so that he'd been smart enough to cover it all up without my ever knowing. That way I'd still have been able to think he was my friend. I'd have preferred the lie.

Marilyn's eyes told me I'd prefer a lie in her case, too. Any secret that had stayed buried that long didn't need exhuming. She opened her mouth to tell me, but I couldn't let her finish that sentence. I wasn't ready for her to move on, so I kissed her.

She kissed me back—not a passionate kiss, but the tender intimacy of two people who have grown old together and accepted the best and the worst in each other.

It might have been more romantic if that fat policeman hadn't stepped through us. A bed would have been nice, too. If we could touch, I was pretty sure we could do other things. For forty years I had craved her touch. To make love one last time would have been a kindness, but it didn't happen.

She ended the kiss and there was no second one.

Marilyn took my hand and led me over to a bench in the little glassed-in bus stop where my bouncers would leave guys who'd had one too many. "I missed you so much," I told her.

"I've been with you for half a century, Eric." She scowled.

"You know what I mean," I said sheepishly. I gestured to her body. "Not like this, not in the same way."

Her expression softened. "That ought to make me angry, but it doesn't. I always find it hard to be mad at you for long."

"Brain damage," I responded.

She almost laughed. It literally rose and fell dead in her throat. The laughter couldn't escape whatever was bothering her.

"Don't joke," she said sharply. "Don't be so much like your old self. It makes everything too hard."

"Good. Let it be too hard," I said briskly, rushing through the words, running them together. "If not telling me will keep you here with me, then don't tell me. I'd rather not know."

"You really need to know this, Eric. I'm sorry." She looked at me, expecting a response.

"No, you aren't," I told her. "You don't have to say anything, but if your mind's made up . . . I've never been able to unmake it."

"Do you remember what happened when you died?" she asked.

"I was driving Roger's car, the brakes went out, blah, blah, blah. What are you going to tell me, that you sabotaged the brakes because you didn't want to marry me?"

"Roger did," she spat out quickly.

I froze. If I'd been in a cartoon, the angel on my shoulder that represented my good nature would have just been gut shot by the devil representing my bad side.

"He wanted me to marry him," she continued. "Roger and I had been seeing each other for months, and I didn't know how to tell you—"

I got up and walked off toward the Pollux, leaving Marilyn still sitting on the bus stop bench. Two of the firemen pointed at the enclosure. Its rear window froze and shattered as I passed through it. I didn't know why it happened. I assumed it was part of whatever ghost powers I'd wound up with, but I didn't give a damn, not then.

"Eric," she called after me. "Wait! You need to hear this."

"Actually, I don't." My voice was calm, but I wasn't. "I was murdered by my best friend *and* my fiancée?" I scoffed. "Nope, didn't need to know that. What, then he got attacked by a vampire and voilà, sucks to be you?"

"No, Eric." She chased after me. I stopped just shy of the middle of the road, didn't turn to face her. "It wasn't like that. I had nothing to do with it. When they called me and told me you were dead . . . I called Roger and he already knew. I went over to his house and he told me what he had done to you and then he showed me what he had let someone do to him."

"He'd become a vampire," I said flatly.

"He said that it had happened three weeks earlier when he'd driven over to Chicago for that conference. He'd met a woman from Atlanta . . . a woman named Gabriella . . ."

"A woman who was really a vampire, and then she turned him." I shook my head, rounding slowly toward Marilyn. "Well, that's just so fucking cute I could puke."

I felt a little tremor of rage, and when I did, I had a brief glimpse of Carl's garage, of my Mustang. I loved that car, an artifact from my living days, a 1964 ½ convertible. I'd wrecked it three days before, but Carl was doing a great job on the repairs. Why I saw it in my mind then, I couldn't say. It was weird.

"I told him to get away from me." Marilyn touched my shoulder, then pulled away as if she'd been stung. "I ran from the house, but he caught me. . . . He pushed himself inside my mind and touched my thoughts. He left something there. He smeared blood on my skin, willed it into a tattoo, a little frog. He said that if I wouldn't join him willingly then I would be his human slave, his thrall."

Thrall. I had one of those. Rachel, my ex-girlfriend's little sister, had damn near forced me to make her my thrall during the whole werewolf brouhaha. But as Marilyn described the process, it sounded pretty familiar, except I hadn't given Rachel any kind of tattoo, blood or otherwise, and Rachel sure as hell wasn't my slave. As far as I knew, thralldom granted the mortal participant protection from other vampires, marked them as protected. It also widened a vampire's senses, allowing them to detect the thralls of other vampires while simultaneously allowing the vampire to sense the location of their vampiric offspring.

"Why didn't you say anything?" I demanded, turning back to face her.

"He wouldn't let me. When you rose and you were stronger than him, he wasn't sure what to do. He'd made me his thrall, and every time I tried to talk about it, the words just wouldn't come out. He'd specifically forbidden me to tell you."

I cursed aloud and saw another glimpse of my car. Ignoring the automotive strangeness, I grabbed the front of her jacket, the ghost leather creaking under my phantom fingers. "What the fuck good does this do me now? Did you tell me just to make yourself feel better? To drive me out of my freakin' mind so my crazy-ass ghost can haunt the Demon Heart?"

"He's been afraid of you for years, Eric, too afraid to kill you, and too afraid to really do anything to me when you were around."

"When I was around? What about when I wasn't around?" I yelled. "What then?"

"I think you already know the answer to that," she told me, resignation clear in her voice. And I guess she was right, at that.

"I'm so glad Willie and his werewolves ate that motherfucker," I ranted.

"That's why I had to tell you," she sobbed. Marilyn tried to put her arms around me, but all the love-struck puppy had gone out of me and I pushed her away. She kept her balance, but I couldn't look at her. "Good! Be mad at me, Eric, as angry as you want, but you have to hear this. You may think you know how devious Roger was, but he's worse. I can't believe I ever thought about leaving you for him! He had some kind of plan to steal your power, to become whatever it is that you are. You're not a normal Vlad. At first Roger didn't believe it, but all the things he did to you, they were part of a test, to convince him, to prove what you were . . . are."

I looked back at her and she wasn't crying. The cadence of her words was increasing, trying to beat the clock. She sounded as if her time was running out, the commercial was almost over and she had to get the rest of her message out before she returned to regularly scheduled programming. "Last night, when I was tied to the chair, I heard them say that you are the rarest of the rare, a king of kings, an emperor."

"Emperor?" I scoffed.

"It has something to do with why your eyes are still blue, why you never went through postmortem syndrome. She said it's like your transformation stopped just before it was finished, and in that gray area, not alive, not dead, and yet not entirely undead, there is a lot of power to be had." In retrospect I should have asked her who the "she" in that sentence was, but I was too caught up in thoughts of Marilyn and Roger to think very clearly.

"Well, la de fucking dah, Marilyn." I tossed up my hands. "What the hell good does that do me now?"

"Because Roger had a backup plan. I don't know what it was, but he was working with . . ." She clawed at her throat, eyes ablaze with terror. "Oh, God . . ." She coughed. "It's coming for me . . ." I tried to help, but my hand passed through her shoulder.

"Marilyn!"

Her mouth opened wide in a silent scream, and then it grabbed her. I didn't know what it was, at first, and then my memories of El Segundo washed over me in a wave. I'd never been on fire so many times in one weekend. El Segundo was where I'd met Talbot, and where I'd met my first demon. Being in the presence of a demon had never bothered me when I'd been a vampire. Now that I was a ghost, its presence burned.

Fear ripped through me, tore at my ectoplasmic brain with tiny meat hooks. A swirling cloud of Marilyn screeched through the air toward its open mouth, her ghostly essence both compressed and stretched, converting her into an unrecognizable blue smoke funnel—a hellish *I Dream of Jeannie* moment. But this was a demon, not a bottle, and that was Marilyn, not Barbara Eden. Where Marilyn had seemed clear and precise to my spirit eyes, the demon was an outline, a hole of blackness in the air. Marilyn, what was left of her, vanished into that void.

The presence turned its attention to me. "Do I know you, revenant?" it asked.

"Give her back!" I charged the demon, certain that I might get sucked into the same vortex, but not giving a damn. Fighting is one thing I'm never afraid of. My hands passed through the creature with no effect. Ghosts can't harm demons, I guessed.

The demon let loose with a series of loud whinnies combined with the sound of a machine crushing ice. It could have been laughter. "Her soul was promised to me, angry one. It is my due for services rendered."

"Let her go."

"I have a contract." The demon moved closer. Supernatural panic forced me to my knees like a two-ton bouncer. The power rolled over me, tried to pound me down onto my face, but I refused to go all the way down. A Mustang's engine roared to life somewhere far away. Beneath me frost formed on the asphalt.

Cops and firefighters screamed. I don't know if they saw me or the demon, but most of them ran. One of them was too close. His life called to me, not like blood, but warmth. The ground rushed up to meet him as his soul tore free and surged into me. The frost on the ground spiraled out from my phantom knees, crusting thickly on the man-made surface.

"Give her back!" Nourished by the firefighter's soul, I forced myself to my feet. His spirit coursed through me, the sensation not unlike the feeling of warmth and fullness I got when, as a vampire, I'd made a fresh kill. *Powers,* I thought to myself. *If I'm a ghost, then I have ghost powers, like freezing the window, breaking it. But will any of them kill a demon?*

"An arrangement might be reached," the demon purred. He sounded mildly impressed. If he was giving in, willing to deal, then it was likely I could hurt him. I just needed to figure out how. "An exchange," the demon continued. "You for her?"

"An old friend of mine warned me about deals like that," I growled. "He said that demons always cheat."

"No prevarication has ever taken place on my part, I assure you, but I do obey the letter of the agreement. It is true that many do not"—he paused—"think through contracts as carefully as they should.

"Marilyn made her deal. The agreement was reached under compulsion from her vampiric master, but the signature is hers. Her soul in exchange for an . . . intercession." The demon moved back, its edges bleeding into its surroundings. "I believe I have a viable substitute, however, and will be able to perform the ritual without using up Ms. Robinson's soul. I'll hang on to her for now, shall I? I hope we meet again, angry ghost. But having collected this lady's soul, I now have other duties to perform, including the intercession of which I spoke."

I lunged for him again, but when I crossed the white line in the middle of the road, I flew apart, my essence bursting into countless little particles of self, the world blurring even more than before. Everything went silent, then dark, until I re-formed, standing in the spot where the bomb had gone off. Nice! Not only was I a ghost, I was a ghost with a short leash.

2

TABITHA:

WATCHING IT HAPPEN

I was half a mile from the Highland Towers, suitcase in hand, when I heard the explosion. Two seconds later I felt Eric burning. He's my sire, the one who made me immortal. He was also the man I'd just dumped. When I walked away from him, I had expected him to chase me, but he hadn't, not yet, and now I didn't know if he'd ever have the chance. I'd walked out on him in the middle of a crisis, one I'd thought he could handle.

I was wrong.

Eric's scream cut through my head; the scent of charred flesh and smoke hit me hard, dropping me to my knees on the sidewalk. The suitcase fell from my hands and my scream matched Eric's. We shouted, not in pain, but in anguish. We shouted a name. It wasn't mine. It was hers. "Marilyn!"

Other vampires screamed the same name. A flash of contact linked us all for a single heartbeat and I saw them—Eric's other ex-girlfriends, the vampires he'd made and discarded, even Greta, his pretend daughter. The connection wavered, and my viewpoint withdrew, arcing up and back from the wrecked remains of the Demon Heart.

Nearby, I thought I saw my sister's face looking out of the doorway of the Pollux, but it wasn't her; it couldn't be. Rachel was dead. It had to be the witch, the one who looked like my sister. A small gold padlock hung from a choker around her neck, glittering in the firelight. She wore the same tight black hip-huggers and midriff top she'd been wearing when I ran into her at the Demon Heart, when she'd been with Roger. The red and blond highlights in her hair echoed the colors in the flames. She smirked and walked back inside the Pollux, removing a jade bracelet from her left wrist as she went, and the vision faded.

My sense of Eric was gone. He was dead. I closed my eyes and blinked back bloody tears.

"Damn it!" My voice was swallowed up by the empty street. Cars passed in the night. In Void City, you don't stop to check on people. You mind your own business, even if the damsel in distress is wearing a low-cut blue dress and filling it well. *I can still go to Phillip*, I told myself. *He'll know what to do.*

I didn't hear the car stop, but when the car door opened, the music snapped me out of it. Rob Zombie's voice rang out, singing strains of the chorus to "Living Dead Girl," and I laughed. When Rachel had died, I'd gorged on chocolate, but that option was lost to me now. The heartbeats of the men in the car hammered in my ears. I was angry, lost—my whole unlife plan had revolved around Eric, making him love me—no, making him realize that he loved me—and it was all gone. Ruined.

"Hey, lady. You okay?" Alcohol-tainted breath singed my nostrils even from ten feet away. I stood up, and there were catcalls. Four men, three in the car, and one on the sidewalk. The car smelled of blood and sweat and fear. A metallic tang mixed with gunpowder and I knew that at least one of them had a gun.

"We don't have time for this," the blond in the backseat muttered under his breath. A wedge of blond bangs hung down over his right eye. "We have what Mistress wants."

"Fuck you," snarled the driver. "We made a big score tonight. Might as well celebrate."

"Look at the tits on that bitch," whispered the other man in the backseat, next to the blond. "Are we going to—?"

"She's a vampire, you idiots," the blond muttered even more quietly, anger glinting in his eyes. "And she's a Queen, at that."

The man on the sidewalk wore a *Void City Howlers* jersey and jeans. He wiped his nose with one hand and stared at me with bloodshot eyes. "You need a ride, lady? We can give you one." He looked back at the car and stifled a laugh. "We can all bunch up."

"Do you have a gun?" I asked.

"Maybe." Mr. Bloodshot Eyes went still and serious.

"Want to get it out?"

He took a step back toward the car, as if he subconsciously sensed the danger. I came forward, stepping under the streetlight. When he saw the blood running from my eyes, the tears of a vampire, he took a breath. "Shit."

The blond stepped out of the car, gun drawn from a shoulder holster under his jacket. He aimed it at the driver. "Pop the trunk."

"What the hell are you doing, Esteban?" Esteban was gorgeous. He wore black slacks, a white dress shirt with an open collar, and a black suit coat. The way he moved made it clear he was used to custom-made suits. Esteban pulled the trigger without blinking, firing through the open window. The driver's brains exploded across the steering wheel.

Mr. Bloodshot Eyes spun on Esteban, drawing a gun from the back of his pants. It snagged in his jersey and I charged him. Vampire speed is one of the best parts of being undead. My fingernails extended into claws, a vague stinging in my fingertips as they grew. I flayed open Mr. Bloodshot's back and ran my tongue along the wound as he screamed. He fired the pistol in his hand reflexively and I sank my fangs into his throat, the brief painful tearing as my fangs pierced my gums completely erased by the sudden infusion of warm fresh blood in my mouth.

"Holy shit!" the man in the backseat screamed. He had olive skin and wore a ratty T-shirt. "Holy shit!" He glanced back and forth between me and Esteban as if he didn't know who to run from. There was a switchblade in his hand. Esteban rolled his eyes. I bent Mr. Bloodshot's neck at an angle so I could watch them both without taking my mouth from his throat.

"Esteban, what the hell are you doing, man?" None of the four men looked older than midtwenties, but the last one in the car looked youngest of all. "We went to school together, man."

"That's why I didn't kill you." Esteban opened the driver's-side door, reaching down to pop the trunk.

A yellow pickup passed by us in the other lane; the wind from its passing ruffled Esteban's hair and the headlights illuminated his dark-blue eyes. Another car swung wide around the stopped car, edging into the other lane.

Esteban reached into the trunk and pulled out a heavy leather satchel, then dropped it on the asphalt. It sounded like the bag was filled with chains or links of metal, but the sides of the bag squirmed as if the contents were alive. I dropped my snack's cooling corpse to the ground.

"What's in the bag?"

"The Infernal Chains of Sarno Rayus, Majesty." Esteban swapped the gun to his left hand. He slipped his right arm out of the suit coat, letting it hang loose as he swapped gun hands again before ripping the sleeve of his shirt at the seam to show me a rose tattoo. "I am Esteban, thrall to Lady Gabriella. I offer you my apology for interrupting your evening, the life of my companion, the vehicle, and its contents, excepting only the chains for which I was sent. In exchange, I ask only your leave to depart this area and deliver to my mistress that which she has requested."

Hunger gone, my fangs and claws retracted. I looked at the vehicle, the dead driver, and I didn't want anything to do with it or the would-be rapist inside. It wasn't that he'd done or said anything overtly threatening, but his scent, a mixture of arousal and aggression, gave him away.

"He was going to . . ." I hadn't even gotten all the words out when Esteban shot the man with the switchblade, the bullet shattering the rear window of the car. Esteban holstered his gun and slid his arm back into the jacket.

"Shit!" I blinked. "You went to school with that guy."

Esteban nodded. "And then his presence offended you, Highness."

"What are you again?"

"Thrall to the Lady Gabriella." He bowed once, looking up at me with a movie star's smile before he straightened. "May I have permission to approach?"

"Sure."

His eyes never left mine as he walked across the concrete. It was reassuring, and I realized that it was meant to be. Eye contact was all I needed to assault his mind and he knew it. Esteban bit his lip.

"Your makeup is running," he said, touching the blood on my cheek. He drew a small plastic pack of wet wipes out of his jacket pocket. "May I?"

"Yeah . . ."

Tenderly, as if I were a sacred object, Esteban wiped away my bloody tears. Using a second wipe, he cleaned the blood spatter from my chin, neck, the swell of my breast . . . all the while watching me closely for the slightest sign of displeasure.

"That's better." Esteban carefully folded the used wipes and put them in his pocket. "I do hope you won't hold any ill will toward Lady Gabriella?"

"No," I whispered.

"Then, if I may?" He gestured to the car and I nodded.

"Just make sure Gabriella takes care of any Fang Fees," I added belatedly. Fang Fees are the vampires' equivalent of parking tickets, but much more expensive. If the VCPD has to cover something up, they find out which supernatural citizen did the deed and submit a bill. Since I hadn't been a vampire for long, I'd yet to be billed for one, and I didn't want to start now.

"Of course."

I picked up my suitcase and looked past Esteban at the people he and I had slaughtered, then walked away, trying to ignore the nausea rising in my stomach. They weren't real people, I repeated in my head, they were just food. Just food. I almost believed myself.

In the distance I heard sirens. Half a block away I watched Esteban light a cigarette, the flash of the lighter revealing a mischievous smirk. Then he walked back to the car and shut the trunk. Seeing him there, standing amongst the bodies as if they weren't bothersome at all, he reminded me of Eric.

"Eric . . ." His name felt good on my lips, but the thought of him brought warmth to my eyes and the tears started again. Most vampires cry blood, but now that I'd fed, there was no blood in my tears, just water, saline . . . whatever tears are made of. That's part of my gift. Unlike all the other vampires I know, I can seem to be human; I can cry, breathe, and even eat. I haven't managed to actually taste anything yet, which makes the actual eating less cool, but I'm working on it.

Talbot tells me that it's not really life, but it feels real enough to me. When I turn it on full blast, I even show up in mirrors. It damps my other vampiric abilities—a lot—but it's worth it to be able to do my own makeup. I couldn't help but think how impressed Eric would have been if I'd simply shown him. *Eric, what am I going to do without you?*

3

ERIC:
BETTER OFF DEAD

The Demon Heart was a lonely place to be. It wasn't completely gone. During the fire, I'd been sure there'd be nothing left, but the central runway, though charred and smoking, still stood. Part of the bar lay on its side across the front sidewalk. I stared down at the twisted remains of the break room refrigerator, watching the mass of melted plasma bags mix with the blood that had once been contained therein. Decades of blood, breasts, and bad art design were gone. The surprise? I didn't really miss it. I couldn't bear looking at it, either, though, so I spent a lot of time watching the Pollux across the street, waiting for the cavalry.

Greta was still out at Orchard Lake, and it was unlikely that she could get back here until morning. Talbot would come waltzing back eventually. He always does. I thought of Tabitha. No . . . Tabitha wouldn't come back to me on her own. If I wanted her, I'd have to chase her. I still wasn't certain if I wanted to do that. Most of the time folks I care about are better off far away from me. I offer my recently blown up and soulnapped former fiancée as Exhibit Ow. Which left me with Rachel, my thrall. . . .

I had half an idea that she'd run off to find Talbot or get some other sort of help. Maybe one of her friends at the Irons Club, the local thrall hangout, knew something about putting explodicated vampires back together again. When the headlights pulled up, I'd convinced myself that it was her until I saw the Void City Department of Public Works logo on the side of the van.

In Void City, most humans don't know about the supernatural. I'm not sure how it all works, but I know there is an enchantment in place that keeps them from remembering all the spooky crap that goes on unless they're into the whole scene. The spell replaces the memory of actual events with mundane occurrences which can explain it all away. The magic isn't always very thorough in the way it creates the new memories, though, so a lot of us hire magicians to do touch-up work. I use a local guy named Magbidion. He's not a member of the guild because he got his powers by selling his soul. Apparently the high-born magical families frown on that sort of thing, so he's an outcast. It also means that he works cheaper than a guild mage and doesn't ask as many questions.

I also use Magbidion when my victims stick around after they die and try to haunt me. He moves them along, no fuss, no muss. The city can't use him, though; they have to pay guild rates. Half of the money taxpayers call graft and corruption is actually money that gets paid out to the guild. In exchange, the guild provides memory alteration service, ghost removal, and whatever else they do, at a reduced rate.

Ghost removal . . . I think not.

The van parked in front of the Demon Heart, and a portly looking goofball with brown hair and a disarming grin stepped out of the driver's side. He wore the same blue jumpsuit that the sanitation workers do. The name tag on his left breast pocket said *Melvin*. He tugged a portable two-way radio out of his right pocket and spoke into it.

"Big Top, this is Mother Goose. I see him. He's a mean mammer jammer, too. You should feel the noncorporeal manifestants he's putting out. Are you sure we want to contain him, not just send him to the great beyond?"

A male voice responded. "This is Alpha-One, Mother Goose. Big Top advises to continue with containment."

Melvin sighed. "Okay, but this is going to cost extra. He's a full-blown revenant."

"Is there a difference?"

"Is there a difference?" Melvin sounded as indignant as a Trekkie who'd just been asked if Spock is the one with the funny ears. "Revenants are an earthbound manifestation of anger and rage. They're capable of class five contact with the natural world: drastic temperature alteration, applied telekinetics . . . These bad boys can suck the soul right out of you. A ghost is just spam mail compared to one of these guys!"

"Just capture it!" shouted Alpha-One.

I floated over to Melvin, and the windows on his van fogged up. "Can my code name be Yosemite Sam?"

He jogged around the van and stood on the other side of the white line in the middle of the road, still talking on the two-way. "I sense a secondary presence as well. Nobody said anything about two. Guild regulations require one mage per ghost present."

"If you were doing this on the books then you could whine to the guild about it, but you aren't. Just capture the damn thing and get it back here!"

Melvin pulled a picture out of his breast pocket and gave it the once-over. He showed me the picture. It was me, Roger, and Marilyn standing in front of my classic Mustang convertible, back when we'd all been alive. My face had been circled with a black Sharpie. "Nice car," Melvin said. "Do you still have it? My uncle had an old '67 Mustang. What kind of mileage do you get on her?"

I let it distract me. His fingers danced in tortuous knots. Words that hummed like wasps in my head cut through me. Never underestimate a mage. A lambent purple coffin-size box snapped shut with me inside. Numbness flowed up my ghostly extremities where I braced against the sides of the glowing prison.

He shouldn't have underestimated me, either. "You ain't dealing with the Stay Puft Marshmallow Man here, you Dan Aykroyd–looking motherfucker!" The cage held for about three minutes, with me pounding on it as hard as I could. I treated it like a workout, punching it over and over again, locking in on the wall of the box closest to Melvin, focusing my rage.

I smelled the sickly sweet mixture of cigarettes and machine oil from Carl's garage. The lights in the garage were turned off; the only illumination came from the high beams on my car. For three seconds I could see the interior as clearly as if I'd been sitting at the wheel. Then multicolored shards of energy flew in all directions as the walls surrounding me gave way.

My vision cleared. Melvin picked himself up off the ground and grabbed his radio. "Alpha-One, this is Mother Goose." His voice contained equal parts excitement and respect, but he wasn't afraid. "Nope! Can't contain him. He tore through Hamnard's Holding Cell like he was opening the fridge to grab a beer. You'll have to pay for a high-end soul prison if you want to snare this bad boy."

"For Christ sake!" Alpha-One sounded irritated. "I thought you were the big man on campus when it comes to ghost crap."

"Tell him to come down here himself if he doesn't like it," I snarled. Tendrils of ice raced along the pavement from my feet to the vehicle. Frost formed on the public-works van.

"Did you copy that, Alpha-One?" Melvin asked. "Subject suggests you come down in person."

"My ass," the radio crackled. "How much for the soul prison?"

Melvin frowned, working it out in his head. "Well, you'd have to call Jimmy over at the local and get official clearance. I can't just do something like that freelance. There's no way I could slip magic of that caliber under the radar with Sheila on monitor duty. If you want to do it next month, when McGibbons is up on the rotation—"

"Forget it," the voice snapped angrily. "Just get the hell out of there. We'll pay you for the site visit, but that's it."

"Not what we agreed on, but okay. Sounds fair to me." Melvin put the radio back into the pocket of his jumpsuit and looked directly at me. His smile was open, honest and indescribably childlike. "I'm done. Would it be okay if I got back into my van now?"

I stepped back, and he climbed in through the passenger's side. The driver's door was frozen shut. He cranked the van and rolled down the window. "I gotta tell ya. I've never seen anything like that before. You had to be approaching a class six physical interaction there when you laid the smackdown on my containment spell. Very impressive. You're the most powerful revenant I've ever seen . . . in fact, I'm not even sure that's all you are."

"Thanks," I said in confusion.

"When they come at you next, they'll try the soul prison route, but I can guarantee you they'll get nonguild labor to put it together. It'll look like a big cat's-eye marble—more than one, maybe. They're wicked powerful, but they'll shatter like glass if you hit them with a rock." He gave me a thumbs-up. "Good luck."

I watched him drive away. Melvin seemed like a good guy. I made a mental note to look him up if I ever got my body back and my own mage wasn't available. He might frown on the whole vampire thing, but aside from the supernatural powers angle, I was betting Melvin wouldn't see much difference in working for a bloodsucking undead monster than for a politician.

Melvin stopped at the street corner and began cordoning off the area. Normal people would see the sign he was putting out as whichever public warning sign they were most likely to heed: *Road Closed, Police Line—Do Not Cross*, or whatever. He blocked off one end of the street, drove back by, and finished up on the other side before speeding off into the night, leaving me alone again.

Or was I? What was it Melvin had said about a secondary presence?

"Hello?" I called out tentatively toward the Pollux. The response was immediate and it came from behind me.

"If you're done fornicatin', consortin' with demons, and chewin' the fat with the locals, son, I'd like a word." The country drawl reminded me of my granddad, a syrupy cocktail of John Wayne and Clint East-wood. Sparkling in the rising sun, a single-action Colt revolver lay beneath the remains of the Demon Heart's runway.

The gun caught my eye when I turned toward the sound. Gun smoke rose from the barrel as I recognized *El Alma Perdida*. In English, the gun's name translates as "The Lost Soul." It had been used by one of my ancestors, John Paul Courtney, in some crazy crusade against werewolves. I'd been shot with it the night before and it'd been stuffed down the back of my pants when I'd blown up.

Manifesting in the smoke like a cowboy stepping through the hazy dawn, a man with my blue eyes and a face a lot like my dad's puffed on the stub of a spectral cigar. Red mud caked his boots and pants, running halfway up his thighs. The buckle of his gun belt displayed a cross. He took a drag on the cigar, smoke billowing out through a multitude of bullet wounds in his upper torso, curling back in as he blew the smoke out through his nostrils. Old blood had turned the red-and-white checkered shirt he wore to a uniform shade of brown, the pattern only emerging at his shoulders.

I guessed this was the ghost of John Paul Courtney, the gun's origi-nal owner. His brown leather duster flapped in an unseen breeze. His head lolled from side to side as he walked toward me, like his neck had been broken. He steadied his head with both hands, snapping it into place with a sickening crack, and took another long draw off of the cigar. The end flared brightly, but the cigar didn't burn down, stuck forever with an eternal puff or two left in it.

"Great, it's the Ghost of Fuck-Ups Past," I said. I wondered if that made me the Ghost of Fuck-Ups Present or the Ghost of Fuck-Ups Yet to Come. The way the morning was going, it could have been either or both.

"Figures you'd talk like some no-account heathen." He ran "no" and "account" together like it was just one word and the way he said "heathen" included an "r" near the end that wasn't supposed to be there. In short, he sounded like I might've if Mom hadn't been from Michigan.

"If I'm a ghost, do I have to have a bad Southern accent, too?" The ghost of John Paul Courtney didn't respond to my question.

Just what I needed, a stick-in-the-mud ghost of some ancestor I didn't give a shit about. Another person might have wanted to ask him questions or hoped he was there to help, but I don't think that way.

"What do you want?" I asked.

"I want Judgement Day to come so I can change my shirt." He stopped a half step too close to me, nearly nose to nose, or rather, nose to lip since he had a couple of inches on me. "I want to see Jesus and find out if I done enough good to keep myself outta Hell, boy."

"Fine." All I wanted was my thrall to come back and fix things, but did I get that? No. I got Hillbilly Roy the Gospel Cowboy. *Where the hell are you, Rachel?* I thought. I closed my eyes. Since Rachel was my thrall, I was supposed to be able to feel her presence if I concentrated, but I couldn't. Whether that was due to a lack of concentration or because I was a damn ghost was anybody's guess. I wanted to know why Rachel wasn't out here doing her job. She knew more about vampire mystic bullshit than I did. Maybe she could get me out of this. I hoped that she hadn't taken off after the explosion. I opened my eyes again and the cowboy was still there. "You wait over on your side of the burned-out strip club and I'll wait on mine," I told J. P.

"I can help you, not that you deserve it." His cigar bounced up and down with the motion of his lips.

"You can help me get my body back? You know that it blew up, right?"

"Your body? This ain't about your body, son. This is about your soul, about your destiny."

"I'd rather have a body, thanks." I tried to re-form myself, rematerialize, coalesce, whatever you want to call it. I reasoned, if I tried hard enough . . . Nothing. I glimpsed my car again and stopped pushing. I didn't need my car; I needed my frickin' body back. "Damn!" I cut my eyes over to the ghost. "Are you in it?"

"Am I in what?" He drew back and cocked his head to one side; something gave, and his head fell over, cheek flush with his shoulder.

"This destiny of mine that you're talking about."

He straightened his head again, forcing it back into position. "I am."

"Then, no offense, but fuck that. I'm not going through the rest of eternity with a cowboy bobblehead bitching and moaning at me about Jesus." If Rachel didn't show up, I knew Greta would come resurrect my happy ass. She's my daughter, vampirically speaking, but it's more than that. To her, I'm Daddy with a capital *D*.

His laughter came from all directions, surrounding me, disorienting. "Suit yourself. You've got the Courtney temper, boy, yes sirree. Like a young stallion with a brood mare's scent in his nostrils. You'll get that pounded out of you soon enough."

"What the hell are you talking about?" I stepped closer.

"Oh, no!" He shied me away with his hat. "You git on, young buck. You need time to simmer down." Smoke curled up from his chest, obscuring his expression. He cleared it with a wave of his hat. "I was just like you in my day, boy. I mean it. Just like you."

Really? He was a screwed-up vampire who got reamed by his best friend, framed for murder, and blown up over a lame-ass real estate deal? 'Cause that's what happened to me yesterday and I doubted he could say the same. "Just tell me what you were going to tell me." I sighed.

"Go ask your demon friend or that fat magician for answers." He spat the cigar out of his mouth. It vanished when it struck the ground, coming apart like smoke. "Just like me," he said. "You'll go to Hell and back before you'll be of any use."

I waited for him to swirl back down into *El Alma Perdida*, like a genie in a bottle. Instead, he flashed, burning brightly with an inner light, and then he was gone.

4

TABITHA:

IN THE PRESENCE OF EVIL

I sobbed, fumbling with my crystal glass as I sat in Phillip's suite at the Highland Towers. Blood wine sloshed up the side. A human wouldn't have noticed, but as the wine ran down the side of the glass, it moved more slowly than real wine would have. A thin residue clung to the surface for a fraction of a second until something, maybe magic, maybe gravity, pulled it down.

"I . . . I'm sorry." I cursed myself for crying, but I knew Phillip didn't mind. Phillip's an old vampire, or so he says. He feels younger when I sense him, but he says that's because he's used magic to make himself more powerful over the years and since he basically rules Void City, I believe him. He probably thought my crying real tears was sexy, miraculous, interesting—any number of things. Once you've been a vampire as long as Phillip has, anything different is good. I'm different.

I reached to put my glass down on a little half-moon table, but missed the edge. The long tapered crystal tumbled and I froze, unable to react with sufficient speed. My vampiric abilities don't work well when I'm seeming human and I had turned my abilities all the way on (heartbeat, body heat . . . the works) to impress Phillip. He righted the glass as it toppled, moved it closer to the center of the little table, and returned to his chair so quickly that I barely saw a blur.

"I just didn't know what to do . . . where to go . . . so I came here, because . . ."

He didn't smile. I was so thankful that he didn't smile. I don't know why, but if I had looked at him and seen happiness, I think I would have exploded, or died, or shattered . . . something. He patted my hand and crossed the room to stoke a small fire. His small wood-burning stove was putting out a lot of heat. I didn't remember having seen it before.

"Tell me everything," Phillip commanded gently.

"Eric died," I whined. My voice was high-pitched and sobbing. I hated myself for it. Trying to stop just made it worse. "I broke up with him out at Orchard Lake . . . He went there because the werewolves were trying to kill him and he wanted it to stop, but they seemed so much like normal people . . . there were teenagers and little kids and old ladies. One of them looked like my grandma. I couldn't deal with it. I told him that there had to be another way, but . . ."

"But he disagreed." Phillip touched my hand, his fingers warm and comforting, his cheeks rosy, like he'd just fed.

"Yes, and then I told him that I hated him." I smiled weakly at Phillip, fighting back the tears. Phillip was being so sweet to me. He leaned forward and I got a glimpse past him at the last person who'd made Phillip really angry. His name is Percy. Phillip keeps him, staked and immobilized, but conscious, in a glass display case at the center of his living room. There is a plaque underneath that I'd read before: *My dear Percy, who serves as a remembrance to all that I do not bluff, I do not make empty threats, and there are indeed worse fates than death.*

Wiping the tears from my eyes, I picked up the glass, staring down into it before drinking. In the sparkle of blood wine, I could see the Demon Heart, my ex's strip club, burning to the ground. I hadn't mentioned that part yet.

"Anyway, I . . ." I could have saved Eric, come to his rescue, and instead I ran off to the Highland Towers to make a point, to make him chase me? I didn't think Lord Phillip would appreciate being chosen as a convenient jealousy device.

"I don't know why I even came here, it's just that you're the only other vampire I know and I thought you wouldn't mind."

"You were right to come here," Phillip crooned. He leaned in closer, the firelight glinting in his pale colorless eyes. In another frame of mind that predatory look might have frightened me, but I didn't give it much thought. "But what, if you don't mind my asking, makes you think Eric has been ended?"

"I felt him burning."

Something about my glass must have bugged him, because he stalked purposefully over to the table, grabbed the glass, and pitched it toward the woodstove, following it quickly with his own. The metal door on the stove opened all on its own, accepting each glass like a hungry pet gobbling down treats.

"I'm tired of the 1301," Phillip explained, "aren't you?" He looked at the bottle and hurled it into the stove. "It said 'Catherine' on the label." He shrugged. "I don't even recall a . . ." Lit with inner mischief, Phillip's eyes widened in recognition. "Oh, yes, now I remember." Looking back at the stove, he smiled. "Fitting end, I suppose."

I nodded noncommittally and wondered what would happen when Phillip lost his fascination with someone. Would a guest be so quickly discarded? Would I? He flipped through a small ledger, his wine list, he called it, and I felt a sudden chill. Not seeing what he wanted, he dropped the wine list onto his chair and, laughing, clasped his hands together. That same impish light seemed to shine behind his eyes as he walked toward me. "Should we be naughty?" he asked.

"In what way?" Phillip scared me when he asked questions like that. His ceaseless good humor and his generosity were treacherous. With him, all of the terrible things seemed distant and avoidable. The past became fuzzy and unimportant, like a movie so bad you could only like it if you watched it with a friend. He muted everything else, overwhelming it with his own presence. For a short, bald, fat man, he managed the Dracula vibe effortlessly.

"We could play the game . . . No, no, we've no time for that now . . . I had almost forgotten." He returned to his chair. "You were telling me about Eric, about feeling him burn. Tell me exactly what happened."

"I was on my way here. The car had broken down and I was walking down the sidewalk when I felt him . . . Eric . . . die. He burned. I can't explain it any other way."

"Fire, you say?" Phillip chuckled in a nasty sort of way. "Burning unto destruction? No. No. No, my dear." He touched my hand. It was so reassuring, I wondered if I ought to sleep with him, you know, out of gratitude, which sounds twisted, but it's how he was making me feel.

"But I felt him die."

Phillip giggled. "Did you?" He stood up. "Well, then, I suppose you had best be on your way, hadn't you?"

"On my way?"

"Back to the Demon Heart," he explained. "That's where I would start."

"Start?" I asked in confusion.

He pulled me to my feet. "Start looking, my beautiful, wondrous, precious creature. Looking. If I know our good little maniac Roger, I assure you that he has no true understanding of the game in which he's become entangled. Even if he does, I can without fear of error tell you that he does not know how to kill the one you love, your sire, the oft-enraged Eric of Void City."

My heart beat twice in my chest. "Eric's alive?"

"Insomuch as a vampire lives, yes, yes. *Vivat imperator* and so forth."

He danced in a circle as he talked, his excitement mirroring my sense of relief. I almost forgot how mad I'd been at Eric.

"That's . . . I mean. Are you . . . Would you tell me how you know?"

"I was quite the mage in my day, you know—alchemical experiments, terrible firestorms, creating new life . . . It was all immeasurably childish, I assure you, but I remember it fondly," Phillip said, sounding pleased with himself. "To see the modern magi of today still puttering about with the same problems I solved in my youth . . ." He clucked his tongue disapprovingly. "Ah, well . . . *dum spiro, spero*, eh? Not that I do, of course, but the sentiment is the same. Surely they'll learn their collective lessons in the end. We all do."

"Huh?"

Phillip's smiled broadened until I was afraid his face might tear at the corners. "Let's call it wizard's intuition. I know of Roger and I am aware of his methods. To burn a vampire in the vampire's own lair is exactly the sort of melodrama that a neophyte like Roger would devise. If I know your sire as well as I ought to know him, I find it hard to believe that mere burning could destroy him for very long. Oh, I'm sure there's something that would destroy him, there's always something, but not fire, not even magical fire. I am an expert on killing other vampires, my dear, and death by burning is far too mundane for your sire."

He scoffed. "You yourself would likely survive a mundane fire. All you would require is blood. Or time."

"What about Eric?" I asked.

"Blood or time," he repeated. "Either will do, but blood is much more expedient."

The wall phone buzzed and Phillip answered it. It was Dennis, the current leader in Phillip's personal game of *Who Wants To Be a Vampire Millionaire.*

"On the other matter, milord," Dennis said warily. "I have done as you requested." Vampires and their servants learn to be very circumspect on the phone. One of the benefits of enhanced vampire senses is that when a vampire can hear one side of the conversation, they can usually hear the other, too.

"Very good, Dennis," Phillip replied. "I've one more favor to ask for the moment; do you have time?"

"I am always at your service, milord."

"Round up one of those little sprayers—like the exterminators use. Clean it out and fill it with a few bottles of whatever I have . . . the 1250s if you want; I'm bored with the whole decade."

He continued giving instructions and I continued to listen, but in the back of my mind something was bothering me. Phillip had said *as well as I ought to know him* when he referred to Eric, but the first time we'd met, he had acted as if he didn't know who Eric was. Why had he done that? So he knew about Eric . . . But why the lie?

"Give it to Lady Tabitha when it is prepared and then drive her out to the Demon Heart, or, rather, the remains thereof," he continued. "She needs to revive her sire and I want to be sure she doesn't spend all night trying to figure out which pile of ashes is his."

"Within the hour, milord," Dennis replied.

"What if I don't want to revive him?" I asked softly.

"Not revive him?" Phillip arched an eyebrow.

"If he's going to be okay . . . I mean, if he's not 'dead' dead . . . then I'm still mad at him."

Phillip encircled my waist with his arm. "I knew you'd be interesting the instant I first sensed you." His eyes sparkled with delight. "Why don't you stay here at the Towers?"

5

TABITHA:

LAP OF LUXURY

Talbot stopped by a week after Eric blew up. I'd wondered how long it would be before one of Eric's little resurrection squad came to check on me. He was dressed, as always, in a smart black suit and a tie that matched the warm rich brown of his eyes. I wanted to reach out and run my hands along the dark skin of his cheek, but he didn't seem to be in the mood.

"I haven't seen you down at the Demon Heart," he said, stepping through as I opened the door.

"Hello to you, too." They were all on Eric's side. The whole group of them, probably . . . all his former employees and friends running around, trying different spells, and spraying blood everywhere . . . It wasn't working. I couldn't bring myself to care why, yet even Phillip continued to ask about Eric.

Why did it matter how long it took him to re-form? He gets so much more waking time than the rest of us, me in particular. Eric is a corpse for a few hours a night, four at the most. Me, I'm dead from an hour before dawn until an hour after sunset. Let him feel what it's like to know that people are running around enjoying immortality while he's stuck, for a change. Even if he lost a whole year, it would serve him right.

I watched Talbot take in our surroundings. The Gryphon Suite had belonged to Roger, but Lord Phillip said that it now belonged to me. Nobody was going to argue with Void City's vampire overlord even if Roger did manage to find his way back from Hell.

"I've redecorated since you were here last," I said, gesturing at the room in general. "What do you think?"

Talbot's eyes took in the decor with a casual flick from side to side. I was proud of it. I knew I wouldn't miss a scrap of the extremely retro office furniture I'd had removed along with Roger's late girlfriend Froggy's awful choice of bedding, an obviously secondhand smoke-scented sofa, and all the rest of Roger's stuff. A week's worth of shopping with Lord Phillip's credit card had given the suite a little long-overdue pizzazz. Dennis promised that an interior designer was coming soon to redo the exterior waiting room. If I was going to be receiving guests, I couldn't very well have them staring at Roger's severe lack of decorating flair.

"I don't think Eric's going to like it," he said brusquely, "but it's very—you."

"Why does everyone care what Eric thinks?" I slammed the door too hard and flinched when one of my decorative plates fell off the wall. Talbot caught it smoothly with his usual catlike reflexes and hung it back in place.

"I'm uncertain what you mean by everyone, but you have a vested interest in making sure that you're on good terms with him if you plan on living in Void City."

"And why is that?" I asked, crossing my arms under my breasts to better show my assets. Since I hadn't been expecting company, I was only wearing a pair of shorts and a tank top. Being undead meant that I no longer needed a bra for support. A vampire's skin and muscles tighten after death, leaving us looking thinner and more toned than we did in life. As big as I am up top, it still does the trick, so for me bras are strictly a "for effect" clothing option. Talbot was normally immune to this type of flirting, but I knew I was an exception to the rule.

"Don't flirt with me unless you mean it," he snarled, eyes glowing green. I'd seen them go slit-pupil and feline, but I'd never seen them glow before. I took it as a sign that I still revved his engine. "Or you might find yourself engaged in the act against your will."

"Maybe that's what I want," I told him. "Maybe I miss you."

"Maybe." He winked. "I think it more likely that you've found out firsthand what a freak Lord Phillip is between the sheets and you don't like it. Has he tried to share you yet?"

"No," I lied. I think Talbot could tell, though. I'd only slept with Phillip once and it had been a mistake. Sex with him was an exercise in the pain-pleasure threshold. He was always biting, pinching, or prodding things that didn't need or want it. It worked out for both of us, because regardless of his deficiencies, he's good with his tongue, but his suggestion for the next night had involved more partners than I was comfortable with. I mean, I'm not a fucking power strip! Since then I'd gone out with him a few times, but other than a little heavy petting, I'd cut him off.

Talbot closed the gap between us, taking up my personal space. "He will."

"Stop," I whispered.

He slipped his arms around me. "Or maybe corpulent little sadists are your thing?"

"What does 'corpulent' mean?"

His fingers slid over my butt, just below the butterfly tattoo, his claws catching slightly against the fabric of my shorts. He brushed my ear with his lips as he answered. "Fat."

"Oh."

"Aren't you going to tell me to stop again?"

"No." I pouted at him. "I need you; I want you. Take me now." My delivery was less deadpan than I'd meant it to be, but he wilted anyway, pulling away from me.

"Fine. Now you are being a tease." He sighed.

"We can do that in a minute," I told him. His fangs came out in his smile when I said that. "First, you should tell me what you came here to tell me."

He sat on the edge of my new daybed and fiddled with the lace coverlet. "I've gotten calls from three of Eric's other children, all on the outs with him. They each called to see if they needed to come back and help."

"So?"

He began taking off his tie. Talbot is built like a bull, all muscled and firm. He caught me watching and bared his fangs. He's not a vampire and he's not a lycanthrope, but I don't know what he actually is. I do know that dominance games turn him on . . . and so do cats.

"He's tried to kill all of them in the past, but they know how this works. Even though they escaped him and even though they'd rather do anything than come to his aid, they know that if he gets pissed about their not helping, then when he does re-form he might take out his frustrations on them."

"Oh, please, what's he going to do? Kill me?"

"Probably not." Talbot strung the tie on the side of the daybed. "But he might take this away from you."

"This? What do you mean?"

"This place. It's yours, right?"

"Yes."

"Then, as your sire, it is also his. Anything you have is his if he wants to claim it. Technically, so are you."

He slid off his jacket and hung it on the bed knob.

"I am not!" I shouted.

"Technically, you are." He unbuttoned the first button on his dress shirt. I wasn't paying much attention, so he stopped. "What?"

"I'm not property."

"You are until you become strong enough to prove you're not."

"Phillip could protect me." I tried to bite it back, but the response was out and there was nothing I could do but stick with it.

"I'm sure he could," Talbot laughed, "and if *One Hundred and Twenty Days of Sodom* is your idea of a good time, then go right ahead."

"One hundred and twenty days of Saddam?" I asked.

"It's a book by the Marquis de Sade; you wouldn't like it. Your horizons are broad, but not that broad."

"You don't know me." I looked away.

"Have you ever met Lady Gabriella?" He ran one claw along the bedsheets.

"I've sensed her. She's got a really cute thrall named Esteban . . . and I know she doesn't get along with Phillip very well."

"Do you know why?" Talbot asked. "Phillip seduced her while she was still a virgin, but not before he turned her."

"So you mean?"

"For her, every time is like the first time." Talbot picked up his jacket and slid it back on.

"That's sick." I winced thinking about it. I thought back to Esteban's manicured nails and the tender way he'd wiped the blood from my skin. No wonder he's so gentle with vampires. "Why would Phillip do that?"

Talbot smiled, showing too much of his teeth. "According to Esteban, Phillip told Gabriella that it would make her his eternal love, always fresh, always new, his immortal virgin, but really, he did it because he was curious and because he knew that in time it would deepen her hatred of him."

"You're lying." He went to put his tie back on, but I stopped him with a touch.

"What?" he asked. "That turned you on?"

"No." I ran my hands across his shoulders, dug into him with my claws. "You turned me on. The story just made me not want to be alone."

6

TABITHA:

THE CAT CAME BACK

I deserved a night on the town. I'd been cooped up in the Highland Towers for over a week. Talbot had kept me from being too lonely, but he wasn't around every night. When he did show up, I'd smell the smoke and ash of the Demon Heart clinging to his skin. Tonight, I was dressed up and waiting for him.

He opened the door and stopped, his eyes raking my body. I'd broken out my little black dress, a tight slinky number with a plunging back that showed off the butterfly tattoo at the base of my spine. The front of the dress showed ample cleavage and if I shifted wrong (or right depending on your point of view), I knew he'd catch a flash of nipple. I'd cut my hair short and the new look surprised him. I waved a pair of six-inch heels at him.

"You're taking me out." I bent over, slipping on first one shoe, then the other, and his eyes stayed right where I wanted them.

"Tabitha," he started.

"If you want me, then we're going out." I slid my hand along his crotch and felt the rigid warmth of him.

Talbot bowed his head, giving in. *Easier than I thought.*

"I don't mind taking you out," Talbot said. He stepped closer, cupping my ass with his free hand. His musky wild scent, not quite human, not quite animal, filled my nostrils as he brushed his lips along my neck. "But it's a bad idea."

"Why?"

"Because I'm a mouser, and though the High Society vamps tolerate my kind, they are never pleased to see us mingle with vampires." His tongue darted along my jawline in a delicate lick, not wet and slobbery like a human tongue, but rough, warm, and grasping. I wanted to feel that touch lower down. My free hand found the back of his head and I pushed him lower without thinking or meaning to and he laughed— the low chuff of a predator.

"And to think you get mad if I do that." Talbot slid a claw across my back, not breaking the skin, tantalizing me. A slight scratch from Talbot would send curls of smoke wafting up from my skin. Done right, it felt erotic, more pleasure than pain, and Talbot always did it right.

"Let me taste you," I said, fangs extended. "Just a little bit."

"No." He shoved me away from him, one hand on my abdomen, and I stumbled, catching myself with the door.

"Why?"

"My blood isn't good for vampires."

"Why not?"

"I've told you before. My claws and fangs are sacred weapons." I rolled my eyes as he spoke. "It's true," he said, showing me his claws. "If I scratched you with these, really scratched you, not sensuous scratches, the wounds would burn. And my blood? The mingled essence of deities flows through my veins. If you took my blood internally . . . ?" He clucked his tongue.

"Ouch?" I wrinkled my nose at him.

"Ouch," he agreed.

"You're so full of yourself." I hit him playfully in the shoulder. He bit back a comment, but I saw it in his eyes. I didn't know exactly what he'd been going to say, but it had been vulgar and very male. "You better be glad you left that unsaid."

"Where do you want to go?"

"Somewhere I've never been . . . someplace high class with dinner and dancing."

"I know a place."

"A vampire place?"

"No," Talbot admitted.

"Then let's ask the concierge."

We took the elevator down to the lobby and I spotted Dennis by the front desk talking with Esteban. Dennis wore a standard suit and tie, while Esteban wore a tailored gray suit, open collared as it had been when I first met him. The shoulder holster was barely noticeable.

"Good evening, Lady Tabitha," Dennis greeted me with a polite incline of the head.

Esteban bowed low, eyes on mine as he moved, forever smiling. "Lady Bathory," he said using the more archaic address for a female Vlad. The satchel from our previous encounter was by Esteban's feet, near the desk behind which Dennis stood.

"Haven't you delivered that already?" I asked.

"My mistress wishes to have it delivered to the Lovett Building." He gestured to Dennis. "And Dennis was kind enough to call me a cab."

"You don't drive?" I asked.

"I'm not allowed to drive at the moment." He shrugged, but a look of genuine regret touched his features. "I was . . . insensitive."

He took the satchel and left when his taxi arrived. The bag jerked toward Talbot as Esteban passed, and Talbot raised an eyebrow in response to the metallic clinking within.

"Sorry about that, Talbot," Esteban called over his shoulder.

Talbot stared after him but didn't say anything.

"He actually said your name." Most people at the Highland Towers acted as if Talbot wasn't in the room and refused to speak directly to him.

"He's not a vampire yet," Talbot murmured. "It pays to be polite when you can't protect yourself." He slapped his hand down on the desk in front of Dennis with a loud slap. "How are you doing tonight, Dennis?"

"I'm doing quite well . . . Highness." Dennis choked on the word, but he got it out.

"Highness?" I asked.

Talbot offered no explanation and neither did Dennis.

"My date wants to go somewhere exclusive and fun." He leaned over the counter, nose to nose with Dennis. "I think she wants to pick a place that will cause a stir, create a scene . . . She wants to get noticed."

"But . . . Highness."

Talbot patted Dennis gently on the cheek. On the first pat, Talbot's hand was human, but with the second pat it transformed. A white glow washed along his skin leaving a covering of thick sable fur in its wake. Each digit on the altered hand terminated in a metallic silver claw.

"I'll make the reservations right away," Dennis stammered. "There is an exclusive engagement at the Iversonian club tonight. Lord Phillip was invited, but his sleep schedule is at its most erratic this evening, and it seems as if he might sleep straight through. I'm certain he wouldn't mind . . ."

"Sounds perfect." Talbot removed his hand from Dennis's cheek and I held it up to mine, rubbing the fur along my skin.

"It's so soft." I felt a warm tingle. "Does it . . . ?"

"Cover everything?" Talbot completed my question. "Yes, but I'm not sure you'd be up for the . . . full Talbot."

"Why not?"

"Mousers have a lot in common with domestic cats and cats require stimulation to ovulate," Talbot said carefully.

"Huh?"

"During sex, a female cat only produces eggs after the male cat withdraws and the . . . spines scratch the walls on the way out."

"Spines?" *Ow.*

"Barbs might be a better word."

"Barbs?" *Double ow.*

"I'll show you later," he promised as he led me to the car.

7

TABITHA:

LASTING IMPRESSIONS

Talbot drove us to Northside, past the trendy shops and the office buildings, into the portion of Void City with an average of one specialty coffee shop per block—occasionally two. We passed Jimmy Chew's where Eric had taken me to dinner for my last pre-vampire birthday.

I didn't need vampiric supersenses to tell that Talbot was stressed out. I just didn't know what was bothering him. His threat to Dennis had been out of character, but even after that, he'd opened up, given me info (even if it had been icky info) about being a mouser. That wasn't like him at all.

Spotlights cut through the night sky, highlighting the garish white walls of the Iversonian on the block ahead of us. Cars lined the street and their occupants weren't human, their heartbeats wrong or absent altogether.

I'd asked for exclusive. Talbot had delivered. He cut around the other cars, forcing his way into the front of the line. The valet didn't even want to let us park. He glared at the two of us through beady-black doll's eyes, gnashing his razor-sharp teeth, the blood-slick cap on his head leaking a tiny stream of wetness into his hair.

"You aren't Lord Phillip."

Talbot lashed out with his claws, leaving streaks of raw burnt flesh on the valet's face. Screaming, the valet fell away from the car.

"And you aren't getting a tip." Talbot had his seat belt undone and the car door cracked open before the valet could respond.

"Park where you want," the valet cried, crab-walking away from the car. "Park wherever you want."

Talbot slammed the door and peeled out into the parking lot. He kicked the Jag into a slide and came to a halt straddling two parking spaces. My door was opening, his hand on the handle before I could blink. Angry masculine scents poured off his skin and he pulled me to him, nuzzling my face with his like a cat.

"You want attention, right?"

"What's gotten into you?" I asked. "You could have maimed that . . . valet guy . . . thing."

"He's a redcap. They eat people." He sniffed me then shook his head. "You really want to make an impression?"

"I want excitement."

"If we go inside," he spun me around and began licking my hair, grooming me between words, "you'll get it."

"What's going on, Talbot?"

"You have to show fey who's boss up front," he said between licks, his voice deep and resonating.

"Stop." I pushed at him, but he tightened his grasp, forcing me against the car with his weight. I felt his teeth on my neck as he growled in my ear and grew. Light from his transformation washed over me and I was being straddled by a leonine beast with soft black fur. A low pounding drum beat against my back, the rhythm of his heart, and then he was off of me, diminishing.

"That should do it."

"What the hell, Talbot?" I whirled on him, claws out, but there was no need. He held out his hand to me, humanoid once more.

"You need to smell like me if I'm going to protect you." I took his hand as he spoke. "There are more than just vampires here."

"I'm a Vlad," I protested. "I can take care of myself."

"Vampires can be destroyed, Tabitha."

"What, and mousers can't?"

"We can, but it's harder to keep us that way. And anyone outright killing me would have to answer to my mother."

"Your mother?"

"You wouldn't know her."

"Talbot," I said plaintively.

"It won't mean anything to you anyway, Tabitha."

"Just tell me her name." I cupped his face and kissed him. "Please?"

"Sekhmet."

"That's an . . . interesting name."

Talbot chuffed. "It's Egyptian. You should hear my given name."

"It isn't Talbot?"

"No," he said patiently, "I just like *The Wolf Man*. C'mon."

We walked across the wide parking lot toward the club. Tiers of neon spelled out the name of the club in staggered wedges: IVER SON IAN descended from the roof, hanging like daggers over an open oval through which alternating bursts of red, green, yellow, and blue light pulsed, casting twisted shadows of the two suit-clad heavies manning the door against the white-layered facing.

"Unlike us, the owner of this club, Iver Richardson, is a true immortal. He can't be slain in the normal sense of the word. They call him 'The Iversonian,'" Talbot whispered in my ear.

"Why?"

We set foot on the sidewalk leading up to the main doors, and the concrete beneath us lit up, pinpoints of warm light marking the surface below our feet. A line wound around the building, but Talbot and I headed for the doors.

"It's a pun. He likes to collect things and the joke is that once something winds up in his collection, he never lets it go—like the Smithsonian."

"What sort of things does he collect?"

Talbot bared his fangs at the two doormen, flashing them our invitation. Up close, their knotted green skin was dry, but shiny like a snake's.

"What are they," I asked, "trolls?"

"As a matter of fact, they are," Talbot answered out of the side of his mouth. The trolls parted, displeasure clear on their gnarled faces.

The music hit us, a wave of bass, shaking my body as it thumped. Men and women, or rather, males and females of varying stripes, moved about the medieval decor, doing high energy versions of classic ballroom dances, but to a punishing techno beat. Creatures I didn't recognize flittered on gauzy wings about the old-fashioned candlelit chandeliers. A fully transformed werewolf with a disco ball hanging from his collar did a hyperfast waltz with a thin-limbed androgynous creature that shimmered, opaque one beat and translucent the next.

I sensed a Master vampire, newly risen and clad in leather bondage gear, having sex in the bathroom with something squat and toadlike—an image I could have done without—but the other vampires gave me no reading at all, meaning they were all Soldiers or lower.

My ears slowly adjusted to the volume of the music, but the scents hurt my sinuses. A bald man in a pinstripe suit, which looked like it had been custom made on Saville Row, cut through the crowd toward us. His overlarge eyes bulged under bushy brown eyebrows that reminded me of the wizard from "The Sorcerer's Apprentice" in *Fantasia*. He stood six foot nothing, and he was not smiling.

"You wanted to make an impression," Talbot reminded me, gesturing at the oncoming person. "Here's your chance."

"He looks angry."

"That's because we don't get along."

"Why?" Talbot's muscles tensed under my fingers.

"That's the Iversonian. He's always wanted to own me and he's always wanted to own a Living Doll."

"*What?*"

"That impression?" Talbot straightened his tie as the Iversonian closed with us. "You're about to make it."

"Talbot!" A crocodile grin flittered across the Iversonian's lips and stuck as if it were trapped there more by habit than a conscious effort. "How nice of you to come uninvited."

The Iversonian's hand jutted out in an offered handshake, which Talbot spurned. "This is Tabitha."

"And she is quite beautiful," the immortal replied, adding a brief bow (or maybe he was just staring down my top) before continuing, "but what makes you think you would be welcome with or without a lovely companion?"

"Two reasons." Talbot held up two fingers. "The first? She's Lord Phillip's newest . . . special friend . . . and she's here using the invitation that you sent to him. It allows a guest. I'm hers and therefore his."

"And the second reason?"

"She's an extremely rare type of vampire, a Living Doll, and I know how much you've always wanted to meet one."

"You wanted to flaunt her in front of me, is that it?" The Iversonian closed his eyes and the hair on the back of my neck stood up. An electric hum rose from his body, only discernable over the music because it was more a feeling than a sound. A short utilitarian sword coalesced in his hand as if the metal were being formed of smoke rising directly from his skin, held together by sparks of lightning.

"A gladius?" Talbot mocked. "Are we in a Ridley Scott movie now?"

"I am not in any sort of movie, Talbot. I haven't attacked you yet, I'm merely preparing to defend myself."

I touched Talbot's arm. "What's going on? I said I wanted to go somewhere for dinner and dancing."

"My bad," Talbot growled, upper and lower fangs extended. "I thought you said you wanted to go where there was dinner and dancing." He indicated the long wooden bar at the back with a toss of his head. The inhabitants ate dishes I didn't recognize, some of them odd colors and others just plain odd. "You can get both here."

"I will not attack first," the Iversonian interrupted.

"Wrong," Talbot spat. "We had a deal. You were to keep the Chains in your collection."

"I never said that." The Iversonian held his sword at the ready. "I only ever said that I wouldn't use them against you."

"Iver, do you honestly expect me to believe that you, Iver Richardson, the immortal who never gets rid of anything, sold the Infernal Chains of Sarno Rayus, a unique artifact for which, I might add, you spent centuries searching, because you didn't want them anymore?" Talbot leaned in close, his lips brushed the immortal's earlobe as he spoke. "Or is it more likely that you sold them because you wanted to get back at me for picking a new person?"

"I was good to you." The Iversonian blurted the words in a whispered rush.

"It's been eighty years, Iver," Talbot said, his eyes pitying the immortal. "You got clingy. You thought I was your pet. But I keep telling people, mousers don't have owners. We pick people who interest us and we hang out. That's it. No guarantees."

Have you ever had one of those moments at a party where you're speaking really loudly, close to shouting, so you can be heard over the noise, and then there's a sudden quiet and you embarrass yourself? That's what happened when I said, "Maybe we should go?"

The music died. Half of the dancers were confused, but the other half, the vampires and the fey, were staring at Talbot, the Iversonian, and me. A finger snap broke the silence and we were fighting.

Talbot seized the Iversonian's wrist, bones crunching as he squeezed. The gladius fell from the immortal's hand and Talbot caught it, impaling the immortal in one smooth motion. Metal flashed in the club's lights as the blade drove straight through Iver's sternum and broke the skin on the other side. He went down and Talbot kept pushing, pinning him to the dance floor, the hilt of the gladius protruding from the immortal's chest like the head of an eccentrically fashioned nail.

"Stay put," Talbot snarled at the downed immortal, then tossed me a savage grin. "Impression time!"

I kicked in the speed, but the fey were faster. Three elves, pointy-eared Orlando Bloom wannabes, with street clothes modded out to look like they'd been made by the costume designers from that movie about a magic ring, charged me, drawing swords from underneath their jackets like the guys in those immortal movies. They left long thin gashes in my shoulders and across my belly, whirling about me in overlapping circles.

More cuts appeared, but they were in the wrong places, not inflicted to do damage so much as to look bad, to hurt. They twinged when I moved, but it wasn't anything I couldn't handle.

Talbot had already gutted two Soldier-level vamps, dust trailing from his claws where he'd ripped out their hearts. "You've got to admit this is better than dinner and dancing."

"I do not. Ow!" One of the elves flayed my cheek with his blade and I caught his wrist with my claws, pulling him to me. He rammed the blade into my chest with a sound like ripping fabric. A stab of explosive pain flared and died in my chest as I tore out the swordsman's throat with my fangs. Mouth open in a silent scream, the elf went down as blood gushed from the wound. I expected the blood to taste different, but it was the same. I spat out the meaty flesh on the floor as one of his friends ran me through.

The one on the left drew his sword out, going for a decapitation, but I pulled the sword out of my chest and parried, forcing his blade into his fellow elf instead. It only worked because I was stronger than he expected and the whole pulling-the-sword-out-of-my-own-chest thing had really caught him off guard.

Quicker than all of us, popping from opponent to opponent like popcorn in an old-style popper, Talbot danced in and out of other fights, one moment rending a troll into flaming green chunks, the next hurling a wailing faun through the ceiling tiles overhead.

Once I orked the third elf, Talbot and I worked as a team. My wounds healed as we fought and by the time the last of the immortal's minions fell, I was sweating blood and glaring balefully at my escort.

"Dinner and dancing," I said.

He shrugged. "Maybe next time."

Noncombatants, human and nonhuman, fled the club as sirens blared. The VCPD rounded up the humans and took them down to the station to have their memories altered "just in case."

"I'd hate to see the size of the Fang Fee for this one," Talbot said.

"Sir?" One of the police officers came over, pad in hand. "Are you Talbot?"

He nodded.

"Then Captain Stacey says this is for you." The officer handed the ticket to Talbot. Crumpling the paper into a ball, Talbot walked over to the Iversonian, who was still stuck to the floor.

"If you pay half the Fang Fee," Talbot offered, "I'll pull the sword out."

8

ERIC:

FANG

Dawn rose over the ruins of the Demon Heart, casting everything into the brilliant light of day. It was the first dawn I'd been able to really watch for over forty years. The sun doesn't take kindly to vampires.

Even though my eyes were only spectral approximations, I was determined to enjoy it. In ghost vision, the sun twirled and danced as if rendered by an invisible painter constantly forced to repaint it in oils of yellow, orange, and burnt umber as it moved across the sky.

Each change was distinct, unique, a succession of masterpieces, each surviving for less than an instant. I'm not a big painting guy, but the scene mesmerized me. The sun vaulted over the Pollux, rumbling through the sky and crashing down on the other side of the Demon Heart in a splash of red, pink, and violet. The canvas changed from day to night—stars, planets, and constellations swirling through the air. Each star pattern I recognized burst into greater focus, writhing and dancing in the night. All too quickly the cycle began anew. Sunrise, sunset, night, disrupted only by the weather, circled in the air with increasing swiftness. Soon the sun zoomed through the air in a smear of color.

Time was passing. Obviously I was out of it, or I would have done something, moved, blinked. Maybe it was the shock of being dead and bodiless. I think that's the real reason angry ghosts can go so long without outbursts. Things start to run together; one hour bleeds into the next. One day. One month. I lost count.

When you're alive, time flies when you're having fun. In death, time flies if you don't grab it with both hands and hang on tight. During my reverie, things changed. People came and left. The remains of the Demon Heart were covered in a light dusting of snow. We don't get snow often in Void City. A half inch of snow on the ground means no school, closed roads, and thousands of tiny snowmen flecked with grass and dirt.

It was the snow that snapped me out of it, that and the sight of a classic Mustang convertible parked on the street in front of me. Not just any Mustang, either—my Mustang. I love that car. Damn were-wolves had wrecked it, trying to get at me over what was really Roger trouble. It had cost me a fortune to have it put back together, but I just couldn't live without it.

My daughter Greta, a blond Amazon, stood next to the car. She had my mechanic, Carl, with her. My Mustang was hooked to the back of his wrecker. He'd finished the repairs beautifully; with ghost-vision, I couldn't tell it'd been wrecked. Between the two of them stood my hired mage, Magbidion, a crazy little magician who was always hitting me up for protection.

Magbidion's hands were cupped over his right eye. He twisted and turned them like a photographer focusing his camera. "Try to start it again," Magbidion yelled over his shoulder. "I think we have his attention."

Carl climbed into the car and turned the key. "Nothing." He climbed back out. "I don't understand it."

"I do," Magbidion muttered. "Assuming his place of power really is his car, then it won't run unless we bring him back. Conversely, if we can manage to start the engine and keep it running, then he'll re-form. He's tied to it—linked. Goddess, but he must love this car." An idea lit up behind Magbidion's eyes, and I watched him dismiss it out of hand. "We've tried everything else. If this doesn't work, then we're going to have to rebuild the whole Demon Heart."

Magbidion is a smart magician, even if he is a little needy. He got his powers from a demon in exchange for his soul. Now that he's getting near his expiration date, Mags wants a little muscle on his side to try to renegotiate the contract. I don't know how many times I've turned him down. If he could get my body back for me, though, then he might have a deal. Heck, I might even make him my thrall.

"We've got to make him mad."

"Shit," said Greta, "if Dad knew that Tabitha was shacking up with that bigwig up at the Highland Towers, we wouldn't need to—"

The Mustang's engine roared.

"I see him," Magbidion shouted.

"She's shacking up with who, where?" I snarled.

Greta ran forward. "You can see him? Can he hear me? Daddy?"

She ran right past me. Some vampires have to be in one of their animal forms to detect ghosts. Others can't see them at all. Greta is ghost-blind. I wish I was.

"We're missing something," Magbidion yelled as the engine died. "I don't know why I was wasting my time on the Pollux. You were right, Greta, he's definitely invested in the car, but we're missing something. What am I forgetting?"

"Answer my question, Mags!" I shouted. "Tabitha broke up with me, what, a day ago, and she's already shacking up with some asshole?"

"Just try to stay mad and give me a few minutes." Mags closed his eyes and sat down on the curb. "The body creation ritual didn't work with the Pollux, because the car is really his place of power . . . But the ritual didn't work with the car, either." He gestured with his hands while he spoke. "Why not? Something must be different about the car. What's different? What is the fundamental difference between a car and a building?"

"Cars have wheels," Greta answered.

"Cars move around," Carl suggested. "You drive them, steer them."

Right on cue, as if she timed it that way, I saw Rachel. I don't know if it was because she was my thrall, but she looked brighter to me, the red of her lips more red, the very essence of what red means. Her smell, a mixture of cinnamon and sex, wrapped itself around me and didn't let go, the first scent I'd experienced as a ghost. She wore hip-hugger jeans, a white crop top, and a black leather jacket. The cold accentuated her bralessness. In her hand she carried a red gas can.

"Cars eat," she said. "Cars run on gas. Vampires have different needs, but they still require fuel." Rachel paused and shook the gas can as she spoke, blood sloshing up the side and seeping back down. "Eric runs on blood. Feed the car what Eric needs and you nourish Eric through their connection." She gestured at me, then at the Mustang. "Nourish Eric and he can rebuild his body. He does it every time he changes into an animal and back, but he needs blood to fuel the transformation."

Magbidion wiped sweat from his forehead with a cotton handkerchief. "I put blood in the car! All over the backseat."

"You put *what* all over the backseat of my car?" I shouted. Staying mad was not a problem.

"But you didn't feed it." Rachel wrinkled her nose at Mags and he stood up quickly, backpedaling. "You don't put the gas in the backseat, you put it in the tank."

"I'm not sure what that would do," he stammered. "Let me clean the car, modify the ritual. There's too much magic wrapped up in the body-creation spell to continue safely. And we'll need human blood, not—"

"It is human blood." Greta, Rachel, and I all spoke at once. I could feel it through the can. I wanted it, needed it, which meant something they were doing was working. If anyone ever asks you what vampires really are, tell them I told you we're a bunch of worthless junkies, eternally jonesing for our next fix. The hunger hadn't been there after the explosion, but it was back now.

"Where'd you get it?" Mags asked.

"Sweetheart Row," Rachel answered.

It was a lie. My spectral eyes saw phantom blood on her hands. She'd washed it away, but the stain remained. She hadn't gotten the blood from Sweetheart Row. Think of The Row as a red-light district just for vampires. For the right price, the girls of Sweetheart Row would give blood, sex, or both at the same time, but the phantom blood on Rachel's hands felt more like murder than a business transaction. More things I didn't want to know.

All the anger about Tabitha subsided. I missed her, but there was no sense beating myself up about it. If she wasn't my girlfriend anymore, why did I give a rat's ass who she fucked? And to be honest, I was sleeping with her younger sister. Rachel is the kind of little sister all boyfriends dream about.

"We're losing him," Mags shouted. "Someone piss him off again. Pour some of that blood on him."

Ignoring his orders, Rachel started pouring blood into the gas tank of the Mustang. Greta snatched the gas can away, the force of her action spinning Rachel around and knocking her to the asphalt. "What do you think you're doing?"

"The car is a place of power for him. He loves it. He had sex with the woman he was going to marry in it. When the car got wrecked, he was as pissed off about losing it as he might have been about losing a child. He has no body. I've sprayed blood all over this damn wreck of a strip club, and none of these ashes are his." Rachel pulled herself up off the ground.

"Whoever planned this," she continued, "completely obliterated Eric's remains. So he can only re-form in his strongest place of power. I went along with you guys on the whole movie theater idea. I told you it wouldn't work and it didn't. The Pollux is just too damn big to be a *memento mori*."

I may not speak many other languages, but Latin I remember from school. *Memento mori*, in English: remember your death.

"A what?" Mags asked.

Rachel's finger pointed at Magbidion, but her eyes looked directly into Greta's. "You had your shot! Now let me try this. If it doesn't work, then we can always go get more blood for the next big idea."

Reluctantly, Greta emptied the rest of the blood into the car.

"Carl's just going to have to drain the gas tank," I said. "You guys are all fucked in the head. This is never going to work."

"Just give it a second, Eric," Magbidion said. At least *he* could hear me.

"Now what?" Greta asked softly.

"We piss him off." Rachel beamed. "We make him want to have hands so that he can strangle us with them. Where is he?"

Magbidion pointed me out to her, but I really thought she'd seen me all along. Hadn't she pointed at me or had I imagined that? I stood in the midst of the rubble where *El Alma Perdida* had been. It was gone. Maybe the Lone Stranger had better things to do and had taken the gun with him. Fine with me.

Magbidion resorted to the equivalent of "yo' mama" jokes, and Greta didn't fare much better, but Rachel knew just how to piss me off. She pulled a sharpened piece of wood out of her purse and jammed it through Greta's heart from behind.

I'm very protective of Greta. I'd brave daylight for her; I've done it more than once. Greta, like me, is one of those lucky vamps who is only immobilized by a stake through the heart, not actually destroyed by it. I knew she'd be fine, but I got mad anyway.

Getting angry doesn't usually hurt, but I felt like a potato being peeled. The Mustang's engine revved. My heart beat once. Beginning with the center of my field of vision, the world unraveled and rewove itself into normalcy. Gone was the surreal vision; in its place, colors and clarity reigned supreme.

"It's working," Rachel shouted.

"Something's wrong," Magbidion said slowly, drawing out the words so that wrong took two syllables. "I told you to let me cleanse the vehicle. The magic is interacting with another spell."

When Greta was a kid, I used to buy her little pellet toys that expanded in warm water, getting bigger and bigger until you could tell what kind of vehicle they really were. That's what it felt like. I've re-formed from ashes before and it doesn't happen the way this did. A piercing scream escaped my re-formed mouth. The Mustang's horn honked wildly and all four tires spun in impossible directions.

Suddenly I was sitting behind the wheel of my beloved Mustang.

Carl's rusty-ass tow truck was a sight for sore eyes . . . and I do mean literally sore. My heart was beating again, while air ripped in and out of my lungs. I wasn't just back amongst the undead; I was really alive!

"Oh, shit!" Magbidion cursed. "Everyone get away from the car!"

Then I was reliving the worst wreck I'd ever been in. I had been coming around the sharp turn on Duggan Road out near Marilyn's house, driving Roger's car, but in this memory, I was driving my Mustang. The warning sign says to take the turn at fifteen miles per hour, but, being speed-limit-sign dyslexic, I always took it at fifty-one. When I died the first time, it had been because Roger tampered with the brakes, and I found out firsthand that if you crash through the guard-rail on that turn and have enough speed going, you have an amazing view of the quarry.

This time it was different. When I get extremely mad and black out, I turn into a large coal-skinned creature with leathery bat wings and glowing purple eyes. Now that I have a thrall, I can turn into it pretty much at will. In the new memory, the uber vamp sat in the passenger's seat, smoke trailing off of his skin as it popped and hissed in the sunlight.

"It's about fucking time," the uber vamp said. It grabbed the wheel, stomped its clawed foot over my own, jammed the gas pedal to the floor, and purposefully steered us through the guardrail and over the cliff. As we soared through the air, the paint job changed from black to red, then the uber vamp faded, leaving me alone to face the sudden stop at the end.

When I hit bottom, I flashed back to the present, but the damage to my car was real. The steering wheel had broken in half, and the steering column was shoved up and partially into my chest. My Mustang had re-enacted the wreck all over the street between the Pollux and the Demon Heart. My legs were crushed in a mass of accordioned metal. Lacerations from the windshield glass covered my face and upper body . . . *Memento mori.* Remember my death. Fuck Latin!

When it was finally over, Magbidion ran for the car and tried to pull me out, so he was up close and personal for what happened next. Later he'd tell me that I was dead for over a minute, but I never lost consciousness. I remember the steering column pulling back, the collapsed roof straightening, every dent and ding popping out smoothly as the whole car essentially fixed itself. My heart shuddered, then stopped, my skin cooled, and I was a vampire again . . . undamaged except for the whole undead angle.

Other than the paint job changing from black to red, my Mustang seemed to be none the worse for wear. I stepped out of the car, and Rachel jumped into my arms, pulling my head toward her neck. I drank; the hunger subsided, and Rachel sagged against me.

"I've missed you," she whispered.

"I don't get it," I said.

Magbidion laughed. "You weren't made in the traditional way, Eric. What happened just now . . . when we resurrected you . . . is that you came back as a human. There is a slim chance with the ritual we used that such a thing can happen, but then another spell intervened."

"What kind of spell?"

"It's so complex, so powerful, that I couldn't tell you. I think it was some kind of curse—very primal and old—probably two hundred years at least."

"And it gave me a supernatural bitch-slap back into the realm of the undead?"

"That's not how I would have put it, but yeah."

I unstaked Greta, kept her from killing Rachel (which wasn't hard once she realized why Rachel had staked her) and sat with the group of them on the snow-covered sidewalk.

"So . . . I wasn't embraced or turned or whatever by another vampire, but by some kind of curse."

Magbidion nodded.

"So I don't have a sire?"

"Yes and no," the mage sighed. His hands twisted around his eye again, but the circle through which he looked was smaller than before. "If I focus, I can usually tell who sired a vampire. When I look at you that way, there is an indistinct figure and I get the impression this person is a vampire. It's as if the curse made you his or her offspring."

"Can you tell who cursed me?"

"No." He focused even more tightly. There was a loud pop, a spark, and Magbidion fell over backward. "Ow." Smoke trailed away from his fingers and he rubbed his eye. "Do you remember tastes?"

I nodded.

"You know how people say that x or y tastes like chicken, but it isn't chicken? It's really duck or alligator or snake?"

"Yeah."

"It isn't magic. It tastes like magic, but it isn't magic. It's cleaner, purer. Maybe it is just a kind of magic I've never encountered before."

"One more question: Why is my car red?"

"It could be a side effect." Magbidion shrugged. "The car was subjected to a great deal of magic, conventional and otherwise. The curse touched it, too, re-creating the accident in which you died. . . ."

He put a hand on the hood. It revved its engine at him, screeched into reverse, and backed across the street. Magbidion hit the asphalt in front of the Mustang and it flicked on its high beams.

"Mags, do not tell me that my car—"

"That's so cool, Dad!" Greta shouted. "You have a vampire car! I always wanted a vampire car! Can we name it Fang?"

"Fang the 'Stang," I grumbled. "Somebody shoot me."

9

ERIC:

PROBLEM NUMBER TWO

Nobody seemed to know what would happen to Fang if the sun hit it, so I parked in the old Bateman's Department Store deck next to Magbidion's RV, where the sun couldn't get at my 'Stang and where Mags could keep an eye on it. Bateman's burned back in the seventies, and I bought their deck since it adjoined the Pollux anyway.

Green, red, blue, and yellow lights dotted the outside of the Pollux and the interior railings. I always decorated for Christmas, and in my absence, someone had done it for me. Usually I would close the Demon Heart and all the girls would come over for a bit of nonworking Yuletide revelry. Yeah, Christmas. I guess my ghostly eyes had stared at the sun for four whole months. I could have stared at it for another eight.

My flocked white Christmas tree stood proud and tall in the center of the lobby, decked in the same bubble lights I used every year. The star, a silver contraption made of tinfoil and popsicle sticks, waited on the edge of the concession counter where Greta put it every year. Whether we were on good or bad terms, there was always Christmas.

Greta's my biggest failure and one of my greatest loves. She made the star for me on our first Christmas together, back when she was still alive. A ten-year-old girl and a sixty-year-old vampire don't have much in common, but we did have Christmas. I don't remember exactly what happened anymore, what her foster parents had done, but I remember that it had been bad and that I'd taken care of it. Afterward it had seemed natural that she stay with me. If I'd stuck to my guns and kept her human, she'd be in her thirties now . . . I think . . . but I hadn't lasted much more than a decade before giving in.

I turned into a bat, grabbed the star with my feet, and dropped it into place (which is exactly as hard as it sounds) before flying upstairs. Rachel followed me up, but I wasn't in the mood for sex and I certainly wasn't in the mood for Rachel. I wanted Marilyn, but she was gone. She was gone and there was something I was supposed to do about it . . . something important. A nagging thought haunted the cobwebbed corridors of my bat brain. It darted between thoughts about what or who Tabitha was doing and hid behind filing cabinets when I tried to look straight at it. I was forgetting something. I'm always forgetting something.

Abruptly, I dropped out of my bat form, landing on my feet, fully dressed. Some vampires can take their clothes with them when they change shapes. I'm one of the lucky ones who can and the process leaves my clothes clean with a fresh-out-of-the-dryer warmth that makes me smile. I snapped my fingers. "Presents," I said softly. "Shit, I've got to get everybody presents."

"Money might be an issue," Rachel interrupted. "Someone closed your accounts."

"Excuse me?"

"Your alias, Eric Jones, was declared legally dead. You left every-thing to Marilyn, she left everything to you . . . To make a long story short, the city tried to claim your assets. Greta bought the Pollux, the Demon Heart property, and the parking deck with her savings, but now she's tapped out. She wouldn't say anything to you about it, I'm sure, but . . ."

Rachel looked shorter all of a sudden. She took two steps back. And now I'd changed into my uber vamp form without realizing it and I hadn't lost control.

Marilyn would be impressed.

"Marilyn." Screw Christmas. Screw the money. I'd forgotten Mar-ilyn. A demon had her soul. A demon that was waiting for me to contact him. How could I have pushed that to the back of my ghostly brain, gotten caught up in the sight of the sun, for months? I hoped he was still waiting. The tangy scent of cinnamon hit me hard enough to make my eyes water, or bleed, as the case is with vampires. I wiped it away with hands that were black as pitch and ended in claws.

Ever since I met Rachel, I've smelled cinnamon whenever she's try-ing to calm me down, convince me to do what she wants, or seduce me. I don't know if it's magic or something all thralls can do, but it an-noyed me that she'd done it in an effort to keep my mind off Marilyn.

"A demon has Marilyn's soul." My voice was deeper, threatening.

"I'm sorry," Rachel told me. She cautiously ran a finger along my bare chest. "Do you know which demon?"

"No . . . a smarmy-sounding one."

Rachel ran her hand much farther south. "You're such a big boy in this form."

"It's hard to concentrate when you do that."

"Then don't concentrate." She stripped out of her top, rubbed her breasts against me. "I don't know any demons, but I know a vampire who would know."

"Not the guy from the Highland Towers," I said churlishly.

It was a moment before Rachel could answer. "No, not that guy. Another guy. We'll go to see Winter." She slipped out of her pants. No underwear there, either. "I've heard that he's very on top of things." As she said "on top" she pushed me back and I sprawled out on the floor. The wings made things awkward; but, like most guys, I could have been lying on a lit cigarette and it wouldn't have bothered me at that moment.

Despite her comment about size, Rachel had little trouble when she climbed on top of me. The way she worked sex into any situation reminded me of a succubus Talbot had saved me from in El Segundo. Rachel wasn't a demon, but she certainly acted like one. Succubi feed on sex, get power from it. Rachel just seemed to get off on screwing vamps.

As we moved together, she kissed me on the top of my head, then again between the eyes, then on my throat. Her soft, wet kisses made my skin tingle, flush with warmth, and feel alive. She placed a fourth on the middle of my chest over my heart and it began to beat. We both climaxed, her left hand resting on my solar plexus, her right hand at the base of my crotch. She guided my fangs to her neck again and I drank. Her blood was rich and full; it had body and flavor, burning my tongue like Tabasco.

Once before, I'd felt little messages broadcasting from Rachel when we were close. Thoughts had danced through my head, pretending to be mine. I heard them again as she lay panting against my chest. "Trust Rachel. Need Rachel. Love Rachel. Be still of form. Be bound of form. Be mine. Be mine."

Cinnamon, the smell of it, the taste of it, surrounded me, just as surely as Rachel's flesh enfolded mine. My heart beat and my lungs drew breath of their own accord. Heat built at my core and my body temperature soared. Blood flowed through my veins as I climaxed again, painfully, and Rachel's eyes rolled up in her head, her legs clamping around me as best she could, her hands pulling at my ass.

"Fuck, yes," she hissed. "Keep going, baby. Come on."

Pushing myself up with my wings, I rolled us over and kept thrusting, my hands on her shoulders, holding her in place. I expected my erection to subside, but it didn't. Purple light from my glowing eyes cast strange shadows on the floor and made her eyes seem to glow a matching violet. As the orgasm hit her, my heart beat faster, and I climaxed a third time, which is pretty much unheard of for me, let alone most men. Maybe it was a thrall thing, some sort of mystic Viagra for vampires.

Every time I asked her about one of her little skills, she said it was a thrall thing. I was going to need a second opinion. Again, I had the feeling I was forgetting something. Something important. I rolled off of her and quickly returned to my normal self, dressed in jeans, a belt, sneakers, and a black *Welcome to the Void* T-shirt.

"I wish I could do that," Rachel laughed as she struggled back into her jeans.

"Do what?"

"The instant clothes changing thing."

"It *is* a perk." As I picked up her top and threw it to her, I remembered. "We're supposed to be doing something."

"We just did," she teased.

"No." I smacked the floor. "I was talking about it right before. What was it?"

"I don't remember."

She remembered. I knew she did. I grabbed one of her nipple rings gently, but firmly. "Don't lie to me."

"I thought you were joking."

More little voices danced in my head. They were harder to hear now, but they were there. *Trust. Trust. Trust.*

"I wasn't."

"We're supposed to go see Ebon Winter at his club, the Artiste Unknown. You wanted to find the demon that took that old woman Marilyn's soul."

I pulled her close and kissed her. She had a hard time returning the kiss in the beginning, mad that I'd accused her of lying, but she covered it up. I'm the kind of guy who would rather not know if all my friends really hate me. If my girlfriend is sleeping around, I'd like her to have the decency to be smart enough about it that I never find out.

"You'll need a tux if you want to talk to Winter," Rachel blurted.

"Does everyone dress like that at Winter's club?"

"No." She fluttered her eyelashes at me. "But we will. If you want to meet Winter, you have to make an impression."

"I don't own a tux anymore. It blew up. Where's Talbot?"

"I haven't seen him."

"He wanders off sometimes." I sighed. "Like a damn cat. He'll be back eventually. In the meantime, I guess you'll have to go rent me one. Do you have the right kind of dress?"

"I still have the green one you bought me, but you'll need to come with me to get your tux."

"Why is that?"

"Because if you're going to make an impression on Winter, it will need to fit well."

An impression? The impression I usually make on most High Society vamps is my boot print on their asses. Now I had to charm some jackass to get information? Shit.

✦ 10 ✦

ERIC:
THE ARTISTE UNKNOWN

For a man who'd just risen from the dead (again), I looked good in the rented tux. Rachel had suggested that I buy one, but I didn't want to eat up the rest of Greta's savings. I felt guilty enough about renting the limo with Greta's credit card, but Rachel said that entrances were important and an undead Mustang did not say elegance. It was her first ride in a limo and I think the only thing that kept her in that strapless green gown was a desire to impress Ebon Winter.

The driver, an oni named Tiko, didn't need to be getting any ideas anyway. Oni are Japanese ogres that eat people. He was big, green, and had a single black horn protruding from his forehead. In Void City, Tiko and his brothers perform public services for the supernatural folks who can afford it and don't want to pay off the cops. They are also the reason that a lot of disappearances go unsolved, thereby avoiding a costly Fang Fee for the supernatural perpetrator. If there's no body, then there's no crime, and, like the werewolves who'd eaten Roger, Tiko and his brothers don't tend to leave any leftovers lying about.

The Artiste Unknown was in a much nicer neighborhood than my club. It looked bigger, more expensive, and in all ways superior to the Demon Heart, except that I could tell just from looking at it that there would be no naked girls inside. Even if there were naked girls inside, they wouldn't be dancing the way my girls had. They'd be covered in silver body paint or disguised as trees or something. Even so, it was quite impressive, a modernistic palace of glass and light and style. I hated it.

As we walked up, a smooth-looking vampire with blond highlights joined the one watching the door. They had a quick discussion and I could tell that the newcomer was not pleased. From the sound of it, the guy at the door really worked security and had just pummeled a prospective guest. I supposed he was used to a far more straightforward job description than being a doorman at this club required.

"I'm sorry, Mr. Andre," the stand-in said. "Klaus said he would just be a minute and that guy wouldn't wait."

The human in question was standing off to one side and his vampire girlfriend was gazing into his eyes with a concerned look on her face. When Andre looked her way, she bared her fangs. "That cretin almost killed Ken."

I stepped forward with Rachel and the female vamp bared her fangs at me. I bared mine in response and "announced" myself.

Vampire society classifies vampires by how powerful they are and any known weaknesses they have, dividing them into Drones, Soldiers, Masters, and Vlads. It has nothing to do with bloodline, but everything to do with personality, the strength of the individual's character. I've always thought of it as a supernatural Rorschach test. I guess being a Vlad is like getting the perfect score. That makes being an Emperor like getting college credit for the course or something. All I know is that I have all the powers in the book and I tend to come back from just about anything, like Dracula.

The lower down the food chain you are, the more your betters can fuck with you. Vlads and Masters can detect each other. We get a mental image, a sense of age from those nearby, and if we want, we can push an awareness of ourselves into a Drone or a Soldier, kind of a big *don't fuck with me* bulletin. That was what I did when I "announced" myself to the three vampires at the door. From their reactions, the girl and the stand-in were both Drones, but Andre was a Soldier. He kept his cool pretty well. I almost liked him.

"Might I be of assistance?" I offered. Social interaction with most vampires is like a damn dance. I knew a few of the beginner steps, but if we started to cha-cha I was going to be out of my league. I'd probably have to start putting undead back in their graves.

I missed Roger, even though he had killed me twice. Roger had been much better at this crap. He'd enjoyed it. He'd liked hanging out at the Artiste Unknown.

There was a reason I'd let him handle all of this stuff before I found out what a murderous little backstabbing power whore he was. God, he'd been good at it, even if he had always been a little sloppy. If you pushed him around, he developed a stratagem and set plans into motion. By the time the last domino fell and you finally saw what was going on, you were already screwed to the wall and crying for mama.

When I get pushed around, I push back. I can't help it; it just happens. I had a feeling that killing off this Winter guy's employees wasn't going to help my situation.

Andre looked into my eyes and smiled. His eyes didn't, but his mouth did; it made me like him a little less. "No, thank you, sir. Everything is well in hand. Go right in, Lord . . ."

"Eric," I told him. "Just Eric. Kind of like Sting, but not."

I offered Rachel my arm and Andre held the door for us as we walked in. The music and the lights hit me all at once, but that wasn't what made me pause. I sensed twelve Master vampires and two Vlads. I couldn't sort them all out, but I thought I recognized one of the Vlads. It was Ebon Winter; it had to be. The second thing that hit me was the people. Over five hundred hearts pushed a few thousand quarts of blood. Most of them were dancing; the varying scents and perfumes, the heightened states of excitement . . . after the calm of being a ghost, it was just too much. I pulled Rachel tight to my chest and buried my face against her neck.

"Shhh . . . ," she said soothingly. Her fingers traced small circles on my back underneath my jacket. "Focus on me. One heartbeat, all yours. One blood, all yours. One body, all yours."

My hands clenched and I grabbed my own forearms, afraid that if I grabbed her, I might break her. Rachel blew softly on my neck, cooing to me as if I were a child, whispering little nonsense words. I smelled the cinnamon that was perpetually on her breath and knew she was up to something. The background noise began to fade; the scents, the blood, my intense desire all slowly abated. Concentrating on Rachel helped. Another thirty seconds and I was able to pull slowly away from her. Her scent was confusing. She seemed excited, afraid, and relieved, all at once.

"Works like a charm," Rachel said mischievously. "Are you okay, baby? I thought I was going to lose you there for a sec."

I nodded.

"How did you do that? Was that more thrall stuff?" I asked.

"I have my ways," she teased. "The principle is similar to what some parents in England did during World War II. Children were having trouble sleeping because of the war, the air raids, all of that, so they learned that if they put the child to bed with a piece of bread, then the kid could sleep at night because at the very least they knew what they were going to have for breakfast."

"I remember that."

"Same thing," she said as we worked our way through dancing couples, some human, some vampire, and most mixed. "It doesn't matter how much blood is out there or how many women, because . . ." She guided my hand to her left breast. "You've already got your prey right here."

I didn't want to think about that, so I changed the subject.

"This Winter guy . . . How would you describe him?" I removed my hand from her breast and took her by the arm. I could smell the alcohol from the bar across the room. More surprising was the aroma of food. The tang of various fried, grilled, and broiled things made my mouth water. The thought of watching Rachel eat was appetizing; there was also the possibility she might actually be hungry. We headed that way.

While I maneuvered us toward the bar through the crowd, Rachel answered me, "He's . . . well, beautiful, like a piece of art or something. Really metrosexual."

I stumbled over the word for a moment, before I realized I'd heard Tabitha use it before. If I remembered correctly, it meant a straight man who had the style and fashion sense of a gay man. That sounded like him. The image in my mind had shown him to be physically in his early twenties. He had carefully ruffled blond hair that reminded me of David Bowie, but younger and more attractive.

Outward appearances can be very deceiving amongst the undead, but from the feeling I'd gotten when I sensed him, Ebon Winter couldn't have been more than a decade old. He felt like the last performance of "Candle in the Wind" or Johnny Colt and Marc Ford's last show with The Black Crowes . . . very late nineties.

"He's younger than I expected." I wasn't used to sensing a large group, but I got the same feel from the others in the room. They were all young as far as vampires go, only ten or fifteen years undead at the most.

We made our way through the club. A circular glass stage moved up and down in the center of the room on a sleek column. Large screens of various sizes showed the action onstage. The two biggest screens had to be fifty feet high and ran the entire length of the walls they were on. A band was onstage—modern alternative, but good. Raw talent was propping them up until they got a little more experience under their belts. If I'd been a talent scout, I would have signed them in a heartbeat.

"He was supposedly turned on his twentieth birthday eleven or twelve years ago," Rachel told me. "I hear it pissed off a lot of people when he was made instead of the competition."

"Competition?"

"His sire is some really ancient Vlad from way back and he only turns two vampires every ten years, a male and a female. I don't know exactly how it works, but apparently the potential vampires have to compete against each other for the privilege. There's supposed to be a lot of money involved, too." The music changed, and Rachel, recognizing the tune, laughed and let go of my hand. She moved in amongst the dancers and joined them. She belonged there, dancing with them to the techno beat. I didn't. Dancing is something I watch others do. The hunger and the presence of so many people began to close in on me again. I gave her a warning look and she stuck her tongue out at me in reply, but came back to my side.

"A lady doesn't leave her escort," I said, quoting Sinatra at her.

She pointed up at one of the walls that didn't sport an enormous video screen, indicating a series of terraced box seats. "Winter is probably in one of those when he isn't onstage. Or he could be in the lower level under this floor. There is a whole second club down there just for his highest paying patrons and their guests. It's called The Velvet."

"Winter? He goes by his last name?"

"Yes." She rolled her eyes at me. "Everyone knows that."

Everyone but me. "Okay, okay. So if we can get down to The Velvet and they let us in, we have a better chance at getting to meet him. How do we do that?"

"I don't know everything." She smiled. "But we'll think of something."

That didn't sound good.

11

ERIC:
DOMINANCE TRAINING

For the next few hours we killed time waiting to be noticed. Rachel and I danced half a dozen times. I know, I know. I don't dance. Don't get me started. We got seats at one of the little glass-on-metal tables near the bar and Rachel ordered an appetizer. The chairs looked—and felt—like they'd been bought for appearance over comfort.

The bartender kept trying to sell me blood. I wasn't buying. I make it a practice never to accept bottled blood from strangers. Not since El Segundo. Instead, I watched Rachel eat.

I don't know why it surprised me, but she had gotten a lot better at entertaining vampires. Little things, like talking through the choice of the next bite of food mean a lot. A good dining companion for a vampire knows how to keep up a dialogue. The façade lets dining instructions be couched within phrases that could pass as normal dinner conversation. "Oh this is all so good, I can hardly decide what to eat next" was code for "What do you want me to eat?" Responding to subtle commands like "that looks like a juicy one" or "have you tried mixing x with y" gives vampires a little control over the meal without making us feel like total freaks.

The appetizer she had ordered was fried mushrooms. The mushrooms were bite-size, but she cut each one in half as she ate and she alternated between using a fork and her fingers. As she bit into each piece, she lingered over the morsel, leaving her lips parted until her teeth actually touched one another. She chewed slowly, savoring the food, letting the expressions accompanying each taste show on her face. Her eyes would half close with pleasure if a bite of mushroom was just right. After the first few she called the waiter over and asked if he could get any horseradish sauce. He did.

When he brought the sauce, she took turns slightly dipping a piece of fried mushroom into it and eating daintily and immersing the entire piece in the horseradish, carefully licking off the excess before it could drip on the table.

There were mistakes. She hurried through a few of the pieces too quickly and she ate more of the mushrooms than she should have before asking if I'd like her to order something else, but I could tell that she had practiced since I'd watched her eat breakfast some four months before.

She must have given it serious thought, studied the voyeuristic nature of vampires in detail. It was as if while I'd been out of the picture for four months, she'd taken a class. I pictured a room full of thralls practicing how to eat for voyeuristic purposes. She would have been at the top of the intermediate class, a real A+ student.

I wasn't the only one who noticed. She was drawing attention. Some of the vamps looked on with the same vicarious pleasure that I did, but a few looked hungry and more than a few of the human escorts looked envious and angry.

"What do we want next?" she asked, looking over the menu. Even with the phrasing of her question, she showed a subtle understanding. Tabitha would have asked, "What do you want to watch me eat next?" That spoiled part of it, but Rachel understood: she asked for advice, not directions. It was perfectly clear that whatever I suggested was what she would order, but doing it this way sustained an important part of the illusion. It allowed an abnormal act to retain a semblance of normalcy.

"I want to get in to see this Ebon Winter guy and then I want to take you out to dinner. Real dinner. Do you like steak?"

Before she could answer my question, another vampire spoke up. "Eat another mushroom."

Rachel shrugged, picked up the fork and looked at me.

I shook my head.

"Make the bitch eat another mushroom."

There was really no way he could have known how touchy I am about how other people treat my companions, particularly my women. The little I did know about vampire High Society told me that an insult to her was an insult to me. That I felt possessive of Rachel even though I knew she had a hidden agenda bothered me, but I tabled that shouting match to myself until I'd dealt with the new moron.

The way I see it, my women take good care of me; they give what I need, blood or otherwise, and they don't make me feel like a monster or a freak. For the most part, I try to take care of them. When I ran the

Demon Heart, I paid for their college, and more. I paid my strippers an annual salary between fifty and seventy-five grand, before tips. They had health insurance with dental and vision. When they left, they knew they could still call on me if they ran into trouble and they knew that I wouldn't call on them unless they'd said it was okay.

Some of them had already called to ask when I was reopening the club. But now that the club was gone . . . I didn't know how I felt about a new one. I don't want to say that I've ever felt like the club objectified women or abused them, because I've always gone out of my way to make sure that the Demon Heart helped rather than hindered the girls who danced in it, but now that I didn't have to worry about filling a rotation . . .

"I don't know," I said, thinking out loud more about the idea of re-opening the club, than the asshole hassling us.

Rachel seemed concerned. "Why don't I just have another mush-room, Eric?"

As I turned to her, I could feel my eyes light up inside. "Do you want another mushroom?"

"N-no," she stammered, "but what's the harm?" I think Rachel was a little surprised at my reaction. She must have been worried that I would go all black skin and leather wings. I was mad, but not that mad. She still had a few things to learn about me.

The vampire with a malnourished heroin addict on his arm had more to learn about me than Rachel did, but he probably wouldn't live long enough. I went from sitting to standing in one pulse of the club's multicolored lights. In the next flash I was next to him. By the third, he was already on the floor with my foot on his throat. I love it when my powers work well. They can be finicky, but they hadn't really misfired since I'd re-formed.

He was much slower than me. "Did you say something?" I asked.

Gurgling at me, he tried to push my leg up and lift my foot.

He was weaker than me, too. I looked at his date. "Would you like a mushroom?"

Happy Boy popped his claws and I broke his neck. "If you cut my tux, I'll end you," I said. "It's a rental." He pulled his claws back in.

His date started to cry. "Please, don't hurt him. He's sorry. Aren't you sorry, Irwin? We'll leave; we won't come back. We'll hang at the park or something."

She was defending him. It made me sick. It always makes me sick to see someone beg. A human pleading for the life of a vampire is even worse. I lifted my foot a fraction, just enough for him to slide out from under it.

"What's your problem, man?" he said, popping his neck into place. "She's just a human. What do you care?"

I grabbed him by the throat and cut him off before he got himself dead for real. Why I cared, I can't tell you. I just did. "The reason you will understand is this: She is mine and I don't share well. I never have. It's a childhood malady. Maybe I had too many brothers and sisters and I have a deep need to indisputably demonstrate my ownership of things."

Anger started building up inside me again and I could feel myself starting to go. Fang's engine roared in my ears, echoing my anger. I wondered if anyone else could hear it or if this was another symptom of the strange bond we shared. If I lost control in a place like this, with so many people around, there was no telling how many might be killed.

Maybe Rachel was right to be worried. There were probably enough Masters and Vlads to take me down, but not before I caused a lot of damage. Irwin's girlfriend looked into my eyes and panicked. "Look at his eyes, oh my God!"

Fang hauled ass out of the parking deck back at the Pollux, heading for me. *It's okay,* I tried thinking at him, *I've got it.* I think he understood because it felt like he was heading back to the deck.

I snapped out of it, as though calling off Fang had taken some of the steam out of my anger. All the same, I was sure my eyes were glowing purple. "Want to see something really scary?" I asked, but Irwin was already dragging his date out of the club. I turned back to Rachel. She was afraid, too . . . far too afraid for someone who'd fucked an uber vamp. She'd almost peed herself. *Why?*

"They're purple, right?"

Rachel got up. "I have to go to the ladies' room."

Biting back a vulgar remark, I walked her to the ladies' room and waited outside the door. While I waited, security headed my way. People watched out of the corners of their eyes. They glanced away when I turned to look at them, but I could feel the eyes upon me. A female vamp came out of the bathroom and I smiled at her. "Is there a no-fighting rule here?"

"No fighting, no killing, no maiming, no threatening of any kind. It's a civilized club," she scoffed.

I glanced around me. Sure enough, there were little signs posted in obvious places that said pretty much what she had told me. The signs were more ornate and so was the wording, but she'd been dead-on. No wonder Roger had never asked me to come here.

I waited for security and made fun of their little plastic armbands in my head. Andre came out of nowhere and joined the goons sashaying in my direction.

"Winter," Andre told me when he arrived, "wishes to thank you for enabling him to win the wager he placed upon your entering the club. As he suggested, you managed to last an entire hour before breaking any of the rules that would cause you to be ejected from the club. As thanks, he would like to invite you and your guest to join him for a pre-ejection drink in The Velvet where he hopes you will be able to restrain yourself amongst those who are your equals, if not your betters."

"Well, fuck you very much," I replied.

Andre was so taken aback that he physically took a backward step.

"He means we'd be delighted," Rachel said as she exited the bathroom behind me. Andre looked at me for confirmation and I shrugged. That was one way to interpret what I'd said.

As he led us toward an elevator, Rachel whispered in my ear, "How many brothers and sisters did you have?"

"None." I smiled. "I'm an only child." *I think.*

12

ERIC:

FIRST IMPRESSIONS

I liked The Velvet. It reminded me a lot of the Pollux's decor. Crimson velvet wallpaper and lamps in brass-backed sconces lined the walls. The sconces' circular rear plates had little snowflakes etched into them. In the Pollux, pentacles had been similarly etched. A collection of intimate booths and vintage-era tables were spread out around a small stage. Dark carpet covered the floors. Wooden railings separated the seating area from the small dance area. There was no bar.

The club could have held around sixty people, but there were only eighteen vampires in it now, each with a human date. Twelve of them were the Master vampires I'd sensed earlier. They were dressed in an array of styles ranging from mob chic to the same metrosexual look Winter sported and they had arranged themselves so that Winter was the center of their attention. One vampire had even pulled his chair around at an odd angle as if he was afraid that showing Winter his back would be disrespectful.

Onstage, Ebon Winter changed songs as I entered. He went into an a capella version of "Love Her Madly" by The Doors and though I disliked him, his voice was like nothing I had ever heard. In comparison, Sinatra's voice had no character and Bowie sounded bland and safe. Wearing matching white leather jumpsuits, the other Vlad and her date sat at a corner booth. Their motorcycle helmets sat on the floor next to them. I stifled a laugh and let Andre lead Rachel and me to a booth a little apart from the rest of them. It was probably a slight of some kind. Maybe it was supposed to give me a message about not belonging. Either way, I was still edgy from the confrontation upstairs and glad of the distance. The only ways I knew to take the edge off involved killing or screwing and neither seemed a likely option here.

Two of the vampires reoriented their attention on me, only to be silently rebuffed by the other vampires. Winter didn't miss a beat, but a flick of his eyes made it clear that the two offenders would have to answer for the momentary lapse in loyalty later. Stupid High Society bullshit.

Each couple was served by their own steward, and apparently there were several chefs hard at work beyond one of the sets of double doors, because delicious smells wafted in from the kitchen. Our server's name was Chad, and I was only mildly surprised when he brought a steak dinner to the table. He brought with it a red merlot for Rachel, which even I could appreciate in terms of color and bouquet. For me he brought a draft beer in a frosted mug. He even set it in front of me as if I wasn't going to have to watch Rachel drink it for me. "Compliments," he informed us, "of the house." I'd had some blood booze once. It had tasted like crap, but I almost asked if he could order me some before I remembered that it had been very expensive and I was on a tight budget.

Winter winked at us from the stage. If he'd been a girl, I would have cherished that wink. Since he wasn't, it made me uncomfortable.

Rachel ate for me and herself at the same time. She did even better than before, and despite the improvement, the show was just for me this time. The other vamps and their dates were too busy watching Winter. I listened to him off and on. I like music to be loud and angry. Skill isn't the most important aspect of it for me. Again, he was great, the best I'd ever heard, but for me, the radio would have been fine. He switched styles effortlessly, making everything work without instruments, going old school with "Lightnin' Strikes" as well as music that was either original or too new to have entered my playlist.

"Are you even listening to him anymore?" Rachel admonished gently. "You'll make him angry."

"I'm edgy. Maybe it's all the not killing people. I'm not used to it."

Before she could comment, the current song ended and soft applause came from the other tables. Rachel clapped, and I joined in halfheartedly. I knew what my problem was. I wanted to get the information I needed from this Winter guy and get the hell out.

Winter flitted over to our booth and beamed at us. "So, how are we doing over here in the rowdy section?" he asked.

"Not bad," I admitted. "My compliments to your chef."

Winter gestured for Rachel to move over and he sat down once she had scooted enough to make room for him. This elicited some shocked looks from the other vamps and some hasty reorienting on their part, as if they wanted to make sure I knew they were focusing on Winter rather than me. Winter was apparently doing us a favor by crowding our booth. "Emil is wonderful, isn't he? Your escort has unique talents, too, wouldn't you say? I almost stopped singing to watch her eat." His eyes flashed red right through the blue contacts he was wearing and then faded, revealing a conspiratorial lightheartedness that rang false to me. I wondered why the light hadn't turned purple when it flashed through the contacts. "What did you think of the performance?"

"It was good. I liked it. I tend to like heavier stuff, though, so I can't really judge . . ."

"Good?" he asked carefully. "Liked?"

"He's not very careful with his words, Winter," Rachel butted in. "I hope you'll excuse him."

"Roger was much better at this sort of thing than I am," I added. "I'm not trying to be an ass."

Winter eyed me carefully and then eyed Rachel. "I suppose we can let it go this once . . . if you'll tell me how you do it?"

"Do what?" I asked.

"Your eyes." As he spoke, he reached up and pulled out a contact, revealing a washed-out-looking iris, a typical vampire eye. I knew immediately what he meant, and it wasn't the funky purple glow I'd sported earlier in the evening. My eyes have always been blue. They were blue in life and according to Marilyn, they are the same color they've always been. "They're blue, really blue. Is it a dye? Some type of implant?"

You'd think he'd have been more interested in what had frightened the folks upstairs when I had started to go off on Irwin, but I gave him the spiel, knowing that, like most, he wouldn't believe it. "If I knew why I still have human-looking eyes, I would tell you, but they've always been that way. To be honest, I didn't even know that they had stayed blue until Roger pointed it out to me some time in the seventies. I haven't done a whole lot of mirror gazing since I became a vampire."

He scoffed at me and rolled his eyes. "Fine, if you won't tell me, then I have nothing further to discuss with you. Andre," he called, "see this plebeian out."

"Wait a minute!" I snarled. "That's it? I wasted three hours and got all dressed up in this monkey suit just so you could throw me out for not knowing how to give you a pair of bright happy blue eyes? I don't think so!"

I put my hand through the mahogany table and Winter flinched. When I tried to grab Winter himself, my hand passed through him. He looked solid, but his body had changed to mist. Movie vampires turn to mist all the time, but I'd never met a vampire who could do it, much less one with control like that. I locked eyes with him instead and was stunned to find myself almost drowning in his mind. I withdrew and he tried to chase after me into my head, but I snarled, announcing myself again, pushing him out. The Master vampires started to casually saunter my way and I turned on them with my eyes aglow.

"I came here for information, not to be deliberately provoked in your club and used as a source of amusement! Why did you bet on me, anyway?"

The Vlad in the Elvis jumpsuit stepped forward. "Everyone knows about the blue-eyed vampire named Eric. We all know that you're supposed to be some kind of badass who's not to be messed with. One of the first things my sire told me was to stay far away from the Demon Heart and farther away from you."

"Mine told me that you killed other vampires for sport," said one of the Master vampires, a short little guy with a shaved head and a Vandyke.

One of the female vamps, an Asian girl with a red wig, stood up. "Mine said you didn't drink human blood. He told me you only drank from your own get. He said that you had special rooms underneath your club where you kept them."

"We were curious," explained Winter. "You sounded monstrous."

"And this made you want to meet me and play mind games?"

As Winter laughed, small curls of vapor poured out of his mouth and around the sides of his face, flowing back into him. He smiled as if reading my mind. "There is beauty in monstrosity, wonder in diversity, and to these simple truths even the gods must confess."

"And we do," the others said as one.

"We are the new gods and you are a titan," Winter explained. "You are powerful, but your ways are the old ways and we are far more powerful together than you are alone."

These guys were nuts! They thought this was a grand adventure, a game to amuse themselves. They could form a great big circle jerk in the parking lot for all I cared, but they could not fuck with me. I turned back to Winter.

"Look, you pansy little fuck! I came here for some information and I'll be damned if I leave here without it. Now I know that you're used to dealing with Roger and other High Society fangs and maybe they buy into this vampires as Greek gods bullshit you've been blowing up your own asses, but here's reality! You're all overgrown corpses that drink the blood of the living to survive. You're not gods! God doesn't want you. If he did, then crosses, Bibles, and holy water wouldn't burn the shit out of you. You can't go out in daytime or the sun will burn you to ash. A stake through the heart will still immobilize you.

"What you are is a bunch of namby-pamby, pretending-drinking-blood-is-like-drinking-ambrosia motherfuckers that haven't come to grips with what sad sacks of shit we all really are! You think being a vampire makes you Tom Cruise in that damned movie, but it fucking doesn't, okay? It just makes you poor dead bastards that can't even eat Doritos anymore without puking blood on the kitchen floor. Now, if fucking with me makes you feel all high and mighty, then bring it, but you better get ready to reap the whirlwind, 'cause I guarantee that the first Lost Boys wannabe that lays a corporeal finger on me or mine will not survive the experience. Now, I want some answers. Either you have them or you don't, but if you do have them, you better give 'em up or I'll fuck you up. Am I crystal fucking clear?"

They clapped. They actually fucking clapped.

"Okay," I began. Closing my eyes, I massaged my temples for a moment. "What the hell are you doing now?"

"I won again," Winter said cheerfully. "You are every bit as amusing as I thought you might be. What was it you wanted to know?"

Rachel looked as confused as I did for once, and since Little Miss Know-It-All was taken by surprise, I felt a lot better about it, too. "Before I tell you," I said, "are there any other bets?"

"That would be telling." Winter chuckled as the others applauded. "I win again."

I laughed in spite of myself. God, I hate vampires.

13

TABITHA:

BUMPING INTO PEOPLE

Pulling up in front of the Artiste Unknown reminded me why dating Phillip was so much fun. This would not be like the fiasco at the Iversonian. Vampires and their human escorts wrapped around the club, a band of wannabes waiting to be told no. Two vampires dressed in suits were stationed at the door at the head of an area cordoned off by red velvet ropes on brass stands, extending all the way to the sidewalk as if one were approaching an award show in Hollywood rather than a nightclub in Void City. Dennis rode next to me, and I leaned close to him, not because I craved his touch or because I wanted him, but to soak up the heat.

"Thank you for coming with me, Dennis," I said as the limo came to a stop. Even though I was pouting, I was glad Phillip had decided to stay in. I could have flaunted my ability to seem alive with Phillip along to protect me, but the more I got to know him, the more he changed from mysterious and cool to short, fat, annoying, and just plain sick.

"Of course, Lady Tabitha. Lord Phillip explained the difficulties making an appearance with Mister Talbot might cause."

"Winter's policy says human escort, not just living escort," I said with a shrug. Dennis's eyes dipped involuntarily to my cleavage, brightening my mood. My dress was tight, black, and sleeveless, cut to make the most of my assets. The diamond necklace Phillip had given me hung around my neck, throwing little dots of rainbow color on the walls. My shoes had an extra inch on the heel that I'd only been able to wear comfortably since becoming a vampire.

One of the vamps, a smooth, casually attractive man in a sharp gray suit, left his station to open my door. This was the side of dating

Phillip that I enjoyed, the glitz, the glam, the not having to dance in some stupid art deco strip club.

Dennis climbed out after me and took my arm just quickly enough to steady me when I sensed Eric. When Eric and I were together, I didn't get a strong sense off of him; maybe because he sired me. Now, though, he felt powerful and strong, way more powerful than I am . . . which shouldn't have been possible since we're both Vlads. His "announcement" made Phillip seem small and not just in a wow-that-thing-is-tiny way.

Eric stepped out the front door and I froze. God, he looked gorgeous! I'd never seen him with his natural hair color before. He had always dyed it black, but tonight it was blond. Maybe he hadn't noticed yet. When had he come back? Why hadn't I felt it? The tux he wore looked like it had been tailor-made for him. I'd forgotten about those true-blue eyes, but they pierced me briefly before taking in Dennis. Eric weighed Dennis with that gaze and found him wanting. I looked away, embarrassed.

Eric glanced over his shoulder and said, "C'mon" to someone behind him. A woman stepped out of the doorway wearing a smirk I'd seen a thousand times. *The witch!*

"It's customary for a man to open the door for a lady," she bantered in my dead sister's voice.

"I was distracted." He nodded in my direction and the woman who wore Rachel's body looked over at me with the exact same glint of mischievousness in her eyes Rachel'd had when I caught her making out with Martin Coleberg in the bleachers at my senior prom. Martin had been my date.

"Hi, slut," she teased. "Where you been?"

Those were the same words she'd used at prom. It was impossible. This woman could not be my little sister. I'd discounted it ever since I'd seen her for the first time at the Demon Heart, but suddenly, seeing her standing with Eric, the innate possessiveness she showed, I knew. It was her, but it couldn't be.

Rachel was dead. She'd died of cancer, wasting away to nothing, and she had not been brave. She'd been angry, hateful, and mad at the world. At her funeral I'd watched Dad, Uncle Tommy, her boyfriend Paul, and three of Mom's friends from church carry her coffin to the family plot, watched as the funeral-home people lowered her into the ground and buried her next to Grandma.

"I don't want a scene." Eric sounded bored with the exchange before it had even really started. "You broke up with me, remember?"

"But—"

"Did he really tell you that you were a moist warm tightness?" Rachel taunted. "I'm his thrall now. He doesn't need your cold dead cunt anymore."

"His what?" I was at a loss, still not wanting to believe that it was really my sister Rachel, still wanting, needing, it to be a trick, an illusion. "He what?"

"Leave her alone," Eric interrupted. "She's still your sister."

Words that I wanted to say, questions that I needed to ask, ran through my mind and bounced off, overcome by the same thought over and over again. *It can't be her. It can't be her. It can't be her.* "You're dead!" is all that I could get out.

Rachel deliberately misunderstood me. "You'd kill your own sister?"

I looked to Eric, pleading with him to understand what I wanted to say. Our eyes met and his mind touched mine. *Shut the fuck up, before you make an even bigger ass out of yourself, Tabitha.* My mouth snapped shut. Eric was my sire, the one vampire whose mental compulsion I could not resist. "Go inside with Toy Boy there . . . What's your name?" he asked my escort without breaking eye contact with me.

"It's Dennis, Lord Eric, but I'm not—"

"If I want to hear more from you, I'll ask you another question. Now shut your yapper."

Only Eric would say "yapper."

"Yes, milord."

"Tabitha here may not be my girlfriend anymore, but she's my spawn, get . . ."

"Offspring," Dennis inserted.

"Thanks. Offspring, and she hasn't tried to kill me yet, so if anything bad happens to her, I'll find you and . . . you're not somebody's thrall, are you?"

"Not at this point in the competition, milord."

"Good. Then I'll find you and kill you. You savvy?"

"I savvy, milord."

Savvy? Eric had been watching too many pirate movies.

"Now. Tabitha, go inside with Dennis and have your fun." His hand touched my cheek. "I've got to go get Marilyn's soul back from some demon. Swing by on Christmas Eve if you want. I'll have something for you." He pulled away. "I'm not mad at you. Now, go."

He's more powerful than me and he's my sire. I had to obey, would always have to obey, even though I didn't want to go into the club anymore. I wanted to ask how my sister was alive. How she'd come back. Had she really gone to Hell like she'd claimed before, when I'd thought her nothing more than a doppelganger? I wanted to know if I could help with the Marilyn thing. She'd never approved of me, but she'd stuck up for me once when no one had any reason to. I felt like I owed her one, but thanks to Eric's compulsion, I had to walk into the club, let Dennis escort me to a booth, and sit down before my mouth would open.

Eric announced himself three more times before I felt him drive away—the final time, all of the other vampires in the Artiste Unknown winced.

"What was that?" Dennis asked.

"Eric was roaring. He does that when he gets angry or overprotective. It's a man thing. You wouldn't understand." A waiter brought us blood wine without being asked, muttered something about compliments of the management, and fluttered away. "When we first started dating, I went to see my parents for a few days without telling him, and he went ballistic. God, how he shouted at me."

"Sounds a little overprotective," Dennis observed.

I wasn't sure anymore. Maybe Eric had just understood the dangers of the world better than I had. Maybe he still did.

"Was that really your sister?"

I wanted to answer him, but Eric's compulsion kept me from talking about it. I was supposed to be having the fun that I'd come to the Artiste Unknown for, before I'd known Eric was here with Rachel. Hell, I had more fun than this at the Iversonian with Talbot, fight notwithstanding. But after a dance and a few drinks, the compulsion eased up enough for me to ask Dennis a question.

"How is it possible?" I asked.

Dennis stared without comprehension. "Lady Tabitha?"

"Rachel was dead, really dead. She died over a year ago. How could she have come back?"

"Maybe it isn't her." A server had brought him a sampler platter of hors d'oeuvres. He'd been eating them slowly for the last ten minutes. He seemed to be really tasting each bite, and it was pissing me off. "It could be a shape-shifter."

"If you take another bite of that food in front of me," I snapped, "I swear to God I'm going to break your fucking neck!" Dennis dropped his fork the way one might drop a poisonous snake. He accidentally tossed it too far to the side and it clattered to the floor.

"I'm sorry, Lady Tabitha," he stammered. "Most vampires find my talent for eating quite enjoyable."

Most vampires aren't stuck being able to eat food, but not taste it, I thought. That subtle cruelty went along with my ability to seem alive. It emphasized the fact that it wasn't real life, just a very clever approximation.

"Just don't," I said. "I don't like it and she's not a shape-shifter. That's what I thought at first, that it was some kind of spell, but—"

"It could have been a construct, a simulacrum summoned to act like your sister."

"Simulacrum?"

"A fake duplicate of a person," Dennis offered.

"Oh."

Maybe. Which would be worse, to have my sister back from the dead and despising me, or to have a weird creature wearing her face?

"No, it was her." Or did I just want her back? Yeah. I did. Even though we hadn't really been friends since puberty . . . I wanted her back. She was . . . is my sister and family is family. "Could it be her?"

"Well, it depends on how badly she wanted to be alive, milady, and how concerned she was about what happened to her soul. Did she know that she was dying?"

I couldn't think about that part too hard. My emotions were too raw. The food I could eat but not taste was still on the table. The music was too loud. Too many hearts were beating all around me. And my mind was filled with lurid images of Eric and Rachel together in bed and on other flat surfaces. "Yes."

The funniest thing of all was that I wasn't mad at Eric for being with her. I knew Rachel. She had gone after him. He wouldn't have pursued her. Eric isn't a go out and get 'em guy. He lets women come to him. What did she want from him? If she could sell her soul, then she might be capable of anything. This was the same Rachel that had dated three different guys at the same time in high school so that she could make one pay for her lunch every day. What would she be capable of now that she'd wrapped herself around Eric's . . . um . . .

"Dennis?" I wished I'd shown Eric that I could seem alive or that instead of walking out on him at Orchard Lake when he went to kill the werewolves, I'd just waited in the car for him. Didn't Eric realize that the only reason I became a vampire in the first place was so that we could always be together?

"Yes?" Dennis looked at me across the table, bored but polite, and I wondered what he thought when he looked at me. Did he see a beautiful woman or did he just think of me as a vampire? Worse than that, maybe he viewed me as little more than an errand—a chore. Was that how Eric looked at me now?

"Why do you want to be a vampire?" I asked.

"I'm not certain I understand the question, Lady Tabitha."

"I mean," I began, "I've always thought vampires were cool. You get to live forever and you get the powers, but now that I have them . . .

I don't regret anything, really, there isn't much point to regretting, but it isn't really . . . I didn't expect it to be like it is."

He was nervous. His heart sped up when I asked him the question, but his eyes didn't give anything away. What must it be like to be a human looking at Phillip or Eric, or me, for that matter? Was it like the spider and the fly?

It hadn't been like that with Eric and me. Actually, it felt more like that after I was a vampire than it had before he turned me. He didn't need me now as much as he did then. I was no longer a source of food and warmth. Life with me had lost its vicarious thrill. Not for long. As a Living Doll, I could eventually provide him almost everything he wanted.

If I hadn't dumped him, that is. God, was I that weak? Was seeing him again enough to make me ache for him even when it was so obvious he'd moved on? He wasn't supposed to be able to move on! He was the one who was supposed to be craving me, not the other way around.

"Power," Dennis answered finally. "Influence. Money. All of those things. Immortality is nothing to sneeze at, but you can still die. You need the money, the wealth, the political influence, and all of the powers just to survive the immortality side of it."

"But, I mean, I don't know. Isn't it . . ."

"A high price to pay?" he asked.

"I guess that's where I was going with that."

He put his hand in mine and the warmth teased my fangs out of their hiding places in my gums. It stung when they cut through the tender tissue, but I didn't wince. Dennis smiled. "Look. I'm a power guy. I've always wanted it, needed it, really, and I've always been willing to do whatever it took to get it. Right now that means that I go through Lord Phillip's glorified hazing, which is fine with me. I do my time as an intern and then I get adopted by the most influential vampire in the city, someone who just happens to be one of the oldest vampires in the world."

I didn't believe him; I guess he could tell by the look on my face.

"Come on, Lady Tabitha. Surely you realize Lord Phillip is more than he appears." When he said Phillip's name he sounded worshipful. "The man is a god. He's still rising, sure, but he is definitely ascendant. He's totally incapable of deficit spending. He owns the police, the fire department, you name it, and the beauty of it is that most of them don't even realize that they've been bought."

Could the same be said of me? Did Dennis think of me as someone Phillip had purchased? Sure, he did, and worse, I thought so, too.

"Are there rules against biting your date in a club like this?" I asked.

"No, milady, but Lord Phillip—"

"Lord Phillip said that I could do what I wanted with you."

His heart sped up again and a bead of sweat rolled down his cheek. "That's true, Lady Tabitha. If something I said offended you . . ."

"Just crawl under the table and lick my shoes," I ordered. "I'll tell you if I want you to go higher." Dennis crawled under the table with a resigned look on his face. How gross. Eric would have told me to kiss his ass. Talbot would have told me off. "Go higher," I commanded absentmindedly. He did. I missed Eric.

14

ERIC:

THE DEMON

We rode to the Pollux in silence and that suited me fine. I'd had enough social interaction for one evening. It had left me tired and frustrated. The last thing I'd needed was to see Tabitha with her dinner or toy or whatever he was. Rachel scooted closer to me in the backseat of the limo, but I ignored her. Talking to Winter and then seeing Tabitha made me want to hit something, break it, smash it on the concrete, and grind it with my foot.

After I turned Tabitha, I'd treated her like crap, because it's what I always do. It's a little like when Humphrey Bogart asked Lauren Bacall to marry him. He told her that she had to decide whether she wanted to be a famous actress or be his wife. He told her that if she wanted to be a famous actress, he'd do everything in his power to help her, but if she wanted to be his wife, then she had to be willing to be with him, travel with him, even if it meant that she had to turn down good roles because they conflicted with his shooting schedule.

Seeing Tabitha again made me realize how much I wished I'd thought to make her the same kind of offer. You can be with me or you can be a vampire. What would she have said if I'd laid it all out for her like that? Instead, I gave her what she wanted and then pushed her away so that we couldn't hurt each other.

Because that's what happens with vampires. Sometimes it happens to the woman first and other times it's me, but one or both parties always wind up betrayed and angry when a young attractive living human comes between them. The warmth is too much of an aphrodisiac and it isn't like Tabitha could have both warmth and immortality. It doesn't work that way.

I shook my head vigorously, trying to wipe thoughts of her and her human boy toy out of my head, but visions of her, the boy toy, and a faceless male vampire clung to my brain like a porno decoupage. In the absence of her vampire fuck buddy's true appearance, Winter filled in.

Winter. Thinking of him brought me back to the task at hand—finding the asshole demon holding Marilyn's soul. Winter obviously knew more than he'd given me, but even Rachel had been surprised when he'd offered me not just a name, but contact information. "His name is J'iliol'lth. He maintains an office at the Lovett Building. Demons adore the Lovett Building." Winter had handed me a business card with a number printed on it.

"Dig a little deeper, darling," he'd told me. "Do your research and by all means, keep your eyes on the demon. They're tricky and you should know that he isn't working alone. Most important, you should know that I had nothing to do with it."

"Nothing to do with what?" I'd asked.

"Exactly." He had laughed in a way that reminded me of golden raindrops falling on my brain. I think I was supposed to be charmed. Instead, I'd been irritated, especially when he'd added, "Now, run along."

Outside the window, Void City blurred past. Seeing me with Rachel had shaken Tabitha. I almost had Tiko turn around, but I didn't know what else I could do. The reasons we couldn't be together were still valid and she'd obviously moved on. If I went back it would just start another scene. Maybe she really was happy with those High Society leeches. It occurred to me that I wanted her to be happy. I rolled that thought around in my brain for a while.

It didn't take as long as I thought it would for us to get back to the Pollux, or maybe I was just too distracted. Rachel's pulse beat too fast. *Nervous or guilty?* I asked myself. She smelled excited, ready for sex, but I didn't trust the scent. Around her that odor was as constant as the cinnamon smell and the little thoughts that weren't quite mine. I didn't want to think about that, either. I hoped she'd just pull whatever scam she was trying to pull without me figuring it out. Ignorance is still bliss.

I felt the Pollux before I saw it, like recognizing an old girlfriend's footsteps in the mall. Certain things felt more real to me since Magbidion and Rachel had brought me back. I felt Fang, too. He wanted to be driven, to hunt.

When we got there, Rachel followed me upstairs to the office. Greta was sitting in my desk chair, typing on the computer. She hadn't been able to keep all of the furniture in the rest of the building when the state had come for my assets, but my office was intact.

"I just reclaimed your e-mail address. I meant to have that done already, but . . ." She shrugged. Vampires get a weird waxy smell when they haven't fed and they're hungry. It takes a few days for me to get to that point, but Greta gets hungry fast. She smelled already. Never turn a human with an eating disorder. You'd think the change would cure the disorder, because you can't gain weight, but it doesn't. It's either famine or feast with that girl and stress makes it worse.

"You haven't fed," I said.

"I wanted to make sure you got back okay."

"You didn't smell like this when the resurrection thing happened, so you can't have gone more than a day. Go eat."

She hugged me. "I missed you, Dad."

"I missed you, too," I said as I returned the hug. "Go eat, but only one person and don't kill them; you can't afford to pay Magbidion right now." I glanced around the room and listened hard. "Where is Mags anyway?"

"He said he wanted to get a buddy of his to pull the info on whoever filed to have Eric Jones declared dead. I told him it was okay if he kept parking in the deck."

She bounded out of my office.

"Take Fang," I called after her. "Run over a cat or something. It'll cheer you up."

"Okay. Cool," she called back.

I picked up the phone, an old-style handset, while Rachel flipped through the CDs stacked on my desk.

"Iron Maiden. Metallica. The Rolling Stones. Are any of these still around?" she asked.

"They are." I pulled the business card Winter had given me out of my wallet and started to dial. Rachel hung up the phone with her finger and leaned over my desk so that the silver rings in her nipples peeked out at me from beneath her dress. "What?" I asked.

"This demon you're supposed to meet, J'iliol'lth? Winter said he was a power broker, but that's not the part you need to worry about. He's a demon, a scary one; I've . . . um . . . heard people talk about him at the Irons Club before."

I was tired of hearing about the damn Irons Club. I moved her hand away from the phone and dialed the number for J'iliol'lth. Rachel wrinkled her nose and stuck out her tongue. She slid past me, grinding against my crotch on her way to the computer.

"Samhain Industries." The voice on the phone was reminiscent of Ebon Winter, curiously androgynous with a dash of civilized disdain. Samhain Industries? Cute, a funny demon.

"How can you help me?" I asked flatly.

"Excuse me, sir?"

"You're supposed to ask how you can help me or how you can direct my call."

"Excuse me, sir?"

"Just let me talk to the demon."

"Excuse me, sir?"

Rachel pulled up a picture of a beautiful girl with lines of piercings laced like a corset up her sides.

"Do you like it?" Rachel asked. "I was thinking about getting one."

I held my hand over the receiver. "It looks painful."

"Sir?" called the voice on the phone.

"Sorry. Look. I need to speak to Jill E. Olth or however you say his name. He may be expecting my call."

"Vampire, human, demon, or other, sir?"

"Vampire."

"Is this issue soul related, ascension based, or other?"

"Soul related." Jesus, she sounded like she was reading from a script.

"Yours or another person's, sir?"

"My aunt Trudy's! Just get the demon on the fucking phone!"

"I don't have to listen to that kind of language, sir."

"You know what? You're in the Lovett Building, right? Why don't I just come down there? I'm sure you've got all kinds of cool wards, but my car recently became undead and I think I ought to see if I can just drive it into the lobby. Then, I think I'll turn into a giant uber vamp and start tearing the place apart. Ooh, or better yet, I'll turn into a revenant and start sucking people's souls out. That would be fun." I don't know why I said that. Turning into a revenant had to be near the absolute bottom of my to do list. Then again . . . I wondered. *Could I change back and forth if I wanted?*

"Hold on a sec."

I turned into a revenant. Done on purpose, it felt as if I were expanding and contracting at the same time, my body bursting and then drawing into the center of my spectral self as my skin went even colder than usual. The receiver fell through my hand to the top of the desk and I changed back quickly, afraid that I might get stuck again. That answered my question, though. I could do it if I needed to do it.

The voice laughed at me.

"You must be the being for whom we're holding Marilyn Robinson's soul." It wasn't the same voice, but it sounded like the same person. He now spoke with a polished, educated accent, almost British.

"Yeah, that's me."

"Then it's my great regret to inform you that you've been speaking to a very talented, but quite mischievous answering imp." The voice changed again. Now it was nasal and annoying. "Call the master's human secretary at the following number." I scribbled the number down, hung up, and closed my eyes for a minute.

Rachel was afraid again. Her body pressed into the left side of the chair.

"Problem?" I asked.

"How are you doing that?" she blurted.

"Doing what?"

She looked stricken, biting her lip rather than answering. I held up my hand in front of my face. Purple light illuminated my palm. With a little effort, I changed the light from purple to red.

"I'm not that mad. I don't know what makes my eyes glow purple."

"But how . . . never mind."

How can I still lose my temper with you doing whatever it is you're doing to try to control me? I thought to myself. Good question.

"Get the piercing," I told her. "Why don't you go get it now, tonight? I want to see it tomorrow."

"It's awfully late."

"I'm sure you can find someone to do it."

"Okay." She sounded cheerful again, but her heart was pounding. She was pissed, but hiding it. If she was a good little thrall, she'd have to go, wouldn't she? But was she a good little thrall? Based on what Marilyn told me, I could order her to do it and she'd have to obey. Something rose up in the hindmost part of my brain . . . something quirky about frogs, or maybe tattoos, then it was gone.

I dialed the number. Someone answered before it even rang. "Yes?"

Rachel moved past me without the grinding.

"I want to set up a meeting with the demon."

"Lord Eric." The speaker sounded like she'd never been happier to speak with anyone in her entire life. "I'm so pleased you called. Lord J'iliol'lth has been waiting to talk to you."

"How soon can he meet me?" And how'd he know my name? I guess he'd had four months in which to do some digging.

"Perhaps this evening around eight?" the voice offered.

The clock on the wall said it was after midnight, almost one o'clock. "No, I want to meet him now . . . this morning, before dawn."

"I'm sorry." Her tone told me everything I needed to know; she thought my request was absurd. "Lord J'iliol'lth has already retired for the evening. We can't all be nocturnal. If you didn't suffer from your condition, of course, then he would be happy to meet with you at his offices in town as early as seven o'clock this morning."

I could hear Rachel changing out of her prom dress in my bedroom down the hall. "Fucking Emperor," she mumbled under her breath. I heard her fingers touch her lips as if she were covering her mouth, having spoken out loud by mistake.

"Where are his offices again?"

"Suite 603 in the Lovett Building."

I scrawled that on my notepad. Everyone in Void City knew the Lovett Building. It was the skyscraper downtown with the big golden dome on top. Rumors said that all kinds of satanic rituals took place there late at night. Obviously, the rumors were wrong. The satanic rituals took place early in the morning. It just goes to show that you can't trust rumors. "What's the window situation?"

"Sir?"

Rachel stopped in the doorway wearing jeans and a T-shirt. She smiled at me and I motioned for her to wait. "The window situation," I said more slowly. "What is it like? Does he have windows in his office?"

"Yes, of course."

"Do they have blinds?"

"Well, yes, sir, of course they do. They were designed by Lady Gh'st'na'kzi herself. They are quite stunning."

"Tell him I'll see him at seven, then, and he'd better be prompt. My assistant Rachel will be with me as well. Is that an issue?" Rachel raised an eyebrow at that, but I held a finger to my lips to keep her from asking any questions.

"No, sir. But if you don't mind my asking . . . won't you be asleep, sir?"

I laughed. "Just confirm the appointment, lady, and make sure he has the damn blinds closed."

She did so and I hung up. It felt good to have a plan. Smiling at Rachel, I put my arms around her and kissed her full on the lips. She returned the kiss passionately before disengaging herself. "Do you mind telling me what I just volunteered for?"

"In five hours I need you to run an errand for me."

"I don't take much sleep, Eric, but even I have to get three or four hours. Otherwise, I'm useless," she complained. "That's the only reason I was worried about getting the piercing tonight."

Sure, that was the reason. I would have believed her if the office didn't smell like a whorehouse running a special on cinnamon-scented panties.

"I think you've told me that before." I walked around behind her, pushed her facedown onto the desk, and helped her off with her jeans.

Later, as she slept, I spooned with her, feeling the faint reverberation of her beating heart against my skin, wallowing in her warmth, in the unconscious rise and fall of her chest as I held her. My fingers traced the intersection of flesh and metal at her nipples. Asleep, there was no cinnamon, no little not-my-thoughts.

"You're making it awfully hard to ignore whatever it is you're doing," I whispered. She gave me a sleeper's sigh in response.

What had been up with the piercing anyway? Why offer to get it if she didn't want it? If I'd been turned on by the piercing, would she have gotten it? I had no doubt that she would have done so gladly, but why? Because it would have enhanced the sex, the attraction? That felt like the right answer. Everything was tied up in that. I disentangled myself and she stirred, reaching back unconsciously not for my hand, but lower. I climbed out of bed. A frown, brief but present, touched her lips before she settled back into her normal circadian rhythm.

I took my clothes with me and changed into them out in the hall, not sure where I was going until I was already in the parking deck near Magbidion's RV. I pounded on the door and was answered by a bleary-eyed Mags wearing nothing but a poorly tied bathrobe.

"What is it?" He clearly wasn't awake yet. "Where's the car?"

"Don't worry about the car," I told him, "and cover up."

He drew the robe tighter, the light of intelligence behind his eyes growing brighter as he fought his way free of the sleep toxins I no longer possessed. "You look intense this morning."

"Yeah. Sorry to wake you. Look, I need to ask you a question."

"As long as it's nothing too complicated." He leaned against the door, not inviting me in. Not that I needed an invitation. Vampires don't.

"What do you know about vampire thralls and sex magic?"

"So you've been thinking it, too?" He smiled.

"Thinking what?"

"That your girlfriend Rachel is a tantric witch."

"Yeah," I lied. "I was thinking something like that."

"Come on in." He stepped clear of the door. "If you don't mind, can you tell me exactly what you did, step by step, when you made Rachel your thrall?"

I told him everything that I remembered, and then he told me how it was supposed to work and I had him write it all down. We ran some tests. Could I sense my vampiric offspring if I concentrated? Yes. Could they tell I was sensing them? Yes. Even if I focused on hiding from them? Yep. Could I sense Rachel? No, or not always. Could I see through her eyes? No.

"It's called the dark tantra," Magbidion said finally. He clarified before I even asked. "Normal tantric magic is about healing energy, divine union. It's healthy and positive, but what Rachel is doing sounds like what succubi use: sex of power, by power, and for power."

"That doesn't sound too bad."

Magbidion balked at that. "She's a human using magic that's meant for demons, very specific demons that suck your soul out through your privates or use sex to control you."

"Is she sucking my soul out?"

"No, or I don't think so. Hold on." Magbidion made a circle with the thumb and forefinger on his right hand, then looked through it at me. "It doesn't look like it, but I can see why she might want to."

"Why is it that? Do I have a really cool soul or something?"

"Um, well, okay, yes, sort of, but I don't think you understand how rare this is. It's like the core of your being exists in a state of grace. There's something else weaving through it, too, a curse or an enchantment. You—"

"Now you're sounding like Talbot." I covered Magbidion's hands with mine, blocking his view. "So I have the York peppermint pattie aura. Whoopee. I don't want to hear anything else unless it has to do with Rachel."

"The short version?" Magbidion said.

I nodded.

"My best guess is that she's trying to control you, but at your power level, I don't know how effective she'd be . . . maybe she could influence your emotions, put thoughts in your head, but very little direct control. She could even leech power off of you, but I don't think it's something you'd miss. I'm talking little dribs and drabs."

"Tell me how it works."

By the time Greta pulled back in with Fang, I felt like I might be ahead of the game.

15

ERIC:

EVERYBODY LOATHES JILL

Rachel approached the Lovett Building a little before seven o'clock. She was dressed in a smart-looking red business suit that showed just a little too much cleavage and way too much leg to be appropriate for the workplace (well, this particular workplace, anyway). The lenses of her sunglasses were also tinted red and the heels of her shoes were three or four inches high.

As many times as Rachel had carried mouse-me in her purse, she should have known to bring a bigger one. I knew she had at least one purse big enough—she'd carried both me and Greta in it after one of our big werewolf fights. While I wrestled her lipsticks, her wallet, her keys, a compact, a pencil, two pens, some Kleenex, a tiny sewing kit, some Band-Aids, a Tylenol bottle, several individually packaged wet wipes, and God only knows what else, I seriously considered throwing out everything that wasn't me. Better not to leave a trail, I decided.

Rachel walked up to the front door and pulled it open. Once inside, her footsteps started to echo. It sounded like the room was big and the floor was tile or marble. It was hard for me to tell. I smelled coffee, donuts, and other breakfast-y kinds of things in the distance. Food court, probably. If I strained, I could make out the sounds of people talking in another large space. There was even a fountain or a waterfall; I couldn't tell which, but I could hear the water.

"Can I help you, ma'am?"

The voice was male and the speaker was taller than Rachel. I guessed it was a security guard from the tone he'd used. He sounded at once willing to help, friendly, and mildly suspicious. Pulling off all three at once as well as he did made me suspect he'd been doing this awhile.

"I'm here to see J'iliol'lth," Rachel told him. "I'm an assistant to Lord Eric. He's expected."

"Is he here now?"

Someone was watching me. I couldn't see them, but as he asked that question, I felt a presence sweeping through the lobby. It was a low but constant pressure on my senses. It brushed the edges of my mind, began to push inward. Nobody had mentioned anything about any psychic checkpoints or mental searches, so I felt no need to cooperate. Using the same technique I used when controlling lesser vamps, I pushed back hard.

The pressure went away, but the presence was still there, flitting about like a gnat, too small to squash but still an annoyance. It was probably that obnoxious imp I'd talked to on the phone.

"Yes, he is with me now. Could you please show us to J'iliol'lth's office or a waiting area with no sunlight?"

"Let me call on up and see."

The guard and Rachel both started walking and I was once again assaulted by the contents of her purse. A zipper tab came out of nowhere and tried to go where no one had gone before. I was halfway out of her purse before I saw daylight and slid back down, landing on top of a compact. I made a mental note to put some kind of thrall compulsion on Rachel and make her only buy really big purses from now on.

By the time we got to J'iliol'lth's office I had discovered a small leather pouch inside a little zippered pocket sewn into the lining of her purse. It smelled like spices and old bones. I couldn't tell exactly what was in it, but I wanted Magbidion to take a look at it. If his suspicions about Rachel were correct, it might be important.

"Greetings, ma'am. Please tell your master he may now appear. The shades are secured. I assure you, the room is quite safe for him."

Rachel turned around and opened the bag carefully. I would have liked to do something impressive—turn into a revenant and try to make it look like I was coming out of her mouth, but for all I knew, I might have eaten her soul by accident. Instead, I leapt off of the top of her purse and landed in my human shape. Both of us turned to face J'iliol'lth.

I was still wearing jeans, tennis shoes, my *Welcome to the Void* T-shirt, and a black leather belt, but I'd added a pair of sunglasses and a leather jacket. The sunglasses would keep our pal "Jill" from noticing the strangeness of my eyes if they went purple again. They were still doing the black-with-purple business off and on unpredictably. I was sure I'd have been able to control my eyes if Rachel would just stop screwing around with me. With her tantric magic or whatever it was.

J'iliol'lth was an ugly son of a bitch. He wasn't red, like I'd expected, and he didn't have little horns or a pitchfork. I always expect demons to look like that, although I've never met one that did. I guess it's some kind of nonhuman prejudice. The confounding thing was how familiar he looked. I couldn't place it.

J'iliol'lth had black skin with small brackish-brown sores that oozed dark green pus. Patches of gray moss covered his skin in an odd approximation of hair and his beady little eyes were transparent except for cloudy brown irises and stark white pupils. Even so, he wore an expensive suit. I guess he thought it would make him look more businesslike. In his case, it didn't help much.

He also had a smell. It wasn't so bad, a touch of mint and a little wintergreen, but he was colder than room temperature and his heart, if he had one, was silent. I try not to trust anyone who doesn't have a heartbeat.

The office itself looked normal except for the window treatments. The blinds were ghastly metal creations covered with a surreal paint job. They were bolted to the wall, drawn closed with a set of chains, and locked tight with a small padlock. Someone was trying to make sure I felt comfortable and safe. Just like a demon . . .

"Ah, Mr. Jones," he began. "How good of you to come, and at such an inconvenient time, too."

"Yeah, whatever," I said, dropping down into one of the two available chairs opposite his desk. Rachel gracefully lowered herself into the other. I stared at one of the motivational posters he had hanging on the wall. It was about leadership and had a picture of a lion. This demon was really going all out to make sure he fit in. "Nice poster," I said sarcastically.

"Thank you, Mr. Jones."

"Eric," I corrected. "No one calls me mister anything. Of course, some people call me asshole or bastard or motherfucker, but I usually kill them. You should probably just stick with Eric."

Rachel gave me a wide-eyed look of warning, but I ignored it. It's what I tend to do with all the good advice I'm given. J'iliol'lth smiled politely. I couldn't tell if he was getting angry yet or not, but my guess was that I could get him there.

J'iliol'lth opened his mouth to speak, but I interrupted him. "So Jill . . . Can I call you Jill? I want Marilyn's soul back and I want it now. I know you want something for it and I'm happy to work with you there, but do you think you could cut all the posturing bullshit and just spell out what you want?"

The moss on the demon's head whitened and the mint smell grew stronger. As he clasped his hands together, they made a slightly disgusting squishy sound. "Eric, please, let's both do our best to be cordial here. I've held on to Miss Robinson's spirit in good faith and I'm quite certain—"

I took off my sunglasses and "Jill" stopped speaking. I caught Rachel staring at my eyes, too. I guess she hadn't seen enough of the purple glow, yet . . . Either that or with her influencing my emotions toward calm, it scared her that I could still get this angry. According to Magbidion, Rachel was using no small amount of mojo to keep me from being able to black out, to force me to stay in control. The only things Mags and I couldn't figure out was why.

"Jill" looked questioningly at Rachel as if he expected her to do something. Maybe it was because we'd told him she was my assistant, but it seemed like more than that. I made a mental note of it and decided to press my advantage, if it truly was an advantage. I popped my fangs.

"Look, Jill, I've been having some anger management issues lately. What's four-month-old news for some folks is two days ago to me, so let's not mince words, okay? Because even though I haven't eaten today, you don't look very appetizing and I don't want to be picking demon out of my teeth. What the fuck do you want in exchange for Marilyn?"

J'iliol'lth regained his composure instantaneously and smiled a toothy white smile. "So you have no problem with the associated costs?"

"I'm not signing anything. I'm not shaking hands and you can't have my soul, what there is of it, in exchange."

He managed to look crestfallen at that and I wondered how much of it was an act and how much was real.

"I'm afraid it is not just a matter of the cost. I'm certain that she's special to you, but Miss Robinson was likely already hell bound. She had long since ceased believing in any sort of deity—"

"Good, then I should be able to buy her off you cheap."

"Normally, yes, in any other circumstance, by all means I would have given her to you as a sign of good faith, but the purpose for which she was intended has rather exacting parameters. To retain her soul as a courtesy to you, I was forced to use the next most compatible soul in my possession, a soul which was a bit more"—he paused midsentence and his eyes flashed—"costly."

Shit. I crossed my arms. "How costly?"

"You see, the ritual in question required a willing sacrifice, a soul

who was aware that he or she was sacrificing themselves for another."
He was positively giddy just describing it. "Self-sacrifice, especially the
sacrifice of one's soul for another, even if the sacrificial soul is already
hell bound, is quite rare. The next most comparable soul I had was a
Catholic priest from oh . . . ten years or so ago, give or take . . . He gave
his soul to save one of his parishioners who'd bargained theirs away to
me. I'd been saving him for a special occasion."

"Fu-uck me," I cursed. "What the hell kind of ritual was it?"

"Normally I charge for this sort of information, but for you . . .
consider it a gift to the vampire who killed my brother, J'hon'byg'butte."

El Segundo was about to bite me on the ass. I killed a lot of demons in El Segundo. Okay, to be fair, Talbot killed most of them, but
he ostensibly worked for me and in the demon world, as in the vampire
world, that made it all my fault.

"Eric." The demon stood up and walked around his desk as he
spoke. "My dear, dear, Eric, I'm afraid your friend, Mr. Malcolm . . .
Roger . . . came to me for an enhancement."

"God, you must be loving this," I said. "What sort of enhancement?"

J'iliol'lth leaned against his desk and looked down at me. I stared up
at him and tried to make my eyes glow red. They didn't. Instead, two
little color-changing dots hit the demon in the pupils and he turned
away quickly. He didn't have eyelids, so he couldn't blink. Interesting.

"Sorry," I said casually, putting my sunglasses back on. "Anger
management. I'm sure I mentioned it. What kind of enhancement?"

"He wanted me to make him a Vlad, like you," he said, walking
back behind his desk. The mint smell went sour, replaced by a rotten
citrus odor. Was that what demon fear smelled like? I could sense that
Rachel was afraid, too. Both of them probably knew more about my
anger management issues than I did, but I wondered if they knew that
I wasn't quite as ignorant as they thought I was. I leaned back in my
chair.

"How?"

"He was going to capture you and bring you to me. We were going to use your essence to 'promote' him to Vladhood." He opened his
desk drawer. "You undid his plot and defeated him when you had your
lupine friends devour him; you should be very happy."

"Yeah, I'm thrilled all right. What does all of this have to do with
Marilyn?"

"We worked out a contingency, an intercession." Just as the final
word passed his lips, the chair I was sitting in sprouted scaly orange
hands that grabbed my arms. Rachel's scream told me hers had done

the same. Smoothly, in one motion, J'iliol'lth drew a gun I recognized from his desk drawer: *El Alma Perdida.*

"You've gotta be kidding me." Bang. The shot rang out. A familiar burning sensation spread through my chest. Silver licks of flame poured out of the wound. J'iliol'lth dropped the gun with a howl, his hand sizzling where he'd touched the butt of the gun.

"Shoulda staked me," I roared. *El Alma Perdida* was made to hunt werewolves. The bullets are magic. If a werewolf gets shot with one of them, the bullet steals its soul. A bullet from *El Alma Perdida* also shape-locks any supernatural creature it hits. As long as the bullet stays inside them, they can't change shape. A vampire can't pop his claws, can't even pop his fangs. Unfortunately for J'iliol'lth, my fangs were already out.

J'iliol'lth said a word I didn't understand and the chains on the curtain vanished, dropping the padlock to the floor where it transformed into a tiny demon with little red horns and a pitchfork—the imp.

Another orange-scaled hand rose up from between my legs. This one had a sharpened wooden stake in its grasp. It stabbed at my heart, J'iliol'lth opened the curtains, and I kicked off of the floor with both feet as hard as I could. My demon chair flipped up and over, but its grip didn't loosen at all. The stake plunged into my chest and bounced off my sternum. I sank my teeth into the only knuckle I could reach and the creature yowled.

"How's it going, son?" John Paul Courtney's voice drawled inside my brain. My mouth was full, but there were plenty of things I felt like saying. "Still fornicatin' and consortin' with demons, I see," the ghost of the gun added. "You could have at least woke up when the demon sent some of his boys to collect the gun. But no, you was jest starin' off inta space."

The back of my head hit the floor and the chair rocked over on its side. Both the demon and I let out "oofs." Sunlight poured into the room and my ankles caught fire between my socks and the jeans. The demon chair's orange scales ignited as the silver flame from my bullet wound touched them. The hand holding the stake at my chest recoiled. I tucked my burning shins up under the demon chair and it howled.

"Fire sucks, don't it?" I snarled. The demon chair let go. "Flame on!"

You've got to question the wisdom of using a non-fireproof demon to restrain a vampire and then opening the curtains. I think J'iliol'lth had intended for me to be staked by the time I caught fire. No such luck. I may be stupid, but I'm not slow. Flame engulfed my entire body as I stood. I raised both hands over my head, clasped them together, and brought them down on the floor. Go, go, vampire strength.

"Someone stop him!" J'iliol'lth shouted.

Fire, pain . . . it causes some vamps to freeze up, roll around on the ground. I catch fire on a semiregular basis. It comes with having a poor time sense and a bad memory. I'm not immune to fire; I'm bored with it.

"But he's on fire!"

"Why didn't you stake him?"

"He caught fire!"

Blinded by flames, I couldn't see anything, but vampire hearing is very good. Somewhere nearby a toilet flushed. Water moved through the pipes. Water was just what I needed.

The floor gave out on my third strike, dropping me to the next level. I ran toward the sound of the moving water, smacked into a wall and punched my way through it, still following the sound. People screamed, cried, and ran, but I ignored them in my pursuit of the water. Another toilet flushed and I burst through the wall and into the ladies' room.

Grabbing the bowl of the nearest sink with both hands, I tore it free of the wall. Water sprayed out of the shorn pipe, dousing the flames. Behind me, a woman backed away, screaming. I needed blood quickly, more than she could spare.

But there was one thing I needed more. I grabbed her throat. "If you can help me get the bullet out of my chest, I won't eat you." She swallowed hard and nodded.

Her waterlogged purse lay on the floor nearby. When I released her, she snatched it up, rummaging through it purposefully. "I . . . I think I have a pair of tweezers."

For me, the healing hurts worse than the burn itself. Vampire nerves stop registering pain after the initial injury. My entire body had been charred. With a sound like two vinyl records melted together and being pulled apart, my skin began to regenerate.

Three dog-headed demons burst into the women's restroom. One of them had an ax decorated with fancy filigree. The second wielded a frost-covered sword. Demon number three just came with claws and a mouth full of sharp pointy teeth. I threw a sink at them to buy time. Everything slowed to a crawl, rivulets of water drifted through the air in lazy streams, and I realized my vampire speed had kicked in. I've never been good at controlling it, but I was glad it had decided to show up.

The contents of the woman's purse fell slowly toward the tile. I spotted the pair of tweezers flipping through the air. I snatched them up with a grin. Some demons have the speed thing, too. These guys didn't. By the time they made it halfway across the room, I had the bullet out.

Can you say uber vamp? I knew you could.

✦ 16 ✦

ERIC:
RENEGOTIATIONS

I walked back into Jill's office in uber vamp mode, holding the frost-covered sword in my right hand and the heads of his three dog demons in my left. Seven other demons stood around the room, not counting the two funky-looking chair demons. Sunlight began its slow sizzle on the ebony skin of my uber vamp form. It stung. I had no idea how long it would take for me to catch fire this way, but it undoubtedly made me seem like a badass.

Jill closed the shades. "If everyone would excuse us, please?"

Rachel ran over to me when the chair let her go, skirting the big hole I'd put in the floor. She moved to embrace me, but I pushed her away. Hunger can do strange things to a vampire, alter perceptions. I couldn't see Rachel's skin anymore, just the veins and the blood coursing through them. My color differentiation faded as well, rendering the world in shades of monochromatic red. I knew if I stayed hungry long enough the perception changes could become permanent.

"I'm too hungry," I explained. "If I feed on you, you'll die."

"I'll order in," J'iliol'lth said casually. He pushed a button on his desk. "Julia?"

"Yes, Master?" the speaker on his desk crackled.

"Could you send a couple of girls up here, please?"

"Right away, Master."

I broke my rule about accepting blood from strangers. Both of the women looked like supermodels. They came willingly, apparently resigned to death. I didn't want to know why a demon like J'iliol'lth kept beauties like this on tap or what he held over their heads. Did he own their souls? How can you tell if someone's soul is in hock anyway? I knew Magbidion's was owed out but it's never been something that I could smell.

After I'd eaten, colors bled back into my vision, but everything still had a tinge of red to it. If I'd drained the girls dry, it might have cleared up immediately, but since there were two of them, I didn't have to kill either of them. The girls were unconscious and I had my unwanted color tint, but I hoped we'd all be fine in a night or two. I also felt more mellow, artificially so, sleepy, too. "Okay, what was in the blood?"

"Nothing that will harm you, I give you my word." His tone made that sound important, believable. "Just a little enchantment to calm you so that we might speak on more friendly terms."

"I don't like being drugged."

"You have my apologies, Eric," J'iliol'lth said with debatable sincerity. "Shall we move to an interior room?"

"As long as it isn't a trap." You have to expect deceit from demons. I'd forgotten, and now I was drugged. I decided I was going to get one hell of a discount on Marilyn, or Jill was going to be on the tooth and claw end of my anger stick. "And I'll want my gun back," I added, pointing the sword tip at him.

He handed *El Alma Perdida* to me and I changed back to my human form, tucking it into the back of my jeans. I pulled the sixth bullet out of the mouth of one of the dead dog demons (where I'd stowed it) and dropped it into my pocket.

"It isn't a trap, Eric. You have my word. I can put it in writing if you like."

"So long as it's nothing that I have to sign and I'm not agreeing to anything." *Bullshit. With demons, it's always a trap. Why else would he have given me my gun back if not to lure me into a false sense of security?*

"Touché," he laughed. "Touché."

Twenty minutes later we were in a plush conference room with leather chairs and a plasma screen television someone had obligingly set to the sports channel. Rachel and I sat down, but not before I sliced into each seat with the frost sword just to be sure.

"What the hell were we talking about?" I asked.

"Miss Robinson's soul?"

"Something else, too." I racked my brain and, very unusually for me, I remembered. "The contingency you worked up with Roger."

J'iliol'lth's mossy covering turned blue. "A vampire can be restored to unlife after destruction once and only once through the willing sacrifice of a human soul." I threw the longsword through the television. It didn't explode like they do in the movies.

"I had his happy ass eaten by a pack of werewolves and you brought him back?" J'iliol'lth stared at the smoke drifting up from the television. "Don't look at the damn TV. Look at me!"

"You're a very expensive guest."

"Get over it, peckerwood. You tried to kill me."

"And you killed my brother."

"Your brother fucked with me while I was on vacation and he got dead. He had a dumb fucking name anyway. Johnny something. Besides, don't you guys come in clutches or something, like flies? You must have a few hundred brothers."

"Eric," Rachel cautioned.

"Give me Marilyn's soul back, right now, for free, or I'm going to tear this building down around your ears."

"That's not going to happen. If you damaged the building enough that I had to leave, I'd drag Miss Robinson's soul with me. You can banish me, but my death would be far from permanent. You are not the only being that is insufferably hard to exterminate. You don't have your mouser here, Eric. You have no leverage."

"Like I give a shit. People try to kill me, unmake me, and screw up my junk all the time . . . or haven't you been paying attention?"

"I assure you, Mr. Jones. No, let us dispense with such foolish pretenses. We both know your true name, don't we, Mr. Courtney? I know that you are the great-great-grandson of John Paul Courtney, just as surely as I know that you do, as you so quaintly put it, give a shit. You care for humans. Your family always has.

"True, yours is a sporadic and capricious morality, but you have one. You're a Courtney. You care. You mean well. You make an effort. That is where we differ." He put his hands on the table between us and leaned toward me. "Go to war with me and you will find that I understand you all too well, where to hurt you, how to make you cry at night. I'm a demon, Mr. Courtney, it's what I do, but," he made a placating wave, "I have no wish to fight with you. As you say, I have many siblings."

He attempted to snap his fingers, succeeding on the third try, and a glowing purple cube rose up out of the table. "She's in there." I reached for the box, but my hand passed through it.

"What gives?"

"I will send her with you, as a good faith gesture, an advance payment for the services you will render. I want you to obtain the Stone of Aeternum for me in exchange."

I jerked the sword out of the TV. "I don't work for demons, Jill. Come on, Rachel. We're leaving." Rachel peeled herself out of her chair and we started for the door. "Thanks for your time, Jill. It's been real fun.

I'll be back with my mouser. If it doesn't work out, you make sure to tell Marilyn that I tried."

"Are you sure you aren't even the teensiest bit interested in being able to eat food again? Bask in the sun? Enjoy the sound of your own eternal heartbeat?"

I stopped. "What the hell are you talking about?"

"It's quite simple, actually," the demon said. "Without a contingency, I'm uncertain that your friend Roger is willing to work with me. He's used his last get out of jail free card and, for him, there are no other routes back to this world if he is destroyed again. Any being may come back once through supernatural means . . . being turned into a vampire, zombie, et cetera." His eyes cut to Rachel for less than an eyeblink and I nearly missed it. "To come back one other time requires the expenditure of a soul, a willing sacrifice."

"And a thrall qualifies?" I asked. "I thought you said she was forced."

"Normally true as well, but it's all a matter of intent." He licked his lips. "Roger didn't force her to sign the contract using his power as her master, he forced her to sign it by threatening you."

Fang's engine roared in my head and the red tinge to my vision went purple.

"He's dead," I said in a whisper. "He just doesn't know it yet." I turned to leave.

"But, Mr. Courtney," Jill said. "You haven't heard my offer."

"What are you talking about, the stuff you promised Roger, the wanting to be a Vlad thing? I am a Vlad . . . you have no leverage," I mocked. "I'm going to go kill Roger and then I'm coming back here for Marilyn."

"A Vlad? Please, Mr. Courtney. I thought we were being honest with each other. We both know that you are not a Vlad, just as we know I can't make you a more powerful vampire than you already are. But I can make you something better, or at least, better as far as you are likely to be concerned."

He stood up. He was taller than me, but from his posture, the extra height didn't reassure him any. "I'm not interested," I said. You can't trust demons.

"Are you sure?" he asked. "I could make you an immortal, Eric, a true immortal. Living, breathing, yet undying; untouched by death, disease, or the ravages of time. You wouldn't be able to change shape anymore, true, but—"

Before he could finish his sentence, Jill was up in the air with my hand around his throat. "You'd better not be lying to me, Jill. You won't like what I'll do to you if you're blowing smoke up my ass."

"I assure you, it is possible. It will only work for you. You are different. For one like you, it will work."

I set him down.

Different. Sometimes I felt different. It wasn't just the eyes. I'd never been a typical vampire. It sounded . . . possible. I struggled to remember something that ghost-Marilyn had said, but it was gone. "Tell me more."

"Indulge me for a moment first," J'iliol'lth said. "What do you remember about how you died?"

"Memento mori," I murmured.

"What?" J'iliol'lth's eyes widened and he drew back. "I assure you I would never ask—"

"Remember your death," I translated. "That's what you want, right? Me to remember it? Well, I do and pretty well, since I just relived it a little while ago. Why do you want to know?" I asked suspiciously. J'iliol'lth walked back over to his seat and lifted a small glass paperweight with a scorpion carapace preserved inside. He held it up so that I could see it.

"Why do I have this?" he asked. "Curiosity. I like to look at it. I like scorpions. We have things like them where I'm from, but they are intelligent and quite dangerous. Here, they are not so dangerous, but look exactly the same. I like having it. It amuses me."

"So?"

"So I want to know because I don't know and because it would amuse me to know."

Sounded very Hannibal Lecter to me. Rachel and I both sat back down. "I was driving Roger's car," I told him. "The brakes went out and it went down into a quarry. When I woke up, I was a vampire."

"So you never knew your sire?" J'iliol'lth asked eagerly.

"No, I always assumed it happened in the hospital or in the ambulance or something."

He put down the paperweight and crossed the room to stand in front of the TV. "And the next evening you rose as a vampire."

I decided not to tell him anything about what had happened when Magbidion brought me back, about the curse, or about Fang. "No, I was dead for a while. Marilyn always said I rose after the funeral."

Rachel looked like a bee had stung her on the butt, but she didn't say anything. Her breathing picked up, her pulse started to race, and I could smell the sweat. There was something very important about all of this and I had no clue what it was, but I wondered if it had something to do with the curse.

"So you rose on the seventh night and—"

"Day," I corrected. "It was in the afternoon. Two weeks later."

J'iliol'lth turned to face me; his eyes glowed a burnt copper color. "By any chance, were you embalmed?"

"I think so," I said. "Why? Is that important?"

J'iliol'lth smiled again. He was always smiling, frowning, and then smiling again. Maybe it was a hobby. "Embalming a person who is going to rise as a vampire stops the process. They die without rising, but you did not die, and in that gray area, between life and unlife, there is much power to be had. You are a Child of Wrath . . . a person who rose as a vampire second and as something else first."

"Horse puckey." John Paul Courtney chuckled in my head. "He's pulling the wool over your eyes, boy. Child of Wrath. Huh, sounds like one of those so-called music groups you listen to."

I should have listened to old J. P., but something about what Jill was saying sounded familiar . . . I'd heard it before from someone I trusted. Hadn't Marilyn said something like that?

I smelled mint again as J'iliol'lth continued, "I think it is very likely that you were murdered, Eric."

"Yeah, I know that," I told him. "It was Roger. He was screwing Marilyn behind my back."

"Even better," Jill crowed. "I think you rose as a revenant, but some unique circumstance caused you to rise as a vampire as well. Sometimes it's a family curse, or it could have been something as simple as a vampire having fed on you in the ER. It's very rare and it makes you exceedingly unique. I've only heard of it happening once or twice every few millennia."

Family curse. I knew Jill made a living by capitalizing on things that sounded right, but it was the little bits that weren't exactly true, the lies of omission, that he used to turn a profit. The thought of being alive again, living in the sunshine forever, made it hard to walk away, even though I still had the feeling a smart man would have done just that.

"What else does it do?" I asked. "I can see why I would want it, but what do you want with this thing . . . the um . . ."

"The Stone of Aeternum," Rachel inserted.

"Right," I continued, "this Stone of Aeternum, what do you want with it?"

J'iliol'lth pretended to consider it, but he already had an answer planned out. The way he spoke, the subtle motions he made as he crossed the room or answered a question, it all had the feeling of something rehearsed, a script or a speech. He knew what I was going to ask him. I had fallen right into the role he wanted me to play. It wasn't a feeling I enjoyed.

"It will only work once per century, but it can grant certain desires of the supernatural. It is within the Stone of Aeternum's capabilities to, under the correct circumstances, elevate a Master vampire into a Vlad or change a normal lycanthrope into an Alpha. Its transmutative properties are substantial," he said with unfeigned avarice. "If one were to possess such an item, the profit would be equally substantial. One could even raise the dead, and not just the newly dead like a Zaomancer can, but the long dead—if the stars were right and the ritual done properly. But, silly me, we're getting ahead of ourselves."

He walked away from the television to put a placating hand on my shoulder and I gave him a look that made him wince. Removing the offending hand, he turned away from me. "Get me the Stone of Aeternum and not only can you have Marilyn Robinson's soul as previously discussed, but I will make you immortal as I have described. You will have enhanced senses, strength, and speed, you will no longer need to sleep, eat, or drink, but will be fully capable of enjoying all three. You can even have children, if you want. You get to retain your soul and you will not gain any hidden weaknesses."

"And all I have to do is bring you the . . . ah . . ."

"Stone of Aeternum," Rachel provided again.

"Right . . ." I stared at Rachel and then continued. "I don't suppose somebody can just buy one?"

"Of course not," J'iliol'lth answered. "I would have purchased it myself long ago, if such were possible. No, the Stone is something that can only be freely given or taken by force. The current owner might be persuaded to surrender it, but most likely you would be required to take it.

"Even so," he continued with a dismissive wave of his hands, "the current owner is a vampire and we all know you have no qualms about killing them."

"Why haven't you tried to take it by force yourself?"

"Because, Mr. Courtney, I must still function in this city. If I sent a force of demons to assault the Stone's owner, it would be bad for business, but if I send you . . . Well, let's say it would be very simple to claim that I had nothing to do with that. You are an unknown quantity."

I stood up. "Who is he and where do I find him?"

"His name is Phillipus and he lives at the Highland Towers."

I nodded. Highland Towers. According to Talbot, that place was a real bitch to get into. I'd have to be creative. But, on the other hand, that was where Tabitha was shacking up with some guy, so I wanted to go there anyway, find out who he was, knock him around.

"One last thing," I said before Rachel and I left. "Someone had my human ID declared legally dead; you wouldn't know anything about that, would you?"

The demon shook his head. "Not specifically, but Roger did strike me as the kind of person who would have taken steps to avenge his own death."

I started toward the door and Jill held out his hand. "The sword, please?"

"Sorry," I said. "This bad boy's mine. Magic sword. Magic gun. I'm starting a collection. All I need now is a spear and magic helmet."

"Fine," the demon purred. "Take the cube, too." He picked it up, a casual arrogance in his demeanor as he tossed it to me. I caught it in my off hand. It felt solid enough this time, cold to the touch. "My secretary will even give you a canvas bag in which to transport . . . everything. But remember this, Eric. I want to work with you. I've gone out of my way to be as reasonable as possible. Working with me on this is a win-win scenario."

I looked at Rachel's tiny purse and bit back my usual obnoxious retort. "I'll take you up on that bag."

I was so on the ball that I even remembered the sun was out. We headed for home, with me squashed in Rachel's purse jouncing alongside a canvas bag (with the Lovett Building's name and logo on the side) containing a glowing purple cube and a magic six-shooter. The sword wouldn't fit, so she had to carry it separately.

Rachel had a hard time hailing a cab while holding the longsword, but not too hard a time. After all, this is Void City.

◆ 17 ◆

TABITHA:

WINTERRIFIC

A single claw sensuously pricked the skin above my sternum before wending its way down my torso, across my belly, and lower. Talbot's touch was masterful, scratching the skin without breaking it. It was a wake-up call that I'd enjoyed yesterday. I glared at the clock. Exactly one hour after sundown. What had everyone else been doing in that lost hour of wakefulness? What . . . no, who had Eric been doing in that hour? It irked me.

"Get off." I slapped Talbot's hand away.

He rolled off the edge of the bed. "What?"

"I'm not in the mood," I said, heading for the shower.

Hi, slut. Where you been? Rachel's voiced echoed in my head. I twisted the shower knob to hot before staring at myself in the mirror. No reflection. I willed myself to appear in the glass.

He doesn't need your cold dead cunt anymore.

"Damn it!" I couldn't concentrate enough to make my image appear.

Talbot poked his head into the bathroom. "You okay?"

"Tell me that I'm beautiful."

"Why?"

"Just tell me!"

He smirked. "No."

My fangs and claws extended of their own accord. Talbot's heartbeat echoed in my ears, but the heat of him was dulled by the shower. "Tell me!" Red light from my eyes cast odd shadows on the wall.

"No," he repeated.

I slammed the door in his face and stepped into the shower. Too cold. My speed kicked in instinctively as I tried to avoid the water. Each frigid droplet stung as it bounced off my skin, then froze, suspended in midair as the universe slowed down. Sometimes the speed is a blessing and sometimes, like when you're standing on a wet surface, it's a curse. My feet went out from under me, sending me backward into the glass shower door.

Shards of broken glass fell toward me in slow motion like little knives. The superspeed was gone before I hit the ground. Talbot threw open the door, scooped me up, and carried me back into the bedroom, leaving a thin trail of blood across the nice white carpet.

"Ow."

"I've never heard of a clumsy vampire," Talbot said. He pulled a large hunk of glass out of my left breast, leaving a jagged stretching tear that was quickly replaced by the tender tingle of regenerating flesh.

"Shut up," I hissed. "It isn't funny."

Did he really call you a moist warm tightness?

Someone knocked on the door and both of us nearly jumped out of our skins. Talbot sprouted claws and fangs as he sniffed the air. A vision of a man leapt into my brain and announced that he was young, not as young as me, but certainly every bit as powerful. He wore clothes that had been made just for him, in shades of blue and white. I normally don't like blonds, but Eric and now this guy were the exceptions that proved the rule.

"I never knock twice," he whispered through the image of himself, "and I'm the last person you want to offend."

"It's Ebon Winter," I whispered to Talbot.

Talbot dumped clean towels over the glass on the bathroom floor and sat me down on the toilet. "Get cleaned up."

"Just a minute," I called. "I'm in the shower."

Five minutes later I opened the door wearing a T-shirt and shorts. I could have prettied up, but I didn't feel like it. Besides, he was on my territory and I didn't want to be ogled tonight, not by him. Winter looked me up and down in an odd, appraising sort of way before gliding past me into the room.

Over one shoulder he was carrying a black garment bag, which he hung from a hook on the back of the door. Every movement seemed calculated. He was the most exquisite being I had ever laid eyes on, but instead of attraction I felt an instant . . . wariness of him. He rotated on his heel in a complete circle, frowned, and glared at me.

"It is important that you understand something." He held up both arms and gestured to the room around him. "This entire room is offensive and I absolutely will not redecorate for you. I loathe it all."

Crooking a finger, he pointed it at Talbot. "Especially that mouser." He shuddered theatrically. "Hideous things, like rats; they really ought to be exterminated."

"Hey!" I began.

The vampire put a finger to my lips. "Do not raise your voice to me, Elizabeth Tabitha Sims," he said pleasantly. "I am enjoyed best as an ally, not an enemy, and I abhor shouting. No harm will come to your . . . servant as long as he behaves himself. As long in the tooth as he is, I'm confident he knows his place."

Talbot leaned idly against one wall, out of the way, and tried to look nonthreatening. It was precisely the same way he acted in Phillip's presence. After our adventure at the Iversonian, I knew why.

My tongue stumbled around my mouth for a second before finally managing to ask, "You're Ebon Winter, from the Artiste Unknown, right?"

"I am Ebon Winter, but you must call me Winter. It's the *nom de guerre* I prefer and I will not answer otherwise. As your sire might say: call me Winter, just Winter. You know, like Madonna but with a dick."

Winter winked when he said the last sentence as if he'd made a clever little jest. I came close to laughing despite myself except that the joke wasn't really very funny; he only wanted it to be funny. What scared me was that that had almost been enough.

"I hope I didn't interrupt you in the middle of anything kinky," he added mischievously. "You must have very broad horizons to take that into your bed." He indicated Talbot when he said "that."

"What? Who the—who the hell do you think you are?" I asked, flabbergasted. How dare he judge me? He'd insulted my decor, my lover, and me personally. I had half a mind to throw him out.

"Although," he caressed my cheek, "you are lovely. Your breasts are a bit large for me, but lovely all the same."

"Who the hell do you think you are?" I repeated.

"I've already introduced myself, darling. Please attempt to focus and I truly will not remind you again about the volume. Let's recap." He placed a hand on my shoulder and steered me toward the front door. "I came in through there. This apartment is hideous. My sire Phillip—I believe you know him biblically—asked me to redecorate your entryway, but you offend me, so I won't be doing so. I'll send Andre around when I can spare him. Keep your pet away from me and put on the clothes I brought you."

"What clothes?" I asked, still bewildered.

"The clothes in the garment bag, dear," he said casually. "Do you honestly believe that I flit willy-nilly about town with luggage in hand?"

"No, I suppose not, but—," I began.

He unzipped the bag and began sorting clothes. He set out a black leather skirt, stiletto heels, hose, and a green silk blouse, leaving the most incredible blue dress I'd ever seen still in the bag. It was sexy yet casual, and I could tell just by looking at it that it had been made with me in mind. He zipped the bag back up and gestured to the rest.

"While you were doing whatever it is you were doing, others were making things happen, love. Now do be a dear and put on some nice clothes. You're making my eyes bleed. They'll look quite fetching— the clothes I mean—and you must promise to take proper care of them. The dress is dry-clean only, and I'll be quite angry if I hear you've been leaving it lying about on the floor. Mommie Dearest has nothing on me and don't you dare put it on a wire hanger, either. I call the dress Isabella. She's an original Winter. Do you like her?"

"I . . . yes," I stammered. "It's . . . I've never seen a dress as beautiful as that—" His eyes narrowed and I quickly changed what I was going to say, ". . . as Isabella."

Still suspicious, I started climbing into the clothes he had laid out. They smelled normal and I hoped Talbot would warn me if I were in danger. They fit perfectly and were utterly flattering. I doubted even Eric would complain. What surprised me the most was the blouse; made for a vampire who didn't have to wear a bra, it gripped and lifted just enough but hung normally.

"Always make sure your tailor has an enchanter on the payroll, darling. They're worth it," Winter told me.

I was a true believer.

Winter walked around me in a circle and shook his head. "No, not *vert* . . . The blouse is the wrong color." He clucked his tongue and lightly touched my shoulder. "Crimson, *s'il vous plaît*." Colors blended across the blouse from my breasts outward and it changed from green to a deep bright crimson. "Darker, *s'il vous plaît* . . . a little more blue, not purple and not red . . ." Responding to his commands, the fabric darkened by fractions until at last he said, *"Merci."*

Circling me once more, he made much more appreciative noises. "Excellent, that's much better. Yes, definitely your color. Of course, that may change as your eyes continue to fade, but contacts can take care of that. Do you have a good picture of your eyes?"

I shook my head.

"I thought not." Winter pulled a photo from his pocket and handed it to me. In the picture, Rachel and I were kids, standing in front of the sign for a roller coaster. Behind Rachel, the *You Must Be This Tall* sign indicated that at last Rachel was indeed "this tall."

"They were a very nice shade . . . a green . . . three on my color scale. I have a fey who makes my contacts; he could probably work you in."

"Where did you get this?"

He laughed. I thought that laugh could take hold of a person and screw them to the wall. If it had been a melody, it would have stuck in my head forever.

"I can get anything."

"Thank you," I said belatedly. "Does the dress change color, too?"

Winter tossed back his head, revealing perfect whiter-than-white teeth as he chortled once more. "It had better, or Melvin will certainly have some explaining to do, now, won't he?"

"Melvin?"

"My enchanter," he crooned. "Have you ever noticed most magically inclined mortals in this city have an M-name? He's a dear little thrall. Most people think that since he does guild work, he's his own man, but in truth, he's all mine."

None of this made any sense. Why would Ebon Winter come out of nowhere and shower me with gifts? The necklace Phillip had given me, the suite of rooms, I understood, but the clothes from Winter were totally unexpected.

"Why didn't I sense you before you were at the door?" I asked.

"Perhaps your exertions left you too preoccupied to detect me? That's one of the reasons I've given up sex. It's vulgar and distracting. Ah, and a word of advice: never use your vampiric speed on a slick surface. Well, perhaps not never, but certainly not until your skills improve."

I know I didn't blink, but he vanished anyway, reappearing beside me, his hands adjusting the way the skirt clung to my body. "Incidentally, given our kind's enhanced senses, you really must remember to use an air freshener. Change your sheets twice a day. Your mouser's scent is all over the room."

"You're avoiding the question," I observed. "Why didn't I sense you earlier?"

Tilting his head to the left, Winter frowned. "Perhaps I am, at that. Though I think it's more a case of you not liking my answer than a refusal on my part to give one. Haven't you ever tried to change the subject when you didn't want to give a straight answer?" He sported a very savage grin. "I'm sorry; did you say you didn't want the clothes?"

"No!" I said more emphatically than I intended. "I mean . . . I would like to keep them. Please. And thank you."

He clapped his hands and kissed me on the cheek. "My, my. You are quite the whore, aren't you?" Winter's eyes sparkled as he spoke. My hand passed through his cheek when I tried to slap him; an intense cold spun up my arm. He could turn to mist! The only vampire I'd met that could do it was Phillip and even he couldn't hold his shape at the same time.

"I'm not a fighter, Tabitha. I never ever fight unless it's utterly un-avoidable and then I never fight fair. Fair fights are for professional pugi-lists and the mentally deficient." He touched my cheek, peering directly into my eyes, his lips a hairsbreadth from a kiss. "I kill. I murder. Remember that and don't be so prudish; everyone is a whore to a certain degree. We all have our price. Mine was immortality."

Words fired effortlessly from his lips, tickling my ears. In an episode of *Charmed*, they'd had a creature called a siren that lured people to their deaths with her song. Winter's voice was like that . . . mesmerizing. "Even so, I have no intent of enjoying your . . . ah . . . girlish charms. I simply wish a favor of you."

"Which is?" I asked carefully.

"I like to make wagers," he said with a smile. "It's a hobby. I like to predict outcomes and I am always right, unless someone . . . How shall I put it so that you will understand?" The charming look vanished and anger, terrible and beautiful, showed on his chiseled face. "Unless some-one fucks things up!" His eyes flashed blue as he spoke, his finger lancing in my direction as if he intended to spear me with it. "You, dearest, have fucked things up for me. Quite unknowingly, you have caused me to lose a bet." And the anger was gone and he was calm again as if he had never displayed it at all.

An incredulous look crossed my face and I eyed Talbot for guid-ance. "And for this you give me gifts?"

"No," he said. There was something in his eyes then, not anger, but the potential for its return. "No, the gifts are either an apology or an inducement. Do me a small favor." He pointed at Talbot. "Send that thing back to its master."

"He's not mine. I can't just tell him to go somewhere and expect him to—"

"Oh, he would go if you told him that his precious Eric had re-turned."

"What?" Talbot demanded. "I was just over there three days ago. I thought they weren't having any luck."

"Didn't I tell you?" I asked, attempting to sound casual about it.

Talbot shook his head, then kissed my forehead on his way to the door. "I kept you safe until he came back, but now I gotta go."

"What? You're running back to him? Just like that? What about us?"

Talbot frowned. "There is no us. You keep expecting me to act human, but I'm not. I never have been. I'm sorry if that hurts your feelings." He scooted carefully past Winter.

Why is it that the only man who was honest and up front with me is the vampire I broke up with?

"What kind of bet did you have?" I asked Winter.

Winter smirked and turned to mist, letting his outer edges blur into wispy trails of vapor. "That would be telling. Besides, I ought not bend *all* the rules. I already had to use a loophole to set things straight. Do you know how hard it is to convince a priest to give up his soul? Fortunately, I'm an exceptional parishioner." He laughed. "The words just bounce right off of your forehead, don't they?" He tapped his own lightly. "My apologies. Enjoy the clothes."

His entire body dissipated as if he had been nothing more than a cloud or a puff of smoke. I picked up the phone and dialed the front desk.

"How may I be of assistance?" Dennis answered.

"I need someone to clean my room and fix my shower."

"I'll send someone immediately," he said cheerfully. "And, milady?"

"What?"

"Lord Phillip asked me to send you to his room when you awoke. He has another visitor that he'd like—"

I didn't let him finish the rest of the sentence. "You tell Lord Phillip that he's a fat, balding, demented little freak and he can go fuck himself." I slammed the phone down hard enough to spider-web the glass-topped end table. That was stupid, but stupid felt really, really good.

18

ERIC:

AT THE MOVIES

Inside the projection booth at the Pollux, modern equipment sat side by side with the original reel-to-reel technology. My *Casablanca* print was gone and so was *Singin' in the Rain*. *The Court Jester* was still there, but only because someone had spilled Coke on the film when they'd inventoried the canisters. Greta pointed at the newfangled digital projector, rambling on about picture quality and noise ratio.

"Does it work like a DVD player?" I interrupted.

"Basically."

"Then it's great. Thanks."

"I got you a selection." Greta opened a filing cabinet. The films inside were all classics, and I saw my two favorites tucked right in front.

"I don't deserve you," I said.

"Yes, you do, Dad." Greta hugged me. "You saved me. I know you don't like to talk about it, but do you remember . . ." She sagged as her words trailed off. My face must have given me away. I felt like a turd for not wanting to listen. She has highs and lows. At her low ebbs, she always wants to talk about our time together when she was human, how much I remember. The truth is, I don't always remember or sometimes I get it mixed up. When we talk, she can tell. It's a bad situation.

"Do you miss Kyle?" She bit her lip when she asked, turned her face away.

"Kyle who?" I wonder if there is a vampire equivalent of Alzheimer's.

"Nothing. Nothing. It's okay, Dad. You just watch your movies." Greta kissed me on the forehead and hugged me again, so tightly that I worried she wasn't going to let go. She pressed a remote into my hand. "I . . . couldn't afford to have the sensor put in professionally, so just point it at the center of the mezzanine and try to ignore the wire."

"Uh-huh."

She opened the door to leave.

"Greta," I called after her. "I really do appreciate all that you've done to hang on to the Pollux for me. I'll pay you back."

Her smile could've made a dead man happy . . . which I guess it did, if you think about it. "It's not an issue, Dad. Just glad to help. I'm gonna go eat again." The door fell closed with a heavy thud after her exit, which left me alone with Marilyn. I loaded *Casablanca* into the glorified DVD player and scooped up the glowing purple cube with Marilyn's soul inside.

Thirty-two minutes into my second run through *Casablanca*, as Ingrid Bergman's face loomed above me on the big screen, I knew what to do. If you haven't seen the movie, I highly recommend it. I always watch it when I have to make big decisions . . . if I have the time. I know people say that *Citizen Kane* is the greatest movie ever made, but they're wrong. I don't care about an old rich guy who dies longing for more innocent times. I live that every night.

Marilyn's cube sat on my left in the front row. *El Alma Perdida* rested in the seat on my right. Pointing the remote control over my head at the mezzanine, I stopped the movie. Blue light from the projection default screen cast the theater in an eerie underwater light.

"I have some options, Marilyn," I told the cube. Who knew if she could hear me, but I hoped that she could. "I can try to bring you back to life. I don't know if you'd be mortal or immortal or undead, but there has got to be a way. If I do that, though, you still won't be in love with me. You'll pity me like you always have, even when you were screwing Roger behind my back and planning to go through with our marriage anyway."

I climbed out of my seat. The Pollux no longer smelled like stale popcorn. Whoever had put it up for auction must have had a cleaning crew come in and do a real once-over on the place. Magbidion's failed rituals on the stage had left an odor of blood, a scent that mixed badly with that of the disinfectant. I considered burning some microwave popcorn to see if it would help, but it was all avoidance.

I knew what I needed to do and didn't like it. My fingers drummed on the wooden stage of their own accord. I couldn't look at the cube. If I could release Marilyn before giving Jill his magic rock, then it meant one of two things: either I was stronger than demon magic (doubtful) or it meant that Jill wanted that rock so badly he would be willing to do or say anything to get his claws on it.

I hit play. Ilsa begged Sam to play "As Time Goes By" and he did. I stopped the movie again. I was wasting time. Roger was out there plotting against me and I was watching old movies. All I had to do, if I believed Jill, was to run on over to the Highland Towers and pick up a magic rock that could make me immortal . . . and I was watching old movies.

"Even if you did come back to life," I told the glowing cube, "even if you did still love me, it wouldn't be the same. Knowing what I know. I mean, I might forget in time. It's . . ."

I seized the cube. It felt warm in my hand. I held it long enough for the warmth to work its way through my fingers and seep into my palm, pretending that I was holding Marilyn's hand, not just her soul in a box.

"I had to save you from the demon, Marilyn." I turned the cube over and over in my hand, the purple light mixing with the blue from the projector and coming out red, which should have been impossible, but you can never tell with magic. "But you're still dead. I talked to Magbidion and he says that's really you in there. He can't tell where you're going to go when I let you out, though. I'll avenge you or whatever, but I can't just keep you here in this cube. I suppose what I'm saying is: I hope you don't burn in Hell, but if you do—it's on you.

"You make your decisions in life, in my case, unlife, and you hope you do the right thing. We never had Paris, but we'll always have . . ." *What? The backseat of a Mustang? Roger? A stolen moment on the sidewalk as cold dead ghosts?* "Aw, fuck it." Marilyn's cube shattered in my hand with less pressure than it takes to crush a soda can.

She hovered before me, bathed in conflicting colors, purple, blue, red, orange. Where the colors touched they disobeyed the color wheel. The blood magic all over the stage didn't mysteriously bring her back to life. She didn't smile at me and float up into the sky with a choir of angels. She didn't even get to haunt the Pollux like I'd secretly hoped.

She screamed, wreathed in spectral flame, and I knew which direction she was headed.

I couldn't watch. The walk back up the stairs to the projection booth took under a second. My speed, activated by the stress, put me into fast-forward, prolonging the moment. Ages passed while I waited for the player to eject *Casablanca*. Marilyn dwindled by fractions while I swapped movies. By the time *Singin' in the Rain* had loaded and begun to play, Marilyn was gone. I sat down in the dark and watched the movie. What else could I do?

I'd gotten to Cosmo's "Make 'em laugh" routine when one of the theater doors opened. It was the wrong time for Talbot to saunter in smelling like Tabitha.

"Hi, slut," I quoted Rachel. "Where you been?"

"You're angry," he said neutrally.

"What gave me away? The eyes?" I pointed to the purple glow. "Yeah, they used to go red more often than purple. I think it's the whole sex kitten mind control thing screwing it all up, but I haven't asked Rachel yet."

"Where is Rachel?" he asked.

"Asleep," I answered. "Humans do that."

"So do most vampires." Talbot advanced down the aisle. Smell is a powerful agent of memory. I smelled fluids on him that Tabitha shouldn't have had anymore. "How long has it been since you slept? Even you need one or two hours of dead time—"

"You smell like Tabitha." I picked up *El Alma Perdida.*

"I've been keeping an eye on her." He tried to shrug it off. "Welcome—"

"And a cock in her," I spat.

"—back." He winced. "She's not your girlfriend anymore."

My anger simmered. "What happened with Tabitha?" A whisper would have been loud in comparison, I spoke so softly.

He didn't answer right away, taking time instead to look around and survey the theater, making sure no one else could hear. "I fucked up, man." The words leapt desperately from his lips and I was just as curious as he was to see how I was going to react to them. "She can turn into a cat, like you can, but when she does it, her heart beats, her body temp rises, and she breathes, okay? She moves like a cat, the whole deal. It's obviously a favored form thing or something like it. The first time it happened, she came on to me . . . It may have been postmortem stress—I didn't think it was, but from the way she tore up my car later, it easily could have been."

"Was she a cat or a human when you did it?" I asked.

Letting his eyes close, he let out a long sigh. Booming, thundering heartbeats resounded in his chest and blood rushed through his veins like it needed to go as fast as it could because in a few moments it was going to stop forever.

"Which time?"

"I don't have to kill you, you know," I said acidly.

"Eric, you're sleeping with her sister." His tone made it clear that he was hoping I'd just let it go. "It's not like you were pining after her."

I walked down the aisle toward him. "That's why I'm not mad at *her.* She can do whatever she wants. Did you know Marilyn's soul got stolen by a demon?"

"No, but I'm sure we can get it back."

"Did that. Broke the containment cube about an hour ago. Watched her get sucked into Hell."

"That's harsh, but what happened to her soul is not your fault."

I cocked the gun. "I know. Did you know that Roger came back from the dead again? That a demon brought him back?" I aimed the gun.

"Shit. I suppose you could've used my help with that." He took off his sunglasses. "Look. Just do whatever you're going to do." He braced himself to accept his punishment. I had no idea what I was going to do. It's not like I was ever really going to shoot him.

"What is that thing anyway?" asked the voice of John Paul Courtney. "Is it a werecat, one of them rakshasa things, or what?" Thank God for interruptions.

I could tell that Talbot saw him, too, the ghostly cowboy sitting front and center in the mezzanine, looking down on Talbot and me.

"He's a mouser," I answered.

"Where I come from, that's just another name for a cat," Courtney drawled.

"Shut the hell up!" I snarled up at him. "They didn't even have penicillin when you were alive. What the fuck do you know about anything?"

"I know a lot about werewolves." He took my ranting in stride. Like before, the more angry I became, the greater the sense of bemusement I got from the ghost. He disappeared between sentences, reappearing on my left. His sidelong glance was ruined when his head lolled over again, but he kept talking. "And I know this. You've got a good soul. It's why your eyes are still so blue." He straightened his head and jammed it back into place, taking a hard, close look at Talbot. "Never seen anythin' like it in all my born days. So since I don't know anythin', why don't you be the one to educate me? What is a mouser?"

In any other situation, I wouldn't have blown Talbot's secret, but I was angry. "Okay, you're right. He's a cat."

"You let a glorified house cat steal your sweetheart?" Courtney jeered.

"Okay, Statler. Not one more fucking word out of you or you're going to be one dead muppet."

"What's a muppet?" Courtney asked. I lost it. Vampires can't touch ghosts, but I'm not just a vampire. Color leached from my skin as the blue glow rushed in when my solidity left me. *El Alma Perdida* was still in my hand.

Talbot went wide to the far aisle, steering clear of me. "Eric, what the hell?"

I didn't answer him. Instead, I popped off a shot at John Paul Courtney and wondered if the bullet would hurt a ghost since ghosts could touch it. The bullet sailed through his stomach and embedded in the ceiling.

"It cain't suck up my soul, boy," Courtney assailed with a laugh. "I ain't no werewolf. You can club me with the barrel, though. Any Courtney can touch *El Alma Perdida* no matter what form they're in. It belongs to the family."

I drifted up as he spoke, my desire to reach him, to wipe the smile off his face, enough to send me into the air. A parody of the song from Disney's *Peter Pan* went through my head: *Just think of a terrible thought. Any evil little thought.*

Ghostflight didn't work like winged flight. I sailed right past John Paul and plunged intangibly through the seats, losing my grip on *El Alma Perdida* in the process. It landed in one of the seats through which I'd passed. Leaving the gun where it was, I tried for Courtney again, again sailing right past him, coming up short of phasing through the ceiling. I rotated in the air to face him.

"You don't want to fight me, son," John Paul said. "I've been tied to that gun and this family for a lotta years. I've fought my share of ghosts along the way and—"

He let out an "oof" as I soared into him, arms wide in a tackle. We plunged through the mezzanine and into the lower seats.

"You cain't kill me again, Eric." Courtney slammed a knee into my stomach and it hurt; the pain was real. I smiled. It had been forty years since being injured hurt properly. Vampiric nerve endings don't register pain beyond the initial injuries. Cut us and it hurts, but the wound doesn't continue to ache unless you tear it open again.

"I cain't rest until the curse has run its course." He punched me twice in the back of the head and I let go with a snarl.

"What curse?" I backed away from him, waiting for my head to clear.

"The one I cain't tell you about."

"Can you guys hold on while I go get some popcorn?" Talbot called.

John Paul Courtney glared at Talbot in shock. "You can really see me? Ain't nobody hardly ever able to see me."

Talbot opened his mouth to reply but didn't bother. I hit JPC square on the jaw, knocking his head back over his shoulders, where it dangled loosely at his back. My knuckles didn't hurt as badly as they should have, but I chalked that one up to John Paul's Nearly Headless Nick syndrome.

"Dude," Talbot exclaimed, partially covering his eyes with his fingers, "that's not right."

Hammering Courtney's stomach with blow after blow, I forced him back through the wall and into the lobby. We stood under the lights in front of the empty concession stand. "Well, what can you tell me, Hopalong, because you popping up to heckle me is getting pretty damn tiresome."

He held up his hand and I waited while he snapped his neck back into place. "I can tell you this." He stomped down on my foot, following it up with a right cross that sent me toward the ticket booth inside the foyer.

"I appeared to you for a few reasons, one of which was this: When you fought the werewolves of Orchard Lake, you didn't use *El Alma Perdida* on them—you showed discretion. They weren't evil. They were God-fearin' folk, skinchangers or no. Later, when you used my gun against Roger, you fired it at evil in defense of the righteous."

He held his arm out to his side and *El Alma Perdida* materialized in his outstretched hand. "That made your business my business," he said as he holstered the gun. "You put yourself on the right path and seeing as how you're Courtney blood, that means I can help you, but it don't mean that I have to."

"I don't want your help," I snarled.

"Then you don't get my gun."

"Fine." I resumed my material form, eyes glowing red. Even the warmth of my newly re-formed clothes didn't take the edge off of my anger. "Keep the damn thing, but don't bother me, either."

"Son," Courtney tipped back his hat and looked down at the marble tile, "this doesn't have to be hard. You know the demon's lying to ya. You know he's up to no good. All I want you to do is take yer foot outta the dern bear trap. Turn aside from the demon's offer and—"

"You don't know me very well, J. P." Talbot walked through the theater doors and we both stared at him.

"You two keep on fighting," Talbot told us, hands up in a placating gesture. "I'm just watching."

"When I see a bear trap, when I know that everybody around me thinks I don't see it, I don't walk around it." I took three steps forward. "I don't skirt the danger. I ram my foot down harder just to spite them. And you know what, John?"

"What?"

"Nine times out of ten, the bear trap loses."

Courtney smiled. "Courtney through and through. I'll be watching, Eric."

"What?" I asked. "You can just be around?"

"I can manifest near anybody that's fired *El Alma Perdida* and to anyone of Courtney blood. I got you both ways, boy." He faded away in the same burst of light as before.

"Guess I'm stuck with him," I told Talbot.

"Yep," came an echoing reply from the disembodied ghost.

El Alma Perdida appeared on the concession counter and I picked it up. "I thought you were taking this?"

"I can't go too far with it anyway," Courtney admitted in a disconsolate tone.

"I like him," Talbot said, grinning.

It was either take a swing at Talbot, too, shoot him, or cut my losses and get on with my bear trap. Since I didn't want to start in on him again about the Tabitha thing, I stepped toward the front doors, stopping with my hand on the glass.

"I'm supposed to go get something from the Highland Towers for a demon," I said. "I'm going to go over there and beat the shit out of people until I remember what it was." I looked at Talbot. "You coming?"

He didn't answer so I moved on.

"Wait. We're doing what?" Talbot burst out of the door behind me. And just like that, I was forgiven for being an ass. I wonder what Talbot sees in me.

"We're taking your car."

"Why?"

"It'll be light out in a few hours. Mine might catch on fire."

"Wait," Talbot asked again, "it might what?"

I opened the front door of the Pollux and sensed Tabitha. "Jesus, I just can't get a break tonight." The click clack of her heels on the sidewalk was the loudest sound. She crossed the street as I sat down on the bench in front of the Pollux. The pad of cat feet softly disappeared toward the back of the theater. Obviously, Talbot didn't want anything to do with whatever happened next. "Coward," I mumbled.

19

TABITHA:

IN HIS ARMS

Snow doesn't last long in Void City. During the day it had mostly melted away, but a small patch was clinging to its icy state in the shadow of the bench, close to the base of the Pollux. Eric didn't seem to notice or care. I'd parked the Lotus Phillip had given me next to the police signs warning that the street was closed. Eric still hadn't redyed his hair. God, my thoughts were jumbled just looking at him. Phillip, Winter, they didn't act like people anymore . . . even Dennis, in his quest to become a vampire, was already so fake. But Eric . . . Eric was still Eric and he always would be. He wasn't perfect, but he was real and without him . . . I could see myself becoming just like the vampires at the Highland Towers, a caricature of me.

"Hi," I said lamely.

"What?" Eric asked.

"Did Talbot—" I stumbled over my words, "make it back okay?" *What do I say to you, Eric? Can we just talk, please?*

"If it's pussy you want, go to a pet store and get your own. Leave mine alone," Eric said.

"What are you even talking about? No. I was just . . ." *El Alma Perdida* rested on his lap. He put a defensive hand on it when he caught me looking. "Why are you carrying that around?"

"Because my magic ice sword is in the closet."

"No, seriously."

"Because if I leave it unattended, someone always finds it and shoots me with it. I need to get a holster." His nostrils flared. "Why do you smell like you?"

I stepped closer. "Who else would I smell like?" *Can we talk please? I think I made a mistake and I don't know how to tell you. I never should have left.*

Eric seized my wrist and jerked me forward, pulling me off balance. He buried his nose in my crotch. Too shocked to act like a vampire, I struggled ineffectively. "What the fuck? Eric, let me go!"

"Every woman has a unique smell. It goes away when you die. You still smell like you. It's . . . nice."

His grip relaxed and I slapped his face. He caught my hand and held it against his cheek. "How'd you get so warm just from feeding?"

My vampire speed wouldn't kick in. I'd been practicing seeming human in the car on the way over and it still had me sluggish. I'd gone full out, heartbeat, saliva, warmth, breath. I'd even eaten a breath mint. My heart beat a few times, little skips as it slowed down. Eric heard it as clearly as I felt it, I could see the surprise in his eyes. I knew I should have waited in the car for twenty more minutes.

"Your heart just beat." Eric put his hand on my breast and my heart beat again. He stood, letting *El Alma Perdida* tumble toward the ground. "I felt it." He caught the gun with his left hand.

"Get off of me!" I shoved him hard, used to having vampire strength, but that wasn't back yet, either. I stumbled backward.

"You did something to yourself. When a vampire feeds, the bones stay cold. You're warm to the core."

"Eric, stop it."

"You smell like more fluids than blood." It was an accusation. He kissed me and I responded. "Even your tongue is warm. You taste alive."

I turned it all back on, body heat, saliva, the works.

"What are you doing?" he asked. "And how?"

"It's my talent. I can be nearly alive." He watched the pinkness creeping back into my complexion. I forced blood back into my veins, made it flow like it was supposed to. Pins and needles ran along my arms and legs. "There's pain in the beginning when I go this lifelike, but it's worth it." I took a compact out of my handbag and showed Eric my reflection. "Do you like?"

"No."

"Yes, you do." I ran my warm hands along his cold shoulders, across his chest, and he shuddered. His skin was like ice, but I didn't mind. I'd warm him.

"This is a bad idea." Eric sighed.

I kissed him tenderly, working my hands under his T-shirt, against his skin. His mouth was warmer, like he'd been inside long enough for the heat to seep in and the cold had yet to leach it out.

No, it isn't. "We're good at bad ideas, you and me." I undid his belt buckle, pulling him toward the lobby of the Pollux. Resistance sparked in his eyes, but he didn't stop me.

"Why are you doing this, Tabitha?" he asked me. I gave up on taking him inside, pulled his T-shirt off over his head. Both sides of the street were blocked off so it wasn't like anyone was around, but I still got a giddy little thrill at the thought of being with Eric out in the open. It felt like the first time I'd stepped out onstage at the Demon Heart. I smiled lasciviously and he took it the wrong way. "What do you want this time? You're already a vampire. I'm broke."

"I've got money."

I kissed him again, painful hungry kisses because even in human guise, as excited as I was, my fangs poked out of my gums a fraction of an inch, peeking through the pink.

"I don't want your money," I said between kisses.

"I do."

His zipper stuck, the metal tab trapped against the upper seam. Eric's fangs grazed my tongue as we kissed. That only ever happens when he's really aroused.

"Something I learned in vampire society. I'm your creation, everything I have is yours, even my body."

"That's bullshit," he said acidly, pushing me away. He stomped toward the Pollux doors, his hands touching the glass before he stopped and looked back. "I don't own you and I don't own any of your crap." He took a few steps back to me. "If that's what you're worried about, you can tell everybody I said you're free or released or whatever the High Society pricks call it."

I shook my head. "But I don't want to talk to them. I hate them. They're all freaks. They don't even act like people anymore. They're not like you." I took his hand in mine. "It's you I want."

"This won't work out," Eric said under his breath.

"Yes, it will." I shrugged out of the magic dress I was wearing; I'd changed into Isabella before driving over, wanting to look my best in a dress Eric hadn't even noticed or cared the least bit about. He cared about what was under the dress. He cared about me. I snapped a fingernail, but the zipper surrendered. Eric wasn't wearing any underwear. The same was almost true for me.

I pressed my breasts against his chest, felt his hands on my ass, his right hand lingering over the butterfly tattoo he'd designed just for me. He didn't need chains, whips, or party favors. Eric just needed me. *I love you.*

"You're not like Phillip at all." *Did I say that out loud?*

I slid my lips over him, like only a woman who doesn't need oxygen can do, but he turned off. He's the only man I'd ever been with who could do that, go from ready to not in seconds when he's angry, sending the blood from one head to the other, tinting the whites of eyes with aggressive red swirls.

"Who the fuck is Phillip?"

I knelt outside the Pollux, only the priceless fabric of Isabella, my Winter original, between me and the pavement. *Why did I say that?*

"Nobody. He . . . I . . . Nobody, baby."

"Baby? Just like that we're back together?" He didn't trust it, shaking his head in a silent *no*. "Look, I won't say that I haven't missed you, that I haven't thought about you. I have, and you doing the warm thing, that's very attractive, but . . ." He reached for his pants.

How do I stop him? "Do you want us to be?"

"Do I want us to be what?" Eric froze in the middle of pulling up his pants.

"Back together."

"Um . . ."

The door to the Pollux opened wide, releasing the pent-up odor of freshly baked cinnamon rolls. In the doorway, wearing a bright red thong and a *Vampires Do It Upside Down* T-shirt, Rachel stared at me with eyes full of hate and a face that was all smiles. "Mind if I cut in?"

"She . . ." Words caught in my throat. The cinnamon made it hard to think, difficult to form words even in my head.

"We could have a three-way, if you want, Tabitha." Rachel's nails, the same bright red as her thong, flickered in the multicolored rays shining down from the Christmas lights. "I don't mind sharing."

"You bitch!" It was a thought, but it came out of my mouth, too. Of their own accord, my fingernails elongated into claws; my fangs slid into place. Goose bumps rose on her skin. She stepped out onto the concrete holding a sharpened stake.

"Bitch? You're the one trying to fellate my master in the street."

"I'm a vampire, Rachel. Don't make me hurt you." The thoughts rushed out of my mouth and it didn't quite feel like they were mine.

"I'm not afraid of you, Tabitha." We moved toward each other. Eric interposed himself between, one hand out to restrain each of us. His right hand touched my breast and his left touched Rachel's.

He squeezed softly, his eyes rolling up, then closing as he announced, "I am now officially going to Hell. I hope you're both very happy."

Rachel giggled.

"How are you even alive, Rachel?" I shouted around Eric. My pulse raced. Being this close to alive came with more drawbacks than I realized. Being a vampire really does take the edge off. No adrenaline to make you freak out. Vampires have something similar, but it doesn't have the kick of the true-blue homegrown chemical nature provides. Eric was old enough to ignore the difference. Going back and forth between states, I lived the difference.

"I didn't want to be a vampire, Tabitha," she snarled. "Not every woman needs to deprive their man of the warmth, the blood, the sex he needs. I'm his thrall. I'm happy to be his thrall."

"That's not what I mean and you know it!" I shouted. "Eric, you've got to know this. She—"

"Hush," Eric ordered, looking me dead in the eye. "Both of you just zip it—for a minute or two. I can't think with you shouting back and forth at each other. It's like a verbal demolition derby, for Christ's sake."

His command sent me right back to mind-control land, so I physically held my hand over my mouth, the rest of my sentence: *was dead and she came back somehow and now she's a witch or a demon*, stuck in my mental queue, unable to be spoken. Rachel winked and touched her nose with her tongue. Eric's hand left my breast. He checked the time on his wristwatch.

"It's four forty-one in the morning," he said. "Rachel, go back to bed. You can crash in one of the dressing rooms backstage. See if Talbot can find you a sleeping bag or a cot. There used to be a couple of rollaways back there, but for all I know they've been sold."

"But, Eric—"

"You're supposed to be my fucking thrall, right? So do it." He cut her off with an angry wave. "Tabitha is one of those early-to-bed, late-to-rise vamps. I want to talk to her before that happens."

Rachel nodded before kissing him, hard and urgently. "Okay, *Master.*" She grinned at me when she said it. "But for every time you fuck her, you have to screw me twice."

"Go inside before something freezes and falls off." Eric rolled his eyes, looking to me like I was his buddy. "She's a pistol. I've gotta . . . tell . . . ya. Right."

We stood in the cold under the flickering Christmas lights on the Pollux marquis, listening to the sound of Rachel's bare feet moving deeper into the Pollux, followed by her talking to Talbot, settling in. Eric motioned me inside and I followed him like a lovesick puppy, my priceless dress in my hand. I followed him upstairs. His bedroom smelled like cinnamon, too, and like Rachel.

"Eric—"

"I don't want to talk about Rachel, Tabitha."

"But—" I began, but he narrowed his eyes and it became a command. I couldn't talk about Rachel, not a word. Maybe tomorrow the compulsion would fade . . .

"I can't explain anything and I can't toss her out. She's my thrall, or she sort of is, if what Magbidion told me about how you make a thrall was right."

But she was dead. She's my sister and I saw her buried. I visited her grave and I . . . I searched for a safe reply, one his compulsion would allow. "Okay. If you won't ask about the guys I was with, then I won't ask about your . . . girls."

"I don't know if we can be together, Tabitha. I'm still the same guy you left."

"And that's exactly why I'm back," I told him.

Eric narrowed his eyebrows. "What? Absence made the heart grow senile?"

"Let's talk about it tomorrow." I nodded at the clock next to his bed. "We're running out of time." I helped him back out of his jeans. We rolled around on the bed for an hour and I did my best to replace Rachel's scent with my own. Just before dawn, as I felt the day catching up with me, we climaxed one more time. Eric panted on top of me and it felt like home. "Are you really going to make love to her twice for every time we did?" I asked.

He opened his mouth, but I never heard the answer. Not every vampire walks the daytime. It hits me hard and fast. My sense of the world went away and I lay cold and dead like the living corpse I'd begged to become.

20

ERIC:
AFTERTHOUGHTS

I found Greta asleep in my office, curled up under my desk with a blanket. A half-intact rag doll was clutched tightly in her arms, nestled between her breasts. Greta's long blond hair spilled over the edge of the sofa cushion she was using for a pillow. Clumps of semidried blood matted her hair. She'd fallen asleep without cleaning up, which wasn't unusual for my little girl.

"Not so little anymore," I whispered. The memory of the first time I saw her stabbed into my brain. I don't like to remember it. My eyes squeezed shut. After I banged my head into the door frame a few times, the memory faded. I went back to my bedroom for a washcloth and towel. The water in the Pollux gets hot very quickly. It warmed up my hands, which made the rest of me feel colder. I let the water soak into the washcloth, then wrung it out so that it wouldn't drip.

Cleaning Greta's hair took three trips back and forth to the sink. Trip number four got the blood off of her face and neck. Her shirt was a goner, so I tore it off. Greta could sleep through the Apocalypse. Her limbs go rigid, too, rigor mortis for the undead, which made getting a clean shirt back on her something of an ordeal. At least there were no dead animals in her pockets this time. I carried her into the bedroom, tucked her in next to Tabitha.

Tabitha.

Hadn't I wanted to turn back around yesterday evening and go back to her? Now here she was and all the reasons that things couldn't work blared loudly in my brain. Rachel could make me feel alive, but I didn't have to have that. If my partner was warm, then that was enough. And now Tabitha could pretend to be human, could wake her body back up. That changed things, but whether it changed them enough to make us work, I couldn't say. Thinking about my love life made me tired. When was the last time I'd slept? Another answer I didn't have.

"Boss?" Talbot called from the doorway. "Eric? I heard you moving around and came on up."

Turning away from my girls, I only slid the door open a crack. I didn't want Talbot seeing Tabitha naked and uncovered on the bed. God, I'm a sap. For all I knew, what we'd just had was nothing more than really good breakup sex, despite Tabitha's words to the contrary. "What is it?"

"Rachel's gone. I don't know when she left; I was catching a few z's. I thought you should know."

"Shit." On a whim, I checked the closet. The magic ice sword was still there where I'd left it, leaving condensation rings on the floor. I should get a better hiding place for it, like maybe a freezer. "What time is it?"

"A quarter to nine."

"Is Magbidion still parked out in the deck?"

"I think so."

"Good. Just a sec." I closed the door. Tabitha's breasts rose gently up and down, each time more slowly than the last. The warmth radiating off of her was three or four degrees lower than a live woman. Watching Tabitha cool down was infinitely more entertaining than what I was going to be doing. Maybe we could work it out, Tabitha and me. I covered her up before I reopened the door. "Can you keep an eye on Greta and Tabitha? I have to go out."

"It's daytime." Talbot put his hand on my shoulder.

"So?"

"The sun?"

"What about it?"

Talbot's quirky smile lit up his entire face. "You'll catch fire."

"Not like I haven't done that before. You worried?"

Talbot doesn't need me. If he did, he'd resent me enough not to care what happened to me. It's a hazard of dealing with mousers. They think like cats. "Just be careful, man," he said, "you look beat."

"You haven't been looking at my aura again, have you?"

"No."

I popped my claws and grabbed his important bits. "This stuff with you and Tabitha is total mouser bullshit, Talbot. You know that, right?"

Talbot shrugged, but I caught the twitch of a grin at the corner of his mouth.

"What the fuck really happened with Tabitha? Was it really just a screwup or was it on purpose?"

"You're not going to hurt me, Eric." The grin was unrestrained now.

I tightened my grip but let go when I realized that it was turning Talbot on.

"Shit, man."

Talbot laughed, long and clear. "Sorry, Eric, but you know how it is."

"Seriously, Talbot. No bullshit this time. Did you string her along on purpose, let her see how inhuman the supernatural crowd really is, just so that she'd come running back to me?"

He didn't answer right away, taking time instead to look around and survey the area, making sure no one else could hear. Who did he think might be listening? "I fucked up, man. I know I already said this, but when she's a cat, even when she's not, the way she acts, the way she moves, it's like she's one of my people. It had been a long time for me, okay?"

Inside my head, it felt like a door opened, just a fraction, and anger that had been hidden away, restrained, flooded forward and Talbot stood illuminated by the red light in my eyes. I seized him by the collar and his grin vanished.

"If you ever touch my girlfriend again to do anything other than extinguish her flaming body, if you ever have any form of sexual relations with her, I will make you a eunuch, chain you to the wall, and pay the oni to eat you like a tortured animal cracker. Do you understand me?"

He took a deep sniff, smelling me, then nodded. I let him go.

"Okay, now don't get mad, but can I ask you something?" Talbot panted.

"Sure."

"A tortured animal cracker?"

I flipped him off. "Feetfirst, asshole. If you want to torture an animal cracker you eat it feetfirst. Everybody knows that."

Suppressing a smile, Talbot coughed. "Why would you want to torture an animal cracker?"

Walking down the stairs, I turned my back to him. "Shut up. Just shut up. Obviously it's a human thing. Just—"

"I don't think it's a human thing, Eric, I think it's more of—"

I stopped at the front entrance and didn't bother to turn around. "Balls ripped off and stuffed in your mouth while you're eaten alive by oni. Don't mess with me today, Talbot. Are you going to keep an eye on my girls or not?"

"I'll keep them safe, Eric." He gestured grandly. "I'll keep the whole place safe."

"Thanks." I stepped out into the sun and darted around the corner. Smoke trailing behind me, I rolled into the protective darkness of the deck. I should put in a sunlight-safe connection between the two, some kind of underground walkway, but I've never gotten around to it.

Mag's RV was still parked where I hoped it would be. *For the luv of God! Sumbudy wash me!* was written in the grime on the side of the RV, but other than that it looked roughly the same as it had the last time I'd come knocking.

The side door on the RV hung open. Eggs and pork chops were cooking on the stove. I rapped on the door with my knuckles. "Mags?"

"Come in, Eric," Magbidion called in an obscenely cheerful voice. In the RV's tiny kitchen, Magbidion wore hemp pants, a white T-shirt, and a black apron. On the front of the apron a mystic design I'd never seen before glimmered brightly. The symbol looked a little like a floppy pentacle. "I'm just cooking myself some breakfast. If there is anything you want me to eat for you, speak up now."

"How do you eat your eggs?"

"Over easy."

"Fried pork chops and eggs?"

"It's my favorite breakfast," he answered. "And I'm in a good mood this morning. Someone tried to blow up my home."

He was showered and shaved. The inside of the RV was spotless, if cluttered. All of the ashtrays had been emptied; there was no porn to be seen. The bed had been made. Even the funky smell was gone, replaced by something lemon scented.

"And this made you happy?"

"Of course. I've known for days that someone was going to try to kill me. The signs and portents were all there. I just couldn't tell if it was the demon who gave me my powers or not."

"It wasn't, huh?"

"No, I think it was that Rachel of yours." Mags flipped hot grease over the top of the eggs with his spatula. I eyed the two chops he had sitting on a paper towel to soak up the excess grease. Even if Jill's deal was bullshit, I was going to give it a shot. He knew just how to tempt me. One quickie ritual with his Stone of whatever and I could be eating breakfast just like Magbidion. Hell, I could eat pizza. "She's as powerful as I thought, but not as experienced, I think," Mags continued.

"What happened?"

"Just a minute and I'll tell you." Magbidion slipped the eggs onto his plate, then forked both pork chops next to them. He sat the plate of food on a little built-in table. "Damn it. I forgot to cook the hash browns."

"I'll do it," I said. "Where are your potatoes?"

"In the freezer."

"What kind of a jackass keeps potatoes in the . . ." my voice trailed off when I opened the freezer. Frozen hash browns? "This frozen crap?" I held up the plastic bag.

He laughed. "You vampires are all such food snobs. I'll microwave them."

"No." I shook my head. "I'll cook your damn potatoes. Eat your eggs before they get cold and if you put ketchup on them, I'm going to kill you."

He frowned. "Is salt and pepper okay?"

"It's fine. Tell me what happened."

I read the directions on the back of the package. Microwave instructions? Nope, don't think so. I was a bachelor in the 1940s. I don't need a microwave.

Some vamps like to nuke their blood, but I can't drink that crap. Literally can't. I have to warm blood bags up in a pot of water on the stove, or just drink them cold. The microwave changes it, my body rejects it—the result is very messy.

"About an hour ago, maybe forty-five minutes, I don't know. My spell barrier was tripped by a fire spell cast with tantric energy."

"Tantric? As in that sex magic you talked about before?" I rubbed a little butter on the bottom of one of Magbidion's skillets, sprinkled in a dash of salt and dumped a serving or so of the potatoes into it. I love hash browns, not as much as I love pizza, but breakfast, God, there is just so much good food that you can eat at breakfast: link sausage, biscuits and gravy, pancakes . . .

"Yes." Magbidion tucked into his eggs. I like eggs, too. He broke the yolk with the fork. Rich and yellow, it ran out over the plate against a pork chop. It's dangerous for any vamp to watch a human eat when they haven't fed yet. Double dangerous for me. I wondered if I bit into Magbidion, would he taste like eggs, pork, and sizzling potatoes? If smell really makes up a large percentage of taste, then maybe.

"Eric?"

I retracted my fangs. "Just tell me what happened."

"My barrier enchantment has a quick wake-up spell keyed to it. When one is tripped, the second goes off. Like dominoes. It's a good spell. I learned it from a technomancer down in Orlando who works for one of the big theme parks. It's the equivalent of five double shots of espresso and two energy drinks. You're so awake your eyes vibrate."

He picked up the pork chop with his fingers and slopped it around in the runny egg yolk. Breading, a perfect golden brown, flaked away to land on his plate.

"I must not eat Magbidion. I must not eat Magbidion. I must not eat Magbidion," I whispered softly.

"Did you say something, Eric?" Magbidion said with a mouthful of food. "Are the hash browns done yet?"

Close enough. I pushed them onto his plate with a spatula. "I need to eat."

"Ah, the short version, then." He slid away from his food, reaching casually under the table. I heard the rough calluses of his fingers rasp against wood. "Fire from her. Counterspell from me. She's very sneaky. I couldn't confirm that it was her, but I think it was. How can I help you?"

"I can't feel her. I was going to track her down, but I can't tell where she is."

"Like I said before, if you had made her into a full thrall, if you'd finished the job, given her the blood tattoo, you would be able to sense her all the time. Tell me how you made Rachel again. Exactly what happened."

"It involved blood, sex, kissing, and me pushing my mind into hers, which hurt. There was nothing about a tattoo or a bunch of words."

"Then you may have formed a connection with her, but it wasn't a bona fide thrall connection and I don't know for certain, but it sounds like it might have given her more power over you than it gave you over her. Of course, you could make me your thrall. Then, you'd know for sure what it feels like. And I'd have protection from the demon in return."

Like I said, Magbidion isn't a natural-born mage. He'd signed his soul away in exchange for his magic and his contract was coming due soon. He'd been after me for years to protect him from the demon in exchange for his services. He was going into his whole spiel, but I barely heard him. "That's just great. All my girls are gone. My club is gone." The hunger roared inside my head; I could hear his heart beating. "I don't remember ever being this hungry, Mags."

"She may have been suppressing your appetite; a proficient thrall could do that. A tantric witch could also do that. I once knew a vamp who was fed illusionary blood for a few days. It took care of all the usual problems, except for the"—I heard his hands tighten around the wooden object, a stake—"hunger." My vision ran to red. His flesh dropped away, becoming a mass of veins. Bump-bump. Bump-bump.

The nearest other living person was Talbot. Tabitha registered, too, and something else . . . cold blood, human blood in Magbidion's fridge. I opened the refrigerator door, grabbed a bowl of human blood covered in plastic wrap. "This is human."

"I was saving that for my next obscuration ritual, Eric. You can't drink that."

"Okay, then," I turned on him, fangs bared, "I'll try not to take too much from you." I moved toward him. He thrust the stake at me; a stake through the heart would only immobilize me, but it still made me mad and I tore the stake away in a flash. Why does the speed always work when I need it not to? Why was I so angry, so hungry? The same feeling that I'd gotten a few minutes earlier, when I'd gone all red-eyed at Talbot, throbbed through my skull like someone had turned on the anger valve in a steady flow.

Fortunately, the speed kicked off again, allowing Magbidion time to do some fast-talking, "Drink the blood in the bowl. You're welcome to it. Be my guest. I can get more. I'll just find another blood whore. Sweetheart Row's full of 'em."

The blood flew out of the bowl and into my mouth, in one long thin stream, defying gravity. Magbidion tried to step back, but there isn't that much room in an RV. "How did you do that? I've only seen that flying-blood trick in Asian vampires."

"I don't know." I was still hungry, but it was enough to rein myself in. "I'm going to go outside."

"Think over the whole thrall proposition thing . . . a magic-using thrall can come in handy," he called after me. "If I were your thrall, you wouldn't have to pay me."

I stepped out into the deck. Fang was parked nearby, his paint job black again, as it apparently was every day from sunup to sundown. Fang unlocked the door for me. I climbed behind the wheel and instantly felt calmer, more in control of myself, too calm . . . as if that faucet of anger had been turned completely off.

Falling asleep in a parked car is a bad idea for a human. It's a worse idea for a vampire who has a lot of people out to get him, but it's what I did. Somehow, I knew I'd be safe with Fang. Twelve hours later I woke up to the sounds of "Second Hand Kiss" playing on the radio. Fang was parked on the upper deck with the roof down and the engine running. My car did a donut on the concrete. The engine revved twice of its own accord.

"I'm happy to see you, too, pal." Okay, I guess I liked the damn undead car. "Let's go hunting and then I've got business to take care of." Fang tore out, leaving a layer of rubber on the deck, screeching toward the lower exit. Heading out into the night with the wind in my hair, I felt more normal than I'd felt in twenty years. When Fang ran over a possum and it didn't come out the other side, I actually laughed. When I'd told Greta to go out and run over some small animals, I'd been kidding.

21

ERIC:

FUN WITH FANG

My undeath is punctuated by things I should be doing. I should have been figuring out where Rachel went. I should have walked over to the Pollux to check on Greta, but she'd done fine for four months without me. She'd really grown up while I wasn't looking. True, she still didn't know how to clean up after herself, but that wasn't a trait she needed for survival.

Tabitha. I should have gone to see Tabitha, listened to her explanations. Did she expect us to be back together and if so, why the fuck did she want me? Fang and I cruised Void City looking for victims and answers. No answers leapt out, but we did wind up on Forty-third Street, locally known as Sweetheart Row. The strip between Third and Fourth Avenues is vampire groupie central, but not the nice, pretty ones like Tabitha or Rachel; the real bottom of the barrel. It's where old groupies that never get their golden ticket on the undeath train go to lie to themselves that they still have a shot.

"Hey, baby. Want a fuck and suck?" A grandma in her late sixties wearing less than was decent or attractive waved at me as Fang and I drove past. Fang slowed and the blood whores began to gather. Either Fang knew what I was thinking, or maybe I'd stepped on the brake. He steered toward the curb, ready to hop it and mow them down, but I veered back onto the road and stopped. Up and to my left in the Bitemore Hotel, the sounds of eight or nine working girls were clear to my trained supernatural ear. The Bitemore was as long-standing a tradition as Sweetheart Row. It used to have a different name, but now *Bitemore* was on the actual sign.

"Hi, honey." The woman speaking to me now was in her forties, but the bloom wasn't entirely off of the rose yet. Someone must have broken her self-esteem in a serious way to drive her so far so fast. "Want a date?"

"What's your name?"

"You can call me anything you want, baby."

"Don't play games with me." I stepped out of Fang. What the fuck was I doing? I had no clue, running on instinct. Maybe Magbidion's mention of blood whores had started me thinking about them. Now that I was looking at Sweetheart Row and the women who worked there, I knew it was wrong and I wanted to fix it, stop it, break it. It's the same feeling I get whenever I step into another man's strip club. Did the 401(k) I'd offered at mine, the health coverage, and the college tuition really make me any better? I liked to think so.

"It's Cheryl."

"Hi, Cheryl. I'm Eric. I'm the crazy asshole who used to run the Demon Heart before it got blown up."

Her heart sped up and I smelled her fear. It was a brief burst of scent and she locked it down fast. Smart girl. Fear makes a vampire want to attack. I closed my eyes, concentrated on the transformation, certain I could go uber vamp on purpose. I grew taller, black as the night sky overhead. The street noises stopped. I announced myself, sent out my vampiric will into the surrounding area. The noises from the Bitemore stopped, too.

"What are you going to do?" Cheryl asked. Her voice sounded tired, beaten.

I didn't know. My actions were becoming more unpredictable lately. Was this a nervous breakdown? Had postmortem syndrome come at last? Maybe it was some kind of aftereffect from the drugs J'iliol'lth had slipped me. No, none of that. If I concentrated, I could feel the valve on my anger tightening as I strained at it. Rachel was doing this, screwing with my head. Which is fine, it's what women like her do even if they don't have magic powers and I think I knew that from the beginning. What I wanted to know was, why?

Gently, with my taloned forefinger I wiped the smeared lipstick from Cheryl's lips. "I think I'm going to kill a lot of vampires," I said in that deep otherworldly voice that my uber form has. Her eyes sparked, an instant of real interest and I think I got a glimpse of the woman she used to be. She'd been strong and brave. I liked that woman, wanted to bring her back, let her have a life again. "Do you have a boss? I think I'll kill him first."

"Why?" she whispered. There was no fear in her now, only something else. I can't describe it, but I think in those few seconds, she'd begun to hope.

"Because I don't like what they've done to you. I'm hungry, and they're already dead, just like me. Who runs Sweetheart Row these days?"

"Are you going to hurt me?"

"Not tonight." Her green eyes caught the light from the streetlamp. "I've been thinking. The other vampires in this city used to understand the whole stay-out-of-my-way thing. When I was in El Segundo, some of them took turns looking after the Demon Heart so that it wouldn't be all fucked up when I got back, so that I wouldn't go ape shit.

"I think they used to self-regulate, keep out of my portion of the city. But lately they've forgotten who I am. They thought Roger had actually ended me. If I was dead and gone, then it was fine for them to let my shit get sold off to the city, but I'm still around, and so is Roger.

"I've decided not to look for him. I'm going to make them bring him to me on a silver fucking platter and if they don't, then things will get worse. If they hurt my people in retaliation, I'll just up the ante. It'll be fun, the vampire equivalent of mutually assured destruction, but to be honest . . . I think I'm a higher tonnage weapon."

"They'll band together," she said breathlessly. "They'll kill you."

I laughed, a deep croaking noise in the uber vamp's body. "I really don't care. That's the difference between us. Who runs Sweetheart Row nowadays?"

"Petey and the gang."

"Is Petey a vampire, demon, or a human?" Jeez, I sounded like the damn answering imp.

"Vampire."

"And where can I find Petey?" I asked. She pointed.

Petey was right behind me. I'd expected a Master vamp, one that I would sense when he walked up. Soldiers like Petey don't even show up on the radar. He rammed a stake into my back, splintering it on my ebony uber vamp skin. Nice safety feature. Petey raked two sets of claws down my back, tearing angry rents in my flesh. Somebody else's blood—my dinner—seeped out of the wounds. Too bad the safety feature that makes stakes splinter on my uber vamp skin doesn't apply to claws.

One of the girls shouted, "Kill him, Petey!" Others joined the chorus, but not Cheryl.

Cheryl mouthed, "There are eight of them," turned, and ran. It wasn't fear that made her run, either, it was prudence.

In stuttering flashes I touched the same level of speed that other vampires get to use all of the time. Petey glared at me. He was a kid. I'd never seen him before; I would have remembered. In his whole gang, nobody looked like they'd been embraced at older than ten. If they hadn't been dressed in modern clothes, I'd have thought I was fighting the Little Rascals.

The fat one stepped in front of Fang, which was a mistake. Darting forward, Fang knocked him flat and rolled over the front of his legs. Fat Boy screamed. Fang's engine revved and the vampire began to slide under the car like he was being pulled in by a strong current.

"Help me!"

The rest of the gang didn't give him a second glance. Only Petey had a set of claws; the others carried switchblades. "You guys are freaking me out," I told them.

A little girl vampire in a pink dress, her hair done up in ribbons and curls, sprinted up my chest and stabbed me in the eye.

"Leave our bitches alone, fucko," she snarled. *Fucko?* Petey clawed at my stomach and two differently weighted kids hit either shoulder, sinking their fangs in deep. The one on the right bit into my shoulder blade and fell off of me, screaming and clutching his mouth. A piece of one of his fangs still protruded from my shoulder. I guess he hit bone.

Dancing in and out of range, they stabbed and bit in tiny microbursts, like piranhas. I snagged Petey by the throat with claws of my own. Two of the kids drummed on Fang with their fists, but I lost sight of what was going on with the car. I had my own rugrats to deal with. Pretty-in-Pink went after my other eye, hacking into my cheek instead. Flipping backward like a ninja, she would have evaded my grasp if the speed hadn't kicked in for a brief second. I caught her by the ankles and ripped her apart.

It was a blow to morale for the little bastards. Petey stopped fighting to cry, tears of blood running down his cheeks and soaking his shirt. One of the kids fighting Fang reeled back in horror, clutching a stump. Fang had chomped him with a well-timed hood slam. Three of the ladies of negotiable volume shielded him as if he really were a helpless nine-year-old boy, not a bloodsucking undead thing. Two more of the gang tried to get away, but the vamp speed had worked up a head of steam and I was firing on all eight cylinders at last. At full speed, I've never seen any creature faster than me as an uber vamp.

Short and thin, a child vampire wearing a hoodie ran right up the side of the Bitemore Hotel. It's not a trick I know, but I do know the "throw a discarded switchblade into the little fucker's spine" trick, so it worked out. It never even occurred to me to fly after him. He fell into my waiting clutches and I beaned another one of the vampire delinquents with the dismembered head of his buddy, still wrapped in the hood. That made four for me. I popped off their heads and ripped out their hearts, just to be sure. Petey still knelt in the middle of the road, bawling his eyes out.

"How many did you get?" I asked Fang. Like he could answer me. He popped his trunk and I walked around back. Inside were the bones of ten or fifteen small animals, and two fanged children. I don't want to know how that works. Fang's dings and scratches were gone, and polished chrome gleamed on his bumpers.

Why couldn't the prostitution ring have been run by a bunch of evil-looking guys with swastikas tattooed on their foreheads? How come I never get attacked by things like that? It's always Bible-thumping werewolves or vampire babies. Okay, and the occasional demons.

A crowd of the bravest ladies of the evening was forming around me. In uber vamp mode, I could clearly see the thin golden veil blocking off both ends of the alley, steering most mortals unconsciously around the street from Third to Fourth Avenue. Petey must have been pretty well connected. He knew who to pay and how much to pay them.

"He killed Darla!" No way that tyke's name had really been Darla. Vision, cloudy, but getting better by the second, returned to my left eye.

"Who provides the spells you use to shield Sweetheart Row?"

"None ya," Petey shouted at me.

"Who is Nunya?" I asked stupidly.

"None ya business!" Without warning he charged, swinging this time not like a vampire, but like an angry kid, pounding on my legs with his fists. "You killed Darla!"

I read somewhere that your emotional development freezes when you become addicted to drugs. Petey made me wonder if the same thing wasn't true of vampires. If you turned a nine-year-old, was he really forever stuck with the emotional maturity he'd had in life? I'd never done drugs and I've lived past thirty, what was my excuse? Was I stuck in some eternal midlife crisis?

A shard of the stake Petey had used to try to kill me lay in a puddle of blood at the edge of the sidewalk. I picked it up, took its measure in my hand, and ended Petey. When he died, the prostitutes screamed in unison. On one of them I saw a tattoo with the words *Petey's bitch* glow brightly and then fade.

The girls of Sweetheart Row were all thralls?

A scraggly looking vamp in an army surplus jacket stumbled out of the hotel. Fresh blood trailed down his chin, dripping on the jacket. "You killed them. The little guys. Why did you do that?"

You know, I can only feel so much guilt for killing a pack of little pimps.

"They were fucking vampires," I shouted. "Maybe you don't get it. Maybe you never got the memo. They were fucking monsters. I'm a fucking monster! You're a fucking monster! The question you should be asking yourself is why should I even feel the teeniest bit guilty about it?"

"Chill out, man." He held his hand out in a gesture that meant *calm down and lower your voice*. "We're all friends here."

"No, we're not." I dropped back down to humanoid, the splintered bit of a stake I'd used to kill Petey still clutched in my hand. "I only have four or five friends: two women, a mage, a cat, and maybe . . . just maybe, one freaky little tantric witch." Fang honked and I added, "And one heck of a car. Nowhere on my list does 'sad little poser in a green jacket' appear." Speed control still with me, I spiked his chest with the stake and watched him explode into a cloud of dust. I love it when that happens. It's so much tidier than the bubbling puddle of rot you get most of the time. "Does anyone know where Petey and the gang kept their cash?"

I turned around. Of the eighteen girls on the street, nine of them had turned to ash.

"What the hell?" I hadn't thought about what might happen to a thrall if the vampire who owned them died. I spun quickly, looking at the other girls. Three others were rapidly going from old to decrepit. Then I understood. Time was catching up to them. But how? Marilyn had been Roger's thrall and she'd grown old and Roger was a Master. Petey and his gang had been Soldiers. Shouldn't Roger's ability to keep his thralls young have been stronger?

The other five girls looked like they might be okay, and Cheryl appeared to be completely unaffected. She walked back, her demeanor much more confident.

"What now?" she asked me. "You got what you wanted. I'm sure some people will be pissed off. Even if we don't stay here, I'm sure I'm not the only girl who has regulars that are a little bit obsessed. They'll track us down. We're going to need some protection. I don't want to be snapped up by the next sadist who comes along just because Petey was pimping me out on Sweetheart Row."

And that, my friends, is exactly why when I eat out, I tend to kill the donor. If she's dead, it's harder for her to stick around and whine. "Hold that thought." More vampires stared at me from the Bitemore, peeking out windows or from the fire escape. Three big vamps in suits that shouted *hired muscle* walked out through the front doors. I don't know if they worked for the hotel or the vampires I'd just killed, but it didn't matter to me. If I was going to send a message, why not send a fucking message, you know? I transformed into the uber vamp again. Two of the muscle-bound morons showed me fang-filled grins. They didn't grin for long.

✦ 22 ✦

TABITHA:

LOOK WHAT THE GANDER DRAGGED IN

The accommodations at the Pollux made me miss the Highland Towers. There was a shower behind the stage near the dressing rooms, but the water smelled funny and no one offered to bring me a bottle of blood wine, mulled or otherwise. Industrial strength cleaner mingled with a background stench of disinfectant.

At least the shampoo from Eric's office was recent. He didn't seem to need or understand the uses for conditioner. I guessed he'd picked the shampoo himself, because it had no strong scent, smelling like soap rather than any herbal concoction or perfume.

After the shower, I put on the magic skirt and top Winter had given me. Even though I had them change color—a blue top, a black skirt—so that no one would notice I'd already worn them once this week, I kept wishing that I'd packed something else. Magic or not, wearing the same clothes is just icky. Rubbing my hair dry with a towel, I nosed around the dressing rooms hoping to find something else to wear. Greta emerged from the one at the far end of the hall, looking hunted. I didn't sense her until I saw her, making her the second vampire I'd met who could do that with their mystic presence. She closed the door behind her too quickly for me to see any specifics, but it looked as though a whole apartment's worth of furniture had been crammed into the small dressing room. Her hands slid across the door protectively.

"This is my room and my stuff." Her fangs glistened as she spoke.

"I don't want any of your junk."

"You want my dad."

"Maybe," I told her truthfully. "I guess I do. I'm really not sure."

"Cut off your head, stuff your mouth with garlic, stake you through the heart with any kind of hard wood, then bury your head and your body in two different plots on consecrated ground. That's all it would take."

"What?"

"You're so unimaginative. I know vampire hunters who would try that method first thing and then you'd be gone forever."

My fingernails stretched into claws. "Is that a threat?"

"No." Greta vanished. The floor rose up to hit me in the face, bloodying my nose, bringing tears of blood to my eyes. Her weight was heavy on my back, grinding me into the cold tiles. Fangs touched my neck and my arms bent backward, broken at the elbows. "This is." She knelt in front of me, head canted at a curious angle. "Hurt my daddy and I'll kill you."

"How did you . . . ow, God!" My elbows reknitted, shifting into their original orientation. The pain was remarkable. It felt . . . it felt . . . like having your elbows broken and then having them jammed back into place. I'd like to compare it to something witty, but it's a unique sensation.

"How did I beat you up?"

I nodded. "I'm pretty fast. I should have seen that coming, at least."

"Daddy is made for strength and hitting him is like punching a brick. You're made for speed and you can do the whole lifelike thing, which is cool; Daddy deserves that. I could feel your body heat from the office last night, hear your heart beat, the rhythm of the two of you. It rocked me to sleep."

Okay, now that was disturbing . . . I wondered if we could get some kind of mystic soundproofing.

"Daddy can do so many things and he has the angry eyes and the uber mode, oh, and the ghost mode, but me, I'm made for killing and I'm hungry all the time. When we're fighting together, Daddy and me, I always make sure to let him look the best, because, you know, he's Dad. It's like when you used to fake an orgasm. You didn't want Daddy to feel bad. I get that. That's why I hope we can be friends."

"Wow." I gushed insincerity. "I totally get that." Our gazes met. My mind darted into Greta's, but her mind was a vacant room, literally. I was standing in a living room. Ozone, tinged with burnt carpet, dominated the room's scent. An undercurrent of blood, sweat, and sex drifted in from elsewhere in the house. The salty tang of the ocean crept in through a broken window. I'd dominated another vampire's mind before. This was nothing like that. Greta had no walls to keep things out, no nice neat ordered core. Walking down a set of stairs came a pretty blond girl, not more than ten, wearing an oversize T-shirt that read: *Daddy's Girl.*

Blood trickled down her left leg. Bruises mottled the side of her face along the jawline. "Greta?" I asked.

"Daddy isn't here right now," she said softly. "Are you my new mommy?"

"What happened?"

"Bad things." Her face was expressionless, but a single tear streaked her cheek. "Daddy made it stop. New Daddy. Old Daddy is upstairs." The girl set her jaw. "You aren't one of Old Daddy's friends are you?"

"No!" I assured her. "No, I'm with Eric."

"Then you must be my new mommy." Little Greta rushed to embrace me, holding me like an anchor, a temple, a safe haven. My God . . .

"Sure. Sure. Okay." I returned the hug, patting her back absent-mindedly. "Mommy's here." What the hell had happened to her?

"I'm sorry I hurt you, Mommy."

"It's okay," I muttered. "It's okay. Your father will be home soon."

"I feel him," Greta answered in the physical world. Breaking the contact, I discovered that Greta and I were sitting on the floor of the corridor, hugging each other. Greta pulled me to my feet. Eric's presence brushed mine. Human heartbeats pounded around him. Five of them. "He brought pets, or maybe snacks!" Greta bubbled. "Let's see which!"

Long blond locks of hair bounced against her back echoing the excitement in her voice. In the rush to get downstairs, she left me forgotten in the hall. I followed more slowly, pausing to straighten my clothes. I'd noticed Eric changing into different sets of clothes without even realizing it, but I couldn't manage that trick yet. I end up wearing whatever I'd been wearing before I transformed or the black dress I'd worn the first time I tried shape-shifting.

"Honey," Eric bellowed from the box office. "You'll never believe what followed me home today."

"Dad," Greta laughed from upstairs. "Don't you already have enough pets? What will Mom say?"

"I was going to tell her they were yours."

"Dad!"

Women crowded around Eric in the foyer, wearing worn lingerie, latex, and Lycra. The smell was disgusting, like sex in a slaughterhouse. Eric introduced them to Greta, his words evading me completely.

"They're hookers!" I blurted.

"Blood whores," Eric corrected.

"We prefer women of negotiable volume," the youngest among them said. She was maybe forty, but she still had spirit in her, the others were older, broken and empty-eyed. "But you can say whore if it means we don't get eaten."

"Where are we?" asked the most senior.

"We're in the Pollux, Gladys," the youngest one told her. "You've got to re-enthrall her." She pushed her finger into Eric's chest. "Gladys has been a thrall as long as any of us can remember. Petey wasn't even her first master. She hasn't got much time left." The older woman sagged physically, her breasts drooping visibly, the curvature of her spine becoming more pronounced as if on cue.

"Can she hang on for another twenty minutes, Cheryl?" Eric asked.

Cheryl sighed. "You don't know how to do it, do you?"

"Just . . . What? Yes, I know how to do it," Eric scoffed.

"Then do it."

Eric held up a finger. "Just fucking wait." He put his hand on Greta's shoulder. "Watch these ladies for me, okay?"

"Sure, Dad."

"Did Rachel show back up?"

"No, Dad."

"I'll be right back." Eric glanced my way for the first time. "Tabitha, just, I'm sorry, just . . ."

"Hi," Greta told the girls. "I'm Greta. I think if you're bad, I get to eat you." She pointed in the direction of the front doors as Eric passed through them. "Anybody want to watch a movie?"

She led the women into the theater, a demented troop leader herding her Hooker Scouts out of the foyer and into the dark. Nope, nothing like this ever happened at the Highland Towers.

23

ERIC:

MAGBIDION'S BARE BUTT

Okay, so I lied. I didn't know how to make a real thrall. Mags had given me a few pages of notes that he'd scribbled down, but I'd never made a real thrall and for some stupid reason, I wanted to get it right this time. I didn't need anyone else to have the same sort of power over me that Rachel had—one was enough.

The concept was simple. Like everything with vampires, making a thrall involved blood. All I had to do was tattoo Mags with my blood . . . somehow push my mind into his to forge the link, then say the "magic words" to seal the deal and claim him. I'm not sure why he had to be naked.

I hadn't noticed it before, but in Magbidion's RV, the bed, when it was unfolded, pretty much dominated the available space, which may have exacerbated the discomfort that I sensed from Magbidion as he removed his clothes. Mags isn't gay, nor does he seem to be interested in women in an actual bumping uglies sort of way. There has to be a term for it, but I tended to think of him as solosexual: a self-sufficient sexual entity having no real need for human contact outside of himself. A vampire can tell these things. Plus, with his shirt off, anyone could tell that his left bicep was bigger than his right and Mags seemed to be a lefty in everything else, too.

Knowing that neither of us was homosexual did very little to relieve my discomfort, either. When Tabitha walked in, I was still hovering over Magbidion's ass trying to copy the butterfly off of the sketch I'd done for Tabitha. Try explaining to your girlfriend that you are copying a tattoo you made just for her onto the lower back of a naked sweaty man . . . It doesn't matter what excuse you use or how reasonable it sounds inside your head or how true it may be, you cannot win. The butterfly had seemed like a good idea. When he mentioned the need for a tattoo, something unique to me, it's what I thought of first. I already had the sketch—I'd designed it. I was pressed for time. . . . Yeah, *embarrassment* is too weak a word.

"Holy shit!" she said when she opened the door. I turned to explain, but she had already closed the door again and retreated.

I went back to what I was doing. "That's just fucking great!" I grumbled.

"You want to go after her?" Mags offered.

"And tell her what?" I asked in exasperation. "It's not what you think. I'm not fucking the naked guy; I'm making him my eternal slave?"

"Slave? My friend, I will not be your slave, so much as a companion, a confidant . . ."

I guess Mags had illusions of freedom. "Who has to do what he is ordered and is bound by an eternal unbreakable mystic link unless his master releases him? Should I go on?"

"Okay, okay. Slave is technically correct, but I still like to think of our arrangement as something special, more an alliance than—"

Definite denial. "And don't say companion. For anyone but Doctor Who, that word has different connotations, especially when nudity is involved. Let me put it this way: Do you want to fight the demon yourself, Mags? Because if I have to listen to much more of your hedging, I'll just try it on one of the Golden Girls in the Pollux and be done with it." He shivered and it really wasn't something I wanted to see from behind. Magbidion naked was something I already hadn't wanted to see, but watching his sphincter tighten reflexively was too much. "Okay, I'm out," I said as I headed for the door. "I am not doing this. Too much naked-man ass for me."

"No, please, Eric," he began.

I turned. He turned. Tabitha opened the door again.

"All right," she started, "I have to ask."

"Please, Eric," Magbidion continued. "You must do it. I need you!" He sounded frantic and afraid. He also sounded like he was begging for something else.

Tabitha put a hand over her mouth. "Oh. My. God."

"This is not happening," I said as I covered my eyes with my palm. Even if Tabitha and I weren't getting back together, this was not the image I wanted her walking away with.

"I'll just leave you boys alone then, shall I?"

"That would be nice," Mags said.

"Okay." I put a hand on Tabitha's shoulder. "Everybody just stop. Magbidion," I pointed to him, "turn around. Nobody here wants to see your twig and berries. Looking at your pale little ass is bad enough." I wasn't looking, but it sounded like he did as I asked. "Tabitha, you've got superhearing. Did you hear what we were talking about or not?"

She giggled and kissed me on the cheek. "That's why I turned back around. Is it mean to have a little fun?"

"Does this mean you two are getting back together?" Mags asked as I uncovered my eyes. He also turned around to face us again. "I don't want to keep you from your . . . festivities. Eric and I were just prepping for the blood whores."

"You are so not helping." I looked Magbidion in the eyes and gave him the universal gesture for *turn around*. He seemed to deflate a moment, but he resumed the position.

"I wouldn't be standing this way if he would hurry up. What's taking you so long anyway? All you have to do is put blood where you want the mark and then picture it in your head. Indecision is one thing, but—"

"Picture it in my head?" I interrupted.

"Yes."

I smeared the blood around on his lower back. "You didn't tell me that. I thought I had to draw it. Tabitha, show me your tattoo."

She obligingly lifted the back of her blouse. It took a few seconds for me to focus, but once I could concentrate properly, the blood on Magbidion's back pooled and sank into his skin. Line by line, the butterfly tattoo on Tabitha's back was replicated on Magbidion's. Red lines slowly changed to the appropriate colors and when it was completed, the entire tattoo flashed brightly one time.

"I mark thee and bind thee," I incanted. "Master to servant. Servant to master. You are mine until I set you free. You are mine. So mote it be."

Of course there was more pain. Why I had thought there wouldn't be, I can't say, but it felt like molten lead had been poured on an open wound and unfortunately, I do know what that feels like. Pretty much the same as having molten lead poured onto healthy skin, just a little more vicious. I bit through my tongue, severing the tip nicely. "Fuck! Damn! Son of a bitch!" I cursed, falling to my knees. And I was fixing to do this shit five more times in a row—lovely.

Magbidion joined the menagerie of people in my mind's eye, only now the vision was clearer, more distinct. Greta was watching *The Goonies* with the survivors of Sweetheart Row. Tabitha felt guilty about screwing Talbot and some fat ass named Phillip, but she did love me. It would have been nice if I could decide whether or not I loved her back. I've been in love before and what I felt for her wasn't the same. Was it close enough? That was the real question.

Rachel, I still couldn't get a fix on, but I could sense her, which was progress. She felt like she was still in the city, but where was anyone's guess. Outside, in the neighboring streets, I felt eight thralls belonging to other vampires. Two of them belonged to Winter, three to a female vamp I didn't recognize, another to a short fat vampire, and the last two to a vamp I'd seen around town but couldn't name. I guess the stunt I'd pulled out at the Bitemore has gotten folks' attention. Either that or I was a very popular person to spy on.

If you added it all together, it was more proof that Rachel had lied to me. It was possible that she was just wrong, that she had, like her sister, read too many books about vampires and had good info mixed with the bad, but Magbidion seemed to think she was too powerful a witch to be so wrong about something so simple. Then again, I had been a vampire for decades and her version had sounded reasonable to me. If it turned out that she was an unwitting pawn in all this, then so much the better, but—not likely.

I felt like I was playing Texas Hold'em with only three cards. I could still win, but everything counted on the flop going my way.

Tabitha knelt next to me and cradled my head against her bosom. Another vampire's scent was there, too, on the diamond necklace. It was a few days old, but the scent infuriated me all over again. What the fuck had she been up to? I couldn't lose my temper about it. Getting mad felt like the right thing to do, but it wasn't going to help me. Instead, I reached down to hand Magbidion his clothes and even though I tried to do it at vampire speed, he beat me to it. "Great!" I hissed.

"What is it?" asked Tabitha.

"Nothing," I told her, "just more of my shit not working right. Mags, get the fuck out of here. Go set up an early-warning system or something. Like the one you have for your RV, but for the whole Pollux."

"But that will take forever," he complained.

"Good," I snarled, "'cause that's how long you belong to me for."

He headed for the door and I beat him to it. The speed kicked in that time and I had no idea why. Mags looked like he wanted to get dressed first, but my expression told him that this was no time to argue. He stepped naked onto the parking deck and I slammed the door.

I spoke, still facing the door. "Go take a shower."

"I just took a shower." She didn't even look hurt. Instead, she smiled at me and got to her feet. "But if you want to join me?"

"Then wash the necklace." I sighed. "It smells like some other guy."

"If you're going to start in on me, remember our deal." She crossed her arms. "You bring up what happened with me and I—"

"Just do it, please."

Smiling the entire time, Tabitha took off her necklace, set it on the dresser, stripped off her clothes, and went into Mags's bathroom. My girls always seemed to leave their clothes lying about on the floor. I've never minded picking up after them. I remember liking that sort of thing even as a human, to have a woman's clothes and underwear just lying about my bedroom. It made normal women seem so brazen. Her panties lay on top of her blouse. I picked them up and sniffed them before hiking over to the Pollux. Yep, it was nice to have her scent back.

24

ERIC:
NEW RECRUITS

Talbot stood next to the stage in front of the wooden elevator that would have raised the old Wurlitzer organ up and down, except that it wasn't there anymore. It had been sold in the auction along with tons of stuff I would never miss. Talbot missed the thing. He and Marilyn had always harbored a hope that I'd play the organ again one day, but I won't. Music aids memory and I don't want the help.

Five women lay on the stage with their tops rolled up to expose their backs . . . except for Gladys who insisted on being completely nude. I went down the line, smearing blood on each of them, willing it into the form of a butterfly tattoo, and this time around I thought to make the mental connection before saying the words again, having been advised by Magbidion that it would ease the pain.

"I mark thee and bind thee," I began. The pain started and with it my range expanded further until I could sense one more thrall, in service to a vampire I didn't know, a vampire with golden-rimmed glasses. "Master to servant." As I chanted, Gladys began to moan and change. Her skin drew taught, the muscles in her calves and buttocks clenching. "Servant to master."

"You're so good, baby," she said between clenched teeth as her hair went from gray to a rich auburn.

"You are mine until I set you free." The others sighed then, in unison, and I realized that it wasn't painful for them. The process was pleasurable. Their breaths came in quick rapid pants. Gladys rubbed her thighs together, rolling her head to one side so she could look at me through those timeless bedroom eyes.

"You are mine," I continued, ignoring my own arousal. Gladys rose up slightly, revealing the curve of her full breasts, a hint of nipple. "So mote it be." They climaxed in unison and Tabitha thumped me in the back of the head but didn't say anything. They were mine, the former girls of Sweetheart Row. My pain built to a crescendo, five distinct spikes of agony and I hit a knee onstage.

They moved for me, as one, but I waved them off. "Wait down there for a second." I gestured at the front-row seats. "Except you, Gladys." She paused and I looked up at her only to find myself eye level with her belly button, the scent of her filling my nostrils.

"Yes, Master." Her fingers curled through my hair and I shuddered as it eased the pain. Note to self: a good thrall is twice as effective and fast acting as aspirin . . . not that I can take aspirin.

"You get some clothes on first and don't call me master."

"Tease," she said with a wink. Her hand left my head and the pain returned. Wait . . . so I was going to have the rest of the girls stand around smelling like sex? What was I thinking?

"Get cleaned up," I called as she headed for the seats. "All of you." I put my head down on the cold wood, ignoring the scent of sex. Red tinged my vision again and the waxy smell in my nostrils was coming from me. After making them, I was running on empty. The magic had used up too much blood.

"Eric?" said Talbot, a note of concern in his voice.

Talbot smelled appetizing, but feeding from mousers is a bad idea as a general rule. "Hungry," I said. Magbidion rolled up onto the stage and shoved his wrist at my mouth.

"It'll be fine, Eric," he said. "Just be careful."

I sank my teeth into his veins and he stifled a hiss. It doesn't feel good when I bite. I'd thought, now that he was my thrall, there might be a flavor to his blood, like with Rachel's. There wasn't, but it did the trick anyway.

When I'd taken enough, I pushed him away from me and closed my eyes, head still pounding. Note to self: when making thralls, do them one at a time. An hour later I opened my eyes. My six new thralls sat in the front row looking a century or two younger between them. Even Magbidion looked younger and healthier, despite the snack service.

Turns out Soldiers slow the aging process when they make thralls, Masters freeze it, and Vlads—or Emperors—can turn back the clock. Gladys in particular was bright eyed and bushy tailed, ready to please. It had been decades since she was a cute young thing; she had probably been around longer than I had, but her beauty was timeless. I could see why each successive pimp running Sweetheart Row had kept her around. She looked like a redheaded version of Marilyn Monroe or Brigitte Bardot, but she was willing to do anything with anyone as long as it was okay with "her daddy." Like I needed another grown woman calling me Daddy.

Magbidion had summoned them all up a set of fresh clothes that he warned would only last twenty-one hours. Talbot had had him burn the others. Greta had supervised showers for the girls and aside from a lack of hair spray, they looked better and smelled better than I was willing to guess they had in the last ten years. My army: five ex-hookers, a glorified house cat, one crazy female Vlad, a greasy magician, my car, and my ex-ex-girlfriend.

I caught Tabitha smirking at me in the back row and flipped her off.

"Okay, here's the deal. Who here knows the trick—" Gladys raised her hand.

"Yes?" I asked.

"I know the trick."

"I haven't even said which trick I'm talking about."

Gladys laughed. "Oh, you might know it by another name, honey, but trust me, I know the trick." Everyone laughed, including me. She was a breath of fresh air.

"Simmer down, ladies," I said affably. Gladys looked over her shoulder. "Yes, I mean you," I added before she could comment.

She winked at me. "Go ahead, sugar. I won't interrupt no more."

"Who here knows the trick where you regenerate blood quickly, so that a vampire can feed off of you multiple nights in a row?"

Four hands went up. Sally, a brunette, laughed out loud. "Gladys can go all night on three Slim-Fasts and eight hours of sleep. I can take three drinkers, more if they just want a taste near the end."

Erin, one of the two blondes, held up two fingers. I'd yet to hear her speak and she wouldn't meet my eyes. Jodi, the other blonde, put her arm around Erin. "She doesn't talk any, but she can give blood a couple times a night. Petey was kinda hard on her, but if you work with her, you might get her numbers up. She's a real good girl and the johns like her 'cause she's quiet. I can do three."

Cheryl was the only one of the gals who hadn't raised her hand. She'd gotten rid of the wig she'd been wearing. Beneath it, her hair was short-cropped and brown. I looked at her and she stared back at me. The other girls were all sexually excited, but not Cheryl. Cheryl smelled angry.

"What?" I asked.

"Nothing."

"Tell me."

"I—" She cut her eyes at the other girls. "I just thought it would be different. You seemed different."

"I am different. Let me explain something to you, Cheryl." I hopped down off of the stage. "This is my theater and that"—I pointed in the direction of the land where the Demon Heart had once stood—"was my club. The women who danced there were my girls. I looked after them. I paid them an excellent salary. I paid for their health insurance. I even put them through college. I didn't do that because I'm a nice man. I did that because it is a fair reward for what I expect from my girls. I expected them to dance their asses off for me for three to five years. They shook their boobs and showed their crotches, but that's only part of it."

"You had your own whores." Cheryl sighed. "I get it. Just tell me who to fuck, Master. Tell me what to charge and I'll do it."

My eyes glowed blue and as I looked into her eyes, she stared back at me defiantly. "You want to leave? I'll let you go right now. No strings attached. No questions asked." She grew still and quiet; I could feel her panic. She was like me, even as a thrall she needed to be in control. "If I wanted you to be my whore," I told her, "I'd throw you on the ground and bang you like a beast and there wouldn't be a thing you could do to stop me." She squirmed uncomfortably in the seat. Gladys's excitement was growing. She wanted me.

"Keep it in your pants, Eric," I muttered to myself.

"Why don't you do whatever you want to with it?" Gladys said. Maybe there is some sort of pheromone I give off . . . an airborne brass monkey or Spanish fly. Whatever it was, it didn't affect Cheryl.

I bared my fangs at her. "I'm a vampire."

"No shit," Cheryl said.

"I don't want to have sex with you." Gladys and the others looked crestfallen, but I kept talking. "I have a girlfriend . . . possibly . . . and I'm really trying to work on keeping it down to me and her, but that's not what this is about." I rubbed my eyes.

Cheryl stood up. "So, you want us to be strippers?"

"No," I said sulkily. "I'm not building another strip club. I built that in the seventies and now that it's gone . . . I don't know . . . I was thinking a bowling alley, maybe. I like bowling."

"Anything, so long as it has balls," Gladys chimed in.

"So all you want is our blood, right?" Jodi spoke up.

I nodded. "Basically."

"Do you have to drink it straight from the source?" asked Erin. "And what vein do you like? Because I don't really like anybody feeding near my nethers. I'm always afraid they're going to bite something that don't need bitin'." Everyone stared at her.

"Well, I *am*." She blushed. Anybody broken just loves me. Maybe like attracts like? The others girls crowded in around her, hugging and smiling, thrilled that she was speaking again. Cheryl asked a question and despite my hearing, I couldn't make it out in the din and excitement, but I heard her reply.

"'Cause he's got a real nice aura," Erin said shyly. Her eyes widened. "I've never seen such."

"You and me both," Talbot whispered.

When everyone had settled back down, I continued, "When I ran the club, all my dancers owed me one unit of whole blood—that's not quite a pint—every fifty-six days. Some of them gave it via the needle and I stored it in the fridge. Others liked to have me take it in person . . . maybe they were into the pain or it fulfilled some creepy vampire fetish. A few did it because they knew I like it better that way.

"Some of my girls voluntarily gave more than is healthy and became anemic; they weren't thralls and they didn't know any tricks. I usually kept around twenty eligible female employees and ate out a few nights a week. If things are going well, I only have to consume about a cup of blood per night. Which doesn't mean that's all I want, but it is all I need. With your unique talents," I smiled at my group, "I might not have to eat out anymore."

I stood and nobody flinched, but, then again, these were professionals. They knew more about the needs of vampires as a whole than I did and Erin's trust in me seemed to work wonders for their morale. I should have shut up, but I went on anyway, to fill the silence. "On the other hand, when the shit is hitting the fan and everyone is out to get me, I require more nourishment. Usually, I get it by killing someone and draining them dry. Even if everything is fine, I still wind up hunting eight to ten nights a month. On most of those hunts, my victim dies. I never feed on Thanksgiving, Christmas, New Year's Eve, or Halloween. I even take my turn protecting folks during the Void City Music Festival. And just so you know who you'll be working for . . ."

I was into the same spiel I gave prospective strippers. From a certain perverse perspective, anything that happened to them if they chose to stay was their own fault. They'd have been warned. "Because of what I am, I murder, on average, roughly one hundred and thirty people a year. I've been doing it for over four decades. The first twenty years I killed someone almost every single night. Sometimes I killed more than that, because I was learning my limits. Overall, I suppose

I have been responsible for the deaths of over ten thousand human beings. Charles Manson can kiss my ass. He has no comprehension.

"Most vampires I know haven't killed a third of the people I have. They either don't have my control problems or they make do with animal blood. And yes, if you're wondering, I have tried animal blood. It didn't work. For me, it has to be human or I just get hungrier. I don't like what I am, but I'm too selfish to let anyone kill me. Any questions?"

Gladys raised her hand and I nodded. She bit her bottom lip, gave Cheryl a sidelong glance, before saying, "Then could you fuck me, like, right now?"

Maybe it was an act, but she knew how to keep things from getting too dark.

"Talk to her about it." I pointed up the row at Tabitha. "I think if we stay together she's going to want things to be mostly exclusive unless it happens on a hunt."

Tabitha raised an eyebrow.

"Things happen when you hunt sometimes," I explained. By her expression, I could tell she understood. I wished that she hadn't. It made her one more woman that I'd turned into a monster.

"What else do we have to do?" Sally asked.

"If I open something across the street, you have to work in it. You'll be paid, I'll put you through college if you want to go, you'll get health care with vision and dental, and you'll feed me. Since you're all thralls, shall we say, experienced with blood regeneration, we'll work up a rotation. I'm sure I'll still hunt some, but this will minimize the damage I do."

"Can I give you mine via blood bag?" Cheryl asked.

"Yes."

"Then you can drink it straight if you want." Her expression softened. "I'm not saying you're all that different," her eyes flicked to Erin, "but I'll give it a try."

"Why are you so nice to them?" Magbidion grumbled. "You hardly know them! Me, you call your slave."

"Because you know I'm kidding," I told him. "They've been slaves too long for me to be sure they know the difference."

"Oh." The mage slunk down in his seat.

"In the morning Talbot will take you shopping for new clothes, linens, makeup, and whatever. Go backstage; pick out a dressing room each . . . any room but Greta's."

"*Talbot* will?" Talbot perked up.

"Yep." I flashed my fangs. "You've got money squirreled away for a rainy day. I'm sure of it . . . and it'll get you off my shit list."

"Okay. Done." Talbot nodded.

"Pick up some bedding, too, sleeping bags and cots or something. Those dressing rooms are small."

"What about me?" Magbidion asked. "Should I just keep working on the early-warning system? I'm going to need blood, oni claws—"

"The girls can help you with the blood, but you'll have to buy the other stuff."

"With what?" He ran his thumb along the other fingers on his right hand. "I have some money, but not what I'd need for a spell that big. To do the whole building I'll need a whole claw, not just a piece of it, and a very expensive ruby—a huge one. Oni are happy to sell their clippings, but ripping out one of their own claws by the roots? For the RV, I used a small ruby, full of flaws, but to do more, I need better materials. On the RV, little gaps are less noticeable, on the Pollux, the gaps would be large enough to walk through."

"I'll work on the money side of things, then. Table the spell until I get back to you. For now, I want you to do a little research. Have you ever heard of . . . Damn. What was it called? The Rock of, no, the Stone of Eternity? I'm supposed to get it from some guy named Phil."

"Phillip?" Tabitha coughed. "Do you mean the Stone of Aeternum?"

I snapped my fingers. "That! The Stone of Aeternum."

"I think a vampire can use it to become more powerful, steal another vampire's power," Magbidion answered.

"You ever hear of it making someone immortal?"

"No. Well, wait. Maybe. I remember a few years ago there was a big brouhaha in the immortal community. One of my friends, Shelley, said that the Council of Elders wanted to locate it."

"Immortal community," I scoffed.

"Oh, yes, they are much more structured and regimented than the vampire hierarchy. They've divided the world into fiefdoms. It's very intricate."

"I don't care about that, just tell me if you think it's possible that the Stone could be used for that."

"I suppose it's possible," Mags admitted.

"Then I'll go get it."

"Eric," Talbot and Tabitha spoke up in unison. An exchange of glances, a silent agreement between them, sent a spike of jealously up my spine, raising the hairs on the back of my neck. Tabitha closed her mouth, letting Talbot continue.

"Lord Phillip is the vampire who owns the Highland Towers, where Roger lived." He did his best to look straight at me, but Talbot's eyes kept straying toward Tabitha. When it happened a third time, he took up a position directly in front of me with his back to her.

"He showed Tabitha a bunch of artifacts he used to elevate himself through the levels of vampiric power. He claims to have been a human wizard who made himself into a vampire to gain immortality. He didn't realize that it would make him a Drone. Since then, he says he has found ways to make himself more powerful. He's a Vlad now."

"Not bad," I said. Suddenly I remembered having heard Tabitha mention this guy. She'd said he was nobody. He didn't sound like a nobody to me. "Did he fuck her?" Why do I even ask questions like that? It's not like I really want to know.

Greta put a hand to her mouth, but said nothing. I caught Tabitha shaking her head in disbelief. I wasn't supposed to bring up her guys, I know, but like I really wasn't going to catch hell from her over Rachel sooner or later?

"Eric," Talbot began.

"She was fucking a vampire up at the Highland Towers, the vampire I smelled on her diamond necklace. Is this Phillip asshole the one who fucked her?" I repeated. "It shouldn't be a hard question unless so many people screwed her while she was with you that you lost count!"

"Yeah, Eric. He fucked her," Talbot told me. "And before you ask, there was no one else, just me and Phillip."

"Holy shit, Talbot!" interrupted Greta. "You fooled around with Mom? What does she have that I don't have?"

"Catlike reflexes," I answered, "and warm fuzzy feline genitalia, apparently."

Greta's eyes widened and she glanced over at Tabitha. "You guys did it as cats? And I thought Dad was kinky!"

"Greta, please," Talbot pleaded. "No, we didn't. It has to do with the way she moves, feline grace . . . Let it go, okay. I'll tell you anything you want to know about it later."

"No, he won't," I said abruptly. "That warning I gave you earlier—"

"The thing with the balls ripping off and the tortured animal cracker imagery?"

"Yes," I said. "It now applies to Greta, too."

"Understood," he said quickly. Greta mouthed the words "tortured animal crackers" and shook her head. Was I the only one in the world who had ever eaten an animal cracker feetfirst because it would theoretically hurt more?

"So, this Phillip, he's got the magic rock I need," I continued. Then I couldn't help but ask Tabitha, "Why'd you leave him?"

"God! He was a freak, okay? He's rich and powerful, but he's twisted. Everything is like a game to him, even people. He wanted to show me off to his special guests in ways even you would never have asked, so I told him to fuck himself. He'd already tried to get me to be the guest of honor in a Victorian-style gangbang. Not that you should even be asking."

I turned Talbot around. "So I should pretty much kill him."

"He runs the city, Eric," Tabitha blurted. "You can't just waltz into the Highland Towers and kill him. He's got magic wards and security."

"Is he awake during the day?" I asked.

"Sometimes," Tabitha answered.

"How hard is he to wake?"

"Pretty hard. Why?"

"That's all I needed to know." I nodded to Talbot. "How long will it take to get there?"

"About twenty minutes," he answered.

"Is there a parking deck or anything? You know what? I have a better idea. I'll head over there in the early afternoon. Are there any good pet-supply stores around here?"

25

ERIC:
PARKING

W e pulled up outside the Highland Towers in Talbot's Jaguar. I trusted the shade in his car enough to just peek my mousey whiskers out of Talbot's shirt pocket. The building was impressive in a monumental Gothic sort of way. Very West Side, but I had to admit that I liked it more than the buildings around it. It wasn't the tallest, but it had a certain architectural extravagance with which I identified.

Talbot pulled into the parking deck. I didn't ask about the key card he used to get us in. I figured that Tabitha had one, too, and I didn't want to think about it any harder than I already was. Despite its normal appearance from the outside, the deck was very vampire friendly. The subtle angling of the exterior wall maximized shade on the exterior parking spots. An interior divide granted access to a second parking area, completely sealed off from the sun, and a covered walkway connected the deck and the main complex.

My little detour to the pet-supply shop had run us later than intended, so Talbot pulled into the covered area. Each parking spot was labeled by suite name. Talbot parked in one of the four marked *Reserved— Gryphon Suite.*

"I wonder how much it set these rich assholes back to outfit this deck?" I asked, crawling out of Talbot's shirt pocket and returning to human size.

"Are you sure you won't let me just go inside and get you in?" Talbot asked again. "Tabitha was given Roger's old suite as a gift. I should be able to get Dennis to let you in past the wards and then you could talk to Lord Phillip."

I picked up the shopping bag from Void City Pets. Inside was a roll-around ball for hamsters and gerbils. I'd spray painted it black. My plan was more fun than Talbot's. Talbot would shut me in the ball in mouse form and then point me toward the Highland Towers. In my new sun-proof plastic ball, I'd roll right up to the wards, go uber vamp, and . . .

"You suck all the joy out of life." I pulled the plastic contraption out of the bag. "The SunRunner Five Thousand, man. It's a cool idea." *Just not a practical idea*, I completed the thought mentally.

"You named the plastic pet ball?"

I sighed. "I *could* just use the walkway."

"You could."

"But busting in through the front door just sounds like fun, Talbot."

"If you say so."

"Okay, you win." I tossed the SunRunner Five Thousand back into the car and stomped toward the interior corridor.

Unlike most parking decks, there was no trash in the stairwell, no stains on the floor or on the walls. Everything was very well kept and the lighting was good. Sand-colored walls were painted with little coral patterns and the floor was a rich brown. The door into the walkway opened easily into a small receiving area. It was carpeted in thick burgundy carpet and the walls were light brown. It was supposed to look welcoming, I guess. Instead, it reminded me of an Italian restaurant I'd taken the living, breathing Tabitha to six months before.

That was when I felt the other vamps. Most of them were sleeping, but a few of them weren't. Fifteen Masters lived here. Their faces blurred in my mind's eye. Some of them were old, others were new, but none of them seemed important. I never get much data off of any vampire, so it didn't surprise me.

It did come as a shock when one of the female vamps stood out. She felt familiar. I'd seen her face before, in the minds of some of the thralls spying on the Pollux. This was their owner, the one who made them thralls. She was asleep. Concentrating on her face made her appear more clearly. She was sleeping soundly, though I recognized one of her thralls moving around in the room. I deliberately reached for more information, a name, anything, and, for once, I got it. The vampire's name was Gabriella, and she was old, far older than me.

Her eyes opened and she screamed. Her panic ripped through the connection and I heard a ramble of thoughts: *Not during the day. He wasn't supposed to be here yet. Good Lord, what if he knows?* before she regained control of herself.

What if I knew what?

Let me in, I thought at her.

Roger is not here, she thought back. *I will have him send Rachel back to you. Please, leave in peace!*

Roger? Huh? I was here for the stupid stone thingy, not Roger. Of course, if he just happened to be in the building . . .

Our contact was severed when I sensed the Vlads. There were seven of them. I wondered which one was Phillip and in response, a balding little man, not a midget but still pretty damn short, swam to the front of my mind. He slept in a huge canopy bed with three humans lying on or next to him for warmth. Two of them were chatting while the third just lay there trying to sleep.

Even after decades of being a vampire, I felt like there was an instruction booklet that everyone else had and that people were purposefully keeping away from me. Previously, when I'd sensed other vampires, I'd known whether they were Masters or Vlads or whatever, and what they looked like. I'd never gotten such good, clear information before.

I heard the sound of Talbot's footsteps on concrete and then he came running down the stairs and into the reception area. "Why did you kick in the super-speed?" he asked. "Are we in a race?"

"I didn't know that I had."

"Let me go in, see if I can find Dennis, and get you permission to come inside," Talbot told me. "Just wait out here. It should only take a minute."

A minute passed, followed by five. I looked at my watch, walked up to the door. There was something there that made the hair on my arms stand up and the back of my neck grow cold.

Reaching out with my left hand, I could feel it, a barrier. It was invisible, but very real. A presence touched my thoughts and then retreated. The double doors ahead of me swung open and the barrier seemed to part like a curtain.

"You are expected," a voice whispered in my mind.

Talbot came around the corner. "Dennis is asleep." A young woman with bleary eyes followed him. "Hannah says she can add you to the system, though. She'll need a drop of your blood."

Hannah held out a golden needle with a crystal at one end. "It's for the security systems," she said and yawned. "That's all. I promise."

"Fools rush in," I cursed under my breath.

She pricked my finger. The crystal turned red, then purple. Her eyes widened and when she spoke next, the words tumbled out too fast. "That's all. Will you be requiring anything else, milord?"

"No, thanks," I told her. "I've got Talbot here to show me around."

Hannah hesitated, but she did comply, wandering off into the complex toward her appointed task.

"Where to first?" Talbot asked.

"You're going back to the Pollux," I told him.

"Why?"

"Call it a hunch. I want you watching over my girls."

Talbot shrugged. "Do you need anything before I go?"

"Leave the SunRunner Five Thousand in the parking place," I told him. "I might need it."

He turned to leave.

"Hey, Talbot. One question."

He looked back at me, waiting.

"Is there something important I'm supposed to know about a female Master named Gabriella? She freaked out when we sensed each other."

"She's Roger's sire?" Talbot said, his answer a question itself.

"So?"

"I know you don't care about the whole who-belongs-to-who thing, but she's a Society vamp and she doesn't know you well. What she does know is that her offspring messed with you and technically, if you wanted to, you could take it out on her for not keeping him in line."

"Thanks." I watched him go, then charged into the bowels of High Society. There is a sickly sweet feeling you get in your chest, a burst of adrenaline right before you jump off of a cliff or stick your hand into a hornet's nest. It's the thrill of the moment, the challenge. I knew suddenly that I wasn't about to walk over to the front desk or find an elevator, grab a house phone and call the concierge, or even go talk to Phillip. I was going to go find Gabriella and make her tell me everything she knew about Roger and Rachel.

"I'm about to whip somebody's ass," I sang under my breath like a little boy. I love those moments of enlightened "I don't give a fuck." If you survive them, later, you even get to look back and laugh. If you're really lucky, you get to do it with all four limbs intact.

✦ 26 ✦

ERIC:
LE DÉMON COEUR

Long ornate hallways and well-furnished sitting rooms took up the bulk of the interior at Highland Towers. Young men and women in bellhop garb manned old-fashioned elevators; each one slid the doors shut moments before I reached them. Talbot's scent had vanished when I crossed the threshold, but I did smell Rachel. I even smelled Roger. It was all quite irksome.

Stained glass windows portrayed mythological scenes at regular intervals along exterior walls. At the end of one huge hallway was an image that grasped my full attention. It depicted an army of vampires marching on a church. The sky was thick with bats and only one knight stood before a hulking black thing that was a pretty good likeness for what my uber vampire form must look like, except this one had breasts.

At the top of the larger tableau, bats were shown to part for rays of sun to shine down on the monstrous vampire. As I studied the scene, the shards of stained glass began to move. Words I recognized as French danced across a scroll at the bottom of the window, narrating the events above. Slowly, the colors all faded to gray and then a title appeared on the scroll: *Le Démon Coeur.*

Seen from the beginning, the dog and pony show was much more impressive. Under the cover of darkness, a lone knight rode in on an injured steed and left his horse dying on the steps up to the chapel. He hesitated, tore off his helmet, and cowered before an immense cross above the door. Baring small fangs, the vampire knight gathered his courage and charged into the church.

Time passed. A stylized sun rose over the church and the white clouds transformed into a churning horde of black bats, blocking out the sun. A female vampire dressed in medieval finery flew into the image from the left-hand side. Thirty vampires on horseback followed her on the ground. She landed before the steps of the great stone church and dialogue in some foreign language flew past on the scroll. Maybe it was French, too, but the font made it hard to read at all. Periodically the stained-glass figure's lips parted and she seemed to laugh.

My guess was that the fancy pants vampire was taunting the one who had fled to the church. A priest in brown robes came out of the church. He held a golden cross before him in both hands. There was more dialogue. Fancy Pants didn't seem pleased by it, whatever it was, and became the winged black beast with which I was familiar.

The vampire knight emerged from the church, snatched the cross away from the priest, and pushed him back inside. Flames engulfed the knight's gauntlets around the base of the large crucifix. The knight walked toward the uber vamp, stopped at the center of the steps, and fell to his knees. His head slowly lifted up to the heavens and more dialogue went by on the scroll. I recognized some of it as Latin.

All of the vampires cast their eyes upward and gold-lettered text went by on the scroll; even I recognized the Lord's Prayer. The knight held up his cross defiantly. Two angels with fiery swords parted the horde of bats. All of the vampires, the knight included, were bathed in the light of the sun. Wisps of gray smoke began to drift up off Fancy Pants, but the thirty vampires with her exploded, and their horses along with them. Fancy Pants had a few words to say and even though I couldn't read them, the posturing led me to believe it was something indignant and threatening—very Wicked Witch of the West.

She exited stage-left in a huff and the knight collapsed in the sun but did not burn. His skin became less pale and he sat up, touching his chest, his teeth. I was betting that he had been given a free trip back to the land of the living—lucky bastard.

More golden text slipped by and the priest came back out of the church, looked at the knight, and fell to his knees in prayer. Miracles will do that to a padre, I suppose. Everything went gray again, the picture returned to the initial image of the knight opposing the uber vamp and her posse. The cross was gone and the knight held a sword in its place, but I just took that as poetic license.

I didn't smell Ebony until she put her hand on my shoulder. She used to work in my club, before it exploded. Lady Gabriella's face was momentarily overlaid on Ebony's own when I looked up at her. "Take this one to refresh yourself," Gabriella's image said.

"Is this the vamp equivalent of offering the guest a Coke?" I asked as I turned.

She was dressed in white lingerie, the kind that showed a lot of leg but didn't really give anything away. She and the outfit both looked expensive. Unfortunately for me, the nose knows. Ebony could give me all the come-hither looks she wanted to and I would still have smelled fear where excitement should have been. In the right mood, it might not have mattered. Sometimes it seems like Little Eric has more say in matters than I do, but not today. She was a distraction and nothing more.

"So Rachel works for Gabriella?" I asked, feigning anger. I would have been mad if I could have been mad. Maybe those drugs of J'iliol'lth's were time-release or it could have just been run-of-the-mill mind alteration, courtesy of my would-be thrall, Rachel. I decided to fake it. "How does that work?"

"I don't know." Panic rose in her voice. She'd seen the club burned to ashes, knew that I'd come back when others couldn't. Here I was, without a scratch and wearing the same damn tennis shoes. She knew what I could turn into if I lost my temper and as far as she knew, she was making me angry. Worse, she knew what I could do just out of spite.

Her eyes told me what they've always told me, that Ebony understood what vampires are. We are one of man's natural predators. We hunt. We kill. We breed. Resignation had its place in her eyes as well. She'd known what she was getting into. Swimming with the sharks is dangerous business. It had been her choice. "The Lady Gabriella didn't tell me. She said to get dressed and come find you, so I came. I'm to tell you that I belong to you now. You can do with me what you will."

"Well, that must make you feel real special." With a big sigh, I patted Ebony on the shoulder. She flinched. "How do I send you back without getting you in trouble?"

"Please, I am for you. Enjoy me." Her hand slid up my chest.

"Get off," I shouted too loudly, spraying her with spittle. Vampire spittle is a little gross if you aren't used to it. Like all of the rest of our fluids, it's basically blood. Little flecks of it dotted her jaw and the front of her outfit. To punctuate it all, my eyes had gone purple. Two telltale violet dots of light appeared on her face.

Ebony's eyes darted to the right and her head tilted involuntarily as if she heard a voice that I couldn't. Her eyes closed and she bit her bottom lip so hard it drew blood. Her heart pumped madly, thundering in my ears. It was so loud and the scent of terror was so great that I nearly missed it when she mouthed, "God, no."

Tiny footsteps came toward us down the hall. There were two of them and I knew without looking that Lady Gabriella had just upped the ante. She'd sent out the mother and now she was sending out the children.

"We're for you now, mister," said a little girl in a white sundress. She was the spitting image of her mother. The boy was dressed in a little suit. Neither one of them was older than six. They weren't thralls, either, just conditioned to obey their mother's mistress. Talbot had been right when he said Gabriella didn't know me. I have a thing about hurting kids. You don't do it. The gang back on Sweetheart Row hadn't been children anymore. In my opinion, I'd done them a favor. These two, however, were still human.

My skin crackled like frying bacon, trying to change into the uber vamp. I fought it. *Don't turn into the uber vamp, you moron,* I told myself, *you'll scare the damn kids.*

I met their gazes, the two little babes, and pushed my mind at theirs. "Sleep," I told them and they both fell into a doze standing up. They wobbled for a moment then collapsed. I caught them, each child by the shoulder, and eased them to the floor. "Makes you feel really important, doesn't it, Ebony? I may have had you dance naked onstage, but I paid you good money, and I never treated you like this, like a whore.

"Your children . . . She sent me your children all dressed up like snack food." Disbelief had replaced the anger in my voice. "What the fuck, Ebony?"

"She's not normally like this, Eric. She's a little demanding, but she's usually so good to the kids and she gives them things that I never could. When their daddy got turned, I didn't know what to do. I couldn't come to you for help because you were . . ."

"Blown up at the time," I completed for her.

"He kept coming over, threatening to turn them, to make them his little forever children, Eric. What could I do? She offered to take care of us, to protect them. I would do anything for my kids!"

Real tears poured down her cheeks. She was on the verge of collapse and the mixture of emotions that was coursing through her sent a nauseating array of smells at my sensitive nostrils.

"One more thing, Ebony," I said harshly.

"What?" she answered, blinking up at me through her tears. I caught her face between my hands and made her look at me. I had no idea whether I could do it or not, but I wanted Gabriella out of her head. I touched Ebony's mind with mine and felt Lady Gabriella in there with us. I ignored her, stuck my thumb in my mouth and wiped the blood onto Ebony's shoulder. Her eyes widened conveniently and I reached for Lady Gabriella's mind. I couldn't leave Ebony tied to the kind of undead thing that would discard her this way and send her children out to pay the butcher's bill.

Pain, merciless and blinding, filled my head, but I kept on pushing.

Ebony screamed. High on her left breast, the rose tattoo flashed brightly before it faded. An echoing scream came from farther down the hallway. My pain was gone and Ebony was sweating through her clothes. My blood formed a tiny butterfly tattoo on her shoulder. Ebony went limp in my arms and as I lowered her to the floor, I said the magic words. "I mark thee and bind thee. Master to servant. Servant to master. You are mine until I set you free. You are mine. So mote it be."

Propping Ebony in a convenient armchair and tucking her sleeping kids into her arms, I announced myself to the whole building. "If anybody touches these three, I'll find you, wherever you are, wherever you run. I'll ram a stake through your heart and then we'll get to be all experimental and find out what it takes to actually make you stay dead! Do you hear that?" Without a clue whether anyone actually heard me, I sat down, stared at the kids and their mom, and wondered what the hell to do about them.

About two minutes later it became clear that someone in the building had gotten my message and taken it very seriously. Elevator doors opened to reveal a young blond man. "I'll be happy to look after them, Lord Eric," he said cheerfully. There were bags under his eyes and he looked like he had gotten dressed in a hurry. It was the same little prick I'd seen at the Artiste Unknown with Tabitha.

"I'm Dennis, personal assistant to Lord Phillip. I assure you they'll be quite safe," he said, and either he was the world's best liar or he was telling the truth. "I'm dreadfully sorry for the inconvenience. Had you called ahead, I should have been quite happy to meet you at the door. Hannah should have awakened me upon your arrival. I'd like to extend my master's regrets as well. His sleeping schedule has become quite erratic over the years and is now completely unpredictable. He's slumbering now; otherwise I am quite certain that he would have come to meet you in person."

"If he's asleep, how did you know that I was here?" I asked.

"Sir Hollingsworth and Lord Giarmo were awake playing Go and when they sensed your ire, they contacted me at once," he explained. "Lord Phillip owns this building and since I am his personal assistant, many of the tenants are used to coming to me with their problems rather than disturbing Lord Phillip himself. Now . . . regarding the young ones and their mother, if you've no objection, I'll just take them up to Lady Tabitha's rooms and have guest services send up a nice nutritious meal."

I nodded numbly, said, "Thanks," and helped him carry them into the elevator. The doors to the elevator closed and then reopened.

"Oh, and one more thing, Lord Eric," he said convivially. "Lady

Gabriella is in the Rose Suite. It's down the hall and on the right. You can't miss it."

The doors closed again and I turned to look down the hallway. Somebody had just been sold out by the management and it sure as hell wasn't me.

27

ERIC:

GETTING TO GABRIELLA

The Rose Suite was hard to miss. A transition from carpet to rose-colored marble began in the middle of the hallway and continued on into a side passage that opened onto an interior courtyard. Gabriella's waiting area was large, maybe twenty feet wide and twenty-five feet deep, not that I'm Mister Fix-it or anything. It was tasteful, in that same extravagant way in which other vampires seemed to approach everything.

Several squares of grass broke up the marble floor and gave the impression of a small yard or patio rather than a reception room. A white wrought-iron table and three matching chairs had been tastefully arranged in the center of each square. Parked at a decorator's angle on the right near the gate was a small tea cart.

Looking up revealed a glass ceiling about a foot below a skillfully painted mural designed to replicate the sky outside. I was willing to bet that the lighting changed to match the time of day, even the time of night. Puffy white clouds slowly drifted across the ceiling . . . definitely magic.

At the back of the courtyard, separated from the front by a gated white picket fence, there was a private stair constructed of the same rose-colored marble. It led up to a doorway, set into a wall that looked like the outside of an old plantation home, windows and all.

So many vampires seemed to spend so much time and money pretending that things are as normal as they were before they became living dead things. In my experience, it just makes things worse. If crying about what you've lost in the middle of the night sounds like fun to you, then be my guest, but this kind of make-believe only makes things worse for me. I'd tried it, more than once. It's nice for a few months, but it sucks every time the happy little house of cards comes down and reminds me that I'm just a bloodsucking undead monster that kills to live.

Gabriella would eventually learn that lesson the hard way: all vampires do, providing they survive long enough. Whether or not Gabriella survived really depended on what I found inside her place and what she had to say about Roger and Rachel and why the hell they were together. It was nice to know that my antics earlier were good for something. Taking out Sweetheart Row and the Bitemore must have been enough to rattle Gabby's cage.

The fence wasn't locked, so I reached over and opened the gate before marching up the stairs. One flight up, the stairs opened up onto a wide platform. On either side of an ornate wooden door were potted plants that went three-quarters of the way up the door, roughly even with the sliding view slot.

A crimson cord with tassels on the end hung next to the door. There was also a gold-plated knocker in the shape of an opening rosebud. I ignored them both and knocked "shave and a haircut" on the door. It's a habit.

Gabriella's rooms must have had excellent soundproofing, because I could barely hear inside. There was movement and a muffled conversation and then the view slot slid open to reveal two blue-gray eyes. A human? My thrall-sense went off like an alarm.

"I am quite sorry, sir," spoke a soft feminine voice. Whoever she was, she wasn't Lady Gabriella, but she did belong to her. Her voice was very pleasant, with a lilting accent. French, maybe? "Lady Gabriella is not at home to visitors this early in the day. Perhaps you could come back after sundown? If you would like, I would be happy to schedule a visit with the Lady Gabriella for another time? For you, sir, I believe that she could be available as early as Friday. To others, of course, her schedule is quite full, but the Lady is always happy to make exceptions for important persons such as yourself."

"No, that won't be necessary. She knows what I want to know and she knows that she'd better tell me. She just sent one thrall and two children to me as some kind of freaky-ass peace offering and now she's got you up here acting like that didn't just happen. Does she think I'm an idiot?"

"*Bien sur que non, monsieur!*" I could barely hear her pulse, but it was racing. "Excuse me, what I mean to say is, of course not, sir. The Lady Gabriella did awaken briefly, overcome as she was by your grand presence, sir, and she immediately dispatched Ebony and her little ones to you as a token of her respect. It is regrettable that she is a very heavy sleeper, however, and lapsed back into the slumber of the immortals shortly after confirming that you had received her tokens of esteem."

She paused and I heard someone faintly whispering in the distance. It could have been Gabriella, but there was no way to be sure. Mystical soundproofing. When the voice resumed, it was shaking. "I have been instructed that should the Lady's offerings be displeasing to you, I am to offer you myself if my demeanor and appearance would be more acceptable."

"What's your name?" I asked softly.

"Beatrice, sir," she answered.

"How would I know if I find your appearance more pleasing if I can't see all of you, Beatrice?"

"I would be happy to reveal myself to you, sir, but I am instructed to make certain that milord is aware of the special properties of the doorways here in the Highland Towers before doing so."

"What special properties?" I asked. As a delaying tactic, Beatrice was doing a wonderful job. I could only hope that Lady Gabriella wasn't slipping Roger and Rachel out the back somewhere while I was chatting up the help.

"All of the doorways to the suites of the Highland Towers are enchanted, sir. When the enchantment is active, there is an impenetrable field of magic in place over the door. It delivers a powerful jolt to any who try to cross the threshold, unless they already possess permission to enter or exit. When I open the door, sir, I would not wish for you to accidentally be injured by brushing against the barrier. It similarly affects those who try to force the door open if they do not have permission to do so."

I punched the door and received a semi-electric jolt for my trouble. Running up my arm, the electric hum set my teeth to vibrating and made my eyes sizzle. I gracelessly tumbled down the stairs, landing at the bottom, my left leg still jerking spasmodically. "Magic s-s-sucks," I said lying on my back. I stared up at the sky and watched some pretty convincing clouds pass by on the ceiling.

Warmth poured down from the sun as it came out from behind the clouds and I was consumed with envy for Gabby's enchanted ceiling. I hadn't felt the sun on my face for decades without bursting into flames—being a ghost didn't count—and it brought a tear of blood to my eye. I wiped the bloody tear off on the hem of my T-shirt and when my leg stopped jerking, I stood up.

"How much did it cost to get the ceiling done?" I called up the stairs. "And why do you keep calling me 'sir'? Shouldn't you call me

'Lord Eric' or something?" I walked back through the gate and picked up one of the chairs, testing its heft. Somebody could get really messed up with one of these things.

I heard the creak of the door opening, followed by the sound of high-heeled shoes on marble. Beatrice was wearing a green velvet dress that looked like it belonged in a Renaissance faire, except that it pushed everything up and to the middle with impressive results. Her bosom wasn't large, but the dress put what there was to good use.

Fiery red tresses cascaded in ringlets down to her shoulders. Her lips had the natural pouty look most women who get Botox injections are looking for and her eyes were a startling blue-gray, like storm clouds. "Please, do not break them, Highness. I have no doubt that you could, but the Lady, she would be so heartbroken. The Lord Winter, I doubt he would come back to redo them for her."

"Since you said 'please,'" I smiled, putting down the chair. "So, you belong to me now?"

"If you wish it, Highness."

"From sir to highness." I walked in her direction and ran my fingers through her hair. She tried to control herself, but she was terrified. It was like petting a skittish colt. Her nostrils flared and any sudden movement seemed likely to make her bolt. "That's a pretty good promotion. Your mistress must think I'm one huge misogynistic bastard. Which I guess is better than being taken for a pedophile."

"I'm certain no insult was intended." She let the words linger on her lips and it dawned on me that I'd been snowed again. She was a marvelous actress and she'd been giving me an Oscar winning performance. She wasn't scared at all. A lot of vamps get turned on by fear and she was trying to seduce me.

"You ever met a female vampire named Irene?" I asked.

"I don't believe so, Highness," she said, trembling. Boy, was she good.

"She was a good actress, too." I looked Beatrice in the eye. "She got even better when she died. Do you mind sitting over there?" I pointed to one of the chairs in the seating area.

"Of course not, sire."

"I'll be right back." I winked.

At the stairs, the door stood open, revealing a room that would have looked more at home in some palace in France a few hundred years ago. I'm certain it would have impressed Tabitha or Roger. It didn't impress me. I just wanted in.

"Okay, Gabby," I called into the room. "I really hope you aren't sleeping, because if you are, then I'm going to feel really stupid."

Windows. Doors. Walls. Magic protects the door, I said in my head, *but magic doesn't protect the ceiling. Does magic protect the walls?* I glanced over my shoulder at Beatrice. She sat obediently where I'd left her, observing me with a carefully indifferent eye. I walked to the window three feet to the left of the door. I held my hand over the glass, concentrating on breaking it open. Sure enough, my palm began to tingle. I did the same thing to the wall and grinned. Civilized vampires go in through doors, and maybe windows. Uncivilized vampires, who don't give a shit what others think of them, who could care less about their place in society, have more options. I punched the wall and my fist went right through it. Score one point for the Neanderthal!

28

ERIC:

LESS THAN NOBLESSE OBLIGE

B its of plaster mixed with traces of blood on my knuckles as I forced my way through the wall. Beatrice choked out a *"Mon dieu!"* behind me, but I couldn't turn to look at her. This had to happen fast. In the movies, when a monster crashes through the side of a building, he gets to do it in one smooth motion. The wall explodes, creating a nice new half oval into which he steps, backlit so that the cloud of dust billowing up about him seems dramatic. No such luck for me. Punches turned to a combination of kicks and shoves with a healthy dose of claws at the end.

Inside, three servants opened fire with crossbows. The first bolt hit a two-by-four on the narrow side and stuck fast. The other two went high and wide, one lancing into my open mouth as I flashed my fangs, then tearing through my left cheek and pinning me for a brief moment as I marveled at an all new pain. None of them got off a second shot before I was all the way in, and by that time it was too late. Their crossbows weren't made for speed loading.

Three humans versus a vampire.

Vampire wins.

Surprise, surprise.

I ran my fingers over the side of my face, but the jagged tear was gone, healed. I tore the third crossbow bolt out of my shoulder without wincing, then looked for Gabriella. "Knock. Knock." I found her in the bedroom, half dressed and moving sluggishly. Her skin smelled of strawberries and the scent was pleasant enough that I had to remind myself to stop being interested. I wasn't here on a date.

Part of what Beatrice said had been true. Gabriella didn't do so well during the daytime. Some vampires are like me. If something bad enough happens, we wake up and we're wide awake. The few times it happened to me, I didn't even go back to sleep. Other vamps just can't wake up at all until they rise the next night. Lady Gabriella was somewhere in between. Moving in stutters and starts, she reminded me of one of George Romero's zombies in *Night of the Living Dead*. If there had been a footrace between the two, I would've put my money on the zombie.

Another human servant sprang seemingly out of nowhere, firing at me with a revolver and screaming, "Get away from her!" He was blond and styled, a real pretty boy. I bounced him off the bedroom wall with a punch to the head and he sacked out like a good little lap dog.

"Esteban," Gabriella croaked.

"Hi, Gabby." Her bedroom was nice. All gold and red with a huge four-poster bed in the middle of it. Heat poured off the bed through some internal wiring system and it was accurate enough that I had to mentally acknowledge the achievement—it felt like body heat. There was the low steady thrum of a pulse, too.

"Don't hurt her." I turned at the sound of the voice, the familiar drawl, exaggerated more by the age of the speaker, the era in which he'd lived, rather than for purposeful effect. John Paul Courtney. "Don't hurt her," he repeated. His body coalesced between Gabriella and me, but this time his form was translucent, lit from within by a wavering amber light that cast an angelic hue upon his bobbleheaded self.

"I don't want to hurt her, you dumb ass," I snapped. "I just want some fucking answers."

"What answers?" Gabriella's voice was thick and slurred. Her face barely moved when she spoke, showing all the expressionlessness of a stroke victim, but on both sides of her pretty face. She stumbled forward, through the specter of my ghostly conscience. As usual, I was the only one who got the dubious benefit of perceiving His Judgmentalness.

Gabriella struggled to stand and I held out my hand rather than let her fall. I smelled more humans nearby. Several of them were women. Their scent was so strong I knew that they had been in the room when I was breaking through the wall. I could feel them in the house, all of those scared little hearts pounding away, all that blood. They had left their mistress struggling with her clothes on the floor and run. I wondered if she had told them to. I smelled two other scents as well: Roger and Rachel. Son of a bitch! They weren't here, but they'd been here last night, and they'd been together.

"So is anyone going to come out here and help you dress or are they all too chickenshit?" I asked.

She managed a brief shake of the head.

"Beatrice," I called over my shoulder. "If you're done catching your breath, get in here and help Gabby get dressed."

John Paul Courtney smiled.

"Oh, hurrah! I made the ghost happy." Once Beatrice took my place helping Gabriella, I stepped back. Her eyes followed me as I crossed the room. My hands traced the top of her dresser and I paused when I reached a set of porcelain horses. Her jaw tightened and her eyes were furious, but she said nothing, still working hard at getting the rest of her clothes on.

"Come on, son," John Paul drawled. "Leave her things alone."

"Get a grip, you nosy ass. I'm not going to break her keepsakes. Damn! You know why I came here. I didn't even know Roger and Rachel had been to the Highland Towers until I smelled them. All I wanted was the stupid magic rock from Lord What's-His-Hype . . ."

I noticed my audience. Bea and Gabby's joint dressing maneuver had slowed to a crawl while the two of them watched me arguing with someone they could neither see nor hear.

"Why can't they see you anyway?" I asked.

"I told you how it works. They ain't blood," Courtney told me, but there was a tremor when he said blood that reminded me of someone. The pain, the tenderness in his eyes when he looked at Gabriella.

"Wait. Wait. Wait." I pointed at Gabriella. She and Beatrice froze, but I gestured for them to continue. "Were you in love with her?"

"Maybe." His maybe sounded more like "meh-beh" and it was soft and sullen. I smiled. "What, you think I weren't living afore I was a haint?" Courtney asked. "We weren't never . . . Aw h—" He caught the *hell* that I saw coming and his cigar appeared in his hand.

"You almost said the h-word."

"I told you we was alike, you an' me. When I was young, my mouth weren't any cleaner than the outhouse behind the saloon, but I changed and so can you." He blew smoke rings at me and smiled, regaining his composure. "Tell you what. I'll tell you all about Gabby and me some time if you really want to know, but for now I'll put this in terms you can appreciate. Each time *El Alma Perdida* finds her way into the hands of my kin, each time certain conditions are met, I can fire her six times in the service of the Courtney line. I can do it, but I don't have to. You honor my request and I'll fire one of those shots on your behalf when you need it."

"What the hell kind of offer is that? I can fire the gun myself, you know."

"Not always," he drawled. "Even you need help from time to time.

If'n you was staked, maybe, or couldn't get to the gun in time . . . or if, say, someone else had aholt of it."

He had me there.

"Could you keep somebody else from firing the gun?"

"I could do either," he agreed.

"Wait," I said. "You said you could appear under certain conditions. What conditions?"

"I told you a few of them, too. You ain't ready to know yet, but the offer stands. Will you take it?"

"We'll see," I said. I should have said "meh-beh," but I didn't think of it in time.

When I turned back to Gabriella, she was clad in a high-collared dress that still showed ample cleavage.

"Better now?" I asked, once we were both seated in Gabriella's sitting room. Beatrice danced attendance on her, a mother hen, clearly worried about her "former" Mistress. Gabriella nodded awkwardly, but with more muscle control than before, a twitch that could have been an attempted smile flickering at the corner of her mouth.

Beatrice brought her a cup of warm blood in a delicate china cup and helped her drink it down carefully. "The blood is the life," Gabriella said artfully.

I was too busy counting doors to pay attention. There were four. Behind two of them I smelled men and metal. Six women cowered behind another door, the Lady's maids, I was guessing. The fourth door seemed devoid of life; it held my attention.

"Good." I leapt across the table and hefted her into the air by her throat. Beatrice screamed. So did I. "Where the fuck are they?"

"Boy, if I could shoot you . . ." the ghost of Courtney snarled.

Why can't you? I wanted to ask, but Beatrice was already speaking. "Please, Master Eric, the rules . . . ," she begged.

"What rules?" I dropped Gabriella on the couch and looked at Beatrice.

"The Highland Towers has certain codes of conduct," Beatrice explained. "No vampire may assault another within any of the private rooms or on the grounds, or they face punishment at the hands of Lord Phillip. Of course, one is always allowed to defend one's self."

"Oh, well, that's fine then." I clapped my hands together. "I'm here to piss him off anyway." I leaned in so close we bumped noses. "I smell Roger here and I smell Rachel. Where are they?"

"I told you he is not here; neither is the woman," Gabriella said deliberately. "I have offered you my two most treasured handmaidens.

I could offer you Esteban, my lover, but I understand he would be of little interest to you."

"This is the Gabby you don't want to hurt?" I asked John Paul Courtney, but he'd gone.

"Who are you talking to?" Beatrice asked.

"Jiminy Cricket," I answered. Esteban stirred, so I put him out with another blow to the head. That was going to smart. Gabby gritted her teeth. I suppose she didn't like seeing her entrée treated so roughly. It was time for another tactic.

I tried to clear my thoughts to calm down, but I was offended by the whole damn thing and it came out in a torrent. "Okay, I have to say this. Do all High Society vamps do this whole 'thralls are slaves to be passed around' crap? What the fuck is wrong with you people? I've got more thralls than I know what to do with already, but they aren't slaves. They are thralls by choice and if they want out, I'd be happy to let them go. I mean, I know that we're monsters and all and I eat people, but come on! You keep offering me people like they're objects. You tried to send me children for a snack. There's no way I'd ever hurt a kid. How do you not know that about me? And how many warm bodies do you think I need to run a bowling alley anyway?"

"Excuse me?" Gabriella's features were becoming more animated as the blood she was drinking did its best to overcome the effects of the daytime.

"You had people spying on me and they didn't tell you about the bowling alley? I'd fire somebody."

"Perhaps I shall. Even so, I am forced to return to the subject at hand. The one for whom you search is not here and has not been here for some time. He will not return until the game is over and the wager decided. If we lose, then he will not return at all. If you are planning to kill me, I ask that you don't. I cannot stop you; I'm too weak. My thralls mean nothing to you—"

"Game? Wager?" I stood up, couldn't stay still any longer, couldn't just sit there and listen to her talk.

"I told Roger that he never should have taken odds against him," Gabriella's voice faltered, then she continued, "but to beat Ebon Winter would have added respectability to his endeavors, legitimized his ascendance, and redeemed him after the Orchard Lake debacle."

"Does this game involve marbles?" I sat back down. Gabriella's eyes followed me warily, but if I wasn't misreading her, Beatrice was amused.

"Excuse me?" Lady Gabriella asked.

"Never mind, just something a guy in a jumpsuit told me the other day." I tapped Beatrice on the shoulder. "Now you see, that's funny. Sometimes I can't remember my own phone number, but I remember what some guy named Melvin was talking about. . . . No, shit, that would have been like four months ago. Wouldn't it?"

"Leave my apartments in peace and never return to them again uninvited," Gabriella said.

"Yeah, that'll work," I scoffed.

"You are a powerful being, Eric—I believe you prefer to be called by your given name only, without honorifics?" She flexed her hands as she spoke as if she were willing the blood she drank to flow into them.

"Yeah," I agreed. "Eric's fine."

"Keep the gifts I've given you. Do not give a thought to the damage you have done to my home, the threats you have made, or the insulting and demeaning way you have dealt with me. You have never dwelt amongst polite society; such lapses in judgment are to be expected, but please do not believe I will be so forgiving if you trifle with me a second time. You may be more powerful than I am, in person, but I assure you I will not be so exposed again." She stood, giving me the mother of all you-may-go-now looks.

"That's a nice offer," I admitted. "It really, really is." Rising to my feet, I gestured to Beatrice to pour me a cup of blood. She did so and I tossed it back in one swallow. "I even like the part where you threaten me. It's nice, makes you seem powerful. For the record, I apologize for busting in here the way I did; it was a bad idea."

"But?" she asked. Gabriella evaluated me, her eyes sizing me up like I was a horse or a side of beef.

Our gazes met and her eyes widened as she felt me slip inside the doorway to her soul just long enough to send a message: *You still haven't answered my question* and then withdraw. It flustered her and in that scant second, her mask of composure dropped and I saw a snapshot of the woman she must have been when John Paul Courtney knew her. Then she was back in control; the strange social vampire she'd become was back in force. Tabitha was right. She'd said the High Society vamps all became caricatures of themselves. The human that she'd been had felt nice, wholesome, virtuous, well-mannered. A lady that a guy like me or, if he'd really once been as much like me as he claimed, a guy like John Paul Courtney, could have pined after from afar . . . afraid that if we touched her, she'd be sullied.

"What time is it, Beatrice?" Lady Gabriella asked.

"Fifteen minutes until one, milady."

"You said you were going to steal something from Lord Phillip?"

I sighed. "Yeah, the Stone of Aorta or something. I'll probably have to kill him for it. He's the fat little bald fucker, right?"

Lady Gabriella had been drinking another sip of blood when I spoke. It shot out her nose, beginning a coughing fit I'd rarely seen a vampire experience. "He is, indeed, as you described," she said after regaining her composure. "That's . . . very industrious. May I ask why?"

"He fucked with my offspring without my permission. He's got something I want. It's Christmas in Void City and I want peace on Earth and ill will toward vampires. Pick a reason. And you still haven't answered my question."

"I'm not going to answer your question, Eric." She smiled when she said it. "So, you aren't interested in Roger?"

"Oh, no. I'm probably gonna kill him, too," I told her. "For one thing, he tried to sell me out to a demon . . ." I let my words trail off. A demon. If Rachel had demon sex magic, then she was supposed to be working for a demon, not for Roger. So why was she with him unless Roger and the demon were still working together?

"Yes?" Gabriella asked, snapping me out of my reverie.

"Since you're his mommy, I won't run down the whole list."

Gabriella looked smug. She'd been smug since Beatrice told her the time. "That is unfortunate. I cared very deeply for Roger. Still, he was an embarrassment for me. In some ways, it is for the best."

What did the time have to do with anything? I was still rolling around the idea of Roger, Rachel, and the demon. Which demon? Was it Jill? He wasn't a succubus, but that didn't mean he didn't have access to someone that could have taught Rachel the dark tantra. "I could make you tell me, you know."

"I don't think you could," Gabriella said. "You've too much of your—would he be your great-great grandfather?—in you. The righteous indignation, the posturing . . . it's all very useful when you're fighting werewolves, but not against vampires. He learned that the hard way. So will you. I have little doubt that you're capable of ending me without ever regretting it, but beating me, torturing me, forcing your way into my mind and stripping the answers from my brain . . . no." She touched my hand. "You could never do that."

She was right. If she'd been a man, I wouldn't have had any issues. Call me old-fashioned, but the idea of torturing a woman, of beating information out of her, made me want to vomit. I've sunk low since joining the ranks of the dead, but not that low.

"Come on, Beatrice," I said as I stood. "We've wasted enough of Gabby's time. She needs her beauty rest."

Beatrice hesitated, lingering at her mistress's side.

"I'm sorry, Beatrice," Gabriella told her. "But I did offer you to him and I'm afraid he has accepted. I'll have Esteban take your things . . . ?"

"To the Pollux," I answered, "across the street from where the Demon Heart was. But don't worry about that yet. I'll send somebody back for them."

We left, and as we walked down the stairs, I was greeted by the sight of thirty-seven thralls packed into the courtyard. One by one, they introduced themselves on behalf of some vampire or other and one by one they offered their assistance.

"What the hell?" I looked to Beatrice for an explanation.

"As far as they know, you broke through impenetrable wards just to question a Master. Combine that with your coming back from an explosion many were convinced would be the end of you and your recent destruction of Sweetheart Row and the vampire running it, I believe the inhabitants of the Highland Towers have sent their thralls around to make sure they aren't next in line for a visit."

I guess announcing myself to the entire building had been a bad idea, though it had certainly managed to stir up paranoia among the Highland Towers residents. A man walked past us carrying a toolbox like none I'd ever seen. He pushed his way through the crowd, opened his box, and began performing a magic ritual near Gabriella's door.

Gabriella stood in the doorway.

"I see, the trouble is right here. Looks like they fouled up the wards when you had the courtyard redone," the man said.

"Thank you for coming so quickly, Maurice."

He smiled at her in a cheerful handyman sort of way. "I get paid to hurry. You're top of the priorities list according to Lord Phillip, right under him.

"Huh, that's weird." He pulled a length of twisted hair from around the sill.

"What is that?" she asked.

"A gaff knot." He walked to the other window and felt around carefully, crossed both fingers, and withdrew a matching string. "It—"

"Fix it first, then explain it," she snapped.

Why the rush? I thought to myself. A thin sheen of bloody sweat formed on Gabriella's upper lip. Why was she sweating?

"Melvin's a good mage, Lady Gabriella, it's not like him to be sloppy like this. A gaff knot is something magicians can use when they are working with a ward they didn't make. It holds the ward back so that they can do surface work, like painting, putting in new windows. He must have just left them up by mistake." He pulled another from around the door frame. "Maybe the wards were interfering with the paint they used on the wall. Was it an eternal mix?"

Melvin?

Gabriella nodded. "Yes, he said it would never need repainting and would be self-repairing—"

As she spoke, the wall began doing just that. Bits of wood, paint, and plaster flowed up the wall like a videotape played in slow reverse.

"It is. All you had to do was pull the gaff knots. It's not like him to miss that, but anyone can make a mistake." He snapped the strings with his hands and gave them to Gabriella. He tilted his head at the same odd angle I'd often seen Magbidion use. "Yep. The wards are in place and the wall should be back to normal in ten or fifteen minutes. Anything else?"

"Will the ward hold even without the wall?"

"Sure," he answered. "It's only selectively permeable at the door, windows, and air vents."

"Air vents?"

"In case owners want to sneak into their own apartment in animal forms," Maurice answered. Maurice . . . mages and their damn M names.

Gabriella smiled at me.

"I believe I will give you a partial answer to your question, Eric." She waited a beat. "One of the two people for whom you were looking?"

"Yeah?"

"She should make it back to the Pollux any time now."

Gabriella closed the door. Two seconds later I felt a terrible screaming in my mind. My new thrall sense told me that they were in pain. The Pollux was on fire. My children were burning and I could smell the smoke, feel their terror. I felt like Obi-Wan Kenobi when Alderaan was destroyed. I was thirty minutes away and that was about twenty-nine minutes too far. One by one the screams began to fade. Greta winked out last. Gabriella was right, though . . . now I knew where Rachel was.

✦ 29 ✦

TABITHA:

BURNING DOWN THE HOUSE

Flames. That's not what woke me up. I think it was the smoke, because the first thing I remember is choking, coughing so hard my lungs burned. Hot air. Too hot and thick to breathe, but I had to breathe. Why did I have to breathe?

"Eric?" I called out.

Heart pounding, I rolled out of the bed and onto the floor, because smoke rises and you're supposed to be able to breathe better on the floor. Blood coursed through my veins as if I were still human. I could even taste the smoke.

"Talbot?"

Whose bedroom was this? I couldn't remember. I didn't recognize it. There was a blond woman, cold and dead, lying on the bed. Greta. Right, Greta was a vampire—Eric's daughter or something. Someone was laughing. The fire was blue, not orange. Why blue fire? Natural gas?

In the doorway I got my explanation. Rachel was laughing, wreathed in flames, but untouched by them. "You should have stayed at the Highland Towers, sis."

"Rachel?" I still didn't know how she'd come back, but the gleam of hatred in her eyes . . . that I recognized. She'd looked at me with those same hate-filled eyes the last time I saw her in the hospital, two days before she died, when she'd begged me to find a way to save her. I'd been at her funeral. It had been open casket. I'd even gone back later to check the grave because my boyfriend was a vampire and I'd been totally scared that something weird would happen to her body. "Rachel! What are you doing?"

She smiled at me before turning away, closing the door behind her. Even over the sound of the flames I heard the lock. Eric had a dead bolt on the door that worked with a key on both sides. I dived for the door with all the vampiric speed I could muster, which was none at all. Sweat ran down my cheek, human sweat. I was stuck. I always had trouble using my vampire powers at their fullest when I'd been seeming human, but it had never been this bad before.

The clock on Eric's wall said it was just after one in the afternoon. I was awake during the day! I pounded on the door. My vampire strength was a no-show, too. I was practically human. Great, my coolest vampire gift was going to get me burned to a crisp!

"Shit!"

On top of everything else, I was so hungry I could barely stand, not blood hungry, either. My stomach growled more angrily than it had when I'd gone on the negative-calorie diet. By day seven, when I couldn't stand to eat any more cabbage soup, it was easier to starve myself.

Fire moved across the ceiling and the walls with a purpose. It curled and twisted, spreading slowly in some directions and more quickly in others as if driven by some sinister intelligence. God, it was hot.

I pulled myself up to my knees. On the bed, Greta's arm was on fire and she still wasn't waking up. I grabbed her foot and tugged her partway off the bed, took another breath, and pulled her the rest of the way down. Her head hit the hardwood floor with a sickening thud and I slapped at the eldritch fire on her arm with my hands.

"Wake up!" I screamed in her ear.

Greta slowly opened one eye, her mouth lolling open before she began to speak.

"What's burning?" she asked thickly.

"The Pollux is on fire!" I yelled at her.

Her head went limp and her left eye slowly started to close, so I slapped her as hard as I could. Pain lanced through my hand and I coughed out an "ow."

Greta opened both eyes and bared her fangs with deliberate threat. I tried to bare mine back, but nothing happened.

"I don't usually wake up so slow," Greta told me. Each word left her lips in a tangle, slurred like she was drunk. "Something's wrong. Is it daytime? So . . . tired."

She leaned back sharply and I shook her awake again. She was heavier than I thought she'd be.

In the distance I heard people screaming, like they were being burned alive.

"Holy shit!"

"Keep it away from me," Greta mumbled, "I'm allergic to holy stuff. Are there any cookies left? Could you eat one for me? I love to watch people eat cookies."

"Cookies?"

"Smells like cinnamon," she continued.

"We've got to get out of here," I told her. The Pollux was old and the wood was dry like kindling. I dropped Greta and crawled over to the door. After kicking it a couple of times to confirm that I wasn't strong enough to open it, I crawled back to Greta and pulled her to her feet. Tongues of fire engulfed the doorway and the smoke was so thick I could barely see standing up. Greta was beginning to doze off again, so I kicked her in the stomach. She snapped at me, but was too slow.

"You need to open that door, or we are both going to burn to ashes," I told her.

She looked at the door and then looked back at me without comprehension. "What door? That's a fireplace."

"What would Eric do?" I whispered to myself. "Eric would turn into something and knock down the door." Not an option for me at the moment. Okay, I wasn't strong enough and Greta wasn't awake enough. I tried to think it through and then the plan hit me. I got behind Greta and shoved her at the door as hard as I could. She hit it headfirst and flames ignited her hair. Hands pulling at her flaming tresses, Greta screamed.

I had never heard anybody scream like that before. Pure terror and agony were embodied in the sound that left her throat and all I could do was hope that she found the presence of mind to stop messing with her hair and knock down the door.

"Please, please, please," I muttered as I crouched down on the floor. Greta took off running in the wrong direction, blinded by pain. She crashed into the shower, rupturing the pipes. My eyes closed from the stinging smoke as the water washed over her. It was almost impossible to breathe and my body didn't seem too convinced that it no longer needed to perform that most basic of functions. Being stuck as a Living Doll was a pretty cruel trick. One, because I didn't want to be human right now and two, because seeming alive was going to get me killed. Coughs wracked my body and I couldn't talk anymore, couldn't stand, couldn't do anything but keep on coughing. A roar came from the shower, and I thought I heard Greta scream a single word. "Out." She charged across the room at the door, fangs bared, and claws extended. The door exploded outward unleashing Greta, screaming, into the hall.

On my hands and knees, I went after her. Outside of the bedroom things looked even worse; the floor was collapsing and the roof was on fire. All of it was glowing a sickening blue.

Greta plunged through a hole, flames trailing from her clothing, screaming all the way down to the first floor. She charged through the wall like a rhinoceros, still shrieking, still burning, heading for the parking deck. If I could get to the deck, then I would be safe from the fire. As for the sun, well, maybe we could stay low and to the middle. Or maybe, like this, so convincingly human, I could even fool the sun.

I looked down through the smoking jagged hole. Below, the flaming wreck of the floor stared up at me. Seeming human or not, I realized I was going to have to jump, as Greta had. Even as I fell, I saw a board sticking up at just the wrong angle and tried to twist out of the way.

Breathing no longer hurt because my breathing had stopped. I had stopped. I lay like a broken rag doll in the middle of the fire, with a two-by-four jutting out of my chest as tendrils of fire licked my body. I didn't catch fire the way Greta had, but my skin blistered and bubbled in the heat.

I'd been shot through the heart once, before the Demon Heart had blown up. Even that hadn't really hurt until the bolt had been pulled out, but being burned hurt a lot. The roaring crackle of the fire reminded me of the winters I'd spent with my grandfather in Vermont. I couldn't close my eyes, but the smoke was so thick I couldn't see anything, so it was easy to picture him in front of the fire, laughing and calling my name.

"Tabitha!" A voice that was not Grandpa's called out from behind me in the smoke. It sounded like Talbot's voice, but smaller. Little padded footsteps ran toward me as my back began to smolder. I was going to catch fire. I really didn't want to; Greta's screams had been, well, awful. Above me, the flooring began to creak dangerously. I was surprised to be so calm . . . must have been the wood in my heart.

Before I had too much time to think about burning to death, I was lifted up off of the plank and carried through the lobby, out through the hole in the wall and into the sun. I couldn't get enough air to scream. Just as quickly, we were in the shade of the parking deck, my clothes still smoldering. Talbot dropped me onto the cement and began patting me all over. "If Eric asks," he said, "I am only touching you to keep you from catching fire."

"Okay," I nodded. He looked around the parking deck and then back at the Pollux. His clothes looked awful. They were actually still smoldering in places. Greta had also made it to the parking deck. I saw her briefly, horribly burned, lying under a parked car.

"I don't suppose either of you thought to grab your cell phone?"

Talbot chuckled exhaustedly. "I think mine is somewhere in the Pollux"—he patted his empty pockets—"next to my wallet, keys, Eric's thralls." Talbot sniffed the air. "Do you smell cinnamon?"

That was the last thing I heard before falling asleep.

✦ 30 ✦

ERIC:
REWIND

Roger just keeps blowing up my shit!" I grabbed the table in front of me and flung it into the ceiling where it stuck feetfirst like a crazy dart.

Several of the assembled humans didn't even flinch. A few even managed to compliment me on my accuracy. Others stared at me with patient wariness. *Is he going to kill us now?* I imagined them asking themselves. I'd already done a number on Gabriella's courtyard. Shards of broken magic glass lay scattered over the courtyard's meticulously tended grass. *I hear when he doesn't know what to do, he just grabs whoever is nearest and forces himself on them. I hope he eats Malloy, I'm so tired of listening to him whine about his master's inner turmoil.* Practiced neutral expressions surrounded me at every turn.

"Is there anything I can do to assist you, Highness?" asked a diminutive man in a cricket uniform. His jaunty little cap looked so funny and he wore it so seriously that I nearly laughed.

"Trouble at home," I told him.

A man from the back produced a bottle of wine that smelled like blood. "Blood wine, Sire?"

"Wine?" I asked.

"It's much like wine, Highness," a fetching young woman in a purple business suit offered, "but it's actually made of human blood, so it's completely compatible with your dietary restrictions. My mistress has also sent a bottle if you'd care to try it."

"Is that anything like blood booze?" I asked. My question was greeted with thunderous assent, that yes, it was, but far more expensive and with a taste that actually resembled wine.

"How many of you brought bottles of this blood wine?" I asked.

Soon seven bottles sat on the table and I wondered if getting drunk would really dull the pain of loss I was trying not to feel. If Tabitha was dead . . . if Greta was dead . . .

I closed my eyes to fight back the emotions and took long, deep breaths.

"Impressive, Highness," offered some dumb brunette, "and quite convincing."

I looked at Beatrice and my voice trembled when I spoke. "What do I say if I don't want to offend anybody, but I'd just as soon they all fucked off?"

No one even blinked as she turned to translate. "His Highness, the Lord Eric, wishes to convey his humble thanks for the gifts and offers of assistance." She fingered a strand of her own red hair, twisting it, the only outward sign of nervousness. "He gladly accepts your tokens of esteem and will be certain to relay more proper gratitude at another time. Unfortunately," she glanced up at the remains of the magic ceiling, the table I'd thrown obscuring the artistic sun overhead, "as the sun shines overhead, the eyelids of the immortal grow heavy and Lord Eric finds himself in need of rest.

"If you'd all leave your cards on the table," she gestured to a little white tea cart that had survived my wrath, "to ensure that the good intentions of your Masters and Mistresses are not forgotten and then file quickly and quietly out of the courtyard, it would be most appreciated."

She clasped her hands in front of her and smiled. Like magic, they filed past and vanished, leaving only little squares of paper and seven bottles of wine to mark their passing.

"Thanks, Bea. Do you mind if I call you Bea?"

"Anything you wish to call me would be—"

"None of that slave shit," I interrupted. "You're a person. What do you like to be called?"

Beatrice scoffed and her full pouting lips drew up into a very brief smile. "Well, my real name is Tina, but Lady Gabriella preferred Beatrice."

"Do you like Tina?" I asked.

She nodded. "But I'd rather keep Beatrice, if it's to your liking, Master. I said good-bye to Tina a long, long time ago."

"Then you're Beatrice. Do you want to go back to Gabby, Beatrice?"

"Sire?" Those beautiful gray eyes of hers lit up at that suggestion, but her expression changed to a more pensive one and she started twisting a lock of hair again, putting the tip of it on the corner of her mouth as she thought. "You wouldn't be offended?"

My laughter was a foreign bitter thing. "I think I'm going to get totally wasted and then act really stupid. If I make it through that okay, then you can come back to me if you want." I stood up and sent the chair in which I'd been sitting up into the ceiling to join the table. It didn't stick, falling back to the floor with a crash. "See, I'm not having the best luck lately. I mean, sure, I did come back from complete and utter obliteration recently, and now my car is a vampire, too, which is cool. It's pretty damn neat to watch him run over stuff . . . squirrels, armadillos . . . other vampires."

Beatrice's mouth fell open. My eyes locked onto a single strand of hair that stuck to her lips when the large lock fell free. "You have a vampire car?"

"It *could* be a zombie car, I guess. It eats meat, too . . . not just blood. Either way, it's definitely undead."

"Really?"

"And that ain't all of it," I said. "See, on top of that, I have to deal with all this trippy shit about me not really being a Vlad, but some legendary one-in-a-million, oh-no-we've-got-to-deal-with-one-of-these-crazy-sons-of-bitches type of vamp."

"Trippy shit?" Beatrice frowned.

"Oh, yeah, I've got trippy shit out the waz. You know how that Ebon Winter guy can turn into mist?"

She nodded. "It's very rare. He and Lord Phillip are the only vampires in the city who can do it."

"Well, I can turn into a fucking ghost, revenant, whatever, and the reason—you'll like this—the reason everybody fucks with me is because when I get really pissed off, I turn into some kind of uber vamp with purple eyes, leather wings, and the ability to control frickin' bats."

Beatrice took a hit off of the blood wine, wiped the top of the bottle and passed it across to me. I took a swig and shook my head. I've never liked wine, but it did taste different from blood and different is good. After another drink I continued, "Only now, one of my thralls, who isn't really my thrall, but some sort of thrall double agent, has been screwing around with me using some sort of sex magic."

I chugged the rest of the bottle. It's easier to do when you don't have to breathe. "Lord, this is nasty! Plus, you really don't want to get me drunk. The last time I got drunk, there was hockey and werewolves."

"You're the guy who killed the Void City Howlers?" she asked.

I opened a new bottle, wondering where my buzz was. "This shit doesn't have any kick at all," I complained.

"Let me see." Beatrice reached for the bottle, examining the label. "It's the cheap stuff." She went through the other bottles until she found one with some guy named Duke Gornsvalt's name on the label.

"Try this one. It's the real deal. Lady Gabriella buys a bottle of his champagne every year for New Year's Eve. When he's done with it, it doesn't even look like blood anymore."

"Really?"

"I heard that he once made a run of blood vodka for Lord Phillip. It took him thirty years to make five bottles."

I opened the bottle. It was a white wine. I hated white wine when I was alive, but the taste . . . it was very different from blood. It also had more kick to it than I remembered wine having. Another swallow and I remembered John Paul Courtney. "Oh, and I forgot . . . I've got a ghostly cowboy hanging around in my pistol." I reached into my jacket pocket and flashed her the gun butt.

"And you say you were obliterated?"

I nodded.

"How?" she asked.

"Blessed explosives."

"Then I'm coming with you." She took my arm and the warmth of her cut through my mood. Body heat will get a vampire every time. "I became a thrall because the world of the vampires was supposed to be mysterious and exciting and so far it's been mostly politics. This is as close as I've come to mysterious and exciting."

Great. Another groupie.

"One thing first, Bea." I held my hand out for the bottle and she slid it back to me. "You don't, like, want to hump me or anything, do you?"

She wrinkled her nose at me. "Um . . . no. Not to offend you, but ewww. You're dead and I'm not a necrophiliac. If I become a vampire someday, then maybe but—"

"Good," I interrupted. "Then you can come along." I stood up and thought about draining the bottle. I wanted to go charging across town to the Pollux, see if I could help, but didn't see the point. If they were gone, then they were gone. Grief welled up and I felt it die, cut off, like water from a spigot.

"Rachel's alive," I murmured.

"Hmmm?"

"Never mind." I put the bottle on the table and gestured at the hall. "I have to wake up Phil," I said tiredly. "If we're lucky, he'll just fucking kill me and put me out of my misery 'cause the Bend Over Festival is starting to wear very thin."

31

ERIC:

STONED

The grain of the wood ran from purple to black on Phillip's door; it was a beautiful piece of workmanship. Dennis came through the open doorway carrying an empty platter that smelled of burgers, fries, and orange soda. I got out of his way. Beatrice grabbed a chair in the lobby and waited for the excitement to begin.

"The children are safely ensconced within the Lady Tabitha's suite, Lord Eric. I have one of the Highland's day-care workers upstairs with them now to make certain they don't get into any trouble while their mother rests."

"Thanks." It's like thralls were stray dogs and I was every mutt's sucker.

"I see you've been admiring our door," he offered. "It's—"

"Brazilian rosewood, I know," I interrupted. "My parents had a bed veneered with it. It's still around somewhere; I'm just not sure what happened to it. Roger would know."

Dennis nodded. "How interesting. Is there anything else I can do for you before I retire? Lord Phillip's sleeping schedule is very erratic and I need to be rested when he awakens."

I grasped his shoulder. "How long is Ebony going to be like that?"

"I don't know." He shrugged. "Did you really break her thralldom by force?"

"Yeah," I said in an aggravated tone. "I guess that's what I did."

"I'll summon the nurse and have her take a look." Dennis headed for the door expecting me to release his shoulder, but I didn't comply. "Was there something else?" he asked.

"Get Phil's happy ass out of bed," I told him. His expression told me that there was no way in Hell he was going to obey that request. It wasn't a request. I knew that I was pushing everything and everyone too far, but I had nothing more to lose. If I stopped to think about everything, I was afraid I'd be paralyzed by my emotions. Maybe that was Roger's plan. Blow up the Pollux and hope I got myself killed when I rampaged through the Highland Towers . . . or maybe he just wanted me to feel like I had nothing left to lose. Marilyn was gone, everyone I knew and cared for had been eliminated . . . That didn't feel like a plan Roger would have come up with, it was too subtle, but a demon . . .

"Look, I know you don't want to and I know that he's going to be angry. You probably think you'd rather die or something, but I promise you"—my voice became a whisper—"if Phil doesn't get his ass in gear, then I'm going to kick in that door and take what I'm looking for."

"The wards here will cut you to ribbons," he told me.

Shoving past him, I walked up to the inner door and twisted the handle. A sensation similar to the one I'd felt upon entering the Highland Towers washed over me and I heard that same ghostly voice from before, the one that let me in the lobby door. "You are expected."

The door opened easily, no sign of a shock or any wards in place, and I stepped inside the room of someone who read way too many books. I smelled blood and death. Three bodies total, I was guessing, very likely the girls I'd seen earlier when I'd done the mental peeping tom thing.

"You may not—" was all Dennis got out before another voice cut him off.

"All is well, Dennis. Do not hinder that which cannot be hindered. I am awake," came a voice from behind a large velvet curtain. The bodies were behind that curtain, and the bed. "*Integer vitae scelerisque purus.* Heh, not exactly, but in a way, I suppose."

"Untouched by life and free of wickedness?" I said by way of translation. "Not exactly, but I really don't give a shit about your delusions. I'm just here for—"

Although he was fat and short, Phillip could move. He appeared before me grinning and in his dressing gown. The curtains didn't even rustle. His smile reminded me of Scrooge's in that movie when he realizes that the ghosts have done their work all in one night and he still has time to make it all right before Tiny Tim gets dead. His whole appearance seemed false. He held a finger next to his nose and dashed across the room and around a corner.

"Aw, I really don't need this crap today, old man. I just . . . Jesus Christ!" A vampire in a glass case stared at me from across the room, a stake through his heart. He was supported by a human-size metal doll stand, only instead of clasping over his clothes like the ones Greta'd had for her Barbies, it snaked beneath the rear of his tweed jacket. The vamp's colorless eyes stared blankly through gold-rimmed spectacles with round lenses. They didn't move, but I felt like he was watching me . . . aware. His expression had been frozen in the midst of what was either a smirk or one of those you'll-never-change-will-you looks that I often get.

He'd become undead past his prime, but his good looks hadn't been eroded. The crow's-feet around his eyes made him look distinguished rather than old. I had him beat there, though. No wrinkles. He had to have been a good ten years or so older than me, physically. With the stake through his heart, there was no way I could tell how long he'd been a vampire. I hoped the bulk of it hadn't been spent in the case.

"My dear Percy, who serves as a remembrance to all that I do not bluff, I do not make empty threats, and there are indeed worse fates than death," I read aloud from the plaque at the base. "You are one twisted dude, Phil, but don't think that means that you can't—"

Phillip reappeared and pushed something into my hand, cupping both of his hands around mine. His earnest gaze met mine and he seemed both utterly at ease and pleased with himself. "The Stone of Aeternum? Yes? Here it is. I wanted to get this out of the way first thing so that we can enjoy our conversation. Would you like some wine? I believe you'll find I have a much better stock than Lady Gabriella. Ah, I almost forgot! How could I forget; I had it made just for you. I hope you'll like it."

He sped past me, through the open door, and out into the hallway. "Dennis! Go down to the cellar and bring up the special black case, the one from Duke Gornsvalt. Be very careful with it, it took him"—he looked me up and down—"fifteen years to manage it correctly. Oh! Oh! And have Brigitte prepare the special menu. Two for him and one for me. Oh, this will be marvelous."

Infectious as his excitement was, I still noticed the way Beatrice's breathing changed when he entered the hallway to speak with Dennis. Her heart rate sped up, not out of control, but different. I looked at Percy and wondered what the poor bastard had done to become a knickknack.

In my hand, I held a small black stone that might or might not really be the Stone of Aeternum. There was no label and it didn't seem very special. It didn't glow and it didn't hum; it just sat there like a rough lump of coal. It was an interesting dilemma; how would I know the real stone? Could I take this guy's word on it?

"So I'm just supposed to believe that you'd give me this powerful magic rock without a fight when guys like . . ." I struggled to remember the name properly, "J'iliol'lth would kill for it?"

Phillip walked back into the room and looked down at his dressing gown. "I haven't even dressed for dinner," he said with dismay. "Just a moment." Darting past me toward the bodies I'd smelled, he slipped behind a large burgundy-colored curtain that hung from floor to ceiling. Several minutes later he emerged dressed in a business suit that was so well tailored it made even him look a little dashing. "That's better. I do hope you'll pardon the delay. One makes preparations well in advance and then when the happy moment arrives, it's always rush, rush, rush. You were saying?"

"The Stone of Aeternum." I held it out to him. "How am I supposed to know it's the real deal?"

"That, I will leave to your own good judgment. Which, if you'll pardon my saying so, you are quite lacking. Good judgment, I mean, and therefore, hopefully you may rely on mine." Nearly floating as he walked, he moved to a large overstuffed chair and sat down. "By all means, be seated. Dennis should be here shortly with our order."

I sat down in the only other chair I saw, giving it a surreptitious kick to see if it was really an orange-scaled demon that was going to grab me. It smelled like Tabitha, though I knew she hadn't been here in days. "The Stone," I said, "seriously—"

"Come, come, Eric, my friend, if I wanted to give you a fake stone, I could have done so. I could have made it quite impressive, with an eerie glow and a subtle hum, a palpable sense of electricity gently pulsing through it, and fixed it up so that when you gazed into it you would have felt a sense of the infinite, the eternal. You would have known, just by looking at it, that eternity was confined within and you would have felt comforted by that fact. I chose, instead, to bestow upon you the actual item. Why should it be so hard to believe? I often bestow items of value upon interesting new vampires when we meet. Like the necklace I gave your . . . the one I gave Tabitha."

"The diamond necklace?" I asked.

"The very same. It has quite a history."

Yeah, I didn't like this guy. He seemed sincere enough, but it seems a lot of clever bastards use truths to tell their lies. Like the chair that still smelled like Tabitha. A guy like Phillip wouldn't have accidentally done that. He wanted to see how I'd react—more High Society bullshit.

32

TABITHA:
I'LL KILL HIM

Rough hands touched my shoulders while I slept. The nicest little dream I would never remember left my mind as I was rolled over. Gasoline and butane mixed together in a noxious chemical odor. I stretched and opened my eyes, expecting somehow to see Eric toweling off in the sink and griping about some new accident with his car. We'd make love and then . . . But the hands did not belong to Eric. A hard-looking mercenary in Void City Police Department SWAT gear crouched over me with one hand on my breast. My heart was still beating and I woke the rest of the way with a start.

"Get off of me!" I shouted, immediately attempting to change into a cat. Nothing happened. There was a barely perceptible tingle, almost as if the part of me that controlled my powers was asleep and trying to wake. . . . So I responded the old-fashioned way, with a knee to the groin. In most places it's not wise to assault a cop, but in The Void, you do what you need to do and if you're in the wrong, then you pay the Fang Fee and move along.

He fell back onto the concrete with a grunt and I pulled myself up and took in my surroundings. A large 3-B stenciled on the wall let me know that I was on the third level of the parking deck, but it didn't tell me where Talbot had run off to or why he'd left me here. Two more cops stood behind me. One had an assault rifle and the other had what looked like a flamethrower, not standard equipment for a task force that is usually cleaning up after vampires, not gunning for them. Both wore headsets and identical crew cuts; neither wore a helmet like the one the man I'd knocked down was wearing.

"Alpha-One to Big Top, we have a possible human bystander here." He paused, listening to someone on the other end, while the friend of his I'd kneed in the groin stood up slowly. He was wearing a headset, too. "She's got a heartbeat, Big Top." He sniffed the air loudly. "Plus the nose knows, you know?"

Didn't the blood on my shirt and the big hole in my chest clue these morons in? Then again, if they were real VCPD, they wouldn't assume. "Possible human" left room for the chance that I might be a shape-shifter. Living doesn't guarantee mundane, not in Void City. I touched my chest, then looked down. I had already healed. There was lots of blood, but it might have looked like I'd been attacked—if you were an idiot.

"Understood. Detaining subject for ID."

"Like Hell," I told them. I saw another three cops sweeping the uphill slope of the deck. The two groups I could see were organized into three-person teams: one man with a spear, another with an assault rifle, and a third with a flamethrower. One would run the spear under a car while the others would line up to shoot anything that came out from under it.

The other team was only one car away from the Le Baron Greta was under and I couldn't tell if there were more on other levels. Eric's parking deck was old school—narrow, circular parking levels wrapped around a central spiral for ascent and descent. Where the heck was Talbot? His powers had been working just fine the last time I'd seen him.

A gunshot would hurt, but fire could do worse, so I charged the one with the flamethrower first, much to the surprise of all three men. Did they think I was going to just stand there—even if I wasn't a vampire—while they called for backup?

On that note, I screamed, "Rape!" When I'd turned thirteen I'd gone from having almost no breasts at all to having the D-cups I have now. One of the first things my mother had done, almost before taking me to buy bras, was to enroll me in a self-defense class. My instructor had said to yell "Fire!" but I figured the fire was old news.

The one with the assault rifle dropped it with a curse and reached out to grab me, but I was already barreling at the man with the flame-thrower. He also looked surprised and tried to hold up his hand to ward me off. I kept screaming "Rape!" and kicked him solidly in the knee. A loud snap let me know I'd done real damage and he went down to one knee.

I screamed "No!" and "Rape!" again, as I turned on the nearest man. He grabbed my left arm and I grabbed his right ear. My defense class instructor had told us that it only takes eight pounds of pressure to tear off the human ear. He was right.

Assault-Rifle-Guy grabbed the side of his head and screamed. Those self-defense classes were worthless against vampires, werewolves, and Talbot, but the basic principles worked just fine against humans.

"Fuck!" yelled the man with the spear. "What the hell is wrong with you, lady?"

The second team headed toward me and I went for the assault rifle. I had no idea how to fire it other than the point, aim, and pull the trigger lessons my dad had given me at age eight. I guess that was Dad's Southern version of gun safety. My hand had just touched the butt of the gun when the man with the spear stomped my fingers and hit me in the temple with the butt of his spear hard enough to cross my eyes. I fell to my hands and knees, a boot on my back between my shoulders.

"Ma'am, we may be moonlighting, but we're still cops. Calm the fuck down. Nobody is raping anybody here."

"Bitch ripped off my ear!" the more injured cop yelled behind me. "I'm gonna kill her."

I heard him charge, his feet slapping the concrete as he ran. A scuffle started behind me between the guys who had run over to help and the cop who'd lost an ear. A third team headed our way, coming from a higher level. I flinched when they passed Greta's hiding place. "What the hell are you guys doing over here?" yelled one of the newcomers. "We ran into two civilians. Our team managed to deal with them without this kind of shit. Mirror test. Pulse. Move on. Mirror test. Pulse. Move on. How complicated is that for you assholes?"

"I woke up and one of them was on top of me," I said with as much false panic as I could muster. "He ripped up my top and he had his hands on my breasts. They were trying to shove something in my mouth to gag me. I don't know what's going on here and I don't want to know, just get them off of me! Don't let them hurt me anymore. I'll do what you want, just stop hurting me. You can have my wallet, my keys, you can even . . . h-have sex with me if you want, but . . . I don't want to die," I said as I sobbed convincingly.

"Shit!" said one of the other newcomers. The name on his vest was *Stacey* and he was older than the others, heavier set, but still in shape. He was bald, with a bushy brown mustache. "I knew it was a mistake to bring you in on this one, Baxter. If her memory needs adjusting, you're paying for it. I don't care how much it costs to put that kid of yours into the Ellery Academy, do you understand me?"

"She's lying, Captain," said the one with the boot on my back. I tried to pop my claws, but the only response was a sharp pain in my fingertips, a pinprick. "We took her pulse and found out she was human, but they wanted us to hold her for ID. Then she freaked out on us."

"Edwards," Captain Stacey snapped. "What the fuck happened? You're supposed to be keeping these new guys in line."

"Look, Captain, I had to take a piss," said the guy who had been holding the flamethrower. "When I came up, Baxter was on top of her with his hand up her shirt and she freaked out. What happened before that I don't know, but I didn't touch anybody any place." His voice trembled when he spoke, somewhere between fear and pain.

"Radio Big Top," Captain Stacey said to the man next to him. "I don't like talking to her."

He complied. "Big Top, this is Bravo-Two, Alpha group has a half-naked bleeding human up here who says they tried to physically assault her. What's your ETA?"

He waited, listening. I missed my vampire hearing. Why wasn't it working and why was I stuck seeming human? Was seeming human the only way I could wake up in daylight? It made sense. Ordinarily, I'd have slept through the whole thing . . . been burned up in the fire. My powers hadn't almost gotten me killed; they'd saved me the only way they could.

"Big Top's walking up the stairs now," said Bravo-Two.

Stacey shook his head. "You guys better hope your story checks out or you're going to wish that Miss Thang here had finished the job she started on you."

"He's hurting me," I complained weakly. "God, my chest . . . I can barely breathe." I started wheezing and choking. Whoever Big Top was, I didn't want to be here when she arrived.

"Baxter, get off of her and step back." Captain Stacey spit on the ground. "She's got two men with assault rifles aimed at her. She isn't going anywhere."

"She's lying," said the man with his boot on my back, but he did take his foot off of me. I scooted quickly away from them and put my back against the concrete riser at the outer edge of the deck. A small ray of sunshine was only inches from my foot. Could I seem human enough to fool the sun? If I couldn't, they'd sure as hell figure out I was a vampire when I caught fire.

I froze and then tucked my legs up against me, hugging them and began to rock back and forth. "Just let me go," I said over and over again, my head buried in my knees. "Just let me go. I won't tell anyone. I'll go straight home and I won't talk to anybody. I'll quit my job and I'll just move and you won't have to worry about me saying anything, just please don't kill me."

"Calm down, ma'am." Stacey frowned at me as he spoke and I

wondered if I'd oversold my performance. "I know this doesn't make a whole lot of sense, but we're sweeping this deck for vampires."

"Feels weird working for a demon, though, Cap," Edwards whispered.

"His money spends just the same," Stacey snarled. "Now shut up."

High heels clicked on concrete and I heard the men step back for someone. I looked up and a woman in an obviously expensive green suit looked down at me. It was Rachel. Behind her, floating in some kind of mystic chains, was Talbot—alive, but gagged. It clicked. "Shit," I cursed angrily. Esteban had been delivering the Infernal Chains of Sarno Rayus to Rachel. They moved like snakes, twisting and altering anytime Talbot tried to shift, the gentle metallic tinkle as the links clinked together providing further proof they were the same chains that had been in Esteban's leather satchel.

"Like the chains?" Rachel teased. "Pretty cool, huh?"

"Shit," I cursed again.

"Did she pass the mirror test?" asked Rachel. She smiled knowingly at me as she asked, winking like this was a big joke.

"We didn't get past the pulse test," Alpha-One started.

"Idiots," Rachel hissed. "What am I paying you for? You always check the mirror first. No reflection means the target is a vampire! End of story. Pulse is second, because we don't want to murder any humans."

Taking a deep breath, I exhaled and then stood up.

Captain Stacey hocked up a bit of phlegm and spit it on the concrete at Rachel's feet. "You aren't paying us for anything, witch." He took a step closer to her. "The demon is paying us to help you find and detain vampires along with the fee to clean up the mess from the fire you started next door."

"Don't get smart with me, Captain."

"Smart?" Captain Stacey walked over to the glowing chains restraining Talbot. He leaned in close, the light from the chains washing the color from his skin, lending him an absurdly angelic glow, and he sniffed the air. "Smart would be if you told me why you're detaining a mouser on a run where we're being paid to gather up bloodsuckers."

"Jill will pay you the extra." Rachel pulled Talbot farther away from him. "But don't worry; I assure you that this female is a vampire."

"Of course he will . . . it's still within the estimate." Stacey spit on the ground again, turning to look at me. "You a Living Doll?" He grinned. "You must have been showing off to the wrong people."

"Rachel." I looked past Captain Stacey. "Why are you doing this?"

"Oh, don't act like you give a damn about me!" she yelled. "You knew all about vampires. You'd read all those books. You'd even already met some of them, found your way past the veil hiding them from everyone. Damn it, Tabitha, you had a passport to immortality in your handbag and you didn't even try to plead my case. You let me die!"

"This is impossible," I mouthed voicelessly.

She touched my face. "Says the undead tramp," she scoffed. "There are ways back, sis. They aren't pleasant," she shuddered, "and they change you, but they're better than the alternative. I do owe you some small debt of gratitude, though. If you hadn't been Eric's little plaything, then J'iliol'lth wouldn't have brought me back at all. He said it made me the perfect bait. A man—a vampire like Eric—J'iliol'lth said there was no way he could resist the wild younger sister. Eric was inside me before we even got back to the Pollux. Easy-peasy."

One of the cops let out a low whistle at that. Another said, "Shit" and looked away.

"Pardon?" I said softly.

"You don't understand where I was or what they do to little witch wannabes down there. I thought it would be tough, sleeping with him, doing this to you, but it wasn't as bad as I thought. He's a very good lover. The power he gives off is intoxicating by itself, but the way he moves—well, you already know about that," Rachel said as she conjured a blue flame in the palm of her hand. It changed from blue to red to green and back again, then settled on purple. "And of course, the deal came with magic, real magic. Do you know how much I dreamed of real magic?"

She always had been more into witchcraft than vampires.

"I do," said a voice from behind her. Magbidion stepped out of the stairwell. He was washed, shaved, and wearing new clothes. It took ten years off his age.

Stacey nodded to one of his men and one of the assault rifles shifted to point at Magbidion. "I only want to talk." Magbidion held up his hands. "I sold my soul for magic, just to taste it, for one real moment. Eric is going to get me out of that deal. He's killed more demons than you've ever met. Let him take care of your problem, too."

The cops exchanged looks. I think things were getting more complicated than they'd been led to believe. Stacey turned to say something to Rachel, but she stepped around him. "I didn't have to give up my soul, old man." She laughed and ran a hand down the outside curve of her body. "Seduce Eric; get him ready for what my employer has in mind for him. And then, when the time was right, use a little bit of borrowed pyromancy to destroy the Pollux. After that, I show up at the appointed place and time, watch the fireworks, and collect my check. I'm free and clear, though I'll still be on retainer."

"Really?" asked Magbidion. "Now, see, that's a lot better than the deal I got."

"You don't know how to negotiate." She chuckled. Six more policemen filed out of the door behind Magbidion. Two of them leveled their guns at him.

"The rest of the deck is clear, Cap," one of them yelled to Stacey.

"Kill the mage," Rachel ordered.

Captain Stacey drew his sidearm with speed that had to be more than mortal, placing it in one smooth motion against Rachel's temple. "You're past your spending limit, witch. Adding the fee for the mouser took you right to the edge of the agreed-upon estimate. We aren't taking on anything extra on credit."

"Damn it, Stacey." Rachel spoke softly, not willing to give him an excuse.

"Your boss could have given you a bigger credit line," Captain Stacey said, "but he didn't. So we're out. We swept the deck. We found your vampire and your mouser and I have a helicopter waiting for me and my men on the roof."

"Jill will—"

"Fuck Jill," Stacey said. "He's a demon. If he didn't like the contract, then he of all people should have known better than to sign it."

"Captain," I said, "take me with you."

"Do you have four hundred and seventy-five thousand dollars in cash?" Stacey asked.

I shook my head.

"Then we ain't your cavalry." His eyes flicked, showing slit pupils. "See you around, Highness." He patted Talbot's chained form as he and his men strode past, the men in the rear keeping their guns leveled in our direction.

"Just us, now." Magbidion made a gesture with his right hand. Rachel did the reverse with her left. Nothing happened that I could see, but Magbidion sighed. "I really should have stayed in the RV."

None of them had my attention. Eric had cheated on me before. It wasn't even really cheating because I'd known about it from the start. I was his, but he'd always needed more than one woman. I had believed it. I'd bought into it. He had lots of women, but I was the special one, I was the one that was his actual girlfriend. I knew he'd been sleeping with Rachel . . . I was even mostly okay with it.

But something else had clicked. "You're the girl," I said. "The one he wanted to pick for a threesome?" It was an offer I'd made him once he'd turned me, before I knew about my ability to seem human, to turn on my body heat, my heartbeat. I'd told him he could pick any one human to join us in our bed. Rachel damned Eric with a smile and my heart stopped beating. For him to sleep with her was one thing. For him to expect me to sleep with her . . . to have even considered it . . . "I'll kill him."

And then I felt them. My powers, like a slumbering beast, a tiger waking from a drugged sleep . . . the tingling numbness was gone. My jaw popped as my fangs slid firmly into place and I relished the pain when they tore through my gums.

I was awake. All of me. Anger was the key.

33

ERIC:

AN EXCESS OF INFAMY

The tantalizing odor of well-grilled beef filled the elevator shaft. Even through the two intervening doors the scent was clear and tempting. Strong food smells still made me salivate on occasion and I carefully closed my mouth and swallowed. A light *ting* announced the arrival of the elevator and when the doors opened, the aroma overcame all other smells. Phillip tapped his fingers together in guileless anticipation. I stood up to go for the door and the older vampire shooed me back into my chair.

"Let it come to you." He licked his lips, leaving a smear of blood on them. "Anticipation is a part of it. Deny yourself the expectation and you will have squandered a portion of the experience. Savor it and you will have realized the potential of the moment. The eternal must maximize all of their experiences to the utmost capacity while simultaneously leaving room for minor improvements, perhaps even arranging flaws. One does not wish to create an experience that cannot be rivaled, for fear that all future entertainments of a similar breed will—"

Beatrice opened the door for Dennis, who carried in a tray with three covered metal plates on it. Behind him, a girl who couldn't have been older than fourteen brought in a cooler and set it down. She opened a concealed closet and withdrew a small table that she placed between Phillip and myself. Dennis set the tray on the table and crossed back to the door. "Will there be anything else?" he asked.

"Thank you, Dennis," said Phillip. "Now out with you." Dennis did as instructed. "You didn't look at the girl," Phillip observed as the door closed.

"She's what, fourteen?" I said, lifting the lid off of the plate closest to me.

"Eleven." Phillip laughed. "Though everyone does guess high. She'll be astonishing when she reaches maturity."

"Yeah, maybe so, but I don't look at them until they are a bit older, you know? Like, oh, out of high school."

"I've offended you," Phillip stated.

"Don't take it personally, most undead do. That's why I have a habit of killing them. So . . . Now what, we stare at steak and talk about pre-teen hotties? Because if that's your idea of a good time, then I'm getting the hell out of Dodge."

"You may go, if you wish," he said sadly. "Take the Stone of Aeternum and do with it what you will. Give it to J'iliol'lth. Keep it. It is of little consequence. It will find its way back to me in time for my ascension. I have foreseen as much."

"You've foreseen it?" I asked. "What're you . . . psychic, too?"

Phillip sighed. "I had great hopes for our meeting. I've prepared for it and planned it; I was just wrong about it. It doesn't often happen to me, being wrong. You might as well take your steaks; I won't enjoy mine without you. When I was preparing their enchantment, every thought I spared to them was of my meeting with you when we could dine on them together. I had forgotten your comparative youth and your flightiness. A result of your unusual circumstance, I have no doubt."

"Unusual circumstance?"

Phillip, who had risen and crossed to the cooler, stopped moving. I didn't need to see his face; I could hear the grin.

"I suppose we could discuss it, but perhaps while we eat?"

"Eat?" I asked. "As in chew, chew, swallow?"

He removed a pair of small brown bottles from the cooler. "The Disinclined Vintage: each bottle lovelessly prepared by Duke Gornsvalt at considerable expense and with unwilling hands." Phillip read aloud the inscription on the yellow label and chuckled. "Duke Gornsvalt was quite wroth with me until I sent him one of those steaks. Shall we try ours? They are growing cold."

I looked back at the steak. "How?"

"I rarely answer 'how' questions," he said as he returned to the table. "I will do so this once because the answer is quite plain: it's magic. What good is magic, to what purpose alchemy, if it cannot ease our burdens, imagined or otherwise?"

On the left side of the plate, there was a fork, on the right, a steak knife. I cut a piece of steak and as I brought it to my mouth, my fangs extended. After a few tries, I got them to retract so I could take a proper bite. It was overcooked, barely pink through the middle, but it tasted like heaven to me. Swallowing was a problem, though; I couldn't seem to get the entire piece of meat down my throat and I gagged.

"You're not chewing it thoroughly enough." Phillip demonstrated, cutting himself a much smaller piece. He put it into his mouth and winced when he bit his tongue.

We got the hang of it, though. My fangs remained a problem off and on throughout the meal; the texture of solid food, the excitement of it, brought out vampiric instincts that I'd cultivated for years. Chewing food is not like riding a bike. After a decade or two, you forget how.

"At the end of this meal, do I get presented with a bill?" I asked.

"Why bother?" Phillip set one bottle of the Disinclined Vintage next to my plate and the other next to his own. "I know you couldn't pay it. The cosmos is insistent on certain things and this is one of them. Vampires cannot eat—not like humans. To turn the laws of our breed upside down in this fashion requires an obscene expenditure of resources. The beer was a bit easier. I could have brought in a more plebian blood brew, but I had Duke Gornsvalt do it because he has a certain talent for exotic beverages and I wanted it to taste like you remember. He did warn me it may cause us to urinate, however, so be prepared."

"Real pee or blood?" I asked.

"I didn't ask." Phillip coughed. "It never even occurred to me. I like surprises."

He watched as I removed the cap and tasted the beer. I'd expected it to taste like blood. I'd had "blood brew" before—fermented blood that packed the same kick as real alcohol. This did not taste the same. "It tastes like camel piss."

"Isn't it supposed to?" Phillip asked in midmouthful.

"Pretty much," I acknowledged.

"This is much more as I had foreseen," Phillip said as he patted the table. "Thank you for fulfilling my expectations."

"Uh-huh," I answered. The beer had more kick than it should have had and the buzz I wanted moved in, taking the edge off. We chewed in silence. I cut the second steak in half, putting the larger piece on Phillip's plate. He was the founder of the feast; I figured that he deserved it.

"But I ordered that steak for you," he said.

"There is no way I'm eating a second steak in front of you, while you have an empty plate," I told him. "Just eat it."

He bristled slightly, but did as I instructed.

When we were done, both our jaws hurt from all the chewing and we sat there in a state of pained, yet satisfactory, fullness. "Tell me what you meant before about my circumstance," I said, breaking the silence.

"I will answer, to the best of my ability, any one question on any subject," he said with a casual wave of his arm.

"Okay, but you have to answer the question I'm trying to ask and not screw me over if I get the words wrong. What I want to know is, what special circumstance? You were talking about the whole uber vamp thing, right? Or maybe the reason my eyes are still blue?"

He took a long pull of beer and finished his bottle. "I was."

"Then tell me."

"It's all in the timing," Phillip began. "With you, everything had to go in a very strict progression. You were murdered. After the crash, you lay there in the dirt. Roger stood there and watched you die before calling the paramedics. He taunted you. You struggled to rise, enraged at your own murder. Given time and opportunity, had you been a normal human, you would have risen as a revenant and Roger's unlife would have become most unpleasant. In time, I feel confident that you would have managed to master your powers enough to eventually catch and end him. I'm not sure his hired mages could have moved you along. Even as you lay there, I could feel your power growing."

"Feel it?" I asked.

"Oh, yes, after all, you were and are a Courtney."

At those words John Paul Courtney manifested behind Phillip's back. His face was twisted with rage. Fangs lowered from his upper jaws—curved fangs, not straight like mine. His mouth opened wider than humanly or vampiricly possible, unhinging like a snake. His fists clenched at his side. He let loose a single angry hiss, forked tongue darting past his fangs, but then gained control of himself, vanishing without another sound. My eyes widened. "Holy shit."

"Yes," he said. "I know all about your family, more than you do."

Really, I thought, *did you know my great grandpaw was a weresnake?*

"You see, even in life I was a wizard, a sorcerer, a magician, an alchemist. It is enough to say that I was gifted with true mystic flair. I have the dubious honor of being the reason why mages who become vampires are hunted down and destroyed by their former allies. They will allow no more like me."

"You upset the apple cart," I said with a grunt of admiration. I like people who disturb the status quo—any status quo but mine, that is. "You're probably the reason guild mages are so touchy about working with vamps in general, too."

"Precisely so." He rubbed his hands together as he spoke, repeatedly flashing that devil's grin he favored so much. "Any being as powerful as you comes to my notice instantly through the web and weave of my magical influence, your peculiar situation notwithstanding. Void City is my domain. If I'm to be completely truthful, I had expected your creation, sensed it, foreseen it, and I had taken several days to prepare.

"My problem was twofold: how to slow your development while simultaneously ensuring your survival? Were you to rise at full strength, your powers intact, you would have realized your potential too quickly to be of use to me—too swiftly to be interesting as well. The timing was dreadful. There wasn't enough, you see."

"Wait." I leaned toward him. *El Alma Perdida* pulled against my jeans as I moved. "So you stole my body?"

"I had no need. It was quite simple to follow your body to the morgue and deal with you there."

"What did you do? Are you trying to tell me you're my sire? 'Cause no offense, but Darth Vader, you ain't."

Shock is the only word I can think of to describe the look on Phillip's face at the suggestion. "Of course not, my boy. No, no, no. Heaven forbid. No, I had you embalmed with a little alchemical concoction which, when applied, destabilized the—shall we call it judgment— under which you found yourself."

"Judgment?"

"Curse, then."

"What curse?"

"The Courtney family curse is a transmuted judgment of sorts. Sins of the father, that sort of thing, very Old Testament. My alchemical concoction delayed the full effects, allowed it to work its will upon you, to bring you back, but prevented the complete attainment of your vampiric nature and hid you from your sire. I'd expected it to last another decade or more, but there was no way I could have foreseen your flurry of activity, the many times you've been reduced to ash. Each time you re-formed, you came closer to your true potential."

"So you're behind *everything* then."

Phillip seemed to think that was really funny; he shook his head as he laughed. "No, my boy. That is another kettle of fish. Trust me when I say you'll figure it all out if you don't get ahead of yourself."

He floated out of his chair and landed in front of the fireplace; the edges of his outline were blurred by wisps of vapor as he moved. His control reminded me of Winter. He took a small box from the mantel. It looked like steel, a very sturdy thing, without decoration. "I want to ascend further and I need your help to do it. Here, take this as another gesture of my goodwill . . ."

He opened the box. Inside, a small journal, burned around the edges, sat silent and alone. The cover read, *Le Coeur du Démon.*

"This is different than the stained-glass thing downstairs."

"I hadn't noticed." Phillip beamed. Before I could ask him to elaborate, he was blabbing again. "If I had left you as you were, you would likely have already confronted your sire. She would have destroyed you or you would have destroyed her and I would be pursuing less amusing roads to victory. Now, she has only just sensed you for the first time. You've created a *memento mori* and she cannot but have sensed its creation. Her mind quests for your mind, but the remnants of my potion make that quite difficult."

"I haven't felt anything. Wait . . . my sire's a *she?*"

"You will and she is. Your sire is unimaginably boring, yet she does represent a singularly rare vampiric accomplishment, one that I can use. I could technically use you, of course, but I never murder interesting people."

"So she, my sire. She just happened to be standing on the side of the road when I was murdered?"

"No, my boy; Lisette hasn't left France in over a century."

"So . . . what . . . I'm the vampire equivalent of artificial insemination?" I shook my head. "Did she use a magic turkey baster?"

"She turned another Courtney into a vampire, a Courtney who begged to be forgiven, to be saved, and he was, but in exchange, the next seven generations of his family had to serve"—he paused, gesturing to the ceiling—"Him."

"You're shitting me."

"I assure you that I am not," Phillip said.

"No wonder Dad was so upset when I dropped out of seminary and enlisted during the war."

"You were the last Courtney male who could have been affected by the curse."

"I think I've heard enough."

"Surely you're curious."

"No, I'm usually not. There are whole worlds of information folks think I ought to be curious about."

Phillip spun in a small circle and jumped back to his chair, where, standing in the seat, he addressed me. "Come, my boy, what could it hurt?" He held out the box containing the journal.

"Shit," I said. It would be stupid to refuse. If Vamp Mom was going to come after me anyway and she was as powerful as all that . . . I considered refusing just to be obstinate. In the end, I reached out and took the box.

"The journal is in French. Do any of your thralls speak the language, or should I provide an interpreter?" Phillip smiled.

"I'm good." I walked to the door. "One last thing," I asked. "You said I'd created a *memento mori*. That means 'remember your death.' I'm guessing that you mean Fang, my Mustang, but what the hell is it?"

"Latin is a magnificent language, my boy, and like so many languages, its phrases may have subtly different meanings based solely on their context. When you think of an Emperor's *memento mori*, it is more accurate to say that the name means 'remember that you are mortal.'

"To achieve their true potential, an Emperor must do two things: create a *memento mori*, a repository to contain the portion of his darkness that he cannot completely control. Usually it's a small item, a necklace, a ring, a pair of spectacles . . . something that can be kept close, because once it is created, the Emperor's powers are tied to it.

"Until an Emperor creates a *memento mori*, his powers are often unreliable. *Memento mori* are also a weakness. Until you created Fang, you could not truly be destroyed."

"And now?"

"Now, if someone were to destroy Fang and to destroy you, then you would no longer be a vampire at all. You would be a revenant and nothing more."

"Good to know." I sighed. "What's the second thing?"

"Postmortem stress syndrome. You still think with your brain and see with your eyes. Even your Tabitha no longer does that. She may not yet have realized it, but she 'sees' with the essence of her being. Flesh is simply a convenient interface."

I said, "Thanks, Yoda," and stepped out into the hall, where I grabbed Beatrice by the arm to ask a very important question: "Do you really speak French?"

✦ 34 ✦

ERIC:
ONCE UPON A TIME

We sat out in Lord Phillip's waiting room while Beatrice read me the brief journal, translating as she went. I wasn't certain how much it helped. It was basically a re-telling of the mural I'd seen downstairs, only this copy had the names filled in. The female vamp's name was Lisette, also referred to as *Démon Coeur*, the Demon Heart. The irony that I'd named my strip club just that did not escape me.

The Knight had a similar name, apparently because he was part of a group of knights called *Le Coeur du Démon*. The Heart of the Demon. They'd named themselves after the monster they wanted to kill. They would stop at nothing less than tearing the Demon's heart from her chest.

They failed. The journal told the story of the last of the knights . . . the one who'd temporarily been a vampire. I couldn't pay attention to all of it; the beer and the food made me sleepy and full in a way that I hadn't been in fifty years. For reasons undetailed in the text, the Knight had given up the quest, moved to America, and changed his last name to Courtney. But I thought I knew why. He'd been afraid either for himself or someone he loved and he ran. On the final page, the author promised to pick up the tale in a new volume documenting the next generation of the Courtney line. The last entry was signed with a single letter—the only indication of authorship throughout the entire work—simply, *P.*

"C'mon, Beatrice." We left and headed toward the Gryphon Suite. "Did Lady Gabriella get all of that?" I asked her.

"Excuse me?" she said.

"She's given you to me, but you're still her thrall, correct? She seems to have a lot of spies, so I'm guessing she could see what happened in there, and she heard what you read?"

"She did see, yes," Beatrice admitted.

"Good. If someone kills you maybe I can bargain with her for the information later. I have terrible memory problems. I may need you to tell me the whole thing again, maybe more than once."

I didn't want Gabby spying on me all the time, though. I also didn't want to rip Bea from her by force as I'd done with Ebony. Was there a third choice? I thought back to the yellow notebook pages Magbidion had given me about thralls. Yep, a thrall could be released by a master or mistress willingly. It was a matter of willpower and saying the correct phrases.

"Is she watching us now?" I asked, stepping into an elevator that was, for once, without a human operator. As the doors closed behind us, Beatrice nodded. "Where are you marked?" Beatrice pulled her top open at the neck and bent over so that I could see the rose on her left breast.

"Release her, Lady Gabriella. You gave her to me and I have accepted."

The rose flashed brightly, then faded. Beatrice grimaced and began to change. Crow's-feet appeared at the corners of her eyes. "Please. If you're going to enthrall me, do it quickly," she said. Her cheeks began to sag and wrinkle as streaks of gray flowed into her hair. I did the deed and watched as the ravages of time faded with only slightly less speed than that with which they had arrived.

I must be better at the whole turning-back-the-clock thing than Gabby, I thought as I studied Bea with a critical eye. Her appearance seemed a bit younger than it had when I'd first seen her—maybe early twenties or late teens. It made sense. Gabby was just a Master and I was a Vlad . . . or whatever.

"How?" Beatrice took two steps away from me, studying her reflection in the metal of the elevator's interior doors. "I'm younger than I was before I became a thrall. How did you do that?"

"Comes from making a whole lotta thralls in two days, I guess," I lied.

The elevator doors opened and we walked through Tabitha's waiting area into the apartment. Ebony's kids didn't look up from the board game they were playing with the Highland Towers' child care guy.

Ignoring them, I pulled Beatrice into the bedroom and closed the door. Asleep on the only bed, Ebony stirred but remained unconscious.

"Excuse me, Highness?" Beatrice said. "Many male vampires like to seal the deal, as it were, with their new thralls." I listened to the sounds of Ebony's kids rolling the dice, moving their pawns along a candy-colored path.

"I thought," I looked at my feet uncomfortably and then looked back at her, "you know . . . ewww."

"That was when I was still in Lady Gabriella's service." Beatrice spoke carefully. She looked at the bed and blushed. "It's been a while since I've been exposed to a Vlad's pheromones without the protection of being a thrall. It shields you, but not from your own master. If your master is sexually compatible, then it is enhanced."

Sitting down on the bed, I patted Ebony's leg casually. "That certainly explains a lot." No wonder all my thralls wanted to hump me.

"And some vampires give off a more powerful . . . compulsion than others. Yours is very . . . intense. I think it should have built up more gradually. You can will certain people not to be affected, if you want."

Unsure of how to do what she was asking, I concentrated on her and thought really hard about her not being attracted to me. "You'll have to tell me when it works."

"That's better," she said after a moment.

"*Cui bono,*" I said, turning back to the problem at hand. "We've got to go to the Pollux to see if anyone is still alive. Do you have a car?"

She nodded.

"How big is the trunk?"

35

TABITHA:

AN UNEXPECTED RESCUE

In the parking deck near the Pollux, I found myself in the middle of a fight between two mages. Magbidion was on my side, Talbot was chained up, and Greta was nowhere to be seen. The sun was shining brightly overhead, but the structure provided ample shade. Rachel had underestimated me, the way everyone always does. I'm not weak.

I wasn't weak when I was pretending to be human and now that my vampire abilities were back, I was truly a force to be reckoned with. Eric was going to find that out when I got my hands on him. What kind of a man expects a woman to have sex with her own sister for his amusement? I understood the thought, the fantasy, but Eric had gone beyond that and my fury drove me much in the same way his had often driven him.

Eric's leather bat wings and black skin weren't in my arsenal, but my own speed, strength, and claws were more than enough. Rachel dueled with Magbidion; the two spell slingers made gestures in the air, spat magic words, and matched each other spell for spell. She could have killed Magbidion any time she wanted to. I could tell from the pouty little half smirk she always got when she thought she'd already won but wanted to run up the score. I crouched, preparing myself to charge. Despite all the things she'd said and done, it was hard to attack. Family is family. I gritted my fangs and charged with a growl. Rachel stopped playing with Magbidion and an arc of electricity struck him from the light over his head. He fell in utter silence and lay still, barely breathing. I slashed at her with my claws and she whipped past me, her feet floating above the ground.

"You're actually gonna fight me, sis." Her eyes widened and went red, the eyes of an angry vampire, and then they went purple—Eric's uber vamp eyes. "How cool is that?" Skin darkening to pitch black, she flexed long talons at me.

"What the hell?" I blinked at her, my mouth agape.

"Every time I make him feel alive." Wings ripped through the back of Rachel's suit, leathery wings—Eric's wings. "I siphon off a little bit of his power." My little sister stared at me across the parking deck, the female image of my boyfriend at his baddest and blew me a kiss.

"Yeah, but how long does it last?" Changing her body was a mistake. I could see her as an enemy. She didn't look like my sister anymore, more like a crude parody. We exchanged blows. I opened a long gash in her suit jacket, exposing the coal-black flesh of her stomach. She moved with the blow going past me, tearing my back, ribbons of my flesh clinging to her talons.

"Long enough to handle you." She clipped my head with a kick and it spun me around, breaking the skin on my forehead.

"That's the only thing bad about this job," Rachel said. I snagged her shoulder, catching cloth from her torn jacket, missing the meat. She backhanded me into the Le Baron. I struck the rear tire, knocking it loose and bending the axle. For a half a second I stared at the spot where Greta had lain prone, but she was gone. "When I'm done—no more Eric."

"What do you mean?" I rolled to my feet, dodged a claw that she'd leveled at my head, and struck her in the head with my elbow. Rachel swatted me with her wings and I slammed into the concrete column at the center of the deck where the spiral allowed cars access between the levels.

"I'll never be this powerful again." She paused as she flapped her wings hard enough to lift herself off of the floor, but the ceiling was too low to allow her much maneuvering room. "Not unless I can find another Emperor-class vampire just lying around. I mean, there are seven, and I even know where to find one of them, but as far as I know, she's straight."

I let her talk, allowing my vampiric metabolism to heal me and hopefully letting her run down the clock on her uber vamp power.

"Then why give up the magic if it's so important to you?" My head wound was gone already, the skin smooth under my fingers. No more wince-producing twinges came from my back when I moved my shoulders.

"Don't get me wrong; I'll still have pyromancy from the demon when I'm free, but it's more of a channeling thing. I need both the demon and the Emperor vampire to mainline this kind of magic."

Blue flames coursed along her outstretched talons and I flinched. *Please don't let me be set on fire again.*

"All healed up?" she asked mockingly. I lunged for her, but she spiraled away through the air and over the deck wall. In the sunlight, she turned to face me, her skin returning to normal, fangs receding. Out of uber vamp juice, or preserving it. Hovering in the air, with her tattered jacket and the backless top she wore underneath, Rachel was more beautiful than I'd ever seen her look, a ragged angel, hair backlit by the sun.

It was one more cruel reminder how much Rachel had paid to cling to life. I'd heard her claim that she hadn't sold her soul, but she was fooling herself. Even so, damnation agreed with her.

"Come and get me, sis." She tossed her hair with a shake of her head. "I'll wait right here."

Talbot floated after her against his will, pulled by the enchanted chains.

"No," I mouthed. I didn't love him or anything, but he had come running into a burning building to rescue me. I didn't want him to die.

"Why do you want Talbot?" I yelled. "I thought you were here to kill vampires."

"There you go, thinking again." Rachel clucked her tongue and shook her finger at me. "Maybe I just want to have sex with him later."

"You're such a whore."

"No, but I do like sex, always have . . . and now I get power from it. Although, technically I didn't have to sleep with Eric. I could have done it with joint meditation or massage therapy; it was just an option I exercised, because let's face it, sex is a hell of a lot more fun. That makes me an *escort*. But you, you shacked up with an ancient perverted old Vlad that disgusted you, just so you'd have a nice place to stay. You fucked him because you wanted what he could give you. So if there's a whore here . . . it's you."

"You're kidding yourself. Phillip was a bad choice, but once I got to know the real him, I told him to fuck himself and left. But you, you can't just quit or your demon pimp will send you back to Hell."

A wave of fire washed through the level of the parking deck that I was on. Rachel's voice called out above the roar. "I was going to let you live, but you talk too much—"

I ran. Flames licked the back of my head, but I didn't stop running. Patting my hair out as I went, I ran down, down, down, and down. What I was going to do when I got to the bottom level, I didn't know, but I hoped I'd think of something.

On the ground level I spied Magbidion's RV and Eric's Mustang. The RV provided the best cover, but there was no way I could outrun

454 ◆ WELCOME TO THE VOID

Rachel in it. I just hoped Eric's keys were in his car. The door was un-locked. I opened the driver's-side door, still trying to guesstimate how long I could last in partial sun. Maybe I could duck down . . . drive with one hand at the bottom of the wheel or something.

"Where ya going, sis?"

Rachel floated down, lifting over the little concrete barrier at the edge of the parking area and landing gently on the concrete. Not bothering to glide anymore, she stalked in my direction, her head tilted slightly to the left as if she were listening to someone else. "The puppet danced just like he was supposed to," she said. "Eric's not coming to save you. He's been kept busy at the Highland Towers. He might be the best lay I've ever had, but mentally he's thick like brick, you know? There's an animal-like craftiness, but he's a total retard."

There were no keys in the Mustang. Frustrated, I punched the steering wheel . . . and things got weird. The radio turned on all by it-self. A heavy metal guitar riff rang out over the speakers, imitating a race car engine throttling up. All of the interior lights in the deck blinked out at once, leaving Rachel illuminated only by the high beams of Eric's Mustang.

"What the fuck?" Rachel and I echoed each other.

The bright white of the car's headlights turned to crimson, casting Rachel in a blood-tinted hue.

"*Memento mori.*" She said the words like a curse, as if they were a stand-in for *motherfucker.* "He cares about her enough for his darkness to intercede?" The last bit I heard only because my vamp senses were back to full, but she sounded hurt.

The Mustang's tires squealed as they turned in place, leaving a layer of smoking rubber on the concrete. It was Rachel's turn to run.

I recognized the song on the radio when the car took off after her. It was "Fuel" by Metallica. Eric's car had his taste in music. Or maybe . . . "Eric, are you doing this?"

Nobody answered, but it felt like him, the angry him, the tall, dark, and purple-eyed him. Rachel leapt out into the sun, hovering just above the concrete barrier. She spun in the air, fingers twisting deftly at the start of what I assumed was the spell that would incinerate me and the car.

The car had other plans. It accelerated, straight for the concrete wall of the deck, bursting through it, clipping Rachel. Sunlight hit the car, but it didn't burn. Flamelike detailing swirled up the hood, along the sides, and the windows darkened from clear to almost black.

The rest I heard rather than felt. A series of crashes and more tire-squealing, punctuated by several explosions that rocked the car, were my best indicators that Rachel was still alive. As the Mustang kept trying to catch her, as its ire grew, I felt Eric again, very muffled and far away, but he was coming. At that instant everything went quiet. We drove for a few more feet before the windows went clear. The Mustang and I were safely within the shadows of the parking deck.

I didn't see Rachel anywhere, but I did see Magbidion, so I hopped out of the car to check on him. The car followed me, rolling over the blood that spattered the deck, leaving nothing but clean concrete in its wake.

Mags was unconscious, but seemed to be otherwise okay. On a hunch, I took his keys and checked his RV. Greta was in there—she'd been cleaned up a bit and carefully arranged on the fold-out bed, covered in a garish orange and pink floral throw blanket. She was badly singed, but I had no idea whether that had been from the burning of the Pollux, one of the creeps' flamethrowers, or one of Rachel's spells. I had a few seconds to wonder who'd gotten her off the third level and how they'd done it without being spotted by me or by Rachel before I heard sirens blaring. The Void City Fire Department had finally decided to give the Pollux their attention. I wondered if Captain Stacey would be with them.

Waiting for dark by myself was pure agony. Magic, tension, or something kept me awake, which was better for security but not good on my nerves. I hauled Magbidion and then Greta over to Eric's Mustang and stowed them inside, then climbed inside myself. I figured we'd be safest there if Rachel came back. I put Greta in the front seat and pulled Magbidion into the back next to me, for warmth. After that I stared at the ceiling and pondered why I wasn't falling asleep.

"That was really Rachel." I tested the idea and the words together. Would I have done what she did to avoid dying? In a way, hadn't I sold out by letting myself be changed? Maybe not the way she'd changed, but just as monstrously . . . She'd sold her services for magic and a second chance and I'd traded my life for a shot at a different kind of life. I understood the desire, but I didn't want to identify with her. Dead and buried, she'd been easier to love.

Thinking about my sister, I finally fell asleep. When I woke, it was to Eric's hand on my arm as he knelt over me. "Tabitha? Baby? Are you okay?"

I was hungry, angry, and depressed. He had bad timing . . . or worse, it had all been planned and I was just as stupid as he was for letting myself be used. Greta was still unconscious. Magbidion was no longer next to me and Eric had brought yet another new girl with him.

Red-eyed and screeching, I tore into him. "Bastard! You've been gone for what? An hour? And you're already fucking somebody else?" He didn't block my claws as they cut his chest.

"I didn't have sex with Beatrice," Eric said, but I wasn't listening. I raked his stomach and it burst open, little bits of meat and blood rolling down his pants and onto my chest. "I didn't have sex with anybody." One strong push sent him into the air. His head hit the concrete ceiling, but he caught himself as he fell and landed on his feet at the back of the RV.

"Tab, listen. Calm down. There has been some really strange stuff going on, and you've got to—"

His eyes were so open, so clear, so intelligent. He didn't even sound like himself.

"Shut up!" I screamed. "You'd fuck anybody! You were fucking Rachel and worse, you wanted me to!"

"I'll admit I did have the thought, but"—he shrugged—"I am a guy."

I leapt up, but my feet slid in the blood and I went back down, catching myself on the side of Magbidion's RV. I came up fast, with a hint of my vampire speed, but not enough to stop myself from slipping and falling again.

"My little sister! I know you don't want to talk about it, but she's back from the dead and working for Roger! And she almost killed us . . . would have killed us if it hadn't been for your car. Where were you, you asshole?"

"I was being blocked. I thought everyone here was dead." He shrugged. "So I handled some other business before coming here to try to trap . . . Wait. Did you say that your sister is *back* from the dead? When did she die?"

Something was slowing him down. He wasn't as nimble as he had been, even after things had gotten screwy. Maybe Rachel was draining him, recharging. On a good day I was faster than him. But with him moving as slowly as he was, it was a massacre. Twice he tried to lock gazes with me, but I'm not stupid—he'd done that to me at the entrance to the Artiste Unknown and I'd had to go through with a really horrible evening just to fulfill the compulsion, going through the movements of having fun, while Eric had gone home with my little sister, with Rachel!

"You bastard! I thought you loved me. I'm so stupid. I really thought you loved me."

"I never said that, Tabitha, but listen—"

Flipping over and behind him, I caught him by the neck as I'd seen him grab so many others. I seized his neck with one hand and his shoulder with the other. It was easy, like snapping beans in the backyard with my momma when I was little.

"Moist! Warm! Tightness!" It was all I could think of to say as I ripped off his head. He started rotting even before I let go of him and I stumbled back. Pulling his head off shouldn't have killed him. The woman with him opened and closed her mouth without saying anything, like the words just wouldn't come.

"You did great, sis!" said a familiar voice behind me. Rachel hovered in the sunlight just beyond the edge of the deck. With a simple gesture, she threw a tire iron at my head. I got out of the way, but as I did so, the tire iron altered direction and instead of striking me, it angled toward the Mustang, smashing straight through the engine block.

A second gesture and Talbot drifted back into view, the chain which bound him slithering across the concrete. As I watched, the links separated and reattached themselves to both imprison Greta and bind Eric's remains. "You see, Tab," Rachel told me casually, "once we had him where we wanted him, we needed someone who could subdue him. Sure, I probably could have done it, but there was always the outside chance that he'd find a way to kill me or stop me. He's really good at that. But once I realized how much he cared for you . . . well, I knew he wouldn't kill you, no matter what you did, especially after losing Marilyn."

"Please let me go," said the woman that had shown up with Eric. "He was going to eat me."

"Get out of here," Rachel told her scornfully. The woman fled and Rachel had us all in her grip. One question I wanted to ask burned brightly in my mind. She'd said subdue . . . Did that mean that I hadn't really killed him? Now that I thought about it, I was sure Eric would survive having his head ripped off. He'd survived holy water, stakes, explosives . . . yup, he'd be fine. Chances were Rachel was telling the truth.

She'd also said he cared for me.

36

ERIC:
DECAPITATED

Okay, I admit it. I knew decapitation wasn't going to kill me. It had never happened to me before, but I'd come back from having no remains at all. The way I saw it, being headless couldn't be all that bad. I hadn't even tried to dodge Tabitha. I used to think that the removal of the head was a reliable way to off a vampire. Of course, I also thought that having Roger eaten by werewolves was going to get rid of him for good. I guess some things just don't work when you're dealing with the high-end bad guys. You see, the idea was to let Tabitha blow off a little steam. I hadn't counted on getting jobbed by Rachel in the meantime.

Rachel loaded us all up into a moving van; my body went into one box (I didn't see what kind) and my head went into a red-and-white plastic cooler. In the box, I considered my options. I couldn't feel my body and, try as I might, I was incapable of speech. Similar to being staked through the heart, decapitation apparently completely paralyzed those that it did not kill . . . Or maybe since I hadn't been through postmortem syndrome, I still thought too much like a human and couldn't wrap my brain around moving something to which I was no longer attached. Either way, I would not be busting my body out of its box and reclaiming my own head. I tried.

When the box reopened and Rachel pulled me out, I looked around as well as I could. We were on the top floor of the Lovett Building. I recognized the big golden dome even from within. From the inside, the dome was semitransparent and the stars shone brighter than they appeared from downtown. The rest of me was already chained up in the center of an elaborate ritual setup. An oddly shaped metal tree held my body upright while one of its branches bore a sharpened piece of wood that pierced my heart. That particular branch was hinged so that it could be folded in or out, removing the stake and then shoving it back in.

A circle of white powder and cat's-eye marbles surrounded the tree. A golden pentagram had been etched into the floor so that the circle of marbles was in the middle. Five little black candles with blue flames decorated the points of the pentagram.

A series of raised bleachers had been arranged around the edges of the dome. They were empty except for the left side of the first few rows. On those rows sat an audience, mostly vampires that I'd seen before in The Velvet. In front of the bleachers was a small folding table with four chairs. J'iliol'lth sat in the left-most chair with two empty chairs to his right. The fourth chair held Ebon Winter.

Winter waved at me and strode over to my head. "Just so you know, I'm here on behalf of my sire to ensure that J'iliol'lth adheres to the rules. As are these," he gestured to the folks in the bleachers, but they didn't even look at him, eyes focused on J'iliol'lth, "fine people. I must say that I'm dreadfully disappointed in you. I abhor losing, especially after all I've done to aid you. You've still time to redeem yourself, however. The ritual doesn't start for a few minutes."

Looking over Winter's shoulder, I saw the bastard who'd been behind everything standing at a podium at the tip of the pentagram. If I'd still been connected to my body, I would have charged him without thinking.

Roger smiled at me from behind his book, a huge cliché of a volume—it might as well have had *Evil Book of Spells* embossed in gold on the cover—and gestured for Rachel to bring me closer. Roger had always been older than me and his vampiric embrace made him look older still. He wore thin reading glasses even though he no longer needed them. As affectations went, it just made him seem more bookish.

"Hey." He removed his glasses and rubbed his eyes. "You almost got me with the werewolf thing. I have to hand it to you, I never thought you'd have the brains to use backup. I always said all you had to do to rule the world was control your temper, your lust, and your tongue. When your abilities become mine, everyone will see how true that statement was."

He looked back at the book and then at my body. "Put his head on his body, Rachel. If I've correctly deciphered your notes, he'll need to be intact for the ritual. It should also help with the smell."

Rachel floated over the circle and placed my head upon my neck. She held my head in place with one hand and raised the hinged limb that held the stake in my heart. My transformation from separate to whole was almost instantaneous. Even my T-shirt was restored. Rachel drove the stake home again and my consciousness blurred; the buzz of the beer and the wine I'd had dropped me directly into the enlightened state of drunkenness where everything seems to make sense even when it really doesn't. Marilyn. Roger. Melvin. J'iliol'lth. Rachel. Ebon Winter. They all danced around in my head.

The cat's-eye marbles were soul prisons. I knew that because Melvin told me . . . Melvin who'd made sure that when I punched through the wall at Lady Gabriella's, there'd be a hole in the wards right where I needed it to be. Melvin who worked for Winter, who'd bet that I could win. I wondered what else Winter had done behind the scenes.

"Check his enchantment." Roger's voice rose in pitch, nearly to a squeak. "Make sure your anger-management spell is in place."

Familiar and friendly, Rachel's cinnamon magic washed over me. "He's fine," she said, then chuckled. "I even put in a little extra buzz. He's feeling no pain."

She walked away and came back out with Talbot, Greta, and Tabitha. They were bound by magic chains that moved across the floor in a serpentine manner. Greta and Tabitha had been staked. Rachel gestured, and the chains released the girls. Rachel propped them against the dome so they would have a good view of my death. The chain extended itself up along the dome as well, hanging Talbot next to them in the air.

My thoughts were slow, but smooth. I ran through my options with no sense of urgency or concern. I had all the time in the world to figure this out. Two minutes was an eternity. I had to find a way to kill Roger that didn't involve moving. I had to save Greta, Tabitha, and Talbot in the process. Then, I needed to kill J'iliol'lth. If I couldn't do any of those things, I still had to make sure that Roger lost.

He'd burned the Pollux and the Demon Heart. He'd been raping Marilyn; he'd made her his thrall so that she couldn't tell me about it. He'd used Rachel to get at me. Rachel. My partial thrall. That gave me an idea. When I'd made Rachel my thrall—or attempted to—the ritual had only worked partway because I didn't make a blood tattoo or say the ritual words. Is there a time restriction on completing the ritual? I asked myself. Or did I just have to . . .

Of course, they'd have to unstake me first or none of it would matter. The way I figured it, the entire reason everything had been so complicated was that Roger had wanted to be certain that I couldn't go Grape Ape on him, lose my temper, and turn into the uber vamp.

"Unstake him," Roger ordered. "He has to be intact for the spell to work. A hole in his chest might be a problem."

Rachel pretended to be aghast. "But Master, he could turn into a revenant and escape." This time, I could tell she was faking it and I think she meant for me to know. Rachel glanced pointedly toward the marbles. Cat's-eye marbles. Soul prisons. With a memory like mine, it's a miracle that I remembered. Maybe it was because Melvin looked like Dan Aykroyd or maybe it was the way he had geeked out over my revenant form, but the words Melvin had said stuck with me, word for word: *"When they come at you next, they'll try the soul prison route, but I can guarantee you they'll get nonguild labor to put it together. It'll look like a big cat's-eye marble—more than one, maybe. They're wicked powerful, but they'll shatter like glass if you hit them with a rock. Good luck."*

My plan didn't require a rock, but it did hinge on someone whose name began with the letter *R.*

"It's a risk we'll have to take," Roger ordered.

Rachel did as he asked, darting out of my reach, stopping just past the boundary created by the circle of stones. Did Roger think I was that stupid? Even without the info Melvin had laid on me, if I could go noncorporeal and escape, then all Roger's preparations made no sense. Unless he needed me to go noncorporeal . . . so that I would be a revenant so that his little ring of soul prisons could trap my ass. All I would have had to do was go ghost-mode and I would have been all Roger's.

For a split second, my rage broke through Rachel's spell and when it did, I saw Fang being unhooked from a tow truck, saw Beatrice pulling a tire iron out of his engine block. I heard the creak of metal as his inner workings slid back together and he repaired himself. In that instant, I knew what Fang was. When I had rage blackouts, the part of me that made decisions when I was so angry that I acted on instinct . . . that part of me was Fang. Somehow, when I'd come back, I'd come back in two pieces. And neither one of me was going to play along with Roger's undead makeover.

Roger. They must have taken the Stone of Aeternum out of my pants pocket before hanging me up on the tree, because Roger held it in his hands over the book. He looked smug. And a smug Roger is a stupid Roger. I needed time for my backup to arrive. Fang felt close, but I couldn't tell exactly how close. Still, stalling wasn't the problem. The real problem was Rachel. I needed her to be closer. Much closer. How could I get Roger to send her over here?

The answer was simple: act like me. As Roger saw me, I was a loud obnoxious dickhead with a soft spot for his friends, a hopeless romantic with no real sense of romance, a guy who'd make life-altering decisions on a whim, a guy who doesn't hold anything back. Fine.

"So," I asked, "Roger—how's it feel to be a fuck-up?"

"Excuse me?" he asked.

"I'm supposed to turn into my ghost form—a revenant or whatever—and come flying at you, is that it? It's a good plan, but it's sloppy, just like you. And it ain't gonna happen. You can't just use the Stone of Aeternum on me and get it over with, can you?"

"Eric, Eric, Eric," Roger tut-tutted, "I have no idea what you mean."

"You really do think I'm that stupid, don't you? Look. This may surprise you, Roger, but I really don't care what happens to me. I'll do what you want, but you have to agree to let Talbot, Tabitha, and Greta go. You have to agree not to act against them unless they physically assault you and I mean no egging them on. No bothering them. No sending other people after them. You also have to reimburse Greta for the cash she paid to buy back my buildings and my stuff. Oh, and you also have to let Tabitha keep the suite at the Highland Towers."

Roger licked his lips, leaving a thin trail of red behind. "She'll have to agree to stay out of my way."

"Fine."

He said, "Done. Witnessed by Ebon Winter, J'iliol'lth, and the others present. Turn into your ghost form and fly toward me."

"One last thing," I said.

"What?" he asked.

"I want to kiss Rachel good-bye."

"I don't know," Roger said carefully. "You might try to kill her."

"Do you need her for the ritual?" I asked.

He bit his lip, removed his glasses, and rubbed his eyes again before putting them back on. "No."

"Then what? You're afraid of me? I'm chained to a magic post here. What the fuck am I gonna do? God, you're such a coward."

"Don't call me that."

"Yes, why call a spade a spade?" Winter laughed. Roger glared at him. "Oh, don't mind me," Winter continued, placing a hand to his chest. "Do what you will. I'm not the one who'll have to live it down. Rabbit Roger, the Yellow Vlad of Void City. It has a certain poetry to it, don't you think?" The audience in the bleachers went off like a laugh track, right on cue to push Roger over the edge. Looking across the room, I noticed Beatrice had slipped into the room unnoticed. She took a seat near some of the others and laughed inconspicuously on cue.

Roger cursed. "Do it," he told Rachel.

"I agree to kiss him and then we're straight? I'm free to go, but on retainer?" Rachel asked. And then I saw Rachel's plan, too, because we both had the same plan. She'd played her part to the hilt trying to make sure that I had enough info to figure it out.

Roger nodded, but she wasn't looking at him. She was looking at J'iliol'lth. The demon nodded, too. He withdrew a thick stack of papers from a metal briefcase and turned to the last page. The vampires around him strained to get a look at it. J'iliol'lth cut his finger letting viscous brown nonblood drip onto a signet ring. He held it poised over the paper.

"The moment you kiss him," J'iliol'lth assured her, "I'll mark your contract fulfilled. The mortgage on your soul will be paid in full and you will be free."

Rachel floated toward me, barely suppressing a smile, and I had butterflies in my stomach. *I can't tell you what to do,* her voice whispered in my head, *but please tell me you've figured it out.* It could have been what remained of the steak and the beer, or it could have been that I was about to bet my unlife on a mouthful of blood, my ability to force Roger out of Rachel's head, and one undead Mustang convertible circa 1964. I normally worry about tests, but I'd already done a practice run on this one, pushing Roger's own sire out of Ebony's head and my faith in Fang was unwavering. After all, if you can't trust yourself . . . ?

37

ERIC:

THE POWER OF SPIT

When you become a vampire, one of the first things you notice, aside from the hunger, is how gross everything can be. You have to be careful licking your lips or you'll leave a trail of blood. Roger did that all the time; it was a basically disgusting habit.

All your bodily fluids are replaced with blood. When your mouth waters, you have to be very fastidious about drool. Bloodstains are hard to get out and drooling blood on your date can be a total deal breaker. When Rachel walked toward me, my mouth filled with what passed for saliva and I let it pool.

She had conditioned me to find her attractive and I did. Her presence was intoxicating and standing in the same room with her was all it took to make me crave her touch, her taste. Floating over the white powder into the circle, she touched my cheek and smiled.

"It's a shame it has to be this way," she said with apparently genuine regret. "You're the best lover I've ever had and I really do like you."

Leaning in for the kiss, she touched the back of my head, ran her fingers through my hair. Her lips parted. Her eyes closed and I spat a mouthful of blood onto her cheek. Shrieking involuntarily, she drew back and slapped my face.

Please, please, please, her thoughts hit me.

I concentrated on the blood, willing it to move according to my wishes. It slid across her left cheek, changing colors, taking the shape I desired: a butterfly. She wiped her hand across her face in disgust. When it came away clean, her eyes widened and she stared at her hand without comprehension until I started saying the words. It was the best acting job I'd ever seen.

"I mark thee and bind thee," I incanted quickly, "Master to servant. Servant to master. You are mine until I set you free. You are mine. So mote it be."

As before, I felt pain, but this time it was a pleasure. Across the room, Roger glared at me. Our eyes met. My mind touched his. *I said you were a fuck-up.*

Roger's thoughts were as slippery as he was. I forced him from Rachel's psyche, trying to keep a grip on his mind with mine. He wriggled free once, but I caught him again and hung on. "Rachel!" I hissed between gritted teeth, "Release me."

It has to be an order, she thought at me. Mentally, I made it a command.

Roger's mouth opened and closed like a fish animated by Art Babbitt. Out of the corner of my eye, I saw Rachel glance at J'iliol'lth, saw her smile when she confirmed that he'd already made his mark on her contract. A single word from her unlocked the shackles, dropping them and me. I slid down the metal tree onto my knees.

"I think you probably need to be mad now," she said and I felt the artificial calm that had been plaguing me drop away. Her soft caress brought my anger roiling back and with it, I saw a vision of Fang, driving up the wall of the Lovett Building.

"Now sic 'em!" I spat. I made that an order, too. . . . Just in case. Rachel giggled and turned on our audience, blue fire at her fingertips.

"He thought his way out of it," Winter told J'iliol'lth with glee. "I win again! Isn't it marvelous?"

Roger's mind was slippery on the surface, strong and ordered beneath. Mine was absolutely chaotic, but I had fought several vampires mind to mind, I'd gone through the thralldom ritual, the real one, more than once, and from the feel of things, Marilyn may have been his only thrall. It gave me power, perspective. Besides, he had it coming from way back.

Roger's fingers involuntarily relaxed and the Stone of Aeternum rolled across the floor. J'iliol'lth dived over the table to get the stone. Beatrice beat him to it. The rest of the audience ran like hell, and a communal scream went up among them as Fang crashed through the dome of the Lovett Building and landed on the middle of the group. Shards of gold-tinted glass rained down on the crowd as "Bodies" by Drowning Pool blared from the Mustang's speakers.

The half-dozen vamps beneath Fang's undercarriage pushed against him as one, only to shriek even louder when the flesh on their hands and forearms ripped free with the sound of tearing fabric. It flattened against Fang and sank into the metal. Inch by rapid inch, they were taken, stripped, shucked, and digested by my *memento mori.*

The ones he missed, Rachel nailed with dots of blue flame that caught and spread. They burned one by one, each adding to the blaze like a book of lit matches.

In the soft blue light, Winter pulled the stake out of Tabitha and pointed her toward Greta. He touched Talbot's chain and gave an unintelligible command. Instantly the chains fell away, rapidly slithering into a neat coil at Winter's feet. Once Tabitha freed Greta, I stopped watching the world outside my mind's eye and turned all my attention on my ex-best friend Roger.

"You can't fight me this way, Eric. You can barely think! You're little more than an animal," Roger said, lashing out at me mentally. I made no effort to defend myself, continuing my charge deep into his psyche. If he wanted to tear holes in my mind, he was welcome to it, so long as I got him, too.

"I let you go the first time. After everything you did, I tried to let you go," I roared. "I would have let you go this time, too. But I had to watch Marilyn burn, not just her body, her soul. I could have made her young again if she'd been my thrall. We could have been together this whole fucking time!"

"You didn't deserve her," he shouted back. "She never even loved you." He was a quick study. Shields popped up around his mind and I battered them down. His mental self manifested armor, a sword, and a shield. My mental self just looked like me. He cut deeply with the psychic sword and blood gushed from my image.

"Didn't deserve her?" I concentrated on what it was like to be the uber vamp, focused on my rage, and sent it at Roger with a roar. Mental-me grew wings and black skin. In my head, I was the uber vamp. Roger shit himself. I guess in his head, his mental version of himself, he was still human.

"The stones, the ones in the circle, are called spirit wardens. I could have trapped you and then elevated myself to Vladhood. Then I could have used your spirit to become what you are."

"Except that you can only ascend once every century," Tabitha snarled. "If you'd ever asked Phillip, he could have told you that."

I blinked and glanced about. I hadn't realized that we were also speaking aloud.

Roger looked angrily at J'iliol'lth and I charged across the pentagram toward him in the physical world, trying to do the same in his mind. He threw himself backward in an awkward flip, but he wasn't close to fast enough once I hit top speed. I felt like a coke-head mainlining for the first time. The rush rattled my teeth and numbed my tongue. Mint assailed my nostrils and I lashed out at the source without taking my eyes off Roger. J'iliol'lth screamed to my left and my hand came back covered in brown goop.

"Wanna know something really scary, Roger?" I shouted. "I'm not even going to kill you!"

I caught him by the neck and snapped his spine, my actions echoing from the physical world into the mental battleground in which we fought.

"You raped my fiancée, murdered her, and sold her soul to a demon!" I reached down, grabbed a fistful of crotch and tore off everything I'd seized. Roger desperately clawed and slashed at me, leaving long bloody wounds on my chest and shoulders.

"You should have stayed dead!" Plunging my fist through his sternum, I wrapped my fingers around his heart. He turned into a frog and squirmed free of my grasp. As he leapt free, he became human again and then went from human to bat, flying for the hole in the dome, flapping toward freedom. "Come back here, you sonovabitch!" I swore, just as a shot rang out from across the room.

Roger burst into flames to the sound of John Paul Courtney's laughter. "Ain't no way I'm gonna sit through another fight with that one." Courtney's ghost blew across the barrel of *El Alma Perdida* and met my eyes. "That's yore one shot. Now git it done."

I dragged the flaming shape-locked bat that was Roger into the pentagram next to the ring of spirit wardens, ignoring the flames that coursed from him to me. His tiny heart popped with all the resistance of a crack whore's virtue. I tore off his head and let it burn. As his body did the same, one of the spirit wardens shone a vibrant green. Roger's remains crumbled into powder. The flames vanished with him.

I picked up the spirit warden and inside, barely visible to the naked eye, a miniature Roger, humanoid, screamed and pounded on the walls of his tiny mystic prison, spectral flames blazing brightly on his back.

Rachel looked over my shoulder and laughed. "Oh my God. I didn't know they worked that way. That is so cool! We should kill J'iliol'lth over one of these, too. That way he can't mess with my—"

"No."

The disgusting demon stood at the top of the ruined bleachers, back to the gaping hole Fang had left there. Beatrice was sitting in Fang's passenger seat. A menacing engine rev made J'iliol'lth twitch, but he stayed put.

"Eric," J'iliol'lth crooned, "you won! Now we can make you a true immortal—"

"No," I said again. "You think I don't know that you did all this? You put Roger out front, your little red flag to make the bull charge, but he couldn't have done this without your help. Him I understand. He hated me. But you did all this for a magic rock."

"I *am* a demon," J'iliol'lth said.

"You get eaten."

J'iliol'lth leapt backward, turning in one smooth motion as filthy, bracken-covered wings erupted from his jacket. I ran after him, the transformation to uber vamp effortless.

"He's getting away," Tabitha shouted.

"Not today." I grabbed Talbot under his arms and took him with me, the two of us shooting through the hole in the Lovett Building's golden dome in hot pursuit of the demon, the cold air of the December evening chilling my flesh, seeping into my bones. It felt like old times.

✦ **38** ✦

ERIC:

DEMONS DON'T GET DO-OVERS

I didn't see him. "Where'd he go?" I shouted. I'd spent more time flying as a bat than as the uber vamp and the uber vamp didn't have radar. The long leathery wings sported by my vampiric form fell somewhere between the wings I sported as a normal-size chiroptera and the wings of a seagull—the membrane didn't stretch and flex the same. My ghost time hadn't provided me any useful practice, either.

"Three o'clock," Talbot answered.

"Where?"

Jill blended in against the cityscape, the dark office buildings in their power-saver modes.

"Now two o'clock," Talbot yelled.

I saw him, a flash of demon backlit by the lights of the Void City Metro Bank building—its windows decorated for Christmas, tinted to make patterns: a candy cane on one side, a narrow Christmas tree on the other. Jill flittered mothlike past the alternating red and white, whipping past the corner of the building. He was too fast, too used to flying.

"Damn it!"

Talbot slapped my bicep. "You've got to get him before he makes it to another locus point."

"A what?"

"J'iliol'lth is a lesser lord," Talbot said. "A Nefario. He can only transition between this plane and his own at mystical loci, like the Lovett Building."

"But we just left there."

"Your car broke the dome. Some loci have to be amplified to function. The dome has to be in perfect condition or it won't work."

"Go team!"

We cut around the bank, swinging too wide as Talbot's weight threw me off and I lost J'iliol'lth. Increasing my wingbeat cycle, I angled upward, giving myself a better view. Void City stretched out beneath us, a city in denial—its lights never bright enough to pierce the shadows of magic that concealed its supernatural inhabitants from their mundane neighbors—the lone city in America where creatures of the night could roam unremembered.

"I've lost him," Talbot snarled.

"Name another place he can escape from."

"The Highland Towers, the . . ." Talbot's words were lost in the wind as I shot toward the Highland Towers, buildings passing beneath me, cars moving along the street completely unaware of the struggle going on above their heads.

"Do you see him?"

"Six o'clock!" Talbot pointed and I spotted the demon and dived. He was making for Lord Phil's snooty-ass home for the tragically upper crust, but he wheeled away as I flew at him, flying higher as he all but vanished against the night sky.

All I had to do was get Talbot close enough to claw and bite, but J'iliol'lth knew that just as well as I did. We flew up until Void City diminished beneath us. J'iliol'lth darted into a bank of dark moisture-rich clouds and I followed, plunging blind into the billowy gray of what might soon be a storm. Maybe it meant we'd have a white Christmas, but if I couldn't catch Jill, I wouldn't be celebrating.

Through a gauzy skein of clouds, I saw Void City as I'd never before seen her—all sparkling lights and wonder, from the newly refinished halls of the Ellery Academy to the condemned church that sat vacant in downtown, more castle than steepled edifice of worship. The spotlights from the Iversonian lit J'iliol'lth for one second in the sky, the light rendering him translucent. I strained up, kicking backward in the sky, raised Talbot over my head . . . and threw him at the demon.

I missed.

Talbot plunged through the night sky in an unerring arc toward the ground. He didn't scream. Arms and legs spread to catch the winds and slow his progress, Talbot looked over his shoulder. "You better catch my ass, Eric."

J'iliol'lth's laughter rang out, that same unpleasant rattle of crunching bass and high-pitched whinny. He followed me down, lighting upon the decorative cornice of a high-rise apartment building to watch. I could have gone after him then, surprised him, and let Talbot fall, but I don't abandon my friends.

"Try to land on your feet, mouser," Jill crowed.

With a muttered curse (I don't remember which one, maybe it was several), I pushed myself as far as I could go, finding the optimum rhythm to the uber vamp's unfamiliar wingbeat cycles, getting maximum positive and negative pressure. In my head, I pictured Talbot as Greta's popsicle star and J'iliol'lth as my Christmas tree. I zipped through the air, seizing Talbot with my legs, carrying him at an angle to slow his fall, then angling up again in an arc. It would have been much easier with bat senses.

The demon moved at the last instant, forcing me to skew to the left or plunge Talbot directly into the concrete that had previously served as J'iliol'lth's perch.

"You really suck at this, Eric," Talbot shouted.

"You want me to throw you at him again?"

"No!"

I did it anyway, twirling him in the air as if I were one of those big East German chicks competing in the hammer toss back in the '64 Olympics. Talbot screamed that time, but it wasn't a curse or a cry of terror, it was one name: mine. I still think he could have snagged J'iliol'lth if he'd have only reached a little harder. I went after Talbot and J'iliol'lth slowed to watch.

Hurtling toward the ground, I caught Talbot again, moving faster. J'iliol'lth didn't wait to see what I would do, winging it for the Highland Towers. I was accelerating again, but the demon had a head start.

"Do. Not. Throw. Me."

"Just one last time."

"No!"

"Fine."

I flew at a downward angle, letting gravity help to increase my speed. Concentrating on the feel of my wings, the ways they pushed and pulled against the air, I searched for the familiar feeling, the optimum wingbeat cycle I'd managed the first time I caught Talbot . . . then I was in the zone. Flying is like jazz. It has a rhythm, a beat, it changes, but when it's done right, even the improvisations sound like they belong. In a race between a moth and a bat, the bat wins. It's simple aerodynamics: bats are faster, more maneuverable, even more efficient.

Realizing he could no longer outrun me, Jill began hugging the buildings, trying to shake me off, but I was used to carrying Talbot and being undead meant my stamina was not a problem.

"Why doesn't he set me on fire or something?" I asked Talbot.

"He can't. Nefarios can channel power into others, but they don't have much of their own."

"He should have carried a gun," I said.

"Huh?"

"It wouldn't have hurt me much or very long, but he could have put a couple of holes in my wings . . ."

We both got quiet, paranoid that having spoken of the possibility would bring it to pass.

J'iliol'lth made it as far as the parking deck across the street from the Highland Towers before I crashed into him at full speed. Three of us—demon, vampire, and mouser—tumbled across the upper deck. Jill came up first, turning to fly when Talbot landed on him in a flash of white. Fully transformed, Talbot stood only an inch or two shorter than the uber vamp. A silver mane, matching the shock of fur at the tip of his tail, stood out in stark contrast against the thick sable fur covering the body of an anthropomorphized lion. The silver hair shimmered, casting a faint light that blended with the ambient glow emitted by Talbot's star emerald eyes.

J'iliol'lth screamed in pain, clutching at the now flaming shoulder into which Talbot had sunk his claws (also silver), the tips sinking down into the bone. Talbot growled, baring fangs that matched his claws, pearlescent luminance escaping his mouth.

"Please," Jill shouted, imploring me, not Talbot. "I'll do anything."

"I already told you, Jill." I took a step forward as Talbot ripped the wings from the demon's back with one casual jerk of his left hand. "You get eaten." I watched as Talbot devoured sizzling pieces of demon. I listened to the screams.

"How did he taste?" I asked.

"Like chicken," Talbot answered, his mouth full.

In spite of everything, I laughed.

John Paul Courtney's ghost manifested on the deck, leaning against a BMW. "Good job, son. You shouldn't 'a made no deal with it in the first place, but you did right in the end." He tipped his hat to me and faded away. *El Alma Perdida* lay on the hood of the BMW next to a western-style gun belt. "Don't forget that I fired that bullet at Roger on good faith, son." His voice echoed in the open air. "You remember the price."

"Ghosts." Talbot shook his head, then went back to licking the flecks of demon from his fur.

"What about your other five shots?" I asked my ancestor.

"One at a time, son. Just remember the price for this one."

Yeah, I remembered the price: no killing Gabriella. Just as well . . . I didn't want to kill her anyway. Lord Phillip had messed with her enough that as long as she left my crew alone, I had no reason to start a fight.

The squeal of tires preceded Fang's arrival. By the time Tabitha, Rachel, and Beatrice had climbed out of the car, Talbot had reverted to normal, bits of J'iliol'lth still trailing from his mouth. There wasn't much left. He slurped up the last few shreds and forced himself to swallow.

"Damn it," Rachel snarled. "You fucking cat, if we could have imprisoned him, I might have been able to keep the pyromancy. Now, I'll be lucky if I can light a goddam match!"

"Good," I whispered.

"I knew there was a reason cats freaked me out," Rachel said, shuddering.

"I didn't know how else to kill him," Talbot explained. "It was the only way to be sure." And that was why I'd kept Talbot with me ever since El Segundo. Oni won't eat other demons. They have a code. They won't even fight them. But if you have a demon that you just can't kill, if you have to be one hundred percent sure that it's dead and gone, a mouser is the only way to go.

Beatrice handed me the Stone of Aeternum. Rachel picked up the gun belt and slid it around my waist. Beatrice handed me the pistol and as I holstered it, Tabitha sighed and turned away. She looked hurt, angry, unable to even meet my gaze. We had a lot to talk about and I sure as hell had things to answer for, but first I had a little unfinished business.

39

ERIC:

BACK AT THE HIGHLAND

Nobody bugged me when I walked into the Highland Towers. Maybe they all knew what had happened. Someone with access to the Lovett Building must have had hidden cameras on the roof, a spy, a crystal ball, even if it was just to let them know that they could rent out J'iliol'lth's office space to some other demon. Then again, there had also been Winter's audience. Those guys were probably tearing up the phone lines yapping, at least, the few that survived Fang's assault and Rachel's flambé action. I stopped off at the Rose Suite and rang the bell to be nice. Esteban answered the door, the bruises around his dark blue eyes eminently recognizable through the door slot.

"Well, you sure heal slowly for a thrall."

"It seems that since my injuries were caused by an Emperor, my mistress's healing gifts—"

"I don't really care, I was just being polite. I'm done now, at least when it comes to you. Where's Gabriella?"

"Lady Gabriella is indisposed at the—"

I took a deep breath and spoke to him in a language I knew he'd understand: bullshit. "Tell the Lady that His Highness Eric of Void City would greatly appreciate a moment of her time. She needn't come outside. We may even converse through the door if she so desires, but I have news of the utmost gravity and I want her to hear it from me."

Esteban retreated and twenty-seven seconds later, Gabriella opened the spy slot at the top of the door. "You sounded almost cordial."

"Yeah, I guess." I cleared my throat. "Roger lost. He's dead and this needs to be the end of it. Come after me or mine . . . threat, threat,

threat . . . You get the idea. Stay out of my way, let it go, and I'll try to steer clear of your business. You lost a son, but he screwed my fiancée, murdered her, and sold her soul to a demon. He destroyed my club and my movie palace, wrecked my Mustang, and tried to suck out my soul. By vampire rules, I ought to come after you, because you knew about it and because you're his sire, but I'm willing to let bygones be bygones if you are. So—are you?"

While she thought it over, I popped my knuckles one at a time and stared at the ceiling. "It will be as you wish, Highness."

"Fuckin' A," I told her. "I didn't want to kill you anyway. It would have made a cowboy I know very unhappy." She coughed and I headed up to Phillip's place before she could say another word.

Phillip's door was already open and I walked right in. The old schemer was sitting at his desk writing in a journal. His pen moved with great speed upon the page, covering the blank white expanse with odd symbols and cryptic notes. He held up a finger, finished his sentence, and met my gaze. *"Acta est fabula, plaudite."*

"No, thanks, I'll leave the applause to others." I reached into my pocket and pulled out the Stone of Aeternum.

"I thought you would bring this back to me." He rose, retrieved a black case, and opened it to reveal a bunch of other little trinkets.

"I'm not sure I'm giving it back to you," I said.

For the first time I got to see Phillip's eyes glow red. It was a quick flash, but I'd seen it. Nice to know I could rattle his cage.

"Can this thing really be used to make me immortal?" I asked.

"It could." He still sounded huffy. "You would need to place it inside your heart."

"Sounds easy."

"And then cure your vampirism while it was contained within."

"How do you suggest I do that?" I asked.

"Violently," Phillip purred, "the same way you do everything."

"I suppose I deserved that. Are we going to have a problem if I want to give it a try?"

"If you haven't accomplished your goal by the time I need the Stone returned to me—"

"I'll give it back to you. You have my word."

"May I do the honors?" he asked. I turned it over in my hand before passing it off to him. *"Ad vitam aeternum, mi amice. Alea iacta est."* He drove his hand toward my chest, pushing the stone into place without breaking the skin. You've gotta love magic.

"That was easier than the way I had planned on doing it," I told him. "What was it you said?"

"To eternal life, my friend," Phillip repeated, "the die has been cast." He winked at me. "I thought you spoke Latin."

"Not as well as you."

Phillip clapped me on the arm. "It went well, then?" he asked. "The confrontation?"

"I'm still the walking dead," I answered with a shrug. "I still have girl trouble, not to mention an undead car. And I'm still broke."

"Not exactly," Phillip chuckled. "I've arranged for your identity to be reinstated. Your accounts have been reopened. I have people trying to reclaim the most sentimental of your possessions. It may take some time."

"Thanks."

"Think nothing of it. In addition, Roger's possessions and monetary resources are to be transferred to you. I did take a small percentage of the total as a handler's fee, but the bulk of the fortune remains."

"How much of a handler's fee?" I asked.

"Thirty-three and one-third percent," he said, looking me over.

"You're a crook," I said with a trace of amusement, "but I'll take it."

"I thought you might." He nodded. "I've also arranged for an additional suite of rooms here to be converted to your use. It's the least we, the residents of Highland Towers, can do, based on the inexcusable behavior of our fellow tenant. Your Ebony is already upstairs with the children. She has awakened. I've sent someone to show Beatrice, Rachel, Tabitha, Magbidion and . . . Talbot the way to them as well."

"I'll probably only stay until I rebuild the Pollux," I told him.

"What about your exotic dance hall?" he asked. "I always meant to go and see it."

Shaking my head, I withdrew the spirit warden containing Roger's soul. "Haven't you heard? I've decided to open a bowling alley instead. Seriously, I have enough girl problems without that place. Besides, Marilyn died there . . . it'd be too weird."

Phillip's eyes followed the glowing green sphere in my hand, watching Roger's impotent rage. "And that?" Phillip asked.

I tossed it to him. "A souvenir. If I keep it, he'll probably get loose or something. Someone will break it or one of Ebony's kids will swallow it . . . I thought you could put it in a little case next to Percy's. It could read *Exhibit B*."

Staring deep into the spirit warden, Phillip shook it vigorously and watched the perpetually burning Roger within dissipate and re-form. "Priceless. I adore it. I'll send up something your young lady will like, a peace offering for you to give to her. We'll speak about the other matter in a few days' time, after you've settled in."

"What other matter?" I asked.

"Your trip to Paris," he said.

"I'm going to Paris?"

Phillip clutched his hands together. "I hope I'm not speaking out of turn, but it does make quite a romantic spot for a honeymoon."

"And who's getting married?"

"Unless I miss my guess, you are, to your young Queen, Lady Tabitha. It's also where your sire now lives. Am I right in assuming that during your fight with Roger, you experienced no difficulties in accessing your vampiric abilities?"

I kicked in the speed, dropped it, kicked it again. "Well, I'll be damned," I swore.

"No, you won't," John Paul's voice echoed.

Phillip glanced about the room. "What was that?"

"My conscience," I told him.

"That's what one gets for asking," he said. "The increasing reliability of your powers signifies a decline in the enchantment that shielded you from your sire, as well as the nearness of your *memento mori*. You'll need to think carefully about whether or not to take the car with you when you go to Paris. The further you are from it, the greater the likelihood that you'll begin to experience a certain amount of unreliability once more."

"Wait. You think I'm just going to go running after my sire just because you told me where she is?"

"To thine own self be true." He gazed up at me, fluttering his eyelashes. "And besides, you are a Courtney."

"You suck," I told him. Phillip nodded, turning back to the little marble in his hand, and I left him happily tormenting Roger. At the very least, I figured that Percy might feel better, knowing there were fates not only worse than death, but worse than his. Phillip would torture Roger in ways I'd never conceived of, and he'd do it consistently until he'd run out of new and inventive ways to make his existence hell. If I'd taken Roger home with me, I would have forgotten about him in a week or two. Roger deserved worse than that.

Dennis met me in the elevator and showed me to my rooms. Bea was up there running interference between Rachel and Tabitha. Talbot sat on an overstuffed ottoman, trying to stay out of it. If I could have done the same, I would have. Magbidion walked in from one of the bedrooms. I thanked him and told him that Beatrice was in charge while Tabitha and I were gone. I made sure Rachel heard me and I took Tabitha by the arm. "Can we go for a ride and talk?" I asked.

"Are you sure you wouldn't like to take Rachel?" It was just more of

Tabitha's shit, but I took it because during the last few days when all the bad stuff happened, even when she'd been ripping off my head, I'd come to understand the truth: I'd never love anyone the way I loved Marilyn, but Tabitha was the only girlfriend I'd had since I died that I missed when she walked away, that I worried about. Maybe what I feel for her isn't love, but then again, maybe it's as close as an old dead man like me is ever likely to get.

"I'm sure." I reached out with my mind and felt Greta in another room nearby, watching the news on television. Ebony was in there with her, groggy, but awake. It even felt like the lights were starting to come back on inside her mind. "Come on," I told Tabitha. "Let's get out of here. Are you hungry? I thought maybe we could hunt?"

"I suppose," she said with reluctance.

40

TABITHA:

NOT A ROMANTIC BONE

Eric took us out in his Mustang, which he introduced to me, finally, as Fang. While Eric was opening the door for me, I gave the 'Stang a surreptitious little pat on the hood, still grateful for its help in the parking deck fight.

Eric and I hunted through the city streets, two predators, a mated pair. I was still angry at him, but he was so sorry, like a little puppy dog, that it was hard to stay mad. Eric had taken me hunting. He never took anyone hunting with him, not even Greta. Would Eric have taken a "moist warm tightness" hunting? I think not. The moon was hidden behind the clouds above us and it felt like it might rain.

After picking up two late-night shoppers, we drove Fang over to the ruins of the Pollux and the Demon Heart. Christmas lights dotted downtown right up to the edge of Eric's property. The last sign of yuletide cheer was a blinking stocking hung over the enclosed bus stop. Not the most romantic setting. I told him as much.

"Not exactly what I'd planned," he admitted. "I meant to be driving out to the old Eighth Street church, to look at the Christmas lights and the nativity scene. Fang wanted to come here, instead."

"We can drive out there later, if you want," I offered. "I understand if you want to look at the Pollux for a while." I wasn't entirely sure if I was talking to Eric or Fang.

Eric hopped out of the car. "Son of a bitch!" he shouted. He ran for the theater, transforming into the uber vamp as he ran, exchanging strides for flaps of his massive wings, flying across the rubble, burrowing deep into the ashes.

Heartbeats.

I got out of the car. Three sets of heartbeats.

He pulled three of his whores out of the wreckage: Gladys, Erin, and Cheryl. They looked badly burned, but the burns were healing. Rachel had set them on fire and left them for dead. Sally and Jodi hadn't fared as well. They were gone.

Watching him fuss over them made me realize something about him. He really does care, not just about me, but about things, people. I don't think I've ever met another vampire who cared about someone they just met, especially humans. Even I don't and I haven't been a vampire long.

"Anything I can do to help?" I asked.

"Testing a theory," he said. He cut through his forearm with his claws, spraying the still cooling blood of the night's kill on his trollops. The effect was impressive, but not impressive enough for him. I could see his disappointment. I think he wanted them to be good as new when the first drop of blood touched their skin. "I don't know why I didn't sense them before," he told me. "I mean, my thrall sense got kinda shorted out when the fire started and everyone started burning, but damn. And the firefighters just left them here . . . fucking enchantment on the stupid fucking city . . . probably didn't even see them."

Or Stacey was there and he didn't care, because he knew you were broke, I thought.

We loaded them into Fang's backseat and sat down on the bench at the bus stop under the blinking light of the lone illuminated stocking. "Damn it," he swore.

"They'll be okay, Eric. Won't they? It seems like they'll be okay." I sat next to him on the bench and put my head on his shoulder. He shrank back to normal size.

"I think they'll be fine," he sighed. "It isn't that."

"What is it?"

"I thought we could do something a little different, tonight."

"Different how?" I asked. Eric put his hand on my thigh and looked at me, really looked at me.

"I needed to do something important tonight." He took his hand off my thigh. I slowly cranked up my body heat; unthinkingly, he put his hand back down. Storm clouds gathered in his eyes and the blue of his irises waxed brighter until they were a deep luminous purple.

"I've only ever done this once before and for all the other ways in which I'm a modern man, I think that I wanted this to stay old-fashioned," his attention shifted to Fang, "if that's okay with you."

My heart stirred within my breast and I closed my eyes and squelched it with all my might. "It's kind of sweet, I guess."

He reached into his pocket and handed me a diamond solitaire. It still smelled like the woman he'd taken it off of, the late-night shopper. She'd been about my size.

"That's your idea of a proposal?" I asked. It was what I wanted, but not the way I wanted it. The little voice in my head was screaming for me to shut up and just be happy, but one thing I'd learned since becoming a vampire is that I'm special. Could I go through eternity with someone who thought handing me a dead woman's ring at a bus stop was romantic? Eric took me for granted and I was tired of it, as much as I loved him.

"I . . . yes." He checked the car again, worried about his thralls. I turned his face back to me with a gentle touch.

"Look at me, Eric. You made me a vampire and then you tried to get rid of me because it made you uncomfortable. Is that going to happen again? Do you really love me or are you just saying that because you lost Marilyn and you need someone to cling to?" As I was talking, my brain kept screaming for my mouth to shut up and my lungs kept trying to start working again. My heart wanted to beat, my blood wanted to pump; I was having a hard time keeping a lid on everything.

"It's not the same love I felt for her, Tabitha. I won't lie about that, but, what I do feel for you—I think it's love, too." He took my hand when he said it and squeezed it tight. "I thought you were dead. When the Pollux was on fire and I felt Greta burning, I thought you were both dead. That's when I knew. I didn't really love Marilyn anymore. I miss her, but only because we were close, familiar. I must have stopped loving her so long ago that I can't remember what it was like."

"I love you, Eric. I love you so much I'm stupid about it. Whatever you want to do, in or out of the bedroom, I want to say yes, just because you want to do it, but I can't let you treat me this way." My lips trembled and a tear ran down my face. From the smell I could tell it was a real tear, a human tear, not blood, and I felt more relieved than I can say. "If we stay together, you can't go screwing around on me."

"Tabitha." He put a hand on my shoulder. "It's like this, when I'm thinking straight, that's fine, but I don't always think straight. Some demon is always using some spell on me. There is always some evil plot. Roger's gone and Jill's destroyed, but Phillip says that I have a sire to worry about, a sire who is as powerful as I am and will definitely want to screw things up for me."

"You just want a loophole so that you can sleep with Rachel." I pouted.

"She's something else that we have to talk about." He sighed. "I know that she did some terrible things, but she did them to get herself out of Hell, to get her life back, and when push came to shove, she did what she could to make sure I figured out how to defeat Roger and that J'iliol'lth was behind it all."

"I know." I chewed my lip. Eric opened his mouth to say something else, but I spoke first. "You don't get to sleep with her," I blurted.

"I know."

"And no three-ways . . . at least not with her."

He grinned and I either had to slap him or kiss him.

We kissed and Eric's hands roamed over my torso in a way that I'd missed since joining the ranks of the undead. We necked the way only vampires can and our clothes made their way to the concrete next to the bench one article at a time.

"We're in a bus stop," I complained.

"I thought you said you wanted to do anything I wanted to do." He laid me down on the pile of our clothes, the corners of my mouth drawn involuntarily into a smirk. I had said that.

"I still want a ring," I said as he entered me.

"I got you a ring."

"A ring of my own." I bit him gently on the ear.

"You'll get one," he promised. "A big one."

"And a church wedding," I added.

"Okay, sure, we'll figure it out."

As we neared climax, I couldn't resist: "Where do you want to go on our honeymoon?"

"Paris," he said breathlessly.

"Why?" I asked.

"So that we'll always have it," he answered.

It was the right answer. "I love you," I told him.

"Thanks," he said. It wasn't what I wanted to hear, but it was enough.

✦ **41** ✦

ERIC:

LOOSE ENDS

About an hour before bedtime, Phillip delivered on his promise. He sent up a new wardrobe of various fashions for Tabitha. Three weeks' worth of clothes, underwear, and lingerie, all enchanted to do this funky color-changing thing. He'd even had everything all wrapped up for Christmas. She loved it and when I tucked her into bed, she was wearing one of her new nighties.

The headboard and footboard were paneled in Brazilian rosewood; it had been my parents' bed. I'd wondered what had happened to it when Dad died. Now I knew. Like so many other things, Roger had helped himself to it. I held Tabitha as she settled in and once she was asleep, I climbed out of bed, went to the phone, and dialed room service.

"Room service," said a sultry female voice.

"I need you to get Dennis on the phone."

"I can't, Sire," she apologized. "He won't arise until tomorrow evening. When he does, I'd be happy to deliver a message for you."

"Arise?" I asked.

"He was selected during the night, fifty or sixty minutes ago. Lord Phillip was very pleased with him."

"I'll bet," I observed. "He'll be missed. So are you the new girl?"

"I might be the favorite for the next round," she admitted. "My name's Wendy."

"What happens to the applicants who fail, Wendy?"

"They are presented to the chosen one as gifts to do with as he or she pleases."

"So Dennis won the guy round and you're hoping to win the girl round, huh?"

"Yes, milord."

"Maybe you can help me after all, Wendy. Is Lord Phillip still awake?"

"One moment and I'll check." She put me on hold and I listened to Prokofiev's *Peter and the Wolf* while I waited.

"He is, Lord Eric," she said when she came back. "I'll connect you."

"Eric, my boy," Phillip said, "what can I do for you?"

"I wanted to call and thank you for the clothes," I told him. "I especially like the way you had Dennis claim he was delivering something I'd ordered months ago. It was a nice touch. I couldn't tell he was lying."

"He's an accomplished liar, that one," Phillip agreed. "He'll make a fine friend and then, after a while, he'll make an even better enemy."

"That he will," I concurred.

"What else can I do for you?" he asked.

"Nothing," I told him. "That's really all I wanted." I didn't sound convincing, but I hung up anyway.

I watched Tabitha breathe for an hour before I slipped out of her room and across the hall to my new suite. Beatrice was watching a cooking show with the volume off and the subtitles set to French, while Gladys, Cheryl, and Erin slept off their wounds on one of the king-size beds. Phil had outdone himself with the suite he'd provided. Five bedrooms, two dens, a kitchen, and three and a half baths were more than I was used to having. There was even an office that looked enough like mine to make me paranoid.

Rachel walked out of the bathroom wearing nothing but an evil grin. She looked kind of weird with the butterfly on her cheek, but she still exuded sex. "I want to be in charge of your bachelor party," she said, running her hands down her body.

Cinnamon hit my nostrils, and from the smell, it wasn't just affecting me. Beatrice was getting interested, despite herself.

"I think Talbot might be a better choice," I told her.

"You think so?" She tugged on the hoops piercing her nipples. "Why don't you let me show you a preliminary outline." Her hands glided down her smooth taut skin to her navel piercing. Shit.

"Put some clothes on," I told her before her hands could go any lower.

"She'd never know." Rachel pouted.

"Not until you told her," I said.

Rachel laughed, sliding into some panties and a baby doll nightie. Not my idea of clothes, but it fit the letter of the law if not the spirit of the request. "Why don't Bea and I put on a show for you." She smiled.

"It's tempting, but no. I do need your help with something, though."

"What?" she asked eagerly.

"I need to find a good jewelry store. I promised your sister a ring." I turned to Beatrice. "You're coming along, too."

Rachel put on some real clothes and we drove out of town toward a twenty-four-hour jeweler Beatrice said all the society vampires used.

As we passed by the city limits I noticed a large billboard in the rearview mirror. It read, *Welcome to the Void.* Beneath it, *City Music Festival* had been painted out. Over that, in red spray paint, someone had scrawled, *We suck.* I wondered if the author was just being vulgar or if he had any idea how true that statement really was. I made a mental note to have Talbot get me a good digital picture before the city had it painted over.

"I want to ask you both something," I said. "Something that's been bouncing around the back of my head for a while now. Normally I don't want to know these things, but this evening . . ."

"What is it?" Beatrice asked.

"Roger made Marilyn his thrall over forty years ago . . ." I paused.

"You don't want to know," Rachel offered.

". . . but Roger was a Master, so she should have stopped aging . . ."

"How much more slowly than normal did she age?" Beatrice asked.

"He doesn't need to know," Rachel said emphatically.

She was right, but this was Marilyn and I was going to know, even if I forgot it, even if it changed nothing. I owed her that.

"I didn't notice any slowdown in her aging process at all."

"Then she was fighting him," Beatrice whispered. "When you fight your master's will, you age. If she aged normally, then—"

"Then she fought him, every day, all day," I said. "That's my girl." Something cold and wet hit my cheeks and when I wiped at it my hands came away red.

Fang swerved slightly to pass over some bit of roadkill. The eerily soft clatter of tiny bones rained down on the pile of Fang's other meals in the trunk, like a morbid rainstick. Thinking of rain made me think of dripping water, which made me think of . . . "Shit!"

"What is it?" both women asked.

"My sword!" Fang hung a U-turn in the middle of the highway, scattering cars and eliciting honks from other drivers.

"What sword?" Beatrice asked me.

"My magic ice sword! I left it in the closet. If some damn fireman stole my magic sword, I'm gonna be so fucking pissed off!"

Red and blue lights flared in my rearview mirror. Just what I needed—cops. Fang's excitement coursed out through the steering wheel, like a horse eager to gallop.

Laughter rang out from the backseat. "Don't you think you ought to stop for the police?" Rachel asked. "Just accept the ticket and let Phillip fix it for you later."

That would have been the smart thing to do, but I didn't want to do the smart thing, and it wasn't just me; Fang didn't want to stop, either. I took my foot off the brake. The accelerator dropped to the floor, my foot still hovering in the air above it.

Fang wanted to keep on going, to tear ass through the city until we lost them. He didn't care about morals or laws. Fang just cared about using his power, having a blast, getting fed. Greta had better take good care of him while I was in Paris. I was going to miss Fang.

"Fine," I told the car. "Go for it."

Fang kicked in the speed and Beatrice let out a loud whoop. I supposed she'd finally found the exciting life. "I forgot to tell you something," she shouted over the wind, the engine, and the radio.

"What?"

"You got a note from Ebon Winter."

I laughed. "A Christmas card?"

"Sort of." She smiled. "It was a gift certificate good for him to redo the interior of the Pollux when you rebuild it."

"That's awful nice of him." He'd done the courtyard outside Lady Gabriella's; there was no telling what he could do for the Pollux.

"He also sent a note." She handed it over the seat to me and I took my hands off the wheel, let Fang drive himself.

It read:

> *My Dearest Eric,*
>   *I hope this missive finds you well. Thank you ever so much for all the fun you've provided me over the last few months. For that I feel I owe you many thanks as well as the following warning: I've bet against you in Paris.*
>
>   *Happy Holidays,*
>   *Winter*

Months? That meant Winter had already been betting on me when I ran up against William and the other werewolves out at Orchard Lake.

Well, Merry Christmas to you, too, you son of a bitch. Fine, you know what, let him bring it. Let them all bring it. Because when it comes right down to it, I'm a badass vampire and I can take it.

ABOUT THE AUTHOR

Photo: © Jonathan Lewis

J.F. Lewis lives in Birminham, Alabama, with his patient wife, two adorable sons, and an ornery Akita. Visit him at www.authoratlarge.com.